Nyria

Unwin's Library

Nyria

BY

Mrs CAMPBELL PRAED

AUTHOR OF

"MY AUSTRALIAN GIRLHOOD," "THE INSANE ROOT," ETC.

T. FISHER UNWIN

LONDON
11 PATERNOSTER BUILDINGS

LEIPZIG
INSELSTRASSE 20

PARIS
3 RUE AUBER

1904

TO MY READERS.

My friendship with Nyria has been one of the most interesting experiences of my life, and I think I may say the strangest; for surely it is not given to many that they should hold converse with a being who lived in the flesh nearly two thousand years ago. Yet such is Nyria's extraordinary claim, borne out by historic corroboration of the events she describes, by a multitude of confirmatory details which she gives, and by the evidence of her own life-like individuality, as she revealed it to me during an intimate intercourse of many months.

Startling as the statement may seem, it is no less true that the whole story of Nyria has been told me by—what shall I say? an entity?—a ghost?—a discarnate or reincarnate soul?—I know not how to call her—to whom is due a series of incidents and portraits which when they touched history I have carefully verified, and which I firmly believe my own imagination would have been incapable of originating. My readers must, however, judge Nyria for themselves. I can only frankly assure them that her story is no invention of mine, but a life-record of which I am the transcriber. In this sense, it is a human document rather than an historical novel.

To explain:—Some years ago, being deeply interested in those questions of spiritual research of which we have heard so much from recent pioneers of thought, I came into touch with a girl of mixed nationality, shy, reticent, modest and unselfish, a child of nature, lacking in education, half puzzled, half frightened at the mystic tendencies in herself of which she was always loth to speak. Owing to her inherent reserve and various other conditions, it was not easy for me to follow up an accidental discovery of her endowments; and but for a chance combination of circumstances which threw us practically alone together in a foreign country, I should have had no opportunity to carry out my investigations. As it was, I saw in my new friend what appeared to be a remarkable illustration of the theory of pre-existence, or—if one prefers so to express it—of the possibility of dual personality. I am not competent to put forward any arguments in support of either theory; I merely relate what fell within my personal knowledge.

I found that when in close companionship with my own mind—which was sympathetic with hers—this girl would go off into a sort of dream-existence, wherein she took on a totally different identity, of which, on resuming her normal consciousness, she had not the dimmest recollection. In these phases, her voice, manner and whole intelligence underwent a change, and she prated—to use Nyria's expression — in a child-like babble, but with plenty of shrewd observation, displaying keen judgment of character about scenes, persons and conversations that she described as going on at the time around her. It was in truth as though she had stepped into a left-off, fleshly garment of the past and had again become in actuality the slave-girl, Nyria, personal attendant of Julia, daughter of the Emperor Titus—in service of whom the girl represented herself as having been associated with many noted personages of that age, and an eye-witness and participator in some of its tragic happenings.

At the onset of my design as Nyria's biographer, perplexity beset me with regard to the form in which I should offer her story to the reading public. To dish it up in mere guise of a novel according to sensational novel-making methods, would be, I thought, to destroy the freshness of Nyria herself and to substitute what I considered a poor exchange. Whereas, to transpose Nyria's narrative from the first to the third person, giving it as far as possible in her own words, but narrowing the historic purview to that of a little slave-girl, might turn Nyria into a kind of mechanical medium for the presentation of the pictures, and suggested an offence alike against technique and verisimilitude. This process, however, I have been compelled to adopt, instead of the more natural one of letting Nyria speak in her own person—a course which her perversity at the beginning of things rendered impossible.

For in the earliest stages of our intercourse, I found that the situation was almost unmanageable, indeed comic, in its difficulty. Realism jostled fantasy in incongruous juxtaposition, and I could bring neither into conformity with art. By no manner of modern reasoning could I persuade the shade of Nyria that she was only a ghost walking a world of other shades which had ceased to exist some nineteen hundred years back. She hinted politely that I must be mad, and flatly declined to regard herself as a ghost. It was vain to assure her that after that lapse of time no disastrous consequences could ensue upon any revelations she might make. She was terrified of betraying either the Christians or her adored "Domina." Not Julia, for Nyria showed few moral scruples concerning Julia, whom she had evidently hated, and who, moreover, she knew to be a shade, since she had assisted in the laying out of that magnificent lady. It was Valeria for whom she feared, and whose name she would not for a long time divulge, because, as she pointed out, there were many people eager to make mischief about so great a personage. I gradually gleaned that the Domina in question had indulged in an indiscreet love-affair, and that her husband was a friend of Domitian's. By slow degrees I succeeded in conquering Nyria's distrust of me, but during the process I had much ado to parry her embarrassing questions. Who was I? Why should I turn up thus in unexpected places—on a spur of the Aventine, in Julia's back garden, or on the steps of Valeria's terrace—wherever I might chance to catch my little ghost in shadowland? Had I no slaves of my own that I should require her guidance? and if I had come in a litter where had I left it? Should she call it for me? How was it, too, that I did not seem able to see anything for myself, but must wait till she pointed it out for me? Whereupon I hit on the plea that I was blind. Her ready sympathy touched, Nyria became tractable, and when she led me down by the goat-track to the city would warn me carefully where I should put my feet to avoid danger. But now arose a new mystification. She was puzzled as to why she could hear me while she could not see me; and the hint that I belonged to an invisible order of beings did not satisfy her. So things went on in baffling fashion, until at last I induced her to give me her full confidence—how, I know not, unless it were by sheer persistency, or by the interposition of some ruler in the kingdom of shades. Or, the fantastic conjecture has occurred to me, could it be that we were picking up strands of two lives that had once been interwoven? Who can say? At anyrate, Nyria ceased ultimately to question my right of entrance into her world, and led me on, scene by scene, in fairly coherent order, through the progress of her short life, while I, taking down her talk almost verbatim, amassed the sheaves of notes from which the following pages have been compiled.

I should here mention that for several years before that time I had been studying the Flavian period for a book I had lately written, and was therefore in a better position to check Nyria's historic and topographic details than I might otherwise have been. To my surprise, I found them invariably correct, though her second and living self had never been in Rome. Once, only, did she seem at fault; this in the case of Marcus Licinius Sura, who was clearly not the L. Licinius Sura of Trajan's reign. History gives no word of Marcus, and I can only accept Nyria's statement concerning his parentage. I believe, however, that Martial's epigram, bearing out Nyria's location of the villa, refers to Marcus, and that likewise one of the two Sura letters, written by the younger Pliny, is to Valeria's lover. For the rest—and the instances are too numerous to be dwelt upon—Nyria's memory justifies itself. As I had carefully tested my subject's modern-day ignorance, I can with confidence assert that she had never read a line of Tacitus, Suetonius, Juvenal, Pliny, Martial or other authorities of the time. I knew her to be absolutely unaware of the existence of Apollonius of Tyana, yet she gave me particulars of him only to be found in Philostratus, and others which I cannot vouch for, but which entirely coincide with what is already known of that Wonder-Worker. Lack of space has, however, compelled me to drop the Apollonius thread, as well as others of interest, in my weaving of the Nyria fabric. The possibility of these being utilised in some later book depends upon the welcome accorded to this sketch of Nyria's life. Sometimes I have asked myself whether the babblings of my little ghost-slave could be telepathic reflections—if I might use such a metaphor—of that which had been in my own mind; but remembering that Nyria often corrected errors of mine, and gave me information I had not at the time ascertained for myself, I cannot give credence to that supposition.

It will be seen that Nyria is not literary. She shows avoidance of allusions familiar even to superficial students of authors of the time, and of modern-day books dealing with the period. These I have therefore purposely avoided in such matter as, for dramatic presentment of the whole, I have been obliged to supplement from my own resources. The matter thus provided has not, however, been great, since I have had occasion to be thankful for the Roman habit of considering personal slaves as automata. In those scenes where Nyria was not present I have relied upon intuition with regard to what I felt sure, from the sequence of events and from suggestions given me by Nyria, must have taken place. In the presentation of Nyria herself, which may seem an idealised picture, I have drawn upon her own naïve and unconscious admissions.

My part, in fact, has been solely that of the literary adapter, for in welding together the various portions of Nyria's narrative and dialogue, and placing them in the manner I thought most effective, I have adhered as closely as was possible to her own method and phrasing. At the last, where she was only able to give me a bare outline of what occurred before she entered the Arena, I have endeavoured to show what it was evident to me that she suffered, and something of the Vision that upheld her before "the tyrant walls of Rome" released what was verily a spirit pure as any ever imprisoned in flesh.

I do not know how far my readers will accept these introductory words for what they are—a simple statement of personal experience. For myself, I should not feel it fair to withhold them. To the world, Nyria cannot prove herself, and I may only bear faulty witness of her. Whether it be derided or no is not my concern. Yet I fancy that there must be many who, like myself, have the sense of some vast evolutionary force pressing behind humanity, stirring spiritual faculties in man as yet embryonic. If this be so, the revelation will doubtless come when the race is ready, as other revelations have come in all ages before. Meanwhile, patient sifting of evidence may find us some fuller explanation of the mystery than those which thinkers are now putting forward under such names as the sub-conscious self, multiple personality, precognition, or pre-existence.

As yet, however, the old question remains—Whence came I, and whither do I go?

R M Praed.

April 1904.

NYRIA

I

The litter of a Roman lady was passing along one of the small streets at the foot of the Palatine Hill—a street leading into the Forum, and apparently an offshoot from the fashionable Goldsmiths' Portico, for it was occupied almost entirely by second-hand jewellers and dealers in silver plate and graven stones of value.

Among these dealers the best known was Stephanus, a Greek freedman formerly in the service of Flavius Clemens, cousin of the Emperor Domitian. He was to be seen now at the door of his shop, a rather short man of extremely powerful build, with a strong, kindly face, and dark, curly, square-cut beard, who was clothed in the plain toga to which by manumission he had acquired the right. He peered out between the heads of a group of loiterers attracted by the sound of shouts from the great lady's slaves as they pushed and struck on this side and that to make a clear course for the litter, calling, as the custom was in Rome,—

"Make a way for the most noble Valeria, wife of the illustrious Valerius Paulinus. Make a way—make a way!"

Stephanus wondered whether the litter was bearing him a customer, for he had recognised the high-born dame's livery, which was a combination of mauve and white bordered with stripes of dark purple, less garish than those in vogue among the followers of the Flavian dynasty. But Valeria, daughter of the late Emperor Vitellius, came from an old aristocratic stock, and preferred refined simplicity.

At that moment a second litter, arriving from the opposite direction, drew up in front of Stephanus's shop and his attendance was required by another patrician lady.

The narrow street was more crowded than usual as the Empress Domitia held to-day a reception at the Palace, which had caused a congestion of traffic in the Vicus Tuscus and the Vicus Apollinus—those two important approaches to the Palatine—so that this road, lying between the two, made a convenient sideway for going and returning guests.

Valeria's slaves, excited by drinks that had been handed round among waiting bearers at the Palace, were shouting more loudly and dealing freer blows than was their habit. One of these strokes descended upon the bare shoulder and arm of a young slave-girl who, apparently lost in dreams, was walking along with eyes downcast, a basket of beautifully-arranged flowers poised upon her head. The Numidian's stave was thick, and the blow so heavy that it drew blood, and a sharp cry of pain and fright came from the girl's lips. She staggered, then with difficulty recovered herself, and in so doing let the basket of flowers fall from her head. Again she cried out, this time in dismay, and, forgetting the smart of her bleeding shoulder, sprang forward, trying to save the scattered blossoms. But it was too late. Already they were being trampled under foot by the crowd, and the basket lay, a tumbled mass of moss and greenery, the exquisite arrangement completely ruined.

Angry tears started to the girl's eyes, and there was a call of "Shame!" from the bystanders when the African, redoubling his shouts, struck her anew, while with his stick he dispersed the crowd.

"Make a way! Make a way!" he continued, "a way for the most noble Valeria, who returns from an audience with the Augusta Domitia."

One of his fellows pushed the girl rudely, and she, recoiling from the touch of his black hand, turned on him a look of outraged dignity befitting a princess rather than a slave.

"How darest thou touch me!" she exclaimed. "The street is free to others as well as to thy mistress, and though I am but a slave, I also am a woman."

The Numidian laughed jeeringly, and so did the huge black bearers of the litter, which after its momentary halt began to move on again, while the slave-girl, her white dress stained with the blood that flowed from her shoulder, stooped to gather up her broken flowers. Suddenly a silvery voice from the litter gave an imperious order, which was repeated even more imperiously by an elderly Greek who walked beside it. The bearers stopped in alarm, and the curtains of violet silk with embroidered bordering were drawn apart as the occupant of the litter—a beautiful lady in ceremonial dress—leaned over the embossed side and looked with vague curiosity at the slave-girl, whose spirited reply to the Numidian had roused her from her high-bred apathy. She gave a gesture of distaste at sight of the bleeding arm, and severely reprimanded the black forewalker for his barbarity.

"The man who strikes a helpless woman for no cause must be beaten himself. Twenty stripes, Chabrias, and let Jumal be degraded from attendance on me and put to coarser work."

The African, whining, was driven to the rear, while Valeria signified that she wished to speak to the girl, who was staring at her in a kind of stupefied admiration.

"Come here, child," said Valeria. "I am sorry that thou shouldst have been injured. These Africans are fit only for the hewing of stones and carrying of marble, but this one shall be punished for exceeding his duty. Accept a coin to buy ointment for the healing of that hurt, and believe that 'tis by no will of mine thou art wounded."

Valeria held forth a gold piece, but the slave-girl made a proud movement of refusal.

"It is impossible, Domina, that I can take money from *thee*."

At the first sound of Valeria's voice she had reddened and then gone pale. Drawing herself up, she stood now beside the litter, a pretty, delicate creature, immature of shape, her blue eyes set in a fair, curiously spiritual face, her small head covered with a quantity of golden hair, long, and with a natural curl—such hair as would have brought a high price in the hairdressers' shops, and which many a fashionable lady coveted.

The slave-girl's eyes, large, soft, appealing, and suffused with tears, gave an adoring look. She had recognised the lady, and there was something so angelic, and yet so sweetly human, in the girl's gaze that Valeria—herself one of the fairest flowers of Roman aristocracy, and ordinarily indifferent to everything outside her class—was strangely stirred. She had a cultured taste for beauty and an intense appreciation of drama. Moreover, she felt in sympathy with the slave's indignant protest against the accepted order of things. Had not she, too, been bought and sold, though in a different fashion? And there was a tenderer thought, too, that gave softness to her manner. Had the only girl-child she ever bore been spared her by the gods, her babe's blue eyes might have looked upon her as did the eyes of this maid. Valeria's voice was less distant when she spoke again.

"But I must make amends for my servant's ill-treatment. Why not take the money?"

The girl's face worked. Her tears well-nigh ran over.

"Because—I cannot—oh! I cannot. It is enough that the Domina should deign to notice me."

Valeria seemed puzzled, though she was evidently touched.

"But thy flowers are spoilt. Wert thou going to sell them?"

"Nay, Domina. I was taking them as a present from my mistress to the wife of Nonius Asprena, who lives on the Cœlian."

"I, too, live on the Cœlian. The distance is not great. Why not go back and gather fresh flowers? Where dost thou come from?"

"From the Aventine, Domina."

"Then thou hast chosen a circuitous road."

"I wished to call at the shop of Stephanus, in order to shew him my handiwork."

"Oh, so Stephanus is a friend of thine! His name is known to me. Well, thou hast hardly time to go back to the Aventine and make up a fresh basket. What will befall thee since these flowers cannot be delivered?"

"I shall be whipped." Her little white teeth clinched upon the slave's underlip.

"Whipped!" Valeria frowned. "Truly unjust. The mischance hath been no fault of thine. And already thou art in pain."

"It is naught, Domina. I can bear pain."

"Art thou, then, often whipped?"

"That is as Julia pleases. But 'tis worth a whipping to hear the Domina's kind words."

Valeria looked scrutinisingly at her. She wondered how much of this was mere flattery, but the blue eyes, showing boundless capacity for devotion, forced her to deem them sincere.

"Come, save thyself a beating, child. Take this gold piece and buy a new basket of flowers from the seller whose booth stands by the Temple of Castor."

"Alas, Domina, I was bidden arrange the basket with mine own hands, that the wife of Asprena might judge whether my skill equalled that of a maid from Cos of whom she boasted to my mistress."

"But the flower-seller by the temple is famous for her taste. Thou mayst yet gain the palm if thou dost say nothing."

"The Domina knoweth that it would be lying. And to lie I cannot—for myself."

"Wouldst thou then lie for another?" asked Valeria, amused.

The girl looked confused. "I know not. I love not to lie, yet it seems to me I would sooner lie than betray one who trusted me."

"Good!" returned Valeria, warmly. "Thy mistress is fortunate to possess such a slave."

"Nay, I would not lie for Julia!" cried the girl. "I would bear fifty lashes sooner. Besides," she added, simply, "Julia needeth none to lie for her. Julia is skilled in lying."

"Thou speakest frankly," said Valeria, with faint sarcasm. "But who is Julia?"

"Surely, lady, there is but one Julia," said the girl. "Julia, the most noble—the daughter of the great Titus, and wife of Flavius Sabinus."

Valeria's brows contracted as though the name brought her disagreeable associations.

"Ah! So thou art a slave of Julia! I should have known, for thy face is familiar to me. Thou must be that barbaric babe whom my sister's husband bought and presented to this Julia. Dost recall the name of Valerius Asiaticus?"

"Ay, Domina, but 'tis long back. Thou art gracious to remember." The girl's hands went to her forehead in a charming obeisance. She had blushed with pleasure. Valeria watched her wistfully.

"What art thou called?"

"They call me Nyria, Domina."

"A pretty name. Well, Nyria, thou needst not fear. I will give thee a letter for thy mistress, explaining this mishap, and praying that thou be not punished for the fault of a ruthless clown. My acquaintance with Julia is slight, but she will scarce refuse when Valeria, the daughter of Vitellius, craves a boon. My tablets, Chabrias."

The elderly Greek handed her a hinged tablet of wood prepared with wax, on which Valeria wrote rapidly with a gold-handled stylus. Then, tying its silken thread around it, she bade the Greek affix a soft wafer, on which she impressed her own seal, carried among other glittering baubles on a slender chain at her wrist.

Meanwhile, Stephanus's customer had gone on her way, poorer by several hundred sestertii, and richer for a small silver effigy of Isis for her specimen table. The goldsmith, again at his doorway, caught sight of Nyria and perceived what had happened. He darted to her side, heedless of the presence of Valeria, and exclaimed indignantly at sight of the sore shoulder.

"What brute hath been laying about thee, little one? By Hercules! To wound a maid!"

"'Tis naught—naught, Stephanus, truly. I am not much hurt," cried Nyria, hushing him, and glancing humbly at Valeria.

"Thou art bleeding! They have dealt thee cruel blows."

"Take in the maid and bind up her arm," said Valeria, with, for her, great condescension. "Consider it my cost. Thou art somewhat of a surgeon I am told."

Stephanus turned and made a rough salute. He was no respecter of persons.

"Thou knowest who I am," said Valeria, haughtily. "Thou tendest my servants when they are sick. Add to thine account the charge for curing this maid's hurt."

"I make no charge for Nyria, lady," said Stephanus, with scant civility. "It hath been my joy and care to tend this maid when aught hath ailed her since first she came, a fledgeling, unto Rome. Haste, little one, and let me wash thy wound."

Valeria stared in some surprise; then, beckoning Nyria, she gave the tablets into her hand.

"Deliver this letter to thy mistress, child, with all due courtesy. 'Twill secure thee from further suffering, I trust. When thou art at liberty come to my house some morning between the fifth and seventh hours, and tell me how thou farest."

Nyria bent in obeisance, and Valeria's litter moved on towards the Forum.

The slave-girl's gaze followed it with the same wondering look.

"Art dazed, Nyria?" said Stephanus, gruffly. "Come in and let me see to thine arm before the wound hath time to inflame. Here is thy basket. Let it be witness to Julia of the accident."

"There is no need," she said, taking the basket absently. "With her own hand the sweet Domina hath written to Julia on my behalf. Was it not gracious of her, Stephanus? And she talked to me—she, the Lady Valeria—almost as though I were one like herself!"

"By Hecate of the cross roads!" exclaimed Stephanus, "art thou bewitched to forget so soon the pain she hath caused thee?"

"Twas not *her* fault," retorted Nyria. "And she ordered that the man should be beaten for having struck me—beaten and degraded from service on her. Think what a punishment! I would have begged that he might be spared, but while she talked to me I forgot all else."

"Thou art indeed bewitched! But those Numidian brutes deserve a lesson. I marvel that Valeria should have stopped her litter on thy behalf."

"Was it not wondrous kind of her?" spoke Nyria, raptly.

"Oh! Ay, and wondrous strange. These proud dames think far more of the whine of a pet lap-dog than of the death groans of a slave. And Valeria, wife of Paulinus, is reputed to care not a jot for aught save herself. Think no more of her, Nyria, for surely she will take no further heed of thee."

They had reached the shop, where a slave stood in charge of the open trays of goods. Stephanus cast a quick glance round the small, low-ceiled place with its precious wares. Then his stiff bearing relaxed, and he turned to the girl with a warm light in his brown eyes.

"Greeting, sweetheart! Praise Hermes, no customer waits, and all my service is thine."

But Nyria, attracted by an odd, guttural mumbling, hurried to a corner, where hung a cage covered with a thick dark blanket.

"Alack! What hath poor Ascalaphus done that thou hast banished him thus?"

"I had like to have wrung his neck," rejoined Stephanus, "were it not that he knoweth thy name, Nyria, and tells me when he doth see thee in the street."

"And is it for such courtesy that thou dost stifle him? Poor friend! Here's Nyria to ransom thee." She tossed off the blanket, whereat a grey parrot from behind chuckled sagely.

"Ho! ho! Stephanus, rogue and robber! Get thee to thy thieving."

Nyria laughed in a merry way, and even Stephanus threw up his head and gave a great guffaw. He had a quick temper, but an equally quick sense of humour.

"I'll have thy tongue, thou lying clown!" cried he. "'Twas thus this bird of hell began when Hippia's litter stopped. Verily he put it into her mind to question the price I asked her. So I threw the cloth over him to stay his evil chatter. Come within, Nyria, and let me tend that wounded arm."

They went through the shop into a room in which was a window that looked out upon a narrow paved courtyard. Here were set plants in troughs and buckets, and along the south-west end of the enclosure some paving stones had been taken up and soil laid, so that creepers could grow up the wall; and there was a border filled mostly with herbs and shrubs used in medicine.

The sun poured down, slanting, across the gap between the Palatine, where Caligula's marble palace towered, and the steep Capitoline Hill crowned by the great national temple to Jupiter. As Nyria sat by the window she could see a glittering patch of its new-gilded dome and the outline of a recently-erected chariot of the Sun, as well as the more ancient horses in marble which surmounted the Temple of Castor. The peace of this place was very pleasant to Nyria, coming from bustle outside. Here the noise of the Forum was deadened by the intervening cloister of the Vestals and the Goldsmiths' Portico behind it, so that the roar of the city sounded like that of ocean surf beating upon a distant strand. Nyria loved this quiet garden court, for often on evil days had she found in it a haven. She knew every plant that grew there, and had helped Stephanus to gather many of them in happy rambles on the hills, when they went to pick herbs for the potions he made for the sick. Stephanus combined with his business as jeweller and curiosity dealer an extensive medical practice among the poor population of Rome.

The freedman now threw off his toga—a badge of Roman citizenship which he took care to wear during business hours—but its cumbrous folds irked him, and he was glad to lay aside the ceremonial garb. Now he stood, a short but powerful figure in his brown tunic, with bare brown neck and arms. Stooping over Nyria, he unfastened her simple, white woollen garment upon the shoulders with the care and gentleness of a woman, and tenderly inspected her hurt.

The Numidian's curved stave had cut through the fair, young flesh, leaving gaping lips upon which blood was stiffening. The sight turned Stephanus's tenderness to rage, and he muttered fiercely,—

"Beast of a barbarian! May the Furies pursue him! I'll try not to pain thee, sweetheart, but I must probe deeply, for who knows what foulness may have clung to thee from the villainous weapon. There! 'twill be but the smart of a moment."

He went into an inner room, bringing back a bowl of warm water, a pot of ointment, lotions and bandages. Deftly he set about sponging the wounds.

"So! not a wince! By Hercules, thou hast a fine courage, Nyria!"

"I had need to have it, Stephanus."

"Poor child! would that I could protect thee. Ha! here I see a fresh mark, and given but yesterday. The bruise has just begun to purple. How camest thou by this?"

"From Julia's hand-mirror, with which she struck me when I set too high the curl above her right ear. Julia likes to hide her ears for they are neither small nor shapely."

Stephanus growled in his beard, but Nyria chattered on.

"'Tis plebeian to have large ears, and 'tis not pretty. The Lady Galla said that Julia's ears resembled those of the god Vespasian's father, whose statue is in the Flavian temple. When folks speak of Vespasian's father, Julia is not well pleased, because his birth was lowly. But in Rome one may become a god even though one's father was a tax-collector. Will the Senate make Julia a goddess because her father and grandfather are gods?"

Stephanus laughed.

"That only Cæsar Domitian may declare. He has pronounced himself a god, and should Julia wear the purple, no doubt she will be decreed a goddess."

"I like thy Greek goddesses best, Stephanus. Julia is so fat, and she hath not the divine air. But she would love to wear the purple. Yet how could Julia wear the purple, seeing the Augusta Domitia liveth?"

"The Augusta may not live for ever," said Stephanus, grimly.

"Domitia is not happy, 'tis said," remarked Nyria. "I have heard from her women that oft she weepeth in secret."

"So wouldst thou weep if thy heart went where thou darest not follow," said Stephanus. "Not that I'd have thee love Paris, little one. Leave mimes for empresses to woo. Look nearer home when thou wouldst love."

"Nay—I know naught of love," said Nyria, shaking her curly golden head. "But I would that Julia would not take me so often to the Palace. Cæsar hath a trick of teasing that I like not."

Stephanus raised his head and looked sharply at her.

"So it stops at teasing, be glad, and trouble not thyself about the doings of the Palatine. 'Tis not well to inquire too closely into the affairs of a family of gods—Roman ones at least. The old gods of Greece were different, in that they had some divine dignity among them, but when one is called on to worship such as Cæsar—faugh!"

Nyria looked down upon him as he bent again, her blue eyes wide and innocent.

"But *thou* dost worship none at all, Stephanus."

"I call on Hermes oft, my dear. He bringeth luck in business, and I need his favour."

"Truly there are no gods so kind as thou art," said Nyria, suddenly laying her cheek for an instant against the dark head on a level with her shoulder.

Stephanus's veins tingled, but he went on with his task, softly dabbing lotion on the sensitive flesh.

"That soothes, doth it not, little one? By Até, it would please me to bestow such a thump upon the breast of Julia—whose skin to thine is as hog's flesh to roses—white roses, sweetheart, such as thou and I have gathered together in summer on the hills." Stephanus's strong hands shook, and his voice trembled as he said gently, "Nyria, tell me, would it displease thee, had I the right to bring thee into my house and provide for thee henceforth?"

Stephanus chose his words carefully, watching the girl as he spoke. Nyria turned on him a look of confiding affection.

"Oh! if only it were possible! How good thou art, Stephanus. I would I were thy slave instead of Julia's—or thou mine uncle, as Cæsar is hers!"

Stephanus shrugged in half-grim, half-humorous fashion.

"Alack!" he said, "I am not Cæsar; and though more than twice thine age, my dear, I have no claim of consanguinity. Still, it might be arranged if thou, Nyria, wert willing."

"Dost mean it, Stephanus? Couldst thou buy me? I fear that Julia would have no mind to sell me. Seest thou—I should fetch a fair price." Nyria reared herself with innocent pride. "I am no ordinary slave."

"Nay, thou art no ordinary slave," he repeated tenderly.

"But art thou rich enough to buy me?" she asked.

Stephanus smiled. "I would offer Julia the whole contents of my shop," he said, "and I have some fine pearls from Britain."

"The Emperor hath given Julia finer pearls than any thou couldst show," promptly replied Nyria.

"I would pray my master and mistress, Clemens and Domitilla, to speak for me," continued Stephanus.

"Julia hates Domitilla. And why dost thou call Clemens and Domitilla thy master and mistress? Thou art free."

"That's so. But while Domitilla lives Stephanus is her slave in fact, if not in law."

"I like thy fidelity," exclaimed Nyria, warmly, "and the Lady Domitilla is well worth it. I, too, could feel like that, but not for Julia. I could be a willing slave to the Lady Valeria. Hath she not a noble air? And is she not lovely, though she seemeth sad. Are things ill with her, dost know, Stephanus?"

"Not as Roman ladies count," he answered. "Valeria hath beauty, wealth, a high position, two sons for the State, and a husband no worse than most, whom she should be able to twist round her finger."

"How's that?" asked Nyria, interested.

"They say that of late Paulinus has become so deeply enamoured of his wife that he hath no eyes for other women. But Valeria scorns her husband."

"Why, then, did she marry him?" said Nyria, simply.

"She had no choice. Vespasian planned the match out of kindness to the daughter of his fallen enemy. The girl was over young to wed, and Paulinus made a jest of her with Eprius Marcellus, Massa and others of his boon companions, saying he must hire nurses for his wife as well as for her babies."

Nyria exclaimed indignantly, "'Tis shameful talk! Whence hast thou learned all this, Stephanus?"

"From her own slaves, who send for me when sick."

"I despise slaves' talk," replied Nyria, loftily. "But thou mayst tell me all thou canst of her."

"Foolish maid! Valeria is reputed the proudest and most heartless woman in Rome—alike to her husband, her children, her friends and her slaves. She hath no lovers, but is unapproachable as chaste Diana in her temple on the Aventine. And now I mind me, by that very token, Marcus Licinius Sura, whose house stands hard by Diana's shrine, questioned me but yesterday concerning Valeria, and was less disdainful than thou, Nyria, of slaves' gossip."

"Marcus Licinius Sura!" said Nyria. "I know him not. He doth not visit Julia."

"Likely not. He who sees beauty in Valeria would pass by Julia's bulkier charms. These Suras belong to the great Licinian gens, though this man's mother was a Jewess, which is no recommendation in these days. He is a fine man—Sura."

"I know him not," repeated Nyria. "What family hath he?"

Stephanus strapped her shoulder slowly as he talked.

"There is Palfurius Sura, who is in Cæsar's favour, and Lucius Licinius Sura, now a follower of Marcus Ulpian Trajan in Germany—a man of parts and substance, with no liking for his cousin on the Aventine, though he fancies much his villa and hath intrigued to get possession of it. This fellow Marcus hath a pleasing way with him, and did interest me, though I found him not a good customer. He drove a hard bargain for a set of graven sardonyx that he gave Salome for a present on the birthday of their son, but 'tis said sestertii are scarce with him. Now, child, thine arm, and I'll anoint it."

Nyria bent forward for the operation. "He is married then?" she said.

"Not so! Salome would sacrifice her hair to ratify the bond, but though Licinius may be a dreamer, as they say, he is yet practical enough not to bind himself with a barbarian freedwoman. To evade her legal claim he sends her each year from his house for the three days and nights enjoined by law—a proceeding that, while it leaves him free, hath brought much trade to the Chaldeans, for there is no limit to the philtres Salome buys from those magicians —yet all so far have failed in their effect."

"Euphena hath some traffic with the Chaldeans," said Nyria.

"Like enough! And how fareth old Euphena?"

"Oh! she doth croak as ever, and draw her signs by starlight on the ground. I marvel that Julia should seek speech with her, but she goeth oft to Julia's rooms, and in her spare moments doth busy herself over the manufacture of potions."

"Tell her I am preparing the berries for which she asked me, and will bring them shortly."

"Methinks Euphena hath found another purveyor of herbs—one Ascletario."

"Ay, ay. I know him. 'Tis a friend of Juvenal's. I have an instrument of his to mend, one with which he studieth the stars. But no purveyor of herbs is he. Ascletario is an astrologer, and wise with the wisdom that some say Zeus writes in the heavens for those to read who can."

"'Tis that which Euphena strives to learn," said Nyria.

"Ay," said Stephanus, lapsing into silence. After a minute or two he spoke again diffidently. "I would thou, too, wert wise, Nyria—not in the teaching of the stars, for a maid needeth not to know aught save such matters as may secure her own happiness. 'Tis of the marriage laws that I would speak to thee—those that concern our station. It is not good for a woman to be ignorant of these. Thou knowest that if thou dost remain long unwed Julia will some day find thee a spouse so that thou mayest bear children for her service. That would go ill with thee—eh, sweetheart?"

Nyria shrank and looked perturbed. "I like not to think of it," she said, in a low, horrified voice.

"Nay, sweet, pardon thy friend Stephanus. I would not brush the bloom from thy tender mind for thou art but a babe thyself. But marriage is a state which every maid must enter upon, and 'tis no prison if love be the jailor. Had I thee here beneath mine own roof 'twould be strange if by some means I could not compass thy freedom."

"But thou art not rich enough to buy me?" persisted Nyria.

"Mayhap. It would perforce depend upon the price demanded. But hast thou never thought that thou mightst marry *me*?"

Nyria shrank anew. "Nay! Nay! I think not of such things, Stephanus. Why speak of them?"

Stephanus heaved a resigned sigh. "I have told thee. 'Tis lest another should snatch thee away where Stephanus may not follow. If he were empowered by Julia how could one oppose the matter? Julia's sanction would be law."

"Nay, nay!" said Nyria, again hurriedly. "Julia willeth not that I should wed—Julia could not spare me."

"Could she not? Well, time will show. I'll not tease thee, child. My chief desire is but to deliver thee from Julia."

Nyria looked relieved. "Yet many a one would be proud to see life as I see it from behind Julia's chair," she said brightly. "Pity me not, Stephanus; save when I am beaten things go not ill with me. All is very grand within our house, and Julia takes me out with her so that I see much that goeth on. And when she needs me not I am free to ramble on the hillsides—among the oaks at the back of the Esquiline, and where the wild flowers grow on that knoll below the garden of Sallust. But one place most of all I love—'tis over the quarries betwixt the Nævian and the Appian Gates. There 'tis wide and open, and naught shadoweth me from the sun. It doth send me many messages, Stephanus."

"Ay, doth it so?" said Stephanus, kindly. "What doth it tell to thee?"

Nyria shook her head wisely, and her little pure face took on an intent look.

"It tells me of a greater god than men worship in Rome. One who liveth behind the sun and yet is everywhere. I feel Him on the hillside, where the bees and butterflies come round me, and the sunbeams kiss my cheek."

"Ay, but they say that malefactors find a hiding-place in those old quarries," said Stephanus, suddenly. "'Tis not fitting that thou shouldst wander thus alone."

"I meet no malefactors, but 'tis not lonely. Many people walk along the path below where I sit. They wear dark cloaks with hoods, and have a gentle bearing. Is it to the tombs they go?"

Stephanus looked sharply at the girl, but her eyes had wandered through the windows to that sunny bit of border where the taller shrubs threw shadows across the courtyard. He contented himself with putting the last touch to his bandage and refastening the clasps of her robe. Then he stood a pace or two from her chair.

"Dost know these people, Nyria?" he said gravely. "Couldst see whither they went?"

"Nay, I look not after them. When one feels God in the sunshine and the wind, one's thoughts go not among men."

"What like hath thy god, Nyria?"

"I cannot tell. But this I know, He is as no other god, for He hath no image, and is higher than the heavens."

"And doth He take count of thee?"

"I know not," said Nyria, humbly. "But I love to think He doth. Stephanus, hast thou heard of any great god like that?"

"I have but little knowledge of gods," said Stephanus, simply. "But long ago, in ancient Greece, certain sages held the belief in one such as thou dost dream of—one mightier than Zeus, to whom the Thunderer was as a shadow. Yet methinks, child, that if this high god do indeed exist 'twere wiser for men to worship one nearer earth, who may more readily be moved by their prayers."

"I, too, have said to myself that whether I weep or laugh the gods care not. But the sun's rays have whispered to me that this great God careth even for a little slave. Yet I fain would know," added Nyria, wistfully, "whether it be indeed so, whether others have found this kindly God, and if such be in truth His nature."

"Thou dost fret thyself with questions that the Flamen Dialis himself could scarce answer," said Stephanus, impetuously. "Here is one who careth for thee and fain would hold thee closer than any god could do."

Nyria rose nervously, dismissing the subject.

"I know, I know, but let me go now, Stephanus. It grows late, and I must be in readiness for the robing. When Julia comes back heated from the Campus Martius her temper is none too sweet. May the dear Domina's letter preserve me from Bibbi's lash," and the girl hugged to her bosom Valeria's tablet as though it had been a talisman.

"Oh! thou art safe for to-night. Julia will not deny the wish of Paulinus's wife, for he is Cæsar's friend. But stay, Nyria, while I give thee a necklace of amber beads which will please thee, for they come from the sea which washes certain shores of thine own northern land." Stephanus stepped into the shop, and Nyria followed him, exclaiming, in childish delight,—

"Are they the yellow beads which the women of my country prize so highly?"

"So 'tis said. Here, little one, dost like them?" He lifted a string of amber beads from a casket and clasped it round the girl's thin throat.

"Oh! Ay! they're beautiful, Stephanus. I'll wear them always if Julia forbids me not." Nyria snatched them from her neck and gloated over the yellow drops, running the string through her fingers.

"A bargain! A bargain!" screamed Ascalaphus from his corner. "Stephanus wants his price."

"Now curse thee, owl! Parrot though thou be, thou dost verily resemble thy name-father," cried Stephanus, swinging round upon his heel. The bird eyed him shrewdly.

"But Stephanus shall be paid," exclaimed Nyria, like the child she was. "Say, shall I give thee three kisses, Stephanus?"

"I like not to purchase thy favours, Nyria, nor that thou shouldst sell them," he replied gently. "Leave such trafficking to Roman ladies." Then, seeing she looked hurt, he drew her towards him and kissed her forehead tenderly.

"There! there! Take that, sweet child, and may Artemis preserve thee. But keep thy kisses till thou canst give them with thyself to him thou choosest as a husband."

Nyria gazed in wistful wonder. "I may not stay," she said, and snatching up her basket with its broken bits of greenery, went to the door, where she turned, nodding lightly.

"Shall I walk with thee?" he asked. "I can leave the shop in charge of Dinarmid, mine apprentice lad, who sits without, and 'tis not till the tenth hour that I am desired to call upon a customer in the Carinæ. Let me take thee to Julia's gate."

"Nay, nay, 'twould be out of thy way, and I had best go alone," she answered hastily.

"Idle excuses!" he retorted, laughing. "Why dost shirk my company, Nyria?"

The girl laughed consciously.

"If thou must know, 'tis because the slaves make mock of me. I am no longer a little maid needing protection. Farewell, Stephanus."

Nyria ran off, and the goldsmith stood at the shop door, watching her girlish form threading the narrow street. As he did so a guttural voice from the corner gave utterance to a well-known proverb, "Many a wise man is but a fool at heart."

The parrot's ribald laughter rang out scoffingly as Stephanus shook his fist at the cage.

"Oh! ay! thou cynic," he said. "But no man is wholly wise when he looks upon the maid he loves."

II

THE house of Julia and Flavius Sabinus stood upon a lower slope of the Aventine, nearer the pomp and bustle of Rome than Valeria's abode on the Cœlian. Julia's principal portico faced the south-eastern curve of the Palatine, and from it could be seen the stately pile of Domitian's new residence that occupied the middle of that hill, while below, to the right, between Julia's house and the Palatine, lay the great oval of the Circus Maximus. To the left stretched the busy Velabrum, and above it the fortress height of the Capitoline, with that gorgeous landmark of Rome, the glittering Temple of Jove.

Valerius Paulinus's villa was placed near the crown of the Cœlian, some distance behind the Claudian temple—that monument of Agrippina restored by Vespasian. The sun shone brilliantly in a blue sky on the morning that Nyria set forth to visit Valeria, but there was a foretaste of winter in the wind that swept over the Campagna from Soracte and the Sabine Mountains. As she rounded the Aventine she passed the walls of an unpretentious villa set among trees, which was an object of envy to various covetous Romans, on account of its valuable site, for it jutted out on a knoll overlooking the Circus Maximus, and from its portico a very good view might be obtained of the chariot races which were run there.

Near a small door set in the wall and overshadowed by plane trees Nyria paused. Close by was Diana's temple, where, beneath the colonnade, realistically sculptured hounds fastened on the limbs of over-rash Actæon. A litter had just left the villa and was moving in the direction of the Velabrum. Nyria waited for it to go by. She knew that this house belonged to Licinius Sura, and felt curious to see the man who admired Valeria. She was disappointed, however, for the occupant of the litter was a woman. Indeed, a moment's reflection had told Nyria, accustomed as she was to the rétinues of persons of consequence, that this plain conveyance, with its under-sized bearers, dressed in a poor sort of livery, and lacking the usual escort of clients and forewalkers, did not befit even a minor member of the great Licinian gens. From it there came a voice that gave an order to the bearers in a tone of indefinable familiarity. Nyria drew her own conclusions accordingly.

and when she saw a handsome, but not high-bred, woman eyeing her with all the scorn of a freed slave, she felt sure this could be none other than that Salome of whom Stephanus had spoken.

The litter went by, and Nyria pursued her way, which branched off to the hinder part of the Cœlian, on which Paulinus's house was situated. She had no great difficulty in finding this, for it stood alone, and was surrounded by large grounds enclosed by a high wall. Nyria espied a carved door set in the wall, and wondered whether she should here seek admittance. This, however, she did not dare to do, but walked on to the public entrance, where an enormous flight of semi-circular marble steps led under a large portico, supported by Greek pillars with sculptured gods and goddesses between. In the centre stood an equestrian statue of more than life-size, representing a man in official robes of state. Nyria thought that must be the effigy of Valerius Paulinus, and decided that he was not ill-looking. Several litters with their attendants were waiting on the sideway, while drawn up at the foot of the steps was one more sumptuous than the rest, finely inlaid with ivory, tortoiseshell and gold, and shaded by curtains of flame-colour and crimson, while round it were grouped a number of chattering slaves. The stairs, portico and vestibule were crowded by eager, seedy-looking men, in togas of the shabby, ceremonial sort worn by poorer clients at their morning visits to patrons. Thus Nyria concluded that Paulinus was about to start on his daily outing. Also, that he was later in his habits than her own master, Sabinus, whose ways were simple and regular. It was not yet quite the fifth hour, or, according to modern reckoning, between ten and eleven of the forenoon. Nyria hung uncertainly about the portico, and presently stole round by the stairway and stood among the statues. The slaves were too busy gossiping to pay any attention to her, and she did not like to ask them questions.

Presently there came a flutter among the shabby-togaed dependants in the portico, started by the better-clad ones waiting in the vestibule. Voices sounded from within, and a train of nobles appeared, richly dressed, their hairless arms sleek as ivory, their perfumed locks and certain tricks of habit and bearing showing them to belong to the most fashionable set in Rome. Nyria recognised some as frequenters of Julia's house. Most of these were Imperial favourites—Bœbius Massa, Eprius Marcellus, Regulus, and others. In the midst walked a person whom Nyria guessed to be Paulinus. He was broad-shouldered, thick-necked, short of stature, but of powerful build. The muscles of his arms and throat stood out, and his skin was bronzed. He wore a thick, short black beard and a heavy moustache, which did not quite conceal a coarse mouth; his face was reddish, the eyes small, the head bullet-shaped—yet he carried himself with an impressive air. A dull red toga of rich material hung in ample folds over his broad breast, but his dress had not that look of exquisite care characteristic of the Roman aristocrat. He had a loud voice with a jovial, authoritative ring, and that he was a very great personage might be seen from the sycophantic manner of his nearest companion—a thin, dark man, with a clever but disagreeable face, to whom he was speaking.

"Two thousand sestertii then, Martial—paid when thou provest my lady's falsity—against a cask of Falernian. But I shall win, for the gods know well that since Valeria is cold as ice she finds it easy to be chaste."

"I take the wager, Illustrious," replied the man called Martial, with a cynical smile, carefully registering it on the tablets he carried.

An unseemly titter went round—Paulinus's laugh the loudest.

"By Jupiter!" he cried, "'tis folly to humour a woman's whims or expect reward thereby. My wife desired a villa away from the noise of streets, therefore I bought her this one, and have ever since been sorry. A man must needs go outside for his amusement, when none is offered him at home. Here am I, a day's journey from the haunts of men—or women either."

Martial murmured some scathing witticism, which was received with applause, and Paulinus resumed: "I had a thought, Martial, that thou shouldst seek me a lodging cityward—neither too open nor too retired—where I may lie of nights when Cæsar keeps late hours. Dost understand?"

"Perfectly, illustrious Paulinus. I know of just the lodging that would suit thee—a stone's throw from the Baths of Daphne. Shall I go to-day and hire it, and wilt thou trust my taste for the furnishing thereof?"

"By the gods! 'tis equal to none when another man pays the count," returned Paulinus with a guffaw, at which all laughed anew, and just then Paulinus's eyes fell upon Nyria.

"Whom have we here?" he exclaimed. "By Eros, a dainty piece of flesh! Observe her hair—it is the colour of a gold aureus."

"Like the yellow tresses of Fabulla with which many a German maid has provided her," simpered Martial. "Wilt sell thy hair, pretty one? For a consideration I'll find thee a market."

Nyria cowered, giving a desperate glance round like a wild thing trapped unawares. She would have flown into the road, but the slaves barred her way.

"Have her up to be looked at, Paulinus," said one of the exquisites. "Last night I wagered Crispinus that I would produce a damsel with hair yellower and longer than the vaunted tresses of his Heliodora. I have won my bet. Here's a curly gold head to vie with the best in Rome. Pretty maid! let me measure the length of thy locks, and for one as a trophy thou shalt have a kiss and ten gold pieces in payment."

Nyria was crimson. Her blue eyes, full of indignant tears, met the amused yet kindly gaze of Paulinus.

"Thou art frightening the maid," he said. "She is scarce more than a child. What is thy business, Yellow Hair?"

Martial, who had been coolly examining her through a crystal eyeglass, exclaimed, "I recognise the girl. I have seen her in attendance on the divinely-favoured Julia. Have a care! She is not such a baby as she looks; Cæsar hath noticed her."

"Ho! ho!" exclaimed the man who had wanted to measure her hair. "That makes some difference. I thought she was a maid from the Suburra."

Paulinus, who was descending the steps to his litter, beckoned, and Nyria approached him timidly.

"Art dumb, Yellow Hair? Thou'st been in the wars, I see." He turned with a snigger to the man behind him. "'Tis well for thee, Martial, to laud Julia's soft thumb, but here, I warrant, is proof that the lady hath a heavy hand as well as a sharp temper," and he pointed to the girl's bandaged arm.

Nyria winced, but stood proudly silent. Chabrias, the Greek, stepped forward and related the story of Nyria's adventure.

"May it please thee, Illustrious, 'tis by my lady's order that the maid is here. Valeria did desire her presence."

"By the gods, a grace which Valeria doth not vouchsafe to her husband," muttered Paulinus. "Thou art honoured, Yellow Hair. Follow Chabrias, who will take thee where thou mayst wait the Domina's pleasure."

Nyria made an obeisance as Paulinus and his train passed down. The nobles got into their litters, which swung along on the shoulders of strong bearers, and there was a rush among the clients of each nobleman as to which should get the nearest place. So, amid clatter and bustle and pompous announcement from the escort, this fashionable procession of a consular Roman wended its way to the centre of business and pleasure.

Nyria followed Chabrias past the vestibule and outer hall, and through the great atrium, which was not so showy as Julia's, but in better taste. Slender Grecian pillars went along two sides of it. Between panels of light-coloured marble on the walls were paintings representing the story of Deianira and Hercules. There were hangings of Babylonian and Indian embroideries, and soft rugs upon the mosaic floor. At one end of the hall stood a small altar with little images and flowers and offerings upon it. Set high on the walls above the pictures were masks of many ancestors; otherwise there was no obtrusive sign of state dignity. In the middle of the hall was a basin of fluted marble banked by moss and plants, and with the petals of blossoms floating upon the water, while, poised on the brim, a marble Hermes held forth his caduceus, with two jets bubbling from the jaws of its interlaced serpents and making a gentle murmur as they fell. There were several statues in the hall; an Artemis and an Apollo stood at one of the curtained archways through which they passed. They went through other apartments and then came on a side court, where Nyria was bidden to wait, while Chabrias went to inquire whether the Domina would receive her. Presently he came back and led her through another wing of the villa to a large marble court partially roofed, and shadowed by a trellis, over which grew creepers—one with large yellow bell-shaped flowers, another with spreading blooms of pale mauve, and a third bearing rich-scented waxen blooms, while late roses climbed up the walls. This court—its entrance framed by a grape-vine from which hung purpling clusters, and guarded by two dancing fauns on pedestals—faced a wide terrace, below which the ground fell, and marble steps led to the garden below. Pale carved pillars of fretwork, and the scent and beauty of carefully-tended flowers, mingling with the murmur of a fountain wherein gold-fish played, formed a most harmonious setting; and amid it all Valeria sat beneath the trellis, looking like one of her own Greek statues, with the shadow and sheen playing upon her.

She was seated in a great marble chair with fretwork back, curved headpiece, and wide arms, on which were purple cushions. Her own arms resting on them showed bare from above the elbow, where the sleeves of her robe were fastened with gold clasps, and her feet, delicately shod, were supported by a cushioned footstool. She wore a stola of finest white woollen material, with a purple border. Her throat and neck were bare. Her skin, soft and youthful, was downy like a peach, yet her features, more Greek than Roman, had a cold, severe look. The lines of her head and throat and of her cheeks were exquisite, and her hair, brown with a touch of gold and naturally wavy, was dressed after the Greek manner, loosely coiled, and held in place by a golden dagger. Her eyes were blue-grey, the iris dark-rimmed. They were full lidded and set beneath low Greek brows.

While she gazed admiringly at the Domina, Nyria became conscious of the sound of music, and of the lilt of a charming little love-song.

"Love's but a child, they say,
Wilful and wild;
Love's always blithe and gay,
For he's a child.
Sweet! hath he been this way,
Or didst thou say him nay?
Send not young love away—
He's but a child.

Love's but a lad, 'tis said,
Laughing and glad;
Many the prank he's led,
He's such a lad!
Where doth he hide his head?
Is't with thy heart he's fled?
Tush! he's too young to wed—
Love's but a lad.

Yet if in quest he's fain
To be thy guest,
Let thy kind bosom deign
To give Love rest.
Heed thou his hapless plain;
Let him not plead in vain,
Lest he ne'er come again
Back to thy breast."

Chabrias stood silent until the song was ended, and then addressed his mistress, announcing her humble visitor. Nyria made a deep obeisance, and waited for the Domina to speak, but Valeria only gazed at the girl absently. The musician, a handsome Greek youth, was about to begin another song, but she signed to him to cease, and he flung down his lyre with a petulant exclamation. Nyria's eyes turned in his direction. Curly black locks, carefully dressed, clustered over the youth's high forehead; there was a faint shade on the upper lip of his full red mouth, and he had great dark eyes of a fixed, morose expression. His appearance was rather peculiar, for his body was marred by a slight malformation—a hunch between the shoulders and an abnormal largeness of the head. Yet, though a mere lad, he was dressed in a foppish manner. Now he half rose, slouching on his elbow.

"Since the Domina wearies of my music I had best leave her to her new favourite."

"I have given no command," said Valeria, and there was displeasure in her cold, sweet voice. "Remain, Gregorio, until it is my will to dismiss thee."

The boy muttered discontentedly. It seemed strange to Nyria that his mistress should permit demeanour so insolent; but in some great houses much licence was allowed to ornamental slaves.

Gregorio glared at Nyria as Valeria signed to her to approach.

"I trust that my request had weight," the Domina said, "and that thou wert not chidden for my fellow's fault."

"I thank the Domina," answered Nyria. "My mistress was pleased by the Most Noble's courtesy. So I was not beaten, and by great good fortune am I released from the duty of attending Julia to Alba Longa, whither she went yesterday with the Emperor. Thus am I here at the Domina's pleasure."

"I see that thy friend Stephanus hath bandaged the arm

well," said Valeria, kindly. "Hast known Stephanus long, child?"

"Since I was a little maid," answered Nyria. "He comes when any of the slaves are sick, and I tend them for him."

"Dost thou, then, often nurse Stephanus's sick?" asked Valeria.

"When they are of Julia's household, Domina, and if I go out with him after my work is done and he sees his sick on the way. Sometimes I help him gather herbs outside the city walls."

"The country must be beautiful outside the walls," said the Domina, dreamily. "The woods should be turning yellow, and the berries red and purple."

"The berries on the arbutus trees are not red yet, Domina; and this year the oaks seem late of yellowing. But 'tis lovely in the woods when one doth gather flowers on the hillsides!"

Valeria smiled sadly. "That I know. I remember, when I was a child in my mother's villa on the Aventine, how great a joy I felt in plucking wild flowers and stringing them into garlands; but they faded quickly."

The lady spoke with regret. Her memory had gone back to the time, shortly before her father's proclamation as Emperor, when Vitellius, harassed by creditors, had pawned his wife's jewels in order that he might take up a command in Germany, leaving her with his mother and the young children to live a retired and impoverished life in Rome. Yet those lean days had been happy ones, thought Valeria, as her gaze wandered over the stretch of mellow, sun-steeped Campagna.

"There are some sorts that do not fade," said Nyria. "If the Domina cares for wild flowers, may I be permitted to bring her a basket? 'Tis said I have some skill in blending autumn tints."

"Nay, 'tis *I* who arrange the Domina's flowers," interrupted the young musician, angrily. "And I, too, have skill. To-day I am devising a decoration for the Domina's atrium of wild poppies and grass mingled with purple trails of nightshade."

"Attend to it, then, Gregorio," said his mistress, curtly, but without enforcing her command, and the boy made no attempt at obedience.

Valeria turned again to Nyria. "Gather me some wild flowers, child," she said graciously, "when next thou walkest beyond the walls with Stephanus."

"I need not wait for Stephanus, Domina," replied Nyria. "He is busy at the shop this season, and I have promised to get him some heads of poppies, with which he doth compound a draught good for bringing sleep to the wakeful."

"That should in truth be a valuable medicine for those who, like myself, find the night-watches long," said Valeria.

"Perchance the Domina would condescend to try Stephanus's poppy draught?" ventured Nyria; but Valeria shook her head.

"I place no great faith in drugs. Of late I have found soothing in the music Gregorio makes for me," and she indicated with a glance the Greek boy, who stood sulkily fingering the ivory plectrum with which he had struck his lyre. Now he eagerly put himself forward.

"Is it thy pleasure, Domina, that I sing thee another song, and that this stranger maid be dismissed?"

"No," answered Valeria, coldly. "It is not my pleasure. Instead, I dismiss thee, Gregorio, and also thee, Æola."

She signed to a young waiting-woman—a shy, pretty creature, scarcely so old as Nyria—who was ostensibly rubbing up some jewellery, but more busily engaged in scrutinising Nyria. She blushed up to her temples and rose, making an obeisance, then went in the wake of Gregorio, who spitefully contrived to jostle her in the doorway and upset the casket she was carrying, while he himself escaped before he could be brought to account for his misdemeanour.

Æola began meekly gathering up the trinkets which rolled out upon the terrace, and Nyria, with the instinct of a fellow-slave, went to her assistance, though Æola seemed too timid even to thank her. Valeria did not trouble herself about the mishap; her attention had been caught by the appearance of another person—a tall man in the brown habit of a secretary, who carried an ink-horn and a roll of papyrus.

"The Domina will dictate as usual?" he asked.

Valeria's delicate brows contracted as she considered a moment, while the secretary placed his ink-horn and roll upon a marble table near, and proceeded to pull up a stool before it. She stopped him with a gesture.

"Not this morning, Phileros. I am out of vein for composition. I know not how to get me into the mind of a captive barbarian queen, seeing that I have never thought to inquire concerning barbarians. Contrive me a way to quicken my dull wits."

The secretary cogitated for a minute, then said,—

"When Pomponius Secundus was working at his tragedies of the times he studied plots and characters from the life, and would frequent the Suburra, and certain regions across the Tiber in furtherance of his purpose."

Valeria laughed impatiently. "Pomponius Secundus was a professional poet, and to men—let alone poets—the world is open. Roman ladies may do many things—which I would scorn to do—but they may not scandalise society by going into the Suburra or across the Tiber in search of literary material. That I leave to Martial, who, they say, draws his wittiest stories thence. I'll consult Tacitus, who is sure to have heard much from his father-in-law, Agricola, about those savage German tribes, such as the Bructeri, over whom Veleda reigned."

Nyria uttered an exclamation of surprise. At the sound of her voice Valeria looked round.

"I had forgotten thee! What is it?" A sudden thought struck her. "Now I recollect, child, that thou art one of those northern barbarians. To what tribe didst thou belong?"

"To the tribe of the Bructeri. May it please the Domina, I could tell her of the Queen Veleda, whom I knew. I was her kinswoman, but I have tried to forget those days, for Julia's slaves used to flout me for having called myself 'princess.' And what matter if I were a princess, seeing I am now but a slave."

"Poor child! Princess and slave!" Valeria sighed. She remembered that she, too, had been a princess. Yet now she sometimes thought of herself as a slave. She turned abruptly to her secretary.

"I have found my model, Phileros. Here is one who will tell me about the barbarians. Thou canst leave us." She dismissed him, and with a gracious smile motioned Nyria nearer.

"Come, child, take that stool and sit by me. Tell me of thy youth among the barbarians, and of Veleda—who is the heroine of my tragedy—and then of thine experience as a captive in Rome. Speak freely, since thou art verily a princess, though a barbarian, and by ill-fortune forced to be a slave."

III

"I HAVE no art of words, Domina, having forgotten mine own tongue, and being uninstructed in the fashion of Roman speech. Nyria can neither read nor write."

Nyria made this confession with touching humility, but Valeria merely smiled.

"'Tis well," she replied. "They say that much knowledge doth make men mad, and if my perception errs not thou hast enough in that curly head of thine. Proceed, small apologist, and think thyself happy if thou dost not know too much."

"'Tis but little I remember, lady. I was young when I first came to Rome—so young that I scarce reached to Julia's shoulder—though in truth the Most Noble is a tall woman."

Faint disdain curled Valeria's lip. "Verily the daughter of Titus is fine of figure," she said, but Nyria was too simple to detect the satire.

"Never had I seen one so magnificent," the girl went on, "but she thought scorn of me—craving thy pardon, lady, seeing it was thine honoured sister's husband who did present me unto Julia."

"I lay no claim to courtesies for Asiaticus," said Valeria curtly. "Thou needst not mince thy speech, child. Where wast thou bought?"

"In the slave-market, where we had been driven with whips. But Asiaticus had seen me on the march. 'Tis all confusion in my mind. There were many of us, and we had been walking among the soldiers for days and days, until it seemed that one had spent one's life in walking. And my feet bled. Then one kind soldier carried me."

"Poor child!" Valeria seemed stirred by the tale. "And thou hadst been snatched from thine own kin?"

"It must have been so—but I do not remember. Nay, even I mind me not of my German name. Mayhap my father and my mother were slain in the war. Our men were brave soldiers and our women noble wives—so I have heard."

"And had all such white skins and such eyes as thine?" asked Valeria.

Nyria blushed, and murmured, "Nay, the men were more ruddy, but the women mostly had yellow hair like mine."

"And tell me of thy country."

"My own land was all a wonderful forest. I have seen none like it here, even in the woods of Aricia, where the Emperor shoots. The trees of that forest were big and old beyond the knowledge of the seers. They had many stems, with spreading arms that dropped over the roots below, so that great archways were formed. My people lived under the trees, and in summer there was no need of a roof, so thickly did the leaves grow. And some of the trunks were hollow, and within were chambers where several persons might abide. But we were happiest in the open, and I think that mayhap that's why I love the woods and the hillsides where there is naught between me and the sky."

"Dost thou believe in any God?" asked the Domina, suddenly.

Nyria hesitated. "I know not. I like not the Roman gods, Domina. But I think there is a God somewhere above all others, nobler than the rest, and Him I long to worship. Stephanus says there was thought to be a god like that in Greece of old time."

"Stephanus speaks truly," said the Domina. "Greek gods are the only ones worth worshipping. But tell me of Veleda."

"Veleda was held sacred to the people, and lived up in a lonely tower, where few saw her; but I was privileged, being her kinswoman. She longed to come down and be as other maids. Most sweet she was, and fair, and wondrous wise."

"For this cause was she brought to Rome and treated to every indignity at the hands of her captors," said Valeria, cynically. "'Tis thus the greatest nation in the world doth spoil her victims, lest they grow stronger than she."

"Veleda is dead," said Nyria, sadly. "She died long since."

"'Twas by her own will," answered Valeria. "Pity her not, 'tis only through death that one may escape captivity."

Valeria's tone was bitter, and the girl gazed at her in wonder.

"Ay, truly, and 'twas hard for Veleda, seeing she had been a queen. But," ventured Nyria, "the Domina knoweth naught of such a state."

"There are many kinds of captivity, my child," said Valeria, noting her look, "and thine—ay, and even Veleda's—is mayhap not the worst. Tell me," she added, "what did Julia say to Asiaticus when first she saw thy face?"

"In truth, Domina, I have heard she was ill pleased and upbraided him, saying she did not keep a nursery and had no use for babes."

Valeria laughed. "Verily! And what said he?"

"That I looked younger than he thought I was, and that if she would have me reared I should prove worth my keep; and so Euphena, the old Ethiopian woman, was given charge of me, and I was permitted to play in the sunshine in the slaves' court. Later on Julia sent for me and asked what I could do. It was not much —only simple embroidering which the women had taught me, and the arranging of baskets of flowers that I had taught myself and for which Julia was pleased to commend me. So then I was bidden help to put wreaths on the statues, and crown the masks on feast-days; and by-and-by I was taken into Julia's rooms, where I held the hairpins for the waiting-maids, and cleaned the curling-irons, and polished the silver taps of the bath—Julia hath a beautiful bath—and the covers of the boxes that hold the pastes and dressings for her complexion. I liked to be in the private apartments," Nyria went on. "Julia's rooms have often seemed to me as though they must be like the dwellings of the gods. It was formerly my duty to turn on the water into the bath and to strew upon it the orange and violet petals, and to mix the scents and lotions in the water—Julia doth love perfume—but now I have been made tirewoman." Nyria spoke as though this was an office entailing anxiety. "Julia liketh her hair dressed high. The Domina doth not care for the Flavian fashion?" Nyria glanced admiringly at Valeria's hair, smoothly waved, and parted with classic grace above her low, broad forehead.

"I think it is hideous," said the Domina, frankly. Nyria thought so too.

"But some admire the Flavian head-dress," she said. "Julia hath many admirers who compliment her."

"And Cæsar many sycophants who deem it wise to follow where he leads," retorted Valeria, unguardedly. But the slave-girl demurely replied,—

"The Domina knoweth that Cæsar's taste is law."

Valeria glanced at her sharply.

"Thou art a wise little maid," she said, "but over young to be a tirewoman."

"'Twas this way, Domina. I had often dressed the chief slaves' heads for the Saturnalia, and once when Thanna was absent, and Samu had been weeping herself sick for her husband, who had been torn from her and sold into Egypt, there was none to dress Julia's hair save the head woman of the draperies, who knew not the art, so that I was bidden to try my skill, and the Most Noble, being satisfied, did appoint me chief tirewoman, which office I have held since then. But Thanna is gone in my stead to Albanum."

"And art thou not sorry to be left behind?" asked Valeria. "The woods lying round that still blue lake of Nemi have always seemed to me most restful."

"I would rather be free in Rome," said Nyria. "Julia will not remain long, for there are no shops there at Alba, and the roads are rough, and Julia careth not for fishing, nor the chase, which hath taken the Emperor thither, so that unless it be his pleasure—"

Nyria stopped, arrested by a shadow that fell across the pavement. It was that of Chabrias, who approached his mistress.

"If it please thee, Domina," he said, "the Honourable Marcus Licinius Sura waits in the atrium and prays permission to offer greeting."

Valeria leaned forward. A flush rose to her cheek as she answered,—

"Bid Licinius Sura enter. I will see him here."

Chabrias retired, and Nyria rose from her stool and moved into the background, waiting for her dismissal. But Valeria seemed to have forgotten the slave-girl's presence. She had shifted her position, and the sunshine through the trellis fell upon her face, illuminating its changing expression. Her eyes had widened, and looked darker because of their dilated pupils, and there was something of girlish yearning in her gaze across the garden towards the Campagna.

Presently firm steps sounded, and Chabrias ushered forward a personage at whom Nyria looked with interest.

Marcus Licinius Sura had given great promise of eminence, having indeed held the office of prætor, but though popular in the last reign he had got himself into disfavour with Domitian. This partly because the good looks, talent and egoism of the man had their aggressive side. Moreover, because Sura had competed too successfully in some chariot races against the Emperor's faction, when it would have been more politic to have let himself be beaten; and also in the Capitoline art contests lately instituted by Domitian, Sura had carried off the oaken crown for poetic composition from an unnamed candidate, who was no other than Domitian himself. These two crimes were enough to damn him in the eyes of Cæsar, but added to them was the suspicion that Licinius Sura held Jewish sympathies—a likely enough thing, as his mother had been a Jewess. There was, in fact, a certain irregularity in Marcus Licinius Sura's birth, though, as his father had lawfully adopted him, this was of small account, and he had duly succeeded to the elder Licinius Sura's property as the son of a legitimate marriage would naturally have done. Still, some slight odium clung to him notwithstanding, and as he was the offspring of the elder branch of Suras, and ranked before his cousins Lucius and Palfurius—pure-blooded Romans—their dislike of him was not surprising. For all these reasons he thought it wise to keep out of public life at present, though the man's somewhat intriguing spirit chafed under an enforced seclusion within the garden walls of his villa on the Aventine. Here he pursued art and literature in *dilettante* fashion, avoiding the Palatine set, but mixing modestly in literary circles. It was at the house of his friend, the younger Pliny, that he had met Valeria.

Marcus Licinius Sura was remarkably handsome, and had a peculiar quality of fascination. Tall and graceful, yet of athletic build, his features of the most refined Roman type, softened by a certain warmth and charm inherited from his mother, he was said to resemble the early statues of the divine Augustus. His skin was clear and pale, and he had dark blue eyes between dark lashes, and brows that shot up abruptly and then took a long curve, giving his face a curiously winning expression. He had dark hair, very curly, his smile was singularly ingratiating, and his manners were those of a man of the world who has acquired polish from travel and the life of cities. In age he might have been nearing thirty. His dress was sober but rich—a violet tunic with toga of deeper hue, and he did not reek of unguents like the fashionable fops who thronged the baths. Now, as he greeted Valeria, his salutation was a model of good taste.

"May I ask pardon, Domina, if I have been too bold, since they tell me that it is not thy habit to hold a morning reception after the manner of many Roman ladies. Business is my excuse for intruding on thy privacy."

Valeria acknowledged the apology with a gracious bend of her head, and Sura drew a roll from the waist-folds of his toga.

"Yet even on that stern plea I should not have dared to ask for the most noble Valeria had not our common friend Plinius—who is called to-day to his villa at Laurentum—entrusted me with this parchment, which he begged me to deliver into the hands of thy husband. It contains, I understand, the report of some special pleadings in which Paulinus is interested. I am sorry to find that I have but just missed him, and with thy permission will discharge mine errand to thee instead."

The plea was a transparent subterfuge. From anyone else Valeria would have dismissed it with haughty indifference. But now the flush deepened on her cheek, and she gave Sura a troubled glance. Her momentary hesitation lent her a suggestion of inexperience at variance with her usual calm dignity, but the slight confusion was overcome immediately, and she looked up at him, smiling gravely as she replied,—

"I will take care that my husband receives the document. Pray do not apologise for thy visit. It is true that I seldom receive in these morning hours, which I usually spend here with books and in dictating to my secretary. To-day, however, I have dismissed him, and for the moment have naught to occupy me."

Licinius Sura laid the roll on a little marble tripod, then diffidently admired the prospect.

"I am not surprised, Domina," he said, "that thou shouldst prefer commune with the Muses to ceremonial visiting and idle gossip. And in truth thou hast consecrated a fitting spot to poetic study. The atmosphere of this peaceful court seems as cloistral as one may suppose the Vestals' nunnery to be. Yet that wide view towards Alba Longa and the hills must lend wings to Valeria's fancy, since yonder lies the home of her own divine traditions, where the goddess Vitellia, wooed by a mortal, gave birth to him who founded the great Vitellian gens."

Valeria received the compliment to her mythic origin with a whimsical but not ill-pleased smile.

"Methought that the grudging historians of to-day had denied our claim to such high ancestry," she said. "But wilt thou not be seated?" and she motioned him to a bench. "I need not say that Pliny's friend is a welcome guest in my house."

Sura accepted the invitation with a courtly bow, and placing himself on the bench threw back his toga, revealing the shapely outlines of his figure. The skirt of his tunic fell in thick folds to the knee, while high dark shoes, bound with embroidered thongs, came up to the calves of his legs.

"I thank thee, Domina, though the privilege thou dost extend to me be on Pliny's merit, not mine own. I am emboldened to hope that thou wilt grant me future opportunity to prove myself worthy—dare I say of thy friendship?"

Again Valeria gave him that quick, troubled glance.

"Friendship is a plant of slow growth," she said. "It doth not shoot up in a single night, nor blossom without careful tending."

"That is true of friendship," returned Licinius; and added, with a half whimsical, half audacious look, "but there is a rarer plant that hath more rapid growth, since it be divinely quickened by Aphrodite herself. The seed of love may shoot up in one morning and put forth a blossom so heavenly sweet as to steal away a man's senses and to warm even the soul of the coldest lady in Rome."

His eyes sought hers. Neither spoke for a moment; then Valeria answered, with an unsteady laugh,—

"Thou hast a pretty fancy, Licinius. Thou shouldst write a poem in praise of this flower of love."

"Ah! Valeria, when love's might is deepest felt words often fail for its expression. Ask thyself if that be not so. 'Twas *thou* who didst inspire the fancy, as I listened to thy voice when first we met on that charmed night at Pliny's."

Valeria started as if recalled by the adulatory note in his speech. She drew herself up, raising her chin in a stately little movement peculiarly her own, and said quietly,—

"A charmed night—truly—one in which the gods made sport of thee."

"Art thou then so cold, noble Valeria? They tell me so, but I can scarce believe it."

In a moment he saw that he had erred. Valeria spoke with dignity.

"Doubtless I differ from other ladies, who find in love their pastime. I prefer the interest of books and Nature."

"And yet some philosophers maintain that by the attraction of atoms, which is surely love in elemental form, this world was created, and that without such attraction Nature would cease to exist," said Licinius, with his engaging smile. "But let me not offend further, Domina. Believe that if I spoke over boldly it was not because I class Valeria among ordinary women, but because I hold her far above them. She can only be associated in my mind with that influence which I consider the noblest and most sacred in the universe."

There was a sudden question in Valeria's eyes, still vaguely troubled, but she answered lightly,—

"Thou talkest so eloquently of love that its mysteries must have been taught thee by a woman learned in them."

"None hath been my teacher, save mine own heart. A man may worship a star, Valeria, knowing it beyond his reach, yet content to gaze and to adore."

"Nay, no modern man would be thus content," she cried. "Such worship died out long since in Greece. If man may not pull down his star he'll turn his eyes earthward and warm himself at lower fires."

"Is that thine experience of men, Domina?"

"No man is faithful—at least in Rome," she said.

"And few women pure," he rejoined hastily. "Ah! Valeria, men would be more worthy were women nobler. And so when I see a woman, who to the tender grace of Aphrodite adds the wit of Pallas Athene, the chastity of Artemis, and the majesty of Demeter, wouldst thou forbid me to adore, seeing that in her I do homage to the very ideal of womanhood?"

His look pointed the allusion; it was admiring, insistent and yet reverential. Valeria avoided his eyes, and her own wandered over the little courtyard, where the sunbeams advanced on the shadows, the wind fluttered the leaves, the climbing roses interlaced, and the drops from the fountain fell with wooing murmur into the basin beneath, while amorous bees hummed above shyly opening petals which held hidden honey. The whole air, languorous with perfume, bore a sense of desire and fulfilment. Valeria's bosom heaved; her lips parted dreamily. Suddenly she straightened herself and her brows knit in vexation. She had become aware of the presence of the slave-girl. Nyria stood in a respectful attitude as Valeria called to her sharply, "Why hast thou remained?"

"The Domina gave no orders. If it please the Domina I will go back to the Aventine," said Nyria, humbly.

Valeria nodded. "Yes, go. I'm glad to see thou cam'st to no harm through my slave's fault. When time serves come again and tell me more of that wild land of thine. My secretary shall write down thy tales."

Nyria made a profound obeisance and was turning towards the house, but the Domina stopped her.

"'Twill be easier for thee to go out by the door in the wall below this terrace. Another time thou may'st enter that way. It is only used by those who come to my private apartments."

"I thank the Domina," said Nyria, and went down the steps.

"A pretty child," remarked Licinius, "and with a look of breeding."

"She is the kinswoman of a barbarian queen," said Valeria. "The hapless Veleda of the tribe of the Bructeri."

"I have always noticed," returned Licinius, "that these barbarians, when of gentle birth, are excellent slaves, and this one's yellow hair should make her fetch a good price in the slave-market. Thou art to be envied, Domina."

"Nay, Nyria is not my slave," said Valeria. "She is the property of Julia, Titus's daughter."

"Then I am sorry for Nyria; and thou too hast cause for regret. She hath a rare devotion to thyself, and would serve thee well. In her I see the look of a faithful little watch-dog."

IV

"Hie thee, Stephanus! Here cometh Nyria," cried the bird whose cage was hung out in the sun at the goldsmith's shop door. "A potion! a potion! The maid looks wan." And the creature chuckled impishly.

Stephanus, seated at the high dresser beneath the window, fashioning a piece of jewellery, threw the parrot a curse and went on with his work. He had been too often deceived by Ascalaphus's announcements to bestir himself over-readily on account of them. But the bird knew his weakness and played upon it.

"May Hades swallow thee, for thou art a lying fiend," said Stephanus, and screwed up his eyes over the stones he was graving. But Ascalaphus continued his unholy mutterings, flapping his wings and dancing about on his perch.

"Haste, Stephanus! Pretty maids wait not long for wooing! A potion! A potion!" he shrieked; then, changing his tone, croaked deep in his chest, "Salve, Nyria!" There was a peal of girlish laughter, and Stephanus threw down his graving tool and darted to the door. Nyria stood by the bird's cage, and Ascalaphus was rubbing his head against her fingers.

"Now I owe thee a sweetmeat for that," said Stephanus to the parrot. "For once thou hast spoken truly. Greeting, Nyria. Thou comest as the light of morning, but I looked not for thee. How is't thou art in Rome seeing Julia is gone to Albanum?"

"She took Thanna to tire her in my stead," answered Nyria.

"And thou hast been nigh two days in Rome and hast not come near me!" said he, reproachfully.

"I had other things to do. 'Twas late when Julia set off, and yesterday I went to the Cœlian as I had been bidden by the Domina Valeria."

"I desire to hear naught of that proud dame," he growled.

"Then thou shalt not hear. See, Ascalaphus rebuketh thee," and Nyria laughed again, for the bird flapped and screeched, catching the word, "A proud dame! A bargain for a proud dame!" "Thou hast best look to thy manners," said Nyria, as she drew Stephanus back into the shop. "What art thou making, Stephanus—something pretty?"

"First show me thine arm," said he. "I will bind it afresh."

"There is no need. Euphena hath dressed it for me. Let me see thy work. A bracelet, is it? I know not those bright green stones."

"They came from the east and were brought thence by Paris, the dancer. They are called chrysoprase."

"Didst buy them from him?"

"Nay," returned Stephanus. "I am paid for the working of them."

"And thou art graving a legend on the stones. Wilt read it to me?"

She had taken up the bracelet, and was turning it about with girlish curiosity. Stephanus leaned over her, a hand on her shoulder, and looked with just pride upon his work. He was esteemed a skilled graver, and lovers employed him often in the fashioning of tokens, upon which he would cut words of sweet meaning in Greek, Persian or Hebrew letters. These he culled from an ancient parchment of designs that now lay unrolled upon the dresser. He would write deep into the stone with his sharp instruments, afterwards tracing the writing in gold. His brushes and gums for so doing lay about on the bench, and the inscription on the bracelet was nearly completed. It went round the pieces of chrysoprase which were strung together by slender gold chains. Nyria tried to make out the characters as an untaught infant might try to spell its alphabet. Stephanus laughed.

"Thou wouldst be clever to read that, little one. 'Tis writ in Persian. Shall I read it to thee? The gods grant thou mayest one day be of like mind with him who made this motto."

As Stephanus translated there was a tremble in his voice.

"'*No crown is brighter than the crown of love.*'

"Ah! my little princess," he said tenderly. "Would that Stephanus might set such a crown as *that* upon thy golden head!"

"Princesses wear not crowns, Stephanus. Crowns are for those who reign."

"Truly, I know a princess who hath reigned right royally since she was ten years old," replied Stephanus. "They name her Nyria, and her throne is the heart of one Stephanus, goldsmith and jewel-vendor in the Vicus Margaritaria at Rome."

Nyria blushed. "Thou art foolish, Stephanus. I am Julia's slave, and no princess."

"Once thou didst tell me different," he answered laughingly. "Dost remember, my little lady, how when thou wert a small child in Euphena's hut, and I picked thee up and kissed thee, thou didst slap my face and chide me sharply for treating a princess thus? That was the day thou camest into this poor kingdom, Nyria." And he laid his hand upon his heart. There was earnestness in his voice, though he laughed again. When Stephanus laughed his great shoulders would shake, and his face would crinkle up like an autumn leaf, and his eyes become small and shiny. Nyria liked him best when he was merry. And she liked that he should call her "his little lady," for though a slave could not be a princess she might be like a lady.

"I have no mind to be made mock of," she pouted. "Then was I a baby, or I could not have spoke so foolishly. Prate no more nonsense, Stephanus, but tell me whose arm will this dainty bracelet clasp?"

Stephanus shook his head teasingly. "Thou wouldst give thine eyes to know, Nyria. But I may not tell thee. 'Tis a secret."

"Now have I not kept many a secret? And even though thou dost sometimes try to hide one from me, the end is ever that thou tellest me all there is to know."

"Thou art a little wheedler! Well, I trust thee not to betray me. And in truth 'tis only mine own wit that hath divined the secret. I have told thee half of it already. Guess. But thou must fly high, I warn thee.'

"'Tis for Julia," she cried at random; but again Stephanus shook his head.

"Alack for Julia, there is one higher than she. Guess again."

"Then it must be for the Augusta herself. Hath Paris ordered it for a gift to Domitia? Oh! Stephanus, 'tis not well."

"Hush thee, child!" exclaimed Stephanus. "A customer cometh. Dost hear Ascalaphus calling? I need not Dinarmid when the bird keeps watch."

"Ho! ho! philosopher," Ascalaphus screeched.

"'Tis Juvenal and his pupils," said Stephanus, looking out. "And with him the astrologer Ascletario."

Nyria glanced with interest towards the door. A strange-looking person had entered in the wake of Juvenal. Ascletario was a tall, emaciated man, dressed in sombre robes, and wearing a peculiar pointed cap. He had dark hair turning grey and a long beard tipped with white. His face was pallid and extremely thin, with hollows in the cheeks and a high-bridged narrow nose; and his large brown eyes seemed to see a great deal as they looked out from under a green shade that protected them from the glare. It was said that Ascletario spent so much time in star-gazing that he could not bear the light of day: and indeed he was so rarely seen in the streets of Rome that his person was quite unknown to most people. He lived on a wild spur of the Esquiline overlooking the Campania, but though Nyria, in her rambles, had often passed his hut she had never seen him there. Only once had she met him, and that was when he was going to visit Euphena in the slaves court at Julia's house. Lingering at the door curious to know what traffic Euphena could have with this stranger, she had gleaned that it was from him the old Ethiopian learned much of her mystic lore. Euphena had come out suddenly, and sharply bade her to go about her business. Nyria would have fled shamed but that Ascletario himself stayed her with a gesture.

"Deal not harshly with the maid," he had said to Euphena. "Young girls are ever eager to draw the veil from Destiny's face." Then he had turned to Nyria, adding, "Be content, little maid, with that which lieth plain before thee. Seek not to discover what the gods have hidden, for with wisdom and knowledge there must surely come pain."

And Nyria, scarce daring to answer him, made obeisance, murmuring, "Yes, sir," and went her way.

Now, Ascletario, going into the shop, courteously addressed Stephanus, who gave him and Juvenal greeting. The astrologer had called for the instrument Stephanus had mended, and Nyria, hiding herself in the shadow, listened interestedly as the men talked together while they examined the telescope which Stephanus had set right. Juvenal was a man of grim expression and plebeian type. He was born of the people and had been a small farmer on the Sabine hills before he came to Rome and turned philosopher. His movements were slow and his manner deliberate. He was rather short and broad of build, thick-set, with a heavy cast of countenance that was framed in coarse, reddish hair and beard.

Nyria had seen him many times in Stephanus's shop, and though reputed to despise women, he was kind to her after a fashion. Juvenal had dropped in more frequently on Stephanus of late, for since, in the previous year, Domitian had expelled the philosophers from Rome, the few permitted to remain were not anxious to bring themselves into notice by orating in the Forums, and Juvenal, though not among the proscribed, had received a strong hint to keep himself quiet, and was forced to abandon his lectures and to turn instead to private tuition. So he employed himself in tutoring the sons of better-class tradesfolk, and when he walked with them through the Forums listening to the pleadings, and discoursing on learned topics, he usually turned in at the end for a gossip with Stephanus, while the boys remained outside amusing themselves in teasing or teaching the bird, and looking at the trays of goods.

It was a sore vexation to Juvenal to be obliged to give up public speaking, for though hard on other people's failings, he was not without his own, and conceit in regard to his gift of oratory was the chief of them. Stephanus used to joke him on it when he first began orating at the corner of the Lower Forum, which led to the Velabrum, and the herb- and fish-markets and bazaars frequented by the slaves—a poor quarter, but having much trade, and being greatly thronged by the populace. Here it was that

Juvenal made his reputation. Later on he moved nearer to the great Forum, and would there mount that rostrum from which many philosophers addressed the people.

Now a higher-class audience gathered to hear him, for the ædiles did not permit food-sellers, hucksters of mean wares, and the riff-raff of the population to linger in the regions which the nobility traversed. Only those who carried their goods—sweetmeats, cooling drinks, fruit, and the like, on trays, might pass that way, and these were not allowed to remain stationary. For round this part of the Forum were public offices, and it was close to the Carinæ, where lived many high persons employed by the State. Hard by the philosopher's rostrum was an office at which any person whatsoever could be hired, from a poor nobleman to fill a vacant place at a dinner-party, to a professional beater for a refractory slave. Matho, the lawyer, had his office adjoining this block of buildings, and he, together with Flavius Archippus, the rogue philosopher favoured by Domitian, Martial, the sycophant poet, Euphrates the Stoic, who had married a patrician wife and who, while he preached abstinence, had the city ransacked to procure dainties for a banquet of twenty courses, with many others, came in for the bitterness of Juvenal's gall.

But perhaps it was Matho who got the most of his vituperation, because Matho, listening from his office windows, and hearing Juvenal's abuse of himself, reported the satirist and obtained a prohibition against him, although he was not able to compass Juvenal's banishment. That was before Matho failed and lost money and clients, so that he had to betake himself to the Lower Forum, at which Juvenal openly rejoiced. Formerly Matho was fat and arrogant and prosperous, wearing a gold signet and purple robes, and reclining in an inlaid litter; but afterwards the skin hung loose on his yellow countenance and his limbs trembled and became flabby, and his small squeamy eyes looked more than ever sideways. Matho was reckoned a sharp lawyer, though he was not always employed on clean work. Most men despised, or affected to despise Matho, but they were glad of his help when cunning was needed, and his word was listened to as the word of informers always is. But, in spite of all, many noble and fashionable persons used to gather round the rostrum of Juvenal, and he gloated in rating them to their faces, and in the name they gave him of "The man with the two-edged sword for a tongue."

Stephanus laughed at Juvenal's stories of his encounters with Matho and the rest of his opponents. It was a wonder, Stephanus declared, that Domitian did not have vengeance on Juvenal for his bold talk. But Juvenal had a knack of escaping by the skin of his teeth: and it was said that Domitian remembered how Juvenal had prophesied good things of him in the beginning of his reign, and for that reason did not call him to account. Juvenal had once held a high opinion of Domitian, believing that he would purify the ranks of Roman society and be a patron of letters, for he was a man of some culture, and thus Juvenal's bitterness against him had its root in disappointment, since Domitian's vices grew apace.

"Methinks, friend Juvenal," Stephanus would say, "'tis wisest not to search out the sins of the great. My time is too well occupied in trying to earn a livelihood for me to concern myself with the mismanagement of public affairs. Poor traders should leave matters of state to the rich and idle," and Stephanus would laugh while Juvenal preached.

"Thou dost make thyself out a shameless dog, Stephanus, caring for nought but thy bone and to bask in the sunshine. Luckily thy deeds speak better for thee than thy words, else wouldst thou not have earned the gratitude of so many bleeding slaves and persecuted freedmen."

"The gods have made me of flesh and blood that stirs at the sight of other flesh and blood in pain. He's not a man, be he Greek or Roman, who, when he understandeth somewhat of bodily pangs, lifts not a finger to cure them. But ills of mind I leave to be doctored by men of mind, and none is better fitted than Juvenal to deal with them."

And Stephanus's eyes would twinkle while Juvenal, flattered by his appreciation, would, maybe, take out a roll of parchment and read some scathing invective he had written against the nobles, or the women, or the priests of Rome. He hated them all. Most of his knowledge of them, however, was bought from slaves, and Nyria knew that slaves who could be bought would as often as not sell lies as truth, and had no respect for Juvenal's sources of information. She smiled now from her corner by Stephanus's work-bench to hear Juvenal growling out a tale of enormities committed at some fashionable entertainment that had lately been brought to his notice, and to which Stephanus, after listening good-humouredly, replied,—

"My friend, if thou wert one of these fine folk thou wouldst take delight in such things too, though at present they appear to thee contemptible."

"I had like to fancy myself one of the lowest beasts of the field rather than share in such pleasures," retorted Juvenal. "Praise Jupiter, I am no hypocrite like Euphrates, nor a low parasite such as Martial."

"Thou wouldst do well to take lessons from Martial," said Stephanus, with a twinkle in his eye, "seeing that great Jove, whom both of ye profess to serve, hath taught him how to pay due reverence to place and dignity, which is what the gods themselves expect."

"Now, by thieving Mercury, who stood sponsor for Martial, I will serve no gods again if *that* be a pattern of the men they favour," swore Juvenal in his unkempt beard. "But it doth make a philosopher wonder," he went on, in more thoughtful tones, "whether indeed these gods who sport in high heaven are worthy of our faith and supplications, seeing that they cannot control men's evil ways, or else choose not so to do."

Stephanus flicked away some dust from a case of gems which he put before Ascletario, who was peering about among the goldsmith's goods, then turned to Juvenal.

"Oh, ay! The gods of Rome find it more pleasant to revel on Olympus than to come down and set things straight in this mad city of the Cæsars. Too busy are they with their own loves and espousals, their quarrelling and their wantoning to trouble themselves over our little lustings. In very truth, were *I* Father Jove, with so shrewish a lady-wife and so large and riotous a family, I should have enough to think of without concerning myself over the grasshoppers that plague the earth."

Ascletario, meanwhile, had turned from the case of gems, and joining the other two, they went towards Stephanus's work-dresser, where Juvenal took up the bracelet and began to examine it with an odd smile on his face. Perceiving Nyria, he gave her greeting, and as the girl rose in response she saw Ascletario's strange eyes fixed upon her.

"Thou art the maid I met in Euphena's cabin—she who did desire to interrogate destiny?" he said in a gentle tone. "Hast heeded my warning, little one?"

Nyria made obeisance. "Yes, sir," she answered; and Stephanus put in eagerly,—

"Of what didst thou warn Nyria, Ascletario?"

"I bade her not pry too closely into secrets that the gods keep hidden," answered the astrologer.

"Ay, ay, but *I* would learn somewhat of Nyria's fate, and who better able to foretell it than the wise Ascletario, whom even Domitian fears."

"Domitian fears all astrologers since the Chaldeans predicted that he should die by violence—as assuredly he will," replied Ascletario, calmly; and as he spoke he looked in a penetrating way at Stephanus.

"I would that I might know the fate of Nyria," said Stephanus again, and Juvenal put down the bracelet and drew closer, for even he was superstitious. "Nay, I ask not what end may overtake her," the goldsmith added hastily—"'tis too far off, pray the gods—but look nearer if thou wilt, Ascletario, and prophesy what her condition on earth may be five years from the present. Will she be wed ere then?"

The astrologer turned his deep eyes on the girl, and did not speak for a moment or two, then he said slowly, "I can prophesy naught concerning Nyria's earthly condition five years hence."

"Naught!" repeated Stephanus. "But at least thou canst say if she will be wed."

"That should be an easy oracle to deliver, for surely so fair a flower is not like to wither for want of tending," remarked Juvenal, with heavy pleasantry.

"'Tis the fairest flowers which are cut down in a storm," answered Ascletario, and there was sadness in his voice. But he would say no more, only adding that no man's prophecy might overset the edict of the stars.

"But a man's arm might, if it were strong enough," exclaimed Stephanus, roughly, and Ascletario replied, with gentle courtesy,—

"Nay, friend, it needs no astrologer's vision to see that this maid hath indeed a right strong arm ready to serve her. Yet, good Stephanus, there are other powers greater still."

"None greater than a true man's love," muttered Stephanus, and as he got out some fresh tools from a drawer in the dresser he contrived to put an arm round Nyria and to whisper in her ear,—

"Fear naught, sweetheart. No storm shall harm thee while Stephanus is at hand."

"Nay, I fear naught," she said simply, meeting the astrologer's regretful gaze. Ascletario changed the subject by complimenting Stephanus's skill and diligence; then, having taken possession of his telescope, he paid for its mending and departed.

Juvenal was chuckling to himself over the bracelet when Stephanus took it from him to continue his graving. Juvenal tapped the goldsmith on the cheek with a saturnine laugh.

"'Tis not news to me that the bauble must reach its destination ere Domitian returns from Albanum. But thou hast time. Didst hear about the monster Adriatic turbot sent up thither, and how Cæsar hath convened the Senate in hot haste for a council whether the fish be cooked whole or cut in pieces. That prodigy will take some time of digestion, as thou mayest for their comfort inform Paris and Domitia."

Stephanus frowned and glanced at Nyria. "I know not of such matters," said he, curtly.

"Nay, it takes a wise man to fathom a fool's folly," said Juvenal, giving another chuckle, which the parrot outside echoed. "By the gods! I know not why Domitian is not contented to divorce the lady, unless it be that he fears the Prætorians or liketh not the fair Julia's way of playing Empress. He sorely lacketh brains. Dost mind, Stephanus, that Paris was first Domitian's favourite? 'Tis but in following her lord's example that Domitia hath learned to love. Thus doth the starling let the cuckoo enter his nest, thinking not that soon there will be no room for himself; and who shall say to whom are due the eggs hatched therein? So not satisfied with being the cruellest knave that ever ruled o'er Rome, Domitian must needs be a fool as well. He resembleth Nero in many things, but not in this, for Nero was no ass in spite of all his braying."

As Stephanus made no answer, Juvenal continued: "For one grain of sense do I give Domitian credit. Did he not keep Domitia so short of money she'd have paid Paris's forfeit at the theatres ere now and fled with him from Rome. As things are, Domitia eateth her heart out at the Palace, and Paris doth fulfil his engagements. Perchance he would not leave them, for Paris loveth his art even better than his mistress. The man's a fool," the philosopher went on, "who maketh any woman his mistress, but he's a worse one that serveth twain, of whom one is a woman and the other ambition, for in that case, of a certainty, he will satisfy neither."

Stephanus had been fidgeting for some time with his tools. Now he said, ill-temperedly,—

"Cease thy scandals, Juvenal. Nyria understandeth naught of these things."

Juvenal turned to the girl who was listening. "Friend Stephanus thinketh that such subjects are unfit for a lady's ear," said he. "But I wager, Nyria, thou dost hear stronger talk within the sacred precincts of Julia's dressing-room."

Nyria made a grimace. "It matters not. Stephanus will tell me all himself when thou art gone."

"Thou art a very catling!" cried the goldsmith. "How can Stephanus keep his tongue silent when thou comest round him with thy wheedling ways?"

Juvenal laughed. "Art thou another fool, Stephanus? I had reckoned there was one less in Rome. But thou dost ill name this maid, for the cat, in Egypt, where they have brought the species to such perfection that they must needs worship it, is counted a very mine of wisdom; and Nyria, methinks, is not so wise as she should be, else would her shoulders suffer less from Bibbi's lash. For the rest, what woman was ever born that knew not how to wheedle a man? Were *I* a law-maker in Rome, I'd decree that all women should be avoided by men till each man had grown as strong as the gods."

"Nay, by thine own showing, Juvenal, a man would be in ill plight before a woman were he no stronger than the gods," retorted Stephanus, scoring with the last words. "Fine game have women made of the gods—ay!—even Zeus himself."

But Juvenal had waved his hand and vanished into the street, where Ascalaphus's guttural farewells followed him.

V

The next day Nyria carried a basket of wild autumn flowers and leaves, on which she had expended much thought and care, and laid it at the Domina's feet. Valeria accepted the offering graciously, and bade Æola put it on a tripod beside her in the room where she sat. Then calling Nyria to a stool near, she desired her to relate again what she could remember concerning Veleda and the Bructeri, so that Phileros, the secretary, might take her information down in shorthand and adapt it later to dramatic purposes. The tragedy had been going ill, it appeared, for Valeria complained that inspiration failed her, and even now she seemed to take very little interest in the halting answers which Nyria gave to the secretary's questions, for her thoughts were wandering elsewhere. This alarming literary task embarrassed the slave-girl, who managed it so poorly that the Domina at length became aware of her shortcomings and dismissed the secretary. He put up his papyrus and inkhorn, venturing a regretful protest, while Nyria begged to try again, but Valeria waved both aside.

"Nay, 'tis no matter. Thou shalt essay thine own hand at the tragedy if thou wilt, Phileros."

The secretary bowed. "As the Domina pleaseth," he answered and went away. Seeing Valeria in an absent mood, Nyria drew near Æola, who was re-threading a chain of gold and coral beads; but Æola was far too shy to chatter before her lady, so Nyria amused herself in looking round the Domina's study. It was not a small room and was very richly furnished—though not gaudily, like Julia's special retiring-room. This one gave a suggestion of simplicity, but it contained many costly things and rare works of art. In the recesses stood bookcases filled with rolls, the ends of the sticks elaborately carved, and even jewelled, while the upper shelves supported busts, chiefly of the Greek poets, and small copies of antique pieces of sculpture. Ceiling and walls were frescoed in panels, and told the story of Persephone. First, the radiant golden-haired girl stretching out her hand for the wondrous many-headed daffodil; then, the earth opening, and the Dark King issuing forth in his chariot with the deathless steeds; and so on, showing the halls of Hades, the eating of the pomegranate seed, the sorrowing mother shedding blight on orchards and cornfields, and at last the return of the bride to the upper world again, fruitful once more during the allotted time she passed upon it.

There was a wide arched doorway in the room, looking out on to the terrace and garden, with glass let in at the top, and heavily-embroidered curtains that could be drawn to shut out draught. On the floor Persian silk carpets were spread; and another archway closely draped led to the Domina's bed-chamber. Sumptuous though it was, the room had a look of homeliness. All the chairs and tripods were of graceful design, and before the windows stood a large marble couch heaped with wadded rugs and cushions, upon which Valeria was now reclining. Near the door, on a tripod, was placed a great mother-of-pearl shell filled with scented water, from which rose a beautiful marble Venus, slightly tinted, while a Pallas Athene, cold and stern, held on her upraised spear a silver lamp. Valeria's literary taste was evidenced by a large inlaid writing-table bearing ink and pens and sheaves of papyrus as well as piles of tablets, while there were flowers and plants everywhere, doubtless of Gregorio's setting, but to-day the youth was not in attendance on his mistress.

After a little while Valeria dismissed Æola and talked to Nyria, but in a preoccupied manner. Her face wore an expectant expression, and she listened to every sound that came from without. Presently she said,—

"Thou dost remember Licinius Sura? I find him learned in the matter of Greece and those writings in which I myself am interested. To-day he is to bring me a record that he hath made of his own travels in Attica and Thessaly. Therefore will I dismiss thee when he cometh. Thou must visit me another day, child."

But the next time Nyria came Marcus Licinius Sura was again with Valeria. He seemed to be a constant visitor. It was about the fifth hour when she entered the garden gate and mounted to the terrace—a sunny autumn morning, full of the scent of lingering roses and late myrtle, the tender shoots of which were turning brown, while the lower rods were yet sheathed in bloom. Valeria was seated in her favourite chair beneath the trellised portico, and Licinius Sura occupied the marble bench near her. He had a scroll unrolled in his hand and was reading from it in his deep musical voice, though he seemed to know almost by heart what he read, for his eyes went more often to Valeria's face than to the parchment that he held.

Nyria paused at the top of the steps, uncertain whether to turn or to proceed, but seeing that Æola sat on the broad marble rim of the fountain, occupied in winding some embroidery silk, she stood close by, waiting until Valeria should notice her. But it was Licinius who first perceived the girl and exclaimed, in a tone half laughing, half vexed,—

"Ah! here is the little watch-dog! Shall I stop, Valeria, while the maid delivers thee her errand?"

Valeria started and her face changed, its eager expression giving place to her usual stately reserve.

"Nay, I pray thee, continue," she said hastily. "Nyria can wait. Seat thyself, child. I will speak to thee presently," and she again bent towards Licinius, while he resumed his reading. Nyria sat down on the fountain rim beside Æola, who nodded and smiled, and at a sign from Nyria took the skein of silk from her knee and put it on the other girl's outstretched hands. Æola did not trouble herself about the poem to which her mistress was listening, or the reciter, and had no eyes save for her task, but Nyria watched the two, and her imaginative mind took in every word of the story.

It was a legend in verse of Xamiel and Xydra—the most ancient of all love-legends, having come, it was said, from a nation that dwelt in Greece at the beginning of days, before the breaking forth of the Great Waters and the re-peopling of the earth. Yet was it a story that through all the ages had never grown old—this story of the princess doomed to sleep on in an enchanted sleep until the god-like prince should come and awaken her with a kiss.

Thus Xydra, the first woman of Greece, beautiful Xydra, slept in Thessaly. And through that sleep of æons—so went the legend—all Nature slumbered with her—great rocks, beasts, and trees that never stirred a leaf, and fields that put not forth blade of grass nor ear of corn. A dead cold world, wherein not even a baby zephyr played to fan Xydra's face, nor stream prattled, nor bird sang to lull her in her slumbers. And now at last, into that strange grim silence, descending from heaven on rainbow wings, there came Xamiel, the god-prince. He bent o'er the sleeping maid and kissed her lips until they kissed him back again; and then he kissed her eyes, which opened wide and blue as violets in the morning, gazing up into the eyes of Xamiel, while low and sweet her voice spake to him.

"Lo, I awake, beloved, in answer to thy kiss. I am thine henceforth, and thus we shall fulfil our joint destiny. For of thee and me shall be born a child from whom will spring the race of Thessaly and by whom shall all the earth be blest."

Then he, passing his arms around her, drew her to his breast; and his mantle dropped and the rainbow wings upsoared, bearing them both through the blue and over Thessaly, leaving behind the cold drear world where Xydra had slept. And as they went Zeus poured heavenly balm upon them, which, falling in dew from his wings and from her garment where'er they passed, swelled into streams by which new verdure unfolded, and gave life to the still rocks and sapless trees and fertilised the earth, making Nature bring forth and all things multiply. So, too, there arose in due time a mighty race of men in Thessaly—fruit of that divine pair who floated higher and higher yet, till they reached those most blessed regions beyond Olympus, of which none but Zeus holds the key. And this the king of gods and men gave to Xydra and to Xamiel.

Nyria knew the legend well—as, for that matter, did Æola, and likewise many a child of Rome. For in the slaves' quarters, as in noble houses, there was told to amuse the little ones a simple version of the love of Xydra and Xamiel. Often had the slaves' wives told it to Nyria when she played round their cabin doors. Only old Euphena the Ethiopian, who brought her up, had laughed it to scorn, saying that in the land from which she came it was thought better to sing the praises of some strong warrior who could count many bloody spear-heads drawn from the bodies of slain foes, or else of a woman who shrank not from dealing death to avenge her honour or the life of a friend. That, she said, was good meat for babes, but that they were not like to thrive on sickly love-stuff such as this. Nevertheless, Valeria seemed thriving well on that food with which Marcus Licinius Sura fed her. For a wondrous new light shone in her eyes, and there had come a soft roundness to her face, which had lost its look of melancholy pride. The change in her seemed to strike Sura also. He threw down the scroll when he had finished reading, and bending towards her said, in a voice that, with its ring of triumph and its suggestion of deep feeling, thrilled even Nyria,—

"Ah! Valeria, methinks that thou, like Xydra, art waiting for the kiss of love to wake thee from thy passionless sleep into the warmth of life that love alone doth bring."

Soon Nyria's brief holiday was over. Julia had now come back from Albanum, and to-day was about to visit Domitian at the Palatine.

Her women had robed her and she was choosing the jewels wherewith to deck herself. The process of choosing them was a matter of moment, for Domitian liked her to wear those he had given her, and they were many and various. Her chief waiting-woman, Æmilia—spare, elegant, no longer young, and with a worried expression tempered by a mechanical smile—was taking out, one by one, chains, bracelets, brooches and head ornaments, from two great golden caskets, held by underlings, while Julia stood in the centre of the room surveying the trinkets critically.

It was a gorgeous room, a mixture of blue and pink and silver, tapestried with splendid embroideries, and canopied in pale blue silk, on which were sewn silver stars. On the floor lay Persian rugs. The bed was of carved ivory, inlaid with precious stones, and a winged Love held back the hangings. A screen of marble fret-work at one end of the chamber, divided off, but hardly concealed the bath and massage rooms beyond it.

Upon marble and inlaid tables were strewn a profusion of boxes, bottles and toilet implements, all richly gemmed. Marble and silver statues, the work of modern sculptors, gave a clue to Julia's tastes, which were not of a refined order. The lady herself was large, florid, magnificent. Her hair, elaborately dressed in frizzed tiers above her low forehead, was in the height of Flavian fashion, but made her head seem disproportionately big, though she was of heroic build. Her face was handsome in a sensuous way, and she would undoubtedly have had an immense attraction for a particular type of man—the attraction of generously-rounded bosom and wide hips, of red lips and bright eyes made brighter by being outlined with kohl, and of a complexion which still had the bloom of youth, notwithstanding that its ruddiness was heightened by paint. Her dress was even more splendid than usual. The stola had a deep embroidered flounce, in colour approaching as nearly as possible to the imperial violet; and draped upon the hips was a silk overdress, worked in various shades—bronze-red predominating—the pattern outlined in gold thread and seed pearls. Above this again, falling in folds from the shoulders, hung the palla, a gorgeous mantle of amethystine purple, also embroidered in gold, while beneath, to cover her neck and arms—for the autumn wind had a nip in it—Julia wore a quaintly-worked jacket with long sleeves of green silk, rucked from the elbow and dropping over her heavily-ringed hands—quite the newest thing in fashionable women's attire.

Julia tried against her green sleeves the effect of several chains, and at last settled on one of huge yellow topazes that went three times round her neck and fell below her waist. With the jacket she could not wear armlets, but she had innumerable brooches pinned about her person, and on her head was a gold coronal that stood up behind the tiers of hair, and to which one of the maids attached a rose-coloured veil of silk gossamer.

In the interval of dressing, scolding and transacting business with the chief steward of her house, Julia had taken her midday meal—an informal repast laid in the private dining-room adjoining her sleeping apartment. Her lunch, however, had not been unsubstantial. Julia's appetite was robust, and she had eaten with relish pickled lamprey, stuffed thrushes, boar's-head brawn garnished with olives, and some marvellous concoctions of pastry and sugar, washed down with copious draughts of Setinian wine. Consequently she felt heavy and was decidedly cross. The topazes adjusted, she nevertheless ordered another goblet of this rich vintage to be brought to her, and then scanning the row of women, called sharply to Nyria, who, her own special duty as hair-dresser having been completed earlier, was waiting in the dressing-room for orders.

"Why dost thou idle there, brat? Do I keep slaves to do nothing? Is that a fitting dress in which to follow me to the Palace? Or wouldst thou compel Julia to wait, while thou dost trick thyself out to attract Cæsar's notice? Let there be no combing out of those yellow curls for the Emperor to pull at. Hold thine eyes lowered, and behave as a slave should, or thou wilt get twenty lashes and shalt have thy head cropped close as that of a malefactor."

Nyria had come forward and stood with her eyes on the ground and her hands folded in an attitude of obedience. Julia's words had stung like wasps, the blood rushed to her cheeks, and she bit her lips in impotent pride.

"Dost thou hear me?" exclaimed Julia.

"I hear, Most Noble."

"Then obey. Go, put on that robe Cæsar sent for thee, for I will not have it said that I dress my slaves shabbily—though the Augustus's generosity does not befit such as thou. Haste, and know that for every minute I am delayed thou'lt answer to the lash."

Nyria flew.

"Command the litter, Thanna," said Julia, and proceeded to issue further peremptory orders to her bevy of attendants, one of which was to desire the instant presence of her husband, Flavius Sabinus. In a minute or two he entered—a tall, thin, gentle-looking man, with long features, a sparse fair beard and mild blue eyes. He looked kind and by no means dull-witted, but he had an oppressed air. Julia held out her hand impatiently for her husband to kiss, while with the other, she waved dismissal to the slaves.

"Hath aught gone amiss, Julia?" said Sabinus.

Julia laughed derisively.

"One might well suppose so, since I want a word with thee. 'Tis a thing of rare happening, eh, Sabinus?"

His sensitive lips twitched at the sarcasm.

"I should be better pleased were matters otherwise between us," he answered sadly. "Thou knowest I have no wish nearer my heart than that we should live in true conjugal union as was once the way of Roman wives and husbands."

"Shade of Lucretia! When was that? In Ovid's age of brass, or before Deucalion's flood? Talk no folly, Sabinus. I hate sentiment; 'tis fit only for such turtle-doves as Pliny and Antæa, and those pious bores, our worthy Cousin Domitilla and her prig of a husband, whom may the gods keep at a distance! Methought we had done with conjugal virtues when I refused to get up of a morning and preside with thee at family worship in the Lararium. Pray, dost thou still practise that antiquated custom?"

"Ay, Julia, and I shall continue that which my father and mother did before me, and which I consider the duty of every Roman parent and householder," answered Sabinus, with all the severity of which he was capable.

"Well, thou art not a parent," said Julia, jeeringly, "so far as *I* know, at least. But even a milksop such as thou, can be a popular consul."

"I would gladly resign the honour," he answered. "In these days 'tis safer not to be a person of prominence."

"Doubtless, but thou dost not flout the honour—if I know it! 'Twas not to bandy words I sent for thee, however, but to tell thee this. The Emperor and Empress dine with us next week. Hold thyself in readiness."

"I should have preferred that thou hadst first consulted me," said Sabinus.

"What about? 'Tis an honour for which half the patricians in Rome are sighing."

"To entertain the Emperor costs more money than we can afford," objected Sabinus.

"Where is my dowry?" cried Julia. "Did I not bring the fortune of an Emperor's daughter?"

"Thou art spending it fast, Julia. I have had it in my mind for some time to remonstrate with thee on thine extravagance—as well"— he hesitated—"as well as upon another matter."

Julia's handsome face darkened with rage. "Thou dost dare too much, Sabinus. I am not accustomed to be remonstrated with. Thou mayst do it once too often."

"I dare for thine own sake, dearest, and for the sake of mine honour. Thou wert an emperor's daughter, but thou art my wife, and my cousin—doubly bound by family tie. I will not believe, Julia, that thou art anything but guileless, but I know Domitian, and thy close intimacy with him hath set evil tongues wagging. While thou wert at Albanum scurrilous writings were affixed to thy statues. The example has been cited of Claudius and Agrippina. To put a stop to this gossip I have a plan to propose."

"Thy plan, then—state it, Sabinus! I knew not that thy brain could conceive one."

"It is that we should both leave Rome and dwell for a time on our Tuscan estate."

"Leave Rome! Freeze on the Apennines! I'll be divorced sooner. My answer to thy plan, Sabinus, is that even now my litter waits to take me to the Palatine."

He looked at her with dumb reproach in his eyes as she struck a small silver gong on a table near and the slaves came trooping in.

"To the litter!" said Julia, "and twenty lashes for Nyria if she be not in waiting."

At these words Nyria advanced with the conventional gesture of submission, making also an obeisance to her master, who, as he was leaving the room, gave her a kindly smile. The girl was dressed in a fine white woollen robe, richly embroidered in floss silk and fastened on the shoulders with silver clasps—a more sumptuous garment than was usually worn by those in her position, but it was the Emperor's gift. She looked very small and childlike and pathetic.

Julia took a last look at herself in the mirror, and then led the way through the great atrium, magnificent with colour, gilding and some fine trophies of war, especially of the Jewish campaign, that she had inherited from Titus. Here, too, was a fine statue of that emperor, before which stood a small gold-inlaid altar with fresh flowers placed daily upon it. This was the only family worship to which Julia lent herself.

The walls of the atrium were decorated in coloured marble and had some rather gaudy paintings depicting, with coarse realism, the enchantments of Circe, while the fountain in the middle, banked with flowers, dropped scented water from the beak of a kingly swan, whose long neck twined amorously over the shoulder and bosom of a finely-sculptured Leda. Chairs of state were placed on a slightly raised platform at the top of the atrium, and other seats of various degrees of honour were ranged about. At the side there opened a chapel with an altar to the Lares, about which hung the scent of incense and of the daily offerings. Pillars of coloured marble extended down the hall, supporting a gallery; and through two draped archways, and at the end of the corridors which skirted the master's study and library, glimpses were had of the peristyle, with its Corinthian columns and plants and statues surrounding a central fish-pond.

Outside, the litter was waiting with its strong Parthian bearers and a retinue of attendants, all dressed in white and red and gold-the Imperial livery, to which Julia by right of birth laid claim. Presently the procession went on its way—an imposing one notwithstanding that it lacked the lictors upon whom Julia set so much store. Before the litter forewalkers went shouting, according to custom, "Make way for our lady, the most noble Julia, daughter of the divine Titus," but there was less need in this aristocratic quarter for the blows and pushes that heralded a great person's progress through the crowded streets of the city. So Nyria, protected as she walked behind her mistress's litter, was not obliged to pick her steps warily—at least until the road dipped into the Velabrum; but here it made a turn and ascended the Palatine across the Clivus Victoriæ, between the old house of Germanicus and the pile of Caligula's palace, to Domitian's magnificent new erection that surpassed all former Imperial dwellings in grandeur. Here, from the Palatine Forum, an immense flight of marble steps led towards the private entrance to Domitian's palace, the state official entrance being from the Roman Forum by way of the street of Apollo.

The great front of the Palace, with its frieze of bas-reliefs and fine pediment, where was set forth a gilded chariot of the sun, typical of the Emperor's divinity, was awe-inspiring to Nyria. Its huge portico and the rows of white pillars gave her sometimes a gruesome fancy that some immense, savage beast, in whose open jaws white teeth glistened, was waiting to devour her. In wake of her mistress's litter the girl toiled up those hundreds of stairs, so many and so steep as to try the strength of Julia's powerful bearers. Occasionally she paused on a platform, of which there were several, where orange trees and oleander and other flowering shrubs were placed at intervals, to take a look back at the city, said to have been turned by Domitian's touch into one of marble and gold. The topmost stage was bordered by beautiful pillars adorned with silver. Sentries saluted as the procession passed under a massive portico into a spacious marble court set with colonnades. Here stood at that time the famous statues of the Danaids. The thought of fifty women who had, all but one, murdered their husbands increased Nyria's childish horror of marriage; but the statues were beautiful and she liked to look at them. To-day, however, she was too timid to give them a glance, for, it being an hour when the Emperor received in state, the court was filled with Prætorians, drawn up in dazzling array, with the sun shining upon their gold-chased helmets and breastplates, and upon the broad curved heads of their lances, which threw out brilliant glints of steel. The officer of the guard gave the word of command, and the soldiers stood at attention, and, as Julia passed, made the royal salute—a slow movement of the lance across the breast to the left shoulder, slower still to the forehead, then in a flourish striking the pavement with a mighty clang of metal as a long blue flash went from rank to rank.

It was a fine salute—more splendid than in the days of Titus, who had never permitted any lances to be used except the short javelins he preferred for warfare. But Domitian liked show, and had instituted these tall lances for occasions of pageantry. Julia held greatly by the salute, finding in it some consolation for the loss of her lictors. This had been a recent concession from Domitian, and she looked upon it as auguring well for future favours.

Soon they were in the Palace itself, but Julia did not alight from her litter till several long halls inlaid with coloured marbles and lined by soldiers had been traversed and they had arrived in a wide ante-room carpeted in the centre, round which many more

Prætorians stood at attention, while a group of officers kept guard before a closed and embossed door, the entrance to the largest presence-chamber. Several of these came forward rendering sycophantic homage to the Emperor's favourite, but one, a tall, fair, good-looking young man, known as Alexamenos, seemed to notice the waiting-maid more than her mistress. Nyria was unaware of his attention. She looked only at the litter in front, or walked with eyes downcast and head bent, so that her hair shielded her face.

Two of the officers went to inquire the Emperor's pleasure, and Julia waited complacently, knowing well that she would be admitted. So came the order, and Nyria, standing close to the litter, held her shoulder for Julia's support in descending, her slight form tottering as that lady's weight rested upon it. The litter-bearers and retinue drew aside, for it was Julia's pleasure to enter the presence of her Sovereign unattended save by one woman, and of late Nyria had been chosen for that duty—why, she could not tell, and was entirely without suspicion that it might be by Domitian's order.

The great doors swung open. Nyria trembled at the vision of scarlet and gold. She could never overcome her dread of Cæsar, who seemed to her less like a man than a beast which might devour her. The lictors, bearing their bundles of gilded rods, who had been standing by the opening, moved apart, permitting Julia and her attendant to pass. Now they were in the throne-room and face to face with Cæsar.

An imposing figure, this lord of the world who chose to rank himself with the gods of Olympus—imposing, not from any natural gifts of person but from the arrogance of his mien and his magnificent attire. He was tall, stout, broad of build, his trunk rather too big for his legs, his head large and bald on the top, with a fringe of reddish hair falling round his forehead and over the gemmed collar that clasped his bull-neck. His features were fairly regular, but spoiled by the unhealthiness of his complexion, which was a fiery red patched with sickly pallor, and was in disagreeable contrast with the extreme whiteness of his thick arms and shoulders. His glassy-looking eyes were set in almost lashless rims, and his pale eyebrows were so thin as to be barely perceptible. He gave an impression of restless melancholy. Yet, when he smiled, his expression was good-natured, and suggested a certain fellowship with humanity.

He had been hearing cases that morning in his Basilica, and his dress was even more than usually splendid. He wore a tunic of brilliant scarlet woven of finest wool, and edged with a deep fringe of gold. It was draped full on the chest and about his knees, and fastened on the shoulders by straps and gold buckles, leaving his arms and neck bare, except for the heavy bracelets and collar, as well as a gold chain with links and tassels of great pearls that hung down over his breast. Falling round him, like an imperial mantle, was a toga, loosely girt, of richest white silk embroidered with gold and many-coloured threads in a large design of birds and fruit.

The Emperor rose as Julia approached—a rare honour—and gave her his hand. She kissed it in effusive homage, and at his bidding took a seat on the slightly-raised daïs, where he sat. Nyria hung back, thankful that Cæsar did not notice her obeisance, as with hands to her forehead she prostrated herself nearly to the ground. Afterwards she retired behind the ring of men who were paying duty to their sovereign. One of these—a courtly-looking person of about thirty, with a pleasant, clever face, who was dressed in a white, purple-bordered toga, and carried in his hand a roll, with a blue seal hanging from it—had been talking to Cæsar and now saluted Julia, bowing from the waist as the fashion was, his hands crossed before him. Julia did not extend her hand to him—in the Emperor's presence that would have been a breach of etiquette—but nodded, as she remarked, with clumsy pleasantry, pointing to the roll,—

"Who ever saw Pliny without a volume of parchment in his hand—save indeed when he payeth *me* a visit?"

"Where Julia reigns, even the Muses retire abashed," replied Pliny, gallantly.

Julia gave him a sharp glance. She admired Pliny immensely, but had an uneasy feeling that that accomplished gentleman was sometimes politely sarcastic at her expense.

Now, however, she could spare him none of her attention, but began whispering and laughing to Domitian, who had placed her on a chair beside him, and was bending towards her, his prominent eyes blinking, his face a deeper red, smiling delightedly at her obvious blandishments.

The courtiers exchanged glances, for gossip was rife about the pair, and Julia's manner seemed absurdly arrogant. In truth there could be no doubt that she had Cæsar completely under her sway. Domitian was at this period in a strange, uncertain temper, and his visit to his Alban Villa had been marked by the most savage eccentricities. It was there that he forced Acilius Glabrio, a man of senatorial rank, to fight naked in the Amphitheatre with a Numidian bear, and though Glabrio's immense strength had saved him, there were dark hints that it would not be for long.

Since his return, Ælius Lamia, the first husband of the Empress Domitia, from whom she had been wrested on their wedding-day, had been ordered to execution; and but yesterday, on the paltriest excuse, Epaphroditus, the Emperor's secretary, had been sent to his doom. Like a wild beast that had tasted blood, Domitian raged for slaughter, and it was in such dark moods as these that the fiercer and more lustful elements in Julia's nature appealed to him most, giving her that strange empire over the world's Emperor which was the talk of Rome. Cæsar fidgeted in his ivory chair, interrupting his low-toned talk with Julia to frown and glare impatiently at the throng of men around, while they in their turn waited uneasily for the signal of dismissal that every moment they expected. Domitian, however, delayed to give it, and, calling up one or two, addressed them on topics they had apparently been discussing.

"These pleadings, Regulus, will go before the Conscript Fathers. I will announce to them my pleasure. Rubrius, concerning this news of the sedition of Civica Cerealis, I have decided to send a trusty general to Africa who will take over command of the Legions. Thou shalt hear shortly of the appointment. As for Valerius Asiaticus—he hath begun the march from Gaul, thou sayest. Let him continue it to Forum Julii, and there await my orders. Some dogs are best kept in the kennel."

Then the Emperor signed to Pliny, and, pointing at the purple-bordered scroll he carried, said, "Thou wilt see to it that the rest of the prætors act upon that mandate. And touching the matter of Agricola's petition—Tacitus hath no doubt advised his father-in-law that the duties of a proconsulate are but ill suited to his years. Thus, I will hear Agricola's petition to retire—yea, I will hear it."

Pliny bowed, and drew back with the customary "At Cæsar's pleasure," and Domitian turned once more to Julia.

"Grant me grace, fairest Julia. Cæsar were an ill father of the State did he not put its business before his own pleasure. Hast aught to say, Norbanus?" as the Præfect of the Prætorians made a movement forward.

"Doth Great Cæsar mind the two Judæan youths that were brought before him in the Basilica this morning—and who remain yet in custody? They who claim to be of the royal house of David—sons of one Jude who calls himself the brother of their Lord whom they do worship. Is it not the will of the August that these traitors be made an example to all blasphemers and usurpers?"

Domitian laughed as if the idea amused him, and Julia cried, in her strident tones, "Hath Cæsar then a rival claimant to his throne? I would I might mete chastisement to him who dares blaspheme our divine ruler."

Domitian laughed again. "That thou shalt do, Julia, but were it on these simpletons, thou wouldst make of Cæsar a laughing-stock. For they are but farming lads with hands horny from the plough—young madmen, not worthy of thy wrath nor mine. Methinks, Norbanus, thy zeal did somewhat overstep thy wit. Cæsar hath little need to trouble himself concerning that Christus of whom they boast as their royal kinsman. For when I asked them of His kingdom,

Julia, they said 'twas not of earth but in the heavens, where at the end of the world, He would appear to judge the living and the dead. It seemed to me that Jove and Pluto had best decide that matter between them. 'Tis not for my treatment. As for the boys, Norbanus, send them back to their farm, and levy such a tax upon its produce as shall keep them well employed to pay it."

Norbanus saluted, not too contentedly. "Great Cæsar is pleased to show his clemency. Yet would I warn the August that this sect of Christians may prove dangerous, for it begins to spread in Rome."

Domitian glared with his prominent eyes. "Find me, then, a worthier example than these two fools upon whom to wreck my vengeance."

"'Tis a strange superstition," said Pliny, suavely, "as are all that come from out Judæa."

"What manner of king or god is this Christus that some of these people worship?" asked Domitian, indifferently.

"'Tis the god with the ass's head, August," replied Norbanus —"the god for which an officer of Cæsar's guard is said to have a liking—that Alexamenos on whom I asked judgment from our own supreme lord-god, the divine Cæsar."

Domitian blinked, as if weary of the subject. "Alexamenos is too good a soldier to be crucified," he said testily. "Moreover, I questioned him, and he denied that he worshipped an ass. Now, sweet Julia, I know thou hast family matters on which to consult me, and it will pleasure me to talk with thee in private for a while."

He made the gesture of dismissal, and bowing ceremoniously before him, the whole company filed out. Domitian gave a curt order to his lictors and the great entrance doors swung open and closed again as the men with the gilded fasces passed forth to keep guard with the soldiers outside. There remained in the throne-room only Domitian, Julia and Nyria. A significant look was interchanged between the Emperor and Julia, but just then Cæsar became aware of the small slave's presence and looked down at her.

"So there is the little Curly Locks!" he said. "Come hither, girl, and let me measure how much thy hair has grown since I saw thee last."

As if to encourage her, he put out his hand with the forefinger curved like a talon. The look of that hand always frightened and yet fascinated Nyria. It was a thick, cruel hand, the skin unnaturally white and hairless, the short fingers, with square nails, carefully trimmed and laden with rings. There was something horrible about the hand, and Nyria could not help trembling as she advanced at its summons. Domitian laughed at her terror.

"By Venus's doves, I will not eat thee. Hast thou not yet

learned that though Cæsar is mighty, and not to be gainsaid, nevertheless he doth not pounce on pretty, good, little girls? Hast been good, Nyria, eh?"

Nyria answered only by an obeisance, for Julia's fierce glance forbade her to speak. She would gladly have retired had her mistress given her permission. But Julia dared not go against the Emperor's whim. Domitian called the girl closer, with rough banter.

"And how long did it take thee to arrange thy hair this morning, Curly Locks? Thou dost grow a woman, I declare." He laid his hand on the girl's bare shoulder. Nyria crimsoned and shrank. Domitian frowned. "What, dost not like being touched by Cæsar? 'Tis an honour slave-girls would compete for—if they might. But I'll wager that with use thou'lt take more kindly to such favours. And what is a woman's soft flesh for but to pat, or pinch, maybe, when she is naughty. Art thou naughty, Curly Locks?—say, shall I punish thee?" He pulled a tress of Nyria's hair so fiercely that she nearly cried, then let it drop suddenly, and pushed her away as if in disgust. Turning to Julia, he whispered something which changed the pout on her lips to a seductive smile.

"Go, girl," said the Emperor, harshly, to Nyria. "I will talk alone with thy mistress. Amuse thyself till the hour has run out—" he glanced as he spoke at the wheel of the clock—"then return and wait in the ante-chamber till thy lady summons thee."

"I would send a message to Domitia," said Julia—"my invitation to the banquet which thou, August, dost deign to honour. It is more politic," she added in a low tone. "I have had words with Sabinus of which I will tell thee. It appears that the plebs insulted my statues while we were at Albanum."

"Be at ease, for the transgressors have been found, and to-night they will be torn in pieces by dogs," replied Domitian, grimly. "Thou art right, however; Domitia had best accompany me. Meanwhile, I have much to say to thee, Julia. I have considered the request thou madest me at Albanum, and may perchance accede to it. Come, we'll talk the matter over."

Julia beamed. Then, bethinking herself of Nyria, she said,—

"Thou hast the letter I gave thee. Deliver it to the Augusta, and inquire from me of her health. Bear her also my excuses for not visiting her to-day. Say that it is by the will of Cæsar I remain with him to discourse upon family matters."

"Cæsar's will is the law of his slave," replied Nyria, with the formula customary before the Emperor. Her hands raised humbly to her forehead, she retired backward from the imperial presence through a small door at the side of the daïs. Then Domitian rose, and, taking Julia's hand, led her toward his private apartments, through an archway closed with curtains of crimson and gold. Nyria was aware of the significant bravado of Julia's message to the

Empress, and regretted being obliged to carry it. She had often felt sorry for Domitia, having on more than one occasion seen her humiliated by Julia.

So the girl lingered in discharging her errand. She knew the Palace fairly well, and asked no questions of the servants she met, all of whom eyed her curiously, knowing her to be the special attendant of Julia.

In order to reach the Empress's apartments she had to skirt round the inner precincts so as to avoid the Emperor's private rooms and the great peristyle lined with mirror-like stone in which he was wont to walk. Passing a less ornate court nearer to the slaves' quarters, she saw a litter waiting with simply-clad bearers, and, coming towards it, an elderly woman, with a young girl, in whom she recognised Phyllis, once nurse both to Domitian and to Julia, and her niece Lavinia.

Nyria made a humble little salutation, for Phyllis was a freed-woman and a person of some consequence in the Palace, where she had a set of rooms and due service apportioned her. She was said to be in Domitian's confidence, and she had a warm maternal affection for him, notwithstanding his faults.

"Thou art in attendance on the Lady Julia?" she said to Nyria.

"Yes, Phyllis: the Most Noble hath audience of Cæsar," answered Nyria, deferentially.

"Thou hast come far from thy waiting-post," returned Phyllis.

"I go with a message from my mistress to the Augusta Domitia," answered Nyria.

Phyllis's lips drew in displeasedly. Gossip said that she hated the Empress Domitia and would gladly have seen Julia in her place; this because Domitia never concealed her dislike and contempt for her husband, and had once said that she owed Phyllis a grudge for not having let Domitian die in infancy—a remark that Phyllis was not likely to forgive.

"Haste then, lest the Lady Julia be requiring thee," and Phyllis passed on.

Nyria pursued her way, and by-and-by found herself at a wide terrace, of which the end near her was screened off by tall orange trees and other plants set in large marble jars, and marking the boundary of the Empress's private promenade. This terrace faced south, so that the sun was full upon it, though here and there a purple awning or a trellis covered with late roses gave shelter from its rays. Nyria knew that Domitia might often be found in this particular spot, and presently she caught sight of her among her ladies.

The Empress paced to and fro with the restless tread which was always a sign to those about her that she was inwardly disturbed.

She looked very distinguished. Her white robes, heavily embroidered in gold, fell becomingly round her thin figure, but though, like Julia's, they were made after the latest fashion, their style was dignified and tasteful, while her hair, curled and arranged in a dark feathery mass upon the top of her small head, was neither overdressed nor disproportionately towering.

Nyria stepped meekly forward, and making the prostration due to a member of the Imperial family, presented the tablets and craved leave to deliver Julia's message to the Augusta. One of the women in attendance took the letter to the Empress, who glanced at it disdainfully.

"The girl may speak," she said in a voice that was shrill but not unmelodious. "This"—and she handed the tablet haughtily to her head-woman—"this requires no answer at present. Thou mayest inform thy mistress," she added, addressing Nyria, "that the Augusta will signify her pleasure later concerning the matter on which Julia hath written."

Nyria again made obeisance, then stood waiting to fulfil the rest of her errand.

"What hast thou to say?" demanded Domitia. "Truly I know not what further subject of communication there can be between Julia and the Empress."

Nyria humbly repeated Julia's message, and as she listened Domitia's lips curled in scorn.

"Say that the Augusta thanks Julia for her inquiry. Tell her that Domitia's health is good. Also, that since it is Cæsar's command which causeth her seeming discourtesy, the Empress accepts Julia's apology."

Domitia's air was royal. She turned and resumed her walk, while Nyria, murmuring reverentially, "The Augusta shall be obeyed," retreated backwards, though the Empress's face was from her, till she had passed the rows of orange trees and out of Domitia's private domain. Presently she heard a slave calling the third division of the hour, and slowly retraced her steps to the little ante-chamber appointed for attendants.

It was some time before Nyria was summoned. Then the doors of the throne-room were again opened, and the lictors with their golden rods ranged themselves within, for the Emperor had returned. Domitian sat on his chair of ivory and gold, while Julia bent to kiss his hand in ceremonious farewell. The lictors had divided in lines and she was passing between them, when Nyria, about to follow her mistress, having rendered the necessary homage to Cæsar saw, to her terror his red eyes fixed upon her. He stretched out his thick white hand and made a clutch at her hair to detain her.

"Here, Curly Locks, put this round thy pretty throat and wear it as a gift from Cæsar."

Dexterously he threw over her head a gold chain that caught in her yellow curls. She turned on him a startled glance, which made him laugh at her. She would gladly have plucked off the chain and flung it at his feet, but that she feared him too much.

Domitian chuckled at her distress and, stooping, whispered in her ear, "Learn to behave prettily, Nyria, and shrink not when Cæsar deigns to touch thee. Put more flesh on thy bones, for shrimps be poor handling, and cease to be a babe. 'Tis time thou left babe-land behind if thou wouldst find favour with Cæsar—which perchance thou mayest. But, on peril of the lash, breathe not a word to thy mistress."

Then he let go her hair, playfully switching it over her face, and Nyria escaped thankfully, her head bent, and her falling locks hiding the smarting tears. She dashed them away as someone came up and spoke kindly to her. It was Alexamenos, the young officer of the guard who had noticed her arrival, and who now made the excuse that her mistress desired attention. Julia commanded that her veil should be adjusted, and as Nyria, standing on tip-toe, drew its folds about her shoulders, she saw that the green silk sleeve of Julia's jacket was fastened by a new brooch of magnificent diamonds. Cæsar had been in a generous mood that day.

Now the great lady deposited her substantial form upon the heaped cushions of her litter, and the stalwart Parthians shouldered their imperial burden. The arms of the Prætorians clanged again in a royal salute, and, to the surprise of the guard, six lictors detached themselves from the bodyguard of the Emperor, and, with their golden rods uplifted, stepped to the front of the litter. Julia's bosom heaved with pride and satisfaction. She put apart the curtains that her eyes might be gladdened by the gleam of those rods and the mace they bound. No woman in the empire was permitted them save the Augusta, and Cornelia, the head Vestal: no man who had not sat in the curule chair. Even in the lifetime of Titus, Julia had but wrested a privilege not lawfully hers. But to-day, her answer to the remonstrance of Sabinus would be the sound of the lictors' rods striking against the door of her house on her return, an announcement of power and imperial favour which the sternest husband in Rome might not gainsay.

VI

Things were going busily in Julia's house. It was the morning of her banquet to Cæsar, and the household, having risen with the dawn, was now all agog—stewards of every grade, wine-bearers carrying dusty amphoræ, gardeners with flowers and greenery, underlings of all sorts, scavengers removing rubbish, servers of each department, all running to and fro, while purveyors from the city were arriving continually with different goods. The caterers had been put to considerable trouble, and the host and hostess to much expense, in collecting throughout the city markets rarities which there was not time to procure from their native homes—sturgeon of the Volga, oysters from Britain, Spanish anchovies, lampreys' roes, the flesh of specially-fed German boars, asparagus out of season, flamingoes' brains, mangoes and young shoots of bamboos from India, and all the other delicacies without which a Roman feast would have been considered incomplete. Then, too, the mimes and singers, who were to furnish entertainment between the courses, had to be hastily engaged, and this was a matter of many sestertii, since such artists as Latinus the buffoon and the incomparable Paris were not to be had—even for the privilege of performing before the Emperor—except at enormous fees. All this had made Julia extremely cross, and caused her to abuse her maids freely. Unluckily for Nyria, she had chanced to offend, and Julia, in a fury, had struck her so heavily with the silver-handled mirror, which was her favourite weapon, that the girl had dropped in a dead faint on the ground, whereat the others carried her to the slaves' court, and left her there to come round as best she could, not daring to stay beside her.

The slaves' court at the back of the house was a big open square, surrounded by small cabins of two rooms—a kitchen in front and bedroom behind it—flat-roofed, and joined together like cubicles, each with a tiny patch of ground divided off also, while along the whole length of the cabins ran a low mud wall. Upon the wall women were leaning, gossiping with their neighbours, or else engaged in some household task. Some were seated on the flat stones set against the wall, idling or doing bits of needlework. Here and there were open fireplaces, at which some were cooking, and about the court there played a number of children—little black Nubians, swarthy Asiatics, brown Arabs and fair-skinned Northerners, who enjoyed the bustle and got between the legs of the carriers rushing about. At many of the cabin doors were crones past work, kept as hut-minders, who basked in the sun with striped blankets drawn around them; and among these the most noticeable was old Euphena the Ethiopian, by whom Nyria had been brought up.

A curious monkey-like figure she was, dressed in a scanty brown skirt and an orange jacket, half buttoned and showing the bones of her neck and her shrivelled breasts. She squatted in the sun, her head bare, its coarse, frizzy black hair tied round at the ends with shreds of red and yellow wool, one skinny arm clasping her knees, the other raised, as in her claw-like hand she held out a greenish brown stone with characters graved upon it, which was suspended from a cord round her lean throat. She was staring at this with her glittering eyes, set in yellow whites, her lips drawn back a little from two black-looking fangs that hung down from her upper jaw, while she muttered in some foreign tongue, scarce audible, over the stones.

"See! the witch is saying prayers to her god," cried a pert, handsome young woman who had just then entered the court by a door separating it from another, on to which looked the apartments of Julia. "Methinks thou hast not got much benefit from thy god, Euphena, seeing that he spared thee neither husband nor child, nor hath given thee aught of comfort in thine ugly old age."

Euphena stopped her incantation to scowl at the speaker.

"Hold thy sharp tongue, Thanna. I have that which is of all comforts the most comforting, as thou mayest know to thy cost, seeing that it is power to work ill on those I hate."

Thanna tossed her dark head and laughed shrilly.

"Thou art a sorceress, as we all know, Euphena; nevertheless I fear thee not. Where is that little fool Nyria? Hath she yet come out of her faint?"

"Here I am, Thanna. Doth Julia send for me?" and Nyria staggered up from a long flat stone, where she had been lying with the sun upon her. She was very pale and her blue eyes had a distressed look.

"Thou simpleton! If thou hadst learned to manage Julia as I have she'd deal thee fewer blows. But 'tis not in thy nature, Nyria, to turn a clout to thine advantage."

"What dost thou want of me, Thanna, since it be not for Julia," said Nyria, wearily.

"Nay, thou owest me something for a good turn I have done thee, for I told Julia that thou wert very sick and like to fall from behind her chair to-night if thou didst not have fresh air. So I bring thee gracious command from our sovereign lady to keep thy puling face out of her sight till thou hast put a smile on it. Thou art free, then, Nyria, till the robing—save for seeing to the flowers on the banqueting-table—and for that thou hast Thanna to thank."

"I do thank thee, Thanna. 'Twas kind of thee."

"And what wilt thou pay me for it?" asked Thanna, coming nearer, her hands on her hips, and a quizzical but greedy look upon her handsome face.

"Nay! I might have known that thou wouldst never do a kindness without bargaining over it. But I have naught with which to pay thee," said poor Nyria, sadly.

"Now, had *I* the favour of Stephanus I should be richer of trinkets than thou art, Nyria. Thou wouldst not find Thanna returning empty-handed from a visit to her lover."

"That I well believe," replied Nyria, with some spirit. "When thou comst from gadding 'tis never without some new kerchief or gewgaw."

Thanna laughed. "How knowest thou that I do not get them in the markets? Yet, whether bought with Cæsar's coin or not, be sure that I pay full price for them. Thou art a moon-brained baby, Nyria, and knowest neither how to trade for thyself nor to value that which thou dost possess. There is a thing that thou hast which is sore wasted on thee, and I'll confess to coveting it."

"What is that?" asked Nyria, puzzled. Thanna put on a wheedling air.

"Surely, Nyria, 'tis sin to waste, and it goes to my heart to see a goodly possession thrown away on one who holdeth it of no account. I'll make a bargain with thee, if thou wilt. Oft have I seen thee chastised for reason of thy stupidity in not knowing how to wile away Julia's mood, when a timely word of flattery would at once have turned the edge of that she-wolf's wrath. I could sometimes save thy skin for thee as I save mine own, and will engage to do it, when occasion serves, if thou in thy turn wilt give me up" —Thanna paused a moment mockingly—"if thou wilt give me up Stephanus," she suggested.

"Cease prating, Thanna. 'Tis *thou* art simpleton."

"Nay, I mean what I say. Stephanus hath a thriving trade and would make a worthy husband. If thou wouldst send me with a message to say thou wilt have no more of him, and that he had best console himself with Thanna, I can answer for it that I could make him turn to me. And thou needst lose nothing, Nyria, seeing that thou carest naught for him save as friend and physician, and I will not deprive thee of either. Say, then, for what thou wilt barter the favour of Stephanus?"

Sick and sore though she felt, Nyria could not help laughing.

"Thou hadst best go to Stephanus thyself and ask him whether he is willing to be bartered."

"'Twould be of no avail without thy word," answered Thanna.

"Thou shalt have, moreover, any trinket of mine that thou dost fancy, Nyria, if thou wilt say the word."

"I care not for trinkets; and if I did, I would not gain them in such a way."

"Then if thou carest not for trinkets," hastily put in Thanna, "give me thine amber beads to pay for the service I have done thee."

Nyria shook her head. "Nay, I may not give thee my amber beads. Now, get away, Thanna; since thou hast obtained me freedom for a while, let me go to the hill-side. There will I consider how I can pay thee."

Nyria let herself out of the slaves' gate and took the winding road towards the Cœlian which led past Licinius Sura's villa. Outside the house two litters were waiting, the slaves in attendance dressed in coarse travelling suits of the kind worn by servants of small farmers or traders, and with no distinction of livery. Thus she judged that it was not Licinius himself who was about to go on a journey. Through the garden entrance—a door set under a small projecting portico, and sheltered by a clump of plane trees, Nyria caught a glimpse of a bowery roof and two figures issuing from the villa with a child between them. Nyria had just time to draw back behind the thick trunk of a plane tree as the child ran forward sobbing. He was not more than three years old, but precocious and singularly handsome. It was easy enough to guess his parentage, for he had the curly hair, the broad brow and dark blue eyes of Licinius Sura, while his complexion was that of Salome.

Licinius Sura looked impatient. He wore the usual visiting garb, with his wine-coloured toga arranged in careful folds, but his companion was dressed for a journey.

Salome called crossly after the child, "Come back, Marcus, and cease crying. Thy tears stir not thy father."

The little boy toddled back, but Licinius lifted him to his breast, gazing at him with proud affection. It was clear that, whether born within or without the law, this son of his owned a large share of Licinius Sura's heart. Salome looked on, her dusky beauty spoiled by sullen anger. Two slaves came out bearing baggage, which was bestowed in the second litter, and now the bearers stood waiting to shoulder the poles. Licinius put down the boy, who began to whimper once more.

"I tell thee thy father doth not want thee, nor me, Marcus," exclaimed Salome, resentfully. "He sends us from him so that he may not be obliged to keep us hereafter."

The boy sobbed more loudly, not soothed by his father's caresses.

"'Tis needful, Marcus, but it means no lessening in my love for thee. Take heart, little man. Thou'lt see Tibur and the great waterfall, and the hill where the vines grow, and it will not be too late for the vintage. See, I'll give thee a coin to buy cakes and sugared almonds."

"And be grateful, Marcus," cried Salome, angrily; "we needs must be content with the crumbs of thy father's favours, since he chooseth to bestow the best of them elsewhere." And then she broke down and sobbed too. "Am I not thy wife in all but that last cruel clause of the law, and am I not the mother of thy child? Give him whom thou holdest dear, and give me a lawful right to the protection of thy roof. My Marcus! Let us stay."

She raised herself, for she was a short woman, and clung to his shoulders.

Licinius kissed her, and she pressed her advantage with caresses. But suddenly he steeled himself and thrust her from him.

"Peace, Salome, peace! Plead no more. My love and my protection are thine and the child's, but 'tis no time in my fortunes for the committing of a further folly. Who knoweth what destiny may be in store? Ask not that which I shall never grant. But calm thyself and depart discreetly. Affright not little Marcus in this way. Thou wilt find Tibur beautiful in autumn, and I will visit thee ere long."

Salome's pleading turned to bitterness again.

"Beware!" she hissed. "Thou mayst drive me forth, and seek thy pleasure as thou wilt, but thou shalt pay dearly for it. Scorn and suffering shall not pass thee by since thou hast heaped them on Salome. She sues no more. Nevertheless, though her hour may tarry late, be sure that it will come."

She took the child in her arms and walked down the path towards the road. Licinius, accustomed to her impetuous moods, took no heed of the threat, but signed to the bearers to bestir themselves. Salome stepped into the litter, they shouldered the poles, and she thrust her head back through the curtains.

"Farewell, Marcus—*but remember.*"

Licinius saluted, smiling tolerantly, and the litter went on. He watched them till they were out of sight on their way towards the Tiburtine gate, and then he walked briskly along the road which Nyria herself was about to take. She followed him at a distance. As she suspected, he was bound towards the Cœlian, and she saw him pause at the villa of Paulinus and enter by the door in the wall which led to Valeria's garden. Nyria now made no attempt to seek an entrance, but passed on sad at heart.

Slowly she walked round the curve of the Cœlian, and heading a valley between that hill and the Aventine, she sought the wild outlying spur below which were the disused quarries. Nyria loved this bit of waste ground. It was a rocky knoll separated by a ravine from any habitations. Upon it grew a few gnarled oaks and some stunted shrubs; but where it was sheltered by an outcrop of rock and faced due south, wild flowers and herbs flourished abundantly and bees found a hunting-ground. The knoll commanded a magnificent view of the Campania and of the distant mountains, with the heights of Præneste to the left, crowned by the great temple of Fortune above its four tiers of terraces.

The landscape beneath the morning sun had an autumnal air, wind-sighs alternating with the rustle of migrating birds. The leaves of the myrtle shrubs were turning brown, and though here and there lingered a rod of cistus, a clump of crimson poppies, or a seeding foxglove, winter was creeping inevitably on. Snow would soon fall and whiten Soracte. Piercing winds would blast the Campania. Leaves and flowers alike must fade. And though roots and stems might put forth new shoots and fresh foliage succeed the old, that which had been scattered by the elements could never bloom again.

A dreary sense of futility oppressed Nyria, though she could not have put her feelings into words. She was conscious that there was no escape from immutable law. What matter that Bibbi whipped and Julia gibed? The slave-girl must fulfil her ordained task till the hour ring for her release. And the world would go on laughing or groaning, as the case might happen. 'Twould all be the same in the end. There was no evading the decrees of capricious Fate, which apportioned good to one and to another evil—indifferent alike to happiness and sorrow. Those who were rich enough might propitiate the gods with offerings, but for the slave, and especially the slave-woman, life held no hope, for the gods troubled themselves not at all about a creature so insignificant. If indeed the gods existed! But mayhap they took their turn like the seasons, living only for a short space. Stephanus said that the gods of Greece were dead. Nyria wondered what had become of the gods of her own forests. Had they died too when Roman conquerors led her people captive? For they, it seemed, were deaf, or blind, or powerless as the others, since they had not rescued Veleda—their chosen priestess-queen—nor guarded their sacred groves from desecration. Were, then, the gods of all countries a delusion? Were there no eternal deities who concerned themselves about human affairs? Nyria longed for an unchanging God-Father who would always listen to the petitions of His children, even if He could not help them much. What matter if one then were lonely and miserable, for this dear great God-Father would see and be sorry and love one all the more. 'Twould be easy to brave trouble if one knew that there was another life afterwards where all would be made right. It was the cruelty and hopelessness of everything that was so hard to bear.

Thoughts like these passed through Nyria's mind as she sat on the brow of the hill, where it overhung a landslip fringed by a few stunted pines. Here were some juniper bushes and wild thyme, monkshood and hemlock, all of which were used by Stephanus in the concoction of his medicines. Nyria, seeing them, wondered why he had never brought her to this spot.

She had seated herself against a rock, whence by peering through the undergrowth at the edge of the landslip she got a view of the Campania, and also of an angle in the zigzag path by which, before the quarries below had ceased to be used, workmen made their way from the poor quarter near the Tiber. Looking down, Nyria noticed, as she had done on former occasions, that people were passing along this path, and she wondered again who they were, and what they could be doing in so unfrequented a locality. Her curiosity quickened, she descended a goat-track till she was stopped by a crumbling bit of wall overgrown with hedge creepers, and peered over it.

These people were mostly dressed in dark clothes, the women with veils or hoods drawn over their faces. Several had gone by, when two men and a woman attracted her notice. One was an elderly man in a grey mantle, with a long brown beard streaked with grey and an expression of singular sweetness and dignity. He was a stranger to the girl, but in the gait of the others there seemed something familiar. Suddenly there swept along a fierce gust, common to the Campania at that time of year, which sent dead leaves flying, and caught the mantles of the men, while it blew aside the woman's veil, so that as the three struggled with the blast their faces were exposed. To Nyria's surprise she recognised Flavius Clemens, her master's brother, and Domitilla, his wife and cousin, daughter of the Emperor's sister. Domitilla's veil had blown against the stem of a pine sapling, and Clemens came to her aid, admonishing her to cover herself quickly. The lady only smiled.

"There is no need to be so careful," she said. "Winds blow at Heaven's command, and not at that of evil men; we may trust the Master to preserve us. Seest thou not," she went on, "this place is deserted, save by our own friends. All Rome is in the Forum, or voting at the Ovilia Septa. I think this early morning hour is better suited to our purpose than the time after nightfall. As thou knowest, Clementus, we dine this evening at the house of Sabinus and Julia, who give a banquet to the Emperor, and our absence might have occasioned questioning, since an invitation to meet Cæsar must be reckoned a command."

He whom she called Clementus smiled as he answered, "Thou art right. The Master Himself said, 'Render unto Cæsar the things which are Cæsar's, and to God the things which are God's.'"

Domitilla having adjusted her veil, the three now moved on, disappearing presently in the curve of the road downwards.

A few more stragglers passed, but Nyria felt too exhausted to watch them longer, for she had had no food that morning, so she re-climbed the goat-track wearily, and seated herself in a dip of the hill-side. Presently she started at the sound of a voice, and looking up, saw Stephanus standing over her, a wallet in one hand and in the other some freshly-gathered roots and leaves.

"Why, little one! what bringeth thee hither at this time of day?" he asked.

"What bringeth *thee?*" she replied. "Methought thou wert always in the shop at this busy hour?"

"There is but little business doing in the Forum this morning," he answered. "Everyone is voting in the Campus Martius, where some election takes place. But what hath befallen thee, my dear?" He laid down the plants and wallet, and throwing himself on the ground beside her, took her hand within his own. The little caress was brotherly, and Nyria did not shrink from it. She told her tale of the morning's disasters. Stephanus listened compassionately. Then, seeing that she was weak and unstrung, he foraged in his wallet.

"Thy pulse is faint. Thou needst food, my child. Eat, then will the world seem less fearsome a place, though, in truth, it giveth thee but scurvy treatment. Nor may I help thy lot, alack! Well! I bide in patience, and will not whimper. Drink—drink, the wine is good, and I have more than will suffice for two." He made her sip from a leather bottle of the red wine of the country that he carried, and nibble a piece of brown bread intended for his own meal. Nyria revived; the food and the sense of companionship brought back her childish light-heartedness.

"But thou hast not told me why thou camest to this place, Stephanus?" she said, leaning against his shoulder. "'Tis mostly by another gate we go to gather herbs?"

"That's true," he replied, "but to-day I needed some leaves and roots of savin, which I thought to find between this hill and the great Dust-Heap."

"Then thou didst not come with Clemens and Domitilla?" she asked.

He gave her a sharp glance. "Why ask?"

"Because I saw them walking down the zigzag path to the quarries. What do they here afoot and unattended?"

"There are often mourning festivals at the tombs," he answered evasively.

"Ay, but I could not see them go that way, though I watched. 'Twas as though the earth had opened and swallowed them up. Others went behind and before, in the same direction. I have noticed them oft, but never have I seen Clemens and Domitilla here. They had one with them called Clementus, with a face so kindly that 'twas god-like. He wore a grey cloak. Knowest thou if he be a philosopher?"

"'Tis a cousin of Clemens," said Stephanus, thoughtfully—"a man of learning. But, Nyria, say to none that thou didst see Clemens and Domitilla passing here afoot and unattended. Harm may be done by idle talk."

Nyria raised herself. "I am not given to gossip," she said. "That I leave to others."

He smiled. "Ay, ay, but there is method in *my* gossip, child. Maids are heedless in such matters, and 'tis not well to prate of the doings of great folk. What Clemens and Domitilla do is their affair, not thine nor mine."

"Seemingly 'tis thine, since thou art so concerned lest it be discovered. Have no fear, Stephanus; I've learned to be silent."

"At least," he said, "be sure 'twas no ill business, since of all women, after thee, 'tis Domitilla whom I hold in highest reverence."

"Worship Domitilla if thou wilt," laughed Nyria, "but 'tis foolish to talk of reverencing *me*."

"I speak but what is in my heart," he said. "For a certainty, Nyria, were wrong wrought on thee, or on my Lady Domitilla, I'd kill the man who did that deed—though it might be Cæsar himself."

"Cæsar!" echoed Nyria. "I'm afraid of Cæsar."

"Hath Cæsar done aught to make thee fear him?" asked Stephanus.

"Nay! nay!"—Nyria reddened from brow to chin—"save to pull my hair and tease, and when I went with Julia to the Palace, not long since, he said mocking words and pinched my neck; and then he gave me a gold chain."

"A gold chain!" repeated Stephanus, fiercely.

"Ay, with a pearl clasp. 'Tis pretty—but I hate it."

Stephanus's brow grew dark. "Do not wear it, Nyria. Let not Cæsar see thee wear it. Thou must not put on the Emperor's gift—dost understand?"

"Nay, I could not if I would, for Julia would be angry, and methinks that Cæsar must know that. But truly I want it not, Stephanus," she added, startled by the ugly look on his face. "Couldst thou sell it in thy shop? 'Twould bring some money, for the pearls are fine."

"Nay, nay, I could not. 'Twould cause trouble."

"I thought the like," said Nyria. "Then will I bury it. Julia will be very fine to-night, and Cæsar will notice naught but her."

This remark seemed to dispel Stephanus's gloom, and Nyria chattered on about the banquet and the guests. Did Stephanus think the grey-cloaked philosopher would accompany Clemens and Domitilla?

"The best of philosophers breed mischief," said Stephanus. "Euphrates the Stoic is the only one welcomed at fashionable tables, and that because he doth not practise what he preaches, but gives good dinners in return; wherein he is wise. A man hath but one life, and had best be merry in it."

Nyria looked at Stephanus doubtfully as he squared himself and took a pull from the wine bottle.

"I must go," she said, rising.

"I'll go with thee," he answered. "I have gathered all the savin and wolfsbane I need, and 'tis time I, too, were back. We'll take the road down the Aventine by the Herb Market, and since thou dost not like to be seen with me, I'll look in on a patient there, and thou shalt return alone to Julia's house." So saying, he slung the wine bottle on his belt, and laid the plants he had gathered in his wallet. But Nyria seemed reluctant.

"I go round by the Cœlian," she said.

"To see the Lady Valeria? She hath cast a glamour over thee." Stephanus shrugged his shoulders in manifest discontent.

"Thou canst reach thy shop that way as well as through the Velabrum," pleaded Nyria. "Walk with me if thou wilt to Paulinus's house. There is a private door in the wall by which I enter."

"Ay, I know—it leads to Valeria's private apartments. I saw Licinius Sura come forth as I passed. He goes fast, that gallant, and one might well suppose that Valeria is not so cold as Diana, to whom she hath been likened."

Nyria withdrew her hand. "Speak not thus," she said quickly. "Valeria is not as other Roman women."

"Time will show," retorted Stephanus. "Take my warning. There can be no true friendship between such as thee, Nyria, and a Roman dame. She but needs thee for some purpose of her own. When she needs thee not her favour will cease."

Nyria's lips quivered, but she disdained to answer. He bade her a gruff good-bye, and the two turned different ways.

VII

VALERIA was alone in her trellised court, the book she had been reading had fallen long since from her hand, and her women, whom she had dismissed, were still unsummoned. There were no sounds to disturb her reverie, but the dreamy hum of sluggish insects snatching the last taste of honey from the summer flowers, and the soft gurgle of the fountain as it dripped from the jaws of a marble dolphin. Valeria sat in the same attitude as when Licinius had left her—one elbow on the arm of her chair, her chin resting on her palm, her softened eyes fixed on space, as her thoughts came and went in a troubled but delicious unrest. Suddenly her body stiffened and her whole expression changed as she became aware of Nyria's approach. Fearing that she had offended by her intrusion, the slave-girl ran forward and prostrated herself at Valeria's feet.

"I beseech the Domina's pardon for coming into her presence unannounced, but I saw no slaves near, and the Domina had said I might enter by that door. I wait the Domina's commands to go, or to remain—as may please her."

Valeria recovered her usually gracious demeanour.

"Rise, child. It pleases me that thou shouldst stay," she said. "I was about to send for Gregorio and his lyre, but thou'lt amuse me better."

Her gaze wandered absently, and returning, surprised the slave's adoring look. The lady smiled.

"Methinks, Nyria, that thou hast some affection for me."

For answer, Nyria kneeled, and in a manner infinitely touching kissed Valeria's embroidered shoe. In a voice choked with emotion she said, "Domina, I would die for thee."

"There! there! I want thee not to die for me," and Valeria patted the golden head and bade the girl seat herself. "I may ask thee to do me a service, Nyria, but thou must keep it secret faithfully."

"Torture should not drag it from me," cried Nyria. "Only tell me, Domina, how I can serve thee."

"'Tis but a small thing—a letter—" Valeria hesitated. "Does not the house of Licinius Sura lie on thy homeward road?"

"Yes, Domina. Is it to Licinius Sura that thou desirest to send a letter?"

"Mayhap, mayhap. 'Tis no great matter, and I have not decided. But thou knowest, Nyria, discretion is a rare quality in slaves."

Valeria fell into dreamy silence again. Presently a man's voice sounded through the open door leading into the house—a loud, authoritative voice, which said roughly,—

"By the gods! have I not the right to seek my wife in her rooms? Where is the Domina?"

Someone answered cringingly, the words inaudible. Valeria had given a violent start, and for a moment was as if petrified, a look half alarm, half repugnance upon her face; then, stooping, she laid an imperative hand upon Nyria's shoulder.

"It is Valerius Paulinus who comes," she said. "Nyria, I give thee a proof of my trust that I could not show to any of my slaves. I do not wish to be alone with my husband. Therefore remain at a little distance—not too far off—until I myself dismiss thee. Dost understand?"

The girl answered only with her eyes, for at that moment a large shadow fell upon the pavement, and she had barely time to retire into the background before Paulinus stepped into the portico—burly and red, and coarsely handsome. He was heated, and wiped beads of perspiration from his brows, while his lips twitched beneath his moustache. There was a look of determination in his small dark eyes sunk in their heavy sockets. Plainly, something had disturbed his mind. He gave Valeria a brief salutation, then, going nearer, stooped as if to caress her, but she turned away her head and his lips barely touched her ear.

"By Juno! a cold greeting!" said Paulinus, with a coarse laugh. "May I perish if I know how to please thee! When a woman refuses her lips, 'tis generally because the price offered is not high enough. What gems will buy Valeria's kisses, since the most costly rubies to be had in the Porticus Margaritaria are of insufficient value? Surely 'twas an ungracious act to return me the necklace."

Valeria smiled distantly. "I sell not my kisses. Are not rubies the favourite stones of Galla?"

Paulinus flushed a deeper red. "Now, I would pardon that speech did jealousy prompt it, but since I know thou willest but to taunt me, the rubies shall adorn Galla's neck at Julia's dinner this evening, and when the world has proof of her complaisance thou wilt repent having flouted my offering."

"Does the world need proof?" returned Valeria, icily. "Martial, at least, has told us that Galla doth not price her favours too highly. Rest contented, Paulinus, for without doubt thy munificence will be bountifully rewarded. But let me hear to what cause I owe this unexpected visit.'

Paulinus's dark eyes looked at her from between their puffy lids in as much puzzlement as wrath. It was not given to Paulinus to understand Valeria. He threw himself upon the marble bench where Licinius had lately sat, and unclasping his toga, flung it to one side, while he stretched out his large limbs so that his knee touched her dress. It incensed him to notice that she flinched at the contact.

"By all the gods! Is't not *my* house to come and go in as I please? Art thou not my wife from whom, if I choose, I have the right to claim conjugal duty?"

Valeria's eyes flashed, but she answered quietly, "Thy right exists in name only. 'Twas forfeited three years ago."

"Three years ago, my dear, the case was different," said Paulinus, ignoring the point of her speech. "Since then thou hast matured, and mine admiration for thee increases. Milk-fed babes were never to my taste, I having always an appetite for spicy food. But one's palate wearies of over-sauced dishes, and a man comes to despise that which he has bought and which may be bought again by a higher bidder. It appears that there is one woman in Rome who cannot be bought—even by her own husband. I like the front thou showest to the world, Valeria, and it hath been my pride to say, 'Praise the gods, if my wife be cold to me at least no other man has found her warmer.'"

Valeria gave a shiver of distaste. Paulinus's voice had softened. He bent towards her, but she sat rigid, and Paulinus, with a discomfited laugh, drew back again. Glancing round he caught sight of Nyria.

"Is that little Yellow Hair?" he cried. "How comes she here?"

Nyria stepped forward and made the customary prostration.

"Send her away," said Paulinus, curtly, to his wife. "I want no other listeners. Be off, Yellow Hair!"

Nyria flushed scarlet, and would gladly have departed, but remembering the injunction she had received, looked at Valeria, who stayed her by a sign.

"My business with the girl is not finished, but her presence shall be no irk to thee. Nyria," she added, turning to the slave, "go yonder—to the steps of the terrace."

Nyria obeyed, but felt uncomfortable at finding that she was still within earshot of the conversation. Paulinus, however, seemed to assume that she was out of hearing, for he nodded sulkily and spoke in intimate fashion to his wife.

"I repeat, I have taken pride in the front that hitherto thou hast shown to the world. 'Twas worthy of the descendant of a goddess and the daughter of an emperor. Judge then of my wrath at learning that this excellent reserve of thine hath abated of late, and that Valeria, of whom 'twas said that her private apartments were as difficult of access as the cella of a temple, now frequently receives in them a gallant of most doubtful reputation."

Valeria winced as though he had struck her, and Paulinus, watchful of her expression, cried, in the language of the amphitheatre, "*Habet!* My words strike home. What hast thou to say?"

"I choose not to answer an insult," said Valeria, with dignity.

"That's subterfuge," cried Paulinus, roughly. "Thou knowest well to what gallant I refer."

She kept scornfully silent, while he continued excitedly,—

"'Twas talked of in the Porticus Europa this morning. That painted rake, Fabulla, started the tale, and Martial, to please her, handed round an epigram that he hid when I came nigh. Then Julia bade him show it to Cæsar, who hailed me mockingly. 'Oh, ho!' said he, 'Paulinus may no longer vaunt himself on having enshrined a new Diana!' And this to me—who have even wagered thee chaste."

Valeria's restraint gave way. "*Wagered!* And on *me!* How didst thou dare?"

"Dare! Why not? Thou shouldst be proud I pin my faith to thee. But I'd have thee know that I'm not pleased to learn this fellow hath been visiting thee while thine attendants were dismissed."

"Hast thou been questioning my slaves?" Valeria said disdainfully.

"What are slaves for but to be questioned?" retorted Paulinus. "'Tis I who have provided them to look after mine interests. The boy Gregorio—"

"'Twas *he*, then!" she interrupted. "I might have known as much. The boy wearies me with his insolent jealousy, and were it not for his music I should owe thee small thanks for having put him about my person. 'Twould please me better if thou didst employ his services as a spy elsewhere."

"Nay, nay," said Paulinus, hastily. "There's no harm in the lad. I only asked him whether thou wert alone. Never has it been in my mind to spy on thee, Valeria, for the good reason that till now I have had no cause. May the gods avert such deeds, since I swear by all the Immortals that now my chief desire is to dwell with thee according to the custom of marriage, providing the State with lusty sons, and with daughters fair as thyself. Tell me—for I know thou didst mourn the girl-child that died—dost thou not desire another daughter?"

Paulinus bent again, and tentatively put out his hand to touch hers, which clasped the arm of her chair. But Valeria made a gesture of repulsion, and clenching her fingers moved her hand away quickly, so that his encountered only marble.

Paulinus muttered furiously, "By Luna! of what use to beseech a woman whose blood is no warmer than Moesian snow?" A moment later, however, he softened.

"The gods bear me witness, Valeria, that I suspect thee not of infidelity. 'Tis true I've pledged my faith on thee, but, by Venus, thou, who art ice to me, shall never melt to another. Understand that. But there must be an end to this difference between thee and me. Thou shalt be my wife in fact, or I'll find means to divorce thee. And in that case, know that thou wouldst go forth a beggar, for though Vespasian gave thee a dowry, he was shrewd enough not to secure independence to the daughter of his old enemy. Now, Valeria, think the matter over. Let thy decision be ready for me by my return to Rome at the end of winter."

Valeria looked at him in sudden surprise. She forgot his threat in the suggestion of his absence.

"Before thy return!" she said. "Where art thou going?"

"To Egypt. This morning the Imperial mandate was given me and my time for preparation is short. I go to resume command for a few months in my old province, for Cæsar, to spite Agricola, who asked the post, and moreover hearing that Civica Cerealis is rousing disaffection in Africa, hath appointed me pro-consul in his stead, with authority to adjust grievances and to report on Cerealis's sedition. The honour is a high one, and I dare not refuse it, though I have no desire to exile myself again."

"I wish thee a fair voyage, and success in thy mission," said Valeria, mechanically. "When dost thou start?"

"On the Ides. My orders to lose no time are imperative. Yet must I, at all costs, make one stoppage, which shall be at Cyprus, to propitiate the Paphian goddess, so that she may kindle in thee desire toward my suit. Truly things have come to a strange pass," he added bitterly, "when a man is forced to sue Venus for the favour of his own wife!"

Paulinus gave a cynical laugh as he deliberately put out his foot and with the toe of his boot, to which the senatorial crescent was affixed, crushed the life out of a hairy caterpillar that crawled along the pavement in advance of three or four of its brethren. Then, in a softened tone, he added,—

"Wilt thou send by me a couple of white doves to sacrifice at Paphos with mine?"

Again she made a gesture of repugnance, but said nothing. He got up and leaned over her so close that she felt his breath, sodden with the fumes of last night's wine, stir her hair.

"Wilt thou have the rubies then?" he asked suddenly. "If I may clasp them on thee for the banquet this evening, and thus give the lie to this talk about Sura, Galla shall have no more from me; and, moreover, I'll bring thee from Egypt such jewels as Antony ne'er gave to Cleopatra."

Valeria thrust out her arm as if to protect herself. "I do not care for jewels," she replied. "To-night I wear my mother's amethysts."

Paulinus uttered a furious imprecation. "Then thou shalt see the rubies on Galla's neck, and if ill comes of thy folly, be its consequences on thine own head." He stamped as he spoke on the mosaic floor, annihilating some more caterpillars.

Valeria sickened. "I beg that thou wilt leave me," she murmured.

He stood irresolute in front of her.

"Remember my warning! For thine own sake," he said, "take my words to heart, lest thou be called upon to leave this house poorer than when thy mother led thee forth from the Palace, on the day of Vitellius's disgrace."

Valeria gave no sign that she felt the thrust, but her face grew whiter, and her eyes stared in a strained manner. Paulinus had turned to leave her, when a lady came unannounced from Valeria's apartments, anxiously observing the scene. She was a woman of about thirty-two, and of a dignified mien. A certain likeness proclaimed her Valeria's sister, but she was larger, of duller colouring, and lacking in Valeria's charm.

"Greeting," she said. "I am but this moment arrived, and was told I should find thee here, Valeria, with thy husband."

Valeria returned the salutation calmly. Paulinus welcomed his sister-in-law with ironic cordiality.

"Greeting, Vitellia. Thou comest opportunely to persuade thy sister to her duty. The gods—and Asiaticus—know that none is better qualified than thou to give a lesson in conjugal obedience. By the way, what news hast thou of that agreeable scoundrel?"

"My husband is on the march from Gaul with his legion," returned Vitellia, stiffly, "and I am informed that the Emperor's command hath been despatched him to await further orders at Forum Julii. I go thither to join him, and leave Rome to-morrow."

"Since thou goest to Forum Julii, send us word, I pray, how our boys fare at the farm," said Paulinus, glancing at Valeria, who made no comment on his reference to their sons. "I regret that thou art leaving Rome, Vitellia," he went on, "for I myself go, at Cæsar's command, on the Ides, to Egypt, to supersede Cerealis, and 'twas my hope thou wouldst have kept Valeria company in my absence."

"I know not if Asiaticus will be sent at once on another command," answered Vitellia. "Mayhap he'll be recalled to Rome. Gladly will I send thee word of thy boys. But why not take Valeria to Egypt? The southern climate would benefit her, and 'tis but right that she should go;" and Vitellia looked at her sister in veiled reproof.

Valeria took no notice of the admonition, but Paulinus scowled openly.

"Look at her!" he exclaimed. "Was ever statue colder? There thou seest a mother who refuses to be troubled with her own children—a wife who careth not one jot more for her husband than if he were a steward hired to keep her in state and luxury—and yet refuseth him his lawful wage. But there's an end to such a one-sided bargain, as I have told her. Either she be my wife in fact, or she ceaseth to be my wife in name. So I leave thee, Vitellia, to put reason into her brain. Pray the gods thou mayest succeed in a thankless task."

Paulinus gathered up his toga, and turning to his wife, remarked, "Count not upon my escort for to-night, Valeria. We shall meet in Julia's atrium."

Then he strode towards the upper terrace, on the steps of which Nyria was seated. He took no notice of her timid obeisance, but passed on and was hidden by a curve in the wall of the house. Nyria looked hesitatingly towards Valeria, wondering whether she might ask leave to return to the Aventine. But Vitellia was bending over her sister; it was useless to try and attract Valeria's attention. Nyria glanced at a sun-dial on the terrace, and the short shadow of the gnomon reassured her. Julia would not yet have returned from the Campus Martius, there would be the mid-day prandium, the siesta, and later, the bath, and the turn of the rubbers and anointers, before she would be required to dress her mistress's hair. It was true that she had to superintend the arrangement of the flowers for the dinner-table, but the under slaves would have everything prepared. So she sat down and waited.

Vitellia put motherly arms round her sister, who, shaken by the strain of the interview, had gone into a fit of dumb sobbing. Gradually she grew calmer, and replied brokenly to Vitellia's distressed questions concerning the difference with Paulinus and his threats of divorce. Vitellia shuddered at the suggestion, and strenuously counselled Valeria to yield to her husband's wishes.

"Thou shouldst go with him to Egypt," she urged.

Valeria shook her head decidedly. "Nothing shall make me do that; besides, he did not ask it."

"But he longs for thee. Canst not see, my dear, that notwithstanding his harsh manner there was love in every word and gesture?"

"Love!" exclaimed Valeria, with a shiver. "Do not desecrate the word by applying it to Paulinus. He doth not know what love means."

Vitellia loosened her arms about her sister and drew back a pace as she replied earnestly, calling Valeria by the name she had borne as a girl and had changed, according to custom, on becoming the wife of Valerius Paulinus.

"Lucia, thou art a romantic dreamer, and hast never grasped the realities of marriage. Thou art full of foolish fancies and dost ask more from life than any ordinary woman dare expect."

"I only ask what should be the right of every woman," said Valeria.

"Little sister! thou hast imbibed the new notions as to women's claims and dues. Our grandmothers, who sat at home and span amid their maidens, did not concern themselves except to mind the house and maintain the honour of their husbands. Marriage annuls personal rights. The wife belongs to her husband."

"I deny it! I deny it!" cried Valeria, passionately. "'Tis monstrous—abominable—that a woman should be forced to give herself to any but the man she loves."

There was alarm in Vitellia's eyes as she listened to this declaration.

"Lucia!" she asked suddenly, "tell me—dost thou love another man?"

The blood rose suddenly, reddening Valeria's pale cheeks. She hesitated, then proudly shook her head.

"Nay! there's none to whom I'd give myself."

Vitellia looked relieved as she sat down.

"I am thankful to hear thee speak so," she said. "It hath been a sorrow to me, Lucia, to be so long separated from thee, but while Asiaticus remained in Belgic Gaul the distance was too great to permit of my coming home. Ever since thou wast grown up I have been almost a stranger to thee, and now that I am in Rome I hear such dreadful tales of the doings of married women that I tremble lest thou shouldst have grown like them. Rome is a terrible place! In Gaul, Lucia, the wives are truer and simpler."

Valeria laughed artificially. "Dear provincial Vitellia! hast thou only just discovered that Roman morals need mending? I should have thought thou hadst found Asiaticus's companionship a liberal education in that respect. But nothing could ever make thee other than thou art. Thou art fashioned on the Lucretia and Arria pattern. But I don't agree with thee that husbands should have the monopoly of vice while wives must be examples of domestic virtue. There! there! good Vitellia, don't look so horrified. I assure thee I am still virtuous, save in my speech and perchance in my writings."

The pain and puzzlement on Vitellia's face gave place to a more confident expression.

"Yes, yes, I know, dearest. Could I doubt that thou hast guarded the traditions of virtue in which our mother and grandmother reared us? But I feared that thou hadst learned to love that man of whom Paulinus spoke—Licinius Sura."

Valeria reddened again, but she answered hurriedly, "Nay, Vitellia, praise Demeter, my friendship with all men is of small account. Thou needst not talk to me of love."

"'Tis a joy to know thee free of heart," returned Vitellia, warmly, "for, that being so, I may more readily speak of thy duty to thy lord."

Valeria made an uneasy movement. Her foot in the embroidered shoe tapped restlessly on the stool beneath it. She listened with a sarcastic smile to Vitellia's admonitory utterances.

The elder woman leaned forward too, laying a capable-looking hand upon her sister's. Vitellia's hand contrasted with Valeria's, which was essentially artistic, with long, tapering fingers and a full palm, the skin velvety, and the nails exquisitely pared and tinted. Valeria noted with a qualm of distaste that Vitellia's hands were not the product of a skilled manicurist.

"Dear little sister," began Vitellia, in her gentle, didactic way, "besides being some years older than thou art, my experience of life and of marriage hath of necessity been fuller than thine. I have learned that 'tis useless for a woman to rebel. One who is mated to a bad husband had best bear her lot cheerfully. She may at least win his esteem, and he will certainly uphold her when he needs her services. Believe me, Lucia, that this is the only way in which an ill-mated wife may retain her rights and secure the respect of her world."

"I care nothing for the respect of my world," petulantly interrupted Valeria.

Vitellia smiled in her superior wisdom.

"Dost thou not? Ah! my dear, I think thy pride would suffer sorely wert thou deposed from thy present position."

Valeria was silent. The shaft had hit its mark. Vitellia went on,—

"Yet, after all, 'tis not that which should be our first consideration. We have to remember what religion requires of us. Our marriages, Lucia, were of the sacramental kind, more binding than any civil ceremony. Every sacred tradition of our race demands that we should faithfully observe the vows we took in presence of the Flamen."

Valeria broke in again with her false-ringing laugh.

"'Tis plain enough, Vitellia, that thou hast been acting the priestess to conquered savages. Nobody cares a sesterce nowadays about those old Quirite traditions. Talk of something more interesting."

"Nay, I must proceed," persisted Vitellia. "I should feel it wrong to leave Rome without having done what I could to bring about a better state of things between thee and Paulinus. Laugh as thou wilt at my provincial ideas, Lucia, but remember that they were those of our grandmother, Sextilia, who was the model of a Roman wife and mother—"

"And died of a broken heart," put in Valeria.

"She died leaving a noble example to her grandchildren," returned Vitellia. "Our mother too—"

"Talk not to me of our mother. Galeria Fundana is dead. If the gods permit, let her rest in peace. 'Tis well for her that death hath spared her my upbraidings. I can never forgive my mother for having cozened Vespasian to sell me to Paulinus."

"Blame not our mother," pleaded Vitellia. "She desired only to secure thy future, and acted, as she thought, to that end. Her pride rebelled against our fallen estate, and she hoped through thy marriage to reinstate our family. Any mother in Rome would have welcomed Paulinus as a son-in-law. Thou art unreasonable, Lucia. Paulinus hath been no worse than many husbands, and is better far than most."

"Ay, better than Asiaticus, I grant thee," returned Valeria. "After all, 'tis not saying much. Yet thou canst not compare our marriages, Vitellia, for Asiaticus had thy love."

"Yes, he had my love," answered Vitellia, sadly.

"And has it still, infamously though he's treated thee."

"I hold my marriage vows sacred," said Vitellia, "and shall never refuse Asiaticus a wife's duty."

"If *I* were Asiaticus's wife he should not breathe the same air with me," exclaimed Valeria. "And yet, Vitellia"—she paused—"I envy thee, for thou hast known what I can never know—the sweet surrender of love. Though it may have been but for a week—a day—an hour, thou hast tasted bliss."

Vitellia's calm features quivered, but she said nothing. Then Valeria broke out passionately, the floodgates of her heart loosened.

"Listen, Vitellia. I'll speak frankly. Thou hast said that thou art almost a stranger to me: 'tis true. If we had been thrown together in the early days of my marriage thou wouldst understand me better, and thy preachings of wifely duty would mayhap come less glibly. Thou wast not sold as *I* was—an ignorant child, driven forth against her entreaties, helpless as a lamb led to the shambles and delivered over unto the butcher. The sin of it!—the shame! Oh! ye gods! how can I forget—how can I forgive?"

Valeria's fingers closed convulsively round Vitellia's, and her bosom heaved under the recollection of that intolerable wrong. The barriers of her reserve gave way. Self-revelations came in a broken torrent.

"Nay, thou dost not know my life. Think of it!—a child, barely fourteen! 'Twas worse than butchery, for the lamb is killed outright, but I—I lived. Having faced horror—with every hope torn from me as the petals of a rosebud are torn away in pieces by some wanton hand—I tell thee, Vitellia, that I was initiated into every coarseness. Neither youth nor innocence were left me. Before I was eighteen I had borne him three children. Then it was told me how he had made his baby-wife the laughing-stock of his friends. He had taken me, he said, only because I was an emperor's daughter and Vespasian had made it worth his while. I was but an instrument, a tool for which he did not pretend to care. At that time I was stupid, and not pretty, and when I plucked up spirit enough to forbid him my apartments, he only laughed, saying 'twas no matter—he was welcome in others. All that he wanted me for was the three children I had given him, in order that he might secure honours from the State. I wished the boys dead, for they have their father's features and his rough ways, and 'tis for that I cannot bear them near me. But my little girl had nothing of her father in her face, and I mourned when the gods took her, and yet was glad. For there in the Elysian Meads no shame, no harm can touch her, and I like to think of her plucking the immortal asphodels and the golden flowers Persephone loved. . . ."

Valeria stopped with a strangle in her throat. There were tears in her eyes, which she brushed away with one hand; the other was in the clasp of Vitellia, who pressed it tenderly. Valeria hurried on.

"*Now*, canst thou understand? I lived my life in loneliness. I grew hard and cold, and learned more and more to despise men. Such contrary creatures are they that it must have been because of my contempt that they began to pay court to me. Then, seeing that I was admired of others, Paulinus discovered admiration for me also—that, too, is the way of men. He deems he may command what he has bought, but, his desire having turned towards me, he is willing to make a bargain, and hath indeed offered to give up Galla if I consent. Thus the position stands. Never since my marriage have I so unburdened myself. What thinkest thou, Vitellia, of my story?"

Vitellia was generous in her sisterly sympathy, and yet there was disapproval in her sweetly monitory tone.

"Poor child!" she said, "my heart aches for thee. Yet what can I say, dearest, save that thou wilt fail grievously in thy duty if thou dost thrust this man back on evil courses. He hath given thee proof of sincerity and repentance, and I would have thee remember that a man resents in his wife proneness to offence. He hath but acted as men will—'tis their nature, as thou sayest. Thou must excuse his past conduct. Nay, do not stir, I know my words are unwelcome, but there is no other manner in which I may advise thee. And I have this more to recommend—re-union would be less difficult under new conditions, away from Rome, and for this reason I repeat that most assuredly thou shouldst go with Paulinus to Egypt."

Valeria wrenched her hand from Vitellia's detaining fingers.

"Go to Egypt with Paulinus!" she exclaimed vehemently. "Thou art mad, Vitellia! I tell thee that I would rather open my veins here and now, than die abroad of the slow torture of his companionship. Dost thou not understand that it was as if I beheld Elysium when he told me that for a while I should be free of his hated presence? Cease thy preaching! 'Tis wasted on me."

Valeria sprang from her chair. Discomfited and alarmed at the result of her pleading, Vitellia rose too, remonstrating feebly. But Valeria paid no heed. There was a wild look in her eyes as she stared round the court. Then she caught sight of Nyria, whom she had forgotten. The slave-girl sat waiting, a conspicuous object in her white dress, and with her fair hair against the marble of the terrace, over which climbed a rose plant with a few late, heavy yellow blooms almost the colour of her curls.

"Nyria!" called Valeria, sharply. "Why hast thou not gone?"

"The Domina bade me wait," said Nyria, tremulously, "but 'tis indeed time I returned to Julia—with the Domina's permission." She humbly approached the sisters. Vitellia scanned her with some annoyance.

"Thou mayst go," returned Valeria, impatiently.

But Nyria hesitated. "The Domina may have forgotten the letter of which she spoke."

Valeria bit her lip.

"I have changed my mind about the letter: there is none," she answered. "Pass out, child, by the garden gate."

VIII

It was later than Nyria expected when she reached Julia's house, and there was more to be done than she had bargained for. Properly speaking, the flowers for the dinner-table should have been seen to, and orders given for wreathing the pillars and walls, early in the morning, for though Nyria was not expected to do the work itself, she was held accountable for the manner in which it was done. But she had felt too ill that morning, and her one thought had been to get into the open air. Now she hurried guiltily to the serving-rooms adjoining the banqueting-hall, to find one of them heaped with flowers already drooping, and the slaves of that department excusing their idleness on the plea that they knew not what design "the Most Noble" had ordered, for all knew that Julia would at once detect and punish any lack of taste in their arrangements, which depended mainly on Nyria's dainty fancy.

At once she set to work, and the hours flew ere she was aware of their passing. The table stewards came in and out, carrying away the vases, while they gossiped about the expected guests, the probable humour of the Emperor, and the latest scandals running through the slaves' quarters of various aristocratic houses. So the afternoon waned—fashionable Roman banquets usually began about sundown—and Nyria found to her dismay that she had not allowed full time to get herself ready and to perform her duties in Julia's apartment before the hour at which the guests were to arrive.

She ran to the courtyard round which the slaves' huts were built. Euphena's hut, where the girl had been brought up, was at the further end of the yard. It was part of Nyria's duty now to sleep in front of Julia's door, but the old Ethiopian had still the charge of her person, and was supposed to make the bath ready, to comb Nyria's yellow hair and to prepare her robes, so that the girl might not spend too much time over her own dressing. To-day, however, it seemed that Euphena was not troubling herself about Nyria's toilet. She was squatting in her doorway, almost filling its narrow width with her lean black form. Before her, on the ground, was a circle drawn in fine white sand, enclosing curious astrological figures shaped out of an ash-like substance that she bound together by gum distilled from berries.

"Mother! let me in," cried Nyria. But Euphena, who was muttering to herself, took no heed, only, as Nyria pushed forward, she drew back on her knees, and stretched out her skinny arms as if to guard her magic ring.

"Mother, I am late. I must bathe and dress."

Euphena darted a vicious look at Nyria and paused in her incantations.

"Seest thou not that I am reading the stars? They do not wait in their places for such as thou. Dost thou think the destinies concern themselves whether a slave-girl be late or early?" And she stooped again and went on with her muttering.

Nyria stamped her foot, half amused, half petulant.

"I must pass, mother. For if the stars will not wait, neither will Julia."

Euphena's eyes shot forth a yellow gleam.

"Julia!" she cried. "What is Julia that she should rule Rome? Ay, I know that Julia's word is law, but even law-givers may be laid low, and as I read, the stars pronounce her doom. Even now the seeds are sown of that which shall destroy the mighty Julia."

There was a murmur outside the low wall of Euphena's dwelling. A number of slaves had gathered and were leaning over it, eager to hear Euphena's reading of the horoscope of their master and mistress. They all hated Julia, and one of the men cried triumphantly, "Well for Sabinus if Euphena's words prove true. Long may he glory in his freedom!"

"Nay, nay. Freedom and Sabinus have no commerce with each other," said Euphena. "A slave is our master—more of a slave than we. Slave to a woman-tyrant, and ere long victim to the next greatest tyrant in Rome." As she spoke thus boldly, other heads craned over the wall and questions were eagerly asked. Many of the serving-men had come, clothed in their new liveries of white and red and gold, which had been given them for the banquet.

Nyria, taking advantage of the stir, pressed into the doorway, and tried to squeeze through it, but Euphena turned wrathfully upon her.

"Woe to thee, little fool! Dost think to defy the stars? Know that thy garment hath brushed the circle and displaced the figures which cast the destinies of Julia and Sabinus. Thus hast thou made for thyself a part in their evil fate."

Nyria plucked her robe from the Ethiopian's fingers, and with a laugh disappeared within. There she made such haste as she could in bathing and donning a fresh white robe, fixing with unaccustomed hands the fillets of gold braid that on state occasions held back her hair. But with all her speed she found, on reaching her mistress's apartments, that Thanna had already dressed Julia's hair, and that a storm of vituperation awaited her. There was nothing for Nyria but to meekly bow her head. Then, gathering up her courage, and taking from Thanna Julia's fan and scent-bottle and various other properties, she followed in the train of her mistress, who scolded one or another all the time, through a throng of hurrying slaves to the atrium, where Sabinus was already receiving the earliest comers.

The great reception-room was aglow with lamps and torches, and was warmed also—for the autumn evening had set in chilly—by fires in ornamental braziers, set on tripods at the four corners of the hall. The embroidered curtains had been drawn apart at the different archways, and the whole range lay open, from the vestibule to the state banqueting-room seen beyond two wide corridors and a peristyle with a fish-pond and pillared colonnade.

Julia took her stand at the upper end of the atrium, by the daïs, where stood chairs, like thrones of gold and ivory, for the Emperor and Empress should they wish to be seated, while Nyria, ready at a moment to obey any imperious sign from her mistress, peered from behind that imposing figure and forgot her troubles in the excitement of watching arrivals, and listening to the bandying of salutations, as many of the guests strolled past her to the peristyle. From there rang the deep tones of men's voices, and every now and then the shriller sound of a woman's little shriek as some venturesome lamprey in the fish-pond leaped up for a bit of biscuit extended by a fair one's hand. Within, the most important of the company waited Cæsar's coming. Here in the scented atmosphere was a confused glitter of lights, jewels and decorations. Between the columns gleamed forms of sculptured gods and goddesses, not always decorous, and enthroned above them all presided the image of Titus, crowned with triumphal bays, and seeming to gaze at certain spoils of Jerusalem which were arranged as trophies round the masks of spurious Flavian ancestors. Upon the altar of Titus incense smouldered, while perfume made the water in the central fountain milky, as it dripped from the amorous beak of the divine swan on to the limbs of Leda, which, by an arrangement of light through an overhead screen, had the semblance of rosy human flesh.

Julia looked very handsome after a full-blown fashion, and was, of course, magnificently dressed. As usual she had overdone her various adornments, but the general effect was gorgeous, and she might not have looked so well had she been attired in better taste. Her ample bust and large white arms were loaded with strings of pearls, chains of pink topazes, and serpent bracelets in many-coloured stones. Other chains girdled her sumptuous waist, while her stola glittered with iridescent embroidery. The frizzed and gold-powdered tiers of her hair were surmounted by a diadem of rubies and diamonds, and her palla, which dropped on her shoulders so as to show the luxurious curves of her bosom, was stiff with gold threads. Her complexion, naturally florid, had been toned by art to the tint of milk and roses, and her full lips, artificially reddened, were parted in a satisfied smile which revealed a faultless set of teeth. Her eyes redeemed the coarseness of her features, for they were really fine, fringed with thick lashes and arched by well-defined brows, and she wore a patch cunningly placed to call attention to the dimple in her cheek. She had an arrogant, yet awkward, bearing, and her self-conceit was evident in her manner of greeting her guests. She did not advance to anyone, as did her husband, who had stationed himself nearer the entrance, and who stepped forward with quiet, courteous welcome as the stewards of the atrium sonorously announced each newcomer, with all proper titles and dignities, making nice distinction between the "Illustrious," the "Most Noble" and the merely "Honourable." Julia was also careful to regulate her salutation according to the social position of her guests, giving her hand to but few, and only permitting those of consular rank to kiss her fingers, while the generality received merely a bow meant to be majestic.

Now, as if in contrast to the high-sounding announcements of other high-born ladies, came that simply of the "Domina Domitilla." Nyria felt a thrill of interest, hoping that the grey-cloaked philosopher might, after all, be of the party. Euphrates, who was a philosopher, was there with his fat rich wife, and the learned Sulpicia and her husband of the Stoic set—why not therefore Domitilla's friend? But the gracious lady, who did not care for the title of Most Noble—which was rightly hers as a near relative of Cæsar—walked alone with her husband, Flavius Clemens. Nyria liked to look at Domitilla. Not that Domitilla was handsome. Her face was homely, with a softly curved nose and a pale, yellowish skin. But her wide mouth had an angelic smile which told of the beauty of peace. Her light brown hair, streaked with grey, was parted in the middle, and simply waved over her ears, making a knot low in her neck. Domitilla never wore much jewellery, and in her hair were only two quaint gold pins. In Nyria's fancy her whole appearance was dovelike.

Then Paulinus passed with Galla, on whose neck hung the famous rubies. Martial, behind her, whispering over her shoulder, was green with jealousy, which he vented in spiteful witticisms. Not so long ago Galla's caprice had been for the poet, and he was divided between fear of offending Paulinus and anger at having been superseded in the lady's affections. Martial carried his tablets ostentatiously displayed, and sometimes scribbled a line, which had been carefully prepared though it appeared the inspiration of the moment. "Ah! Galla!" he murmured. "'Tis cruel to expose thy charms seeing that I am too poor to purchase a kiss. Mercenary one, are my lips henceforth to go hungry?"

Galla laughed and fluttered her jewelled fan. Attention was now attracted to the entrance as the stewards called out pompously, "The most noble Valeria, wife of the illustrious Paulinus."

Nyria's heart bounded with satisfaction as she noticed in what stately fashion the daughter of Vitellius comported herself, sweeping on without the flicker of an eyelid in the direction of her husband and her rival. She bent in haughty salutation to her hostess, apparently not perceiving Julia's half-extended hand, and Nyria radiantly took to herself the little smile Valeria threw backwards as she passed, giving place to Pliny and his timid young wife. Antæia had only been married a month or two. She was hardly out of the hands of her tutor and had never before left her mother's home under the Apennines. She trembled with fright at Julia's banter, for it was her first meeting with this redundant lady.

"Oh! dimples of Cupid!" cried Julia. "So this is the country innocent who has captivated our elegant Pliny. She looks as though she had fed on cream and honey, and would faint at a naughty word. Hast brought her pap-bottle, Pliny? And how dost thou propose to teach her the language of fashionable Rome?"

"With the example of the divine Julia before her," returned Pliny, with a courtly bow, "Antæia can scarce be slow in learning to take her place among the ladies of Rome."

"He is teaching me Greek," put in Antæia, with a shy, adoring glance at her husband. "And 'tis by his wish that I have a tutor for rhetoric."

Julia burst into loud laughter, and Pliny broke in,—

"Meanwhile she is an ignorant little country mouse, and terribly afraid lest the great Cæsar should notice her. Of thy kindness, gracious Julia, tell me that thou hast not placed her at dinner in too alarming company."

Julia looked cross. "As to that, I wanted thee, Pliny, at my end of the table, but this infant would scream at our talk. So I wash my hands of ye both. If people will bring babies to dinner-parties they must look after their charges themselves."

Julia turned brusquely to greet some fresh arrivals—the magnificent Nonius Asprena—ex-consul—and his beautiful wife, who was said to be the most graceful woman in Rome. Antæia looked as though she would like to go home, but Pliny reassured her with a tender pressure of her hand, and Valeria spoke kindly to her, so that Antæia's bird-like face grew bright again. She had evidently tried to make herself appear fashionable, in order to do credit to her husband, whom she considered the cleverest and greatest man that had ever lived; but her head-woman was apparently not an artist, for a simpler fashion would have suited Antæia's hair better than the towering head-dress favoured by the Flavian ladies.

Then Nyria's eyes turned again to Valeria, beside whom all

other women seemed commonplace. Her dress was the loveliest and the most harmonious in the room—a stola of softest white silk falling in Grecian folds, and embroidered in blending shades of heliotrope, and a palla of mauve worked with silver and lined with violet that fell round her like a regal mantle. Her small head was poise liked a lily on its stem, and her naturally wavy chestnut hair was arranged in classic bands, held back by a coronal of large amethysts tipped with pear-shaped pearls. Round her long throat was a collar of amethysts and pearls, and her beautifully-shaped arms, bare to the shoulders, whence hung open sleeves lined with violet and edged with white fur, were clasped above and below with bands of amethysts and pearls connected by thin gold chains. Below her bosom was a stomacher of the same gems, and an amethyst girdle terminating in pearl tassels circled her waist. The amethysts were of specially fine colour and the pearls matchless. They were the jewels which Galeria Fundana had pawned to provide thé debt-ridden Vitellius with necessary funds for taking up his German command, and, to his credit be it said, they had been faithfully redeemed on his return to Rome as Emperor, and were finally presented by Galeria Fundana to her youngest daughter on Valeria's marriage to the Tribune of the Prætorian Guards.

Paulinus looked specially well to-night in his flame-coloured tunic and toga of deeper hue. His brick-red face turned in unwilling admiration to his beautiful wife. The man was cut to the quick. Never yet had he failed to win a woman, and the failure was a wound to his pride. So cold, so distant, so unapproachable, and yet so perfect, Valeria seemed to soar above him, a living witness to his own inferiority. Do what he would, he could neither subjugate nor humiliate her. There was but one way in which he could revenge himself, and that way he hesitated to take, for in so decisive a measure as divorce he would for ever separate himself from the one woman he desired and was forced to respect. Moreover, in spite of his threat of appeal to Cæsar, it was not easy to dissolve a sacred marriage, especially when two sons were the fruit of that union. He must have proven cause for so drastic a step. And Valeria was proverbially chaste. He pictured the accomplished Pliny pleading against him. As for that ill-natured gossip about Licinius Sura, it was impossible to believe that Valeria could demean herself to any vulgar intrigue. The sweetness of her smile as she talked to Pliny made Paulinus's blood boil in strange tenderness, and he took a step with the half intention of accosting and apologising to his wife. But Valeria's gaze, straying round the room, encountered his, and there was in it such cold disdain that he retreated, furious though abashed. Valeria looked from her husband to Galla, and back to him for a moment, then slowly withdrew her eyes, and again talked to Pliny in her most friendly and interested manner. Paulinus supposed that they were discussing books—a subject in which he was not competent to join. Often had he writhed at the thought that Valeria despised him for his lack of learning. Many times only Pliny's exquisite tact had saved the situation, when Valeria had shown too plainly that she regarded her husband as a coarse Bœotian in comparison with the cultured people she gathered round her, and on whom she delighted in exercising her own Attic wit. He could hear that she was now talking in Greek to Pliny, and presently she had collected a little circle—the Stoic blue-stocking Sulpicia, with her meek husband, Calenus, Euphrates gesticulating after the manner of an orator, Fronto, that rich patron of learning, and Tacitus, the highborn essayist and historian with his mild, reserved manner. Paulinus knew that Tacitus admired Valeria, and also that Fronto did, and ever so many more of the most intellectual and highest esteemed men in Rome. But he was not jealous of any of them: he only envied their learning, because it appeared that learning came foremost with Valeria. And in Paulinus's rough soldier youth it had not been thought necessary that a Roman should salt his discourse with quotations from Homer and Æschylus.

Now there was a craning of heads and a flutter in the assembly when it was known that the Empress's arrival preceded that of Cæsar. Sabinus, warned by the stewards, went to the outer hall to receive Domitia, and even Julia, in compliance with the social rule, made a feint of advancing a few steps when her husband reappeared conducting the Augusta.

Domitia looked thin and worn, as though she were scarcely able to support the weight of her ceremonial robes, and the brightness of her restless eyes intensified her appearance of delicacy.

"Domitia will be pleased to hear that Paris recites to-night," observed Julia, maliciously. "In truth," she added with a meaning laugh, "one had need secure the Augusta's presence, or have access to Cæsar's treasury, in order to induce Paris to forfeit his engagement at the theatre."

An amused murmur ran through the bystanders, and Domitia seized the advantage which Julia's clumsy speech had given her, with an adroitness scarcely to be expected.

"I am glad to know," she said in sarcastic, high-pitched tones, "that Cæsar pays for the entertainment of Julia's guests. That is as it should be when the Empress is one of them."

Julia reddened, and began an angry retort, but Domitia, small and stately, had swept on, for once a victor.

Presently the arms of the Prætorians clashed in the vestibule, and the rods of the lictors rattled against the lintel, for Cæsar had come in state.

Sabinus hurried forward and the company parted, leaving a

roadway down which first Julia passed, curtseying profoundly to the Emperor as he approached. Domitian extended his hand, which she kissed, and raising her with marked favour, he walked up the room by her side, ignoring Sabinus, who fell meekly behind.

Domitian—as tall and superb as Julia—looked an emperor in his tunic of vermilion heavily fringed with gold and a toga of the imperial amethystine hue, bordered also with gold. On his head was a chaplet of laurel leaves in emerald and gold, while immense chains of precious stones fell over his bulky person, the portliness of his trunk contrasting with the thinness of his legs. His red face and crimson vestments made his neck and arms appear unhealthily white, and there was something repulsive in the pale pink patches that came and went upon his cheeks and forehead.

Always of uncertain mood, there was a brooding expression on Domitian's face to-night from which those present drew ominous auguries. None could avoid a feeling of apprehension. For, only a few days ago, Rome had been horrified at the condemnation of Senecio and Arulenus Rusticus, and people were beginning to ask themselves what man of consular rank would be the next victim. Nevertheless, those of the Palatine set who thought themselves secure in Domitian's favour—such as Eprius Marcellus, the blind Messalinus, led by his body slave, the blustering Carus, Regulus the witty but unscrupulous barrister, and others of their kind, pressed round Cæsar, hailing him as their lord-god, and tendering him homage given to a deity. Paulinus alone dared to treat Cæsar as though he were but a high-placed mortal. Truckling subservience was not in Paulinus's nature, and perhaps the only thing in him of which his wife approved was his easy manner to Domitian. Valeria herself held aloof, making merely the customary curtsey.

Now the playing of an orchestra without gave the signal for dinner, and there was a general movement in the company, Julia walking with Cæsar, Sabinus and the Empress following. Nyria watched them pass. Domitian was frowning, and his short-sighted eyes blinked along the lines of attendants, as though he saw something which displeased him. Julia plucked at his sleeve and forced his attention until he listened as she talked.

As soon as the Emperor and Empress had passed, Nyria flew through a side door and round by the serving-rooms so as to gain her position at the back of her mistress's chair before Julia and Cæsar took their places. Again Domitian blinked displeasedly at the files of slaves in their liveries of white with broad scarlet and gold facings, scarcely to be distinguished from those of the Emperor's own men, who stood close to his chair. This, as was usual on such occasions, had been brought, with the Empress's seat and the imperial drinking-cups, from the palace. Domitian's was a gorgeous throne of ivory, with arms in shape of dragons' heads carved in gold, and with a high back formed of the outstretched wings and interlacing beaks of two golden eagles. A gold-fringed canopy was fixed above it, but this Domitian, flushed and hot, crossly ordered to be removed.

The Empress's chair, at the further end of the table, was such as she preferred, straight-backed, high and stiff, slenderly fashioned of ebony, and beautifully inlaid with mother-o'-pearl. The master and mistress of the house had their chairs of honour placed respectively beside the Emperor and Empress. For the rest, cushioned lounges to accommodate three, with an occasional seat for one pushed between, extended along the table, up which the guests were ushered by the stewards as they filed in.

Nyria looked down the banqueting-hall, proud of its grandeur, and specially of the arrangement of flowers and fruit for which she was responsible. She delighted in the vast room with its many-coloured marbles, its wreathed pillars, its beautiful mosaics, and the massive sideboards resting on monsters in silver and jade, and holding enormous salvers, great embossed flagons, jewelled vases, cups and lamps from Egina, and figures in Corinthian brass, treasures of workmanship both ancient and modern. The whole was illuminated by huge torches set round the walls in gold and enamel brackets, which, being prepared of certain resinous substances, gave out a smokeless and peculiarly brilliant flame. These lights seemed to converge towards a raised stage on one side of the room, which Cæsar's place fronted, and which was framed and banked with flowers.

Very beautiful was the marble table down which Nyria gazed—it was one of Sabinus's most treasured possessions, for it had been made for his grandfather, the first wealthy Flavian, who had had it hewn out of one of the famous Phrygian quarries and shaped and polished in Rome. It was a great table of many slabs—to-night all in requisition—and of the deepest pink in hue—the colour of a rose's heart, with veins resembling blood running through its surface. Its rosy glow shone up through mother-o'-pearl dishes on gold stands, and was reflected in the low, flat, silver lamps, containing scented oil from the Lebanon, on which floated coloured wicks that gave a soft fairy light. The rose shade tinged, too, the vessels of engraved glass and the cups of amber and of murrhine ware, while it lent an appearance of living flesh to the group of marble naiads rising out of a bed of lilies that supported a fountain of wine in the centre of the table. From this the wine rose in a sparkling shower through silver tubes so cunningly devised that the spray, playing crosswise, mingled and fell into mother-o'-pearl basins at the four corners, without wetting the table or disturbing the central reservoir of a rare vintage kept for toast-drinking at the end of the banquet.

Domitian was making irritable movements, flicking his fingers after a habit he had of killing flies, or when waiting for game to be driven before his bow. It did not take much to rouse the tiger in him, and clearly something had given him offence. The moment was an awkward one. Guests were slow in taking their places, and it was not etiquette to begin serving until all were seated. Domitian glared at the army of slaves, and Nyria shrank into the shadow of Julia's ample person, praying that Cæsar might not turn his eyes on her. Julia herself looked uncomfortable, for her efforts to divert the Emperor met with small response. She beckoned to the chief wine-bearer, and by a sign bade him fill the Emperor's cup. It was his own goblet—a large one of chased white onyx banded with gold and gems. The wine was strong. Domitian quaffed it at a draught, and his cup was discreetly filled again. The Emperor's brow cleared. He paid no heed, however, to the ceremonial libation that preceded dinner, though Sabinus looked questioningly at his august guest and then at his wife. For Domitian, being of highest rank, and as Pontifex Maximus, should, according to the usage of strict houses, have poured the libation in company of his host and spoken the prayer to the gods. But though Sabinus held to religious customs, and usually, when the banquet was a small one, himself performed this act of devotion, he dared not press the matter this evening.

So Vibius, the chief steward, formed the wine-bearers into line, when the guests had placed themselves, and, heading the procession, went to the great silver shell, with a drain beneath it, prepared for the purpose at the end of the hall. Then, holding a huge wine flagon in one hand, and a gold cup in shape of a funnel in the other, he poured the wine, reciting, in a loud voice, these words;—

"To the great Jupiter who bestoweth all good things: to Ceres, Earth-mother, from whose fruitful womb they issue: to the generous Bacchus, who blesseth the glad juice of the grape—we offer praise and honour in this libation of that which is given for our benefit and enjoyment. Be it poured forth."

IX

"I TRUST that Cæsar finds the wine to his liking," said Julia, deferentially. "It was purchased in his honour, and is Cæcuban—in bottle long ere Nero razed the vineyards."

Domitian lifted his cup again and drank, rolling the wine in his mouth with the air of a connoisseur.

"Not so bad—not so bad," said he. "Nay, 'tis good wine—better far than I should have thought Sabinus had the wit to choose."

Julia laughed. "Oh! my lord! dost think I would permit Sabinus to choose wine for Cæsar's drinking? Sabinus is but a poor wine-buyer, and there comes no liquor to my table which I have not myself sampled."

Domitian gave her a leering smile.

"By Bacchus! I might have guessed as much," he said. "Sabinus hath water in his veins, and could have no taste for generous wine. But Julia's blood is of richer quality, and needs the best vintages to keep it warm and full pulsing."

Julia wriggled delightedly, satisfied that things were now going right.

The slaves trooped round, staggering beneath the weight of silver dishes and distributing incentives to appetite—cunning little fishes dressed with rue, tiny sausages smoking on silver gridirons, livers of geese prepared with truffles, devilled dormice, brains of flamingoes and many other pungent dainties, the tastiest of which Julia pressed upon Cæsar, whose temper seemed to improve in proportion with his appetite. He deigned to nod affably when Martial, craning to attract the imperial notice, loudly apostrophised a giant sturgeon.

"See," he cried, "the barbarian river yields to our lord-god its choicest progeny! Such a rarity should never be seen save at a feast to the divine Augustus."

Mountains of food multiplied, and so did weight of bullion. One silver platter was changed for another, and costly bowls of scented water, with exquisitely woven napkins, were passed again and again. Here was sufficient precious metal to furnish a treasury, for Flavius Sabinus was noted for the magnificent plate he had inherited.

Domitian's eyes gleamed covetously, and he remarked, in a manner intended to be jocose, but with a darker meaning in it,—

"'Tis a pity that so much treasure should be locked up in a private house instead of being turned to the beautifying of Rome. Were Sabinus's head ever to become forfeit to the State, his possessions would prove a good haul for the Emperor."

Julia replied with saucy promptitude, "Thou dost forget, my lord, Sabinus would leave a widow. 'Tis *I* who should claim his possessions."

"And remain thyself unclaimed!" retorted the Emperor. "In that case, were *I* the reigning Cæsar, I would not leave the most valuable asset without an owner."

Julia giggled, and dropped her handkerchief, which obliged Nyria to come closer that she might pick it up. Julia had a way of dropping things, and it was Nyria's duty to restore them, so that the slave-girl could never stand far from her mistress.

"It may be, my lord, that my wishes in the matter of ownership might not coincide with those of Cæsar," said Julia, emboldened to pertness.

"Julia should have learned that I am not one to force a lady's inclinations," he answered. "Nevertheless, I dare wager Cæsar's signet that Julia's wishes will not go counter to mine." He bent closer and whispered. Julia ogled him from behind her thick black lashes.

"Divinity, there is no keeping even the secrets of a woman's heart from the all-comprehending Cæsar."

Domitian blinked, pleased at the flattery, and pressed her large white arm.

"The change of owners should profit thee, beautiful Julia, for if Sabinus gave thee silver plate, Cæsar can give thee gold."

"Oh! Cæsar, thou art scarcely kind to laugh at my poor plate," murmured Julia, in affected reproach. "Can I do more than give the August of my best?"

"Oh! oh! I do not say thou hast not given me of thy best. Hitherto I have had no cause to complain of thy generosity," said Cæsar, with a meaning look. Julia glanced to each side of her with an air of bravado, for the Emperor's words had been audible in a lull of the talk close by. At the further end, however, Sabinus was courteously engrossed with the Empress, though occasionally he threw a humble, questioning look at his wife. Galla kept both Martial and Paulinus in play, and Pliny, while he surreptitiously held his young wife's hand, was talking interestedly to Valeria. Eprius Marcellus, on Julia's other hand, clearly expected nothing from his hostess, and equally, the old general, Agricola, on Domitian's left, did not look for imperial favour. It was a wonder why he had been put in that place of honour. His son-in-law, Tacitus, seated lower at the table, would every now and then look up uneasily, for it was no secret that Agricola, lately returned from Britain, had been refused the pro-consulship which was his due, and that he was out of favour at the Palatine. Tacitus feared disaster in to-night's apparent honour, for it was Domitian's humour to caress his victims before he struck the fatal blow.

Julia hurriedly turned the conversation, asking Domitian whether the brackets for the torches, which she said had cost a pretty penny, were pleasing to his artistic taste.

The Emperor muttered some indifferent comment. He had his brooding look again. Domitian's moods were incalculable. Suddenly he jerked his head round to give an order to one of his own men behind, and caught sight of Nyria. His scowl changed to a grin, and the girl was terrified lest he should speak. But just then Agricola made some diffident remark about the splendour of the decorations, and Cæsar cried,—

"As thou sayest, worthy Agricola, here is a feast for Cæsar's eyes as well as for his palate. Yet one great error hath been made, for the prettiest thing in the room has been put behind my head, so that one must needs have eyes at the back to see it."

"What is the thing of which Cæsar speaks?" asked Julia, tartly.

"'Tis Nyria," answered Domitian. "Little Curly Locks—the choicest bit of beauty here to-night."

All near turned to inspect the slave-girl. Julia looked furious, and Domitian, to appease her, made it appear that he was but jesting.

"Curly Locks should have been put in the middle of the table to hold up the wine-fountain," he said. "'Twould be a pretty punishment for a naughty little slave-girl. I'll warrant her as white and shapely as any one of those marble nymphs."

Eprius Marcellus put up his eyeglass on the bridge of his hawk nose, and leaning over the back of the couch stared at Nyria, who would have been glad had the mosaic floor opened and swallowed her.

"German—by her yellow hair!" he said. "And who dare say that Cæsar is not best judge of all things German? Did I understand that the Most August challenged comparison of this maid with Myron's marble nymphs? But of that how can we decide unless she stand unrobed?"

There was a roar of laughter, which Cæsar led, though he put out his hand as if waiving the suggestion. Nyria, in an agony of shame, would have stooped down behind Julia's chair for protection from the men's insolent gaze.

"Leave the brat alone!" cried Julia, angrily. "Too much notice hath been taken of her looks, which have naught out of the common. As for her shape, a flea is fat compared to it. But 'twould seem that Cæsar hath ever admired skinny women," she went on, in a low tone, turning to the Emperor and glancing from him to

Domitia at the further end of the table. "At least," Julia added audaciously, "if we may judge by his choice of an Empress."

Domitian frowned at first, then burst into a savage laugh. He murmured something in Julia's ear, and Nyria saw her mistress's fine shoulders, from which she had cast her gorgeous palla, shake with malicious merriment. They were discussing Domitia. Presently the Emperor spoke louder. "But see," he said, "Sabinus hath actually brought a smile to those peevish lips. It seems that he is better company to Domitia than thou dost find him."

"The two are well matched in wits," said Julia, with a shrug, for it was Julia's foible to consider herself clever.

But the Emperor's interest soon began to flag again. Unluckily there came a wait in the serving, and Julia sent Nyria with an imperative message to Sabinus, bidding him reprimand the slaves.

Then Nyria noticed that Domitian was scowling down the line of attendants resplendent in their red, white and gold, and the sight of them seemed to increase his ill-humour. His body twitched, and he blinked angrily at Agricola with his watery, short-sighted eyes, muttering something which Nyria did not hear. The old general, who had been too long among barbarians to play the courtier to a tyrant, innocently fanned Cæsar's wrath.

"Ay, Sabinus maintains a fine family of slaves, my lord—worthy the kinsman of a Cæsar. And I perceive that Julia has the Augustus's permission to use the imperial livery. One may easily see that this is a princely household."

"A princely household indeed!" said Domitian, in sarcastic accents. "Too many princes are not good."

Julia turned, scenting trouble. "What else should my household be but princely, seeing that its mistress is a princess?" she said. "And since also it is Great Cæsar's pleasure that I have the privileges of an emperor's daughter."

Nyria detected a note of anxiety in her voice, but she smiled bravely at Domitian with her full red lips and her bold black eyes. Almost unwillingly, it seemed, he yielded to their fascination, for though he was wrathful he did not vent his displeasure upon her.

"Thou mayst be an emperor's daughter, Julia, but Sabinus is no emperor's son. And when I ordered thee thy lictors I gave no permission to him that he should dress his slaves in the livery of the Cæsars. Mark me," he added, in those soft, dissimulating accents which boded ill for the offenders. "As thou knowest, my nature is over gentle in the matter of affronts, yet it might be held by the Senate that such presumption savoured of treason."

Tacitus and Agricola exchanged glances, and Eprius Marcellus murmured faint applause. Julia answered meekly,—

"Indeed, my lord, the liveries are no copies of Cæsar's. If the

Most August would condescend to examine the facings, he would see that they are fashioned quite differently from those of his own slaves. How could there be thought of treason in one to whom Cæsar's person is sacred as that of Jove?"

Domitian gave her a searching look. "It sounds strange in my ears to hear Julia plead excuses for Sabinus," he said jealously.

Julia, once more confident, shrugged and smiled. "'Tis for myself I plead, not for Sabinus, Divinity," she replied. "There would be small purpose in blaming that good nincompoop, seeing that 'tis *I* who direct the affairs of my household; and that being so, I suppose that I must take the consequences." She looked very handsome and defiant as she spoke, and Domitian chuckled, apparently pleased with her answer.

"Come, come, that's not a fair division," he said. "If Julia hath the labour, 'tis but right that Sabinus should shoulder the results. For by the marriage laws of Rome a wife's debt is that of her husband, and the man must pay the penalty of his partner's mistakes."

Julia shook at him her fingers twinkling with rings, and cried banteringly, "Fie on thee, Most August! Cæsar's views on the rights of husbands and wives are more advanced than that. Society in Rome will be vastly improved when the greatest of the Cæsars sets about reforming the marriage laws."

Domitian surveyed the company with a cynical smile. He was not without a certain shrewd humour.

"May Hercules aid me in my task," said he, "for 'tis like to be a heavy one. First must all ill-matched unions be dissolved, and they are many. Mine and thine, Julia, head the list. Therefore I had best begin with thee and me, leaving each of us free to mate as we please a second time."

Julia's eyes told what thought was in the minds of both. But Domitian had not forgotten his grievance about the liveries.

"Nevertheless, Sabinus must be bidden change his colours," he said curtly; "unless he choose that the Senate's voice shall settle the matter."

"Cæsar knows that the Conscript Fathers have re-elected Sabinus to the consulship?" said Julia, in a peculiar tone.

"Sabinus may be consul once too often," returned Cæsar, darkly. "The Senate is but Cæsar's mouthpiece."

The banquet had gone through its heavier courses and lighter business was at hand. All the time musicians had been playing and a couple of actors had given a recitation, of which small heed was taken. Then a troupe of gymnasts appeared, and some performing monkeys drew languid attention. The best artists would not come on till after the toasts, which were about to begin. Now the chief steward, Vibius, conspicuous by his broad gold chain, and holding a long-handled silver ladle in one hand, and a handsome bowl in the other, advanced between the guests to the wine-fountain, and dipped the wine from its reservoir into the smaller vessel he carried. At the same time Nyria brought her mistress a cup of the costly murrhine ware and placed it before Julia, with a pair of ivory pressers and a dish of particularly large purple grapes. Julia selected the ripest bunch, and squeezed the grape-juice with the pressers into the goblet. Then Nyria handed her various bottles of essences and different kinds of spices, which Julia blended with the grape-juice, presenting the beverage to Cæsar. The little ceremony was reckoned a personal compliment to the Emperor, though he was seldom known to take the cup from any hand but Julia's. Indeed, at most houses where he dined, Domitian kept his Prætorians round him in the banqueting-hall. Under Julia's roof, however, they remained outside, and, except the official who tasted before the Emperor, only a row of lictors stood guard behind Cæsar's chair, sufficiently far off to allow space for the table-stewards' service.

It was Julia's fad to mingle this drink herself, and she knew how to make it seductive and potent, for after he had quaffed the cup a change was observed in Domitian. He grew more peaceable, and upon his haughty, frowning face there came an expression of voluptuous lassitude. Having filled the guests' goblets, Vibius stood forth importantly, and struck with his wand of office a little metal disc he held, calling the toast of the evening.

"Noble and illustrious Flavius Sabinus: most noble Clemens; Lords, honourable gentlemen and most noble ladies, glasses are charged. It is your humble duty, as well as your highest privilege, to drink to the greatest of the Cæsars. Hail! August Domitian!"

Sabinus rose to his feet, also most of the men, and a few of the lesser ladies, who were anxious to curry favour with the Emperor. Valeria sat erect and indifferent, giving only the conventional gesture of homage. Domitilla bowed with a serene smile, and everyone turned to Domitian, saluting him. The men waved their right arms, holding their glasses high, and all cried,—

"We drink to mighty Cæsar. Hail! August Domitian!"

The Emperor leaned over the table and blinked and bowed lazily. At the toast of the Empress, which followed, he neither drank nor smiled, but, immediately it was over, signed to the toast-master, and turning to Julia raised his goblet, saying, "I drink to thee, most noble Julia."

Cups were refilled, and there was a shout, "To the divine Julia!" And Julia grew redder and showed her white teeth in broader smiles. After which the steward called for the health of the Illustrious Flavius Sabinus, Consul Elect.

In Rome, after each health, the drinker turned his goblet upside down upon the table, and the slaves came with napkins to ensure that no drops of the last toast mingled with the new. For that would have been an evil augury, betokening feud and bloodshed. Now Nyria was not the only one this evening who noticed that, when about to drink to Sabinus, Domitian had fresh wine poured into his cup before the dregs left from the last toast had drained from it and been wiped away at the brim, as the custom was. Many, seeing this, shivered with superstitious dread.

The rich after-dinner wine flowed copiously, though, when the health of Sabinus had been honoured, people drank as they pleased, paying no particular attention to other toasts, for the greatest dancer and singer in Rome—Paris, the adored—began his performance.

Curious eyes went to Domitia, and Julia, pointedly drawing Cæsar's attention to the Empress, laughed and murmured behind her fan.

Domitia sat very still, her haggard face tense, while for once her bright, dark eyes ceased their restless roving and her thin hands, which had a way of fluttering about her bodice or clutching nervously at her ornaments, remained folded in her lap. From the moment that Paris made his appearance her gaze never left the stage, and the actor seemed to show his consciousness of the Empress's presence by the sedulous manner in which he avoided looking in her direction—except when, as he entered, their eyes met, and then his step faltered, and through the brownish tint of his skin the red blood showed, while Domitia's lips twitched involuntarily, and she sat white and rigid as a corpse.

Paris appeared to-night in the character of Bacchus, vine-wreathed and naked save for the dappled fawn-skin that girt his loins. It was his most popular part among the Romans, for it showed the perfection of his form. Paris was tall and handsome, with tapering, well-covered limbs, a Greek head, and a skin pale brown in tint but flushing at times to a soft red. His hair was brown and curly, and he had great brown eyes full of expression. He carried a lyre, and as he played it he sang and danced, making long, rhythmic movements in time to his music. He was even more famed for his singing than for his dancing, and his glorious chest-notes, deep, rich and sweet, had gained for him the epithet of "honey-voiced." His performance usually began with a song and ended with a dance. He stood quite still now, and drawing his hands across the strings sang the story of Semele, thrilling men's and women's nerves with the passion and sorrow of it. The lyre gave low, ecstatic wails; and now a new key was touched and sadness changed to exultation as he sang of the god who came to avenge his mother's memory, and by inflicting madness to prove his godship.

"Evoe! Evoe!" he sang. The lyre dropped out of his hand. From behind the scenes came a wild Corybantic measure—the clash of cymbals, the clanging of tambourines, the shrilling of Phrygian flutes, echoes of the Dionysaic mysteries long since abolished in Rome.

Leaping to the sound, a sort of divine fury seized upon the dancer. He was as one possessed with the spirit of motion. His beautiful body quivered in the torches' light, his eyes glowed. He flung himself into frenzied postures, each one of incomparable grace. His feet twinkled over the polished floor that reflected his form in fantastic shadow-shapes. He seemed the poetry of gesture and movement embodied. He danced—danced as though he were dancing life and soul away. Now he tore the vine wreath from his brows, and it whirled with him as he whirled. Then it swung loosely in his outstretched hand. The music slackened; it grew softer. The dancer lifted his feet more slowly, and yet more slowly. They hovered above the floor, poising each moment higher as though they needed no solid support. The wreath fell; the arms were raised in an attitude exquisitely ethereal. He seemed to be floating backward—to be melting into air. The music was but a dreamy murmuring. One long sweet note—he was gone.

Shouts of his name recalled him. He came to the front of the stage languorously, his gaze fixed on space. The storm of applause seemed to shake the banqueting-hall. People stood up and flung gold, jewels, flowers—anything they could readily reach—at his feet. Several men—Pliny among them—came up and put coins in his hand. Others took off their gold armlets and chains. Women threw brooches, necklaces—trinkets of all kinds. But the Empress offered him nothing. Only her eyes never left him as she sat cold and very quiet, the muscles of her throat looking strained.

Nor did Julia give him any thanks—but that was not Julia's way. When she was displeased people knew it, but if things prospered that was only her right. And Domitian appeared of the same mood. He sat indifferently smiling, his cruel, white hands on the arm of his chair. Julia whispered to him and he gave a sneering nod. They both looked towards Domitia. Then Julia spoke in a loud voice to the dancer, who was gathering up his tributes and laying them on his lyre.

"I congratulate thee, Paris, upon the honours my guests have paid thee," she said, and Nyria knew from her voice that she meant mischief. "Yet there is one of them," Julia went on, "whom thou apparently hast failed to please, and without whose approval thy success must be incomplete. How is it that to-night Paris has received no sign of favour from the Empress?"

Everyone present understood the sting of malice in Julia's speech. The red blood showed through Paris's brown skin, and his eyes flashed. He bowed silently.

Domitia looked very white, but still sat motionless, staring in front of her, and Pliny, addressing Sabinus, made a valiant effort to cover the incident.

This, however, was not to Julia's mind. She whispered again to the Emperor, and Domitian laughed, and leaning forward said, in his most arrogant tone,—

"Cæsar deputes the Empress to present Paris with a token of their joint appreciation. What jewel does Domitia wear to-night that will be a fitting mark of imperial favour?"

Domitia's face was deathly, but she made as though she had not heard. Domitian was having his goblet replenished, and might have let the matter pass had not Julia willed otherwise. She signed to one of her house-slaves and bade him take Cæsar's orders to the Empress. The man delivered his message, and Domitia eyed Julia for a second as if she could have killed her. But she was frightened and nervous. Then, seeing that the Emperor meant to be obeyed, she hurriedly raised one arm to her neck, where she began to unfasten a string of pearls. But Domitian stopped her, calling, in a voice of thunder,—

"Take not off the pearls I gave thee. Present Paris with the bracelet of chrysoprase which is on thy right arm."

Domitia clutched at the bracelet as though she could not part with it, then reluctantly she undid the clasp and it fell down over her wrist—a chain of large green stones graven in letters of gold connected by small gold links. With the Emperor's red eyes glaring at her Domitia was forced to take off the bracelet, and she was about to hand it to Vibius, the steward, who stood behind Sabinus's chair, when Domitian again stopped her.

"By Cæsar's pleasure Paris shall have a yet greater compliment. Come thou, Domitia, and clasp it thyself upon his arm."

Like a cowed creature Domitia rose and went slowly down the large room to the platform. She was compelled to pause in front of the Emperor's chair, which was placed to command the best view of the stage, and there at his feet to clasp the bracelet herself on Paris's wrist. Rebellious, but impotent, Paris knelt on the platform before her, and a swift tremor seemed to pass through him as the Empress's cold fingers touched his arm.

"Treasure the token, good Paris," sneered Domitian. "The favour of an Empress should bring thee luck," and he grinned, his thick red lips drawing back from his white teeth like those of an animal, while Julia threw herself sideways in her chair and laughed outright.

Other performers came. Latinus, the celebrated buffoon, and then a set of Jew women, dark and curious-looking, with long noses and coal-black hair and pale faces, who sang mournful songs of their own country, and who got engagements only because they were a novelty in Rome. It was a dreary business—some playing on harps and the rest wailing strange harmonies, beating their knees the while and swaying their bodies from side to side. Domitian found them not to his taste, and pulled a wry face.

"Here's a dish of sour plums, like to give me a pain inside. I would now have something more cheerful," said he; and at this Nyria could not forbear laughing.

Domitian must have heard her, for he turned round.

"So, Curly Locks! Thou art thinking that thou couldst sing better than that. And I warrant thou couldst, even though thou hadst a cold in thy head. Try, child, try."

Confused and frightened, Nyria sought shelter behind Julia again, but the Emperor leaned back, and, as she held her head downcast, put out his hand and jerked up her chin, saying, in rough banter,—

"'Tis not the custom in Rome, Curly Locks, for pretty women to hide their faces—no matter what their rank may be. And I find no need for thee—a little slave-girl—to set a new fashion."

Julia looked round then, wrath upon her face, and he saw that he had offended her. But the soothing effect of her Eastern cup was wearing off, for Cæsar had since drunk deeply of strong Cœcuban and Falernian, and was in the mood to be provoking.

"Come on, Curly Locks," he cried. "Come round here. My footstool is big enough for my feet and a shrimp of a maid as well."

Nyria threw a wild glance of appeal at her mistress, but Julia looked straight down her nose, her lips pursed sulkily, and that meant that she was very angry indeed and would give no aid to an innocent offender. Besides, though she was furious with Nyria, she dared not defy Cæsar. Nyria would have moved away, but the Emperor caught her dress and again bade her sit on his footstool.

"May it please Great Cæsar, I would rather stand," said the girl, desperately. Luckily for her, Cæsar's attention was diverted at the moment by a fresh band of mummers that sprang on to the stage. These were negroes, who gave a comic show, making a prank of swallowing serpents, and swords, and scorpions, and twisting their bodies into all manner of ridiculous contortions. Domitian soon wearied of their feats and fidgeted, flicking his fingers irritably.

"Have we nothing livelier," he said, "than this horse-play for boys?"

Julia retorted crossly, "I am sorry, my lord, that I do not succeed in entertaining Cæsar."

"Not so—not so, Julia. I am greatly entertained—by thyself most of all."

Then he turned round again and pulled Nyria forward. "Here's a lazy little wench who should do something for her keep. Curly Locks must have learned tricks from the women of her own land."

"The slut, my lord, declares herself a princess," cried Julia, jeeringly.

"So! so! Curly Locks!" Domitian held Nyria by a strand of her hair, and she stood reluctant, and crimson with shame. "Then it should be easy to show how a German princess robes and unrobes. First, I see, she paints her face," and he flicked Nyria's cheek, making it redder. "Hast got the receipt for those blushes, child?"

Just then Julia, leaning close to the Emperor, caught the gold fringe on her bodice in his armlets, and as he unhitched it he looked her up and down admiringly.

"Thou dost surpass thyself to-night, beautiful Julia. Was it Nyria who clad thee so bravely?"

"Nay, for the minx was late in coming in," said Julia, angrily.

"Why, how was that, Curly Locks?" asked the Emperor.

"May it please Cæsar, the Most Noble gave me permission to go out, and I wandered on the hillside."

"My lord wastes his kindness upon the brat," said Julia.

Domitian pushed out his long, red underlip and gave a peculiar nod. "In thine interest, dearest Julia—in thine interest only. Cæsar, who is the father of his people, hath concern for the welfare of the humblest, and would fain discover for what the girl is suited. Therefore let her act, or sing, or dance, and show Cæsar of what she is capable. Begin, Nyria."

The tears started into Nyria's eyes, and she made a terrified obeisance, not knowing how far he was teasing.

"My lord, when Cæsar commands, his slaves must obey. But the Most Noble has ordered these players, who are the best in Rome, to perform before the Emperor, and if Cæsar be not satisfied with them, how can I, the meanest of slaves, please him better?"

"We will see! we will see!" said Cæsar. "I think I guess the reason of Nyria's lateness. Was she not fooling with the players—Paris, maybe, or Latinus, the clown, who loves a pretty face. Tell the truth, girl."

"My lord, I spoke not with the players, and, indeed, I hastened over the decorations and should have been in readiness for the Most Noble, had I not—had not I been stayed."

Nyria stammered. She feared to bring censure on the old Ethiopian. But Domitian pressed her.

"What stayed thee, child?"

"May it please Cæsar, 'twas at Euphena's door that I was stayed."

"Who sawest thou at Euphena's door?" he asked. She hesitated again, and he repeated the question.

"Euphena sat at the door, my lord."

Cæsar's eyes twinkled meaningly. "I know not who Euphena may be, but the name should be that of a woman. Else would I have construed 'Euphena' into 'lover.' Now, speak straight, shrimp. Was none but Euphena there?"

"None, my lord. I had to bathe and prepare myself for the Most Noble's presence, but Euphena—would not—could not—let me pass. Euphena was—she was—" Nyria halted, realising that she was telling tales.

"Answer," said Cæsar, sharply. "What was Euphena doing?"

"May it please Cæsar, Euphena was reading the stars."

He drew himself up at that, his mouth agape and his eyes widening. For Domitian believed in the lore of the stars.

"Ah! so we have an astrologer in the fair Euphena—a maiden priestess, mayhap," he muttered, "like the virgin Veleda." He turned to Julia. "Produce Euphena," he said.

But Julia shrugged her great shoulders vexedly.

"How shall I produce Euphena? Does Cæsar think that I know the name of every slave and underling in my household? It appears that the converse of slaves is pleasant to Cæsar."

Domitian repeated imperiously,—

"Produce Euphena."

Julia, seeing that she had overshot the mark, yet unwilling to concede the matter, put on a cringing tone. "My lord, how shall I produce the slave? For aught I know, she is a street beggar, or perchance a slave of another household."

Now Nyria knew that Julia lied, seeing that Euphena had been summoned several times of late to her mistress's apartments. But she had small time to speculate on Julia's falsity, for the Emperor called her to him.

"Little one, canst *thou* produce Euphena?"

Sorely frightened, Nyria looked at Julia, but received not a glance.

"If it be Cæsar's pleasure," she answered. "But Euphena is—" she stumbled. She had been going to say "old and ugly," but changed it to "Euphena is shy," for Nyria was sure that Cæsar would scoff at Euphena's black face.

"Shy!" repeated Cæsar. "Is she, then, a young and lovely maid, with yellow hair and turquoise eyes like Nyria?"

"Nay, may it please Cæsar," said the girl, "Euphena is—" and again she stopped. Cæsar laughed aloud, while Julia maintained a sulky silence.

"It seems that this Euphena is somewhat of a mystery. She whets my curiosity. I will see her for myself."

"As it may please Cæsar." And with an obeisance Nyria drew away, hoping that one of the other slaves would be sent for Euphena. But Cæsar called her back.

"Hold, Curly Locks! Thou sayest Euphena was reading the stars. How could that be when the sun had scarce set and the stars were invisible?"

"My lord, Euphena knoweth their places by day or night, for she has much strange lore. Euphena says that she can best read the fate of a married pair when their birth-stars are in a certain conjunction, the hour of which may be in sunlight or in darkness." Then Nyria would like to have bitten out her tongue when Domitian asked quickly,—

"Whose were the fates that Euphena read?"

But the girl answered as the words came, "The fates of my master and of the Most Noble, may it please Cæsar."

"So, ho! Dost hear, Julia? Art thou not anxious to know what Euphena and the stars said of thee?"

Julia's brow grew darker, and she pouted. "I listen not to slaves' babble," she said.

"That is left for Cæsar," returned Domitian. "Haste, Nyria, and bring Euphena hither."

The girl sped, daring not to disobey, though she guessed that Euphena would flay her for reward. The same thought struck Domitian, for he stopped her before she had reached the door.

"Come, stand again beside my chair, child. So small a maid might easily be lost sight of. The steward shall fetch Euphena," and he nodded curtly to Vibius.

Nyria crouched behind Cæsar's great chair of gold and ivory, for she dreaded to face Euphena. There was a stir in the room when it was said that a diviner was coming who had foretold the fates of Julia and Sabinus, for among the fashionable people of Rome there was much private consultation of Chaldean soothsayers.

"Now we shall hear State secrets!" cried someone. Others said it was not wise to unveil futurity; while those eager for an augury left their couches and, amid talk and laughter, pressed nearer the upper end of the banqueting-hall, where it was expected the sibyl would enter. So they waited in expectation of Euphena's coming.

Julia sat silent, and, as she plied her big fan of green and gold feathers tipped with red before her face, Nyria saw by the movement of her hands that she was exceedingly wroth, and said to herself,—

"There will be more strokes for me to-morrow, and, alack! I am sore of skin already."

Presently Euphena was brought in between Vibius and Bibbi—

the slave-lasher—a Moor with white blood in him, and the strongest man in the household. Each had hold of an arm, but dropped it as they approached, and pushed Euphena up before them till she fronted the Emperor's chair, now drawn sideways from the table. And there stood the little old black woman, defiant, her head reared, her yellowish eyes gleaming, and her arms crossed before her. She had on a scarlet petticoat and an orange-coloured jacket unbuttoned at the throat, where, on a cord on her bony chest, there hung the stone which most of the slaves firmly believed to be an instrument of her witchcraft. She made no obeisance to Cæsar, but looked straight at him and then at Julia. And Nyria wondered yet more, for Julia's eyes shrank and quailed before the scorn in Euphena's gaze, so that one might have fancied that Euphena was the princess and Julia a frightened slave.

X

DOMITIAN stared at the hideous old woman, then burst into a laugh which was echoed on all sides. Everybody was astonished and inclined to mock, for the surmise Domitian had hazarded having got about, the company had expected some fair priestess of the German nation.

"So *thou* art Euphena?" the Emperor said, eyeing the Ethiopian from her ugly head to her withered ankles. "The beauteous Euphena! Nay! but thou art miscalled. Europa thou!—like to that loveliest maid of Tyre whom the father of gods and men bore off to Crete. Too beauteous thou art for mortal lovers! Such fairness should tempt Jove himself once more to come a-wooing," and Cæsar laughed immoderately, the company catching his merriment till even slaves guffawed. All but Julia, who gave no laugh. The Ethiopian glared fiercely, but held herself erect, looking proud and stiff. "So thou art Euphena!" repeated Domitian.

"Thus in Rome men call me," she answered in her guttural voice. "But I am no Roman woman."

Again there was a burst of laughter.

"Nay, thou art no Roman woman, lovely Euphena!" scoffed Domitian. "How could we find such fairness in any Roman woman?"

"Fairness is but skin deep," replied Euphena. "Look for fairness, Cæsar, in those who lead honest lives, and not on the faces of Roman women. Nevertheless," she went on, "beautiful I was when Roman robbers stole me from my kingdom. And what I once was, that I am, and that I shall be ever. Therein lies a deeper truth than thou canst understand, oh! Cæsar."

"Ho! ho! So thou wouldst teach Cæsar?" said Domitian.

"Truly, a thankless task," returned Euphena. "Yet could I teach Cæsar many things that 'twould be well for him to learn."

The slaves exchanged horrified glances, and Nyria stood aghast, expecting that no less than fifty lashes would be ordered Euphena. But her audacity amused Cæsar; for, at least, there was variety in it, and he only chuckled.

"That is as it should be," he said, "since thou hast been sent for in order that thou mightest instruct Cæsar, as well as these noble lords and ladies, in certain things of which they are as yet ignorant. For I suppose thou wilt admit that others in Rome are ignorant besides the Emperor?"

Euphena looked at him unabashed. "No man is so ignorant as he who thinks there is naught for him to learn. Domitian hath been wont to consider that there is naught of importance in the universe save that alone which he holds of account. Let me tell him that he is but as a child counting for treasure grains of sand."

"Well! well! We will grant that we know nothing, and that thou knowest all things," said Domitian, with impatient tolerance, "for this night, at least, if thou canst prove thyself learned in the wisdom of the heavens. So, fairest Euphena, expound to us the book of Destiny, and fear not to speak boldly, for I pledge thee the word of Cæsar that, no matter what thou sayest, thou shalt go unpunished."

Euphena smiled disdainfully and asked, "What wouldst thou that I should tell thee?"

"That which thou wast reading to-day by the light of the invisible stars," said he; "unless thou hast better means for casting an augury?"

"Means are many, and all good in their fashion. But the book of Destiny is often closed to man; even when a page lies open, none but those with eyes to see may read what is written thereupon."

"So! Then, if thou hast eyes to see, interpret to us the writing. First, I desire to know the fate of the Most Noble."

Julia shrank suddenly, for Euphena's eyes were fixed upon her.

"The Most Noble!" repeated Euphena. "Whom meanest thou?"

"Thy mistress, Julia, woman," said Cæsar, angrily.

"My mistress, Julia, hath no right to the title of Most Noble, except it be granted her of courtesy and by the favour of Cæsar."

"What dost thou say? No right!" cried Cæsar. "Hag! Witch! I pledged the word of Cæsar that thou shouldst go unharmed, but I bargained not for insults to thy mistress."

Euphena ignored Domitian's rebuke and replied, quite calmly,—

"Cæsar demanded a page from the book of Destiny on which Julia's fate is written. Be it so. Is it of the past, or of the future, that Cæsar desires to hear?"

There was a murmur among the guests, but all kept silence when Cæsar spoke.

"Begin at the beginning," he said. "Tell what auguries welcomed the birth of Julia, most noble daughter of Titus."

Then Euphena stood back a pace, and folding her skinny arms on her breast, half shut her eyes, showing only a line of yellow-white between her drooping lids. Presently she spoke.

"Auguries that boded no good—portents of lust and bloodshed—loomed at the birth of Julia, daughter, not of Titus, but of Croton, the scavenger, and Marcia Furnilla, Titus's wife."

Domitian started forward in his chair, his face red, his eyes glaring, but Julia cowered back, her fan before her face. Many of the company stirred and touched each other's sleeves, while amid smothered cries of reprobation rose the hiss of meaning whispers. Euphena went on, heeding nothing.

"Over the cradle of Tatiana, only daughter of Titus, there hovered the presage of untimely death. Tatiana passed away in infancy, but yonder sits Julia, the scavenger's child, no daughter of Titus, but offspring of his lowest slave."

The buzz of voices in the room grew louder. People talked among themselves, and thoughts went back to a scandal in Rome hushed up at the time by Vespasian, but which had leaked out later on when Titus divorced his wife. Julia, whose fan fell for a moment, looked the image of baffled fury. Domitian was the first to recover himself, and laughed in affected incredulity.

"No daughter of Titus!" he exclaimed. "Here indeed is entertainment provided for us that we had not cause to expect. Excellent Euphena! thy fancy is winged as thy face is lovely. Thou dost promise well, fair diviner. We asked for amusement and thou hast made a fine beginning."

"'Tis more than can be said of Julia," rejoined Euphena, imperturbably. "She, whose father wallowed in mire, did not in truth make a fine beginning, though she stands near the throne of Cæsar—ay, and would seat herself upon it."

There was dark meaning in Euphena's words. Julia furled her fan and laid her hand on the Emperor's arm.

"How can Cæsar listen to the harridan's lying talk?" she cried. "This Euphena is the scum of some slaves' quarter, and not fit to appear in the presence of the Most August. Dismiss her, and let worthier performers show themselves."

But Cæsar shook his head. "Nay, the witch diverts me. I would hear to what length she dare go. But mark me, black hag," and he turned to Euphena, "though I have given thee my word for thy safety, I cannot guarantee it at the hands of thy mistress. Julia deals with her own slaves as she doth will, so take heed lest it be commanded that thy tongue is slit and thou thyself sold as a beast of burden in the slave-market."

Euphena faced the two dauntlessly. "My tongue shall not be slit," she said, "nor will Julia send me to the slave-market. The old Ethiopian is too useful for the high-born Julia to dispense with her services. While Domitian reigns in Rome, and Julia holds his favour, Euphena will be needed as an instrument to carry out the decrees of destiny."

"Cæsar is proud to share in such faithful service," sneered

Domitian, but there was a troubled note in his voice, and his eyes dropped before Euphena's contemptuous stare.

"Go on, woman," he muttered. "Tell us further of the Most Noble, whose fate, since according to thee it began so low, should now be all on the ascendant."

"On the ascendant, surely, as the world calls climbing," replied Euphena. "And higher yet will Julia climb, until she has reached the very steps of the throne."

"Ah!" The sound came with a quick indrawing of Domitia's breath. She had come up with Sabinus, and both were listening intently.

"And then?" asked the Empress. "Then will Julia gain a foothold?"

"Rome's empire is vast, and the arm of Cæsar mighty," Euphena went on. "But the realm of shades is vaster, and the power of death more mighty still."

"So the supreme control of life and death will not be granted to Julia?" asked the Empress again in a strained, eager manner.

Euphena answered slowly, "Life and death shall lie indeed within the grasp of Julia. Nevertheless, those hands which have done much violence will tremble in the hour of their own doom, and when snatching at the pleasures of life shall close only on the portion of death."

Julia shrank back, huddled, with a frightened look. Sabinus moved beside his wife's chair as though he would put himself between her and danger, while the Empress watched her rival with hard, bright eyes full of hate. Julia caught the look, and exclaimed,—

"'Tis a pity the witch should spend her evil tongue on me when Domitia's fate remains untold. Here we shall have more pleasant hearing, for if the Empress be the greatest lady in Rome, is she not also the kindest, the most amiable and best beloved by her subjects and her slaves? We all know Domitia's favour can only be won by merit, for her noble soul scorns low aims and abhors tyranny."

Julia had got back her spirit, and everyone present understood the irony of her words, for Domitia's ungenial ways and bitter speech had made her one of the most unpopular of Roman empresses.

Euphena seemed to be weighing her as she answered,—

"Domitia doth indeed abhor tyranny, and thus it is that by her aid Rome shall be freed from its tyrant, so that in years to come the Roman people shall tell how Domitia's voice urged the assassin to drive his dagger home."

Now it was the Empress's turn to shrink back with a shudder; her eyes, always restless, threw round her a wild, startled look—

the look of a prisoner behind bars who hopes, yet fears, to be set free. She stood twisting her unquiet hands in and out of the gold fringe of her palla, and biting her lips nervously. Many of the company glanced apprehensively at the Emperor, thinking that he would order punishment to the utterer of so daring a prediction. But it did not appear that Domitian applied Euphena's words to himself, or perhaps the wine he had drunk and the Eastern drug had dulled his perceptions, for he sat saying nothing, a fatuous expression on his bleared red face.

Now Julia, seeing that her guests pressed forward, bade Euphena exercise her prophetic wits on some of these, and as she spied that Valeria looked interested, she called her loudly by name, bidding her come closer and hear what happy fortune the gods had in store for her.

"For," she said, "Valeria hath a sad air, which is but natural since Paulinus goes shortly to Africa, and the Fates should recompense his devoted wife for so heartbreaking a separation."

Whereat Martial broke in fulsomely, praying the gods that Valeria might not be induced to accompany her husband and so leave Rome to mourn the extinguishment of one of its most brilliant lights.

Julia laughed. "Does not all the world know," she said, "that Valeria's health will not permit her to take sea journeys, and that regard for her, forces Paulinus to leave her lamenting."

Paulinus's brow grew dark, and Valeria paled and stiffened, saying distantly, when urged by Julia to test the Ethiopian's skill, "Nay, I think the gods are gracious in keeping the future hidden from our eyes. For my part, I have no desire to raise the veil they have dropped before the gaze of men."

At that Euphena took up the word. "Thou art wise! Remain ever thus wise—since for thee, above all women, it is happiest that the veil should not be lifted."

"Not so! We will hear what thou hast to say of Valeria," cried Paulinus, roughly.

Euphena did not answer. It was as though a spell had been cast upon her, for she stood staring into space, her arms clenched tightly upon her breast and her lips moving inarticulately.

"Speak," said Julia, imperiously. Once or twice Euphena tried to speak, but only made an indistinct muttering. Then suddenly words came to her, and she loosed her arms, pointing a bony finger at Valeria.

"The sword of love shall pierce thy breast, that never yet has known love. In vengeance shalt thou cause him whom thou lovest to be slain, and thou shalt deliver unto the beasts one for whose faithful love thou shalt hereafter yearn in vain. Thou who hast scorned love—unloved shalt thou wear out thy days, and at the last unloved shalt thou die. And Rome shall fall, and the Wheel of Life shall turn, not once but many times; and souls shall float through ages on the ocean of Time ere the dead drift back to thee again and thine expiation be complete."

Valeria listened unflinchingly, a faint smile on her lips, though her face was very pale. Nyria watched her, straining from behind Julia's chair. A deathly hand seemed to clutch the slave-girl's heart. The lights and people blurred into a confused mass, of which Euphena alone stood forth plainly, her bony finger still pointed at Valeria, while her eyes looked past as at a vision in space.

"I see a feast of blood, and above it Cæsar enthroned in purple and gold. I hear the shouts of a multitude greedy with the lust of carnage. I hear the tramp of gladiators and the voices of the doomed acclaiming their destroyer. I hear the wails of women, the groans of the dying, the roaring of wild beasts—"

And as Euphena spoke giddiness came over Nyria, and a deadly fear and sickness caused her limbs to totter, so that the whole room swayed and became shadowy mist, out of which there seemed to troop and spring the shapes of beasts of prey—lions and tigers with panting red tongues and fiery eyes. Closer they pressed around her, and their hungry roaring was as the thunder of a mighty wave that engulfed her senses, and she knew no more.

When she came to herself she shuddered at the sight of Bibbi, the lasher, who was pouring water upon her forehead, while Vibius held a cup of wine to her lips, saying that Cæsar had sent it. Nyria drank the wine and felt better; the beasts were gone now, and the lights blazed smoothly as before. After all, it was not strange that she should have fainted, for she had eaten little all day.

The men put her on a marble stool, against a pillar near the platform, and Domitian nodded at her in the friendly way which frightened Nyria. But she was relieved now she saw that they would not scold her, and began to take an interest again in what was going on.

Euphena was talking to Flavius Clemens and the Domina Domitilla. These two must have been called up by the Emperor, for Nyria had heard from Stephanus that Domitilla disapproved of all manner of soothsaying, and would never herself consult the diviners. She stood now with both hands on her husband's arm, a pained but serene look upon her gentle face. Those standing round, however, had a discomposed air, as though they liked not what they heard, but Cæsar chuckled evilly. It was he who now spoke.

"The witch has told me naught about my household. Let me hear of the boys, fair Euphena—Vespasian and Domitian, sons of Clemens and Domitilla, whom Cæsar hath chosen for his heirs. Will they prove good rulers of my Empire when, in fulness of time, the gods call me to my place amongst them?"

"The boys will rule no empire wider than their own souls," she answered.

"Ho! ho!" laughed Domitian, not ill-pleased. "Thou meanest, then, that Cæsar will have a son of his own to sit after him upon his seat? This, hag, is the one fortunate augury thou hast yet given."

Just then Sabinus leaned over and said a word to Julia, thus bringing himself to Cæsar's notice, and Domitian called out, "By Pallas! I had forgotten that the blackamoor was reading Sabinus's fate as well as that of the most noble Julia. Tell us, then, oh! sport of Hades, what the stars revealed to thee concerning thy master and his house."

"Alas! Naught but what bodeth ill," said Euphena, with a motion of her head towards Sabinus. "Few and short are the days in which my master shall rule his house, and when the head is stricken the house shall fall and night shall cover its ruins. Yea, even now the bloody cloud overhangs Sabinus—and not alone Sabinus, but many another who banquets here to-night." She stretched out her arms, seeming to compass the assemblage. Her lean form was shaking and her fingers pointed at the walls, where, amongst the wreaths and torches, she seemed to see lurking dark and dreadful omens. Then she drew in her arms with a sinister gesture of finality.

"Woe!" she cried. "Woe to the godless and to the godly, since the good must suffer with the evil, and not till all is accomplished may justice be fulfilled. Woe to Rome!—to the city in which terror reigneth—for where death comes at the lifting of a tyrant's finger how shall there be peace? Nevertheless, rest satisfied, shades of Sabinus and Flavius Clemens, of Ælius Lamia, of Senecio and Rusticus, of Arretinus and Agricola, of Metius and Glabrio, and Licinius. Let thy manes be content. For he who slew thee shall himself be slain, and by treachery and bloodshed shall Cæsar go to his last account. Woe to thee, Domitian! The stars have spoken, and thou knowest thy doom."

There was a moment's awful silence, and then a great stir and confusion in the hall. People rose from their seats, pallid and angry, expostulating eagerly.

"Treason!" shouted Norbanus, the Prefect of the Prætorians. The lictors stepped nearer their master, their golden fasces raised, and all eyes turned to Cæsar.

Terrible to behold, he could scarce speak for fury. His face turned crimson, and then to a corpse-like white, his mouth foamed, the veins in his thick neck stood out. He half got up from his chair and lifted his arms menacingly, while a torrent of imprecations burst from his lips. Every moment it was thought that the guard would be summoned, or the lictors bidden to lead some present to execution. Euphena alone stood undaunted, caring nothing for the storm she had raised, and no one dared approach to take her unless Cæsar gave the word. But Domitian's fury seemed more against his host and the company—even Norbanus, the Prefect, whom he accused of neglecting his duty in permitting traitors to be at large. Each consular and senatorial personage shrank back, and was silent, for none knew upon whom this mad dog of an Emperor would turn his teeth, and some would have propitiated Euphena, seeing that the tyrant seemed disposed to propitiate her also. For they whispered to each other, "She hath uttered the prophecy of the Chaldeans, which Domitian feareth."

Julia, looking towards the old woman, seemed to avoid her gaze, and, pressing close to Domitian, tried in an undertone to soothe his savage mood.

"The black impostor doth but play upon thy superstitious fears," she said. "My lord knows what foul things she spoke of me, and if I, a weak woman, paid no heed to the vile croaking of this gutter-scum, how should the mightiest of the Cæsars give credence to her malicious babble?"

Domitian listened. Then quite suddenly his mood changed and he broke into a laugh.

"A fine entertainment!" he cried; "to bid Cæsar to a banquet and provide a fortune-teller to predict him an evil end!" and he made pretence at scoffing; but Nyria, from her stool against the wall, felt thankful that Cæsar seemed to have forgotten her part in the producing of Euphena, for she saw plainly that he was much disturbed in mind. So, too, was the whole crowd, and none even glanced at the stage when, at Julia's sign, some comic pantomimists came on to make a diversion. People would have liked to leave the banqueting-hall, but that, of course, they could not do till Cæsar gave the signal, though the reigning consul present took advantage of his privilege, and of a trumped-up message conveyed by his own servant behind him, to plead urgent public business and crave Cæsar's permission to depart.

Flavius Clemens and Domitilla were almost the only ones who did not appear discomposed. They moved about among the guests, talking in their gentle, dignified way; and Sabinus, too, was calm and gracious. He came round before the Emperor, and Nyria thought that perhaps he was going to apologise for the untoward incident and to suggest Euphena's removal; but he only spoke with pleasant courtesy, asking whether it was Cæsar's pleasure that the dice-tables should be brought, and saying that he hoped Cæsar had not found the Ethiopian's prophecies too wild and wordy for his liking.

Domitian looked at his cousin for a moment in a furtive, reflective kind of way that was always ominous.

"Truly, worthy Sabinus, the performance hath been of a sort to make me merry. Mayhap, however, there are those who will find less cause for laughter when the end of the play has come."

Sabinus only bowed, and was retiring, when Domitian stopped him.

"Stay. The Senate, I understand, is well-disposed towards thy consulship, and thou wilt enter office in the January kalends."

"By the favour of Cæsar I am thus honoured," said Sabinus, simply.

"I am told," proceeded Domitian, "that there is a division of opinion upon certain reforms thou dost wish to institute, and it may be that I have not done wisely in sanctioning the appointment of my valued kinsman to a position wherein there is danger."

Sabinus looked the Emperor straight in the face and replied, in firm accents,—

"My lord! Flavius Sabinus, like other men, can live but once, and die but once. In that he has ever sought to comport himself after a manner befitting his gens, I pray thee of thy favour to grant him an end that shall equally befit the name he bears."

Then, with a grave and respectful bow, he drew back and gave a command to the chief steward. Presently wine from the fountain was ladled out afresh, and slaves brought round dice. Cæsar roused himself from a low-voiced colloquy with Julia, and grimly bade Agricola stake for a pro-consulship—by which Tacitus guessed that disgrace, and not a pro-consulship, would be his father-in-law's portion.

Domitian took no further notice of Euphena, who stood, her arms crossed, contemptuously and menacingly. Bibbi, the beater, and another, waited near for the sentence of lashes that they expected to be given forth; but it came not. Domitian seemed engrossed with the dice, and delivered no order for punishment. By-and-by Julia looked across at the Ethiopian.

"Thou hast done enough," she said curtly; "thou mayest go."

Euphena walked out untouched.

XI

NYRIA did not dare to go back to Euphena's cabin for her night-clothes, for she feared to face the old woman; so, when the time came, she merely slipped off her outer robe and rolled herself in her blanket to sleep, as was her habit, outside Julia's door. All the guests had gone, and Julia was in her dressing-room preparing for the night. It was not Nyria's duty to help in the unrobing. From this ceremony the upper slaves were released, with the exception of Æmilia, the head-woman. She superintended the under maids, who thus graduated for the more difficult task of arraying their lady for the day.

When the other maids had been dismissed, Julia, remembering that she had left her scent-bottle in the atrium, called Nyria to fetch it. The girl groped her way along the passages to the great hall, which was deserted and dark, except for a few night-lamps always kept burning. Even the fountain was turned off, and the shapes of Leda and the Swan looked ghostlike in the gloom. But from an opening at one side of the atrium there came a stronger ray of light. The chapel of the Lares was softly illuminated, and as she crept by Nyria saw Sabinus in a reverential attitude before the altar, praying to the household gods. He seemed deeply in earnest, and his uplifted face had an expression of mournful resignation.

Nyria stole past, pitying her master. She would have liked to say prayers for Sabinus, but knew not to what deity to pray, So she went back, and stretched herself again in her blanket at Julia's door; and then, full of futile longings, she dropped asleep.

When she awoke next morning she did not run out, as was her custom, to dress at Euphena's cabin, for she was still afraid to meet the old woman; but, against all rules, washed her face in Julia's bathroom while Julia still slept, and combed out her hair sacrilegiously with one of Julia's combs; then, putting on a wrapper of Thanna's that she found, waited in the loggia outside Julia's dressing-room till her mistress should require her for the head-tiring.

Julia's rooms faced west, therefore there was no morning sun on the steps of the loggia; and feeling chilly, Nyria stepped out into the courtyard, surreptitiously sunning herself, when her heart stood still for a moment at sight of Euphena coming from the slaves' quarters. She trembled, but the Ethiopian looked indifferently at her, and only bade her tell Julia that Euphena waited.

"But I wait myself, mother, to be called for the hair-dressing, and till then I may not take thy request to the Most Noble."

"'Twill serve," said Euphena, sharply, and sat herself on the steps, clasping her skinny arms round her knees, and gazing sombrely over the courtyard.

"Thou art not angry with me, Euphena?" Nyria asked.

"Angry!" exclaimed the old woman. "And with thee! How canst thou make Euphena angry?"

"Because I spoke of thee to Cæsar, and he sent for thee to prophesy. But truly, Euphena, I thought not what would follow."

"One does not expect babies or fools to think," returned Euphena. "Tush, child! Fret not thyself over so small a matter. Take my word—thou wilt have greater cause to fret by-and-by. Whether thou hadst spoken of me or not, I should have been sent for to Cæsar's presence, for 'twas willed that he and his lawless wanton should receive a warning of their doom."

Nyria sat mute and frightened, and Euphena, unfolding her arms, stooped and drew on the ground a figure of a bier.

"So! A fine corpse she will make," muttered Euphena. "And thou and I, Nyria, shall dress her for her funeral pyre. 'Twill repay thee, child, for the many stripes thou hast received at her bidding, and for the blows she hath dealt thee with her own hand."

"If thou dost mean Julia, mother," said Nyria, "I wish not to see her dead."

"Dead women cannot strike. As well become used to death, child, for thou wilt some day have to face it grimly enough."

At that moment Thanna appeared, beckoning Nyria, who ran into the dressing-room and made obeisance.

"May it please the Most Noble, Euphena waits without," she said, and, taking the combs and pins from Samu, she shook out the false tresses with which Julia augmented her own locks.

A shrinking look crossed Julia's face, but she shrugged her shoulders petulantly, and sat down before the large silver mirror which a negro dwarf supported, and bade Nyria proceed with the hair-dressing.

"Let Euphena enter," she said, and Nyria fumbled with the combs, thinking Julia would dismiss her waiting-women, but her mistress turned crabbedly upon her.

"Get on, Nyria! Must I wait all day?" And Nyria began combing out the thick hair till it hung in a great black cloud round Julia's head.

One of the women had gone to bring Euphena, who now stood within the door.

"Well," said Julia, "what is thy business, blackamoor?"

Euphena answered, "I have but forestalled the Most Noble's pleasure in summoning me."

At this audacious reply Julia turned her head and caught sight of the other women-dressers standing by, one folding a robe and one polishing a silver toilet-vessel.

"Go, ye gaping fools!" she cried. "Do I need all the females in my household to listen when I choose to speak to one of them? Begone, Æmilia, Samu, Thanna, and take the black boy with ye."

The dwarf propped Julia's great mirror against a marble tripod, and they all went away through the curtains, though Nyria knew quite well that Thanna, at any rate, would stop behind them and listen. As her own name had not been mentioned she went on brushing, expecting every moment to be dismissed also. But Julia gave her no order, only turning fiercely to Euphena.

"Thine errand, hag of Tartarus," she said, "and be speedy over it."

"The Most Noble may address her slaves as she pleaseth," returned the Ethiopian, "but a day will come ere long when Julia, reputed daughter of Titus, will cry for Euphena to save her from hell's torments, and it may be in vain."

Julia blenched. "Well, well! No matter. What madst thou tell all those lies last night, old fool?"

"I tell no lies," said Euphena. "Destiny writes her fiats on the heavens, and I am the stars' mouthpiece. I was bidden by the gods to warn thee, Julia, while yet there is time and opportunity for thee to undo thine evil deeds. Once, twice have I saved thee. A third time the potion may be of no avail but to destroy thee. Take or leave the warning as thou wilt. 'Tis no affair of mine."

"Insolent slave! Knowst thou not that I can have thee stripped and lashed in the Forum till the paving-stones are black with blood?" hissed Julia.

"I know that Julia dares not strip and lash Euphena," answered the slave, boldly. "While the Most Noble hath need of a Wise Woman's knowledge, that Wise Woman's skin is safe. Julia knoweth that none is wiser than Euphena. Therefore Euphena fears not Julia."

Julia jerked her head forward, so that her hair was pulled from Nyria's hands, and she glowered at the old woman. Then, abashed by Euphena's gaze, she dropped back in her chair, and said, in a cowed way, "What dost thou want of me?"

"What should I want, since the Most Noble provides so lavishly for her slaves?" answered Euphena, sneeringly. "I would but remind Julia of her promise. The last time that I succoured thee thou didst swear by the steps of Cæsar's throne to grant me freedom."

Julia, recovering herself, laughed mockingly. "Not yet! Not yet! I still have need of thy services. Not till Julia mounts the throne may Euphena look for her freedom." Then her voice changed. She leant forward again, speaking low and huskily.

"Euphena might herself hasten that day of manumission, for were a certain potion to do its work upon Domitia well and quickly, then might the Wise Woman claim even more than freedom for her reward."

Euphena drew back a step and shook her head, smiling with malevolent cunning. Julia hastily bent to a table near her, on which stood a large silver casket, open, and crammed with trinkets. She picked up a long gold chain set with emeralds, that hung half out of the box, and threw it at Euphena.

"Take this," she said, "and consider of the matter."

The old woman's eyes glistened with a miser's greed. She made a snatch at the chain, and, fingering it, gloated over its glittering length.

"Truly I will consider the matter, most noble Julia. Here is a gift worthy of an emperor's daughter, and jewels gleam as brightly on a dusky neck as on a white one. Be assured that I will consider the matter. Yet do thou reflect," and she drew closer, and almost whispered in Julia's ear, "'tis not Domitia alone who stands between thee and Cæsar's throne."

Julia looked at the woman swiftly, then her eyes dropped, but she said nothing. Euphena gave an elfish chuckle, and cringed mockingly, with bent knees, before she departed.

After the Ethiopian had gone Julia remained very quiet for several minutes, while Nyria curled and twisted and reared the pile of her hair. Evidently the lady was in deep thought, for she did not even admire herself in the mirror, nor scold Nyria for driving a hairpin too tightly or not adjusting a love-lock. Presently she drew in her body with a shiver, then, bursting into a laugh, she stared at her image in the expanse of polished silver, and muttered strangely under her breath. Nyria, giving touches to the little ringlets at the nape of Julia's neck, caught one or two words here and there.

"Paris might serve . . . . and yet a potion would do better—for the dead come not back to confound . . ." And presently, . . . "The other? Bah! A flick that would kill a fly will be enough . . . it should be easy to sway the Senate . . . . By aid of Kore, queen of hell, and Euphena, blackest of her satellites, the path of Julia will be cleared of obstacles . . ."

Nyria wondered what meaning lay under her mistress's utterance. Deep in her own thoughts, Julia had forgotten the presence of her waiting-maid, but that was not to be marvelled at, for slaves counted but as automata. Now Julia bade the girl remove her wrapper, and standing up before the mirror preened her neck, well pleased with the sight of herself. Her face had been carefully tinted—that was Thanna's work—and her eyebrows pencilled. Altogether, she was pranked for conquest.

"I am at my best!" she exclaimed. "Do I not look well, Nyria?" and she turned exultantly to the slave.

Nyria was startled at the appeal, for though Julia frequently referred a matter of the toilet to Æmilia, her head-woman, she would usually have scorned to question one of the younger maids. Thus the girl had no response ready, and this angered Julia.

"Speak, brat. Or is my beauty such that it strikes a barbarian dumb?"

"Assuredly the Most Noble is looking well to-day," faltered Nyria, but Julia was not satisfied.

"Thou art faint in thy praise. If 'twere that pale gowk, the daughter of Vitellius, thou wouldst have found something warmer to say."

Nyria bent in silent obeisance, and Julia, still preening herself in the mirror, laughed again sarcastically.

"Bah! I care not! The daughter of Vitellius may boast of a Cæsar's blood in her veins—which yon black slanderer denieth me—but, by Bacchus! what a Cæsar! Yet there would not be many minds, I imagine, as to which of us would look best on the Imperial throne." She turned again to Nyria.

"Should I not make a fine empress, brat?—a finer one than that skinny kill-joy who flouted me last evening."

Nyria made another obeisance. But if to please Julia she spoke slightingly of Domitia, Julia was quite capable of denouncing Nyria for treason to the Empress should a fit of temper or motives of policy prompt her to do so. So Nyria merely answered,—

"Nay, Most Noble. How should a poor slave judge on so great a matter?" at which Julia sniffed, half angrily, half disdainfully.

To-day she took Thanna with her to the Palatine, but Nyria was not jealous; she was amused by Thanna's pride in the occasion. She helped to arrange round Thanna's head and shoulders a red veil with an embroidered border that Thanna said she had bought from a Jew pedlar in the city and had paid for with kisses—boasting how cheaply she had obtained her purchase. Whereat Nyria cried shame on her, declaring that she herself might give her kisses, but assuredly would never sell them.

"What, not even to Stephanus!" retorted Thanna. "How camst thou then by thine amber beads?" And Nyria blushed and ran away.

That night Sabinus and his wife dined alone in a small room off the atrium. Julia was curt and scornful, as was her wont to her husband, but Sabinus tried to interest her in his courteous fashion by the recital of his day's doings. Julia, however, seemed indifferent, merely making a few snappish remarks, and eating fast and drinking much the while. Nyria, as she stood behind her mistress, listened vaguely to the talk, not understanding its drift, but feeling deeply sorry for Sabinus. He had been, he said, at the Senate House most of the morning, having been summoned to explain his views concerning reforms he wished to introduce during his term of consulship. And this summons had surprised Sabinus, for he had understood that Cæsar supported these reforms, and that the Senate could be in no doubt as to his opinions.

Julia pricked her ears now, and Nyria also became more attentive to the conversation, as Sabinus went on to say that his proposed measures advocated the granting of greater privileges to slaves, so that it might be easier for them to gain their freedom. It appeared that the question had provoked new and unexpected discussion, and that some of the Senate who had previously agreed with Sabinus were now of a contrary mind. Some adverse influence had been brought to bear, and Sabinus wondered greatly how this fresh opposition had been started, seeing that Domitian had nominated him for the consulship and that the Emperor's word was paramount in the Senate. He inquired of Julia if she were aware of any change in Domitian's sentiments, and whether there was likelihood of the Imperial favour being withdrawn from his candidature, for it was not an unprecedented occurrence that a consul-elect should at the last be debarred from entering upon his office. Julia tossed her head and shrugged disdainfully.

"Hast thou not already understood that Cæsar's favour is uncertain as the winds?" she said. "One had better make the most of any crumbs that he may throw—but take them as small earnest of any future meal." Then she leaned over the table and spoke to her husband in a cajoling manner. "Give me credit for a far-seeing policy, Sabinus. Thou didst find fault with me for seeking Domitian's favour, little knowing that 'twas for thine interests I worked. If Domitian prove thy friend thou hast Julia's good offices to thank."

Sabinus's gentle melancholy was dissipated. His face beamed as he bent to Julia, venturing to touch her hand. Some broken emotional words came from his lips, of which Nyria caught but few.

"Oh, Julia! if that were so 'twould be naught to me whether I became consul or not. 'Tis *thy* favour which I desire, not that of Cæsar, nor of the people."

But Julia repulsed him angrily. "Cease such sentimental drivel," she said. "Refrain from folly and proceed with thy dinner."

Sabinus drew back instantly. He was profoundly hurt, and showed it as he helped himself, with small relish, to the dainty dish offered him by Vibius, and of which Julia partook with gusto. He ate in silence at first, but at length made some casual remark concerning his brother, Flavius Clemens, and the Domina Domitilla.

"I hate that woman," said Julia. "A puling, meekfaced hypocrite."

"Nay, now, that's not the way of Domitilla," put in Sabinus.

Julia sneered. "Domitilla is the worst of hypocrites. Knowest thou not that she belongs to the secret sect which follows Christus, the malefactor, and *that* while parading in Rome as the mother of future Cæsars. Oh! Domitilla knoweth well how to practise underhand and rebellious rites!"

Sabinus flushed and looked perturbed. "Thou art surely mistaken, Julia," he said. "It cannot be that Domitilla is given to underhand practices. In certain matters of conduct I know that she holds different opinions from some Roman matrons, but every woman hath a right to regulate her own life. And concerning that sect to which thou sayest she belongs, I am told that the followers of this Christus are orderly, law-abiding people, asking only a right conceded to Egyptians, Chaldeans, and even Jews—the liberty to practise their own religion in peace."

"Who hath told thee all this?" asked Julia; but her attention was diverted at the moment by her favourite delicacy, a stew of sow's teats garnished with truffles. After she had finished Julia's thoughts seemed busy, for a cynical smile dipped the corners of her mouth.

Presently Sabinus looked up from his plate.

"Speaking of that sect, Julia, hast thou ever heard of one Clementus, a holy man of note, who is reckoned head-priest among them?"

Julia shook her head while she picked at some dressed almonds in a mother-o'-pearl shell near her.

"Nay! I know naught of priests," she said, munching as she spoke. "They are but poor company, and I prefer to consort with men of wit; or, if I must be acquainted with dullards, give me fools of substance who have somewhat to bestow on their friends. But priests are neither rich nor amusing—nor worldly-wise, else would they not be priests."

"Priests may possess greater wisdom than that of the world," said Sabinus, thoughtfully. "I would not cry scorn upon the faith of any man though it differ from my own; and to me it seems that this Clement hath a wondrous spiritual understanding."

"Enough to find an advocate in thee, it appears," sneered Julia. "Where sawest thou this miracle of wisdom?"

"I have met Clement at the house of Flavius and Domitilla," replied Sabinus, simply. "He is distantly connected with our family, and therefore I, too, should be glad to show him hospitality."

Julia made a face of disgust and answered tartly,—

"This house is mine as well as thine, remember. *I* have a voice in the dispensing of hospitality here. Receive this Clement among thy clients in the morning if thou wilt—or thou mayst even ask him to dine. 'Tis no matter to me, since I shall not appear.

I advise thee to be careful, however. Domitian hath no sympathy with that secret sect of Christus; and whether or not he oppose thee in amending the laws, he is likely enough to disapprove if thou dost entertain one known to belong to a band of blasphemous conspirators."

"Nay, nay," put in Sabinus, hastily. "They have their own god, 'tis true, but there's no question of blasphemy against the gods of Rome."

"Oh, well," said Julia, carelessly nibbling at an almond as she looked at him with regal unconcern, "whether a man worship a foreign god, or none at all, is naught to me. Nor, I fancy, is it any serious concern to Domitian. But he hath a superstitious leaning to the gods of our country, and, being Cæsar, is bound to protect them. Take my word, Sabinus, he will have his thumb on these irreligious plotters ere Rome is much older, and that might be unpleasant for thee. In any case, I do not see why thou shouldst trouble thyself to entertain this Clement. The Flavians are a big brood, with too many hangers-on clamouring to have their pockets and their stomachs filled. Let others of the family do it, say I." Julia quaffed from a big goblet of wine, and set it down to be replenished.

"I'll not be concerned with these low friends of thine," she said. "Men call me the divine Julia, but even a goddess may burn her fingers if she meddle with Cæsar's whims. Should danger overtake thee, Sabinus, remember my warning."

"Nay, I have done no wrong," said Sabinus, gently. "Domitian knows well that I seek no other gods than those of Rome. Though they forget me—and I sometimes think they do—yet will I serve them faithfully, for they are the gods of my fathers, and should be the gods of those that come after me. But, alas! I have no sons to sit in my place." He spoke so sadly that Nyria hoped Julia would say something kind to him, but she only laughed derisively.

"For my part, I thank the gods that they do not continue a breed of nincompoops. Thou hast no spirit, Sabinus. Hadst thou been more of a man thou mightst have ruled—who knows?—thou mightst have ruled even *Julia*."

She threw herself back in her chair and laughed at him scoffingly.

Sabinus answered her in quiet rebuke.

"I have no desire to rule in such fashion, Julia. To my mind there should be but one law to govern husbands and wives—the law of mutual love and respect."

"Shade of Numa! hear thee," shrieked Julia. "Such notions might have suited Egeria, but certainly not a woman of the days of Domitian."

XII

Stephanus, having got wind of Euphena's prophecies, soon made a pretext to visit the slaves' court, where he might hear particulars of the matter.

He found Nyria sitting outside Euphena's cabin, mending a torn robe, while the old woman did some task within. It was getting towards evening. Julia had been to the Palace that afternoon with Thanna again in attendance, and Nyria was now waiting her summons to the Most Noble's dressing-room. She told Stephanus straightly all that had happened, but he, not content, went in to confer with Euphena. Presently he came back looking perturbed, yet eager.

"Little one," he said, "supposing it were true that Julia should die shortly, what fate would be thine? They would sell thee, Nyria, and it might be to even a harder mistress."

"I would pray Sabinus to keep me," answered Nyria.

"Euphena prophesies evil concerning Sabinus likewise, and though I put small faith in such predictions, yet would I fain secure thee, Nyria, from any chance of harm. Give me the right to protect thee, little one." He looked down on her yearningly, but Nyria laughed.

"Thou needst not fear for me, Stephanus. Since Euphena be so wise she can foresee danger, and will guard us against it."

Stephanus shrugged his great shoulders.

"I laid that question before her, but it seems that a seeress's power fails when the matter concerns herself, or one close to her, and that Euphena can see naught of her own fate or thine, for she only shook her head when I asked her of thy future."

Nyria glanced across the garden strip to Euphena, who had now come to the door of her cabin, where she was sitting, her bony arms clasped round her knees, her dim old eyes in a fixed stare before her, not heeding Nyria and the goldsmith, nor the other slaves pottering about the court. She was in one of those mystic moods when she gave strange utterances.

"She hath the fit upon her," whispered Nyria. "Ask what thou wilt, Stephanus, and she will answer thee."

He led the girl to the cabin door.

"Euphena!" he said. "Here is Nyria. Tell me what thou seest of her fate."

Euphena's gaze did not move, but she spoke, and her voice was low and deep.

"Take thy hand off her, Stephanus. Thou art staining her with the blood."

Stephanus snatched his hand from Nyria's shoulder, where it rested, and examined it.

"There is no blood on my hand, mother."

"Nay, but there *is* blood," she answered, "and 'tis dripping on her robe. Stand back, Stephanus."

Nyria shuddered, and Stephanus stepped hastily back.

"I understand thee not, Euphena," he remonstrated. "I have not spotted her robe. What is ill with the hand?" and he held it out.

"The hand will shed the blood," said Euphena. "But woe to him who wields the dagger, and woe to her for whose sake the blood is spilled. Woe! woe!" she cried, rocking herself to and fro. "For not love, nor riches, nor the will of the Cæsar may save the maid in her hour of doom."

Nyria gave a little cry, half laugh, half sob, and Stephanus looked startled.

"Is it for the sake of Nyria that my hand shall shed blood? Well, help me, gods!" he cried gruffly, "for so it should, were Nyria to suffer wrong."

He stooped forward, his eyes red in the dusk as they searched Euphena's face. The Ethiopian only rocked and moaned. Suddenly she ceased. There was a faint shifting of her eyes and she seemed to listen.

"Speak, mother," repeated Stephanus. "What dost thou hear?"

"I hear the tramp of the Prætorians," she answered slowly, "and the shouts of those that hail a new Cæsar. But nearer still I hear a sound as of many winds roaring in a forest—louder and louder it grows—'tis the roaring of hungry beasts."

Stephanus straightened himself and seized the girl's hand again.

"What hath this to do with Nyria?" he asked

"Sin and suffering do not end with the doers of evil," replied Euphena. "The innocent bear the burdens of the guilty."

"Yet Nyria shall be safe," said Stephanus, "for my arms shall shield her."

"Nyria shall be safe when she hath passed the portals of pain—yet not in thine arms, Stephanus. Nyria will rest in the embrace of one stronger than thou art—even as death is stronger than life."

"Thou liest, old hag!" cried Stephanus, stormily, and he caught the girl to his breast and kissed her in sight of those in the court. "Now, by all the gods of Greece, this thing shall not be. Hap what may, I'll save thee, Nyria, or die in the saving."

Nyria drew herself out of his arms vexedly. She was angry

with Stephanus for having kissed her thus. She minded the slaves' tittering much more than Euphena's direful prognostics.

"Thou dost forget thyself, Stephanus. As for me, I shall be in sore danger of Bibbi's whip and of Julia's tongue if the Most Noble finds me not in readiness. From these thou canst not save me," and she would have run away but that he detained her.

"Be my wife, Nyria," he said so earnestly that she was compelled to listen. "Come to me, my dear, and I will guard thee against anything and everything—even Julia herself. The gods know that thou needst a protector. Think over it, Nyria, I beseech thee."

"Euphena hath turned thy head with her silly auguries. Let me go and I promise that I will think of it. I can say no more. Farewell." She put her palm lightly on his mouth to silence him, but when he kissed it passionately she fled without another word.

In the weeks following, which were those preceding the Saturnalia—that great festival of Roman slaves—no important events occurred in Julia's household. Life flowed on in its ordinary course for Sabinus, except that he became daily more immersed in State business and spent longer hours at the Senate House. Yet though there appeared no outward cause for apprehension, he looked more and more worn and anxious as the fateful kalends of January drew near when he and his colleague would be ceremoniously installed as consuls for the coming year.

During this time Julia went often to the Palace, but since Domitian had taken so much notice of Nyria she made excuses to take Thanna instead, and Thanna was delighted, for besides getting a new robe she turned things to her advantage in other respects. Nyria was indeed thankful at the change, since now she had many afternoons at her disposal, some of which she spent with Stephanus, accompanying him on his rounds to tend the sick, or gathering simples outside the city walls. But since he kissed her outside Euphena's cabin, Stephanus had become an importunate wooer, who, when he did not talk of love, discoursed at length on the Roman laws of marriage.

Several times Nyria went up to the Valerian Villa on the Cœlian. Paulinus was gone on his Egyptian command, and Æola told Nyria that her mistress spent much time on the south portico, apparently reading a book—though the parchment remained scarcely unrolled—and denying herself to all visitors, save Marcus Licinius Sura. Twice when Nyria went to Valeria's house Sura was there conversing with the Domina, and Nyria left, seeing that her presence was unwelcome.

The first time she was met on entering the garden gate by the young Greek musician. He sat on the steps gloomily nursing his now silent lyre, a dark cloud upon his handsome face and vindictive fire in his eyes.

"Yah! Go home," he snapped. "Thou art not wanted here."

But she took no heed, and went in, only to find the Domina engaged with Sura, and so returned almost immediately. Gregorio still sat on the steps watching for her, and made his malign comments.

"Well, who was right? Did she want thee? Now, 'tis neither thee nor me, but a worse one who is her favourite."

Nyria looked at him, startled.

"Oh, thou needst not stare! 'Tis true. Thou wouldst scarce believe how oft he comes. And Paulinus away! Think of it! And *she* said to be the proudest lady in Rome. But I will be even with them. 'Tis no unmeet thing for a noble dame to favour a youth of her household. But to take a lover from outside—a stranger, and he no blue-blooded Roman, but best part an alien—that's another matter. Yah! But I will be even with them. Paulinus shall know when he returns."

And as he said that Gregorio drew his lips back over his gums, showing his teeth, and made a hissing noise like a venomous snake.

"Paulinus shall know," he repeated. "Then we shall see who is master here—the rightful lord, or this half-breed dog of a Jew."

Nyria did not answer, for she would not discuss Valeria with the lad, but she was alarmed. This was not the only time Gregorio said such things. He would have spat out his jealous rage on anyone with whom he dared to speak of his mistress. Once or twice, when Nyria met him on the road, he stopped and hissed, "Did I not tell thee I would be even with them? Paulinus shall know"; and as Nyria made to go on he cried, "A fine-weather friend thou! Dost thou not care to hear how things are with us?"

But Nyria shook her head and proceeded on her way, and that enraged Gregorio against her. She disliked the boy, in spite of his well-featured face. He had a way of drawing his eyebrows together in an evil frown, while he watched furtively what was going on, and Nyria soon discovered that he had a habit of listening behind doors and spying at corners. So she did not take much notice of Gregorio, but, after several unsuccessful visits, gave up going to the villa, and took to wandering on the hillside alone, walking with the goats on their tracks, climbing over the ridges, and up to rest on the knoll that overlooked the quarries. Frequently, towards evening, she saw the same string of cloaked and hooded people that she had seen before, and would hide herself again behind the piece of broken wall and watch them as they passed and disappeared.

She became much interested in these people, and decided that they must be going somewhere for religious worship. She wondered what sort of god they worshipped. They never carried his image in procession, nor did they seem to like processions, for, though following not very far one from the other, they had little converse together, and evidently did not want to attract attention. More than once among them she saw the Domina Domitilla and her husband, and the philosopher in the grey cloak, whom Nyria guessed to be that holy man of whom Sabinus had spoken. She greatly longed to hear him speak again, but he always passed swiftly by.

Most afternoons now, when free to do so, she went up to this outlying spur. Sitting solitary on the hillside among the gathering shadows, with the streets of tombs and the great stretch of Campania before her and the sun setting over the hills, she thought many thoughts that did not come to her amid the stress and toil of daily work. Nyria loved the sunset hour, especially in autumn. She had a fancy that it was the earth that was setting, and not the sun. She felt as though the earth were sinking gradually into sleep, while the sun drew down night curtains, so that she might slumber in gentle security. And it seemed to Nyria that always behind those night curtains of deep blue sky, through which the star-glory gleamed, there was Someone very great and high and wonderful waiting to say good-night to the poor, tired earth—Someone who waited and watched and would not go away, as a nurse or a mother might wait and watch by the couch of a little child.

Then she would go and stand on the brow of the knoll, and when the soft night breeze swept her face she fancied that it might be a fold of that great Someone's veil brushing her cheek. Nyria wanted to say good-night too, and to feel that even one so small as she had a share in the tender watching which this great Being gave to the weary earth. She was often so tired at night, and there was no one who cared whether she slept or sobbed on her mat by Julia's door—except Stephanus, from whose displays of affection Nyria shrank. It was another kind of love for which she longed. But in her very saddest times, when she was most dejected and sore with stripes, she never lost the sense of that great Someone behind the sky, and used to wonder, child-fashion, if that were God.

Nyria would have dearly liked to have a god of her own to whom she might say her prayers. A slave's lot is limited, but there was a good deal that she might pray for—not to be beaten so often, and that her poor master might be more happy, and that Stephanus should prosper and grow content without wishing to marry her.

She had various whimsical ideas about Stephanus. For one thing, she knew that she would like him much better if he had no body—if he were a spirit with wings—if they both had wings, and might float away to the golden west and into another world. That made her laugh, for she could not imagine Stephanus a spirit—Stephanus, with his big shoulders and thick beard, and the quick way he had of laughing and of crinkling up his eyes when he made a joke. There was something absurd in the image of Stephanus floating in air. He was too big and heavy. And wings would not grow for the wishing. Besides, if it came to that, Nyria thought she would rather float out to the golden west without Stephanus.

She longed to go through that golden gate and the red wall of sky. Of course there must be something beyond. There was always something beyond—everywhere. Juvenal said so, and quoted the words of other learned men to back up his opinion. It was probable that if she could fly through those gates of red and gold she would find something wonderful—a temple or a palace, perhaps, finer than the palace of Domitian. Involuntarily Nyria made obeisance. How should she, a slave—who could question no command nor leave her mistress's service unless it might be at the Saturnalia—how dared she dream of flying to a golden region where lived One far greater than Julia and mightier than Cæsar himself. For Nyria felt sure that if there were one Supreme God anywhere He must inhabit that region beyond the sunset glory. And yet she had a fancy that He was not too high or distant to take notice of her, a slave—else how was it that she so often heard His Voice call her—"Nyria."

There were other voices that she heard when the wind was rocking the tree boughs, making the leaves chatter and the grass whisper softly, and where the flowers lifted up their faces, giving and receiving messages. Those voices told Nyria many things as she lay along the ground beneath some oak or olive. Or better still, when the sun shone down on her and sent warm, tingling thoughts all through her being. She dared not stay long in the sun, for that was forbidden because it would spoil her fairness. Nyria had to keep her skin white, else what would be the use to Julia of having a yellow-haired slave to enhance, by contrast, her own dark comeliness? Sometimes, however, she defied the edicts of Julia, and would hold out her arms to the sky, and it was almost as though the sun were a god and she were saying her prayers to him. But it was not only on the hillside that she heard this wondrous Voice—sometimes, on wakeful nights, when she lay rolled up in her blanket at Julia's door she heard it. And then it would call her, in a gentle whisper, sweet and clear—just call her softly, "Nyria—Nyria."

When first she heard it she had started, thinking that she was summoned, but when she searched she found no one who had called, and as she grew more accustomed to the sound she became sure that it was no human voice.

Often she longed to answer, but what should a little slave-girl reply to One so great? When Julia sent for her, or Cæsar deigned to call her, there was naught for her to do but go with folded hands and, bowing herself, await their orders. Now she would have bowed herself gladly, but there was strangeness in so doing when she saw no one. So she could but open her heart and listen and wait.

And as she waited tender thoughts would flow into her—forgiving thoughts of Julia, even though her poor little body were sore from the lash; and earnest wishes for her master, Sabinus; loving thoughts for Valeria; kindly thoughts for Stephanus—for anyone with whom she had to do. It was not hard to think kindly of people after she had heard that voice.

But it was on the hillside at even that this high Someone approached nearest to her, and as she stretched out her arms to the setting sun, and the sky curtains dropped, slowly enfolding the earth, and all the noise of the day was hushed, then Nyria seemed to hear that Voice saying,—

"Some day, Nyria, thou shalt see my Face."

XIII

It was mid-December and the Saturnalia had come—that one period in the year when the Roman slave was his own master—when he might do as he pleased, provided he did not run away altogether. It would not have been much use if he had, for he would certainly have been caught and brought back again, and woe betide him afterwards! In the Saturnalia, however, he might refuse all service to his master, even though high pay were offered him for it, and he could not be punished unless for an offence against the State. It was wisest, nevertheless, that he should not make himself disagreeable to his lawful owner, for if so he would surely be beaten when the Saturnalia was over.

It may seem strange that the Roman nobles, who thought of none but themselves, should have submitted to being uncomfortable during this time. But the Emperor and Senate dared not interfere with the Saturnalia, for feeling about it ran so strong that there would inevitably have been a popular rising were it abolished. Besides, it was a religious festival, inaugurated by solemn services in the temples of Saturn. Many of the slaves went to these observances, and the testimony of the priests counted in their favour should they get into difficulties with their masters. And that was a very usual occurrence, for masters and mistresses did not like being left to fend for themselves, and bad masters would try to extort service, though subject to a fine if there was no legal loophole of which they might take advantage. It said something for the probity of the Senate that any restrictions should be enforced on slave-owners. Notwithstanding, it would be a very venturesome slave indeed who dared to defy his master.

Good masters bought the attendance of certain of their slaves during Saturnalia, and some by favour permitted the slaves thus detained a holiday of equal length later in the year, but these were an exception to the general rule. Sabinus was the most indulgent of masters, and, consequently, his slaves adored him, and saw that his house did not suffer during the Saturnalia. The same could not be said of Julia, who was hated, and whose handmaids were thankful to escape in the time legally allowed them. Æmilia, the head-woman, was married, and always went with her husband and two children to her father's farm near Tusculum. Samu, Thanna and the rest went about their own business; and even Euphena sometimes took a holiday away from Rome. Thus it had almost always happened that Nyria—who had no ties and no friends except Stephanus, in whose house it was not fitting that she should stay—remained the only toilet-woman to attend on Julia. She, too, would have liked a holiday in the country, but she did not care to spend Saturnalia with the slaves left in Rome, dancing and rioting in the Campus Martius, which was then given up to them as a place of amusement. Nor did she care to attend the feasts which the household slaves held sometimes in their own quarters, aping the customs of their master and mistress, and waited on by the underlings. On the whole, she preferred to drudge for Julia.

Drudgery it was indeed, though the Most Noble had small cause for her noisy grumbling, for Nyria worked trebly hard that her mistress might miss nothing. But in Euphena's absence she had to see to her own clothes, and get her food, and to keep the cabin clean, in addition to her work in Julia's chamber, which was no light matter. Sabinus's men, however, were kind in filling the ewers and vessels needed for Julia—the oil cans with perfumed olive oil for her lamps, and the other scented oil for her body and for her hair, and they would polish the great silver mirror and the fittings of Julia's bath when the Most Noble was out in her litter. Her own bearers were gone on Saturnalia, but Sabinus contrived to hire a set for her use, and mightily she scolded about the way they shook her, so that it was poor pleasure at such times to be in her company. It was perhaps because there was no one but Nyria to attend her that she did not visit at the Palace as often as usual, or, if she did, went alone.

One evening, some few days after the Saturnalia had begun, Julia was entertaining a small party at dinner—an unusual event in most houses during the festival—but it was Julia's boast that the Saturnalia made no difference in her household arrangements, and that she could bid her friends welcome to a properly-tended board then as at other times. This was true enough, but it was thanks to Sabinus's forethought and to the affection his slaves had for him, not to any consideration on their part for Julia.

Nyria followed her mistress to the atrium and stood behind her in the dining-room, bearing fan, and scent-bottle, and others of the fal-lals which Julia used. But the slave had neglected to provide her with a pocket-handkerchief, believing, indeed, that it was in her mistress's hand; and it happened that one of the lady guests—who were of Rome's most fashionable and dressiest set—began talking of the new embroidered flax kerchiefs, imported from Persia by a certain dealer in the Vicus Tuscus, and comparing them with others that might be bought cheaper and better, she said, at a shop in the Forum. Whereupon Julia defended the dealer in the Vicus Tuscus and would have produced her own kerchief to show its superiority, had she not discovered that it was missing. At that she sharply reprimanded Nyria, and bade her go and fetch it.

Nyria accordingly went back. Julia's apartments were in darkness, save for a single silver lamp which swung from the arms of a marble boy. This gave but a faint illumination, and the room seemed full of shadowy shapes as Nyria entered. One, more definite than the rest, uprose from the steps of the wide window that looked on the portico, half disappearing among the folds of the curtains, which swayed in the night breeze. A quavering little voice came forth.

"'Tis I—Æola. Do not fear me."

Nyria laughed—there was something comical in the suggestion that she might be afraid of Æola.

"Nay, I fear naught save Bibbi's whip, and Cæsar, and Julia. But what bringeth thee here, Æola?" she asked. Then remembering that doubtless Æola was having holiday, and had merely come down for a gossip, Nyria picked up Julia's kerchief, which she saw lying on the floor.

"Come an hour hence, Æola. I am still in attendance and may not delay;" but as she turned to go Æola cried,—

"Thou must delay. Or rather, thou wilt not delay, but come back with me at once, for Valeria is ill of fever and calleth for thee."

"And thou hast left her?"

"What else could I do? I only am in the house. These three days none have been nigh her bedside." Æola shook like a frightened child.

Nyria listened, thinking rapidly. Her first intention had been to crave Julia's permission that she might accompany Æola and see to Valeria's needs, knowing that at Saturnalia time Julia would have no legal right to prevent her. But, hearing that the case was urgent, she made up her mind to run no chance of delay, and seized Æola's hand, drawing her to the window.

"Come, haste with me," she said; and the two ran down the steps and across the courtyard. They met one of Sabinus's men, who was bearing a flagon of wine and some fresh-got snow. Nyria stopped him while she said,—

"Crispus, I pray thee, when Julia calls for me tell her that Nyria claims the Saturnalian rite and is gone, but that she will return."

She was speeding away, but the man cried out jokingly,—

"Oh! oh! So little stay-at-home hath found wings at last! Doth Stephanus send for thee? Who is his messenger?"

He caught at Æola's veil and tried to peer beneath it, at which Æola screamed, but Nyria pulled her along, and Crispus laughed the more.

The girls did not pause till they had got through the side gate by which the slaves came in and out. Here Nyria asked,—

"Art thou afraid to go into the city, Æola?"

"Nay, nay," answered Æola, though she still trembled.

"Dost know the house of Stephanus?"

"I know the street," Æola said.

"Then haste thither and say that Nyria needs him at the villa of Paulinus on the Cœlian. Bid him bring with him his bitter potion and such things as he deems well for one sick of fever. And if he be not there, Æola, remain an hour for him—nay—remain until he comes."

"But, Nyria—" Æola hesitated, and blushed rosy-red in the darkness. "How can I wait in the house of Stephanus at night? 'Twould not be well, Nyria."

"'Twill not be well with Valeria if thou dost not," answered Nyria. "Thou or I must run the message, and since Valeria needs me it should be thou. So prate no more, but go."

Æola made no further difficulty, and the two parted just below the brow of the Aventine.

Nyria found Paulinus's villa in darkness, save for one swinging lamp that feebly illuminated the great portico. She entered by the garden gate. Æola had left a little vessel with a wick burning in oil at the steps of the door leading into Valeria's sitting-room, but the room itself was in gloom. Nyria groped along, through an ante-chamber curtained at one end, until she saw through the opening in the curtains another feeble glimmer of light. A low moaning sound made her heart beat in alarm. Valeria was calling,—

"Nyria! Nyria! Oh! where is Nyria? Why does no one come? Nyria! Water! Give me water."

Nyria pushed through the curtained archway, and passing another smaller waiting-room for slaves, lifted a second curtain and found herself in the Domina's sleeping-chamber. It was lighted with two or three lamps, one held by a Cupid of gold and ivory above the sumptuous bed, draped in white and gold, where Valeria moaned and tossed.

Nyria ran swiftly to the couch. "I am come, Domina. Nyria is here."

Valeria looked strangely at her with bright, wild eyes, and said, as though she saw no one, "Why don't they send for Nyria?" And then she made a feeble sign for water.

Nyria held a cup to her lips. Then the girl wiped some grapes and gave them to her, and squeezed the juice of an orange, which Valeria took, seeming quieter. Æola must have had hard work, for everything was orderly, and all that Valeria might want was placed on a tripod by her bedside—fruit, that however looked somewhat bruised, and water that had evidently been iced; but the ice had melted, and when Nyria touched the ewer it seemed hot, though not so hot as Valeria.

Presently the Domina grew restless again, and began to mutter to herself, and to pluck at the embroidered coverlet with her thin hot fingers.

"Is there no one I can trust?" she cried. "Nyria could be trusted. Why does not someone send for Nyria?"

It made Nyria's heart ache to hear her. She knelt by the bed, and taking the burning hands in hers tried to still them.

"Nyria has come, Domina. Nyria is here."

Valeria stared at her, then turned her head away. Seeing that it was of no use to explain, Nyria only tried to make her charge more comfortable. She took off the coverlet, and drew up the sheets of fine linen, and combed Valeria's tangled hair over the embroidered flax of the pillow. And as she was doing this very gently, Valeria caught the slave's hand and held it to her cheek, murmuring, with inexpressible tenderness,—

"Dearest! do not leave me."

"I will not leave thee, Domina," the slave answered, and bent over her. But Valeria's mind was wandering. Who was it for whom she called? Oh! if the delirium could be stilled! If Stephanus would but come! Nyria was going forth to watch for him, when a sound made her turn, and she saw that Valeria had risen and was leaning on her bed, her hair all about her shoulders, and her hands clasped upon her bosom.

"Marcus!" she called in loud, clear tones. "Come back. Why wilt thou go when thou knowest that 'tis only thee whom I need? Leave me not—or if thou must, then—" Weakness suddenly overcame her, and she fell back against the bed. Nyria flew to her assistance. At that moment there was a step in the ante-room, and Æola came through the doorway. Behind her loomed a broad figure that Nyria knew to be that of Stephanus.

"Help me, Æola!" she cried. "The Domina has fainted."

Æola ran in, looking pale and terrified, her long hair and veil wet with night dew, so that Nyria guessed that she had not waited in Stephanus's house, but by the door outside. She did her best to raise the Domina's head while Nyria held her body, but the task was beyond the girl's strength, and Nyria cried, "I cannot do it; let Stephanus come."

Stephanus entered hurriedly, and, taking the Domina in his strong arms, he laid her in her bed as if she had been a little child, and drew the sheets gently round her. Then he held Valeria's wrist for a minute.

"Nyria," he said, "go, fetch my bag from the ante-chamber;

and thou, little one"—turning to Æola—"seek me ice or snow, and linen."

Nyria brought the leather wallet in which he always carried his instruments and bottles of medicine, and watched while he measured a few drops in a glass and forced them between Valeria's teeth. Meantime Æola, who had fetched some linen, stood hesitating and timid.

"Will not Nyria come with me?" she said. "I am afraid to go to the ice-house alone."

Stephanus jerked his head at Nyria, saying, "Do thou go," in the short way he had when occupied with something serious. Æola took a swinging lamp, and a large glass ladle and a bowl, and they went outside and round the house to the snow-cellar. It was made under an embankment of earth in the garden. Stone steps led down to a heavy door, and beyond that was a further door, still heavier, and swung on metal clamps, so that the girls had to put down the lamp and bowl, and pull with all their might before they could get it open. A rush of icy air came out as they stepped within.

"Fix the door, Nyria, lest it slam and we die of cold," cried Æola, who was frightened in the tomb-like place; and Nyria put a block of wood into the aperture, while Æola's lamp cast wraith-shadows as she went towards the great stone vats in which the snow and ice were kept. There was no ice left at all, and not much snow. Æola, as she ladled this out, explained that the steward had told Valeria a fresh supply was required, and that the ice ships were even then coming up the Tiber; but she had paid no attention, and the Saturnalia falling immediately after, there had been no one to see to the matter.

Stephanus was cutting bandages and spreading them upon the bed when the girls went in again to Valeria's chamber. He had already wrapped damp cloths round the sick woman. Now he laid the snow in bands of linen, and placed these upon her forehead and wrists and ankles, for the fever was very high. Then he asked Æola for milk, and she ran to get it; but even of this there was not much, for the milk-sellers, like other tradespeople, were slack of calling in the Saturnalia.

"Now," said Stephanus to Æola, leading the girls into the ante-chamber when he had ministered as far as might be to Valeria, "tell me how this fever came upon the Domina. I took thy breath away hasting up the hill, but fear not—all will be well with thy mistress if we can but get the fever down. How came it?"

"I know not," said Æola; and she began to tremble with cold now that her excitement and terror were over. "My mistress hath not been well this two weeks past."

"And yet she permitted all her slaves to go on Saturnalia when she might have kept enough to serve her!" exclaimed Stephanus.

"My mistress troubleth not herself about such matters," said Æola. "I think she scarce remembered that the Saturnalia was approaching." Æola stopped and glanced in a troubled way at Nyria.

"Thou needst not mind telling," said Nyria. "Thou knowest, Æola, that I would die to serve Valeria, and Stephanus is my friend."

"Who needs must die too, if needful, to serve the lady—eh?" put in Stephanus with a laugh. "Have faith in me, Æola."

"I can tell little," answered Æola, hesitating. "Lately Valeria hath seemed sad, and to care for naught but—but the visits of—"

"Speak, Æola. This is no time for secrets—the visits of whom?"

"Of Marcus Licinius Sura," replied Æola, and covered her face with her veil, for Æola was a modest maid, and though young, she, as well as Nyria, knew to what such intimacies were like to lead.

Stephanus made no answer, but went back to the bed and stood looking down upon Valeria in silent thought. He touched her temple with one finger, and Nyria saw that it burned still to his touch.

"There has been mental trouble here, as I thought," he said. "What doctor hath visited her?"

"None at all, Stephanus. My mistress said no word, and how could I judge for whom to send?"

"Nay! So thou didst judge there was but one doctor in Rome, and that Stephanus!" He patted her shoulder with a smile. "I commend thy judgment, Æola. Nevertheless, another doctor must see Valeria, for it is not fitting that the wife of Paulinus should be attended only by one unregistered as I am. Hath the lady no relatives at hand?"

"None, I think," said Æola. "Paulinus is not returned from Egypt, and the Lady Vitellia is absent also. Were she in Rome it would be well;" and Æola gave a sigh. It was plain that she liked Vitellia.

"There is small use in the Lady Vitellia if she be not in Rome," said Stephanus, putting his things together in his wallet as he spoke. "When doth Paulinus return?"

"I know not," replied Æola; "but 'tis said—"

"Ay—go on," put in Stephanus. "'Tis said—what?"

"That the Domina desireth not his return; and thus Paulinus is not like to hasten it," and Æola blushed and hung her head.

"Since there is none to whom we may appeal," said Stephanus, "we must e'en do our best unaided. I will stay till sunrise. I must then go home to leave word with Dinarmid. Afterwards will I bring up such things as are needful, and call in Archimenes, who is of best repute for dames. We must have the first physician in Rome, I presume, to attend the most noble Valeria. Now, do ye sleep in turn. I shall lie outside. Is there a rug or blanket I can have?"

"Oh, I will get thee one, good Stephanus," and Æola ran out.

"I shall remain within call," said Stephanus. "Let Æola sleep as long as may be, for she may have to be alone to-morrow night. In Saturnalia 'tis hard to hire even a watcher. All Rome is off its head."

"Have no care, I shall be here," said Nyria, and Stephanus came closer to her.

"Thou hast a spirit that I like, Nyria. But why keep it only for yonder noble lady? I would, my dear, that thou didst hold thus loyally to poor friend Stephanus."

"I do hold to thee, Stephanus," and she put her hands into his outstretched ones.

"According to thine own rendering, Nyria, but not as I should wish." And then he drew her closer. "Say, dost think Stephanus hath done well to-night? Did not Stephanus come at once on Nyria's bidding?"

"Ay, but Stephanus would have hastened to one sick if another than Nyria had bidden him. This I know, for Stephanus always doeth well." She put her head down, and laid her cheek on his hands, for at that moment Nyria loved Stephanus dearly.

"Then, Nyria, give me a reward," he made answer. "See, we are alone, and if Stephanus hath done his best to serve thee, let thy lips grant him token." Nyria looked up and saw that he was all flushed and trembling. This did not repel her at the moment, and she lifted her mouth frankly to kiss him. But he drew his head back, and looked full into her face with a gaze of yearning tenderness.

"'Tis not such cold lips that I desire to kiss," he said. "Sweet thou art in all ways, Nyria, but most sweet as the woman I love, and which it seems thou dost scarce know thyself to be."

Nyria laughed lightly. "If thou wilt have none of my kisses, Stephanus, thou hast no cause to complain," and she drew herself away. He would have caught her again, but just then Æola called softly from the doorway,—

"I have brought thee a wadded quilt, Stephanus, from the rooms of Paulinus. 'Tis one that Gregorio lieth upon there, and Gregorio liketh to make himself comfortable. There is a pillow, too."

Stephanus stepped to the door and took the bundle of wraps ruefully.

"Thou wouldst have been kinder, Æola, to find me some blanket of Paulinus's, however old, for he is a man, while Gregorio is a poltroon. I like not the feel he giveth his things."

"How canst thou expect Gregorio at his years to be a man?" said Nyria.

"The lad is older than thou thinkest, Nyria, and hath many faults of manhood, though but few manly virtues. A pest on his garments. They have the savour of his sour tongue," and Stephanus made a wry face at the cosy coverings Æola had brought.

"Shall I fetch others? But I got the best I could," she said, disappointed.

"Nay, child, I was but joking. If evil spirits have lain here Stephanus's arm is strong enough to sweep them hence. There is no room beside Stephanus for what he willeth not to have. Get thee to thy slumbers, Æola. Nyria will watch first, but she must sleep before the dawn." And Stephanus strode to the ante-chamber, carrying the bundle with him. He laid himself down outside the further curtained archway, so that he should not disturb the maids.

Valeria seemed to sleep. Presently Nyria changed the snow bandages as Stephanus had directed, and when she became wakeful gave her milk to drink. But though Valeria looked at the watcher, Nyria saw that she did not recognise her. The girl sat very still as Valeria slept. Her eyes went round the room noting the luxurious details of its furnishing—the embroidered hangings in mauve and silver, the white Persian carpet, the inlaid chairs and tripods, the great silver mirror nearly as big as Julia's, the toilet-table with gold and silver appurtenances and caskets of jewels—almost as many as Julia had. But the room displayed a delicate refinement that made it wholly different from Julia's gorgeous apartments.

At one end, facing the bed, was a small alcove or archway, over which hung curtains of pale violet with silver fringe, and Nyria wondered what lay behind them, concluding that here probably was the entrance to a private study. Nyria might have supposed that the curtains hid an altar dedicated to some venerated god, but she fancied that Valeria cared naught for gods.

Valeria looked very ill as she lay with the shaded lamp throwing death-like shadows upon her face. There were deep circles round her eyes and mouth, and the nose was blue and pinched, while every now and then the forehead would twitch, or the restless fingers pluck at the sheet. Nyria decided that she would go early to the Aventine and get a change of clothing, and attend to Julia's robing, and that then she would come back and stay all the time with Æola. Julia could not prevent her doing so, for was it not the Saturnalia? And it would be time enough to think of Bibbi's lash when Bibbi was there to administer it. She wondered how Julia had managed for herself, and whether she had sent someone else for her kerchief. Nyria was reminded of this kerchief as she shook out her dress at last, before lying down in Æola's place, by seeing the embroidered square drop from her sleeve where she had tucked it in running up the hill.

"Julia will chastise me if she knoweth I have taken it," thought Nyria, for Julia was ever one to think the worst of her slaves. Still, she could but scold, and so Nyria laid herself down to sleep, and did not wake till after the sun had risen.

"Stephanus hath just gone," said Æola. "He will return as soon as may be with the best doctor he can get. But thou, too, wilt come back to me, Nyria?"

"Ay, ay, I will come back," said Nyria. "I would not leave thee, only 'tis but right I should tell Julia."

"Thou wilt not let her keep thee?" pleaded Æola.

"She cannot," retorted Nyria.

"But thou dost not often claim the Saturnalia?"

"Never before, that I remember, for more than one day; but that is all the more reason why Julia should grant it me freely now."

"Stephanus said he would send up what was needful," added Æola. "Stephanus is very good, Nyria."

"Ay, he is very good. Is he not Stephanus?" said Nyria, proudly.

"He loveth thee very dearly," said Æola. "But thou dost not love him, dost thou?"

"Nay, what is love?" said Nyria. "I think I love Stephanus; but he is not satisfied. Thou and I, Æola, are over young to talk of love, and over busy too."

Æola shook her head. She was brushing out her hair, which was brown and curly, and hung prettily round her little pale face.

"Nay, I think, Nyria, 'twould be sweet did someone love me as Stephanus loveth thee. Mother Lævina, who brought me up, doth sometimes say, 'Thou'lt have a lover soon, Æola.' Yet none doth come."

Nyria laughed. "One will come, maybe, ere long. Meanwhile, take care of thyself, Æola, since there is none else to take care of thee, for I must go."

XIV

JULIA was awake, and hearing movements in her dressing-room, she called out to know who was there.

"It is Nyria, Most Noble," answered the slave, and entering, made her obeisance.

Julia sat up in bed, with ruffled hair, looking very red and big and angry.

"So! thou runaway—thou hast returned. And what hast thou to say for thyself?"

"Most Noble, it is the Saturnalia."

"And what has that to do with thee?"

Nyria bowed, with her hands to her forehead.

"I am a slave, rendering a slave's service, and, as such, I may claim a slave's dues."

So wroth was Julia, that for a moment or two she could not speak. Then a torrent of abuse broke forth.

"Is that what thou hast to tell me? Insolent hussy! Dost realise that thou art lower than the least of my slaves, and in no way entitled to their privileges? Thou art a barbarian—bought as babe, and tended at my trouble and expense. Is *this* the return thou wouldst make for my generosity?"

"Most Noble! I have indeed tried to serve thee faithfully," answered Nyria, humbly. "But last night—" She stopped confusedly.

"What about last night?" screamed Julia. "There is naught thou canst put forward for thyself that will make me think less ill of thee—and so take warning, Nyria."

"Then, Most Noble, I will not seek to persuade thee, for time presses, and I came but to say that for the rest of the Saturnalia Nyria's services are needed elsewhere."

Julia crimsoned deeper with rage.

"Nyria! *My slave!* Her services needed elsewhere! How darest thou speak so? I forbid thee, girl. Dost thou hear? I forbid thee to leave this house. Dost thou hear?" she repeated, as Nyria made no answer.

"I hear, Most Noble, Nevertheless, the custom of the Saturnalia is in Nyria's favour. I have ever served thee, as I said, and claimed no due. This time—oh! this time, Most Noble, I pray thee let me go."

Julia fell back on her pillows and laughed in scorn.

"A pretty way to sue!" she cried. "First to defy me, and then, finding that fail, to pray thy due—thy due, indeed! . . . Go, get the bath ready, girl."

A stubborn look came into Nyria's face, and she shook back her yellow curls as she turned.

"I go, Most Noble," she said; "and I will attend thy dressing as thou desirest, but I may not stay for long. I have asked thee of thy grace to grant me that which is my right, and if thou wilt not, then Nyria must take it."

She moved a step, but was stopped on the instant. Julia had sprung out of bed and caught her by the shoulders. The Most Noble's face was inflamed with fury, and her great limbs were quivering in her rage. She shook Nyria violently, and, as she did so, the embroidered kerchief dropped from the girl's sleeve. Julia pounced upon it.

"How! What is this? My kerchief! Thou hast been stealing, jade, and, by Mercury, this is the cause of thy flitting. Thou hadst the design to pilfer my goods!"

"Most Noble, I have taken nothing. The kerchief was in my sleeve because I had placed it there last night to keep it for thee. It is the kerchief thou didst send me for from the banqueting-room."

"Why not have brought it back to me then, if thou wert honest? Be done with false excuses, Nyria. Thou shalt have twenty lashes for this. I keep no thieves in my household."

"Oh! Most Noble, I am no thief—indeed, I am no thief." Nyria's heart sank within her, for, did Julia cause her to be beaten, it would delay her, and she would be unfit to help Æola nurse Valeria, for the sentence was severe. Ten lashes raised weals, but twenty would bring blood. Nevertheless, Nyria's pride would not let her stoop to ask mercy of Julia. However, it was Saturnalia. Bibbi was away, and who was there to lash her? Nyria breathed more freely. Maybe Julia had given a threat that she would be unable to carry out.

She went about her work, preparing for the robing, and Julia, securing the kerchief, bade her hasten, dealing out more abuse.

"There will not be much spirit left in thee to work with when I have done with thee, girl!" she cried tauntingly. "Methinks thou wilt consider twice before going forth holiday-making in such a plight as that wherein I shall leave thee. If thou canst not serve Julia, assuredly thou wilt not be of much use to anyone else."

Nyria tried not to heed, but went on with her work, though her heart beat fast the while. She could have thrown down what was in her hand and run away, for outside the gates no one would have any power to touch her. But, if she did that, things were likely to go harder with her later on, and she hoped to propitiate Julia by helping her to dress and doing her hair nicely.

Alas! Nyria did not yet know Julia. The Most Noble said no more until she had had her bath, and had been rubbed and anointed, and partially dressed. Her face had been tinted, her hair arranged, and she sat at her table, the silken wrapper round her shoulders, when suddenly she turned and bade Nyria strike the silver gong which carried to the outer atrium. There were different notes for the summoning of slaves in each department. Presently one of the men came, and, raising the curtain, made an obeisance. It was Crispus, Sabinus's chief body-steward. Julia asked him sharply whether Bibbi was in the house. Crispus shook his head, smiling slightly.

"It is the Saturnalia, lady."

"Now, may the Saturnalia perish, and may all the gods wreak destruction on these besotted holiday-makers. Who is in attendance here to do my bidding?"

"Crispus is here, Most Noble," and he mentioned two or three others besides himself, as well as some underlings; they were Sabinus's servants. Julia interrupted him fiercely.

"Which hath the strongest arm?" she asked.

Crispus turned up the sleeve of his tunic, and with modest pride held out his own for inspection. It was brawny, and covered with hair, unlike the sleek arms of Roman nobles, and the knots and veins stood out upon it, for Crispus had the physique of a gladiator.

"My arm is strong, lady," he said.

"Good! Then go, whip Nyria."

Crispus looked at the girl, who had shrunk behind a tripod.

"Nyria, Most Noble?"

"Ay, Nyria, dolt—did I not say Nyria? Give her twenty lashes. She hath been dull and slow of late in attending to my affairs—though sharp enough, it seems, in minding her own. Last night she stole a kerchief from me—one of my best, embroidered in Persia, and like to fetch money, as no doubt the jade thought. The lash will warm her blood, and mayhap keep her from thieving. Twenty strokes, mind. Take her to the whipping-post."

Crispus shook his head and slowly turned down his sleeve again.

"Thy pardon, Most Noble, but I whip not Nyria," said he, and a thrill of joy went through the unhappy girl.

Julia glared at him. "Didst thou not understand that I gave thee an order?"

"Ay, lady, thou didst give me an order which no law of Rome compels me to obey."

Julia began to threaten him, but stopped short, checked by Crispus's steady gaze.

"Go, fetch me one less squeamish than thou art," she said shortly.

The man made his obeisance, and, dropping the curtain, went away. Julia turned to Nyria.

"Do what thou hast to do, but move not out of my sight," she said, and watched Nyria put away the brushes and combs and fold the various garments scattered about.

The girl saw that Julia was eager to carry through the beating, and now with a shiver she realised that if such were Julia's will there was small hope that it would be averted. It was true that, according to Roman ordinance, her mistress might not punish her for going away during the Saturnalia, but alack! she might have her whipped for stealing, and that in seeming clemency. For it was a decree that by favour of the master or mistress a slave might be let off with twenty lashes at home for a first criminal offence. Otherwise, a culprit would be taken to the public prison, and in due course be dealt with more severely according to the law. That would be shame intolerable, and how could Nyria disprove the charge of theft, seeing that the kerchief had been found upon her? But she was shrewd enough to guess that Julia would not wish to lose her services now that she had no other handmaids, and would choose the lesser penalty if she were really bent on punishment. So the only hope lay in Bibbi's absence, and in the chance that the other men would refuse to beat her.

It seemed a long time to Nyria as she went about putting the room tidy and rubbing the bottles and caskets, while Julia sat fanning herself. When Julia fanned herself like that in cool weather one might know that she was extremely angry. Her eyes followed Nyria's every movement as if she feared that the girl would try to escape, and she made her push back the curtains between the bathroom and dressing-chamber, and bade her set down, outside the door, the pails that should have been carried right away for the cleansing. And now Nyria wished that she had run off when Julia was still in bed and the chance hers, for it appeared clear that her sentence would not be remitted.

Then Crispus came back; he stood within the curtains and bowed himself.

"May it please the Most Noble, I can find no one in the household who will use the lash to Nyria."

It did not please the Most Noble. She raved at Crispus, demanding whose slaves were these, and by what right they refused her orders. Crispus seemed about to reply hotly, but changed his mind, and merely answered, with a quiet smile,—

"'Twere best, Most Noble, that the slaves should speak for themselves."

"When 'tis *thou* who hast set them the example of insubordination!" stormed Julia. But she dared not say much to Crispus, for he was a skilled servant, and very necessary both to Sabinus and herself now that Vibius was away.

"Summon here the household," she said. "We shall soon see who is master."

Crispus withdrew again, and Julia made Nyria remove her silken wrapper and pull out her robe behind her as she took her position on the steps of the wide window leading to the loggia, where the slaves were brought before her. They came presently across the courtyard—it was there, on a little raised platform, that the whipping-post stood, within sight of Julia's apartments—and they bent in rather a defiant manner. Julia cast her eyes along the row.

"Dogs!" she said. "Sons of the lowest, and sweepings of the slaves' quarters, how dare ye reject the commands of your mistress?"

"We are Sabinus's servants," they answered in a breath, and then Crispus came courageously forward.

"Most Noble," he said, "thou knowest, by the laws of Rome we are compelled to obey him who has bought us, and that he, being our master, we may not reject his commands lest vengeance overtake us. But the Most Noble—great and high though she be, and the lady-wife of him whom we serve, hath not bought us, neither is she entitled to our service save at the command of Sabinus, our master."

Nyria wondered to hear him speak thus, knowing well that should Julia appeal to her husband, Sabinus, however averse to having a woman-slave beaten, would certainly not deny Julia in any matter on which she had set her will. The girl could only conclude, therefore, that Sabinus was likely to be detained at the Senate House, which afterwards she learned to be the case, the man who spoke having attended his master there. Still, fearful as to the issue, she held her peace, and, as she expected, Julia demanded fiercely,—

"Where is Sabinus? Fetch him hither immediately."

Now it was extremely ill-bred in a Roman lady to speak thus of her husband to his slaves, but Julia did not mince courtesies when she was angry, nor in truth was she ever lavish of them as regarded Sabinus.

The man gave a string of clever excuses. His lord was out, and had left orders that he would be late of return; and when Julia asked his whereabouts, for she had evidently a mind to send after him, no one could tell whither he had gone. The Most Noble, nonplussed for the moment, folded her arms across her broad breast and beat her hip irritably with her long-handled fan.

"Insolent beasts! Do ye think to thwart me? I say that Nyria shall be whipped, and that before the sun has reached its highest point in heaven. Now, have ye a will to defy me further, or is there one of ye who will go seek me in the Forum, or at the office in the Carinæ, Balbus Plautius, the public beater, for it seems to me that 'tis he who can best do my work. And if he too be brain-sodden and keeping Saturnalia like the rest of mad Rome, then bring me the ablest lasher to be found in the Palæstra."

At her words horror did indeed strike Nyria. To be lashed by a public whipper was shame such as had never yet befallen her. It was bad enough to be whipped by Bibbi, but at least he was of the household. At thought of a hired beater curling his lash around her naked body she made a shuddering movement backward, which Julia interpreted as an attempt at flight; and turning furiously, seized the girl with her own hands, and held her as she called out,—

"Am I to be obeyed in my own house, ye scum, or will ye let the thief escape outside the gates? In that case, I warn ye that a ten times' greater vengeance shall fall on her when once this cursed Saturnalia is ended."

A shiver of repugnance passed over the men, and Julia, seeing their indecision, ordered them imperiously to bring the ropes and lash Nyria to the post.

She pointed across the courtyard to the whipping-stake, which told its own gruesome tale, for by marks worn in the wood at different heights it could be clearly seen where both men and women had been bound for punishment.

A black look came over Crispus's face, and he seemed inclined to interfere; but two of the men, almost strangers to Nyria, had stepped forward, and one hastened to fetch the ropes, while the other put out his hand to lead Nyria away. But the girl, though too proud to cower before Julia, would not let him touch her.

"I will go with thee," she said, "if thou layest no finger on me; but do so, and I will bite and scratch like any wild cat."

Julia heard her, and laughed derisively.

"So, so, my pretty Nyria! my dainty waiting-maid! Cæsar's curled darling! thou treatest us to fitting language, truly! Out, then, wild cat, and let us see thy downy fur laid bare."

Nyria drew herself up with her princess air, and as Pheidias—that was the man's name—did not again attempt to touch her, she followed him across the courtyard, while the other slaves made the ropes ready to bind her at the wrists and ankles. Crispus followed, as if he would have snatched her back; but Julia's eyes were upon him, and he could only mutter angrily,—

"Set those nooses slack, and see that they cut not the maid's skin. Hounds that ye are!"

Pheidias laughed. "Fine words fly thick," said he. "Who shall we obey, since Julia calls us dogs if we do not her bidding, and Crispus dubs us hounds when we fulfil our lady's orders?"

"A curse on thy ready tongue and hands!" said Crispus.

"Thou wouldst do better to stand in the maid's place than to permit chastisement on such a child."

Julia called sharply to them, asking which one was going to seek the whipper; and Pheidias bowed low.

"If it please the Most Noble, I will find out Balbus Plautius," he answered, for Pheidias, being new in the household, feared Julia. Not so Crispus, who said gruffly in the man's ear,—

"Mind—the beaters are all out, keeping Saturnalia like the rest of Rome—that is if the great god do not deem them too unworthy to take part at his festival. A pest on their calling! And mark me—if thou dost bring other word than that, thou scurvy, bloody-fingered knave, I'll have a strip of thy hide for every lash that leaves its line on Nyria!"

Pheidias only shook himself, saying shortly, "A slave lives but to obey," and departed on his errand.

He was a considerable time absent, and Julia, seeing that Nyria had been secured to the post, went indoors again. The other men withdrew, and hung round the corners of the house, talking together; while Crispus, who had gone to the slaves' hut, returned carrying an earthen flagon with a cup in one hand and a small jar in the other. Nyria did not see him approach the whipping-post, for her eyes were fixed on the entrance gate, and she was wondering whether Pheidias would come back with the beater, or if by chance salvation would reach her by some unthought-of means; wondering, too, how Valeria fared in Æola's inexperienced hands. Anxiety for Valeria tugged at the girl's heart till it seemed as though she must pull the ropes through her flesh in a passionate effort to escape. But she knew that such effort must prove unavailing, and she cared not that idle watchers should see her struggle. Crispus came close to her as she stared blankly, her thoughts on the Cœlian.

"Art thou magnetised, Nyria?" he said. "Truly it doth appear that thou art in that bewitched sleep which conjurers cast over birds and serpents upon which they would work their will. Well for thee, child, were that so! Poor maid!" he exclaimed, as Nyria, starting, turned her frightened eyes upon him. "Art very troubled, Nyria? Cheer thee—for if the scoundrel brings a long lash, I will cut off the half of it when he is not looking. And see! Here is one of Mother Euphena's ointments, which, if thou dost rub into thy skin, will render thee hard and impervious to pain. She reckons it one of her finest secrets, and I know 'tis good, for she gave me this before my great fight with Amphiabus, that my body might be insensitive to that big beast's fists."

Nyria answered nothing, and Crispus, setting down the cup and flagon, removed the lid of the jar, and showed it to her half full of Euphena's ointment. Then with a small pointed piece of wood he put some upon a leaf that he had plucked and held it out to her.

Nyria shook her head. He looked at her compassionately.

"Thou art stupefied, poor maid. Now, all plagues rest upon that pest-spot, Julia's head. She is the worst disease the gods have ever sent among men. Thou needst wine, child, to restore thy wits. I will give thee some. Come—drink."

He poured from the flagon into the cup, and handed it to her, but Nyria pushed it away.

"I am afeard, Crispus, lest thou hast put a drug into the wine."

For Nyria knew that the slaves had a custom, when condemned to be beaten, of taking beforehand, if it were possible, some drugged wine or vinegar, that had the effect of dulling their senses. This sort of intoxication was not likely to be detected, for after the lashing the victims were too stupid and sore from pain to be able to move themselves, and generally had to be carried from the whipping-post. Then the drug would often cause unconsciousness, or induce sleep, in which their suffering might be temporarily forgotten. Nyria did not want to be drugged, for she desired to keep her brain steady, so that as soon as she was fit to walk she might go back to the bedside of Valeria.

"Hast thou put anything in the wine, Crispus?" she asked.

Crispus half smiled and began to utter a denial, but when Nyria looked at him earnestly he stopped short and answered her,—

"Now I could almost say a plague on thy truth-loving nature, Nyria, for I cannot tell thee lies. Behold, there is but a grain or two at the bottom of the cup."

Nyria took the vessel out of his hand and emptied its contents on the ground. After wiping it well with the edge of her robe she held it to him again.

"Wilt thou spare me another cup of thy wine, Crispus? Indeed, I will take it thankfully. But I want no drug."

She looked at the gate as she spoke, and a cold horror suddenly overswept her, for just then she saw Pheidias enter, and with him a great ominous figure, shrouded in a dark cloak. This person followed Pheidias to the steps of Julia's apartments and there made obeisance, though Julia was not visible. Pheidias went up to the door. At sight of the two Crispus interposed himself to screen Nyria while she drank, and as soon as she had finished the cup he snatched it from her and concealed it in his tunic.

"There, hearten thee, child, if thou canst. Crispus's hand hath been powerless to save thee, but thou hast all his sympathy. I would rather bear on my shoulders the brute's lashes—and I know him well, cursed son of a public executioner—than that they should fall on thine."

"Thou art very kind, Crispus. I had never thought thou wouldst trouble thyself for such a matter."

"Dost think because a man be light of tongue and ready to sport when he hath leisure, that his heart must needs be hard as stone? But see, Nyria, thou hast not used the ointment. Quick, dip thy finger, and spread it on thy breast and shoulders. Or wilt thou let me spread it for thee?"

"Nay, 'tis too late, Crispus. Julia would see, and then thou knowest my lot would be fifty lashes instead of twenty."

Reluctantly he secreted the jar, only just in time, for Julia was looking towards them. She stood upon the steps, and spoke to the huge man in the cloak, which, at her bidding, he threw back, disclosing the whip he carried. It seemed a very long lash, and he drew out from a side-pocket several lengths of knotted cord which could be fastened on if a more severe punishment were required, or if the victim were a tall male slave, for whom it was necessary to use a longer lash. When, however, he saw that the culprit was but a little maid, round whose slender form a long whip would coil many times, he put the extra pieces back, except one, which Julia insisted should be substituted for the end he had at present. The whip handle was in joints that fitted the one into the other, and he busied himself in adjusting these while Julia gave him his directions and said she would herself count the strokes.

Pheidias conducted the beater to the whipping-post. Another slave was called up, and he and Pheidias stationed themselves on either side—a usual precaution in case the victim should struggle to escape.

Crispus turned his muscular body, as strong though of lighter build than that of the beater, and addressed him menacingly.

"Thou art Balbus Plautius," he said, "and hast chosen a calling well suited to thine ancestry. Now I, Crispus Sabinus, am waiting for my freedom, which it hath been foretold me shall shortly be mine. And having cultivated a good arm and a stout leg, it seemeth to me that the profession of gladiator will fit me finely, and that a tussle with thee in the arena might well advance mine interests. Look therefore to thy training, friend, for assuredly the day will come when Crispus shall pay thee back in heavy score the lashes thou bestowest on yonder little maid."

Balbus Plautius shrugged without answering, and took up his position with arm upraised, signing to Nyria that she should unloose her garments. And now came the dreadful moment.

When a woman-slave was beaten, two or three of her fellow-women invariably attended to perform such kindly offices as were permitted. But to-day there were none to help Nyria, and it seemed to the hapless girl that already the men's curious eyes gloated over her shame. Pheidias and Euginus pressed forward officiously as she tried to unfasten her robe, but Crispus thrust them back.

"She is at the mercy of one beast," he cried, "in the name of pity and justice let her be free from others!" Then, seeing that the poor little trembling hands fumbled vainly, he asked, "May I, Nyria?" and she let him undo the clasps at her shoulders. But he turned away as the garments slipped to her waist, leaving the upper half of her girlish form uncovered save for her abundant hair.

Balbus had poised himself, and there came a strange hissing sound in the air and the sense of a serpent's sting. No serpent had ever bitten Nyria, but it went into her mind that a serpent's bite could be nothing compared with this. That would be but a small puncture, whereas the lash fell in a long, quivering line that stung her from head to foot and yet was but the beginning of the torture. She had folded her arms across her breast. Women always did that, knowing the exquisite pain of a cut on the bosom. It was a common trick with an ill-disposed beater, since this part of a slave's body being ordinarily covered he was free to lash it, while any disfiguring mark on the face, neck or arms would bring down upon him a reprimand and stamp him as a clumsy workman. Thus it needed practise to let fly the lash upon a woman so as to avoid such exposed parts, the more so because she would naturally try to protect herself with her arms.

Now there came a thin, burning pain all round Nyria's body, and another, and another, each one sharper than the last. She lost count of them in the wave of terror and shame that overwhelmed her at the thought that her remaining garments might be cut away by the lash and leave her whole form bare to the brutal gaze bent upon her.

Just then she heard Julia call out, "Hold, good Balbus!"

Julia, though she treated her own slaves like dogs, was civil of speech to anyone outside her household who might serve her better for a fair word. Nyria lifted her head dizzily in the half-hope that her mistress's heart had softened sufficiently to grant her grace. But such was not Julia's intention.

"Twist that hair up on the maid's head," she called out. "It hinders the stroke. And see that the arms are raised. By what right does the mean-spirited little wretch keep them lowered?"

Balbus dropped his whip and came near to execute the command, but Nyria shrank from him.

"Thou needst not," she murmured, and tried shudderingly to bind her hair and pile it together on her head. She had no skewer to keep it fast, and fearing that it would fall and make Julia still more angry, she looked appealingly at Crispus. He gave her the bit of pointed wood that he had brought with the ointment, and with that she pinned the tresses and held up her arms as she was bidden.

The lash fell again, and again, and again—like a dozen fiery snakes hissing and springing and coiling round her defenceless bosom. She shut her eyes, bracing herself in a supreme effort to endure without a sound, for Nyria's pride would not let her shriek for mercy. Yet she knew that there might come a point at which she could bear in silence no longer. Hitherto fifteen strokes were the most she had ever received. After twelve she knew that the pain became intense, for each lash drove into gaping flesh. It was a bright day and standing in the sun in her terrified waiting for Balbus's coming had already made her feel sick. Now the sun was like a warm mantle enfolding her, but the deadly sickness was overpowering. As it were in a dream she heard Julia's voice counting "fourteen—fifteen—sixteen" slowly.

At length Nyria felt a curious stiffening all over her and a kind of singing in her ears, and she was glad, for she knew that it was the faintness coming. Suddenly everything grew horribly black. She opened her eyes for an instant to see the lash wriggling just over her head against a purple sky. Her face was wet, the air seemed dropping blood. Across the courtyard Julia's voice sounded further and fainter. Then something slipped away from under her, and Nyria felt herself falling . . . falling . . . falling . . .

She had dropped, but not to the ground. The ropes holding her to the post ran up against her broken flesh, but mercifully she was past sensation. The beater paused. He had given all but two stripes and Julia had gone within to get the money for his payment. Balbus flung down his whip and looked with some compunction on his work.

"'Tis a shame!" he said, and would have loosed the bleeding form from the cords, but Crispus, snarling fiercely, bade him keep his hands off the maid for they had done her harm enough.

Still Balbus bent over Nyria, and while Crispus tried as gently as he could to slip the nooses from her limbs, the beater muttered,—

"Had they told me I was wanted for such a job they might have fetched another in my stead, for Balbus Plautius is no butcher, and 'twas a butcher that was needed here."

Nevertheless he went up and took his money from Julia, making her a low obeisance. For that was his living.

XV

When Nyria awoke to consciousness she was lying on the straw bed in Euphena's back room, whither Crispus had carried her. There was a pillow under her head and a wool covering spread over her. But when she tried to move she grew sick again with pain. She had a smarting weal down her temple. If Bibbi had made that mark, she thought, he would have been punished in some way. Bibbi was too big to be beaten himself, and besides, a whipper was never whipped—at least among household slaves.

The room was very dark. It had one tiny window, but over that the curtains had been drawn, leaving but a glimmer of light. Someone had stretched a piece of cloth on the floor beside the bed and laid thereon a cup with wine in it and some pieces of light cake, of a kind that the slaves made for themselves. Nyria looked round in the gloom and saw that she was alone. She raised herself painfully. Her whole body was stiff and aching, and she could feel great cuts across her upper arms and her shoulders, while her back and bosom were all bruised and sore. By turning herself a little she could see some of the stripes. Someone had wrapped her round in a white cloth and had spread ointment on her wounds, but she shuddered at the sight of the sheet, which was stained horribly with grease and blood. As she was thinking what now she could do, the curtain between the front and back rooms was pushed aside, letting in more light, and Crispus peeped in. He entered when he saw that she was sitting up.

"How art thou, Nyria?" he asked. "Thou shouldst not stir thyself, child."

"But I have to get about my business, Crispus," she answered.

"A truce to thy business! Dost thou not remember that this is the Saturnalia, and not even that she-wolf, Julia, can make thee work?"

He came and knelt down close beside her. "Thou hadst best have taken some of the drugged wine, Nyria," he said, "for the gods have been hard upon thee. Drink this," and he lifted the cup to her.

She hesitated before sipping it. "Thou hast not put anything in it, Crispus?" she asked anxiously.

"Nay, of what avail to drug thee now?" And then she took a long drink.

"Truly no, it would not do to drug me now, for I must be upon my feet," she said. Then a blush overspread her face and neck and she pulled the sheet round her. "I am 'shamed before thee, Crispus."

"Nay, then, thou needst not be. For if Julia would not remember that thou too wast a woman, Crispus hath not forgotten it. Think no shame, little friend, for there have looked no eyes on thee save these of mine, and for once Crispus was blind."

Nyria wept and he soothed her gently.

"There, there, child! Suppose to thyself that Crispus is but a dotard without sight or sense. And this, too, thou mayest think on, Nyria—I had a little sister once."

Nyria remembered that he had lost his sister and had grieved sore after her. She smiled at him through her tears.

"I am grateful to thee, Crispus, though words are poor payment," she said. "Wilt leave me now, for I must robe myself and be gone?"

"Whither goest thou?" he asked, rising to his feet. "Thou art not fit to enter on any fresh adventure."

"But I must," she said. "Do not try to stay me, Crispus."

"Since I cannot, mayhap Stephanus could," he answered. "I would have fetched him to thee, but I feared to leave thee with no one near save those scoundrels who took part against thee. Seeing, too, that thou wast suffering only the fruit of yonder fiend's cruelty, I knew that Stephanus himself could do but little, and thought it best to remain at hand till thou shouldst waken. But if thou needst a messenger tell me and I will do thy bidding."

"Nay, I need no messenger," she replied. "I go to the house of Valeria, wife of Paulinus. She is sore smitten with fever, and hath but Æola, the youngest of her handmaidens, to tend her."

"And was that where thou didst stay all night?" inquired Crispus.

"Ay, and to-night too Æola will need me. Detain me not, Crispus."

"It seems that I but waste words on thee," he said kindly. "But I'll go with thee, Nyria."

"Nay, I would have thee stop and make my excuses to Julia when she sends for me—as send she will," said Nyria.

"She hath done so already," and he gave a gruff laugh. "Julia hath sent twice to summon thee, and each time I answered that thou wert unconscious and, for aught I knew, at the door of death."

"Julia would care nothing though she slew a slave," said Nyria, but she did not speak bitterly, for such was Julia, as those well knew who served her. Crispus went out, bidding Nyria call if she needed help. But first he fetched a jar of water that he had warmed in readiness, and a pile of soft rag which he had routed from one of Euphena's cupboards. The wounds hurt dreadfully when she tried to draw her garments over them, but at last, after brave efforts,

Nyria finished dressing and went out into the slaves' court. Crispus sat upon a low mud wall, smoking one of those long pipes with herbs in which the slaves surreptitiously indulged.

"I sought Sabinus, and he hath released me for this evening," said Crispus. "Look not so fearful. Julia is not my master, remember. Behold, here are thy bearers, for 'tis a little noble lady who fares forth to visit the great Valeria."

A litter was being borne across the courtyard—one of a kind that traders and such folk hired on the outskirts of the Forum.

"Oh, Crispus!" Nyria cried. "How shall I repay thee?"

"Sabinus advanced me a few sestertii, which was enough, for we shall not need it long. He is a good fellow, Sabinus, with a kindly heart and a gentle soul, and he is worthy a better mate than that sharp-fanged she-wolf of his."

As they crossed the outer courtyard Pheidias met them with a message from Julia demanding Nyria's presence as soon as she was able to stand. Crispus, signing to her to be silent, took upon himself to answer it.

"Tell the Most Noble that by grace of the gods, who are kinder than men, Nyria is able to rise, but not fit to work. Therefore she attendeth Saturnalia according to the law of the land, and is now on her way to give thanks in the temple."

Pheidias laughed. "The gods know thou liest," he said lightly, "but methinks they will care naught," and he let the litter pass on.

"Oh! Crispus," said Nyria, distressfully, "thou shouldst not lie, even though the gods care nothing."

But Crispus also only laughed, and they did not talk much going up the hill, for Nyria was weak, and suffered from the slight jolting of the litter. Moreover, she wished to keep in reserve all the strength she had. At her request the bearers put her down by the small gate, where Crispus paid them and sent them off. It was now about sundown, and the shadows lay black, though there was a band of reddish light westward.

"Thou wilt take this," said Crispus, handing Nyria a package he had brought with him. "'Tis a little flask of wine and some bread and meat; 'twill give thee strength. Here cometh someone," he added, as there was a fumbling at the gate latch. The door opened a little way, and Æola peered out.

"Oh, Nyria, thou art here at last!" she cried. "I was wondering what had chanced to thee. The day hath seemed so long."

"I was kept," Nyria answered. "How fares the Domina?"

"But poorly. A great doctor hath been to see her. Moreover, the Lady Vitellia hath returned of a sudden, and came hither at once, though she knew naught of my lady's illness." Æola now saw over Nyria's shoulder another face, and drew back.

"This is Crispus, my good friend," said Nyria. "Salute him, for were it not for his kind aid, Æola, I might not have been able to return."

Æola blushed up to the roots of her hair, and made a salutation meet for a lord, for Æola was inexperienced and knew no difference between strangers. Crispus bowed, well pleased.

"It hath been my happy portion to bring thy friend to thee," he said, "and I am more than recompensed."

"Thou art kind, sir," replied Æola, timidly.

"Nay, 'tis thou who art kind, maiden," said Crispus. "And thou wouldst be kinder still if thou didst not so plainly show that thou findest me somewhat of an ogre."

Æola grew redder, and stammered. Nyria pulled her by the arm through the portal.

"One moment, Nyria," called Crispus. "I will come hither to-morrow about this hour to learn how thou dost fare and the lady thou befriendest. Perchance, if thou art not free to speak to me, this maid will honour me with a word."

Nyria nodded. "Ay! ay! Come, Æola," and the girls went in.

"I told the Lady Vitellia about thee, Nyria," Æola said breathlessly, "and she bade me bring thee to her presence as soon as thou didst come. Enter, but tread softly, for Valeria sleeps."

Nyria's heart craved for sight of Valeria, but she waited in the sitting-room, which looked strangely desolate. Presently she was summoned to Vitellia, who, seeing that she moved with pain and difficulty, asked first what had befallen her. Nyria was covered with confusion, for it was one thing to bear a whipping bravely in sight of her fellow-slaves, and quite another to betray her shame before a noble Roman lady.

"Hast been in trouble?" asked Vitellia, kindly.

Nyria answered meekly, "May it please the Domina, I have been under correction."

Vitellia drew aside the girl's robe and looked at some of the marks on her shoulders.

"It may be that thou wert in fault," she said in that gentle, though severe, voice of hers, "but assuredly others have likewise erred."

Nyria looked up, emboldened by the compassion in her eyes. Vitellia went on.

"Æola telleth me that thou art skilled in nursing. Art thou free to serve Valeria for a while, or doth Julia demand thine attendance?"

"It is the Saturnalia, lady," Nyria replied. "Last night I claimed my due, and came hither, and by the right of Saturnalia I have come again."

"Thy liberty is bought at a bitter price, I fear," said Vitellia.

"Nevertheless, listen, and I will tell thee what the doctor said of my sister."

She quoted then the opinion of Archimenes, a physician of considerable repute in Rome.

"Archimenes was brought hither by a certain Stephanus," she added. "A friend of thine, it seems, since he spoke naught but praise of thee. This Stephanus appears to be a good doctor himself, though not duly qualified to practise as such. Thus declared Archimenes, who spoke of him as one wasted upon his own calling." Nyria bowed in silence.

Then Vitellia gave her a written list of directions that the great doctor had left, but Nyria shook her head over it, and nearly cried as she put it back in Vitellia's hand.

"What troubleth thee, child?" asked Vitellia.

"I cannot read, lady," replied the girl. "If it would please thee to say over to me the great doctor's orders, I can engage to observe them faithfully, but I am a poor, ignorant slave. The Giver of Wisdom hath not vouchsafed knowledge of letters to Nyria."

"He hath vouchsafed thee other knowledge, if I judge aright," said Vitellia, kindly. "Come closer then, child, and I will read thee the doctor's directions." She recited them slowly, while Nyria committed them to memory as she had been wont to do with those of Stephanus.

"Now tell me what thou must do first," said Vitellia, and Nyria answered her, repeating the list with such accuracy that Vitellia showed surprise.

"Truly if thou canst not read with thine eyes, Nyria," she said, "thou hast in thy little mind a scroll upon which one may write indelibly. Now I will leave thee, for I have come a long journey and must take rest. Thou and Æola will watch in turn. But tire not thyself, for thou too needst care."

"That matters not, lady. I am here to tend Valeria, and will give her my faithful service."

"What hath my sister done, I wonder, to win thy young heart?" said Vitellia. "Valeria was not wont to sow seeds of love broadcast."

"Valeria is—Valeria, oh, most noble lady! and it is my pride and joy to serve her," answered Nyria, as, making obeisance, she went towards the inner room.

Valeria was stretched so motionless that swift terror seized Nyria. In her anxiety she hardly dared to breathe. The deathlike pallor and the blue shadows on Valeria's face made it sharp and unsightly, but a faint movement of the chest told that she still lived. Later in the evening Æola crept in, and the girls talked in whispers. Æola told Nyria how she had served Vitellia at supper. Vitellia had had some food fetched in, but she had not brought her own women, who were busy putting in order their mistress's mansion on the Esquiline in readiness for the arrival of her husband, Valerius Asiaticus. It appeared that Vitellia had not been able to meet him at Forum Julii after all, but had been waiting in the north of Italy till he should have received certain promised commands, delayed in the sending. Now he was with his legion marching by another route, and was expected any day in Rome. Vitellia had said that she might be able to stay only a short time in Valeria's house, for her husband would require her, and, she added, it was the duty of a good wife to remain with her husband.

"Methinks a good wife must have many duties," remarked Æola. "But doubtless if she loved her husband that would not matter," and Æola looked askance at Nyria. "In what way did he befriend thee, whom thou callest Crispus?" she questioned shyly.

"I cannot tell thee that story now," replied Nyria, who did not relish Æola's chatter. But Æola was curious about Crispus, and would not be put off.

"Well, then, he was very good to me, and salved my sores, and saved me in all that he could," she said. "'Twas through him that I came hither so comfortably, else should I have had to crawl up the Cœlian."

"But who is he?" asked Æola. "Serveth he Julia?"

"Nay, he serveth *not* Julia," and Nyria laughed softly, remembering how that morning Crispus had defied Julia. "'Tis not Crispus's way to serve Julia when Julia's commands are not to his liking."

"In truth he seemeth too great a lord to serve," murmured Æola.

"Thou art foolish, Æola. Crispus is but one of Sabinus's dressers, and attendeth also at the table, for Sabinus liketh his wit and merry humour. 'Twas he who pulled our veils last night. Dost remember?"

Æola crimsoned, and Nyria saw that she remembered very well.

"Crispus laughs at everything and everyone, save folks that are in trouble," continued Nyria. "If thou wouldst win his favour, Æola, pull a long face and be faint and weary. Weakness is the road to Crispus's heart, as Nyria knows, for hath she not trodden it?"

Æola looked at herself in Valeria's long mirror, shoving back the curls that lay on her forehead and drawing her features into solemn shape.

"My face is round," she said. "I cannot pull it long, and there is naught weak nor ill with me."

She stood before the mirror, turning her small body and lifting her hands above her head so that she made a pretty figure. Valeria always dressed her maidens in soft, bright colours, and Æola wore a robe of rose, bordered with white, that became her well.

"They tell me I am but a babe," she said. "Sometimes it seems to me that my thoughts grow higher than my head. Yet they are not high enough to reach the favour of"— she paused a moment and blushed, adding, below her breath, "Crispus. He would ne'er look at me, thinkest thou, Nyria?"

"He looked at thee enough this evening," returned Nyria. "But be silent, Æola, or else get thee gone. We must not talk while Valeria lies asleep. Go, sleep thyself, or Crispus will not like thy weary face."

"Thou saidst that weakness was the road to Crispus's heart," pouted Æola.

"Ay, but that road stoppeth at its outer door. Crispus, like the rest of his kind, would let none but a fair face enter that inner sanctuary where men enshrine what they call love."

"'Tis thou who talkest folly, Nyria," retorted Æola, her cheeks aflame, but not ill pleased at the banter. "Without doubt he is over grand to think aught of a maid like me;" and Æola slipped away.

Nyria remained watching, and twice the time came to give Valeria medicine and food—milk with drops of Archimenes's in it, and an egg lightly beaten. She took the first half sleeping. The second time, as Nyria put her arm beneath the pillow to raise the sick woman's head, Valeria caught at her hand and kissed it, murmuring, "Marcus! Marcus! . . ."

It made Nyria's heart bleed to hear her, and she wondered how this Marcus could have served her seemingly so ill. Valeria's eyes rolled restlessly in an unseeing stare. Then there came sudden strength into her voice, and she cried,—

"Marcus, why art thou so unreasonable? In spirit, at least, am I not wholly thine? Have I not given thee more than ever I gave before? There is none to divide thy kingdom with thee. Thou dost reign supreme in Valeria's bosom."

Half raising herself, she clasped her hands before her and gazed wildly across the room.

"Marcus!" she cried again. "Beloved! Oh, come back to me. Come back! Thou wilt not leave Valeria thus? Ah, come!" and her voice rose to a wail. "Have I not said that where'er thou goest I would go—that I would cherish all thou holdest dear? Command Valeria as thou wilt."

All this she said, and much more, sometimes speaking quickly, sometimes slowly, and dropping her voice now and then to a note that pierced Nyria's heart. Knowing not how to soothe her,

Nyria stood in sorrow, when she heard a muffled tread and the movement of a robe, and saw that Vitellia was beside her.

Vitellia stepped to the head of the couch and laid her hand on her sister's mouth as if she would silence her ravings. The slave-girl drew back into the shadow until Vitellia called "Nyria!" and she came forward.

"Thou hast nursed fever before?" asked Vitellia.

"Ay, lady."

"Then thou knowest that many a one, like my poor sister, prateth of matters that have no reality, and are sore afflicted by what is in truth no more than evil fancy. 'Tis but a dream that distresseth Valeria."

She paused and looked questioningly at the slave, who repeated,—

"'Tis but a dream, lady."

A sigh broke from Vitellia's lips. "A dream that might easily assail even Valeria."

Nyria bowed her head in silence, though she knew full well that Valeria's dream was no fevered fancy.

Vitellia looked earnestly at her sister, who had become quieter. Then she turned again to the slave-girl.

"Remember," she said, "maids may chatter of things that are of small moment, but 'tis not seemly for a watcher to prate about that which she heareth or chanceth to see in a sick-room."

Nyria was cut to the quick, but she answered nothing. Vitellia went on.

"I hope thou art a wise maid and dost understand."

"I am Nyria, lady. Am I not a slave?"

"But thou art not Valeria's slave," said Vitellia, surprised. "A handmaid should be true to her mistress, but she may not be compelled to be faithful to another."

"I am Nyria!" repeated the girl again. "I render naught but faithful service. Naught shall pass from me that may injure Valeria."

"Thou couldst not injure the noble Valeria," replied Vitellia, haughtily. "Nevertheless, it is not well that the name of one so highly placed should be bandied about in Rome. I trust thee, Nyria."

She laid her hand on the girl's shoulder as she spoke, and, seeing that the slave winced, added kindly,—

"Poor child, thou hast been hurt and shouldst have rest. Thou shalt sleep at dawn, Nyria."

Valeria had sunk into a comatose condition, and Nyria only roused her to administer food and drops according to Archimenes's directions. Towards morning Æola came to do her share, and Nyria got some sleep. Thus they watched by turns.

Vitellia conferred with the great doctor when he paid his visit as to how the nursing had best be managed, for it proved impossible just now to hire attendants. Vitellia had only two women with her, and these were needed at her house. Æola wept when Vitellia spoke of sending for them to help, and begged that she and Nyria might be permitted to serve Valeria alone, knowing that strange maids needed more tendance than their mistresses. Vitellia did not contest the matter, for she did not wish her women to hear Valeria's ravings.

A messenger had arrived that morning to say that Asiaticus would reach the walls of Rome on the same day. Vitellia went home in order that she might be prepared to welcome her husband. In the afternoon, when she had gone, Æola summoned Nyria to speak with Stephanus, who waited in the ante-room. He looked grim and sad; and when she would have taken him to Valeria's chamber he shook his head.

"'Tis not for Stephanus to attend on the most noble Valeria," he said, "now that she hath passed into the hands of a registered physician. I came that I might doctor *thee*, Nyria. Show me thy wounds." And he made her unrobe, cursing, and gnawing his beard as he looked at her stripes. Crispus had told him what had happened, and Stephanus was grieved and wroth. He swore all sorts of vengeance against Julia, yet he seemed likewise angry with Nyria herself.

"Thou art a fool to endure such treatment," he cried, "seeing that there is a good home awaiting thee, and an arm strong enough to protect thee—even against Julia."

He spoke so harshly that Nyria whimpered, for she was still sore and her nerves were shaken.

"Blubber not like a babe!" cried Stephanus, gruffly, "but act as a wise woman should who knows her friends and will abide by their counsel." Then, seeing that she wept the more, he kissed her wounds, and all his wrath turned against himself.

"'Tis enough to bring madness on a man beholding of such wrong," he said. "The gods are not content to have young things killed publicly on their altars, but must needs allow baser sacrifices in the privacy of Roman households, where neither justice nor mercy may make themselves heard."

And so he grumbled on while he deftly dressed Nyria's sores with fresh ointment and linen bandages that he had prepared. He had brought with him also a flagon of wine, and, pouring some out, bade her drink, adding, in surly accents, "Though it be not so rich a brand, mayhap, as that which thy friend Crispus provideth. Since when hast thou drunk Crispus's wine, Nyria?"

"Since yesternoon, when Crispus gave it me," she answered.

He looked at her sharply. Stephanus had a trick of screwing

up his eyes till they seemed like gimlets when he wanted to probe any matter to the bottom.

"Ay, so he told me. Dost thou oft take favours from Crispus—eh, Nyria?"

"I took many yesterday," she replied. "'Tis by favour of Crispus that I am here, alive."

"Now, that is untrue!" exclaimed Stephanus, roughly. "I own that thou hast been brutally beaten; but there's better stuff in thee, Nyria, than to die like a dog beneath the lash. But I would learn more of this Crispus. What doeth he following thee about?"

"Kind things, else would he not be Crispus. Abuse not my friend, Stephanus. If thou lovest me thou dost owe him much."

"Can I, then, count thy debts mine, Nyria?" Stephanus asked quickly.

"Ay, if thou wilt help me pay them, instead of scolding me for naught," she answered sobbing.

"Nay, nay, little one!" and he put his arms round her tenderly. "May the day never dawn when Stephanus shall scold thee. But it makes his blood boil, Nyria, to think that another standeth closer to thee than himself."

"None standeth closer than thou," she said. "Crispus is but Sabinus's body-man and steward, as thou knowest as well as I do. Dost remember the story of little Loyella, that sister of his, and how she was sold away from him and took half his heart with her? 'Tis that makes him kind to maids. But bend low, Stephanus, and I will whisper thee a secret. I think I know a maiden who, did he offer her the other half of his heart, would perchance accept it."

"So long as the maiden be not Nyria," said Stephanus, looking hungrily into her face. "Thine eyes are blue and clear as the skies of Greece, child; let no falsehood darken them."

"I am not false," she answered. "If thou wouldst use thine own eyes, Stephanus, thou mightst discover the maiden for thyself, since she lives not a league from here."

Stephanus dropped his arms in no good humour, and began to put his salves and lint back into the wallet, while Nyria fastened up her robe. His glance fell on the untasted cup of wine which he had poured out for her, and he grew angry again and would have emptied it on the carpet had she not stayed him.

"Better water the thirsty ground outside," she said, smiling. "But if thou wert to ask me prettily, Stephanus, mayhap I would pledge thee in it."

Delighted, he held the cup to her lips, and she quaffed. Then suddenly he drew it away and kissed her mouth, wet as it was with the red wine.

"Fie! that was rude," she said.

He laughed, and Nyria saw that he had recovered from his bad temper. She crept across to Valeria's door and listened, but all was quiet within. Returning again, she went out with Stephanus to the terrace where the Domina had been wont to sit beneath the rose-vine, now all bare and withered. But there upon the edge of the steps sat Æola, laughing and blushing; and who should be below, leaning on the parapet, but Crispus.

Stephanus flared up anew.

"How now!" he cried. "Here comes that scoundrel courting thee again. Well, if thou favourest him, Nyria—"

"Hold thy peace!" she interrupted. "Seest thou not that he hath no mind for thee nor me?"

Stephanus's mouth went into a large round O. He shot a quizzical glance at Nyria, and, pouncing forward, whistled in Crispus's ear,—

"By Eros and Mercury!" he cried, "'tis one thing to rob a man of his mistress, and another to come stealing the heart of a child." And he vaulted the parapet and was gone towards the gate before Æola and her companion perceived that they had been spied upon.

XVI

SOME days went by, during which Nyria scarcely dared to leave Valeria's bedside. At last the great physician sent for Stephanus to give his opinion on the case. Nyria was amused to see him puffed up with self-gratification at having been called by the distinguished doctor.

It was said that Archimenes had no great learning in his profession, but sucked the brains of other people, taking the credit thereof, and that he relied chiefly upon his soft tongue and courteous manner, which gave women confidence in him, but that when all was said and done Nature cured his patients. He was nevertheless reputed the second best physician in Rome. Celsus, who served about the court, and had much skill in the treatment of men, was counted first, but Archimenes was in great favour with women, and when any grand lady in Rome fell ill, Archimenes was always called to her.

Archimenes was a large man, bland and benevolent, who girdled his robe loosely about his ample chest, and carried a number of pouches containing powders and pills, and sweetmeats as well, for he had a fashion, which endeared him to the aristocratic children of Rome, of producing a sugared violet or a bit of preserved fruit to lay on their tongues when called to see any ailing among them, and thus make them look at him.

"'Tis plain Archimenes hath taken thy counsel," said Nyria to Stephanus.

"Ay! ay!" he answered, and went on,

"I have dissuaded Archimenes from the letting of blood, for I hold that too much healthy blood is let in Rome already from the bodies of beaten slaves. The gods, sated with so lusty a stream, are not like to be appeased by a poorer flow from sick folk's veins."

"Thou art Juvenal's mouthpiece!" cried Nyria. "Such speeches are never thine."

"Well! well!" laughed Stephanus, "what doth that matter, so they be good hearing?"

But Nyria went on sadly,—

"What wilt thou do if Valeria doth not grow quickly better?"

"Then," said he, "Archimenes will consult with Symmachus, who stands next of repute in Rome. But I doubt if the mighty Symmachus will meet Stephanus."

Symmachus would certainly have disdained to meet Stephanus had he known that he was a mere slave-doctor, and by trade a goldsmith. Perhaps, however, Archimenes suppressed the fact. Symmachus lived in a fine house, keeping a number of slaves himself, and exacting large fees, and had Valeria been other than the daughter of a Cæsar or the wife of Paulinus, Domitian's friend, Symmachus would probably have paid less attention. As things were, he was ready enough to come to her, and since Archimenes laid stress upon Stephanus's skilful treatment at the onset, which, he said, had saved her life thus far, Symmachus could not in courtesy to his colleague refuse the consultation. So Stephanus was bidden to meet the two doctors, and it was Nyria who admitted him into their presence as they waited in the ante-chamber of Valeria's bedroom.

Symmachus was very different in appearance from Archimenes, being lean and spare and saturnine of aspect, with a peaked beard and narrow dark eyes that had a trick of closing themselves, only opening wide in a sort of affronted look when he considered that due deference was not paid him. Nor was his manner courteous to those beneath him as was that of Archimenes, for he took no notice of Nyria and did not rise to greet Stephanus or to show him any civility, which made Stephanus redden and roused Nyria to anger, since Stephanus was their equal for the occasion. Stephanus afterwards told Nyria that the interview had been stormy. For Symmachus advocated bleeding, which Stephanus stoutly opposed, advising remedies that the other two, under protest, consented to try, but which brought down the fever. Symmachus did not often come after that, and never again met Stephanus. Archimenes had conduct of the case, and Nyria looked forward to his daily visit and the pleasant greeting he always gave her.

"Well, and how are we this morning?" he would say, drawing her into the affair, though she was but a slave.

Once, while she was making some readjustment of Valeria's bed, the robe slipped from her shoulders and with it the bandage, and Archimenes's eyes noted her weals and scars. He made no comment while he was occupied with Valeria, but after he had given all his directions, he called the girl to him and turning back her sleeves, said, "What have we here, little one?"

Nyria glanced affrightedly at Vitellia, who made answer for her.

"Nyria hath been in trouble. The hurt was painful, but she feels it less now."

"Ay, lady," Nyria said. "The hurt is naught."

But Archimenes had undone the bandage and was setting it straight, and he saw plainly enough what was the matter. He patted the girl's head kindly, and said,—

"There beats a brave heart in this small body. Hast many sores such as these, my child?"

Nyria grew red, and was silent. Again Vitellia spoke for her.

"Nyria is proud," she said, "and will not speak of what ails her. Moreover, she hath her own doctor."

"So!" said Archimenes. "And who is he?"

"Stephanus, may it please thee, lord," answered Nyria humbly, deeming it right to address Archimenes as though he were of noble station.

"Good Stephanus!" said he. "Thou couldst not have a better doctor, nor Stephanus a braver patient. He hath dressed the arm well, but take care, child, that the bandages be not loosened, or they will abrade the sores and cause an inflammation."

Nyria made obeisance and moved away, but as she did so she saw Archimenes glance meaningly at Vitellia, and heard him say, though he lowered his voice,—

"A lashing that I'll warrant was undeserved, Domina."

"Alas! I fear 'twas the mouth which ordered it, rather than the hand that was in fault," said Vitellia.

"There is one of the crying shames of this fine city," said Archimenes, shaking his head. "Of what avail for physicians to try to alleviate suffering when its people fall upon each other like beasts? It is as though the gods meant Rome to learn wisdom only in destroying herself."

"I fear that much must be laid to the charge of Roman women, if all that I hear of our society be true," said Vitellia, sadly. "In yonder poor child's household the mistress orders punishment that many a man would shrink from inflicting. If women would but learn gentleness, and practise their wifely duty, there would be less trouble in Rome."

Archimenes placed his large hand upon his heart, and made her a courtly bow.

"Nay, Domina. Had men more true manhood, women would quickly follow the nobler example set them by their mates."

Vitellia only smiled in her gracious but austere fashion as Archimenes took his leave.

Now Nyria's conscience soon began to smite her on the score of Julia, and as soon as she was well enough to walk so far, she went down to the Aventine to see her mistress. It was a rash proceeding, but she knew that Julia would be inconvenienced without any women to attend her during the Saturnalia, and Nyria would willingly have gone every day for the robing could she have been sure of getting quickly back to Valeria.

She entered by the slaves' gate into the quadrangle of now deserted huts, and there at the door of her own she saw Euphena, who squatted in the sun, nursing her lean knees after her wont, and who, when she saw Nyria approaching, screeched out not unkindly,—

"Little fool, what dost thou here? When the fly hath escaped from the spider's web he had best remain at a distance, lest the angry spider catch him again and suck his blood."

"If Julia be the spider," said Nyria, "she hath bitten me so oft that a bite more or less mattereth little. Moreover, I am sorry for her now, for none will serve Julia for love, and 'tis hard she should go untended."

Euphena mumbled crossly,—

"Julia hath sent for me to serve her, and if she threaten me I have but to tell her I will go serve Domitia. Why shouldst thou pity Julia, fool? Hath she not gold in plenty to pay her way to the grave, and beyond that even *thou* canst not follow her."

Nyria felt like to laugh at sight of Julia, for she had a quaint appearance in ill-assorted garments, and Euphena had dressed her hair after the manner of the Ethiopians, looped down over the ears in funny plaits tied with bits of coloured silk, and here and there a bead. Julia looked depressed and had not even heart to be wrathful.

"So 'tis thou, Nyria!" she said. "Sawest thou ever such a fright as Euphena hath made of me—though I pay her well. Go, fetch the combs, and get me fit to receive my friends once more. I have been obliged to deny myself to everyone, and most of all to Cæsar, for who could care to look at Julia in such a guise as this?"

And she plucked at the rags of silk in her black hair which she could not disentangle—so tightly had Euphena braided them.

"Thou art an ungratful brat," she said, while Nyria tired her, "since thou canst leave me to the mercy of that black-skinned hag who talketh ever of death and the dungeon. How know I that she doth not plot to compass my end?"

"Nay, surely the Most Noble need not distress herself," replied Nyria, who was unplaiting and combing out Julia's matted locks. "'Tis impossible that one so lowly as Euphena could compass harm against the great and mighty Julia whom fortune hath favoured with everything she doth desire."

Julia sighed, and was silent. She seemed preoccupied while Nyria dressed her hair. Presently she said,—

"'Tis true that Euphena, limb of Hades as she is, hath dealings in witchcraft, and one never knows whither they may lead. . . . . But the hag is good and faithful, Nyria," added Julia sharply. "And mark—say not that I have laid a word of blame on Euphena." By which Nyria saw that Julia was afraid of the old Ethiopian, and that she clung to Euphena in spite of her grumbling; and that puzzled the slave-girl.

When Nyria had finished dressing Julia's hair, the lady said,—

"Thou speakest wrong, Nyria, in prating of the mighty Julia having all she doth desire. What woman hath her dearest wish? Julia rose and looked at her great comely shape in the mirror. "I am beautiful," she went on. "Yea—and I have wit to guide me along a difficult road. But I have not the power that should be mine. I am not the Augusta—neither it seems can I lay claim to willing service such as that thin-faced jade whom thou adorest can command—even from those who are not her slaves."

Nyria drew back with a formal obeisance.

"Craving the Most Noble's permission, I will now return," she said. "I came but for an hour, and may stay no longer."

At this Julia's anger burst forth.

"Craving my permission, brat!" she cried in fierce sarcasm. "Dost dare to mock me?" And seizing the silver hand-mirror, she dealt Nyria a blow with it that made one of her wounds break out fresh bleeding, so that the girl was glad to escape as speedily as she might. She refrained afterwards from coming again, until the thought of Julia's head tired Ethiopian fashion, oppressed her with so great a pity that she went down to dress it as often as she could, and Julia, being defenceless in the matter, received her without further abuse or hard words.

So the first half of the Saturnalia went by, and Nyria wondered that there was no sight nor word of Licinius Sura, who, had he known of Valeria's illness, would surely, the girl thought, have come to ask after her. Nyria concluded from this seeming neglect and also from certain words Valeria had uttered in her raving, that he must have been absent from Rome. And so it proved, when at last he made his appearance at the Villa.

He let himself in at the private gate one afternoon when Nyria sat alone on the terrace steps. She had watched nearly all the night by Valeria's bedside, and was weary after her vigil. Her midday meal, too, had made her drowsy. Vitellia often sent up viands from her own household—soup with lentils and nourishing paste in it, stewed kid and meal-bread. And Crispus brought many tempting baskets of fruits, decked round with leaves and beneath it meat and olive cakes and such homely dainties as were popular in the slaves' quarter.

So to-day she had eaten well, and was dozing in the sun, her head against the marble steps, her yellow hair all unbound about her shoulders, and a pretty picture she made. Presently a voice aroused her from slumber, crying softly in her dreams, as it seemed, "Xydra . . . Xydra . . ."

She started up and rubbed her eyes bewilderedly. The voice went on in gently mocking tones,—

"Xydra! Golden-haired, sleeping Xydra! Doth she wait the embrace of her rainbow-winged lover?"

Nyria knew the voice, though it had never before addressed her thus. She stared in dazed fashion to right and left, then close to her in the angle of the steps she saw the face and form of Marcus

Licinius Sura. A handsome face and form—too slender for Nyria's fancy, since, if she had a choice, it was in favour of stout-built muscular men like Stephanus—though she had never gratified the poor fellow by telling him so. But Sura was not a dandy. His arms were not too white, and his legs showed brown and knotted between the high boot and the skirt of his tunic from which his toga fell back in carefully pressed folds. He was looking at Nyria intently, his pleasant eyes gleaming with interest and amusement, a smile widening his clear-cut mouth.

"Ah! now I see," he said. "'Tis no sleeping princess of a fairy tale, but the little watch-dog maid—she whom they call Nyria."

The girl arose and made her obeisance.

"What dost thou here?" he asked. "Hath the most noble Valeria added to her staff of waiting-women? I warrant she saw there was but one faithful watch-dog in Rome, and must needs beg, purchase, or steal her. But seeing it is the Saturnalia, a pretty girl like thee should be dancing and making merry in the booths at the Campus Martius. Where are the rest of thy fellows disporting themselves?"

"I know not, lord," said Nyria. "I wait on the most noble Valeria here while I am free, for she is sick."

"Sick!" he repeated; and his face darkened. "'Tis not unlikely. I told her it would chance if she were not wise. But I trow," he added, "that wisdom and Valeria are not mates. In what way is she sick?"

"With the fever, may it please thee, lord," Nyria replied.

"Now, by Libitina, it doth *not* please me," he exclaimed. "The fever, indeed! Is it serious? Who hath seen her?"

Nyria gave him the names of the doctors, putting Stephanus first, as seemed to her but fitting, seeing that Stephanus had been the first to tend the Domina.

"I know not this Doctor Stephanus," said Sura sharply. "But Rome goes on apace, and there may well be stranger physicians. A Greek, by his name, who hath sprung into prominence of which Licinius Sura in his hermit's life knows naught. As for Archimenes—'tis but an old woman with a woman's faddish fears. Symmachus is sager, but he is not in charge, thou sayest?"

"The Lord Symmachus came twice or thrice," said Nyria.

"By whose bidding?" asked Sura. "Who taketh command here, seeing that Paulinus is away?"

"The Lady Vitellia," replied Nyria, and told him of how Valeria's sister had come back to Rome.

His face changed. "Well, now, 'tis time for all who be not saints to pass without, for their room is better than their company to Vitellia. Is she within?"

Nyria shook her head. "Not so, lord. The Lady Vitellia cometh but once a day. Most often 'tis towards evening."

"Then haply—" he said, and paused. Thrusting his hand into the pouch men wore at their belts, he brought forth a handful of coins, and selected one therefrom.

"Say, child, thou hast service for gold pieces, I warrant. Couldst spend one upon sweetmeats or gewgaws?"

Nyria shrank back. "I am well supplied, lord," she answered proudly. "'Tis to Julia's household I belong. I serve the Lady Valeria by special favour, and need no money for the serving."

"Thou art different from the rest of thy sex," he answered, coolly putting back the coin within the pouch. "I'll rebuke thee not. Licinius is none so rich that he can spare coins to fling to unwilling maids. But I would see thy mistress. Wilt bear her this message? Say, Licinius waits without, and craves to know if his pleasure be her own."

Nyria shook her head, and answered sadly, "Valeria knoweth naught of any man's pleasure. She sleeps a sleep nigh unto death."

A sudden sickness seemed to seize Licinius, and he sat down on the steps staring on the ground. "But she speaks at times, perchance?" he asked.

"Ay, fevered words, my lord."

"Hath she said aught of me?"

"She hath spoken much of one Marcus," said Nyria, looking straight before her.

For a minute he made no answer. Then he took his tablets and stylus from his vest and laid them on his knee.

"Nyria," he said, "if I should write a few lines to Valeria, wouldst thou deliver them when the fever leaves her?"

Nyria hesitated. She felt that here lay a crossing of the roads, her "yea" pointing one way, her "nay" another, and she knew not to what disaster either path might lead. For herself she cared not. But how would it be for Valeria? . . . Then she seemed to see Valeria's pale sharpened face upon the pillows, as when she had watched it through the night, and to hear the low rambling sentences which now and then had broken her stupor. The burden had always been of Marcus. Nyria knew full well that this letter from him would be as balm to that tortured heart. It was not much to do—to bring comfort to her whom she adored; and she answered, "Yes."

He nodded gloomily. "Sit there and wait. I will give thee the message when 'tis finished."

She obeyed him, and sat in the sun as before, silent, while his stylus travelled rapidly over the slips of waxed ivory. Presently he laid them together.

"Hast thou a morsel of silk to bind these, and somewhat with which I may seal the knot?"

Nyria got to her feet.

"Ay, lord," she said, and went into the house, bringing back a taper of wax and a strand of violet thread from Valeria's work-basket.

He looked at the silken skein as though he recognised it, and there came a gleam of tenderness over his face as he tied the silk round the tablets, sealing it with Valeria's stem of violet wax and his own signet. But his hand shook so that a drop fell on the ivory edge.

"I want no prying eyes to read my missive," he said, smiling as he gave it to her. "Dost understand, Nyria? Can I trust thee?"

"None ever found they could not, lord," she answered.

"I believe thee. Thou wilt guard the letter?"

"As Valeria's self," she said; and placing it in her bosom, made obeisance and left him.

A day or two later Licinius came again. It was Æola who met him on the terrace, but he asked for Nyria, who went out, not too well disposed towards him. He questioned her eagerly, scarcely believing that Valeria was yet too ill to have sent him a message. "The physicians say she hath trouble on her mind," Nyria said.

"She needeth another doctor," he replied. "See, little watch-dog, ask Valeria, when next she knoweth thee, whether it would not pleasure her to have the learned Doctor Marcus by her bed-side?"

He gave a meaning laugh, but Nyria stood silent.

"Thou carest for Valeria, dost not?" he asked.

"Yea, lord," replied Nyria, stiffening.

"Then thou wouldst not withhold from her that which would make her well?"

"Nay, lord, that would I not do," she answered.

"Whatever it might be?" he questioned.

"Whatever it might be," she replied.

"Good! When Valeria hath sense to know me, bid me to her bedside and I'll cure her." And with that he turned on his heel, not seeming to need an answer, but Nyria was in no mood to give the one he wished.

XVII

THE day after that another, and even less welcome, visitor found admittance at the garden gate, and presented himself on the terrace outside Valeria's apartments. This was the youth Gregorio.

He came round the corner of the house in a sly, suspicious way, his large, handsome head thrust forward, and his knees bent in a slouching, cat-like walk. He looked excited. His full red lips hung apart, and his great dark eyes rolled bright and moist in their sockets. He had had his hair dressed at a barber's, and it was oiled and parted on one side in a bunch of glossy curls. On his head was a wreath of paper flowers, in imitation of the costly garlands that Roman lords wore at Bacchanalian feasts. With some suggestion of gallantry he carried a bouquet of tastefully-arranged flowers.

Gregorio scowled at Nyria, and would have passed into Valeria's rooms unbidden, had the girl not stepped resolutely in front of him, saying, "Thou canst not enter."

"And who art *thou*, to deny me entrance into this house, where I am of the family and thou thyself but a stranger?"

"I am tending the Domina," said Nyria. "'Tis the Lady Vitellia who hath put me in charge, and there is no other of the household for thee to question, save Æola, who acteth according to my directions. Thou hadst best do the same, and be gone."

"I go not at thy bidding," said he, showing his teeth.

"Then thou wilt go at the doctors' bidding," returned Nyria. "There are two within, and I have but to call and they will hear me."

Gregorio faltered, and stood still, shifting the bunch of flowers in his hand. "I brought these for *her*," he said in a more subdued voice.

"The Domina shall have them when she waketh," said Nyria. "But she is sore sick, knowing naught around her; and thou must go, Gregorio."

The boy looked at Nyria from under his brows in a cunning fashion. She saw that he did not believe her statement, and that he was in two minds whether to obey her or to make a disturbance at Valeria's door. Evidently the last idea predominated, for he advanced with a threatening gesture. But just then Stephanus spoke from behind, having come out unseen at the sound of a strange voice.

"Why is this ruffian annoying thee, Nyria? What doeth he here?"

Gregorio went green with rage.

"I am of the Lady Valeria's household, and have a better right than she to be here," he said angrily. "I came to bring my lady an offering."

"Thou canst leave it," returned Stephanus, shortly. "Nyria will see that thy lady hath it when she is better. Now, get thee gone to thy Saturnalian orgies. From thy look I should say that they have not agreed with thee over well."

Gregorio glared at Stephanus as if he would have killed him. He drew back, his whole body quivering, and his large head moving slowly from side to side.

"Set down thine offering and get thee gone," said Stephanus again sternly.

Gregorio stooped as though to lay the flowers on the steps leading to Valeria's sitting-room, but suddenly snatched them back.

"She shall not have them from any hands but mine!" he cried; and going to the edge of the terrace, flung them far into a dusty court below the slope of lawn. Then he turned fiercely on Nyria, hissing from between his teeth,—

"Yea, I go now at thy bidding, but mark me, Nyria, some day thou shalt go at mine. Dost hear, thou evil, white-faced slut? Thou shalt go—ay! and thou shalt not return."

And so saying, he departed.

Gregorio went back to his lodging in a state of malignant animosity against Nyria, against Stephanus, against Valeria, and against Licinius Sura, to whose influence he attributed Valeria's recent preoccupation. He sat nursing schemes for vengeance, but towards evening he got tired of sulking in his garret, which was too high up for him to get a view of what was going on in the streets. During Saturnalia there was always a run upon lodgings in the Suburra, for many of the upper slaves in great households liked to hire apartments and ape, after a fashion, the ways and amusements of their masters. Thus it was not for lack of means that Gregorio was housed so little to his liking, for the youth was fairly flush of cash, both Paulinus and Valeria being generous to their dependants. Their household was conducted on lavish principles, so Gregorio, who had a great idea of his own importance, was able to gratify his taste in the matter of clothes, and might order himself a new mantle and tunic, as it pleased him, from a tailor in the city, with whom Paulinus held a running account for his slaves' habiliments. Gregorio spent much of his spare time at this man's shop, and took infinite pains over the colours and cut of his garments, choosing those which he considered most becoming to his style of looks. He had replenished his wardrobe before the Saturnalia, and it can be imagined that a youth of his type let loose in a demoralised city was not likely to be at a loss for amusement.

As he looked out from the door of his lodging-house upon the bawling, roystering crowd, wending its way to various disreputable places of entertainment, the idea suddenly occurred to him that he would shame Valeria by taking his lyre and performing in the public streets—a thing no respectable householder would countenance in his slaves, even at Saturnalia, and which would be considered utterly derogatory in the pet musician of so aristocratic a lady.

Gregorio laughed to himself while he donned his smartest mantle of crimson and gold—he had a passion for bright colours—curled his hair anew, tied up his lyre with ribbons, and went forth into the thoroughfare, taking a street that led along the better part of the Suburra, where it made a sort of border-ground between the stately Esquiline and the Carinæ and certain disreputable haunts of pleasure. It was a custom of street-singers in this region to perform in front of inns and drinking-booths, but such musicians were regarded as scum of the city, and unfit for decent citizens to hold converse with. Gregorio was well aware of this, but it added zest to his adventure. So he went on in a kind of triumphal progress, playing and singing with such skill as had never before been known in a place like this. Presently he came to a longer stop before a big eating-tavern, all the windows of which were lighted up, and which were thronged by freedmen and upper-class slaves in holiday garb, and gaily-dressed women with painted faces and gold-powdered hair, disporting themselves. Gregorio took up his station under a flaring torch opposite, and striking his lyre, began to sing. Soon he had attracted a crowd around him, and in the balconies and at the open windows of the eating-house gay parties hushed their talk and laughter in order to listen to his song. Gregorio came closer and doffed his cap. When coins had rained upon him he went on singing again, with so much effect as to attract the attention of one of the keenest critics in Rome—a man wearing a mask, and shrouded in a dull-coloured hooded cloak, who was hovering about the different tables, quaffing a beaker of wine here, having a throw with the dice there, mingling jauntily in the conversation, and occasionally drawing apart to make surreptitious notes on tablets that he had held partially concealed by the folds of his cloak. This was none other than the poet Martial, who was on the prowl for high-flavoured witticisms with which to adorn his epigrams and amuse his distinguished patrons.

An anomalous figure in Roman society was Martial, a contemptible, brilliant, spiteful dog, yet with more power than might have been supposed. Most people hated him for one reason or another; some feared him, but many encouraged him because of his cleverness, his sharpness of repartee, and his knack of telling amusing stories, though his way of entertaining each set of patrons was with ill tales against the others. How it was that he did not come to grief among them was known only to the gods who protect malevolent wits.

Like Gregorio, Martial happened to be in need of distraction from jealous vapours. He owed Valeria a long score of grudges for having always shown herself indifferent to him. Nor had he quite overcome his bitterness against Paulinus for supplanting him in Galla's facile affection, since, though Paulinus had gone away, Galla continued to show herself tired of the poet, whose devotion she did not find sufficiently profitable to retain. Poverty pressed on Martial, and it was with a view to raising money that his thoughts turned vaguely to the wager Paulinus had once made with him concerning Valeria. If he could at any time extract two thousand sestertii from Paulinus it would be a pleasant addition to his slender purse, which he not infrequently augmented in a manner that would scarcely bear strict investigation. At all events the sum was worth playing for.

Now, recognising Gregorio, Martial saw a possible thread that he might pull to his own advantage. The poet never spared pains to amass private information which might bring him profit. It was chiefly in this manner that he gained a hold over his patrons, thus procuring himself many a benefit; nor did he mind how mean were the instruments he used so long as they served his purpose. Pursuing this end, he often disguised himself in order to visit these convivial haunts where unscrupulous slaves could be induced to chatter freely about the concerns of their masters and mistresses. Thus he learned many a secret which he turned to account. So when he had identified the street-singer with Valeria's slave musician, Martial, leaning over one of the tavern balconies, did not throw down denarii after the manner of other revellers, but waited till Gregorio had gathered up the coins at his feet and, bowing his acknowledgment, was about to pass on in quest of further excitement. Then fixing his mask, and drawing up his hood, the poet went down, and as he tapped the young man on the shoulder slipped an aureus into his hand with a friendly word. For though he would never have wasted a sesterce in charity, Martial was always willing to pay when he saw a prospect of getting back more than his money's worth.

"'Tis a small guerdon to offer so incomparable an artist," he said. "By Apollo, I am open to wager that desire of fun and not greed of gain hath brought thee masquerading here to-night. I warrant thou art better accustomed to sing before Cæsar and his friends than before such an audience as thou mayst find in the Suburra."

Highly gratified, Gregorio saluted his unknown admirer, and gaily accepted the imputation that he was some great professional out upon a frolic.

"It would seem, sir, that I am not the only frequenter of palaces who plays the mummer to-night," he pompously returned.

Martial laughed, tickled at the boy's effrontery. "Well said

But thou art not as cautious as I am. Thou shouldst wear a mask after my example, for such a face and such a voice are not like to go unnoticed, and that might lead to unpleasant complications."

"Oh! all eccentricity is excusable at the Saturnalia," replied Gregorio, loftily.

"Among festival-keeping slaves, but not for thee or me," rejoined Martial. "May I suggest, however, that thou hast fatigued thy voice sufficiently for this evening, and that after so much exercise thy vocal cords should need moistening? Wilt honour me, sir, by being my guest at supper? I know of an eating-house not far from here, which, though unpretentious, provides an excellent meal and sound wine. I have recommended it to many a young patrician of my acquaintance who, like myself, would see life yet hath not the wherewithal to see it always from the senatorial benches. Come," and he linked his arm within that of Gregorio and drew him on, out of the crowd that assembled round him. Nothing loth, the boy submitted, flattered, and a little bewildered at the easy manners of his new acquaintance, who, he thought, could be no less than a lord himself. Martial chatted on.

"'Tis a place, too, which ladies do not disdain to enter. There are private rooms where one may give a little supper-party and be no worse the next morning in health or reputation, where, mark thee, I whisper it in thine ear, some of those most welcome at the Palatine have condescended to accept my humble hospitality—even the great Valerius Paulinus. Thou art perhaps acquainted with this friend of the Augustus?"

Gregorio hesitated, unwilling to admit that he was but a slave in Paulinus's household, yet realising that it might be well to make a virtue of necessity lest he should be found out in due course. They had by now turned into another street leading towards the Tiber, having crossed the upper end of the Flaminian Way, and were skirting the Campus Martius, all alive with torches, whence came the shouts of Saturnalian roysterers.

"Since thou visitest Paulinus," said Gregorio, "I may as well tell thee, good sir, that he was pleased to charge himself with my bringing up, and that the Domina Valeria, having a taste for music, taketh pleasure in my talent and hath prayed me to remain near her."

Martial again laughed. "The worse for thee, perhaps, friend, since mayhap it debarreth thee from a public career. I know these great ladies and that they will not let go a young client who chances to please them until they have had their fill of his brains and blood. Nevertheless, thou mayst consider thyself fortunate, for many a patrician would pay well for thine opportunities. 'Tis as I have said in certain writings of my own—philosophers and artists are they whom the gods and women favour. If I mistake not, my young Orpheus, thou art Greek by birth, perchance a philosopher, and have made for thyself an imperishable renown. I would not say that, like another mummer we wot off, thou mightst have won the regard of an empress, for there are those who'd say thou hast done better for thyself in gaining the favour of Valeria."

Gregorio gave a snarling sound, that might have been interpreted according to the listener's pleasure. Martial chose not to heed it.

"Lucky dog!" said he, and nudged the youth humorously. "That is a lady whom I hold in most profound esteem and admiration. The Tenth Muse, I've heard my friend Pliny call her. I would I were in thy shoes as regards her favour. But we'll discourse with thee upon her gifts and her charms over a goblet of mine host's best Falernian, for see, we have arrived at our destination. A picturesque hostel, is it not? that should commend itself to thine artistic eye."

Gregorio looked up and effusively praised his friend's selection. It was a high house overlooking the Tiber, with an entrance on the street between a couple of well-grown orange trees, hung with ripening fruit, under which were set some small tables. The place was gaily illuminated and draped with green, for the walls were overgrown with winter creepers; and from every open window and balcony streamed the light of numerous oil lamps. The landlord came forward obsequiously, and presently the two found themselves in a great terrace-like room, partly closed with jalousies, and where many tables were laid, at which men and women were supping merrily. An orchestra was stationed at one end of the room, and some acrobats performed on a stage in time to the music. Martial chose a table away from these, placed in an abutting window, and overhanging a narrow embankment, along which foot-people passed to and fro. Below it lay the river—a turbid, yellow flood—upon which the lights along its banks, and from the house, cast wavering, fantastic reflections. The Jewish quarter opposite lay shrouded in evening mist, with only a feeble glimmer here and there making protest, as it were, against the Pagan celebrations. Up and down the sluggish stream glided great shapes of market barges, and galleys used in work of the city, with a twinkling lamp at the prow of each, giving them a strange, phantasmal appearance; while in contrast to them were pleasure-craft hung with coloured lanterns, from which came the sound of music and jollity. Over the whole scene lay a suggestion of mystery and romance, while within the light laughter of gay women, the music on the stage, the contortions of the acrobats, and the hurrying slaves, only seemed to intensify this effect. Gregorio had never before been to such a place as this, admitted on equal terms with the other guests, who were chiefly the better class of tradesmen, with a sprinkling of impoverished nobles among the ladies of pleasure; and his imagination was stirred, and his self-importance inflamed by his surroundings. The fare, too, was rich and attractive—little fishes steeped in olive oil, cold spiced meats and pasties, highly-seasoned sausages smothered in sauce distilled from honey and cloves, and a speciality of the place—sucking-pigs dressed with cream and onions, and very tasty. Besides these and other viands there were piles of fruit, fresh or preserved in syrup, with sweetmeat-strewn cakes, and plenty of red wine, that was surely not Falernian, but Gregorio did not know the difference. The whole repast had for the youth an air of luxury that appealed to the sensuous and artistic side of him. So, too, the conversation of his host, whom he thought delightful—a man evidently of fashion—witty, satirical and, what charmed Gregorio, with no airs of superiority save those natural in an older man. Martial interlarded his discourse with words of wisdom befitting one whom pleasure had sated, and gave friendly advice to Gregorio as to a youth before whom all the golden doors of opportunity were open, assuring him that with such a face and such a voice he need never sigh for lack of a mistress. Then he led the boy on cleverly to talk, and soon discovered Gregorio's morbid passion for Valeria and his jealousy of Marcus Licinius Sura—all of which was so much grist for Martial's mill to be kept in reserve till occasion came when he might use it.

Meanwhile he plied the youth with heady wine, and when they brought pipes of a new kind, with curious bowls and long-painted tubes, in which a certain Eastern drug was inhaled through water, thereby producing a delicious intoxication, Martial taught Gregorio how to smoke one of these, till he became doubly drunk, and there were no bounds to his indiscreet revelations. When the time arrived for them to leave the tavern, Martial admitted to himself that he had spent not only an amusing but a profitable evening, and, before parting with Gregorio, he ratified the friendship by inviting him to a little supper-party in a private room at this very hostel which the poet was giving to some persons of note, and arranged that Gregorio should bring his lyre and perform before these important guests.

That was Martial's way of returning the hospitality he received in great houses. His invitations were always couched in cringing terms. He could not afford, he said, to offer his patrons the state and luxury they had at their own tables, but should they care to see a phase of life which perhaps might interest them with its novelty, he could promise them at least a wholesome meal, witty conversation, good music, and maybe a pretty face or two to grace the board. Ladies of Galla's station he could not, of course, invite to such festivities, but there were others who would be only too glad to come and enliven the party.

Gregorio accepted this invitation with incoherently-expressed gratitude, having barely sufficient wits to comprehend it. Martial took the precaution, however, of writing down the date and address.

Then, removing his mask, he showed the youth who had been his entertainer.

XVIII

NYRIA scarcely stirred from the sick-room. All her thoughts and hopes were bound up with Valeria. Again Licinius Sura came and prayed her to admit him, which she stoutly refused to do until Valeria could command him herself. Licinius went away ill content, leaving Nyria very sad. Vitellia, too, was sad; and Æola would have been sad likewise if Crispus had not often come to cheer her.

Now it was the last day of the Saturnalia. On the morrow Valeria's women would be back again, and Nyria must go to Julia. She looked so pale and miserable that Vitellia had bidden her go forth and get some air. That afternoon, therefore, she went out while Valeria slept and Æola was left watching by her side. The girl wandered round above the gap in the Cœlian to that lonely knoll overlooking the deserted quarries and the long stretches of tombs.

It was a grey wintry day—banked-up clouds on the horizon and driving wrack overhead, with fantastic shadows floating here and there on the hills—a day when one might well have fancied the shades of dead men were let loose from their graves and roaming the earth, as so many Romans believed they did. Often had Nyria listened to tales of this or that man's wraith passing down the street and in and out of the shops, following some living being and leading him to mischance. It seemed always an enemy, Nyria noticed—there was no story of anyone's steps being dogged by departed lover or friend. Knowing that the Romans prayed to the manes of their ancestors, she had sometimes laughed to herself at hearing how the fancied sight of a spectre would send a pack of Prætorians flying with swift heels. Weaklings, indeed, would be those conquerors of barbarians in combat with the dead, though strong of arm and courage against fleshly foes.

To Nyria superstitions mattered naught, since she prayed neither to god nor ghost. Yet as she mounted the hill, with the mist-shapes fleeing before her, she might have been moving amid a troop of shadows.

The girl sat down in a little hollow near the brow of the hill, where she cowered against a clump of cistus, scarce lifting her eyes from the stony hillocks about her. On one of these, near where she sat, there grew a brier bush, with still a few red-brown leaves upon it and some withered berries, and it seemed to her that this poor plant was a symbol of Valeria's own life. Once that brier bush had been beautiful, and had borne fruit and sunned itself graciously.

But now part of it was torn from the root and broken. Some fierce goat, mayhap, had trodden it down and gnawed it. The poor bush had not recovered, and now winter had brought nipping blasts, and sunshine was scant, and the berries were dropping off, shrivelled and dead. As these thoughts went through her mind, tears gathered in Nyria's eyes and rained down her face. While she sat there, sobbing dismally, a voice said to her,—

"Why weepest thou, little maid?"

She looked up, and there stood before her him who was called Clementus, and whom she had seen with Flavius Clemens and Domitilla passing along the winding road to the quarries. The same grey cloak fell round him, fastened by a jewel at the throat, which was set in a quaint scroll-work, simple and yet uncommon. He had a flowing beard of brown, in which grey hairs were mingled, and large, kindly eyes of melting blue. His nose was thin and high-bridged; large, too, and giving to his face a look of dignity. His mouth was most gentle in repose, and gentler when he smiled, and his brown hair, parted in the middle and thickly streaked with grey, fell in waves downward on each side of his face, and was combed back behind the ears, curling on his shoulders just below the neck. His throat was bared, and showed thin, with full veins that throbbed when he spoke, and his breast, too, heaved, as though he felt deeply the things that he said. But at first he stood silent, his purple under-robe gathered in his arms, and the long grey cloak falling to his sandalled feet.

"Why weepest thou, little maid?" he said once more.

Nyria rose then, realising that this was a living man who spoke to her. At first she had fancied that she might be looking on a picture. For, when out on the hills by herself, she was wont to see visions and strange forms flitting round her that would sometimes seem human and sometimes of elfin shape, but she did not fear such apparitions, for they never did her any harm. She answered simply,—

"Sir, I mourn for my lady, who lies sick unto death."

And with that she covered her face with her hands, for saying those words had brought the truth more vividly before her.

"And wouldst thou save her?" said Clementus, kindly.

"Ay! Would I not?" she answered. "But that, alas! is not for Nyria to do, seeing that there are three great doctors who have done all in their power and, so far, have failed."

"And thou art Nyria?" said her questioner.

"Ay, Nyria, sir," she answered. "I am but a slave."

"And who is thy mistress, maiden? She should rejoice in having such a faithful heart to serve her."

"Julia is my mistress, sir," Nyria answered. "But I weep for Valeria, wife of Paulinus."

"Valeria!" said Clementus. "What is she to thee?"

"My friend, if I may call her so, seeing that she is not my mistress and hath been wondrous kind."

"Kind! To thee?" he asked. "Valeria is not wont to be kind."

"So men say, sir. But few men know Valeria."

"She hath at least one champion. Sit thee down, little maid, and let us talk a while."

Nyria nodded, for she could not speak.

The priest or philosopher, whichever he might be, sat down on the knoll beside her.

"What wouldst thou do to save the Lady Valeria?" he asked.

"Sir, I would give my life for her."

"Thou needst not give thy life, maiden, but give thyself to Him who holdeth all things in the hollow of His hand, and He, perchance, shall save thee thy friend, by reason of the love thou bearest her."

"Who is this of whom thou tellest?" cried the girl. "Ah, sir, I pray thee trifle not with Nyria! A poor maid with a breaking heart is not fit sport for gods or men. Say, who is He that can save Valeria? Liveth He in Rome?"

"Ay, in Rome, but not in Rome only. His habitation is higher than the heavens, for His glory is above them all, and earth is His footstool."

Nyria thought this must be some emperor even greater than Domitian, and she marvelled who it could be. She knew that many rich and noble strangers came to Rome, and it was not likely that she, a poor little slave, should hear their names, especially since she had seen less of Stephanus, who was the mouthpiece of all the news that went about the city.

"Sir, I know not of whom thou speakest," she said humbly.

"Nay, but thou shalt know, Nyria," answered Clementus. "Hast thou ever prayed?" And this question confounded the girl.

"I know not to whom I should pray, else would I have prayed for Valeria." And again she besought him. "Oh, thou art kind and good, and if thou couldst see into my heart thou wouldst know that I would gladly have laid it on each temple altar in sacrifice for Valeria if the gods that dwelt there would but aid her. But the gods of Rome—" and she paused, not knowing of what faith this lord might be.

"Speak on, little maid!" he said. "The gods of Rome—what thinkest thou of them?"

"Sir, they help no man. They feed upon the sacrifices, mayhap —or the priests do—'tis all the same. But of what benefit are they? One saith to me, 'I worship Apollo;' and another, 'I worship only in the temple of Jupiter;' and another, Bacchus; and another, Athene. But who are these gods? What are they? What do they? Sir, I have heard much of the gods, yet it cannot be that they have power to heal, else why do they permit so many to suffer and yet care naught for the pain and sorrow with which Rome is filled?"

Clementus's hand held hers closely.

"Child," he said, "many wiser than thou have asked the same —ay, and will ask until the kingdom of God shall come among men. Nevertheless are we trained by this present life that we may be crowned with the glory of the future. Sorrow and suffering there must be, for man is evil, though goodness is eternal. Yet mayhap Valeria shall be saved. Wait here for me whilst I depart for a little while and am alone."

Leaving her, he walked to the brow of the hill and stood looking out into the sky. His tall, grey figure showed dark against the pale light, but there grew in the west, whither he faced, a faint glow which spread and deepened to rose red, until a beam of it seemed to touch him like a shaft of flame. He bowed his head and remained in spiritual commune, while Nyria's heart beat high with hope. Then Clementus came back, and, standing before the girl, spoke.

"Question thyself, Nyria, concerning this that thou desirest. Were it given to thee that she whom thou lovest should regain all that illness hath taken from her, and yet that life to her should mean suffering and sorrow to thee, wouldst thou still desire it?"

"Sir," she answered, folding her hands upon her breast and looking up at him, "would Valeria be happy?"

"Earthly happiness might in a measure be Valeria's portion. Yet an aftertime of pain may be decreed for her. That thou canst not save her, if it be her destiny, for certain things lie beyond the power of men to control. The gift of life is one of these, but seeing thou hast centred thy soul upon this boon, it may be that thy desire will be granted thee, for the Father who is pitiful in all things lovingly bestoweth His favours on them that draw nigh unto Him with a single mind."

"Then, sir, let life and happiness be granted to Valeria. I'll gladly bear what comes."

"Thou art brave, child," said Clementus; "but thy strength shall not fail, for He that is stronger than the nations shall be thy succour. Love covereth all things, and prayer out of a good conscience doth verily deliver from death. Behold, Nyria, if thou wert in the presence of Cæsar, or of some great potentate able to command all things, and if thou wert about to ask him for Valeria's life, how wouldst thou word thy prayer?"

"Sir, I should kneel at his feet," she cried, casting herself down and stretching forth her arms to the skies, "and I should say unto him, 'Oh! great lord—thou in whose hands are all powers of life and death, seeing that by thy will is life granted to us or taken away, I beseech thee, listen to Nyria, and bestow upon her who so sorely needeth thy favour this boon and blessing, that Valeria may know health again, and that happiness may shine upon her. And this, not because Nyria craveth it of thee, but for thine own sake and of thy mercy, that we who pray may learn to praise thy great and wonderful bounty.'"

Nyria forgot everything but Valeria and that supreme Cæsar of whom the stranger spoke. Would he listen to her prayer?

When she stopped there was silence—a long, deep silence. The wind came sighing in the brier bush, and looking up Nyria saw the western sky as though it had opened into one glorious sheet of gold. But across it ran a crimson streak like a stain of blood. She turned round. Clementus was kneeling too, close by her side. He put his hand on hers and said,—

"Nyria, thou hast prayed, and He to whom thou prayest has heard, and will answer thy prayer."

XIX

Clementus talked very kindly to Nyria as they left the knoll and walked down the hill together. He spoke as none else had ever spoken to her, and the girl opened her heart to him freely. Presently they came to a place where the path was steep, and he put out his arm to help her.

"Sir, I know the road," she said. "Even the goats are not better climbers than Nyria."

"Whose goats are these, Nyria?" he asked.

"I know not, sir," she answered. "They belong to many lords in Rome, and some to farmers. They who have no pasturage for their herds do send them forth to browse upon these mountain sides. And some there be—rich lords—who bid their herdsmen bring the flocks hither, since the herbage is in places very sweet."

"And who tendeth them, Nyria?"

"None, sir," she replied. "Oft have I wondered that they lose not their way, nor meet with mishaps among the rougher passes of the hills. Sometimes have I found a little goat that hath lamed itself and bleateth sore, and I have borne him in my arms and sought out the herdsmen—since some of them I know—till one should claim it, for I like not to think of the goats wandering alone. But the herdsmen come at stated times and drive them into a fold which they do furnish in some secluded part, and there they examine them to see which shall be slain for food and which shall be saved for the breeding; and if there be any evil ones among them, these are set aside from the rest."

"Ah, Nyria! So these herdsmen know their work, though they come but seldom;" and the stranger was silent for a minute as they went down the track. Then he said, "And, Nyria, who tendeth thee?"

"Methinks I am like one of the little goats," said Nyria, "save that there is no herdsman to tend me, or if there be, he is long in coming."

The kind stranger asked her many questions, and led her on to talk of her inmost thoughts, until at last she told him of that which she had never spoken about to anyone—even of the Voice that came to her, and of that which the Voice had said—"Some day, Nyria, thou shalt see My face."

Clementus listened attentively.

"Knowest thou who spake thus to thee?" he asked.

"Nay, sir, I know not. Oft have I wondered if it might perchance be one of the gods. For many say that they speak—each through his chosen symbol. Bacchus in the vine, Athene in the olive, and great Jupiter in the thunder. But I hear the voice of Him that speaketh to me in all these things and in many more besides."

Then the stranger paused upon the hillside, and drawing her hand up between his folded palms, he laid it on his breast.

"Nyria, hearken to me," he said. "That which thou hearest is the voice of the one great God who is as much greater than those of whom thou hast been told as the sun is greater than the stars—ay, as much greater as the sun is than the diamond glints thou seest in a dewdrop or on a leaf. Blessed art thou, my child, for none save the great God Himself hath revealed this unto thee. He is above all, Nyria, yet He is everywhere and in everything—in the shining of the sun, in the whisper of the wind, in the arching colours of the rainbow, in the little face of a flower. And He is in thee also, Nyria. Thou hearest Him through all these signs and sounds, but thou wilt hear Him oftenest speak in the silence of thine own heart."

And as Nyria listened to these words it seemed to her that there was indeed an echo throbbing in her heart. No words it spake, but softly cried upon her to give herself to the teaching of this stranger. She looked at him and said, "Sir, tell me of this God."

"Ay, thou shalt verily learn of Him," Clementus answered. "For the Master willeth not that any be lost of His little flock, of whom thou art surely one. Thou wilt not deny the Lord, Nyria, when He calleth for thee?"

"But, sir, I know naught of Him, save the promise which hath so often rung in my ears that some day I should see His face."

"And if that be not enough, little maid, behold He giveth thee further assurance by the mouth of His servant Clement. When thou wert pleading for Valeria's life wast thou not willing to pledge thyself wholly unto Him who should save her whom thou lovest?"

"Truly so, sir," she answered. "Hath this wondrous God indeed power to save the life of Valeria?"

"Soon shalt thou see," answered Clement. "Thou didst call upon Him, Nyria, and He is never deaf to the prayers of His children."

Nyria was silent. It seemed to her terribly presumptuous that she—Nyria, a slave of Julia's household—should have dared to lift her voice to Him who ruled earth and heaven—who perchance was the Great One that drew the curtains of night over the tired face of the earth—yet who most surely must be He that spoke thus sweetly to her own heart.

Then said Clement, "Abide His mercy, Nyria, and 'according to thy faith it shall be unto thee.' Those words were uttered by the Master who came among men to teach us of the great God, the Father whom He knew, and of whom we on earth have but dim knowledge. Nevertheless, we too shall some day see the Father's face. Now I must leave thee, child. The Spirit of the Father Himself worketh in thee, and at His own good time He shall claim His own. Then shall none snatch thee from His breast, Nyria, poor, lonely little lamb! In the Divine Fatherhood thou shalt find all thy need fulfilled, and when danger and distress shall come upon thee, as come they must, that Voice shall be thy surest counsel, and thou shalt follow whither it leads."

"But will Valeria live, sir?" questioned Nyria, clinging to his hand.

He stooped and parted back her curls.

"Ay, loyal little heart, Valeria will live, and she shall owe her life to thee."

And it was of these last words more than of any other he had said that Nyria thought as she ran down the hill and through the valley, and so up the Cœlian. She could not but believe in this great diviner. But she remembered that Sabinus had spoken of Clementus to Julia as a holy man, of good repute among the Christians. Now, Nyria had heard of the Christians as an accursed sect, and she could scarce believe that Clement was one of them, supposing that the great God of whom he had been telling her would not have dealings with such evil folk. Nevertheless, Clement had said that his God was the God of all men; and if that were true, if in His greatness He had stooped to win one so humble as herself, might He not reckon even the Christians among His children? But she had small time to consider the question, for she soon reached the Villa.

Out on the terrace steps sat Æola, with Crispus beside her. He had brought a basket of winter fruit, and some gay scarlet blossoms which Æola was twining in her hair. She looked very happy, her brown eyes big and starry, and a rosy flush upon her cheek that vied with the blossoms' hue. It seemed that she could not twist the flowers in her tresses to her liking without the aid of Crispus, who was forced to wreathe them for her, and most tenderly he did it. So absorbed were the two in each other that neither saw Nyria as she went by, too full of gladness even to blame Æola for leaving Valeria's chamber.

Nyria ran into the room where Valeria lay sleeping peacefully. Æola had left the silver lamp burning at the head of the bed, and Nyria fancied that the Domina's face looked less sharp and shadowed. There was a delicate flush upon her cheek—no burning patch left by the fever.

Nyria kneeled at the side of the couch and leaned her head against it in sheer joyfulness. She whispered, "Domina! Thou shalt live! Life and happiness are thine, dear lady. Oh! haste thee to take these glad gifts for thine own."

Valeria smiled faintly in her sleep. The words seemed in some way to reach her consciousness.

Nyria folded her hands together, and out of the fulness of her heart her gratitude overflowed.

"Dear God—from henceforth Nyria's God—I thank Thee, oh! I thank Thee! and behold, I am Thy slave."

"Nyria!" said Valeria, softly, "to whom art thou speaking? Is anyone here?"

"None other, lady, save—" Nyria paused. She was about to say, "One whom thou canst not see," but Valeria's gaze looked confused, and the girl saw that she would not understand; so, bending over her, the slave smoothed the pillow and went on gently,—

"Nyria is here, dear lady. She hath watched long beside thee. But now thou art better. See, the fever is gone;" and she slipped her fingers into Valeria's palm, which felt cool to the touch, as it had not for many a day.

Nyria swiftly poured a cup of milk from a vessel of it that stood warming near the brazier, and now she added some drops of Stephanus's famous soothing potion.

"Domina," she said, "I have news to give thee. News of great comfort. All will henceforth be well with thee."

"How can that be?" asked Valeria.

"Thou shalt hear, dearest Domina. As I walked on the hillside one met me who is skilled in divining, and who, seeing me sad, questioned me of my sorrow. So then I told him how thou wert lying sick and suffering. Then sought he the mystic knowledge that never faileth—for thus, as thou knowest, the augurs say. And he bade me take heart, for that thou wouldst assuredly recover and claim the happiness which awaits thee."

"Happiness? Happiness for Valeria? What happiness can come to me?"

"Nay, I know not, Domina. He but bade me believe, and we prayed together to the greatest of all gods—He who is able to grant all things, and who never faileth to hear prayer. He it is who shall send thee that which thou dost most desire."

Valeria received this child-like announcement with an incredulous smile. But for the first time she was strong enough to take the cup herself from Nyria's hand, and she drank a long draught. Then she gave it back to the girl, sighing softly.

"If this God would send me here and now that which my heart doth most desire, then, Nyria, would I believe in Him. . . . Ah! Who cometh there?"

She had started up in her bed, uttering a faint cry, and her eyes were wildly gazing across the room. A footfall had sounded in the ante-chamber, and at that moment the heavy curtains that hung over the doorway were parted and someone stood between the folds.

It was Licinius Sura.

He spoke in his musical tones, mockingly, yet with a ring of passion.

"Nyria refuseth me admittance," said he, "so I must needs seek my own way unbidden."

Valeria held out her arms.

"Oh, Marcus! Comest thou indeed? Now are life and joy assured me."

And Nyria went out, leaving them alone together.

XX

NYRIA sat on the steps of the terrace while Licinius Sura was with Valeria in her room. Presently Æola stole up out of the dusk, and sinking down beside her, laughed and chattered in a conscious way, then fell into silence, and sighed. Nyria paid her small attention.

"What aileth thee, Nyria?" said the younger girl. "Thou art dull to-night. Didst thou not hear when I told thee that Crispus said there had been grand doings down at Julia's house—men coming and going, and lords from the Senate in converse with thy master, who hath taken office as consul, and made his sacrifice to Jove in the great temple—yet all the time bearing himself in a sad way."

Nyria answered testily, "Love is a madness that maketh all men fools. What right had Crispus to speak to thee, Æola, of the affairs of his lord?"

"Nay, we meant no harm, Nyria," said Æola, meekly. "Thou knowest Crispus trusteth me. So dost thou—or so didst thou once."

"Hush, Æola!" cried Nyria, hurriedly. "Here are the Lady Vitellia's bearers. Alack! Alack! What shall I do?"

Nyria rose agitatedly, and all manner of fears raced through her mind. "Now show me, Æola, that thou dost deserve the trust which, as thou sayest, I have ever given thee. Be wise, and do as I bid thee—no more nor less. See—the Lady Vitellia cometh. Hasten to her litter—keep her in converse. Let her not approach Valeria's room until I shall return. Understandest thou?"

"Oh! how harsh thou art with me to-night," whimpered Æola. Then, seeing that there was something serious in hand, she added hastily, "Nay, have I ever failed to do thy bidding when thou didst charge me? The Lady Vitellia shall not pass till thou comest again." And Æola drew her head-stole closer and ran down the steps, while Nyria sped to Valeria's room. She ran across the ante-chamber, coughing as she went, in order to give sign of her approach. It was presumptuous to enter unbidden, but no other course was open to her, so she drew the curtains apart and bowed herself between them, seeming not to see the pair who were in each other's arms.

"Domina, the Lady Vitellia cometh," she cried, breaking in upon their happy murmurs.

"Vitellia!" exclaimed Valeria, with a sharp note of terror in her voice. "Alas! Marcus, thou must leave me. . . . But how? Nyria, which way cometh my sister?"

"The Lady Vitellia cometh no way, Domina, until I give her entrance. Æola stayeth her upon the steps."

"A pretty pair of conspirators, by all that's loyal to love!" cried Licinius, laughing. "Well done, little watch-dog! I'll credit thee with wit."

"But, Marcus! Marcus!" cried Valeria, clinging to his arm, the red mounting in her cheeks. Nyria saw that, were not her excitement allayed, this visit of her lover would do harm instead of the good for which the girl had fondly hoped.

"There is the other entrance, Domina," she ventured. "The Lord Licinius can, if he will, follow me, and I will lead him out by the great atrium. The Lady Vitellia's bearers are waiting at the Domina's own steps."

"Well spoken, watch-dog! Come!" cried Licinius. Nyria went forward, and he was about to follow, when Valeria's faint voice sounded among the pillows. Though Nyria looked not back she seemed to see Valeria raise herself, her arms extended, and all the passion and pathos in her poor white face, which had paled from red to deathly pallor.

Licinius turned and caressed her. "Nay, I must leave thee, sweet. Yet 'tis but a foretaste of bliss. Content thee till I come again, Valeria."

"But the risk—the risk!" panted Valeria as she lay in his arms.

"Had Hercules any thought of risk when he faced the fateful maidens in his quest for the golden fruit? I am no Hercules, dearest, for I flee before thy sister. In very truth, Valeria, 'twould need a doughty warrior to confront the glance of Vitellia's eye. I must go, beloved, but it sufficeth that thou hast bid me come again."

"I said not so, Marcus."

"Nay, *this* is permission enough—and *this*—and *this*," he answered; and in the silence that followed Nyria knew that he kissed her repeatedly. "Get thee well, Valeria, else will thy grand new doctor have failed in his dear task."

"But me thou wilt not fail, Marcus—not again?"

"Beloved, have I ever failed thee? Ask thine own heart. This soul of mine may have refused to let its limbs bear my body to thy feet—for Licinius Sura is not without a conscience, though thou hast well-nigh lulled it to sleep. But be assured that I will mutter a requiem over its grave ere it shall part me long from thee."

Then he followed Nyria. She led him out swiftly, running on before him through the passages, for she was afraid lest Vitellia should grow impatient. In the outer atrium she paused, and, pointing to the entrance door, said,—

"There lies thy way, lord. Haste, and none need know thou hast been here."

"Good!" he answered, drawing his mantle about him. "I see,

sweet Xydra, that thou'st been brought up in Rome to some purpose, and 'tis fortunate for one who so far is in thy debt. Come, I will reward thee, pretty maid!"

Nyria glanced at him vexedly, thinking to see him finger his wallet again, but he held out his arms instead.

"Thou dost despise gold, I know. Therefore I offer thee that which even gold cannot always buy."

The blood rushed to Nyria's cheeks.

"Shame on thee, sir!" she cried, for she knew full well what he meant. "Not for this did I bring thee hither."

"Scarcely," he said, with a laugh. "'Twas to escape the scorn of that immaculate Vitellia, and I am beholden to thee, little watch-dog. Let me pay my debt and plunge myself yet further in thy favour. A touch of those ripening lips—they are not ripe yet, thou knowest, Nyria—would taste sweet in passing, and not one be aught the wiser."

"Nay, lord—but twain the greater fools!" said she, bending low before him, and jerking her chin away as he placed his hand beneath it to lift her face to his.

"Power of Venus! shed some softening spell upon this marble maid!" cried he, with a merry laugh, which, lightening his face, made him seem so comely that Nyria, notwithstanding her indignation, could not help admiring his looks. "He who sets forth to win thee, Nyria, will surely need wisdom—and courage too. I wish him joy of his adventure." And Licinius Sura swung his mantle over his shoulder and disappeared through the doors of the atrium, while Nyria ran with burning cheeks back to Valeria's side of the house.

Vitellia was pacing the portico listening to Æola, who poured forth a lengthy history of Valeria's ailments.

"Ah! I rejoice to see thee, Nyria," said Vitellia, kindly. "Doth my sister sleep? Æola hath been giving me but a poor account of her."

"The Domina awaits thee, lady," answered Nyria, making a low obeisance, with the hope that she might thus conceal her crimson face. "Will it please thee to enter? She is better, methinks, this last half-hour."

The lady followed her through the parlour and ante-room, as Nyria, entering first, whispered to Valeria that her sister was coming. Valeria nodded but said nothing, for that was not her way. Then Vitellia went in, and Nyria came out and met Æola.

"Have I done well, Nyria?" asked the little maid, whose wits had been on the stretch.

"Ay, over well," answered Nyria, ungraciously. "Thou needst not have said Valeria was lying at the door of death."

"But was she not?" asked Æola, astonished.

"She hath departed therefrom," replied Nyria, pettishly. "If thou hadst not been love-making with Crispus in the court thou wouldst have known how much better she was."

"The gods be praised!" said Æola, devoutly. "I care not for thy cross words, Nyria, but I grieve for thee. Hadst thou a Crispus of thine own thou wouldst not be so hard on lovers."

By-and-by the Lady Vitellia came out and called Nyria to her in the ante-chamber.

"Æola is a good child," said she, "but ignorant. I'll take thy word, Nyria, before that of any other. Verily, thy tending hath brought good fruit.. 'Tis well indeed with Valeria to-night. Almost I should have said that a physician more skilled than those who are attending her had been but lately by her bed, for there's new life in her eyes and her voice hath gained strength."

"Yes, lady," Nyria answered meekly, and said no more. It irked her sore to take the boon of Valeria's life from Licinius Sura. But, having pledged herself to barter anything for the health of Valeria, it did not seem fitting that she should question the means by which it came.

According to custom, the Saturnalian revellers had all to be back in their places next morning, and now it was to the head dresser—a staid, efficient, but disagreeable woman—that Archimenes gave the chief care of her mistress when he learned that Nyria had to leave. The doctors came early that morning, and their talk was more cheerful than usual.

"Truly a resurrection," said Archimenes. "And right good testimony to thy skill, Brother Stephanus, and to the careful tending of yonder wise little maid."

Stephanus was much gratified, for great Roman doctors never said "Brother" save to one of their own professional status. The pair conferred together in high good humour; and presently Archimenes bade a kindly farewell to Nyria and left, but Stephanus waited, in order to walk with the girl to Julia's house.

Nyria went in to bid Valeria farewell. The Domina put out her hand and caught that of the slave-girl.

"Art going, Nyria?" she said.

"Yes, Domina. Thou knowest the Saturnalia is over and Julia will be sending for me. Moreover, there is naught to keep me, seeing that thou art on the mend," Nyria answered sadly.

"But thou canst not go until thou hast given me my letter," said Valeria eagerly, "from Licinius Sura, who bade thee guard it for me till I should be able to read it. What hast thou done with the letter, Nyria? Keep it not from me." Her hand tightened on Nyria's, and she shook the girl's arm impatiently.

"I have it here, Domina," Nyria answered, and she brought the missive forth from an inner pocket next her breast, where she had secreted it. Valeria almost snatched the tablet from her hand.

"Ah! 'tis well—'tis well," she cried, and broke the seal, having no eyes save for the letter.

"Shall I go, Domina?" asked Nyria, fearing she should be late.

"Yes, yes, child, go, I need thee not," Valeria said absently as she turned over the second tablet.

Nyria straightened the coverlet over her feet, and stooping, kissed them; but Valeria took no notice, and the girl went out with an aching heart, for a kind word from Valeria would have helped her to bear the other payment which Julia was sure to render.

Stephanus took her bundle, and as they walked down the hill together Nyria told him how she had met Clementus on the previous day, and much—though not all—that he had said to her.

Stephanus did not seem over-pleased at the encounter.

"Ay, Clementus is a Christian," he said in answer to Nyria. "No Christians cross my threshold."

"But supposing that I became a Christian, Stephanus," she said, slipping her hand into his.

He looked down upon her tenderly.

"Ah, there's a different matter! My threshold is for thee, Nyria, to cross as mistress of my house when thou wilt. It only waits to have the flax bound round its posts and the wine and meal poured upon its bar. But I have no faith in Christians. They are neither honest men nor sound knaves. As enemies or friends I want them not."

"But Clementus is cousin to Clemens and Domitilla."

"Ay! The cousin of Clemens and Domitilla may command Stephanus's fealty, but to Christians he owes naught."

Nyria did not pursue the subject, for they were drawing near to Julia's house, and the girl's heart was full of apprehension as to what might greet her there.

Presently Stephanus said, "Thou art grave, Nyria. Is it because thou fearest to face that she-wolf? May the gods defend thee from her teeth! Say only the word and Stephanus will make it his office to see Sabinus this evening on thy behalf."

Nyria shook her head. "Methinks, Stephanus, that I am not for marriage," she answered.

"Tush, Nyria! Every maid is for marriage that hath the chance to wed. Wouldst wither and grow old unmated, dear?"

"Methinks I never shall grow old. Old age ne'er comes before my mind as it doth to other girls. Even Æola fears, as thou sayest, to wither all unwed. But I—nay, Stephanus, marriage would not content me."

"'Tis a goodly ceremony, Nyria, and should content any honest maid of womanly feeling. I like not to hear thee talk so, child. At times thou seemst unnatural."

"Maybe I am," said Nyria, with a sigh. "I love so many things that other maidens care not for, and have no taste for that which gives them pleasure. I love the sunshine, and the wind, and the flowers. Ah! Stephanus, I like the sun and wind to woo me. Right goodly lovers are they—lavish with their kisses, yet not lingering overlong lest they should be scorned."

"Verily, thou art but a wind spirit thyself, Nyria," he said, "or haply some daughter of the sun. Beware, lest the god Apollo come to woo thee. Ill stories are told of maids who love the solitude of woods and hills, and yet who die in shame."

Nyria smiled sadly. "I am no child to be affrighted with such idle tales. But here we are at the house. Talk no more of wooing. I have worse matters to contend against."

For Nyria was terrified at the thought of going back to Julia, since the end of the Saturnalia meant the day of reckoning. "Oh, Stephanus!" she cried suddenly, "I wish thou wert my father or my brother."

"Now the gods forbid that bargain. 'Tis not such I'd be to thee," he answered, wrapping his arms round her. "Embrace me, Nyria, for who can tell when I shall look upon thy face again once thou hast passed beneath the rule of Julia—hardest task-mistress in Rome."

Nyria let him kiss her, then she mounted the steps of the gate. "Farewell!" she said, and waved her hand, but sobbed a little as she left him.

At Euphena's door she dropped her bundle. There, as usual, the old woman sat, glowering in the sun.

"Julia hath a fine dish of hot broth prepared for thee," she cried as Nyria hastened past.

Sounds of turmoil reached her ere she got to the steps of Julia's apartments. The waiting-women were shrieking, and Julia's voice, raised in high wrath, sounded above their lamentations.

Samu darted out as Nyria ascended to the loggia, and the girl thought she must be drunk, for she was lurching this way and that, with great red marks of blows on her face. And now Julia herself, with an uplifted brush in her hand—no mean weapon, for the back and handle of it were solid silver—followed close on Samu's flying heels. The unhappy slave tumbled against a pillar, which stayed her progress, just as Julia caught sight of Nyria and stopped in her beating of Samu to yell a string of abuse at the newcomer.

Nyria put her hands to her forehead and made the obeisance. Well was it for her that she did so, for Julia threw the heavily-weighted brush at her head, but by stooping at the moment Nyria avoided being stunned. Her missile having failed in its mark, Julia flung herself forward; nearly falling over Samu, who, seeing that her assailant's attention was diverted to another object, uprose swiftly and scurried out of sight, while Julia, like a tower of storm, bore down on Nyria and caught her by the hair.

"Here, thief, truant, sneak and traitress! So thou hast dared return? Thou shalt have a warmer welcome than thou hast bargained for. Oh! none shall be so well received as Nyria. Hath thy skin healed yet, brat? 'Twere better that it had not, else Bibbi shall have the labour of laying it open again. Come, come—compel me not to claw thee along by this mass of yellow tow. Get to thy feet, hussy!"

But Nyria tried in vain to stand, being held too close by her hair, and Julia pulled the girl with all the force of her strong arms across the loggia and into the dressing-room, where she stood panting after her exertions. A wild figure she looked, half clad, her black hair touzled, her face and neck hot and bloated after the bath, and] so lacking in dignity that Thanna, who had been taking lessons in impudence from Saturnalian associates, burst into a fit of riotous laughter and began making grimaces at her mistress. Julia, catching her in the act, turned infuriated upon her, but Thanna, leaning against the inner doorway, did not stir.

"Thou clownish slut!" cried Julia. "Thou pantomime trollop! Hast been training with the street mimes? Art practising thy ugly faces to go out and win a few denarii before the drink-shops in the Suburra? Go, get the dressing-things and set thee to my head-tiring."

"Of a surety thou dost need it," mocked Thanna. "'Twill be a day's work to comb out the rags and tags that are knotted in that horse's mane of thine. Euphena is a fine hairdresser, ha! ha! Methinks that Julia hath set a new fashion in Rome" And Thanna shook anew.

Julia, crimson with rage, would have dashed at her, but refrained. Thanna guessed what was in her mind. She saw that Nyria was to be beaten, and knew that Julia would not wish to deprive herself of the services of both her best hairdressers. So she made a mocking salutation, saying, with insolent familiarity,—

"Let it be peace, Julia. The end of the Saturnalia is a sad time for us, though to thee, doubtless, a cause for jubilation. Grudge us not our few poor days of pleasure."

Julia glared at her, and Thanna, suddenly dropping on the ground in low obeisance, went on, in servile accents,—

"When thou art Empress, oh, most mighty Julia! I pray thee extend the Saturnalia. Then will Thanna spend hers in offering sacrifices upon thine altar, since thou wilt be a goddess then."

Julia, half mollified, flung Nyria by her hair towards Thanna, and retorted,—

"Thou art an impudent baggage, but useful. Do thy duty, Thanna, and I'll say no more. Get the things for my robing, and bestir thee. But first 'tie this jade to the hook and bid one of those lazy drabs call Bibbi."

Thanna moved leisurely to obey the order, but Nyria exclaimed, in sore wrath,—

"I'll stand beneath the hook, Most Noble, and Bibbi must beat me if 'tis thy will, but Thanna shall not touch me!"

"What use to answer her thus?" whispered Thanna. "Give her a dose of flattery and there need be no hook for thee to-day, nor whipping either. Come—I'll not tie thee tight."

"Thou'lt not tie me at all!" cried Nyria, walking to the hook, which was one set high in the wall at the end of the dressing-room. Here Julia would sometimes keep an offending maid tied half the day, or longer, when she chose.

Nyria put up her hands to twist her hair round her throat, so that Thanna should not catch it, and took her place beneath the hook, but with that expression on her face even Thanna dared not touch her.

"Cease chattering," called Julia, seating herself before the mirror. "Thanna, bring the washes for my face and leave that slut alone."

Bibbi grinned when by-and-by they took Nyria out to the whipping-post.

"Art pleased to meet thy friend again?" he cried; and when Thanna and Æmilia stripped her to the waist he came closer and critically examined the weals on her shoulders.

"Thou hast been having pleasant feeding this Saturnalia, Nyria," he said. "These are no marks of Bibbi's lash."

"But those that come will be," she answered sharply. "Get on if thou must."

"Nay, I like not to hasten. 'Tis a delicate task, and needs skill. Also, I'd fain know that I retain thy good fellowship."

"'Twere kinder to get to thy work," said Æmilia. "Prate of good fellowship another time. Art ready, Nyria?"

The girl nodded, setting her lips tight, and the lashes fell.

They gave her only ten this time, though twelve had been ordered. But Nyria lost count at the last three, and did not return to herself until they were dragging her to Euphena's cabin.

The old woman rose from the doorway to give them entrance. As she saw what had happened she cried,—

"What! Nyria again!"

"Yes, Nyria again," answered Æmilia. "'Tis shameful to beat such a defenceless lamb. But Julia knoweth naught of shame."

"Thou hast seldom spoken more truly," Euphena returned. "Many a time hath Nyria been carried forth fit only for the burying. Yet never fear, pretty one. To-day again shalt thou escape the bier. But when death in truth doth come to thee, there shall be no carrying forth and no burying."

Nyria heard the words, and wondered dizzily what Euphena could mean. But she was in too great pain to care. Æmilia brought some ointment and wiped the wounds with a soft rag. Then she gave Nyria some warm milk to drink before she went to tend her little ones and to get her husband's mid-day meal. Euphena, too, was called away, so Nyria lay alone. At last she dropped asleep, and when she awoke it was drawing on to late afternoon, and Thanna sat beside her, doing some plaiting work, of which she was fond, for Thanna was clever with her fingers.

"I am come to give thee some news, Nyria," she said.

"For what dost thou wish to bargain it?" inquired Nyria.

"'Tis no time for bargaining," returned Thanna. "We are all agog with what hath happened."

"What is it?" asked Nyria, feebly. "Is Samu ill from Julia's blows?"

"Samu? Nay, her skin is thicker than thine. I saw her cooking sugar cakes in the sun an hour ago. Guess again, Nyria, but go higher in thy guesses."

"Hath aught ill chanced to Sabinus?" asked Nyria.

"Sabinus is of small account," replied Thanna. "There is one greater than Sabinus in the household, and she it is who suffers."

"Not Julia?" cried Nyria, opening her eyes, for Julia was never ill.

"Yes, verily, the great Julia. Is not that somewhat to make thee sit up? Julia's tantrums this morning have been too much for her. The Most Noble hath not lately chased us round the rooms, remember. Methinks she exercised herself too severely with her brush on Samu and in dragging thee by that yellow mop of thine." Thanna bent nearly double, laughing.

"But what is wrong with Julia?" Nyria asked.

"The gods alone can tell, unless Euphena, mayhap, could throw some light upon the matter. I have always said that a wise waiting-maid knoweth how to make herself useful, and how to be of no use. Now—thank the gods!—I am no use in illness," and Thanna shook her head with a waggish air.

"Thanna is useful, oh! most useful," she continued, "when there is anything gay and cheerful going on—to be in attendance at the Games, or on a visit to the Palace, then is Thanna in high demand, seeing that she hath observant eyes and a witty tongue. But now that the goddess Julia is laid low, not even Thanna can avail her. I offered,—oh! to be sure, I offered—to remain and nurse her—for is not Thanna devoted to Julia?—but Julia ruleth not the household to-day. 'Tis Euphena that holds the reins of our most noble lady's government. And quoth Euphena to me, 'Get out, thou baggage,' which was rude of her. But since I was very willing to get out, I took no heed of her manner of speech. 'If thou wert Nyria,' said Euphena, 'I could put thee to some account, but thou art only fit for masquerading,' which I say was rude, even though it be true. 'Get thee gone,' quoth she, 'and if Nyria be fit, send her hither.' But thou art not fit, art thou, Nyria?"

"Nay," answered Nyria, smiling faintly. "Nyria is sore sick, but hopes Euphena may not come hither herself to see."

"Euphena dare not to go the length of Julia's girdle from her bedside, for the great Julia doth desire to be well, and that soon—I heard her say as much—and she hath strange confidence in Euphena. I know not what the power is that Euphena hath over Julia," said Thanna, thoughtfully.

"Hadst thou deemed the secret worth discovering thou wouldst have ferreted it out ere this," retorted Nyria.

"Why, like as not," answered Thanna, "if there were money in it. But Julia's whimsies are but empty bubbles. This one will vanish when she is well. Never yet did I know a sick mind that was worth physicking. Give me healthy folk to deal with."

And Thanna got up and tucked away her work in a little gay-coloured bag she carried. "Thank the gods that they themselves do favour jollity," she said, "else would this earth be a dull old place. But as they made it—oh! is there not life and to spare, if one might but have a taste!"

"Thou art never satisfied, Thanna. The taste of such life as Rome hath to give is ever in thy mouth."

"Bah! No more than can be put on a spilikin. I want a mouthful—and not one, but many. Thanna will have lived in vain if she do not get her fill before she dies. Shall I bring thee thy portion at the supper hour? Things are dull outside, for none will talk save of what may hap should Julia die."

"Should Julia die!" repeated Nyria. "Julia is not like to die, is she?"

Thanna shook her head. "I know not, nor do I care. Haply a change might better our state. Dost think I would remain a slave for ever?" cried Thanna. "Not I! Or, if I must, at least I'd serve a man. For a man's slave may be his mistress, then in truth is she a fool if she remain his slave. But cease chattering, Nyria. What a gossip thou art!"

"Thou must indeed be badly off for company to stay with me," retorted Nyria.

"A truce to that impudent tongue, else will I bring thee no supper," laughed Thanna.

"If thou wilt not, then will Crispus," answered Nyria, "should he hear that I am laid low."

"Ho! ho! Hath it come to that? Crispus, forsooth! But I

would look higher than a steward or body-servant. What saith Stephanus to such a rival?"

Nyria answered shortly, "Crispus is no lover of mine."

"Nay, we are all like that when we begin," said Thanna, cynically; "ere long thou wilt be counting thy lovers on both hands. But thou didst make a good beginning in Stephanus, Nyria, and I advise thee not to take up with one whose highest ambition is to be a gladiator. Leave such to the ladies of Rome. 'Tis well that noble dames do fancy gladiators, seeing that their husbands, sons and brothers fall therefore to the like of us." And Thanna sauntered out.

Nyria anointed her sores, and presently Thanna brought supper for both. Julia, it appeared, was better, and Æmilia had been allowed entrance. Also, related Thanna, a messenger had been sent to the Palace. That, however, was no rare occurrence.

Later, Nyria obeyed a summons to attend Julia, who was on her couch and looked unusually pale. When Sabinus returned from the Senate House he sent a message asking to see her, at which Julia remarked, with a scornful laugh, that were she not already sick the sight of Sabinus's face would make her so. But she admitted him, and Sabinus entered, full of concern and deferential as was his way with her. He had said only a few words of affectionate solicitude when a missive from the Palace was brought to Julia—a purple-bordered scroll sealed with Domitian's signet. Julia read it beneath the eyes of Sabinus, who looked longingly at her, but asked no question.

As she read a smile of satisfaction came over Julia's face, then a petulant look. She remained silent, the scroll curled up in her hand, pondering deeply its contents.

"I trust there is naught here to trouble thee, Julia," Sabinus said gently.

"If all the world would mind its own business and leave me to mine I should have little enough to trouble me," answered Julia, tartly, and as he leaned near her, his hand upon the head of her couch, she shoved him crossly back. "Hast thou naught to occupy thee, Sabinus, that thou dost come hanging about me?"

"Not at this hour," he replied. "My business for the day is over, and it is to this time I look forward, Julia," he went on tenderly, "since it brings me to my home and thee. To-night it grieved me to sup alone, and I made but a hasty repast, for I sorely missed thy company."

"'Tis a pity the gods did not implant like tastes in our breasts," grumbled Julia, sarcastically. "There is small sense in having given Sabinus a longing for Julia's society when on Julia they bestow no similar desire."

Sabinus stood upright and looked down upon her sadly.

"Thou art hard, Julia," he said; "but I will not believe thou dost mean the half of thy shrewish speeches. 'Twould be sad indeed if a pair mated as we are should seek their best joys apart. How will it be, beloved," he went on, deeper feeling stirring him, "when death hath closed upon us the gates of upper earth and there stretches before us both the long road of that life beyond, which those whom the gods have united must needs traverse together? There can be no worldly pleasures to distract us then, Julia. Should we not therefore seek some happiness in each other now, lest when that day doth come no joy at all be left us?"

Nyria, sitting by the curtained doorway, could not help hearing all that passed. Tears of sympathy for Sabinus came to her eyes as Julia, looking up from the pillows, laughed derisively.

"Korē bear me witness 'twould be a dull road indeed that I had to travel alone with thee. Why prate of such things, Sabinus? I am sick of all this talk of death. It hath been dinned into my ears too much of late."

"Truly," said Sabinus, with a melancholy smile, "the wings of death hover over the land, and many have the gods summoned to Hades."

"The gods!" cried Julia, derisively.

"Ay, since the reins of life and death may not be given unrestrained into the hands of any man, though in truth it doth appear that Domitian is in a measure permitted to guide them," said Sabinus. "And seeing thou dost guide Domitian," he added slowly, "why shouldst thou fear death, Julia?"

"I fear not death, thou gloomy owl!" she retorted, sitting up on her couch angrily. "Get thee gone. Thou shouldst hire thyself out as a mourner. I am not one to make prayers, but if I were, I should supplicate the gods that when they summon thee hence I might of their charity be permitted to make my journey free from such croaking company."

Sabinus sighed heavily. "Hast thou a heart of stone, Julia?" he said in sharp reproach.

"I had like to have no heart, nor brain, nor body if I listened long to thy maudlin whine," she cried. "Get thee gone, Sabinus. Seest thou not I'm sick, and this dark-omened talk doth fret me?"

He was touched on the instant, and said, remorsefully,—

"Nay, I should have thought of that. The gods give thee better health, dearest;" and he stooped tenderly and would have kissed her hand, but she made an irritated movement and pushed his head away.

"If 'tis only through thine intercession that I may gain the gods' good gifts, Sabinus, then shall I be poorly provided, for thou art too great a fool even to obtain aught for thyself. In order to get me good health I must first have peace. None of my slaves come slobbering over my hand. Why shouldst thou?"

Sabinus stood upright, and there was acutely wounded pride in his tone. "I am thy husband, Julia, not thy slave. Know this, for I have played the part of slave to thee too long," and with that he turned on his heel and left her.

Nyria lifted the curtain for him to pass, and he went without a look behind him. Julia uttered a startled ejaculation. She raised herself on her elbow and stared after him with a puzzled face. Then she gave a mocking laugh, and cried,—

"Haste thee, Nyria, look without—was that the Lord Sabinus who passed?"

Nyria obeyed the order, though she knew it was given satirically.

"It was the Lord Sabinus, Most Noble," she answered.

"Verily, methought he had been metamorphosed from a mouse into a lion," said Julia, and sank back, laughing hysterically.

XXI

NEXT day a large concourse of nobles and great ladies gathered in the Campus Martius, the usual proceeding immediately after the Saturnalia.

During the holiday time, considerable parts of the field were given up to the slaves' amusement and patricians sought their recreations elsewhere. But as soon as the vulgar revelling had ended, Government officials came in to sweep and redecorate the place, and games were held which the Emperor and all the fashionable set of Rome attended in state, bringing with them even larger retinues than was customary, as if to emphasise the fact that they had re-taken possession of the park. There was a certain irony in the sight of these troops of slaves, who only a few days back had rioted proudly on that very spot, now cringing and bowing in abject servility at the beck and call of their masters and mistresses.

Contrary to Euphena's advice, Julia insisted on going to the Campus Martius; and her magnificent litter, with its brawny forewalkers—the coveted lictors preceding them—and its attendant slaves made a goodly show in the procession of notabilities that wound along the Flaminian Way, turning in by the great Porticos of Europa and of the Argonauts towards a large oval enclosed by trees and fantastically-clipped box-hedges and planted with irregular beds of shrubs and flowers which divided off the stretches of velvety turf where wrestling matches and various games of skill were played by trained performers.

Here the populace was not admitted, but the Plebs crowded outside, and strained over the barriers, eager to catch a glimpse of Cæsar and his friends.

Nyria, with Thanna and Samu, walked close behind Julia's litter, and as it crossed the field loud shouts from the multitude, the clattering of armour and a blare of trumpets announced that the Emperor was arriving with his body-guard of Prætorians.

To-day Nature's mood had changed. Only a light sprinkling of snow on Soracte remained to tell of that wild weather when the cloud-shapes had roamed like ghosts over the hill-sides. It was one of those clear winter days when the cypresses stood out as if hewn in green marble, and the pine needles and ilex were drawn against a sky so deeply blue that it seemed to hold the innermost secrets of infinity. And in the solemn cypresses, the sombre oak-groves, the shadowy slopes of olives across the Campagna, as too in the frowning heights of that ancient Sabine region beyond, there was a strange oppression of tragedy, heightened here, where at a little distance the Flaminian Way merged into a street of tombs.

In contrast to that suggestion of tragedy and death, dazzling sunshine bathed the domes and spires of the city, dancing on the Tiber—except where blocks of high dwellings made black reflections on the water—illuminating the gorgeous buildings that tipped the seven hills and the many marbles of the Porticos, and making the barbaric colouring of the Temple of Isis close by, appear garish in its brilliance.

There was little wind, but sometimes a long balmy breath would stir the palm-fronds and make a silvery gloss on the olives. Then the air would swell with the scent of roses and violets and mignonette, of cassia and mimosa, and many southern blossoms with which the flower-sellers heaped their booths. And notwithstanding the nip of night-frost and the late gust of snow, carefully-tended beds of carnations showed perfumy heads, and camellia shrubs were pillars of white and pink blooms, and yucca spikes reared their waxen bells, and all manner of bulbs shed fragrance. This was part of the magic of the scene—the mystic blending of mirth and tears, of materialism and poetry, of gloom and glory which, from the beginning of its history, has made up the enduring spell of Rome.

The great pleasure-ground was at its best, and presented a glittering array of colour and sheen. The crowd, where it massed under the trees, was like a tangle of tropical bloom. On the fringe where it circulated, there was an effect of enormous walking nosegays, as slave-girls held gay parasols over the heads of their ladies, or screened them from the glare with long-handled feather fans, while little groups moved from place to place looking at the various games. These were the more energetic of the assembly. Others, lazily inclined and established under the trees, were content to witness such performances as came within their view.

There was a grand stand in the Imperial enclosure, splendidly tapestried, and its pillars wreathed with flowers, but it was scarcely used, for on an occasion like the present, when no chariot-racing was going on, people met to show themselves in their pomp, to make love and to plot together, rather than for the sake of looking at the sports. Domitian set the example of having his litter placed on the lawn so that he might change his position according to his pleasure, and everybody else did likewise, casting aside formality and strolling about as they pleased.

Julia never cared to use her feet when she could be carried. Moreover, to-day, notwithstanding liberally-applied rouge, she looked far from well. She did not get out of her litter, but had it brought up beside that of Cæsar, and leaning over its cushioned side talked to him long and animatedly. But he scowled, and once Nyria heard him say curtly,—

"Prate not loud enough for all Rome to hear."

Julia cast a contemptuous glance at the body-guard drawn up near him and cried, "Then send this vermin away," which angered Domitian, for it was his foible to make himself popular among the Prætorians, and he reprimanded her for her lack of courtesy.

Julia sulked silently till Cæsar signed to the chief of the officers that he should draw his men back, whereat Julia gave command to her own people, and Nyria retired with the other women.

Thanna liked nothing better—short of eavesdropping on great personages—than to witness games, and so gladly went off as far as she dared to amuse herself after her fashion, while melancholy Samu, on whose face were some violet marks bearing witness to the weight of her mistress's silver brush, sat hugging her knees. Nyria moved a little way from her and sat down too, gazing with half-seeing eyes now at the litters of ladies and their accompanying gallants going to and fro, and at the figures of men and women on foot passing and repassing the clear space kept by the lictors round Domitian and Julia, and now at a set of ball-players, as with wondrous grace and agility they tossed their gay feather balls from hand to hand, under and over their arms and above their heads, so that the bright-coloured globes looked like a number of fantastic insects whirling in air.

The soldiers of Cæsar's guard were grouped together beneath the trees at a little distance, and presently Nyria, attracted by the quick flash of gold-bossed armour, saw Alexamenos, the fair-haired young officer, step forward in her direction.

Nyria smiled and greeted him pleasantly, for she often received courtesies from him. At first they talked idly of the games, Alexamenos's gaze lingering admiringly on her face, her robe and hair. Presently he said earnestly,—

"Tell me, Nyria—hast thou power in thy household?"

Nyria knew what he meant. It was Fashion's freak just then for many a high-placed lady in Rome to make a boast of being under the influence of some pampered slave. She shook her head.

"In our household none have power save one, and that is Julia."

"Alas! I feared so, and her dominion stretcheth even to the palace of Cæsar," said Alexamenos.

"Likewise over all the men in Rome," put in Nyria. "At least, so 'tis said."

"Nay, Julia may rule the fools, and perchance the knaves," exclaimed Alexamenos, "but not the men of Rome."

Nyria tossed back her curly hair. "What is the difference? No men let women see it."

"Thou knowest better, Nyria," he replied gravely. "Julia doth not rule the soldiers. Were her finger to be laid on the backs of the Prætorians there would be a rising among the legions."

"Then Domitian doth not rule the soldiery," retorted Nyria.

"Domitian Cæsar ruleth them," he answered, "though not Domitian, the tool of Julia. But let us cease to bandy words. There is somewhat I would say to thee—secret and important. When wilt thou hear me?"

"Thou canst not say it now," replied Nyria, who saw by certain signs of restlessness that Julia would soon call her maids and bearers.

"Then wilt thou meet me to-night by the lower gate in the wall outside thy house and let me speak with thee alone?"

"I make no such meetings," answered Nyria, coldly, and folded her mantle closer round her. "Let me pass, Alexamenos."

"Oh, misunderstand me not!" he murmured beseechingly. "I beg this grace of thee for a weighty reason — the safety of Sabinus."

Nyria's feet were arrested. Her eyes had been bent on the ground. She raised them and gave Alexamenos a searching look.

"Doth danger then beset Sabinus?" she asked in a low, hurried tone.

"Ay, so closely that methinks Sabinus hath never known danger until now. Yet thou and I may save him yet, Nyria, if thou wilt lend thine aid."

"My life is my master's," said Nyria, simply. "Therefore I will do what thou askest me. Only mind thee this, Alexamenos—if thou makest mock of me—"

"Makest mock of thee!" he cried. "Oh, Nyria, trust me, for in very truth there is no thought of mocking in my heart. I hold thee far too dear."

He caught the edge of her robe, and raising it, stooped as if he would have kissed the hem. But at that moment a laugh sounded from the company of Prætorians who, unnoticed, had been watching the scene and joking at the expense of their comrade. Nyria snatched away her robe, and flew with crimson cheeks towards Julia's litter, while Alexamenos reared himself angrily, his breastplate and his shoulder-pieces clicking, and strode back to his company. He gave the word to stand at attention, for Julia was bidding Cæsar farewell. She looked in happier mood as the bearers picked up her litter and bore her, 'mid obsequious leave-takings, away along the sward. Her train of slaves fell into rank, and Thanna and Samu took their places behind Nyria, who kept her eyes on the ground while they passed the body-guard with Alexamenos at its front. She did not look up till the procession had reached the outskirts of the field and was going by a railed-in space where gladiators were allowed to practise and the public to witness their trials. Then, at a nudge from Thanna, Nyria looked across towards it, and saw Crispus among the performers, leaning against the rail just within. He was stripped but for a loin-cloth, and the muscles of his body stood out, his firm flesh shining from having been rubbed with oil. He smiled and nodded at the women, seemingly well pleased with himself, and then went to his turn at wrestling.

Julia took her dinner in a small triclinium that evening. Sabinus was detained at the Senate House, and did not return till she had almost finished her repast, when he made a poor pretence of going through the courses which Crispus and Vibius brought back and pressed upon him.

Julia interrogated her husband closely as to the debate that day and the opinions of the Hundred; and though he disliked discussing State affairs in general hearing, he was forced to answer that the debate had gone against him, and that a great majority of the Senate was opposed to the reforms he advocated.

"Was Domitian at the Senate House?" Julia asked, looking keenly at her husband.

"He came for a short time on his way back from the Campus Martius," answered Sabinus.

"And did Domitian support thy vote?" she said, with a sarcastic curl of her lip.

"'Tis not Domitian's way to support me," he replied; and added, "I have wondered that he should have favoured my election to the Consulship, since a word from him could have ruined my chances. It seems as though he raised up only to destroy."

Julia laughed softly as she ate some fruit.

Nyria was now dismissed to go to her supper, and hurried out, not waiting for food, but sped fleetly to the lower gate, gathering her robe close, and peering round to make sure she was not observed.

Alexamenos waited in the shadow of the wall, where a bench was set a few feet beyond the gateway.

"Ah! Nyria! I thought thou wast not coming," he exclaimed.

"Nyria never fails to keep her word," answered the girl. "Only bonds could hold me back after I had pledged myself. But be speedy, Alexamenos, for I have no time to dally."

"Thou art niggardly, Nyria. 'Tis not oft we have a word together."

"Thy way and mine lie different roads," she answered shortly.

"Thy way doth sometimes bring thee to the Palace, yet never do thine eyes lead thee to where Alexamenos stands."

Nyria made an impatient movement.

"If 'twere thy business to attend on Julia thou wouldst be wiser than to let thine eyes play truant from her chair."

"Is that the reason, Nyria?" he asked wistfully. "Alas! I fear not, since never have I had a sign that I might seek thy company. Thou art a little vestal. But expect not soldiers to be more than men."

"I know not much of either," she said. "We do but waste speech, Alexamenos. What wouldst thou with me?"

"'Tis a serious matter," he answered. "But first, if I can do aught to save thy master, Nyria, thinkest thou that he will grant me a reward?"

She drew back vexedly. "I like not such bargains," she said. "Sabinus is not one to forget a favour, and be assured that he will recompense thee for any service thou dost render him."

"And *thou*—wilt *thou* reward me, Nyria?" exclaimed Alexamenos, fervently. The flickering light of a torch set above the gate illumined his eager face as he tried to take Nyria's hand. Just then a little mocking laugh sounded on the other side of the wall. Nyria recognised the tinkling tones as those of Thanna, and knew by the click of the gate that followed the laugh that she must have been spying on them.

Nyria snatched her hand away from Alexamenos's grasp, and cried, in low, indignant tones,—

"Haste with thy business. Thou sayest Sabinus stands in danger, and yet wouldst bargain to save him! I thought better of thee, Alexamenos."

"I did but jest," he answered meekly. "Yet I fain would win thy favour, Nyria."

"Then tell me speedily what ails my master," she said. "What trouble is like to overwhelm him?"

"'Tis trouble at the Senate," he answered darkly. "They seek to charge Sabinus with treason, though naught else can they find of which to accuse him than that he hath too much at heart the interests of the Plebs and slaves. But 'tis enough. Thou knowest, Nyria, that Domitian rules the Senate. Listen! Draw nearer and let me whisper, for walls have ears, they say, and there is no alley in Rome without an echo. Nay, I will not finger thee. Thou mayst trust me." He folded his arms behind his back, and Nyria crept closer to him, raising her head, while he stooped to whisper.

"Domitian hateth Sabinus, and would remove him from his path. This further I may say. Were Sabinus to die, the next to suffer would be the Empress Domitia herself. Now I like not Domitia, for she is sour-tongued and spare of civilities; nevertheless, she is the Augusta, and should be sacred to her subjects, though she be not so to Cæsar."

"But tell me what present danger threatens Sabinus," put in Nyria, agitatedly. "In what guise will it come?"

"The same danger which hath threatened others as great as he. One so high placed as Sabinus cannot be slain by open force, nor stabbed in the dark by some assassin. In the seeming cause of justice will he suffer. Dost know, Nyria, that one who, wearing Cæsar's uniform, betrayeth Cæsar's secret command hath earned the penalty of death? Yet hear this—Soon shall I be bidden to take Sabinus prisoner. Once charged as a traitor to his country's laws, who shall save him?"

"Thou!" murmured Nyria, wildly. "If 'tis thy task, Alexamenos, canst thou not see he be not harmed and afterwards release him?"

"'Tis impossible," said Alexamenos, shortly. "I must fulfil my duty. Sabinus should flee. Tell him there are foul plots breeding against him. Hint not the source whence the news hath come, for no good would be gained were I destroyed and another sent in my stead. But should Sabinus escape I will engage that none shall know whither he hath gone, and when the soldiery are in search of him 'twill be a strange mischance if he be found. He must take ship," Alexamenos whispered rapidly; "there are boats now in the Tiber, in any one of which he would be safe, disguised—vessels that trade along the coast, so that he can land further down the country, or, if he choose, go hide himself in Gaul till things improve. These are bad times for Rome, Nyria, but though Domitian is young, he may not reign for ever. Nero was but a little over thirty when his power came to an end," added Alexamenos.

"Are there then those who would do away with Domitian as they did with Nero?" asked Nyria, breathlessly.

"Nay, I know not—nor would I dare to tell thee if I knew. Yet of this be assured—tyranny may not endure, for only justice and mercy are eternal."

"Thou dost speak a new thing," said Nyria, shrewdly.

"It may seem so to thee, Nyria, for I have learned many new things of late. 'Tis not the will of God that ill-doing shall prosper in the land. When thou hearest of oppression and wrong, know that 'tis the work of men, not of God."

"Of which god dost thou speak?" she asked with interest.

"Of Him who is the God and Father of us all," replied Alexamenos, reverently. "Of Him who sorrowed so, beholding how sin and suffering filled the world, that He sent down His only Son to be a sacrifice for erring mankind."

"Now, who was that?" exclaimed Nyria. "Speakest thou of him they call Zeus or Jove? I never heard that he did so serve his son."

"Because thou hast not heard the message of glad tidings and peace to all the world which was sung at the Saviour's birth," said Alexamenos, gently gazing down at her.

"Then 'tis true that thou art a worshipper of strange gods," said Nyria.

"I am a worshipper of the one true God and of Jesus His Son, but not of those images which Greeks, and Romans, and barbarians alike set up and call divine—as though wood and stone and metal could hear and answer men's petitions."

Nyria drew a deep breath of awed surprise, for she thought that this god of Alexamenos must be that great Someone whose benignant presence had overshadowed her on the hillside—that All-Father of whom Clementus had spoken.

"Thou hast said things of which I would fain speak to thee again," she murmured, "but now 'tis of Sabinus we must think."

"Ay, Nyria. Urge upon him that he flee immediately. Only bid him say no word to Julia. The least sound of this to her and he is lost."

"And yet he doth love Julia," replied Nyria, regretfully.

"Men have loved viler things. For my part, I fain would love only that which is pure and lovely."

The young officer's eyes sought hers, as though there was much more that he desired to say.

"I know not if Sabinus will listen to me," said Nyria, troubled. "Canst thou not urge him, Alexamenos?"

"Nay. My duty as a soldier of Cæsar forbids me. But Sabinus hath money and devoted slaves at command. He himself will know best how to act. This, however, thou mayst say. Bid him seek the ship *Goat and Star* on the Lower Quay. The master of her comes from Phrygia, and is a kindly, honest-hearted fellow whom he may trust. Moreover, seeing that Sabinus can make it worth the captain's while to hoist anchor at once, by this time to-morrow night he may be well out in the stream if he so chooseth."

Nyria thought out the matter quickly.

"I like not the task, Alexamenos. 'Twill be difficult of accomplishment. Not that I fear my master, but that I know not how to obtain speech with Sabinus without the knowledge of Julia—unless, indeed, one of his own body-servants should aid me." But Alexamenos would not hear of this.

"How knowest thou that the man may not betray the story?" he said. "Then Sabinus would not escape, and worse mischance would follow, for I should be charged before the tribunal."

"Oh! thou dost not know Crispus—him I should employ," Nyria expostulated. "He is good and true, even as thou art, Alexamenos, and I would trust him as myself—or as I would trust thee."

"Mayhap this Crispus hath the same reasons as I for desiring to serve thee," said Alexamenos, gravely. "In that case thou mayest indeed put faith in him for the moment. But what faith would he keep should he find that thou didst favour another?"

"I have favoured none," she said petulantly. "'Tis no time to talk of favouring. If thou wilt not trust me I can do naught."

Alexamenos was silent for a moment, then he said quietly,—

"I will trust thee, Nyria. I have no other course. But I pray thee to use all the caution thou canst command. Remember, 'tis Sabinus's life—and not that alone which is at stake."

"I'll do my best," she answered. "Fare thee well, Alexamenos."

"Fare thee well," he said, "since go thou must. May all powers of good be propitious to thine enterprise. For in very truth, if it fail, thou wilt see me in Sabinus's house too soon for thy pleasure, or for mine."

XXII

Nyria slipped through the gate and put up the latch. There was no sign of anyone in the outer yard, but in the slaves' court, lights were burning, and men and women lounged about the doorways chattering, as was their habit after the evening meal. A little crowd had collected before a cabin at one end of the court, and loud talk and merriment proceeded therefrom. It was there that Thanna lived with the widow Samu. Thanna was given to complain of Samu as a dull companion, and when twitted with her own gossiping propensities would retort that when she wanted a laugh she had to go out for it. To-night it appeared that she had attracted some laughter to her own door, though Samu looked melancholy enough —a huddled figure crouching in the dim glow of an oil lamp within. The lamp shed its faint light upon a row of amused faces stretched over the mud wall outside, while Thanna stood upon the threshold of the hut, her hands on her hips, and gabbled shrilly. Her talk elicited every now and then some sniggering comment from her listeners, and Nyria, drawing nearer, heard Crispus call out,—

"Thou'lt get ulcers on the tip of that scandalous tongue of thine, Thanna. Such plague-spots, remember, are like to come and shame the lips of liars. For that Nyria could stoop to idle courting in the lane is a tale I'll not believe."

"Ho! ho! my lord champion!" shouted Thanna. "Dost never go a-courting thyself? Or is the maid thou courtest of so spotless a reputation that she doth scorn to meet thee at dark in the shadow of a wall?"

"Now, Diana hound thee for a spy, Thanna! Thou revilest saints whose sandals thou art not fit to tie," cried Crispus. "Hold thy peace. Or, if thou must needs prate falsehood, do it to those who'll listen. I'll have no more of thy slander." He turned, and, as he did so, met Nyria coming towards him. "Here's Nyria to answer for herself," he exclaimed.

"Ay, so she shall!" cried Thanna. "Were Alexamenos's kisses sweet, most simple, saintly Nyria? And dost thou need a messenger to carry to Stephanus the news that thou has pledged thyself to another wooer? Or wouldst thou combine the merchant with the military in thy lovers and retain the services of both? Thou'rt a pretty deceiver, and a miserly one too, since thou wouldst not give up thy claim to Stephanus, notwithstanding that I offered thee a good price for his favour. But now, perchance, Stephanus himself may have a word to say in the matter."

Nyria stood silent, amid the laughter and jeers, then she sprang forward, crying out,—

"Thou art a lying hussy, Thanna, and I'd scorn to answer thee but that thy sneaking ways are more than one can endure. Thou wert spying on me from the gate, and that I know, for I heard thee come. But though thou didst see me talking with Alexamenos, 'tis no reason thou shouldst suppose that we were occupied as *thou* wouldst have been."

"Oh, I suppose nothing, Nyria," said Thanna, folding her hands in mock humility. "I know naught, and, by Diana, I'd scorn to spy. I was but passing up from the great gate, whither Julia had sent me to see if a messenger she looketh for were coming from the Palace. How should *I* know on what weighty affair thou and Alexamenos might be conversing? But seeing it was not such light dallying as Thanna doth enjoy, thou'lt tell us, wilt thou not, what was the business ye were whispering to each other?"

"Nay, that I'll not," answered Nyria, tears of vexation rising in her eyes.

"Tease not the maid," said Crispus, gruffly. "Thou'rt a vixen, Thanna. Hold thy peace."

"Alack! alack! I am not in high favour as thou art, pretty Nyria. Hard words fly at Thanna, though soft ones circle round Nyria. But then she is of much account. 'Tis not every wench can prate on State business with an officer of Cæsar's guard. This secret matter on which Alexamenos and Nyria do busy themselves is not for lowly ears like thine and mine, Crispus."

Nyria was about to retort angrily, but suddenly it flashed upon her that it were better for Thanna to believe she had been love-making with Alexamenos than that her secret concerning Sabinus should be put in jeopardy. So she began to bridle, though with an ill grace.

"Nay, now, Thanna, may not any maid but thyself pass a few compliments with a man? Why should I not listen when a Prætorian so well-liking as Alexamenos pauseth to speak to me?"

"Yea, why not? Why not, indeed?" laughed Thanna. "Why not? Oh! only because Nyria hath held her head too high for such unseemly ways. Nevertheless, I did misdoubt me sore of Nyria."

"It appeareth, then, that thou knowest Nyria better than she knew herself," said the girl, stormily, for she hated to play the hypocrite. "At least," she added, "being born a woman, I have leave to change my mind and manners, even as thou sometimes dost."

"Oh, ay!" ejaculated Thanna, with a note of surprise. "But what will Stephanus say?" and her laugh was echoed by the group of listeners. Nyria turned to Crispus, who stood silent.

"Come away," she said. "I want a word with thee, Crispus. Let us leave this hive of wasps to buzz as they please."

"Are two lovers not enough for thee, Nyria?" called Thanna as Crispus and the girl strolled away together. "Must thou have a third freedman at thy feet?" And again the loiterers took up the laugh, some in good will, some enviously, for it was known in the slaves' court that Crispus would soon be freed.

Nyria and he went out by a gate that shut off the slaves' huts from a wide space round the end of the house. Along it a torch was set here and there, lighting the way to Julia's apartments on one side and to Sabinus's on the other. Nyria looked timidly up at Crispus and saw that his face was very dark.

"What meaneth all this talk, Nyria?" he asked sternly, and her heart sank, for she saw that he had half believed Thanna's insinuations.

"It meaneth this, Crispus," she answered bravely. "Ill portents do shadow our house, and there be direr deeds in the wind than such nonsense as Thanna doth accuse me of. Be patient with me and listen. I have much to tell thee."

"In truth, I had not thought of thee that thou wouldst play the common light-o'-love," he said, relieved in mind. "Look thee, Nyria, Stephanus is worth more than all the gaudy Prætorians who may come doffing their helmets thy way."

"Stephanus is worth more than most men," she replied. "But 'tis not of him that I would speak." Her voice lowered to a whisper. "I have learned a great secret this evening, Crispus—a deadly secret. Oh! be silent and listen. Take me where none can hear."

"Come this way, then," he said, and led her from Julia's rooms round by the darkened windows of Sabinus's apartments. "Now thou canst speak freely. Art cold, Nyria? Thou'rt shivering."

"'Tis fear. I fear for our master, Crispus. Sabinus's life is in danger," she answered in low, quick tones. "There's a plot in the Senate against him. Domitian seeketh to destroy him for love of Julia. And more than this"—she raised herself to his ear—"the Augusta Domitia will be next. Domitian willeth that Julia shall share his bed and throne. Now, Crispus, what thinkest thou of that?"

"What I have always thought," retorted Crispus. "But I looked not for it to come so soon. It doth seem that Julia groweth impatient. Mayhap these megrims of hers have something to do with the hasting of Domitian's vengeance. How hast thou learned all this, Nyria?"

"Alexamenos told me. He is a brave man and true, and he would fain save Sabinus if it be possible. Oh! Crispus, thou wilt keep faith with us?"

"Have I ever done aught to make thee think differently, Nyria? What wouldst thou have of me?"

"That thou shouldst break this to Sabinus and persuade him to depart in hiding. There are vessels in the Tiber by which he can make his escape." And she poured out all that Alexamenos had told her.

"'Tis no easy task, Nyria," said Crispus; "thou art better fitted for it than I. Sabinus hath a strange stubbornness, for all that men think him but a reed. Perhaps none know this stubbornness as do we who are about his person. Yet he might listen to a maid. Hast thou courage to divulge to him thyself this tale of dread?"

"Yea," she answered, trembling, "I have the courage to tell him. But 'tis not fitting, Crispus, that the tale should come from me."

"As fitting as that it should be of my telling," he said. "Yet I like not to put it on thee, Nyria, for thy life may be the forfeit if Julia learneth aught of this. And with all his kindness, and a certain wisdom of his own, Sabinus is a very king of fools where Julia is concerned."

"My life is naught," returned Nyria, excitedly. "If my life or that of Sabinus must be the forfeit, why, better mine than his."

"Thou little fool!" said Crispus, in rough compunction. "Thou must save thine own skin if thou wouldst save Sabinus's. But 'tis unmanly to ask from a girl that which I myself would shrink from doing. Look, Nyria—I will speak first to Sabinus, but if he will listen best to words of thine, thou shalt come to him to-morrow before he leaves for the Senate. He will not then have seen Julia, and thou wilt have a better chance to persuade him. The gods grant it, for good men are scarce in Rome. Long may Sabinus live and prosper, though it be not in the city of his fathers. In the morning I'll contrive a word with thee. Now, say no more to-night. Get thee to thy slumbers, else Thanna and that crew will be saying evil things of thee and me."

Nyria's heart was in a flutter next morning as she did her part in the business of head-tiring and robing her mistress. Julia was late of rising, and seemed languid, but her spirit was indomitable; and to-day, in spite of her evident weakness, there was triumph in her manner. She had herself dressed most carefully, and in the middle of her robing Euphena came—as she often did—with a potion, which Julia drank. As she swallowed the draught a flush rose to her cheeks, deepening the rouge, and heightening the glitter of her eyes. She got up from her chair as if the medicine had given her new strength, and surveyed herself complacently in the long mirror. Then she turned to the Ethiopian.

"See, Euphena, thanks to thee—for all thy croaking—Julia hath cheated death and disaster.'

"Let not Julia boast," answered Euphena, grimly. "Death is an ill fellow to cheat; and when one thinks to have evaded him, lo! he appeareth."

"If it be true, Euphena, as some say," quoth Julia, lightly, "that our souls have come out of birds and beasts, sure 'twas a raven—or a frog, mayhap—that thou hadst for grandfather. Croak more cheeringly if thou canst."

"How shall one be gladsome when the shadow of death hangs already upon the house?" replied Euphena. "Thou thinkest to escape it, Julia—and perchance thou wilt—since men and women are but playthings of the Immortals, and none may act as umpire among the gods, or foretell the outcome of their frolicking. Yet mark thou this, Julia. None ever cast a net who ran no chance of being himself entangled in its meshes."

Julia made a pouting face, and turned again to the mirror.

"I should run a small chance of being cheered if I listened long to thee. Thou canst go, hag. I have no further need for thee."

"Not yet, pretty one," whined Euphena. "But thou wilt have need of me when the winding-sheet lies ready and the savour of the spices mounts to heaven. Even now, meseems, the gods do twitch their nostrils, scenting that sweet savour." And Euphena went out.

Julia was in an uncertain mood this morning. She made her women bring forth the most gaudy of her clothes, trying first one embroidery or gaily-striped silk against her face, then another, and piling on jewels, only to take them off again. Nyria made excuses to leave her to Thanna, who served her best at such times, and who would turn Julia's variableness to her own advantage; for when Julia crossly threw aside some article of apparel, saying she did not wish to see it more, Thanna took good care she never set eyes upon it again, and thus acquired many a garment, and sometimes even a piece of jewellery, out of which she made a fine profit.

Meanwhile, Nyria ran to Sabinus's apartments, in obedience to a summons from Crispus, who met her, and whispered encouragingly,—

"Take heart of grace, Nyria. 'Tis not in Sabinus to hurt a fly. I told him there was a tale afloat rumouring ill to him, and gathering that 'twas of serious import he bade me fetch the one from whom I had got the story. In truth, Nyria, I think Sabinus is like to be persuaded by thee. For gentle though he be to all, yet to a woman he is as a ship that doth answer to its helm. The gods grant, little pilot, that thou mayest guide yon poor ship to some safe harbour." And Crispus pushed her towards Sabinus's room.

"I'll keep the door," he said, and lifted the curtain as Nyria went in and made a low obeisance to her master.

"Why, Nyria, is it thou?" exclaimed Sabinus in surprise. "I looked not to see thee. Come hither, child. What wild fancy is this thou hast culled?"

"May it please thee, 'tis no fancy," Nyria answered shyly, drawing near, but not lifting her eyes from the ground. "Oh! may it please thee, Sabinus, 'tis true that danger doth threaten thee. Thou knowest how that death hath been rife in Rome, and one hath told me that 'tis my master—thee, dear lord—who hath now been singled out."

Sabinus did not answer. The silence was so long that at last Nyria raised her head and saw his face—pale, sad, but strangely calm.

"Is that so?" he said slowly; and she bowed herself in agonised assent.

"Death comes but once," he said, "and none shall say Sabinus shrank from meeting it."

Nyria had fallen upon her knees at his feet, and she caught his hands. "Oh! may it please thee, lord—" she cried. "Even now the dogs of death may be upon thy steps. Oh! save thyself, Sabinus—for thine own sake—for Rome's sake!"

He shook his head mournfully, and his fingers closed over hers.

"For mine own sake, Nyria, I would not flee, seeing that death may give me greater joy than I have found in life. And for Rome's sake, why should I flee? If Rome doth murder her sons—then in death they must bow to her will."

"But, lord!—but, lord!—" urged Nyria. "If not for thine own, nor for Rome's sake, be it for the sake of those that love thee. Carest thou not?—carest thou not?" and her sobs choked her.

"Nay, child!" he answered very gently. "I am grateful indeed. Yet why should I care to live? Sabinus hath striven to serve his city well, and, like a true lover, or like an obedient son, he must accept whatsoever reward she chooseth to send. In truth," he added, "the spirit of Rome is capricious as the favour of a woman. Her kisses are given only to slay."

"But, lord, there is yet time," pleaded Nyria, Alexamenos's counsels crowding her mind. "Behold, vessels lie in the Tiber, any one of which would serve to bear thee into safety. One I know—the *Goat and Star*—hath a loyal master mariner on board, who would not see injustice done without putting forth an arm in defence of right. Thou hast but to hasten in disguise down to the Lower Quay. Crispus is thy faithful slave, and I—even I—would aid thee if thou wouldst permit."

"Thou art a faithful child, Nyria, that well I know," he answered. "But Romans do not flee when danger threatens. Do not weep, little maid. I am strong enough to bear whatever fate shall befall. Now I must haste me to the Senate. Fear not. None shall hear thy tale." He raised her to her feet. "I am indeed fortunate in having such service rendered me," he said. "And 'tis for such as thee and Crispus that Sabinus will be called upon to suffer. For know, Nyria, the only charge they can lay upon me is that of oversetting my country's laws, in that I have tried to make them easier for the lowly among her servitors."

And Nyria in her distress felt that here stood the noblest of Rome's servitors. Sabinus's thoughtful and unsmiling face was paler than usual, but there was unwonted strength in every line of it, and high purpose in his eyes. He was fully dressed, even to his toga, and round his neck and shoulders, falling to his feet, was the broad purple band, the sign of his Senatorship—the laticlave.

Again she pleaded, recapitulating Alexamenos's advice, imploring him anew by every argument she could think of to save himself. But to all her entreaties he only smiled and shook his head.

"I ask not who hath told thee this, Nyria," he said in answer to her reiterated assurance that the news had come from a reliable source. "Whoever gave thee thine information would not like his name to be known. But tell him, whoe'er he be, that Sabinus thanks him for his warning, and takes it in right good part. Nevertheless, 'twould not be well that I should avail myself of it. A Senator I am, and as a Senator I must abide by that which the Senate doth decree. Ill would it be for Rome did those who are set to guide her erring counsels forsake their task."

He put his hand kindly round Nyria's shoulders and pressed her to him.

"Weep not, little maid. Thou art a brave child; but thou'lt have to be braver yet. Maids who live in Rome in these days must needs have courage to face the storm-clouds that gather over our hapless city."

Nyria could only gaze at him with streaming eyes. Sabinus made a step to the door and called, "Crispus!"

The curtains opened and Crispus stood between them. He glanced from Nyria to his master, and his face fell, for Sabinus was adjusting his toga and badge ready to go forth upon his official duty.

"Thou wilt attend me to the Senate to-day, Crispus," he said. "'Twill be the last time I shall command thy services." And then he strode through the doorway, pausing a moment as a dozen or so of slaves came out from the waiting-room and bowed as he passed. He turned to them and said, "Take ye all heed, and be witnesses. From to-day Crispus is free."

And Crispus made obeisance, and followed sadly in his master's steps.

Julia was giving a small banquet that evening to half a score or so of guests, which was well for Nyria, since it kept her mind and fingers occupied. Soon after Sabinus had gone forth there came up from the market the little brown-skinned boy who usually brought flowers on such occasions, with great baskets of violets and white blossoms to be arranged for the feast. To-night one of the medium-sized dining-rooms was to be used—not the state banqueting-hall—yet still there was much for Nyria to do in superintending the decorations, and the boy went to and fro many times to bring up all the flowers needed for the wreathing of the pillars and the design she made of white and purple for the dining-table. So the day wore on and Nyria was deep in her task when Æola came in shyly and told her the news from the Cœlian. The Domina, she said, was much better, but seemed occupied in mind. Nyria did not ask many questions. Æola was excited about Crispus's freedom, and disappointed to learn that he was at the Senate House, so that she could not see him. She had small thought for any other matter, and stayed but a short time, having errands to do in the Lower Forum.

Towards evening Julia rose from her couch and made a sumptuous toilet. It was blue that night—a brilliant blue in royal tint, made of soft thick silk embroidered in deeper shades with red and gold intermingled, in large designs of dragons' heads and flowers. Her under-dress was of lustrous white gauze caught in a golden girdle, and falling in close folds over her full bust, where it was bordered with gold, and so to her feet, edged with a heavy golden fringe. Her sandals were of gold, the straps gemmed with blue stones. Round her neck hung ropes of rosy coral and of pearls, and her hair was tired very high. Upon her forehead, set in a gold fillet, she wore an enormous ruby that Domitian had given her. It shone with a deep red fire, and had the look of a large bloody eye. There was something about the jewel sinister and terrifying to Nyria's fancy, like Domitian himself.

Hurrying along to the atrium behind Julia, the girl caught sight of Crispus, and he whispered to her that their master had only just returned. The guests were arriving, and Sabinus was already in the atrium receiving them with his gentle, somewhat formal, courtesy. He was still in the clothes he had gone in to the Senate House, and wore his broad purple badge of office. For this he apologised, saying he had been kept late in the courts by public business and should have delayed the meal had he waited to change. They went into the dining-hall and the feast proceeded merrily enough, save for Sabinus, who, though courtly, was grave and preoccupied.

The banqueters, with the exception of Plinius and Nonius Asprena—who were both present without their wives—belonged to the most riotous of Julia's friends, and the company was for the most part of the kind that Julia delighted in—women independent of conventional shackles, and men who flattered her grossly and hung upon her favour in order to secure that of Cæsar. The talk was noisy and scandalous, and Pliny's delicate humour, usually applauded, withered in the rank atmosphere. There was, nevertheless, an air of restraint about Nonius Asprena and one or two other Senators present, and a marked avoidance of political topics. Nyria, standing behind Julia's chair, noticed that, notwithstanding her laughter and gay sallies, she fanned herself feverishly, and drank more wine even than was her custom—always a sign with her of mental perturbation.

Suddenly, towards the end of the banquet, Nyria caught a sound that made her heart beat in wild alarm. Crispus heard it too, she saw, for he stopped in his serving, and the silver dish he was carrying almost fell from his hands. Sabinus heard it also, for he bent forward, and his face took on a listening look.

The sound came nearer, subdued, but regular and distinct. It was the tramp of soldiery. Now it ceased a moment, and then came the muffled clang of spear-butts on the stone without.

Sabinus signed to Vibius, who was holding a wine flagon behind him, and said, in low, clear tones, "Go, see who cometh."

As Vibius went out Julia half turned her head, while her voice broke uncertainly in what she was saying. But it was only for a moment. She picked up her sentence and laughed and joked with the man next her more loudly than before. Conversation flagged, however, and the guests exchanged looks, scenting that things were wrong. When Vibius returned everybody left off speaking. The steward walked up the room and bowed low before his master.

"May it please thee, Sabinus, Alexamenos waiteth without. He hath brought a mandate from the Emperor."

Sabinus's hands were resting on the table. He rose slowly, steadying himself by them. "Bid Alexamenos enter," was all he said.

The breathless pause continued. Nyria clung to the back of Julia's chair for support in the sick horror that came over her. Even Julia ceased her jerky motion of the fan, and there was silence until Vibius came in again, and behind him Alexamenos. The Prætorian held his helmet in one hand, in the other a purple-bordered scroll bearing Domitian's seal.

"Greeting, oh, Sabinus!" he said.

"Greeting, Alexamenos!" replied Sabinus. "What is the Emperor's pleasure?"

"Cæsar sendeth thee this. Read for thyself," said Alexamenos, and, bending his knee, presented the mandate.

Sabinus took the scroll, and with his stylus broke the string. He unrolled and read it through, not a muscle moving, then half rolled it together again. No word came from him, but, lifting his face, he looked at Julia; and to Nyria, who was watching him intently, there seemed a special purport in his gaze. Julia's face she could not see, but Crispus said afterwards that she stared at Sabinus as if he had cast a spell upon her. Then she recovered herself, and cried out sharply, "What saith the Emperor?"

For answer Sabinus laid the scroll upon a salver beside him, and handed it to Vibius.

"Take that to thy lady. 'Twill perchance interest her," he said. Then his eyes went round the assembly, and he made reply to the questioning looks turned towards him.

"My friends, it is the Emperor's command that I be conveyed hence by four quaternions of soldiers to the Tullianum, there to await his pleasure."

A murmur ran round the table, partly of indignation, partly of curiosity.

"What hast thou done, Sabinus?" cried one man, with a harsh laugh.

"I have served my country and my people. 'Tis for this Domitian fain would serve me now," said Sabinus, simply.

He paused, and put out his hand for his toga, which lay across the back of his chair. Crispus gathered it up and placed it on his shoulders, stooping to settle the folds. Sabinus looked in a blind sort of way round the room. Then his attention was caught by the crowd of slaves who pressed in at the door, their faces full of alarm and trouble. His gaze went from one to the other tenderly.

"My children—" Sabinus's voice broke, but he began again quickly. "May the gods protect ye all," he said. "For though man be evil, the gods are ever good—" Again he stopped, and, putting his hand to his waist, felt the hand of Crispus, which was arranging his toga. Sabinus laid his own hand upon it, and looking down, saw the bent head beside him.

"Ah, Crispus, my son!" he said, and, holding Crispus's hand, drew him upward and looked at him affectionately. A sudden thought seemed to strike Sabinus.

"The papers, Crispus. Let them be fetched."

"Not now, oh, not now, lord!"

"Ay, Crispus, *now*, lest it be too late. Are they prepared?"

Crispus nodded, and Sabinus gave an order to one of the men near to call the chief secretary. This person was even now in the doorway, and he went immediately for the documents. Sabinus turned to the Prætorian.

"Thy grace, Alexamenos," he said. "Thy grace, and that of Domitian, for a moment while I secure the freedom of this faithful son of mine. Truly no Roman need call himself childless who hath such loyal hearts as these to give him devotion."

Alexamenos bowed. He had spoken no word since he delivered the Emperor's mandate, but stood, helmet in hand, his uncovered head bent, waiting Sabinus's pleasure.

Then there came a stir at the door, and the slaves parted to let the secretary pass through. He bore the papers and a pen and ink-horn, and laid them on the table beside Sabinus, who pushed away his drinking-cup to make room for them.

"Come, Crispus," he said cordially. "Do thou read over my shoulder and see that these letters be without fault, so that they secure thee that which thou deservest."

Crispus could not speak, but he drew near as his master bade him, while Sabinus wrote his name beneath. Then, looking along the guests, whose eyes were all upon him, he asked,—

"May I crave the kind indulgence of two of my friends that they will put their hand to this paper and witness a traitor's signature for the freedom of an honest man?"

Plinius and Nonius Asprena rose immediately, and, coming up, signed the deed. When Plinius laid down his pen he put out his hand, which Sabinus took, and in silence the two men embraced. Crispus received the deed upon his knees and drew away, putting it within his tunic; and then Sabinus, while Alexamenos followed close behind him, went round the table towards Julia.

"Fare thee well," he said. "Some day thou'lt know who loved thee best."

Julia stared up at him in a frightened way. She had sat motionless with Domitian's scroll in her hand. Now her eyes dropped before her husband's gaze, and she answered hurriedly,—

"Oh, cease thy sentiment! Thou art unnerved, Sabinus. 'Tis but some freak of Domitian's. Thou'lt be back to-morrow."

"To-morrow!" he repeated. "Who can count upon to-morrow! Yet never wish I to return, Julia, till thou wilt welcome me."

He bent nearer to her uncertainly, holding out his hand as if he would have taken hers, but Julia shrank from him.

"Go! go!" she cried. "Go, if thou must. I—I am not well. This play-acting doth upset me."

And, in truth, she looked faint as she sank against the back of her chair.

Sabinus still held out his hands, but, seeing that she made no movement towards him, dropped them, and said sadly, "Fare thee well, Julia." Then, looking from her, he became aware of Nyria, who stood behind her mistress, sobbing bitterly. He put his hand gently upon her bowed head.

"Take courage, little maid," he said. "The gods send no trial without the strength to bear it. I would that I had bethought me of thy freedom, Nyria," and he spoke to his wife once more.

"Julia, wilt thou grant me one last request?"

"What is it?" she murmured pettishly behind the folds of the handkerchief which she was stuffing into her mouth. She seemed to be on the verge of hysterics.

"Wilt thou give Nyria her freedom? I ask it of thee."

Julia, glancing up at him, for a moment appeared inclined to accede. Nyria's heart beat high with hope. But Julia answered sulkily,—

"I promise naught. I'll think of it."

Sabinus gave a long look at her, and then at Nyria.

"The gods will protect thee, child," he said. "For they are gods not only of the rich and free, but also of the poor and slaves."

Nyria stooped down at his feet and wildly kissed the border of his robe. Then, even as she fancied that his hand still rested on her head, Sabinus was gone.

XXIII

NYRIA ran out among the other slaves, many of whom realised that they gazed for the last time upon their beloved master. The great atrium seemed full of armed men, who were drawn into line below the fountain, which played on musically from the beak of the divine swan over the marble limbs of Leda. There were four quaternions of soldiers—a goodly escort. Sabinus, as he entered their ranks, cried but one word,—

"Farewell!"

The Prætorians closed in quickly, and saluted with their short lances—no imperial parade this—and Alexamenos gave the word of command. Thus went Sabinus forth from his house. He marched between the files of soldiers, and he turned not, nor looked back, for his face was fixed as the face of one who beheld that which others might not see.

When he had gone and the tramp of the quaternions became more and more muffled, the slaves still stood about the atrium, some weeping, but for the most part in awe-stricken silence. Presently Julia's voice sounded from the doorway of the dining-room.

"Where went those dogs?" she shouted. "Idle gapers! what is it ye would see? Hath no mandate from Cæsar ever before come to this house?"

And at that some of them shuddered, for never before had there come such a mandate as this.

Nyria ran back at Julia's call, and Julia struck her sharply over the mouth with her fan, crying, "A pretty thing, truly, to grant freedom to such as thou, who dost but stare about thee for some new thing to idle over." The blood spurted from Nyria's lips, for the fan was of carved ivory and had cut deeply. But she stanched the bleeding as best she could, and took her place again behind Julia's chair, while the guests settled themselves anew and the stewards went on serving—hurriedly pouring the wine and handing the fruit, for it was near the end of the meal. Julia drank and talked freely, but her voice faltered at times and her laugh was not easy.

The guests for the most part responded to her sallies, but none spoke of Sabinus. Only Plinius, usually so urbane and self-possessed, appeared at a loss how to comport himself. His place was at Julia's end of the table, and at first he hesitated to sit down, and when he did so, half rose again, and took up and fidgeted with the pearl and silver knife set for fruit as though he hardly knew what he was doing. Vibius filled his cup and he drank off the strong wine almost at a gulp; then when Julia rallied him upon his silence he drew himself to his feet and made her a courtly bow.

"I pray thee, have me excused, Julia," he said, and without further apology prepared to leave the table.

Julia looked at him, flushing angrily, but the eyes of Plinius were fixed upon her in something so like scorn that her own fell before them; and he, throwing his toga over his arm, bowed again, and left the room.

Crispus attended him to the atrium, and Plinius, recognising the man, turned there and spoke to him.

"So thou art the fellow who hath just been freed?" he said.

"Yes, lord," answered Crispus, with an obeisance. "My freedom was promised me long since, and Sabinus hath never failed of his word."

Plinius sighed heavily. "We shall not see his like again," he said, and Crispus bowed in silence. "What art thou called?" asked Plinius, "and what dost thou seek to do with thyself?"

"Crispus Sabinus is my name," replied Crispus. "I am training in the school to be a gladiator."

Plinius looked thoughtful and shook his head.

"'Tis a pity that good men should make sport for evil ones in the arena," he said. "They are ill-advised, friend Crispus, who are tempted by the gladiator's spear and net. Deeds of prowess are done, no doubt, in the amphitheatre, but to what end?"

"To the end we all must reach, lord," answered Crispus; "and if a man can make a death that is well in the eyes of the world, 'tis surely something."

"So some men say," returned Plinius, "yet I trow the gods laugh." Crispus arranged his toga for him, and asked, "Shall I call thy litter?"

"Of thy courtesy, yes, friend," Plinius answered, with a smile, as if to remind the freedman that he might not now ask of him a slave's service.

"'Tis my pleasure, lord," replied Crispus, equally courteous. "But wilt thou not await the mimes? Julia hath as usual some fine entertainers."

Plinius shook his head. "This is no longer a house for honest men to visit in. Seeing that trouble hath befallen the master and host, it ill befits his guests to remain and laugh at the pranks of mimes."

Crispus made no reply, except to bow his head mournfully, and went out to call the litter.

"Thou wilt soon be going hence thyself, good friend, wilt thou not?" said Plinius as he stepped into it. "Well can I imagine that one would serve Sabinus for love, but to remain in the house whence he hath been driven out is no part, I take it, for a loyal servant."

"Nay, lord," Crispus answered. "Nevertheless, I would remain long enough to see whether Sabinus doth return."

"Sabinus will not return," said Plinius, gravely. "Thou and I, friend Crispus, will some day follow him whither he hath gone, but the gods grant it may be by another road."

So saying he waved his hand, and was borne off, the torch-men preceding him, and Crispus went sadly back to the atrium. It was on the morrow that Crispus told Nyria what Plinius had said, when they found opportunity to talk and to put together such bits of information as they had gathered concerning Sabinus. All the slaves were gleaning what they could that might throw light upon his fate, for a household ruled over by Julia alone was no pleasant prospect. But there was little to be learned, though Crispus went down into the city and made all inquiries possible. Such doings were always veiled in mystery, and no public announcement was ever given till notice had been read in the Senate that a traitor had paid the due penalty for his offence. This, Crispus said, would be the first definite news they should get of Sabinus.

Thanna's anxiety about her master took the form of assiduous attention to Julia. For Thanna guessed that Sabinus's disgrace was but the prelude to Julia's elevation. Now, were Julia translated to the Palatine, she would in all probability sell some of her slaves, and Thanna had no desire to serve a lesser lady. Therefore she affected immense deference and devotion to Julia, even overcoming her antipathy to folks who were sick and sorry, for Julia was neither well nor cheerful, and became more and more peevish and uncertain of humour as the days went by without bringing her any comforting assurance from Domitian. Cæsar came not near the house, deeming that it would go against him were he to visit too hastily the wife of one whom he had condemned as a traitor. But Julia did not understand his policy, nor was she able to control her impatience. Messenger after messenger she despatched to the Palatine without effect, till at last Domitian himself sent her a scroll which so enraged her that, after reading it, she flung it from her and did not inquire for it further. Thanna secreted the scroll, and its contents soon ran through the slaves' court and roused a good deal of speculation. Domitian, it appeared, had rebuked Julia severely, bidding her be patient and learn that there were fitting times and seasons for Cæsar's visits, and that this was not one of them. The whole tone of the letter was not calculated to sweeten Julia's temper, for in it Domitian showed her plainly that he was the Emperor and she merely the woman he chose to favour. And

Julia had already discovered that, highly susceptible to her personal influence, Domitian was much less easy to manage when they were apart.

One day Nyria, being sent on an errand into the city, contrived to call on Stephanus, hoping that he might have gathered information about Sabinus; and while she was talking to him the Domina Domitilla came—not in her litter, but walking, unattended save by a handmaiden. Stephanus hastened, bowing low, to welcome her, and gave the handmaiden a seat at the door, while Domitilla went with him to the inner room behind the shop. Nyria would have withdrawn, but Domitilla stayed her, and began questioning Nyria concerning her master. Domitilla spoke with much feeling.

"It seems that the Christians are not the only ones to suffer in this most unchristian city," she said. "But though ill beset Sabinus, so that his place here may see him no more, still his soul shall not suffer condemnation, for he hath served truth and goodness, though he called them by the names of false gods, and in his sore strait the Master whom he knew not will surely uphold him."

Nyria stood with face downcast, not knowing how she should reply, and Domitilla went on kindly,—

"Thou standest in need of comfort thyself, child, as do we all in these days of darkness and sorrow. Wilt come with me, Nyria, and I will take thee where thou shalt find light and solace for thy soul?"

Nyria looked up at her wonderingly, but Stephanus broke in, "Thou knowest, Domina, that the paths in which thou and Flavius Clemens walk are beset with thorns."

"Ah! friend Stephanus, the Lord give thee greater faith," she answered. "At times like this, when dark deeds of terror are rife, then verily do men and women need the Light which alone can lighten the world."

Nyria wondered what Domitilla could mean, but Stephanus shook his head and answered,—

"Thou art gracious, Domina; and I would that Nyria were like thee in all things—save only this."

"Thou too, Stephanus, shalt be one of us some day," said Domitilla. "Haply the hand of this little maid shall lead thee." Then, rising, she drew her palla round her, folding it crosswise about her throat, and looking earnestly at Nyria, said, "Thou art fair, child, and young, and in thy youth and fairness thou shouldst give thyself to Him who died for thee, for 'tis the young and the fair that we desire to be the first-fruits of our harvest to the Lord."

At these words Stephanus put out his hand and drew Nyria to him, not loosing his hold even when he went with Domitilla to the door and bowed her on her way. When she had gone he looked at the girl passionately, and cried,—

"Of a truth, Nyria, thou art the first-fruits of my heart. But if this God demandeth such as thee to be sacrificed unto Him, then is He no better than the gods of Greece and Rome, who open their rapacious maws for all they can obtain." He went back to the inner room, but Nyria followed, asking him,—

"Where is it that the Lady Domitilla wished to take me?"

Stephanus appeared to be much occupied at the moment and did not reply. Then suddenly he said gruffly,—

"How should I know? Thou art over-curious, Nyria. It ill beseemeth a maid to busy herself thus over the sayings of any chance lady that doth come by. Things had like to have gone better with thee if thou hadst wasted less time and thought upon Valeria."

Nyria opened her eyes wide, surprised at his tone.

"But, Stephanus, thou canst have naught ill to say of the Domina Domitilla, for thou dost love and serve her."

"Ay, none better," he replied. "But *thou* needst not, Nyria."

"Nay, Stephanus! She did address me kindly, and I would learn whereof she spoke, for she said that she would lead me where I should find comfort for my soul. And these are troublous times, in truth, and one needs comfort," Nyria added wistfully. Stephanus, who had been listening, suddenly came round towards her with arms outstretched.

"Here is comfort," he said. "Here, child, in my heart is more of rest and solace for thee than thou wilt find elsewhere."

Nyria put her hands in his to avoid the clasp of his arms.

"Ay, that I know right well. Nevertheless, methought 'twas the service of that greatest God of all, of whom Clementus spoke, that the Lady Domitilla meant; were that so, I would beseech her that she'd lead me to Him."

Stephanus's face darkened.

"Be assured there is no comfort in the service of any god, Greek or Roman," he said roughly, "or even such as Him whom the Domina Domitilla doth serve."

"Ah! then 'tis true—she hath indeed her own most favoured god!" exclaimed Nyria.

Stephanus looked intently in the girl's face before he answered her, and then he spoke jerkily.

"'Tis not the part of a faithful servitor to betray his mistress's secrets. But seeing that Domitilla told thee half as much herself, and seeing that thou art loyal and that I feel to thee as though thou wert myself, I'll tell thee, Nyria. Canst keep thy lips closed upon this matter?"

She nodded. "Thou knowest Nyria. Trust me."

"Ay, there's naught with which I would not trust thee," he said, and kissed her fondly. Then, keeping his lips to her ear, he whispered, "The Lady Domitilla is a Christian."

"Verily—one of that strange sect?" cried Nyria.

"Yea, verily. Now be satisfied, and ask no more."

"Nay! but if it be *that* which bringeth so beautiful a peace into her face, why shouldst thou forbid me to question, Stephanus, since I, too, desire peace?"

"The creed of the Christians is not for such as thee. There's too much danger in it for the poor and lowly-placed. Leave it to such as are strong enough to protect themselves."

"But I have heard said that 'tis best fitted for the poor and lowly-placed, and that for them 'twas first taught," she urged. "Oh, Stephanus! long have I desired to learn more of this faith—ever since I met Clementus on the hill."

"Him they call the bishop—ay," answered Stephanus. "A goodly man without doubt—one that both Clemens and Domitilla greatly favour—seeing that they desired to charge him with the training of their sons." To turn Nyria's thoughts, the goldsmith went on talking of the two boys, Vespasian and Domitian, whom Cæsar had adopted and given over to Quintillian to educate. "Well will it be for Rome," he said, "when the sons of Clemens and Domitilla rule the Empire, for children of so good a mother cannot be aught but good themselves."

Nyria drew closer to her friend coaxingly.

"I too would be good, Stephanus, and I love the Lady Domitilla," she said. "Wilt thou not take me whither she would have me go?"

"Nay, I'll not lead thee to what may prove thy destruction," he answered. "Domitilla is a great lady and may do as she will. Thou art but a little slave-girl whom Stephanus can only protect by such means as lie in his power."

"Hast thou ever been to that Christian place of worship thyself, Stephanus?" she asked.

"Now I'll have no more of these questions, Nyria," he replied, holding her to him.

"I see thou dost not care for me, Stephanus," retorted Nyria, tearfully, drawing herself away.

He growled and eyed her ruefully. "Thou art the light of mine eyes," he broke forth, "the one true goddess of my soul. If the law of Rome or of the old Greek faith should bid Stephanus worship Nyria, that would he do right willingly, though men say he bends the knee to neither god nor man. And yet thou sayest that he doth not care for thee. Thou *knowest* that he careth for thee, Nyria. Thou dost ill requite his service with such speech."

"Nay, I meant no harm, Stephanus," she said penitently, dismayed at the storm she had aroused. He put his arms around her again.

"Wilt thou be my wife, Nyria?" he cried. "Often have I asked thee that question. Say 'Yes' to it and then will I answer whatsoever thou dost ask of me."

"If thou wouldst bargain, Stephanus, I'll go elsewhere with mine inquiries. We have talked enough of marriage."

"Not enough it seems to bring us to the temple steps. 'Twere wiser to talk less and to get ourselves made one."

"Marriage is not for me," said Nyria, decidedly. "I have no wish to be wed. My chief desire just now is to find out whither Domitilla would have taken me, and to whom."

She said no more, but began to arrange in a basket some small packages she carried, while Stephanus went to the door and stood looking out with his back towards her. Presently he turned round.

"Thou wouldst beguile even Cerberus," he said. "If I do favour thy request, Nyria, wilt thou then look more kindly on my suit?"

Nyria smiled at him, well pleased, but shook her head. "I make no pledge, Stephanus. For I never break my word, and therefore will I not bind myself."

"Things of air and sunshine cannot be bound," he said. "Methinks thou art verily some white fairy of the hills or a spirit such as they that do haunt the temples. Thou'rt no human maid, Nyria. Nevertheless, I'll trust thee, for I am liker to win thy favour if I serve than if I deny thee. Thou canst not be hard-hearted long."

Then he gruffly promised that he would see the Lady Domitilla, and, if it were her pleasure, would meet Nyria that evening upon the steps leading from Julia's house to the foot of the Aventine, and would take her then whither Domitilla should direct.

When Nyria reached home Æmilia met her outside the loggia and told her that Julia had sent an imperative summons to Phyllis, Domitian's nurse, who had therefore come down from the Palace and was now with Julia. Phyllis did not often visit the house, and had obeyed Julia's mandate on this occasion seemingly against her will. Æmilia described her as having the air of a mourner and looking sad and perturbed. It was not difficult to guess the reason of the summons, for Julia hoped, no doubt, to learn through Phyllis something of Domitian's mind. Julia was worrying herself into a fever, said Æmilia, and had taken to her couch, where she lay, none knowing whether she was feigning sickness so that word of it might reach Cæsar and perhaps bring him hither, or whether she were really in bad case. Nyria sat down with Æmilia on the steps of the loggia, over which the westering sun was shining, and they talked on the matter in low tones.

"Mayhap Phyllis will prove a better medicine for her than Euphena's potions," said Nyria.

"I care not to speak ill of Euphena," said Æmilia, glancing round to be sure none else were listening, "but it doth mistrust me that she should give so many potions to Julia, whereby she seemeth not to mend."

"Say naught against Euphena," whispered Nyria. "She doth make me suffer when I so much as think ill of her. But what harm can these potions be? Euphena purchaseth them of Stephanus. He is not like to sell her aught that might do mischief."

"Nay, she doth concoct them herself," answered Æmilia. "Methinks they are no bought drugs, but stewed berries she hath gathered, and of which she alone knoweth the secret."

"None can tell," murmured Nyria. "But it would profit her naught to serve Julia ill."

"Hush thee," said Æmilia, softly. "Here she cometh," and at that moment they saw Euphena prowling round the corner. Her head was bent forward, and she had a searching look in her eyes. Drawing near to the door of Julia's room, she peered through the curtains, then hearing voices came back to where the two sat.

"Whom hath Julia with her?" she asked.

"'Tis Phyllis," answered Æmilia. "Didst thou not see her bearers?"

Euphena laughed maliciously. "The day will come," she said, "when Phyllis—ay, and Julia herself, would gladly enough set foot to earth if they could. Why should they be borne, forsooth, when I must needs stagger along as best I can?"

She unfolded her blanket, which she carried across her back, and spreading it over her, sat down on the steps. None of them spoke. Presently Euphena turned round, drawing her thin lips back from the gums, so that her two black fangs gave her the look of a hungry animal. "What gentle thoughts do occupy your brains, my dainty ladies? Ye are cheerful company," she said.

"We look to thee for cheering, Euphena," replied Æmilia, with a deprecatory laugh.

"Ay, verily, I will cheer ye. . . . I will cheer ye with gay doings. Ye shall see as fine a funeral pageant as ever ye did set eyes on. Prepare ye for the passing of this great one to the realm of shades, so that, with all right reverence, as beseemeth her ancestry, ye may bid her farewell and a lucky journey."

Æmilia shivered.

"So she hath sent for Phyllis," said Euphena, jerking her head towards Julia's room. "Much comfort may Phyllis bring. But 'tis ever so," she mumbled. "The minds of those that near their end do cling to their beginnings."

"Thou art taking good care of Julia, art thou not, Euphena?" Æmilia asked anxiously.

Euphena's laugh was like the rattle of uncooked peas in a pan.

"Oh, ay! Am I not the servant of the gods, whose pleasure it is that Julia shall be well tended? Fear not. She shall lack for naught. Right merrily shall she be sped upon her way."

"I scarce like thy talk, Euphena," said Æmilia, diffidently. "Dost mean that Julia is sick unto death?" And then, at a little sound behind, she stopped, and turned to see Phyllis standing close by outside Julia's doorway.

Phyllis held her veil half before her face, as though the lowering sun dazzled her. It was a dark veil, and her robes were dark also, so that, as Æmilia had said, her appearance was like that of a mourner. She looked down upon the women in an agitated way. Euphena, in her orange bodice and brown petticoat, with the striped blanket falling from her lean shoulders, raised herself slowly and glared at the newcomer.

"Hast seen thy nursling?" she asked. "A beauty, is she not? She'll make a handsome corpse."

Phyllis nervously tightened her veil. She took no notice of Euphena, but asked Æmilia, with all the dignity she could command, though in a voice that vainly strove to be calm,—

"What saidst thou?—That the most noble Julia was sick unto death? Such words are ill-omened, and might, perchance, but for the mercy of the gods, bring their own fulfilment. Yet, by the blessing of Æsculapius, thy lady doth seem more at ease. Pray Jove she may live to wear the robes of her desire, and to rule many years over those who are dirt beneath her feet!"

"A fine saying indeed!" screamed Euphena, in derisive anger. "We are better born than Julia! Dost hear, thou daughter of a small wool-merchant? Ay, better born, verily, are we. Hast not yet learned that many a princess doth serve in bonds? One yonder" —she thrust her hand at Nyria, who had risen, terrified, to her feet— "poor fool of a babe, who will walk blindfold into the snare that Destiny hath spread for her. And one here"—she struck her withered breast—"the grand-daughter of great Candace, before whom thou shouldst abase thyself."

"Nay, I meant not to offend," said Phyllis, cowering before the force and fire in Euphena's voice and eyes. "But such talk is not fitting so near the presence of the divine Julia."

"The divine Julia!" screamed Euphena. "Have done with such false tales, thou life-long deceiver. Who took the babe and swore to Titus she was putting into his arms the daughter of his own loins? Ay, and who paid the dirty wretch that stole about the Palace, and had naught of this world's goods to serve him save his comely visage, which he ne'er learned to wash till she, who should have been Augusta, did look on him with favouring eyes?"

Now Euphena's screaming brought a bevy along from the slaves' court. First Thanna came, twisting up her hair, which she had been washing and drying—and as she ran, crying over her shoulder to those behind,—

"Hither! hither! Haste! who would hear Euphena hold her own? . . . What shall we lay on Euphena? . . . Some may back Phyllis, but for myself I stand up for the honour of the family. . . . Thy tongue is sharp, Euphena. . . . Stab her with it. . . . See thou dost make marks, Euphena. . . . Again! . . . again! . . . Give her somewhat that shall be hard of digestion . . ."

Meanwhile, the combatants faced each other. Phyllis, stung to feeble retort, was trying helplessly to silence her assailant, and then vainly appealing to the throng of slaves, who picked up Thanna's jests and threw in laughing comments.

"Hush! hush! I cannot stay to hear such insults," Phyllis cried at last. "Will no one call my bearers?"

But none went, and all seemed to have forgotten that the tumult might rouse Julia.

Euphena squared herself, two yellow flames leaping from her eyes, and her two fangs gleaming. She tore her bodice open and exposed her dusky, shrivelled breasts, yelling fiercely,—

"Ho! Thou art proud of thy nursling, thou rearer of monsters. I, too, had a babe—lawful seed of mine own spouse, and no spawn of the city's scum. And lo! that she-wolf thou didst rear slew my nursling, for by her commands was I put to such labour that the milk dried up in these breasts, and I had none to give my little babe. That monster of thine—wallowing in the plenty of her ill-gotten riches—did refuse me a coin to provide milk for my starving child—mine own offspring, untainted by sin, of pure blood and royal descent. Oh! thinkest thou, wretched wheedler, who would seat on Cæsar's throne this offspring of a scavenger—this wanton, who fleeth the embraces of her rightful lord to riot in gaudy lust—thinkest thou that I, Euphena, Libyan princess—will e'er forget how thy tigress sold away from me my spouse, and ordered my babe's body to be thrown upon the dustman's cart and carried with other refuse—so she said—without the city? Nay! nay!" shrieked Euphena, "Julia shall have the royal funeral that was denied my babe. But while my little one doth lie in peace, awaiting the queenly state another life shall bring her, thou, Shade of Julia! shalt wander unresting, having nowhere to lay thine head, which did aspire to Cæsar's crown, and finding no companion but him from whom, in horror and remorse, thou wouldst escape, till even he whose love drew him to thy side shall leave thee to that desolation which is the direst punishment of evil-doers."

Phyllis had shrunk back trembling while Euphena raged, and silence had fallen even upon the troop of jeering slaves, when suddenly all eyes turned towards the doorway, where, wrapped in an embroidered robe, tall, large and flushed, clutching at the wall for support, stood Julia.

"What mean these unseemly sounds?" she cried. "How dare ye, sweepings of the earth, disturb my rest?"

Phyllis turned to her and held out her hands, shaking with agitation, for she could not speak. Euphena, her whole manner and bearing changed, crept whining to Julia's feet.

"Well mayest thou ask, oh! Most Noble, what these unseemly

sounds do mean. Here's Phyllis—Phyllis, who is so devoted to thee, divine Julia, yet who hath in strange unwisdom been exclaiming at thy condition—wondering what ill thou hast done that thus the gods do visit thee with so much sorrow, seeing that thy dear lord, Sabinus, hath been taken from thee, and that thou art sick—very sick—ay, sick, she said—sick unto death. Did not she say—*sick unto death?*" said Euphena, looking round upon them all, and clinging the while to her mistress's robe. But none answered her.

Julia looked down upon her silently, then tried to draw her skirts away.

"Thou hag of hell!" she said slowly, "the gods alone know when thou liest."

"Nay, nay," whimpered Euphena, while Phyllis sobbed dumbly behind her. "Sick unto death—that was the word. Or, at least, meseemed it was the word. If none spoke it, some *thought* it—and thou knowest, Julia, Euphena's mind can read the thoughts of men."

She looked up with her glittering eyes set in their yellow-whites, and again Julia seemed fascinated and silenced before her. The other slaves were drawing back, fearing to be punished if they remained, yet eager to see what would follow.

The Ethiopian went whining on.

"Fair Julia, the wisdom of Euphena tells her that thou art sore disturbed by these sad and unseemly happenings which are like to work thee ill. Get thee to thy couch, gentle Julia—most sweet and stately Julia — and Euphena will come and tend thee. . . . Euphena will sit beside thee, and charm around thee such spirits of succour as shall best serve thee in thy need."

So saying, with leering, up-turned face and coaxing gestures, Euphena guided her mistress back within the doorway. Julia walked as if under a spell, not even the sound of Phyllis's sobbing seemed to rouse her. When she had passed within her chamber, and the doors were securely closed upon her, Euphena came back for a last gibe at Phyllis.

"Oh! thou false hypocrite!" she hissed. "Thou lying nurturer of bloody whelps, Euphena bids thee take her warning, lest a worse evil befall thee than that which already hath come. *Who* mixed the cup for Domitia last night? *And who drank it in her stead?*"

Phyllis gave a piteous moan and drew down her veil over her face, as a man called out,—

"'Tis true enough. The Augusta was nigh poisoned, but ere she took the cup she summoned Phyllis's niece, Lavinia, and commanding her to drink, the maid dropped dead."

There was a horrified murmur in the crowd, but Æmilia, shocked at the scene, signed to her husband, one of the table-stewards, who came up at that moment, and bade him conduct Phyllis to her litter.

XXIV

JULIA was lying upon her couch almost in darkness, for only one lamp had been lighted, and that not near her. She moaned and tossed from side to side, yet seemed to be half sleeping, and on the floor at the foot of her bed squatted Euphena, her hands clasped round her knees, and her eyes fixed in that curious way which made them appear as though they were looking at the tip of her nose.

Nyria, peeping through the doorway, would have withdrawn noiselessly, but Euphena glanced up and signed to her to wait in the ante-chamber.

Presently the old woman came forth softly.

"None are needed to attend Julia to-night," she said, "save Euphena."

"But if Julia be sick thou wilt need help, Euphena," whispered Nyria.

"Nay, child. Go thou, take thy pleasure," replied Euphena, grimly, "if pleasure it be to walk along a path that leads thee to the gates of Hades."

As she spoke Euphena came closer and laid her bony claw upon Nyria's arm, looking up at her intently, for the girl was taller than the bent, shrivelled form of the old woman.

"Thou hast been a good little maid, Nyria," she went on, more gently than usual. "I would fain accord thee thy due. Mayhap Euphena hath seemed over harsh with thee, but 'twas more than flesh and blood could stand to have a strange child thrust upon this bosom bereaved of its own babe. Yet that was Julia's wrong, not thine. Thou'st always been good to Euphena, and in truth thou art made of different stuff from the idle chattering crew who blow with every wind of favour, and will acclaim Cæsar to-day and his successor to-morrow. See now, Nyria, I would save thee, if it be not too late. Go not forth to-night whither thy desire doth lead, and perchance thou shalt escape the doom that is in wait for thee."

Nyria stared at the old woman in doubt and wonder.

"Thou art stiff-necked, Nyria," said the hag, more sorrowfully than in anger. "Have thy will, but when danger doth encompass thee, remember that Euphena would have held thee back."

Euphena moved a pace away, and Nyria, shivering, found her tongue.

"I was but going down the hill, Euphena—" She stopped in confusion.

Euphena picked her up sharply.

"There's no need for thee to tell Euphena that which she hath not asked. By all the stars on high, Nyria, dost think I need to read men's secrets on their lying lips? Thine is plain to me, but matters naught. Go in peace, and may the God thou wouldst serve protect thee."

She pointed her bony finger to the outer door and Nyria went forth. The girl caught up a cloak that she had left outside and hastened through Julia's court down to an entrance from which a long flight of steps led to the public road, skirting the lower slope of the Aventine. At the foot of these steps Stephanus waited, and she ran almost into his arms.

"Say, Nyria," he cried, kissing her, "what hath lent wings to thy feet? Alas, my dear, 'tis not poor Stephanus, I warrant. Thou dost not hasten thus to me."

She laughed and slipped her hand in his, but he felt that she was trembling.

"Hath aught affrighted thee?" he asked.

Nyria did not care to tell him of the old woman's warning, so she only said that Euphena was in one of her strange moods, to which Stephanus replied, "Had Euphena lived in Greece long ago she would have been stretched upon the ground, and left there to see whether the gods would feed and save her. In truth she is an evil thing, and I like her not near thee, Nyria."

But Nyria remembered that Euphena had spoken kindly to her, and answered,—

"She hath strange ways, but so have all wise people. Look at Ascletario, how strange a life he leadeth."

"Ay, but he doeth ill to none, and is ever courteous."

"Euphena doeth no ill. 'Tis but her talk," said Nyria.

"One cannot tell," Stephanus answered. "Ill things are told mayhap of those who deserve it not, while others who work mischief have yet the wit to shut men's mouths upon their deeds."

He fell to silence, and Nyria fancied that he might be thinking of the Christians, of whom it was said that they slew babes and had riotous love-feasts and kept no laws. Yet Stephanus must know the untruth of such reports, seeing that the Lady Domitilla was a Christian. She asked his mind on the matter.

"Thinkest thou if these things were true I'd take thee amongst this people?" he answered harshly. "Nay, Nyria, have more faith in Stephanus. A set of mad fanatics they may be, but peaceful and law-abiding citizens nevertheless. The greatest ill I've heard of them is that some will not bear arms for the State. And in very truth, with such a country to fight for as Rome, which rewardeth only those that be in Cæsar's favour, 'tis no great matter for wonderment that they should refuse to serve her. Moreover," he added, "the Christians pride themselves upon giving back good for evil; and I grant they do that which they avow. I am not with them," he said with a laugh. "For myself, I had rather show a stout pair of fists to one that injured me than I would sit me meekly down and bless him."

"But thou art not a Christian," said Nyria.

"Not I—save in so far that any sect to which my Lady Domitilla doth belong must needs have from me some measure of tolerance. But now that *thou* wouldst join in with them, Nyria—what shall I say?" and he clasped her hand tighter. "Must every Christian be dear to Stephanus for thy sake?"

"Leave me first to judge of them," she laughed. "It seems, Stephanus, that if all Christians be like the Lady Domitilla and the Lord Clementus, then would I fain be one of them, for I'm in sore need of peace."

"Now why," he answered, bending quickly over her. "What wouldst thou have of peace that thou dost not find in the arms of Stephanus? Behold, they are open and aching for thee, desiring only that thou shouldst rest forever within them. What peace had like to be so sweet as this, Nyria?"

"Thou art very dear to me, Stephanus," she replied. "Greatly do I love thee, and, in truth, thine arms are kind to rest in. Nevertheless, it seems to me that 'tis not love like thine I need, but one greater far that shall envelop all my life and lift me to heights of understanding of the which as yet I only dimly reckon."

Stephanus gave a sort of angry grunt. "I know not what to make of thee, Nyria. If thou wert other than thyself I should say that thou hadst set thine affection upon Cæsar and wouldst fain queen it in Rome."

She shuddered. "'Tis no love of Cæsar that I would have," she said. "Thou dost not understand, Stephanus; and how shall I show thee?"

"In truth I know not," he answered gruffly. "I would that thou wert more like ordinary maids, Nyria, with but the simple craving for motherhood and care of husband and home. Then would it be easier for Stephanus to fulfil thy need."

"What can I do, Stephanus?" she answered, distressed. "I made not myself."

He was touched at once by the note of trouble in her voice.

"Thou art a changeling, as I've told thee many times," he said, half laughing and wholly tender again. "Since none kept record of thy parentage, Nyria, perchance thou didst spring from the union of a god with some strange northern woman. For half of thee is not of this earth at all, but seems to find its joy in things ethereal which mortal men do look for only when they be translated to the gods' abode. For mine own part," added Stephanus, "I should not hail the change with over much delight. To me the joys of earth—of sun and wine, good food, prosperity, and, sweeter far, the kisses of mine own wife and babes—were dearer than any bliss Olympus might afford."

Stephanus sighed, and Nyria kept silence, not knowing what to say. They had been going down the steep narrow short cut to the city, and its darkness gave him excuse for holding his arm around her. But now as they got into better-lighted and more populous streets she fidgeted within his clasp and made him loose his arm with a poor attempt at a jest.

"Thou art like a young bird, Nyria, that would try its wings. Some day, mayhap, this little fledgling will fly back to the soft nest of Stephanus's embrace."

"Mayhap," she said. "But let me fly now, Stephanus. All things that have wings desire to fly."

He teased her no more, but she let him hold her hand, as did many a man that of his maid, while they walked, and it was almost needful when they passed through the Lower Forum and among the markets and workmen's haunts in which the crowd was rough, though they skirted the more respectable part of the Suburra. Higher towards the Campus Martius, where inns and places of entertainment fronted the river, the thoroughfare would have been gayer and less decorous, but here they passed along a fairly wide and decently-kept street that ended near the wharves and had high tenement houses and citizens' dwellings, as well as a few shops. There were fewer of these, however, at the other end. This was not a favoured spot, the banks being flat and the Tiber liable to overflow. Nevertheless, there were some solidly-built houses down here, and it was towards these that Stephanus led her.

Only two or three people walked in the same direction, among them the veiled figure of a woman attended by a waiting-maid. This made Nyria suspect that she must be a person of distinction, and when Stephanus quickened his pace she scarcely needed him to tell her, as he did in a low voice, "'Tis the Domina Domitilla."

They followed on her steps, and coming close behind, Stephanus spoke, at which the lady turned and half drew her veil from her face, showing that it was indeed Domitilla.

"Ah, greeting, friend!" she said; "and is this the little maid?"

She put her hand on Nyria's shoulder, and walking at her other side conversed softly with Stephanus till they paused at a tall house—the last but one in the street, where it gave upon a narrow embankment with the dull stream beyond. Domitilla struck in a peculiar way on the door, and it was opened at once by a young slave-boy. Domitilla led Stephanus and Nyria into a room—a poor sort of place that seemed parlour and sleeping-chamber in one, for a bed stood in one corner, and there was a table with a few chairs, while on the further side was another door.

A few minutes later this opened, and there entered a man bearing a lamp, which, as he stood, cast shadows about him. He was tall, with a brown beard tipped with grey sweeping to his chest, and a grey cloak; and when Nyria looked at these she recognised Clementus.

Domitilla went forward and knelt before the bishop, craving his blessing. It seemed strange to Nyria that a lady of high repute in Rome and of noble station should stoop thus before a man—her husband's distant cousin; but she saw that Domitilla greatly reverenced Clementus. Stephanus came forward too, and bowed. Clementus spoke graciously to him. "Ah, friend, welcome! Nevertheless, I would that it were for thine own sake that thou wert here to-night."

Stephanus made a gruff little murmur. He did not wish to be discourteous, that was plain, but 'twas equally plain that he was ill at ease. Domitilla struck in, "I, too, would that were so. It hath been my most earnest prayer that Stephanus—faithful friend as he is, and one with Flavius and myself in all things save this—should join us too in the service of the Lord."

Clementus answered gently,—

"Remember, sister, that the Master said, 'Other sheep I have which are not of this fold.'"

"Yes," returned Domitilla. "But the Master added, 'Them also I must bring that they may be one with me in my kingdom.'"

Stephanus stood silent and awkward.

Clementus came nearer and saluted him in brotherly fashion.

"Whether or not, friend Stephanus, thou art most gladly welcome, since, like one of the Master's own shepherds, thou hast brought a lamb into the fold."

The bishop moved towards Nyria with outstretched hand as though to place it on her head, but Stephanus stepped quickly before him, and at last found his tongue.

"May it please thee, Clementus, Nyria knoweth naught of thy teaching. But the favour of my Lady Domitilla hath pleased and flattered the maid, so that she would give me no peace till I should bring her here, as the Domina did desire. Therefore are we come. Nevertheless, Nyria is no Christian."

Stephanus spoke confusedly and with some sourness, but Clementus looked from him to Nyria, indulgence in his eyes.

"Methinks thou art not wholly justified in that thou sayest, friend. Though Nyria be no Christian, most surely is she one of the Lord's lambs for whom a place hath been prepared. And if she have learned but little of our teaching, yet somewhat she doth certainly know—and of myself likewise." He put out his hand

and took both of Nyria's; and standing so, turned smiling to Stephanus, who answered glumly,—

"Yea, the maid hath told me that thou didst meet her on the hill and speak words of comfort to her when she was sore troubled by a private sorrow. For that I thank thee, Clementus, though had Nyria come to me I would have striven my best to ease her pain," said Stephanus, sadly; and added, "Notwithstanding, Nyria hath no knowledge of thy faith save such as thou didst give her."

"Nyria knoweth more than we suppose, friend," returned Clementus. "For the grace of God is like the dew which cometh upon the fields, and as the dew sinketh into the earth and maketh it bring forth grain, so the heavenly grace doth enter men's hearts, filling them with bounteous refreshment and bringing forth sweet fruit. Nyria, in her wanderings on the hillsides, hath, methinks, been taught by Christ Himself, who is ever with them that are lowly of mind."

Stephanus made no answer beyond an impatient sound in his throat, and walked away, standing with his back towards them, as if deep in thought, while Clementus raised Nyria from her knees, where she had fallen before him, and bade her be seated. He placed himself in a large wooden chair with arms, near to Domitilla, and Nyria drew up a stool to his feet.

"Say, Nyria, wilt thou be a lamb in our little flock?" he asked.

"Ay, if it please thee, lord," she said diffidently.

"We use these terms," he explained, "because the Master used them—He who came down from heaven and entered into flesh for the shepherding of the world, so that by-and-by, in that great day when the Lord's flocks are numbered, they shall be as the sand of the sea, or as the hairs of thy head, Nyria," and he softly stroked her curls. "Yea, even without number shall they be. Now dost thou see, little one, how it is we would fain call all sheep into the fold?"

"I will be a lamb to go within the fold, may it please thee, lord," she answered. "Shew me the door at which to enter."

"Yea, verily, that will I, Nyria. The door is baptism, whereby all thy sins will be washed away, and thou shalt be pure and clean as the wool of some unstained lamb."

At that Stephanus turned round on his heels abruptly, and went towards them.

"May it please thee, lord, the maid prateth nonsense," he cried. "Nyria hath never committed sin."

"Truly, friend Stephanus, we are all born in sin," said Clementus, "Nyria as well as the vilest evil-doer."

Stephanus again made that rough sound in his throat, but

seemed to find no words, and Clementus went on speaking to the girl.

"Nevertheless, Nyria desireth not to sin—of that I am sure, and by the merit of Him who died for her she shall sin no more."

Stephanus looked at her with a baffled expression in his eyes, but, seeing she took no heed of him, turned away. Nyria's eyes were fixed on Clementus. She listened eagerly, not quite comprehending his meaning, but feeling that his words sank into her soul, even as he had described that the dew penetrated dry ground.

"Lord, who was it that died for me?" she asked.

Clementus gazed down at her tenderly, and again stroked her hair.

"'Twas in very truth the Son of God Himself," he said. "He who cast from Him His glorious estate, and came down to dwell among men, living as the poorest, and suffering as the most sorrowful, He is the Good Shepherd who gave His life for His sheep."

"But wherefore did He die?" asked Nyria. "Did men sacrifice Him to other gods? And if He was indeed God, could He not save Himself?"

"Thou dost echo the cry which hath rung many a time," said Clementus. "He was indeed God, yet He chose to sacrifice Himself at the hands of men, that through His death we might inherit eternal life."

This seemed most strange and wonderful to Nyria.

"Eternal life!" she repeated. "Life in the sunshine! Life without pain—without beatings—without sorrow! Life for those who suffer, in which their sufferings shall cease? Say, lord, dost thou mean such life as this?"

"Yea, truly, Nyria, such life do I mean. For even if pain and sorrow come upon us here, the Lord Himself hath suffered them and will help His children to endure. And though death overcome this body, and worms eat this flesh, yet shall the eyes of thy soul behold thy Redeemer ascended unto the right hand of His Father, where all power and dominion are His."

As Clementus spoke Stephanus made a quick movement towards Nyria, but she looked at him rebukingly.

"Peace, I pray thee, Stephanus," she said. "Thou canst not talk here, for no god of whom thou hast told me hath done so great a thing as this. 'Tis a stranger, sweeter story than any I ever heard." Stephanus was silenced, and Nyria turned eagerly to Clementus.

"Thou knowest, lord," she said, "the service of a little slave can be but of small account, yet is Nyria faithful, and fain would serve this Shepherd-God with all her heart."

Clementus smiled at Domitilla.

"Verily, out of the mouth of babes He hath perfected praise.

It seems to me that here we have one who may be received without delay."

"I will be her sponsor," said Domitilla. "Flavius and I will present her—unless, indeed, thou wert thinking of immediate baptism, Clementus?"

At these words Stephanus seemed as if he could contain himself no longer. He had been pacing to and fro in the small room, and now he stopped and faced Domitilla, addressing her beseechingly.

"Domina! may it please thee and the Lord Clementus," he said, "I pray thee give the maid time. Nyria knoweth naught of this ceremony of baptism. And to permit an ignorant child to pledge herself at the shrine of a strange deity for purposes of which she hath not learned, is surely no better than that most savage custom in old-time temples of sacrificing innocent maidens to appease the wrath of lustful gods."

"Stephanus speaketh truly," interposed Clementus, as Domitilla was about to answer him. "Such, friend, was not mine intention. Notwithstanding, I grieve to see in thee this spirit of opposition to the maid's chance of gaining eternal life. It is not within thy power to withhold her when the Master calleth. Yet, seeing that Nyria hath long looked to thee for council, and is dear to thine heart, 'twould be better for the maid, and kinder, if thou couldst bring thyself to regard the matter through her eyes instead of by the light of thine own maimed understanding."

"Craving thy leave, lord," replied Stephanus, "'tis because the maid is dear to me that I like not to see her thus sacrificed. For myself, I am a plain fellow, and have had small dealings with gods of any kind, saving Hermes, upon whom, by custom, one doth call in business. Yet meseems there's none of them—Greek, Roman or Christian—that can be of much help to man or maid in their way through life."

Clementus put out his hand as if to stay Stephanus's speech.

"Blaspheme not, friend," he answered, though in mild accents. "Say what thou willest of Roman gods, or of those of thine own country, but before me at least thou mayest not speak ill of the Master whom I serve."

"Nay, that I would not do, out of courtesy to thee, Clementus, and respect to my Lady Domitilla. Nevertheless, what the maid needs for comfort and guidance is a strong arm to shield her and a loving heart wherein she may abide."

"No arm is so strong, nor heart so loving, as that of Him whom we call Master," said Clementus. "Thou canst safely trust Nyria in His keeping."

But Stephanus shook his head.

"Sir, I know naught of the Christians' God, nor would I listen to the idle tales which designate His worship as fouler and more unseemly than the vilest ancient rites. Enough for me that my Lady

Domitilla is a Christian. 'Tis not for that I would prevent the maid from being one of ye. But thou knowest, lord, what terrible fate hath overtaken certain Christians, and who can say it may not fall on others? Moreover, Nyria is made of stauncher stuff than most maids, and if she pledgeth herself to worship this unknown God, neither Greek, nor Roman, nor Cæsar himself could turn her from Him."

Clementus smiled in approving fashion.

"Verily, friend, I feel that Nyria is of the nature we need amongst us. Such faithful service should be given to God and not to man."

The baffled look returned to Stephanus's face, and his eyes sought Nyria's pleadingly, but she was gazing up at Clementus.

"Oh, my lord!" she cried, "heed not Stephanus. 'Tis because he careth thus that he feareth for me. But I would have thee know, lord, that I can bear pain, and if aught of suffering befall Nyria for the Master's sake, she hath strength to endure."

"I believe thee, child," said Clementus. "And by the strength that shall be added unto thee, Nyria, thou shalt bravely sustain the faith. For though thou art as a lamb in the midst of wolves, the Shepherd Himself has said, 'Let not the lambs fear the wolves though they rend them in pieces, for the wolves can only destroy their flesh, but I will save their souls alive.' Wherefore, Nyria, fear nothing, for by water and by blood Christ shall make thee His own. When the waters of baptism have flowed over thy head, then shalt thou be received into His fold; and if He call for a mingling of thy blood with His, rest assured that thou too shalt go where He is gone, for that blood-stained portal is the further door that leadeth unto eternal life."

Then, seeing that Stephanus stood sad and silent, Clementus turned to him.

"Nyria's heart is wholly the Master's," he said, "therefore it is of small account how soon she be signed with His sign. Take back the maid with thee, Stephanus, and bring her again if thou wilt—or bring her not if thou dost so desire. It matters not, for the Lord knoweth them that are His. When His voice doth call in the wilderness of the world, they that hear shall answer Him. Then must all other voices needs be silent."

Stephanus said nothing, but stepping forward he took Nyria by the shoulder rather roughly, and pulled her to her feet, she clinging the while to Clementus.

"Send me not away from thy presence, lord," she implored.

"Nay, Nyria, 'twould avail naught, since of a certainty thou wouldst seek the Master even as Mary followed Him who was her heart's dearest. Assuredly I will see thee again, but go now, for I would talk with the Lady Domitilla."

Clementus laid his hands on her head and blessed her, but

Domitilla kissed the girl's forehead. Then Nyria went out, and Stephanus behind her.

On the way home Stephanus talked much in a surly way, but Nyria scarcely answered him, for with Clementus's blessing there had come to her so great a peace that she dreaded lest any words should drag forth from her breast the heavenly assurance which now lay within it. When they reached the narrow alley leading up to the Aventine, at which their ways naturally parted, she would have had Stephanus turn along the Forum into his shop, while she sped alone to the steps of Julia's gate. But he was angry at the suggestion.

"Art thou, then, going to shelve me, Nyria?" he said. "Wilt thou thrust thine old friend on one side for this new fancy? Truly, I thought better of thy constancy."

At last they came to the flight of steps leading to Julia's courtyard, and there he caught her in his arms and strained her to his breast.

"Am I to lose thee, Nyria? Is this new sect to snatch from me my best treasure?"

She laid her head upon his shoulder.

"I go not away from thee, Stephanus," she said, "even though I try to follow Him of whom Clementus spoke. Mayhap thou wilt some day follow Him too."

"Nay, nay," Stephanus answered gruffly. "I have humoured thy every whim, Nyria, till it seems to me that I am but a fool for my pains; but I'll not follow after thee in this mad chase."

Thus, for Stephanus's sake, she felt a little sorrowful, but the peace within her made all seem well. From Julia's apartments she saw a feeble glimmer through the windows of which the curtains were still undrawn. She went on round the end of the house, past the whipping-post, to the slaves' court. There she stood at the door of Euphena's hut, and looked back at the great villa, which rose up very black, and very white—white where the starlight struck any projecting wall of marble, and black in the shadow of pillared recess and loggia.

The night was clear, and Nyria raised her eyes to the sky, which was full of stars. She was thinking of what Clementus had told her—how the Son of God had come down from His kingdom above to suffer death among men. Then she wondered if all the heavens were paved with silver and gold, and if those glittering stars that she beheld were bits of the bright flooring shining through. She remembered that Clementus had said she should see Him there one day, at the right hand of His Father, and she yearned to put up prayer unto Him whom she had chosen to be her God. She had no altar, and no flowers, and no offering to bring; but, standing there alone in the light of the stars, she folded her hands upon her breast, and in a hushed voice said,—

"Lord! teach me to pray."

XXV

At the first glimmer of dawn the next morning Nyria, wrapped in her blanket, went out into the court to get some water from the fountain, when Crispus passed her with his own blanket folded about his shoulders. She asked him if he were going to the Gladiatorial School.

"Not yet," he said. "The school doth not open for another hour or more. I go to gather news of Sabinus, if that be possible."

"Hast heard aught of him?" she asked.

"Naught, save that he is still in prison and doth stand in peril."

"Oh! 'tis hard," cried Nyria, "that with so many to serve him none should be able to stir a finger on his behalf!"

Crispus took his hand from under his blanket, and Nyria saw him clench his fist, the veins standing out.

"By all these vaunted gods and goddesses," he cried—"these heartless powers who gambol with the griefs of poor mankind—and especially by those that favour vengeance—I swear that if one hair of Sabinus's head be hurt I will extort payment for the injury—ay, with the life of him who caused the wrong, no matter how long this retribution be delayed."

So saying, Crispus passed through the gate.

The thought came to Nyria that his vow was not such as Clementus would have approved. "For," said she to herself, "if the Master of the Christians, who is now my Master also, did endure suffering at the hands of men, and took no vengeance for it, then surely ought we to do the same." But since it was for redress of Sabinus's wrong, and not his own, that Crispus would exact payment, perchance it might not be counted against him.

Nyria went back with the water to the hut and washed and dressed herself, and then she hastened to Julia's door. There was silence within. Putting off her shoes, the girl crept to the antechamber. Euphena squatted there alone, her eyes fixed in that curious way of hers—the pupils small and bright, and the whites very yellow.

"Hast thou been up all night, Euphena?" Nyria whispered.

The old woman rubbed her eyes vehemently. "I shall have time enough to sleep," she said.

"How fareth Julia?" asked the girl.

"Julia sleepeth," Euphena replied. "Trouble not thyself about Julia. Let her sleep while she may."

"Nay, I grudge not her sleep," said Nyria. "But hark! 'Tis no easy slumber." Julia was moaning distressfully.

"Go—see," said Euphena. Nyria went on tiptoe to the bed-chamber. Julia lay beneath her rich coverlet, with the pale blue and silver hangings at the head of the bed shadowing her. There was a lamp burning close by, but the grey dawn stole in at the window. Julia's eyes were shut, and she appeared to be sleeping, but every now and then she would turn slightly and moan as if in pain.

Nyria went back to the Ethiopian.

"What is wrong with Julia? There is a change upon her face, and I like not the sound of her sleeping."

"Heed her not," said Euphena. "She is but dreaming—as men call it, not knowing what dreams be."

Nyria got herself some food, bringing some also for Euphena. Then she went out again and sat upon the steps of the loggia, waiting till the other women should come. The ghost-like grey of dawn grew lighter, and a pearly tint crept over the sky. The stars had gone, and Nyria wondered what the change was like in heaven when day broke and the dark curtain of night was drawn from above the sleeping earth, giving place to one of rose and blue. From where she sat Nyria could not see the sun rise, but she could watch the reflection of its coming—first a faint, pink, purplish flush upon the livid arch of sky, and then a sudden redness which shot up behind the house, deepening and spreading far overhead, until even the western heaven before her caught the glow and flung it back like flaming banners. It was a stormy sky. As Nyria watched it she could still hear Julia moaning in her room, and longed to fetch her something that might ease her pain. But she knew not what to get, and feared to ask Euphena. Presently Æmilia and Samu came round the corner of the house with their blankets over their heads and shoulders, for the morning was chilly. As they stood talking to Nyria in low voices, suddenly there came a piercing cry from inside the house, and the three, throwing down their blankets, rushed through the ante-rooms to Julia's chamber.

Euphena was there before them, and stood with crossed arms at the foot of Julia's bed looking at her, but she spoke no word. Julia had raised herself to a sitting posture. Her face was flushed and excited, and her eyes, large and round, stared out of her head as if in horror. She shrieked again, and indistinguishable words of panic came from her lips.

Samu hung back, dismayed. Even Æmilia looked frightened. Only Nyria ran to the head of the bed and tried to soothe the distraught woman. At the sound of her voice Julia clung to the girl, almost crushing the bones of Nyria's hand in her frenzied grip. Nyria put her other arm round Julia, for she shook all over and seemed in need of support.

"'Tis Nyria, Most Noble!" cried the girl. "Dost thou not know Nyria?"

A great sweat had broken out all over Julia, soaking her night-robe. The drops stood upon her forehead, and her hands were wringing wet. She grasped the girl's hand tighter, and muttered wildly. But presently she turned to her as if a veil had fallen from her eyes, for there was the light of recognition in them.

"Oh, Nyria, is't thou?" she said. "Oh, I have had such a dreadful dream!"

"Dreams are naught, lady," Nyria answered soothingly. "Lay thee down again and rest."

But Julia would not let herself be lowered, nor would she loose her hold, so Nyria signed to Samu for pillows, and propped her up so that she could see her women round her and know that she was not alone with her spectral dream.

Euphena had been warming some milk at a brazier by the doorway, and now brought it to the couch. Nyria tried to induce Julia to drink it, but she had seen Euphena hand the cup, and waved it angrily aside.

"Nay, I will have naught that that hell-hag hath touched," she cried. "Do thou get me some fresh milk, Nyria, and warm it for me here, where I may see thee do it. But bid Euphena begone."

Nyria looked doubtfully at Euphena, who had moved back to the doorway and was watching all that went on, but who paid no heed to Julia's command. Nyria feared to order her away, and so was forced to leave her there while she fetched the milk.

Euphena kept her eyes fixed on Julia, and took no notice of Nyria as the girl pushed past her and ran hastily out through the courtyard to the sheds, where the new milk was stored. There she filled a fresh basin. But first she threw away the milk that Euphena had given her, and found at the bottom of the cup a white powdery sediment, which roused in her a frightful suspicion that Euphena might, indeed, be bent on poisoning Julia. But as she went back Euphena met her, and laughed, seeing the brimming bowl of fresh milk.

"Thou little fool!" exclaimed the old woman. "Dost think Euphena would risk her own life by depriving Julia of hers? There's no need for that. Euphena is but a servant of the gods, and Julia shall go when the gods call her, not at Euphena's sending."

"Yet, come not in again, Euphena," said Nyria. "Thou seest Julia is affrighted at thee."

Euphena gave a grim chuckle. "I have told Julia that I leave her now, seeing that she needeth me no more. But the hour will come ere long, Nyria, when thou and I shall perform a welcome service for the great Julia, since she who thought to become

Empress of Rome is bidden to the court of a more mighty monarch than even Domitian Cæsar."

Nyria did not answer, but hurried in and warmed the milk, as Julia desired, in a vessel placed on a lamp by her bedside. After she had taken it, Julia seemed to grow easier both in mind and body. But she would not let any of her women, except Euphena, leave her room. She gave them all orders about the doing of one thing and another—the preparing of her robes and of her false tresses, of her jewels, the arrangement of some ornaments for her hair, and the mixing of different perfumes in her bath. But when the time came to rise it was impossible that she could take her bath or be properly robed, for when she tried to put her feet out of bed she was too weak, and sank back upon her pillows again. So the women straightened her bed as she lay in it, and Nyria and Thanna brought sponges and scented water and washed her as best they could. They tired her head also, decking it with the ornaments; and Æmilia, at her command, fetched silken, gold-embroidered wrappers to choose from, and dressed her in the finest, adding the jewels that Julia chose, so that she made a brave show when she was done.

But then she was too tired to move, and when she was lying quiet she showed terror again, moaning and gazing strangely before her. Once she raised herself, and, turning upon a group of women who were standing about the doorway, asked them,—

"Is your master in the house?"

At her question the women glanced at each other and shook their heads, not liking to answer. Then said Julia, with her old imperiousness,—

"Speak—ye dolts, where is your master?"

She fixed Thanna with her eyes and Thanna looked at Nyria, who signed to her to reply, so Thanna stepped forward, quaking.

"The most noble Julia knoweth that at Cæsar's orders our master, Sabinus, was taken hence three nights agone."

"Three nights agone!" Julia repeated and turned on her pillow. Then she asked mutteringly, several times, "Whither did he go? Whither went Sabinus?" But no one answered her.

And as she muttered the fear came on her anew. She started suddenly and clutched at Nyria who was nearest, staring like a madwoman, so that Thanna said afterwards she was glad that it was Nyria who stood there and not she.

"Oh! Nyria, I have had such a dreadful dream," Julia said again, moaning. "But 'twas only a dream, was it not, Nyria? Didst thou not say 'twas naught?"

"Ay! lady—dreams are naught," Nyria repeated soothingly.

But Julia shuddered and went on muttering, "Oh! I have had such a dreadful dream!" while she pulled Nyria closer to her.

"Most Noble, 'tis said that if a dream be told the spell of it is broken," said the girl, thinking to ease her. "Tell Nyria what thou didst dream." Julia hung upon her hand.

"Ay, will it break the spell? Then will I tell thee, Nyria. Methought thy master entered at the door and spake to me. And there was a wound upon his shoulder nigh to the throat, from which the blood spurted . . . And he spake . . . oh! Nyria, he spake . . . " and she fell to fresh shuddering.

"Ay, lady, what spake he?"

Julia went on in a low, harsh murmur. "This he said . . . he said 'I am not come to bid farewell, for, Julia, I'll be here again. When the sun shall hang low in the sky, 'ere yet the night cometh, or the day be gone down upon this deed. Then . . . then . . . ' saith he, 'I'll fetch thee, Julia, and thou shalt go with me whither I be bound. For 'tis lonely crossing the shadows of the river, and the Ferry-man waits . . . ' Ah! Nyria!" and she shrieked aloud. "What meant he? Oh! what meant Sabinus?"

"Most Noble, 'twas but a dream. Did not the Lord Sabinus leave thee then?"

"Ay, he left me, but as he passed he turned and looked from over his bleeding shoulder, and said he, 'At sundown, Julia, will I come.' Now whither went thy master—whither went he?"

"Lady, I know not," faltered Nyria; and Julia looked questioningly at the other women, muttering petulantly, "Whither went he? Will none say?"

All were silent. Then Thanna stepped forward daringly.

"Most Noble, naught hath been heard of Sabinus since three nights agone. Yet cheer thee, lady, for he went at the behest of Cæsar."

But Julia scarcely heeded her.

"Why doth not Domitian come?" she cried. "I would he came to-day. Send messengers to the Palace, Nyria—send two or three, one after the other, if the first be not enough. Bid them say that Julia would fain have word with Cæsar now, ere any further waiting. Tell Cæsar that Julia brooks no more delay."

At that moment there came in a noise from outside, a noise of steps and of voices murmuring. The women in the doorway moved uneasily, not daring, however, to go forth and see what had caused it till Julia gave the word, and presently Julia, hearing the stir, turned on her pillow.

"What mean those sounds?" she asked. "Look without, Æmilia, and ask who cometh. Mayhap"—and she flushed excitedly—"mayhap 'tis a messenger from Cæsar."

Æmilia bowed and went out. All within waited in silence while the distant murmur swelled like that of lamentation. Presently Æmilia came back, looking horror-struck and sorrowful, and she gazed at Julia but did not speak.

"Well, woman?" asked her mistress, harshly. "Hast no tongue? Wherefore did I send thee forth? Speak, speak." And as Æmilia hesitated Julia shook a quivering hand at her and cried, "Speak—if thou wouldst not wholly madden me."

Æmilia bent low and said, "Most Noble, one stands without who beareth news of Sabinus."

"Bid him enter!" cried Julia. "Bid him enter!" and her voice went off in a harsh, high note. "Enter—dost hear?—without tarrying. I fain would hear of Sabinus. What, am I not mistress in my own house? Bid him enter, woman. Why standest thou gaping?"

Æmilia, fearing to gainsay her, went at Julia's bidding. When she returned a man followed, with his mantle folded crosswise on his head after the manner of mourners. As he lifted his face after making obeisance, Julia gazed at him for a minute without speaking. Then she said slowly,—

"Thou—art—Crispus?" And Crispus bowed.

"Hast brought news—of—Sabinus?" asked Julia.

"Ay, lady," returned Crispus.

Then Julia seemed to recover herself.

"Well, what is it? Whither went he? When doth he return?" She put her questions quickly and impatiently.

"Most Noble," said Crispus, solemnly, "Sabinus suffered at dawn."

"What meanest thou?" cried Julia, shrilly, and she leaned forward, catching the side of the bed with her hands while she glared at him. "How meanest thou?—Sabinus suffered—suffered *what?*"

"The death penalty, lady."

Whereat Julia shrieked aloud, "Thou liest! *That* was not Cæsar's will."

"I know not if 'twere Cæsar's will, lady, but 'twas at Cæsar's command." And Julia fell back upon the bed and turned her face to the wall, saying never a word.

Crispus bowed low again, and withdrew, his mantle over his head. The women, seeing that their mistress lay as if stunned, stole out after him one by one, eager to hear what he had to tell, and Nyria alone remained with Julia, who did not speak nor move.

She lay thus through the long hours. By-and-by someone came in and brought Nyria food. It was Æmilia, who offered to take her place. But Nyria shook her head and stayed with Julia.

The day wore on. It had turned dark soon after the redness of the morning, and a lamp had to be kept burning in Julia's chamber. Clouds drove over the sun, and there fell a drizzling rain, so that mist covered the city. Julia lay quite still in the shadow of her blue and silver hangings, and Nyria could not tell whether she slept or if she were busy with her own thoughts, for she uttered no sound save an occasional moan. Æmilia came again later and made Nyria go with her into the loggia for a few minutes while Samu kept watch just within Julia's door. Æmilia had an awed look upon her face as she bent to Nyria and whispered,—

"Euphena doth say she will depart at sundown. If this be so, Nyria, methinks 'twill be her dream that bringeth it about."

"There will be no sunset, for the sky is black," replied Nyria. "We can make her think the hour hath passed before it comes. See, I'll shake the sand from the hour-glass."

The messengers had not yet returned from the Palace. Afterwards Nyria learned that Domitian had kept them. As the afternoon waned Julia was fed with more milk, and she seemed better for it and began to doze peacefully. Seeing her quiet, and that it was now near the close of day, Nyria shook the grains from the hour-glass, and, putting it back in its place by Julia's bed, stole forth again into the loggia, content to think that Julia was sleeping.

The women were gathered upon the steps with their mantles drawn over their heads, and lower down in the court many slaves talked in groups, none caring to go about their ordinary business, for all were sad because of Sabinus. Nyria sat down beside Æmilia.

Presently Euphena came round the corner from the slaves' court, bent, and peering before her as was her manner. She looked all over the assembly and smiled, with her lips drawn tight, so that her two great teeth showed hanging from her upper jaw.

"A fine company!" said she. "Julia will have a fair off-sending. So ye fools, who flouted Euphena's prophecy, art waiting for its fulfilment? Believe ye—*now?*"

None of the slaves dared answer her: but some looked up at the sky and said 'twas senseless talk to prate of sundown since no sun was to be seen, while others remarked, with a feeble attempt at jocosity,—

"Nay, were a messenger to arrive from the Palace saying that Cæsar was about to visit her, Julia would think naught of the hour, but would order torches to be lighted, and send for her dressers and tirewomen to make her ready for Domitian's pleasure." Others again said,—

"Lo, Nyria hath emptied the hour-glass so that Julia may comfort herself that the time hath passed and the Shade of Sabinus gone alone across the Styx."

Euphena laughed scornfully.

"Nyria is never over-wise," she said. "But though Nyria may empty the sands from the hour-glass, not thus readily will she scatter the wrath of the gods, who wait their own appointed time for the pouring forth of vengeance."

So saying, Euphena sat her down upon the steps, and all were silent, while the hour drew on when the sun should have been setting. Close towards that hour there came a break in the dark clouds westward. Streaks of red appeared, like bloody fingers drawing back the curtains of mist, and as it parted before the slaves' wondering eyes, there came in view the sun—a great ball of fire, dropping slowly—slowly—so slowly that the eager watchers drew deep breaths of fear, not knowing what this might portend. Lower sank the sun, and lower, till it almost touched the line below which it should disappear.

Those sitting on the steps of Julia's loggia could see it well, through a break between the Capitol and a block of high buildings, where the ground lay low along the Tiber. The women's eyes strained towards the fiery globe, and the men-slaves standing below looked likewise after it. Thus none saw nor heard that which came behind them till Euphena touched Nyria, and the girl, hastily turning her head, beheld Julia—Julia, whom she had left sleeping and too weak to rise, yet who now had traversed the ante-rooms and who stood, pallid and terrified, within the doorway.

Nyria sprang to her feet, and would have gone to Julia's support had not Euphena held her back.

"Lay no finger on her," said the old woman. "These be matters of the gods' ordering, and not for thee nor me to meddle with."

Julia looked at the setting sun. Her gaze went straight before her, over the heads of those below. The crowd divided and drew apart, like a flock of frightened sheep, on either side, as though they feared lest the glance of Julia's eyes should fall upon them. But she gave them no sign of recognition. Like a sleep-walker she moved a slow step forward, muttering, in hushed, complaining tones,—

"Ay! . . . ay! . . . I come . . . I come . . ." she said. ". . . But whither goest thou? . . . Not there, Sabinus! . . . Oh! not there!" she shrieked on a sudden. . . . "'Tis dark! I will not follow thee."

She stared spell-bound, and then again fell to muttering remonstrantly. And now it seemed that she was compelled against her will, for she came further, pace by pace, reluctantly across the loggia, with her hands outstretched, as though she were blind, or beheld only him that beckoned her.

"Thou wert ever a fool," they heard her mutter querulously as she passed the group of women who cowered against the pillars. ". . . Why wilt thou not go alone, Sabinus? . . ." Then she paused, and threw up her hands as one who needs must obey.

"Peace! peace!" she cried aloud. "Touch me not . . . For I will come. Ay! . . . ay! . . . Sabinus! . . . Ay! I come. . . ."

And in a moment, none of her women knowing what would chance, Julia fell along the marble pavement at their feet.

Her head but just escaped the edge of the steps. None durst go near her, save only Nyria and Euphena. But when Nyria ran to raise her, Euphena dragged the girl away.

"Let her lie," she said.

And even as Julia lay there, and the women huddled together in shivering silence, and the men-slaves crowded to the foot of the steps, there was a sound of lictors' rods striking and the great gates swinging open; and there came a litter, with men in the Imperial livery, which was borne round to the side of the house.

Before it walked Parthenius, one of Cæsar's chamberlains, who, seeing the throng at the steps, strode up and addressed Æmilia, whom he knew to be the chief of Julia's women.

"Say to the Most Noble that Cæsar sendeth greeting, and a litter, which waits to bear her to the Palace."

But Æmilia drew her hand across her face and did not speak, and when Parthenius saw that all looked blankly at him he repeated, more insistently,—

"Say to the Most Noble that Cæsar greets her, and would have her know that Imperial business hath detained him, else would he have been here ere this to learn how his kinswoman fareth. Acquaint Julia with the Emperor's pleasure."

Again no one spoke. Then Euphena went towards him, bending low, and said,—

"Since these who are more highly placed in the household find no words in which to answer thee, Parthenius, then will I. Tell Cæsar that Euphena, whom he will remember, sendeth greeting and word of his most noble kinswoman, who would doubtless grieve that she is not here to comply with the Emperor's request. But Julia hath been called hence."

The Chamberlain was surprised.

"Called hence! Whither? And by whom?" he demanded.

"By her lord, Sabinus, whither he hath gone," replied Euphena.

Parthenius started, and drew back, turning pale.

"The passage of the Styx is lonely," said Euphena, "and Sabinus did desire that his loyal and tender spouse should bear him company upon the way. Wherefore Cæsar will understand that his command for Julia's presence comes too late."

Then the Chamberlain, seeing that a thing dire and strange had happened, cast his eyes around the scene in search of further explanation. They fell upon the body of Julia, over which Nyria bent, a silken veil in her hand, with which she was about to cover the dead face.

Parthenius staggered. "What? *What is that?*" he cried.

Euphena glanced down. "Oh, that!" she said. "'Tis naught. 'Tis only somewhat Julia left in passing."

XXVI

The dead Julia lay in lonely state within her blue and silver room. As Euphena had foretold, it was she and Nyria who dressed her for the burning. The other women would not touch the body lest Julia's manes should haunt them.

Nyria, too, would gladly have refused to aid in that last robing. But when she saw that Euphena would have decked Julia out in gorgeous finery, overloading her with unseemly trappings of incongruous colours, Nyria's sense of propriety forbade that the dead woman should be thus made mock of at her last ceremonial. So she herself tired the thick black hair as she had been wont to tire it, and brought forth a rose-tinted silken robe embroidered with silver, and wrapped Julia therein over a soft stola of shining gauze that had once become her well. But Euphena placed upon her forehead the great ruby that was like a blood-red eye, and wound ropes of precious stones about her neck, covering her besides with all manner of gauds. "For," she said, "when Cæsar visiteth her, 'twill pleasure him to see that she doth still cherish his love-gifts."

Then, as soon as the body of Julia was prepared and laid out on the silver bed beneath the silken hangings, Euphena sent messengers to Cæsar, bidding him come, for that Julia was ready to welcome him.

But Cæsar came not, and though Euphena sent again and again he took no notice, so that the last day arrived without his having entered the death-chamber. Then Euphena loudly cried scorn upon him, and going out from Julia's room, she spat upon the ground and said,—

"This, and this, for Cæsar's devotion, and for the lusts of men. Shame to him that he will not, when the spirit hath passed hence, look upon the fleshly envelope of her whom he professed to love."

But some said that Domitian had a superstitious dread of seeing the body of Julia, and some that he grieved keenly for her loss; some, again, that he was disturbed at news of a revolt in Sarmatia and was so busy calling in his generals and making preparations for war that he had not time to indulge his grief. Moreover—though this was told in whispers—there were rumours of a scandal among the vestals, concerning which Domitian, as Pontifex Maximus, was bound to institute strict inquiries. His former revival of the Scatinian law against such crimes compelled him, and perchance he thought thus to draw attention from his own violation of the moral code. And so Cæsar came not to the house on the Aventine, but merely commissioned officers to make the necessary arrangements and to take command of Julia's estates, which now belonged to him instead of, as some had hoped, to Sabinus's brother, Flavius Clemens. For it seemed that Sabinus had left a will giving everything he had to Julia. Therefore, since she had survived him, though but for a few hours, and had some time previously caused a will to be made by Matho the lawyer, in which she bequeathed all her possessions, and any that she might inherit, to Domitian, Cæsar became Julia's lawful heir, and her slaves, with everything else, were now his property.

Consternation filled Nyria. She had never thought of anything so dreadful happening to her as that she might be claimed by Cæsar; and she wildly prayed Æmilia to hide her if it were in her power, and so keep her from falling under Domitian's notice. But Æmilia said that he was not likely to trouble himself personally about Julia's slaves, and this seemed true, since no summons came from him. He did not even attend the burning when it took place down by the Tiber. And this was much commented on, though some imputed it as merit that he should put State concerns before a family sorrow. It seemed as though he desired to forget Julia, for the story went that, walking on one of the terraces of the Palatine, and seeing a great smoke rising below, he inquired whence it came and whether Rome was ablaze again. Whereupon those around told him that it was the flame of Julia's funeral pyre, and the smoke of the resin and spices offered to the gods upon it; at which Domitian—so 'twas said—turned away and went hastily within.

Now, while Julia's body lay in state, Euphena sat on the steps outside, and scarcely ever left her post, while such as desired went in to look at the show. Some of the slaves were sore afraid, not of death—for that was a common enough sight among them—but of Julia dead, seeing that when she was alive they had so dreaded her. But, being curious, they would crawl in little companies up the steps and peer between the curtains till one braver than the rest took courage and led the way within.

It was because of the charge Euphena had seemed to assume that Vibius and others of the upper slaves laid blame to her when, on the morning of the obsequies, it was discovered that Julia's body had been robbed in the night of its jewels, saving a few rings too tight on the fingers to be removed. Some of the under-slaves were thought to have done the deed, and it was said that Euphena should have set a proper guard. But none would stay near the death-chamber unless they were well paid for it, and such payment had not been provided. The State officers had sealed up Julia's coffers, leaving only a certain sum to Vibius for carrying on the slaves' allowances of food and firing and other necessary expenses. So, as there was not any member of the family in authority, none cared to probe the matter.

Fearing lest Cæsar's attention should be called to her, Nyria shut herself up in the cabin when Julia's body was carried forth, and did not see the forming of the procession. There had been discussion among the upper slaves as to whether permission should be asked to follow the bier, as was usual among the attendants of a noted lord or lady. In this case, both master and mistress having died, all the slaves were under ban of the law, and might not quit the premises, except by favour and under control of soldiery, till the time when they should be sold by public auction or else delivered over formally to their new owner. Æmilia, as head dresser, gave it as her opinion that Julia's women should not demand the privilege, for, she said, the pretence of mourning would be shame rather than honour. Vibius, on the other hand, declared that for the sake of Sabinus, who would have wished it, the upper men ought to go, and prayed them for this token of respect to their dead master's memory. Some consented, to the number of perhaps fifty, but of the women only Euphena went. A gruesome figure she was, with flat cakes of mud upon her head, while in her skinny arms she bore a bundle like the form of a child. Her fellow-slaves did not know what the bundle could be, but Æmilia, who stood with Nyria in the cabin and watched the old woman pass out, shuddered and said,—

"She meaneth it for the image of her own dead babe, by whom she willeth to call down vengeance on the shade of Julia."

Thus it was that of the retinue of handmaidens that had made obeisance to her, Euphena alone attended Julia on that last occasion when she was borne through the streets of Rome to the rattling of lictors' rods and the clang of Prætorians' spears as they gave her a parting royal salute.

Now came a time of miserable suspense for this great disorganised household that had a head no longer. The most irksome part of it to the slaves was their isolation from the outside world, since without legal permit none might issue forth or enter in at the gates, which were kept guarded day and night. These restrictions, usual to a greater or lesser extent on the death of the owner, were rigorously enforced in the present instance, on account of Sabinus's popularity among the lower classes of Rome, which made it advisable to guard against any chance of a rising, or at least of augmenting the public disaffection against Domitian — particularly because of the foreign revolt and also the ferment in Rome in regard to his rigorous treatment of the Vestal Cornelia, whom later he ordered to be buried alive for breaking her vow of chastity.

Meanwhile, the slaves' quarter at the great house on the Aventine resembled a hive of disturbed bees. Sabinus, desiring to protect the slaves' interests, and knowing the difficulty they had in keeping from being pilfered any birth-papers or money or goods they might have acquired in service, had a custom, rare among masters, of reserving in his strong-room a compartment wherein any slave might deposit things he cared for. These were in the custody of Sabinus himself and of the head steward, and were at stated times checked in their presence and that of the owners. The theft of Julia's jewels had made the slaves suspicious of each other, and having now received back from Vibius, in the presence of the lawyer's officers, the papers and other valuables that had been consigned to Sabinus's keeping, they were naturally anxious as to the safety of their goods, which they packed in chests, bag, or bundle, and scarce left for a moment.

Thanna went about with most of her finery on her person, trying to bargain for other things she fancied. Euphena did not leave her hut, but sat glowering in the doorway and drawing magical figures before it. Nyria herself had nothing of any value except Cæsar's gold and pearl neck-chain, which she had buried in a corner of the hut, and Stephanus's amber beads. She had not seen Stephanus since the evening before Julia died, and though he had been angered then, Stephanus's anger would not last, she knew, but Nyria thought less of Stephanus than of Valeria. The girl longed and hoped that Valeria would buy her, but she became uneasy as time went on and a notice had been read in the slaves' court that by order of Cæsar they were to be put up at public auction in the Forum on a date specified some few weeks later. In one sense the proclamation came as a relief, for it showed Nyria that Cæsar did not intend to claim her for his household, but in other respects it increased her anxiety, for now intending purchasers might obtain an order to view the slaves, and it was terrible to be inspected, not knowing who might take a fancy to her. Soon after the proclamation the lawyer came round with his clerks and the officers who were to conduct the auction, in order that the list of the slaves, giving particulars of their looks and acquirements, might be checked under his supervision. Matho had been Julia's lawyer and undertook the legal business of the sale, which some of the greater men of law might have thought beneath them. But Matho—though at this time he had not fallen from prosperity—was ready enough to do anything which might bring him into favour with high-placed clients. He paused now before Nyria, examining her, and remarking that she would fetch a good price. At Euphena he simply scoffed. But Euphena smiled with equal scorn, which seemed strange, seeing that though she might be a sorceress she must go to auction like the rest.

It was a day near that of the sale when many chamberlains and chief stewards of great houses had already been to inspect the slaves on behalf of their masters and mistresses, and Nyria was sick within her because none had come from Valeria. The poor girl was wondering how things would fall out, when Vibius told her that Alexamenos had arrived with an order to visit her. Nyria's heart sank, fearing he might have brought a summons from Cæsar. But the Prætorian was bent upon his own business. Cæsar, he said, was at Albanum, where, he told Nyria, the Senate was just convened to consider what sentence should be passed on the Vestal Cornelia.

But at mention of the word "sentence" Nyria's thoughts reverted to Sabinus. She asked what manner of fate had overtaken her master. Alexamenos shook his head.

"Inquire not, Nyria. 'Tis better not to know."

But Nyria broke out, "Shame on thee, Alexamenos! Wherefore didst thou not save Sabinus?"

"Sabinus refused to save himself," the young officer answered. And as she continued to heap reproaches on him he said, "Thou dost not understand, Nyria. While I yet owed no obedience to Cæsar in the matter, 'twas within my power to cause warning to be carried to Sabinus. But when Cæsar's command came upon me there was naught for me as a soldier but to obey."

"Even though it were the command of a tyrant and dealt death to the best of men!" she retorted.

"With the nature of the order I have no concern," he replied gently. "My office is not to judge Cæsar, but to obey him. I grieve greatly to have hurt thee, Nyria," he went on, "for, alas! it bodeth ill for my success in the errand upon which I am come."

Curiosity prevailing, she asked him what his errand might be, and he told her that, having been favoured by Cæsar, he was now in a position to purchase her, and that this he desired to do—not as a slave, but in order that he might make her his wife.

"If thou wilt wed me, Nyria," he said, "I will demand thee from Cæsar. He will not deny my request."

But the mere idea of being brought to Cæsar's remembrance filled Nyria with a blind terror which she could not confide to Alexamenos.

"Cæsar would not think Julia's handmaiden a fitting wife for his favourite officer," she said.

"That rests between Cæsar and me," replied the Prætorian. "'Tis our affair—not thine. Do thou but let me speak for thee, Nyria."

"Nay, I have no mind to wed, Alexamenos. I am over young."

"I, too, am young. But one is never over young for happiness—and I can make thee happy—that I know. But sorrow is like to befall thee if thou dost go with the rest to be bought by the highest bidder."

"What should I look for but sorrow? 'Tis a slave's portion," Nyria answered.

"Thou art no ordinary slave. I have heard of thy lineage, and in truth one has only to look upon thee to know 'tis noble. As my wife I could greatly improve thy case, even though it might not be to the state befitting thine ancestry. Nevertheless, the Prætorians are a power, for since Cæsar ruleth Rome, be it whispered that the Prætorians rule Cæsar. Haply I should rise to be Tribune of the Guard. 'Twas the office held by Valerius Paulinus when he married Vitellius's daughter. Sweet, if I stood where Paulinus stands, wouldst thou not wed me, Nyria?"

"Nay," she answered. "Hast thou not said the Prætorians rule Cæsar? And yet thou didst not save Sabinus!"

He laughed disappointedly.

"That is woman's reasoning. The Prætorians are Cæsar's safeguard, and since men must live we earn our wage. Cæsar were not Cæsar did the Prætorians rise against him—yet, being Cæsar, we are sworn to obey him while he reigns. As for poor Sabinus—had he been given choice of death, or further life as Cæsar's puppet, methinks he would have faced the sword unhesitatingly. Life held no great joy for Sabinus. He is happier now."

Nyria nodded through her tears, and Alexamenos went on,—

"We, who believe in mercy and justice beyond the tomb, cannot doubt that Sabinus hath entered into a kingdom of peace. But give me hope, Nyria. If I should send to purchase thee might I then make myself a place in thy heart?"

"A slave may not dictate to her purchaser," Nyria answered coldly. Then, as he made an impetuous gesture of dissent, she added, "Nay, Alexamenos, leave me to my fate and seek some likelier maid to be thy wife."

"Never shall I seek another," he said dejectedly. "Thou hast roused in me a feeling that I had not thought to bear a maid, seeing I loved best my sword, until the Master revealed Himself in my soul, showing me all things—even Cæsar and my duty to him and to my country—in new colours. Ah! Nyria! 'twas of the Master that we spoke on that sweet night when it seemed to me there was somewhat in thy heart which would turn thee to the faith I hold so dear. Couldst not thou become a Christian, Nyria?"

And here Alexamenos put forward a plea of greater weight with the girl than aught else.

"Thou, too, then, art a follower of the Lord Clementus?" she asked.

"Not of him only, but of One far greater—the Lord Christ Himself. Oh! Nyria, wilt thou not follow Christ with me?" Alexamenos clasped her hands. "The road that leadeth to Christ is for many strewn with stones, and hard to tread, but for thee, sweet maid, my love shall make it easy. Thou and I, blest in our union, as Christ blessed the marriage of that happy pair in Cana of Galilee, shall walk together whither He hath showed the way, seeking Him in His own heaven—a fairer place, Nyria, than Greek Olympus, where the old-time gods are said to dwell."

Nyria drew her hands gently away from Alexamenos's clasp.

"Thy talk is fine," she said. "I fain would follow Christ, by the guidance of Clementus, whom I find a gracious and godly man, and one that hath much in his teaching for the which I have always longed. But I had like to go alone, Alexamenos. To me it hath ever seemed that I must tread the way of life alone—though in truth no road is lonely when Christ doth lead and the Lord Clementus guide. In the matter of this closer companionship that thou dost desire, methinks 'tis not for Nyria."

Alexamenos looked down at her in passionately tender reverence.

"I understand," he said. "Nyria's pure soul would shrink from such companionship were it with one whose heart and mind were not such as her own. But to be united in Christ!—oh, Nyria!—" He caught her hands again and pressed them against his armoured breast. "Surely, sweet, that would be better far."

"I know not," she answered. "Nyria knoweth naught of love."

"But Nyria might learn," he said. "And oh, 'twere joy to teach thee! With Christ's blessing, Nyria, let me be thy teacher."

Now Nyria was touched by this devotion, for Alexamenos was of a goodly countenance—just the man to take a maid's fancy were her thoughts set on mating. Yet she released her hand again, saying, "Some there be, Alexamenos, who learn such lessons quickly; and others who all their lives remain dullards. Thou hadst best go hence, for Nyria is a dullard."

Just then Vibius came up with a visitor who wished to look over the slaves, and Alexamenos went sorrowfully away.

Later in the day Nyria was sitting outside Euphena's door, when, looking up, she saw Stephanus gazing at her over the wall.

"So thou hast come!" she cried, not too graciously, for Euphena had been howling upbraidings at her for keeping Stephanus away.

"Ay, I've come," he said. "And soon enough, methinks, Nyria, seeing that by thy welcome thou dost not need Stephanus's protection in the ills that befall thee."

"No ills have yet befallen me," she responded. "I'm safe enough and look not for misfortunes."

"Perchance thou'lt speak differently when the sale is over," he retorted.

"Now, why be wroth with me, Stephanus?" she said, rising. "How know I that some kind and noble lady may not purchase me?"

"There be not many such in Rome," he said.

"I had a mind to ask thine intercession with the Domina Domitilla," she said, smiling. "Dost think she'd buy me, Stephanus?"

"I know not. But she'll not have the chance if I be able to prevent it. Thou mayest walk the way to ruin, Nyria, if thou wilt, but think not that Stephanus will drive thee thither. The Domina Domitilla doth lead the life she chooseth; Stephanus is but her steward, and may not say yea nor nay concerning it. But Stephanus is more than that to thee, Nyria—or would be if thou wouldst permit him."

And then Euphena's voice called shrilly from the hut, "So thou art here at last, laggard! Hie within, I have somewhat to say to thee. Do thou stand without, Nyria, and see that none disturb us."

Stephanus hesitated, but Euphena called again crossly,—

"'Tis worth thy while, good goldsmith. I've a bargain for thee."

"As well to humour her or we'll have no peace," murmured Stephanus, and he stepped inside the hut, and Euphena banged the door after him.

Nyria stood leaning by it. She could hear the buzz of voices within. Euphena and Stephanus seemed to be arguing hotly. Presently Euphena screeched out,—

"Thou art a fool to waste thy substance on fruit that will ne'er drop into thy mouth. Nyria is for no man. Those that desire her will find themselves embracing wrath and bloodshed."

Acting on an impulse, Nyria pushed open the door and stood before the pair.

"I warn thee," she said, "thy speech doth carry."

Euphena stooped as if she would hide a glittering pile that lay on a wooden-legged stool between her and Stephanus. Then, seeing that only Nyria was there, she cried,—

"Enter, since thy word hath weight with this fool, and add it unto mine. But shut the door behind thee, else shall we have the whole household hither."

"What wouldst thou of Stephanus?" asked Nyria.

"Gold!" said Euphena, "and I offer him good value in return. Now, Nyria, look."

She pointed to a pile, which was of jewellery—rings, chains, bracelets set with many gems, and various articles of gold and silver besides. Nyria saw on the heap that long chain of gold and emeralds which Julia had given Euphena, and she saw also some of those same ropes of precious stones and other ornaments that she had herself helped Euphena to place on Julia's dead body.

"How camest thou by these?" asked the girl. Euphena shrugged her shoulders.

"Gifts! gifts!" she answered. "Gifts for long and faithful service. Gifts from Julia living, and gifts from Julia dead."

"Then *thou* wert the thief!" cried Nyria, quickly, turning on her.

Euphena spread her arms over her jewels, glaring like some beast disputing its prey.

"Brand me!" she exclaimed. "Go, spread it abroad that Euphena robbed the corpse. Say that Euphena hath been laying by a store of gems wherewith to purchase her freedom! But the vengeance of Euphena shall follow thee. Think twice before thou courtest it."

"Nay, I have no wish to betray thee," answered the girl. "Of what avail would that be? Do as thou wilt. 'Tis naught to Nyria."

Euphena laughed elfishly. "Thou art wise," she said. As she turned over the jewellery, Nyria saw amongst it her own gold chain set with pearls, the gift of Cæsar. Euphena noticed her glance of recognition, and lifted the shining thing on her skinny forefinger.

"A pretty gew-gaw, is't not? Found in a most strange hiding-place!" She pointed to the corner of the hut where Nyria saw the flooring had been displaced. Then Euphena turned to Stephanus. "A fine lot, worthy goldsmith. Name a good price. That thou surely wilt, since Nyria adds her persuasions to mine."

"What is thy will, Stephanus?" put in Nyria.

"Euphena doth desire that I should buy these things," said he, "but I tell her that I have not the money. There is Onesimus in the Porticus Margaritaria, who is richer than I. He, doubtless, would speedily conclude with her for the purchase."

"Dost dream I'd have Onesimus hither to see these gems," growled Euphena. "Why, man, he'd beat me down to half their value. Nay, thou shalt buy them of me, Stephanus."

"Woman, I tell thee 'tis impossible. I have not the money—and if I had, there are other ways in which I choose to spend it."

"How willest thou to spend thy money, friend Stephanus?" whined Euphena, mockingly. "Shall I tell thee? Is't not to purchase Nyria in the slave-market? Is't not for that thou hast been putting a claim on all thy goods, so that if more gold pieces are needed thou mayest have them forthcoming?"

"Hermes alone knoweth how thou hast learned the truth," replied Stephanus, sulkily.

"Well, save thy pains," she returned. "For if thou wert to bid three—ay, four thousand sestertii, still wouldst thou be outdone. 'Tis not to thee that Nyria will fall. Yet fret not that urgent soul of thine, Stephanus—the maid is safe as yet, and the road which she shall walk will be of her own choosing."

Stephanus scowled at Euphena from under his pent brows.

"Come now, friend," she cried, "leave the purchase of Nyria to others, seeing she doth not desire to be thine, and grant unto poor old Euphena the means to buy her own freedom. Do this, and thou shalt not suffer for it. Thy business shall prosper. Gold shall flow into thy coffers, and ne'er be lacking when thou requirest it. Haply, Stephanus," and Euphena put on her whining manner again, "haply some day hence Nyria may need thy help e'en more than now; then the money thou shalt have paid Euphena will bring thee in good interest, and stand to Nyria's advantage in her hour of dire extremity."

Stephanus's eyes were screwed up into bright needle points under his heavy forehead, but he shook his great shoulders and straightened himself.

"Thou art a cajoling hag," he said. "Thou knowest well what part of a man's nature to touch with thy sharp tongue. But I'll not do this thing. Nyria may be mine or no, but she shall never stand in the slave-market without a friend to bid for her. And were I to buy thy gems, Euphena, she'd run a chance of that. Yet I tell thee what I'll do. Give me yon load of gauds—thou canst surely trust Stephanus—and I'll take them down to the Porticus Margaritaria and find thee a buyer. It need not be known whence they came, for in the trade none would question Stephanus. Dost agree?"

Seeing that Stephanus was not to be stirred from his resolution, Euphena began to wrap the things in a bag whence she had taken them. "I'll hold Nyria as hostage," she said crossly. "Bring me back a fair sum, Stephanus, over and above what will purchase me, —and of that thou canst give a good guess—else will harm come to Nyria."

"I'll guard the things well," he rejoined, "and within an hour or so I'll bring thee the best price to be got for them."

Stephanus shouldered the bundle she gave him, which now Nyria saw looked like the one Æmilia had supposed to be the effigy of the babe borne in Euphena's arms at Julia's funeral. It proved to be a package made with pockets, in which the jewels might be placed according to their value, and was cleverly arranged and sewn. It weighed heavily, for in it as well were richly-chased armlets, and anklets and girdles of solid silver, together with several of Julia's dressing utensils and silver ornaments from her room, which Euphena had secreted. It contained also certain discoloured trinkets that Euphena must have rummaged for among the ashes after the burning to augment her store, and doubtless for this purpose she had followed the body. When Stephanus was gone Euphena barred the outer door, and pushed Nyria through the curtains into the little back chamber.

"Stay there," she said. "Think not thou shalt escape before Stephanus brings the price of Euphena's freedom. Nevertheless," she added, half laughing, half sneering, "distress not thyself, Nyria, for another fate awaits thee, with which Euphena may not interfere." Then she set herself down in the front room to bide Stephanus's return.

The time seemed long to Nyria. Evening came on, and they set the torches in the slaves' court. Euphena lighted her lamp, and crouched on the floor beside the stool on which she had placed it. Nyria, watching her from behind the curtains, saw long black shadows dance about her as the wind blew in at the cracks of door and window and stirred the murky flame of the lamp. A strange, evil thing she looked. By-and-by Stephanus tapped on the door, and Euphena hastened up to open to him. Then she called to Nyria, bidding her go outside.

"Thou art free now," she said, "for well I know that Stephanus's wallet is full of gold pieces. Wert not afraid to walk up from the Forum with so much money upon thee, good Stephanus?" she asked cheerfully.

But he curtly stopped her talk.

"Sit thee down, old dame, and count thy gold," he cried. "I want not to waste more words on thee."

Nyria pulled the door to behind her, but through the crack she could hear the clink of coin and the murmur of their voices as Stephanus rendered account of his commission. It was not many minutes, however, before he came out, and putting his arms round the girl as she stood outside the hut, he held her close to his breast. "Yon old sorceress hath secured herself against adverse happenings," he said. "Ah! Nyria, would that I could secure thee."

XXVII

EARLY on the morning of the sale the slaves of Julia and Sabinus were drawn up together for the last time in the large slaves' court of the villa on the Aventine, and here inspected by various officials, who saw that they were properly dressed and prepared for the auction. They took their places in the order of sex and service. The under slaves were put foremost, then the upper men, according to their household rank, and the women according to theirs. Those who had young children were permitted to keep them, but boys and girls of a saleable age were taken away from their parents and placed in the class to which they should belong. Heart-rending scenes ensued. In the case of husbands and wives who had not been wedded in the same grade of service, the couples were parted, and had small chance of being sold together.

Nyria had no anguish of this sort to face. As chief tirewoman she ranked only beneath the head-woman of the draperies, and kept close behind Æmilia. This woman's husband was of the same class as his wife, and was therefore permitted to walk beside her, that opportunity might be given them of being bought in couple—for the division of married pairs, though it seemed so inhuman, was not done in cruelty, but merely to preserve order among the groups offered for sale.

Euphena remained in the rear of the women, holding herself proudly aloof and showing no perturbation. Those who had time or attention to spare from their own anxieties wondered at this, but none save Nyria knew that the old Ethiopian was carrying enough gold to purchase her freedom. Nyria herself had only a small bundle, which she bore upon her head, and so was able to take charge of one of Æmilia's children. Æmilia's face was strained and anxious, but neither she nor her husband said much, and the pathos of their silence was greater than that of the noisy lamentations which came from others.

About sunrise the whole company was driven in long lines down the streets to the city, some fifty officers or thereabouts walking beside them, for Julia's household was a large one, and had the slaves chosen to revolt they might have given trouble. Most of them, however, had been bred in service, and were not of the type to make any futile attempt to escape. Crispus was in the Forum waiting for their arrival, and this not out of scorn—which frequently drew freedmen thither—but that he might minister to their wants as far as he was able.

It took some little time to arrange so large a number on the space allotted round the rostrum and the adjoining pedestal, on which all in turn would stand. The under slaves were massed together without regard to grouping or convenience, but the upper ones, and especially those among the women who were likely from their appearance to fetch a good price, had each an apportioned space to sit or stand in, as they chose, so that they need not be jostled by the rest, and in order that possible buyers might examine them freely.

The exposure was the most trying part of the ordeal to the women, for while the sun was still low, and especially in shadow of the houses, the cold was bitter. It was imperative that the clothes they wore should add to, rather than detract from, their appearance. Hence they were not permitted to wrap themselves in their warm blankets, and only few possessed sufficiently gay mantles. Then, as the hours advanced, the sun, even at this time of year, poured down with so great strength that the very paving-stones became hot, and from the crowding and lack of breeze many got faint. Even Nyria, who loved the sun, found it overpowering.

It was a long, weary time of waiting. Nobles in Rome never rose early, and such as were engaged with clients needed their chamberlains and chief stewards to be in attendance during the morning audience. These functionaries always had the buying of under slaves, and for that reason the lower ones were put first, perhaps in twos and threes, according to the class of work they were accustomed to—gardeners, scavengers and such-like being often bought by freedmen and farmers in the Campagna, some of whom had camped for this object in the Forum over-night. But the selling of the better class of slaves seldom began before the fifth hour—at this time of year nearly eleven o'clock. Even in the case of upper slaves, lords and ladies did not usually come to bid, but having viewed them beforehand, and made their decision, would send a deputy to conclude the purchase. Or, if they were persons of note, and had not taken opportunity to view before the day of sale, they would not wait for the auctioneer to mount the rostrum, but would settle the matter with the legal representative of the owner before the slaves were put up. Thus a slave might be purchased privately on the spot, without knowing anything about the transaction, and this added considerably to the uncertainty and anxiety felt by the helpless living merchandise. At any moment a slave might be directed to withdraw from the rest and to follow his new master's pleasure.

A sale so important as that of Julia's household was likely to attract a good many fashionable people into the Forum, and the seller expected brisk bidding. The chief of Julia's women were placed in favourable positions, and ordered to show themselves to as great advantage as possible, carefully grouped in such a manner as to enhance each other's appearance, and to present an attractive variety. Nyria, being specially valuable on account of her fair skin and yellow hair, was given a prominent place, and to her regret was removed from beside Æmilia, neutral of colouring, to a space next Thanna, who, with her clear brown skin, red lips, bright eyes and black hair, was distinguished by a certain flashing comeliness. Thanna had dressed herself in her gayest apparel—a striped petticoat of many-hued silk, and her red embroidered veil—and there could have been no more effective contrast to Nyria in her simple white robes, with her golden curls unbound about her shoulders. So greatly prized was yellow hair in Rome, that an ugly slave might sell well if she possessed it; and poor Nyria was like to curse her hair that day because of the notice it brought her, and the rude speeches made by those who desired to finger it—which, however, the officers in charge permitted none to do. Thanna did not mind having her hair or anything else about her commented on, if it were with admiration; and she changed her head-tiring several times in the day, having brought a little mirror, which she fixed against the stones, and by its aid coiled up her tresses with bright skewers, or rolled them in great plaits down her back. Nor did she object to exhibit her person in different attitudes, and would spring alertly to her feet, or recline in any posture that was required to show off her shape, making Nyria blush by the pert answers she returned to those who remarked upon her. Nyria suffered sorely, both from Thanna's sprightly self-assurance and from old Euphena's scathing wit, for she was placed between the two. Euphena was described in the inventory as her foster-mother, and for this reason, or probably to heighten the effect of Nyria's lily-fairness, the Ethiopian was put next her. A crowd pressed round them, hooting and laughing at the old woman's hideous face and the scornful speeches that she threw freely among them, giving back jeer for jeer, till Nyria could have sunk into the ground with shame.

Before the beginning of an auction a noisy rabble was wont to collect—usually the very scum of Rome. Those who might be of the lowest grade, upon whom a proud, well-kept slave would ordinarily look down with the utmost contempt, were now at liberty to taunt at will the unfortunate creatures about to be sold, and who had usually no spirit to retort upon their scoffers. And when a slave was led off, the rabble would cry sharp speeches afresh—some envying him if he chanced to have been bought by a master of good repute, or gibing if his purchaser were a skinflint or of lower rank than his former owner. Euphena, however, gave back as good as she got, which only made matters worse for Nyria. So things went on until the actual bidding began.

Now the auctioneer mounted his rostrum, the idle loiterers were thrust back, and those who meant to buy pushed their way to the front of the ring. Matho, the lawyer, took his seat at his desk, on the lookout for any great personage strolling along the rows of slaves who might come up and bid privately for the purchase of one of them. Matho had his two clerks on lower desks beside his own, and a little army of messengers to do his bidding. So, too, had the auctioneer, and there were besides officials of both, whose duty it was to walk round among the better sort of slaves and see that none suffered injury or discomfort. For this, which was perhaps the most humiliating day in a slave's life, was also that on which a slave of position found himself of most account. Once the money had been paid down for him it mattered to none but his new master what became of him, but until then it was necessary that he should appear at his best, and to ensure this, no reasonable request that he might make was disregarded. Some of the women made the most of their opportunity and begged various comforts—a cup of wine, a cushion to sit on, a screen to shield them from the glare—and their demands were duly complied with. Had Nyria put forward the plea of injury to her complexion she would have been accommodated with a seat under cover, and anything else she might have chosen to ask for. But she was too proud to do this. Æmilia also—who though of less account in one sense, because her youth was past and her beauty faded, had nevertheless the claim of her position and talents—held herself haughtily silent. Æmilia desired naught but to remain with her husband and children, and as the critical time approached her worn features grew more tense, and the look of agony in her eyes deepened.

Nyria watched many of those whom she knew being sold and led away. Pheidias went to a master said to be severe on his slaves. Bibbi would naturally have been classed with the upper household, and being a muscular man of great strength was likely to have been in request, but a deputy from the public office near the Carinæ, where a staff of beaters was kept, came early and examined him, and his purchase was arranged by private treaty, so that Bibbi became the property of the State. Before he departed, while his papers were being made out, he sauntered round, declaring that his former companions would regret his lash. And this was true enough, for most of them would rather have gone under the lash they were accustomed to than that of a stranger.

"Take heart of grace, Nyria," cried the great brute, jocosely, when he came to her. "Like enough some day a beater will be sent for to perform his office upon thee, as was Balbus Plautius. Then will Bibbi see that 'tis himself who serves Nyria."

Nyria took no heed of the laughter that followed this witticism. She was craning through the throng to see whether anyone likely to buy her was approaching, and if there was any sign of Crispus, who, to please her, had been walking round the Forum taking note of all those that came that way. Alas! there was no one from the Valerian villa, and when Crispus told her that he had seen none of Valeria's household, Nyria's courage began to fail her and the poor girl was ready to weep. As the tears welled into her eyes, and her heart felt as if it would burst, Nyria saw Stephanus shouldering his way towards the rostrum.

He had a bag in his hand, which the girl guessed held gold, while on either side there walked one of his fellow-goldsmiths from the Porticus Margaritaria—Onesimus and another—to vouch for him if required, for, being only a freedman, Stephanus had to put down all his money for a purchase, or to bring witnesses to his word.

He bade his friends stand back while he went up to the ring of slaves, and Nyria saw a smile on their faces as they pointed to her and whispered together.

"So thou art unclaimed yet, Nyria?" said Stephanus, his blustering manner ill-concealing his anxiety.

"Yes," she answered absently, her eyes straining past him.

"For whom art thou looking?" asked Stephanus, gruffly. "Dost suppose that fine lady on the Cœlian will bethink her to send and purchase thee? Nay, Nyria, thou'st yet to learn that when Valeria needs thee not, she'll ne'er cast e'en her old shoe after thee."

Presently there came a shifting movement in the moving crowd which swelled the Forum and converged towards the slave-market—a serrying together as if to clear a road-way. Down the space Nyria could hear the tramp of drilled feet and see the flash of soldiers' helmets and lances as they marched along. Some legionaries were going, 'twas said, to meet a general who was arriving in Rome, and Nyria caught the name of Asiaticus as that of him who commanded the detachment, but just then someone came up to examine her, and Stephanus was forced to draw back in a fever of alarm. He had already been to Matho, offering to pay the reserve put on Nyria, but the lawyer would not suffer him to bid until she should be put up from the rostrum. For, being yellow-haired and well-looking, they hoped to get a large sum for the girl. Besides, what could Stephanus want her for, save as wife or mistress, seeing that he was unwed, and for such idle truck, said Matho, contemptuously, she should not be taken from her betters. And this infuriated Stephanus, there being already bad blood between them, on account of Juvenal, who was himself strolling about the Forum. He came and talked to Stephanus, who had stationed himself as near Nyria as he dared. The satirist said a few kindly words to her.

"Had I the money, Nyria, I'd purchase thee myself—or I'd join forces with Stephanus so that we might share thee—eh? And how would that please friend Stephanus?" And Juvenal laughed. But Nyria only hung her head, for to her it was no laughing matter, and in her misery the poor girl wondered that Thanna could disport herself as she did.

Æmilia and her husband sat silently close together and hand in hand, each with a child in one arm—the strained look on Æmilia's face growing to one of dumb terror.

The hour came at last for the principal women to be sold. Now Euphena made her way through the ring to the lawyer's desk and began to speak. Matho called angrily to her to get back to her place. But Euphena stood firm, saying stoutly that the law was upon her side and that she claimed to be heard. Then Matho bade her come closer, and rudely demanded what she wanted.

Nyria, who was watching, expected to hear her spit forth some of her insulting speeches; but the old woman bent herself and whined in servile tones that she did but desire to purchase her own old body so that she might have a few years of leisure in which to serve the gods before they called her hence. As she spoke she leaned upon a stick, and seemed to shrink to naught, till she looked older and uglier and skinnier than any had ever before seen her.

Matho ran her over with his sharp eye and asked sneeringly how much she was prepared to pay for herself.

Euphena named a sum. Nyria could not hear what it was, but judged by Matho's face that he was surprised at the amount. He asked the Ethiopian, in rough, suspicious tones, whether she had come by it honestly. To which Euphena answered, still with whining civility, that the law did not require her to state how she had earned it, but that she was ready to count out the sum before him if he would have the paper drawn up for her freedom.

Matho questioned those who had been watching likely purchasers while they looked over the slaves, but all reported that no one had cast more than a glance at Euphena, and that it was improbable there would be any bidding for her.

"Nevertheless, I have a mind," said Matho, "to put thee up and see if any better price be offered." But Euphena cringingly reminded him that the law protected an ancient slave, who, if she could procure a certain sum, had that right to her freedom; and she proceeded to count it out before him, taking the money from a bag she carried in her breast, and gloating over each gold piece as she laid it down, while many standing round made amused comments.

"Verily thou hast done well for thyself," said Matho, looking at the purchase-money, which lay in a glittering pile on his desk. "Thy mistress must have been a generous lady."

"Yea! yea!" purred Euphena. "For was she not the most noble Julia, and grudged her slaves naught, as her women here will testify." Euphena turned with a flourish of her lean black arm towards the row of Julia's dressers, none of whom dared gainsay her.

Thanna nodded, laughing, for Thanna knew that she looked well when she laughed, with her white teeth glistening in her dark, handsome face. She knew, too, that a man standing near was watching her. A fine-made man, but his was not a noble countenance, although he wore the symbols of senatorial rank. He stepped across and addressed Thanna.

"Didst thou, too, find thy mistress generous, and did she give thee this—and these?" He pointed to the embroidered veil and some gilt pins in Thanna's hair.

"I earned them by clever and faithful service," replied Thanna, promptly.

"Clever women are seldom faithful," he retorted.

"Ah! that depends, my lord," answered Thanna. "Give me what is worth my faith and I'll be faithful."

"Art tired of serving dames?" he suggested.

Thanna beamed and nodded, saucily clasping her knees. "Try me, lord; I'd give thee faithful service," she said.

"I have no lady-wife for thee to deck," he answered shiftily. "What else canst thou do?"

"Try me," she repeated. "Thanna is but young yet. Give her time, and test her."

Just then another nobleman, also wearing the senatorial insignia, came up.

"Thou art a fool, Regulus," said he. "Get thee hence. Why burden thyself with such cattle? Take thy pleasure more cheaply, man. The girl will cost thee a good sum, and when thou hast got her thou'lt tire of her in a week."

Thanna, hearing him, lifted her chin and addressed the air.

"That would be strange indeed! None ever tired of Thanna yet—nor should, if Thanna knew it."

Regulus turned with a sheepish laugh to his friend.

"Now get thee hence, Marcellus, or thou mayst be tempted to bid against me. I am minded to try the girl. If she suits me not I can put her in the next big sale."

"Oh! ay, thou canst. But thou wilt not," said Thanna, mischievously. "See, my Lord Regulus," and she bent before him as he turned back to her again. "Let Thanna look to the preparing of thy garments if there be naught else for her to do. There must be a hole in that pouch thou wearest, for I see a paper sticking forth. Lords that carry papers in Rome should guard them carefully, lest secrets be betrayed. Perchance thou wouldst do well to employ Thanna as thy messenger. A tongue doth sometimes serve better than a pen. For what is written all may read, but that which is spoken none shall hear save as the speaker willeth. I pray thee, purchase Thanna. 'Twould be a good investment at the price."

"By Hercules, I believe it would!" answered Regulus with a keen look. "But hark thee, girl; if I find thee valueless thou shalt go into the next auction held here."

"I'll take the chance," said Thanna, shewing her white teeth. Regulus came nearer. "Is all that hair thine own?" he asked.

Whereat Thanna pulled out the pins and let it fall in a dusky shower round her.

"Stand up," said he. She rose obediently, and turned herself slowly round, her hands on her hips, to shew her shape, then thrust her face forward coquettishly.

"Art satisfied, lord? Fear not!—thou shalt find profit and pleasure here. Thanna is young—thou'lt get her date of birth on the paper—but she is wise beyond her years."

"Verily! a man is like to make more amusement out of thee than in a week of festivals," exclaimed Regulus. "I'll buy thee, girl. What is thy price? Dost know?"

"Nay, lord," returned Thanna, meekly. "But it should not be dear to him who holds so many of the private purse-strings of Rome."

"Thy speech is smart," said he, with that keen yet shifty look. "But be careful before whom thou dost prate when once thou art mine."

"Seal Thanna's lips, lord, and thou alone shalt break the seal," she said, and bent low before him with all her hair covering her like a sumptuous veil. But as she did so Nyria saw her shoulders shake and knew that she laughed.

"Who is thy purchaser, Thanna?" Nyria whispered as Regulus turned away, and Thanna, rising triumphantly, watched her new lord approach the lawyer.

"'Tis the great Regulus," she said proudly. "One had like to know naught of Rome who hath not heard of Regulus," and then she began swiftly to get her things together. "Matho may be a sharp lawyer," said she, "but he will need his wits when Regulus deals against him."

Nyria remarked that it had not appeared to her that Regulus looked particularly clever, but Thanna exclaimed, "Dost not know that they who are truly wise be wiser than to bear wisdom on their faces? Thou art right in this though, Nyria. Regulus is not so wise but that Thanna can make him wiser."

"I had rather have been bought by a lady," said Nyria.

"Oh! wouldst thou!" retorted Thanna. "Well, each to her own taste! I have had enough of working for a woman; I would fain now have women work for me."

And with that she stood up and smoothed down her garments

and rearranged her veil, having twisted her hair anew, so that she was prepared for the Lord Regulus when he came back with his friends Marcellus and Massa.

"Now," said Regulus, "art ready, girl?"

"Ready to follow whithersoever my lord leads," promptly returned Thanna, with a low obeisance.

"Ay, be civil," said Regulus. "But I am not one who likes over much sugar with his porridge."

"Sugar is but for babes," said Thanna, softly. "Thanna is accounted a good porridge-maker, lord, but she putteth spice in hers."

Massa nudged Marcellus, who gave a cynical guffaw, and Regulus grinned.

"I see we shall not be dull," he said. "Come then, Thanna, take thy belongings and follow me."

Thanna picked up a light parcel containing some of her clothes. But there still remained a small box on which she had been sitting. She looked at this and then at Regulus.

"Surely," said she, "the Lord Regulus will supply a slave to carry the baggage of one he doth favour."

The lords behind laughed loudly.

"Thou hast thy work cut out for thee, Regulus," cried Bœbius Massa; and Eprius Marcellus remarked, in his slow, cynical way, "Thou'lt have to furnish thyself with a new household to wait on this Lady Thanna."

"The girl is right," said Regulus. "Who would ask a woman to carry such a weight?" And he signed to a porter from among a knot of those always hanging about the Forum touting for jobs. Half-a-dozen rushed up clamouring. Thanna selected the likeliest, and delivered her trunk to him with a haughty injunction; then she gave her parcel to another fellow, bidding both follow her, all of which Regulus and his friends watched amusedly.

"She will be choosing thy bearers for thee next, Regulus," said Massa.

"And I warrant they'll be a wise choice," rejoined he. "Seest thou not that the girl hath brains and judgment? She's just the sort I need. Art thou not, pretty maid?" and he nodded affably to Thanna over his shoulder.

She dropped a pert little curtsey, and while Nyria marvelled at her brazen bearing she bade her late companions farewell.

Meantime Stephanus's temper, never mild, was no sweeter for the long hours he had had to wait. While he was worsening his cause with Matho by angry expostulations, Crispus brought a jug of fresh milk to Æmilia's babes, and some little sweet cakes such as were sold on the trays. As he talked, there sounded again the tramp of soldiery and the blare of trumpets. The helmets of the soldiers shone in the sun as they came down one of the streets leading from the quays. So loud was the cheering that a fear struck Nyria lest it might be Cæsar passing that way, and she begged Crispus to see if it were and bring her word. But he told her that it was Valerius Asiaticus, who had gone with a band of soldiers to welcome his brother-in-law, Paulinus, just returned from Egypt, and that the two were now being borne in their litters round the end of the Forum.

Seeing a sale of slaves was in progress, and being told it was of Julia's household, Paulinus, eager after his absence for the sights and news of Rome, had himself set down from his litter; and he and Asiaticus, with only an attendant or two to clear their way, walked along through the slave-market talking and laughing together; Asiaticus was perhaps the taller of the two, with a great square beard, a thick thatch of hair, and a face less red and less open than that of Paulinus. Not so jovial either, for at this moment Paulinus seemed to be beaming all over with rough geniality, and was seemingly well pleased at finding himself in his own city again. Nyria caught sight of them, and a wild hope shot through her. Oh, if Paulinus would buy her! He might, perchance, could she only get word to him that she was here. She gazed at him with such longing in her eyes that Crispus said teasingly,—

"Wouldst have a word with the great Paulinus, Nyria?"

"Ay, that would I," she answered earnestly. "Oh! I beseech thee, Crispus, try and draw him this way. Would it be too much if thou shouldst say that Nyria prayeth he will speak to her?"

Crispus hesitated. "Why now, I scarce like to do that," he said. "And yet I know not why Crispus, being free, should fear any man, victorious general or no? Cheer thee, Nyria, I'll ask him if I can."

Crispus went off into the crowd. But Nyria, fearing to lose the opportunity, flew out from among the slaves, and passing in front of the lawyer's desk waited only to say that she craved Matho's permission to wander a pace or two, pointing in Paulinus's direction, and ere she was answered had already gone.

Matho, but just returned from his midday meal, at which he had drunk some strong wine, was less quick-witted than he might have been earlier in the morning, so that Nyria was almost out of sight before he turned to his clerks, saying,—

"What did the yellow-haired maid demand? Speed after her, lest she go too far."

A scribe pursued her through the crowd, which parted to let her go, people fancying that she was a runaway slave and that by giving her a start they might prolong the excitement of the chase. But Nyria soon paused, for up the roadway Paulinus and Asiaticus were approaching, their litters borne behind them, while at the corner of the street the soldiers filed off in an opposite direction.

Nyria rushed forward and cast herself on her knees in front of Paulinus. He, talking with Asiaticus, did not at first perceive her, but stumbled against her form, his armour clanging as he made a false step, and the edge of his short mantle brushing her head.

She caught the fringe of his tunic beseechingly, and he, looking down, exclaimed,—

"Why, what have we here? By Venus and all her nymphs! A pretty welcome back to Rome!" And putting out his hand he swung Nyria to her feet, holding her by the shoulders before him.

"'Tis Yellow Hair!" he cried. "Why, little maid, didst know me?"

"Ay, lord," she murmured, scarcely able to speak. For now that she had reached him strength seemed to fail her, her breath came gaspingly, and her eyes filled with tears.

"Art in trouble, child?" he asked.

"Nay, lord—not since thou hast come," she answered.

"Since *I* have come! Ho! ho! What wouldst thou of Paulinus?" And he put his arm round her and drew her protectingly to his side. "Speak, little one. Be not frightened. I am no Minotaur, ready to devour beauteous maidens that sacrifice in my honour. So, since thy worship must surely be in mine honour—and most prettily is it tendered—what wouldst thou in return?"

"Lord, buy me!" she cried.

"*Buy thee!*" he repeated with a chuckle. "By Eros, thou art a tempting purchase. Art for sale, little maid?"

Nyria nodded. It was as much as she could do to choke down her sobs. All the morning she had borne herself bravely, but the strain had become too great. She saw the road of safety opening before her, and the thought of being driven from it utterly broke down her fortitude. She shook all over in the effort to control her hysterical weeping.

"Hush thee, child," said Paulinus, patting her shoulder kindly, "or else blubber freely and relieve thyself. Women are mostly better for a sound lament. When thou hast swallowed thy tears explain this matter."

Asiaticus said something that Nyria did not catch, but, judging by Paulinus's gruff retort, she guessed it to be a sneering remonstrance.

"I trow, indeed, *thou* wouldst not trouble thyself. But since the maid hath appealed to me she shall have my succour. Ye gods! is it not worth while to spend a few sestertii for such a welcome home as this?" Nyria stooped to kiss the hem of his cloak, knowing no other way to express her gratitude. Then Paulinus noticed Crispus standing interestedly by.

"Canst tell me aught about this maid?" he asked.

Crispus made obeisance. "May it please thee, Illustrious, the maid is called Nyria, and both she and I were slaves to Julia and Sabinus, whom the gods have called hence. Sabinus gave me my freedom, but Nyria is about to be sold in the market yonder to the highest bidder."

"So, ho! Is that thy tale? And thou wouldst that Paulinus bought thee? Say, little maid, is this thy desire?"

Nyria humbly bowed herself, wiping the tears from her face with a corner of her robe.

"And now I mind me," Paulinus continued, looking at her carefully. "Thou didst win the favour of Valeria, who is spare in such bestowings. To be sure, I'll purchase thee and present thee to her. Come, Yellow Hair, we'll see him who hath the selling of thee. But," he added, shaking back his mantle, and glancing once more at her ere he strode on with his hand on his sword, "be sure thou bring'st me luck, Nyria."

At that he gave Asiaticus a nudge with his great elbow, and said, leaning towards his brother-in-law,—

"There be some—eh?—who, landing on the ground of their forefathers, would haste to offer sacrifice in the temple. But 'tis no secret that of all goddesses I'd sooner sacrifice to Valeria: and since doves she will have none of, nor jewels either, this little maid shall make me a road to her heart."

Asiaticus laughed loudly. "The road to a woman's heart is scarce worth the seeking," said he. "'Tis like that silly game where one follows a clue through a labyrinth only to find at the end that naught is hidden there."

"That may be true of other women," returned Paulinus, shortly, "but 'tis not so of Valeria."

"Thou thinkest thus because thou hast not penetrated far into thy lady's mind," scoffed Asiaticus. "Now, *I* have some sort of experience by which to judge of Valeria, seeing that I have wandered over every inch of that well-tilled field—the heart of her fair sister."

"As well compare a lily to a field daisy!" cried Paulinus. "With all due deference to thee, Asiaticus—for, mind, I like Vitellia well—but thy wife is made of different stuff from mine."

"Women may all be made of different stuff," said Asiaticus, with a shrug, "but I find a palling similarity in the patterns by which Jove turns them out."

By this time they had reached Matho's desk, to which the scribe sent after Nyria directed them, and Paulinus thrust the girl forward and demanded to know her price.

"The reserve is a thousand sestertii," replied Matho, servilely. "But the maid is to go to the highest bidder."

"The highest fool!" exclaimed Paulinus. "Thou old thief of a lawyer! Thou darest not gainsay any man whose word is worth a button on his armour and who'd offer thee a fair price for her. Come now, what wilt thou take?"

"I have told thee, Illustrious," said Matho, fawningly. "The maid is reserved at a thousand sestertii. But with that face and that yellow hair she is well worth three, which is what we hope to obtain for her."

"By Mercury! thou hast his own audacity. I wonder thou darest sit there in the sun lest thou be shrivelled up."

Paulinus laughed angrily, then looked at Nyria and pulled her hair, but not unkindly.

"Dost hear, Nyria? Didst mean to break Paulinus's exchequer in putting this obligation upon him? I'll warrant Valeria may think thee worth that much, but what shall *I* say?"

Nyria gazed at him in piteous pleading, not knowing if he expected her to answer, but seeing that he did, she murmured faintly, "Oh, buy me, lord!"

"Ay, that I will," he answered. "But not at this old thief's price. Come, come, a thousand sestertii, Matho, and thou art well paid."

Just then there was a shoving and pushing in the crowd that had gathered round, and Stephanus came, with his two friends behind him, for, by the laws of sale, now that someone had offered a price he was privileged to put forward another.

"Twelve hundred sestertii!" he cried.

"Twelve hundred!" exclaimed Paulinus, eyeing Stephanus in surprise, while Matho nodded to the newcomer. "Who art thou that darest to bid against me?"

Stephanus said nothing, but watched to see Matho register the sum he had offered.

"Well, if thou dost say twelve," added Paulinus, "I suppose I must say fifteen."

"Two thousand!" added Stephanus.

"Two thousand five hundred!" Paulinus followed on quickly. "and no more nonsense, Matho. Write the maid down to me." He strode forward, putting his hand on the desk. "I know not who this fellow is," he went on, "but we are not bidding publicly. The maid is not being put up from the rostrum, and I demand that thou dost sell her to me by the law of private treaty. I'll pay no more than that. Put her up to auction if thou darest!"

Matho cringed before Paulinus's bullying manner, for he knew that Paulinus was a man of note in Rome and a friend of Cæsar's.

"Yea, lord—yea, lord," he answered hurriedly. "This fellow—the worthy goldsmith, Stephanus, did desire the maid. But being only a freedman, and unmarried—and the reserve on her so high, seeing that she hath yellow hair and is like to take a lady's fancy" —Matho stumbled over his words, sedulously addressing himself to Paulinus and ignoring Stephanus and his friends—"why, 'tis not fitting he should have her. But she will suit thy noble lady well."

"Prate not of thy betters," stormed Paulinus. "Give me a pen and I'll sign for the sum. I have no time to waste here with thee all day." He scrawled thickly on the parchment which Matho handed him, and left the desk, saying,—

"Come, Yellow Hair, thou and I are both glad to quit this spot, I warrant."

Paulinus strode off a step or two, and was caught in a knot of welcoming friends. But Nyria looked at Stephanus, who was leaning against a corner of Matho's table. His face was so white and strange that the girl's heart smote her, and she ran to him. As she did so the bag of money that he held dropped, jingling, to the ground.

"Fret not, Stephanus," Nyria whispered. "Thou knowest 'tis Paulinus that hath bought me, and I shall be so happy in his household. Grudge me not. Only smile on me again."

Stephanus looked at her blankly. His two friends were talking in low tones behind him, when Juvenal, in his long philosopher's cloak, who had been standing by, watching all that passed, came up and laid his hand on his friend's shoulder.

"Tush, Stephanus," he said, "'tis but justice—the justice of Rome. Didst think that *thou'd* be heard—thou who art but a server in this city and not one of those that rule? Cease mourning, man—cease. No maid is worth it."

Suddenly Stephanus thrust Juvenal and the two goldsmiths aside.

"Begone! begone!" he cried huskily, his arms outspread before him. "I would be alone."

With head bent down he pushed his way through the throng. His friend's regretful gaze followed. Then Juvenal slowly picked up the money-bag.

"Verily," quoth the philosopher, "he whom the gods would afflict, they do first madden—thus to make the matter surer."

XXVIII

NYRIA had to haste in the wake of Paulinus, for he took long strides, and she feared to lose sight of him. When she reached her new master he was talking to Plinius, who, with his young wife, was strolling round the slave-market.

"Yes, I am come to buy a head dresser for this little lady," Plinius said. "Hers is too fine for Antæia, who would fain have one of simpler tastes. I misdoubt me of Julia's women, but haply among the lesser maids we may find one who will be kind to this little shy mistress of mine."

"A maid I have just purchased may advise thee," said Paulinus. "Here, Yellow Hair, where hast thou got? Thou art so small, thou little flea, that if thou dost hide thee beneath the hem of my cloak, how am I to find thee?" And he swung Nyria forward. "Dost know if there be one among Julia's women who can serve the purpose of Plinius and his lady?"

"Yea, lord," answered Nyria, promptly. "But she is wed, and much desireth to be sold with her husband."

"That is but natural," said Plinius, smiling. "I can make room for the fellow if he have aught at his finger-ends."

"May it please thee, lord," said Nyria, "Æmilia's husband is a table steward, and hath served Sabinus's person."

"So much the better," answered Plinius. "Show us the couple, little maid."

Nyria joyously led the way to where Æmilia and her husband sat. Matho was just pointing her out to be brought beside the rostrum, and there was a wild look on Æmilia's face. She and her husband glanced anxiously at the party approaching, and, rising with alacrity, answered all that was asked them. Plinius conferred for a moment with Antæia, who seemed pleased with the pair.

"That's done, then," said Plinius. "Place thy chattels together, good folk, and be ready to follow. . . . And thou, little maid," said he, handing Nyria a gold aureus, "there's for thy commission."

Nyria took the gift gratefully, and when the lords and lady had moved away she threw her arms round Æmilia, from whose face all strain and fear had passed, and kissed her. Thus they parted.

At the edge of the Forum Paulinus called his litter.

"Thy little limbs will scarce keep pace with my bearers," he said to Nyria. "Jump in, Yellow Hair! There's room for thee."

The girl flushed up at this condescension. "Nay, lord, it is not fitting. Nyria can run."

"But Nyria need not run," he answered. "Thou hast had but a poor time in the past, if I remember rightly, Yellow Hair. For once at least thou shalt ride like a lady."

He made her get in first, and she curled herself up with her bundle beside his feet. Then the bearers hoisted the poles and they went along, round below the palaces and the Gardens of Adonis, past the great new amphitheatre, and up a curving road to the Cœlian.

Paulinus rode with the curtains raised, and the sweet afternoon air was refreshing after the heat and noise of the slave-market. It seemed to Nyria almost as though Rome had changed during these last weeks of confinement and gloom. Winter was gone, and there was a foretaste of spring in the scarce-opened clusters of blossom on the blackthorn, and the pinkish tinge of the almond rods. The sun slanted in beneath the cover of the litter, and its warmth crept into Nyria's heart.

"Thou art a piece of sunshine thyself, Yellow Hair," said Paulinus. He had been shouting remarks to Asiaticus, who was carried behind, and now noticed Nyria's face. "Hast never ridden in a litter before?"

"Once only, lord, since I was a babe."

"And when was that once?" he asked. Encouraged by his questions, she told him how Crispus had hired a litter to bear her up the Cœlian, and his reason for so doing.

"Poor little maid!" said Paulinus. "And that because thou wouldst serve Valeria at the cost of a beating. Methinks she might in return have sent a steward to purchase thee."

"Haply, lord, she knew not that we were to be sold," faltered Nyria, eager to excuse her idol.

"Haply not," he said, "seeing that Valeria liveth for the most part in a dreamland of her own, where thou and I, and such-like common fleshly folk, Yellow Hair, do not exist—save to serve her." There was an angry ring in his laughter.

Presently they reached the great entrance to the villa, and were borne up to the vestibule, where they were set down. Paulinus sprang out, and Nyria walked after him as he passed between bowing slaves, who had congregated quickly. A steward preceded him to the ante-chamber of a room in the central part of the house, which adjoined the apartments of both master and mistress, and here he drew aside the heavy curtains over the doorway, dropping them behind Paulinus, who left Nyria standing in the ante-chamber.

In a few minutes Asiaticus arrived and went in too. Snatches of talk reached Nyria. She heard Valeria's voice, very cold and sweet, inquiring after Paulinus's health and his journey in courteous fashion; and presently that of Vitellia saying,—

"Now, thou dost doubtless desire, Lucia, to be alone with thy spouse. Asiaticus and I will depart." But Valeria interposed pressingly. She hoped, she said, that her sister and brother-in-law would remain and partake of the evening meal with Paulinus and herself; at which Paulinus remarked that a good dinner would be welcome, since he had fed chiefly on dried meats aboard the vessel; and as for Egypt, there was naught but sand wherewith to season one's food.

"I shall enjoy a tasty dish or two and a cup of old wine in which to pledge thee, ladies. Truly, 'twill be a pleasure to dine again with such fair faces before me," he added in high good-humour.

"But I had forgotten!" he exclaimed. "I came not alone. There is a lady with me whom thou must receive graciously, Valeria. Her talk, as she sat with me in my litter, made the road seem short, even though it led to my wife."

"Who is this dame?" inquired Valeria, coldly.

"I'll show thee," laughed Paulinus, and Nyria heard his armour ring as he strode across the room and flung wide the curtains.

"Enter," he cried, "enter, thou blue-eyed, golden-haired nymph of Venus, and bring some fire from her altar to hallow this domestic shrine."

"Why, 'tis Nyria!" exclaimed Valeria.

"Ay, Nyria—she, whom it appears, hath served thee well, and whom thou hast served less kindly in leaving her to be put up at the common rostrum. Yet glad was I of thy neglect, since it gave me the chance to present her to thee myself," said Paulinus.

Valeria's lips twitched, but she answered courteously,—

"I am pleased to receive Nyria." Yet she took small notice of her new property, who drew shyly back, for Valeria seemed absorbed in keeping her sister at her side until the two lords withdrew to Paulinus's part of the house. Then Valeria led Vitellia to her own apartments, while Nyria followed the ladies. Æola was sitting in a small court which they passed, and Valeria bade her take Nyria to the slaves' quarters. These were somewhat differently arranged to those at Julia's, and rather less numerous.

Nyria delayed there no longer than she was obliged, but hurried back to the house, where she waited at the door of Valeria's dressing-room until the ladies emerged, and she took her place behind them as they went towards the triclinium, a small one near the great atrium.

Paulinus and Asiaticus, each attended by a slave, came forth, and meeting the ladies, walked with them. Peering through the curtains was Gregorio, but when he saw Nyria he showed his teeth in an evil grimace and, dropping the curtains, disappeared into Paulinus's apartments.

Nyria stood behind her mistress's chair as she had been accustomed to do at Julia's. The table was a costly one, of rare African wood, and so finely polished that the dishes of fruit were reflected in it; but there was none of the garish magnificence in which Julia had indulged. The wine was poured into glasses richly chased, but colourless, and very different from Julia's gemmed and tinted goblets. The silver vessels, too, were of simpler design, the whole service quieter and in better taste.

Valeria looked very lovely. She wore a dress of pale grey silk, with much embroidery of silver and small pearls. Round her waist was a girdle of silver, and her sandals were silver with purple thongs, while on her shoulders her robe was clasped with ornaments of silver set with pearls. Her hair, knotted in her usual Greek style, had only a silver fillet; and her throat and arms were bare. Her manner, though gracious, was preoccupied, and she ate little, and drank her wine sparingly, mixed with water. Asiaticus made frequent pretexts for a fresh toast, whereat Paulinus rallied his brother-in-law on seeking excuses for his cups.

"I see, Asiaticus," he cried, "that thou dost not drink without some pledge, nor wilt thou ever pledge thyself without a drink. Methinks that drinks and pledges are both good in their way, but I require no plea for a glass; nor, with my lady-wife before me, do I need any excuse for a pledge." He raised his cup to Valeria and smiled. But though she answered courteously, Valeria seemed ill at ease.

Asiaticus had his glass refilled, and drank to her also, coupling her name with Paulinus's in terms of coarse wit. Presently he called another toast, saying, with his harsh laugh, "I drink to the union of husbands and wives, for to be separated from one's faithful spouse is doubtless one of the worst ills the gods can inflict. Praise Juno, however, my lady, being of like mind, doth rarely punish me with this privation."

Paulinus winked at his brother-in-law and laughed riotously, but Vitellia's smile was forced. The sentiment seemed not wholly to her taste, though it was the one she preached. The dinner was not so long nor so sumptuous as at Julia's, but there were many good dishes, and Paulinus praised Valeria for having remembered his favourites.

The corners of her mouth curled as she answered, "'Tis a small matter, my lord."

"Like enough," quoth Paulinus. "Yet the dishes taste sweeter, Valeria, for having been thy thought;" to which Valeria answered nothing. Paulinus, from his large chair, talked greatly during the meal, he and Asiaticus having much to say of their different deeds in Egypt and in Gaul, and also concerning the coming war, in which, it appeared, both were to have commands. For this it was that Paulinus had been recalled, Civica Cerealis having been given orders to open his veins in Egypt, and one Metius Rufus appointed pro-consul in his stead. Towards the end of the banquet, however, conversation flagged, and Paulinus's glance fell on Nyria.

"So there's thy new toy," he said to Valeria. "Little Yellow Hair, dost know how a good slave is fashioned?"

Nyria only blushed, and Paulinus went on jestingly, "Thou shouldst be made of springs, of which none but thy mistress should know the secret. Hast eaten aught since thou didst enter the Lady Valeria's service?"

Nyria shook her head. "Nay, lord."

"Then since Valeria hath not bound thee over, we'll do it now by ancient rite;" and turning to a steward behind him, Paulinus said, "Go, fetch the meal." Then, signing to another, "And thou, fellow, fill the glass. Nay, not that vintage. 'Tis too strong for the maid. Thou wouldst not that we should carry thee out afterwards, eh, Yellow Hair?"

Nyria laughed uncomfortably, for she saw that Paulinus meant to go through the old ceremony by which slaves bound themselves in faithful service to their masters. It was a custom long fallen into disuse, though tales were sometimes heard of young slaves being had up in drinking revels and made mock of in this manner.

Paulinus bade the girl come round beside him at the table, and put the bowl of meal into one of her hands, and the wine in the other, and drew before him a ladleful from the great salt-cellar with which to sprinkle her lips. She looked anxiously at Valeria and was relieved to see that her new mistress was not angry, as Julia would have been.

"Now, Yellow Hair, we'll hear thee take thy vow," said Paulinus. "By the bread—" he prompted. "Get on, little maid. Dost know the words?"

"Oh! ay! lord," whispered Nyria, half frightened, half amused.

"By the bread—" he repeated; and she took him up.

"By the bread, fruit of the earth, that buildeth life in man—"

"And by the salt," he said.

"By the salt that is the savour of all things—"

"And by the wine—"

"And by the wine that cheereth man's heart—by all these things which give him strength and render his service staunch—and chiefly by—"

Here of a sudden Nyria paused, for she liked not to call upon any Roman god, and the choice of a divinity was left to the slave, who might swear by any favoured one.

"Well, who is thy fancy, Yellow Hair?" cried Paulinus. "Wilt swear by Venus, or by Artemis, or by that playful god who doth hide himself in guise of a child while verily he hath all the wiles of manhood? Say, is it by Eros, little maid, that thou wouldst take thy vow?"

"Nay, lord," murmured Nyria, "but by the greatest God of all."

"Thou art not modest," laughed Paulinus. "Now, Jupiter, list to the maid's oath and register it eternally!"

Then Nyria turned to Valeria and spoke with deep earnestness.

"By the greatest God of all I vow to serve thee faithfully—my hands—thy hands; my feet—thy feet; my lips, too, thine—that I may truly do thy bidding, and that if my life be demanded of me, that too I may render up for thee, since I am no more mine own, nor any man's, save only thine. I pray thee, hear my vow."

"Well done, Yellow Hair! Well done! Drink the wine;" and Paulinus would have tossed it down her throat himself had she not sipped as was her duty, and also tasted a mouthful of the meal; then, having laid the salt upon her lips, he leaned back in his chair and seemed satisfied.

"Many a vow is taken in jest," said Vitellia, gently. "But though this old Roman one be of small account nowadays, verily I believe that Nyria will keep her word—even to the death."

Valeria bent forward as Nyria set down the bowl and laid her hand upon the slave's.

"'Twas well done, Nyria," she said. "Go now to my rooms and await me."

Nyria went straight to the Domina's apartments. The place was all deserted, for the women were at their supper. She had taken nothing herself since early morning, save the taste of meal and sup of wine, and felt in sore want of food. But no one brought her any, and she dared not go in search of it.

Before very long Valeria came in, closing the curtains behind her. She walked quickly across the room, her robe shimmering as she moved like a silver cloud.

"Nyria," she said, and the girl saw that her heart was beating fast, "I have somewhat for thee to do to-night. Canst thou be swift and silent?"

Nyria bent at her feet. "Trust me, Domina."

"'Tis well," Valeria said. "Wait while I write," and, going to the table, she took a tablet and stylus and wrote rapidly, binding her letter with ribbon and wax. Then she gave Nyria the packet.

"Veil thy head and face," she said. "Take some old cloak of mine. Let none know who thou art, but haste thee. Speed down the hill till thou comest to the house of Licinius Sura. Enter by the smaller gate, and get thee through the court round the house, when thou shalt find a door with a trellis over it whereon a jasmine grows. There is a window set in the wall close by, and thou shalt see a lamp burning. Rap thrice on the door—a single, soft knock with thy knuckle—and to him that openeth give this despatch.

Wait then and see what answer there shall be, and bring it back without fail."

"I will not fail, Domina," Nyria answered.

Valeria turned into the bed-chamber and brought out a soft grey cloak with a hood that covered the girl from head to foot.

"Be swift and sure," she said, "and seek me when thou dost return."

Nyria made obeisance and hastened away, through the anteroom, down the terrace steps to the little gate in the wall, her hunger forgotten. She sped along the Cœlian road, then up the bend of the Aventine, perceiving in the dim distance the great house of Julia, wherein now was darkness darker than the night.

There were two entrances to Licinius Sura's villa, and she knew the one of which Valeria had spoken—a smaller door set in the stone wall thickly over-arched with trees. Nyria closed it carefully behind her, finding herself on a path that led to the building and round one end of it. She went slowly on, looking for that window in which should be set a lamp. This presently she saw, and stopped beneath a porch over which grew a plant that might have been a jasmine. Here she rapped with one knuckle, as Valeria had told her, three times upon the panel.

Scarcely had she done so when there was a movement within. A shadow crossed the lamp, and the door was swung open a foot below, so that Nyria, standing on the raised step, seemed more than her height. A man's form was before her, the lamp behind him, and his face in shadow. But she had no time to distinguish who it might be, for of a sudden he caught her in his arms and, pushing back the hood, rained fervid kisses upon her face and head. She would have cried out had she dared, but, remembering Valeria's order to be silent, she only tried dumbly to release herself. As she put forth her hands to thrust the man back he drew her into the room; and then, as the light shone upon her hair, he dropped his arms and laughed, saying,—

"Whom have we here? Verily, there's some mistake."

"Nay, no mistake, lord," replied Nyria, seeing that it was Licinius Sura. "I bear this to give to thee."

And, bending, she offered him Valeria's tablet, which he took from her hand but did not look at, his eyes being fixed on her face.

"Yea, verily, a mistake on my part, little watch-dog," he said. "And yet methink not wholly a mistake. For Eros ordained that those kisses thou once didst scorn should be given thee some day; and lo! thou'st had them in full measure. Is't not so, Xydra of the golden hair?"

As Nyria did not answer he cried, "Have the gods sealed thy tongue? By Venus, they shall not seal thy lips!" and he put a hand beneath her chin to draw her nearer.

But Nyria contrived by curtseying to evade him.

"Lord, I am Valeria's messenger, and as such should be sacred to one whom Valeria deigns to honour."

Licinius laughed. "Well said, little watch-dog. I see thou art a citadel not to be captured by any common arts of love. And thou art right—he whom Valeria deigns to honour should bear himself in nobler fashion."

Then he moved away, wrenching the silk that bound the tablet.

"This is ill news," he said, scanning Valeria's letter. His brows darkened as he turned the waxen sheet. "So Paulinus hath come back! And the great god of destiny doth stretch an arm betwixt his villa and the luckless house of Licinius Sura. Ah! well-a-day!" Nyria made no reply, nor did she change her position, while Licinius walked to a writing-table and took up a stylus, flicking it meditatively against his mouth. Then he sat down as if to write, and then re-read Valeria's letter. Now he flung the stylus from him, and pushing back his chair turned round.

"Tell Valeria, little watch-dog, that Licinius fears to write. No offence to thee, child. 'Twould not be well that any words of mine should fall within Paulinus's paws. Now, hear my message. Say to Valeria that which she doth already know. Tell her Licinius's love and loyalty are hers, and that there standeth naught between us save such obstacles as she herself doth raise. But that 'tis safer for Licinius to keep his distance, even by note of hand. Nevertheless, this house is free to Valeria. Bid her come when she will. The door and Licinius's heart are alike open to her. Canst remember, Yellow Hair?" Standing before the girl he picked out a strand from her curls and held it up. "Verily, a love-lock!" said he. "How many of these hast thou given away?"

Much displeased, Nyria shook herself free. "I'll bear thy message to Valeria, lord," she said formally.

"And one word more. Tell Valeria that Licinius may not be here long. That, I warrant, will bring her flying."

Nyria said nothing, but drew her cloak over her head, and with a swift obeisance went out at the door.

"Thou mayst tell Valeria too," called Licinius, softly, after her, "that she hath chosen a speedy messenger, one who will not delay, no matter what be the temptation."

His mocking laugh sounded behind Nyria as she ran out, angry with him, angry with herself; and had Valeria been other than Valeria she would have been angry with her as well.

The girl went warily as she neared the villa, lest any should be observing her. She entered at the little gate and passed up the terrace steps unseen. But as she approached the door of Valeria's apartments Æola came running out, and by the light of the hanging lamps Nyria saw that she was frightened.

"Oh, Nyria!" she gasped, "I have been searching for thee. Whither hadst thou fled? But tell me not now, only come—come quickly."

And she hurried Nyria along, scarcely giving her time to remove the cloak she wore. Of a sudden there sounded a voice loudly raised.

"Paulinus is in there," Æola whispered, pointing to the curtains of Valeria's sitting-room; "ay, Nyria, Paulinus!"

"Well, what of that?" retorted Nyria.

"But Valeria desires him not," answered Æola, all a-quiver with dismay. "The Lady Vitellia and her lord have left, and Paulinus followed Valeria to her rooms, and went not at her word of dismissal—ay, and said he would not go. And when he saw me he bade me leave them. But Valeria bade me stay—"

"And wherefore didst thou not stay?" inquired Nyria, sharply.

"How could I when Paulinus ordered me hence? Oh, Nyria, hearken! What shall we do?"

"*Do!*" said Nyria, drawing up her small form with decision. "Go thou to bed, 'tis all thou art fit for. I'll seek my lady." And Nyria ran across the room.

With a loud-beating heart she bent herself between the curtains and entered, making another obeisance as she advanced. But neither husband nor wife noticed her. Valeria was supporting herself with one hand on a marble table, whereon were silver knick-knacks and small weapons from foreign parts. Close before her stood Paulinus, his face flushed, the veins on his forehead swollen, and his great knotted arms extended. At sight of him Nyria shrank. This was not the Paulinus who had treated her so kindly. He seemed some monster, and Valeria gazed in horror at him. Her hand, moving over the table, caught at a dagger that looked like a toy, the handle set with gems, but the blade fine and deadly. She snatched this up and held it to her breast.

"Come no nearer," she said, "come no nearer, or I strike."

XXIX

"Dost think I'd see thee slay thyself?" exclaimed Paulinus. "Thou'rt mad, I say. Drop that weapon and let me still thy fears." Valeria stared at him with fixed eyes, repeating, the blade upon her bare skin,—

"Come no nearer—come no nearer, or I strike."

Then Nyria ran forward and made obeisance at her feet.

Valeria's glance fell upon the girl, and all her body seemed to relax. "Ah! Nyria," she cried, holding forth her hand which held the dagger, and as she did so it slipped to the floor. "Nyria—"

"Ay, Domina. I am here," and Nyria sprang up and tried to support Valeria as she, too, fell.

"Remain, Nyria . . . remain," she murmured. And then a shiver went through her frame, her head fell back, and Nyria saw that she had fainted.

The girl laid her mistress on the ground and drew a cushion beneath her head while Paulinus bent over her.

"By all the gods!" he said aloud, "Pygmalion was better off than I, for his love did warm his statue into life, whereas mine, it seems, doth but turn this woman into stone."

There was exasperation and yet remorse in his voice.

"My lady hath but recently been ill, lord. As yet her strength hath not returned," said Nyria.

He bent his eyes upon her broodingly. "I should have thought of that," said he. "Such fragile women are not fit for men to touch. Call help, Yellow Hair, and bear thy lady to her chamber. Did she feel Paulinus's arms around her she'd wake to fright again. 'Tis evident that my wife's rooms are no place for me."

And he strode away. But as he went his glance fell on the dagger which Valeria had dropped. Stooping, he tossed it, with a fierce oath, to the other end of the room, where it lay embedded in a carved wooden stool that it had chanced to strike. Nyria found a silver whistle which Valeria always wore for the summoning of her slaves, and putting it to her lips, blew sharply. Æola came running in, and Nyria bade her summon assistance.

But after Valeria had been borne to her chamber, and they had put hot bottles to her feet and poured strong spirits between her teeth, or tried to, since she kept them clenched, and she still lay without giving sign of life, Nyria left Æola beside the bed and ran through to the rooms of Paulinus. There he was, pacing to and fro, talking to Gregorio, who fluttered like some gay bird beside his master, swinging the folds of his tunic and tossing a long feather that he carried in his hand, while he prated to Paulinus, doubtless breeding mischief, Nyria thought. But she hurried in and prostrated herself before her lord.

"May it please thee to send for Archimenes, who is the doctor that hath attended Valeria and will know best how to treat her, for my lady hath not regained consciousness."

Paulinus stopped in his walk and swore freely, asking,—

"Hath this Archimenes attended thy lady for long? How was she ill? What brought about the fever?" and other questions. Nyria told him all she could.

"Archimenes doth but pander to the whims of nervous women," said he. "Nevertheless, since he hath restored Valeria to health before, 'tis doubtless best he should see her now. Go thou, Gregorio, and summon this physician. Bid other messengers likewise seek him wheresoe'er he may be found."

Gregorio's eyes flashed as he answered sullenly,—

"I'll send someone to take thy commands." His insolent manner angered Paulinus.

"Thou'lt serve them on thyself, thou painted jackanapes. See to it that thou doest my bidding—and right quickly. Dost think I keep thee for naught except to caterwaul? Hasten!" and Gregorio sprang away, his face black as night.

Nyria was leaving the room when Paulinus stopped her.

"I'll seek the doctor myself," said he. "Say, Yellow Hair, where shall I find this Archimenes? And if I find him not, who else is there I may command?"

Nyria told him where Archimenes lived, but hesitated to answer his second question. Paulinus, seeing her embarrassment, waved her off.

"Go back—go back, child! Attend to thy duties; I'll find a doctor for Valeria."

"May it please thee, lord, I know one who is good and wise, though he be not registered," said Nyria. "He served Valeria before. If it please thee I can send for him."

"Ay, send for him—go, send at once. I myself will seek this Archimenes." And not waiting to don his toga, Paulinus hurried off.

Nyria was alone at Valeria's bedside when the great doctor arrived. She had not called the other women, for it was not Valeria's custom that they should attend her at night.

Archimenes looked grave as he bent over the bed.

"I like not to let blood," said he. "But at times it is needful, and this is one of them." So with a sharp instrument he made a puncture in Valeria's arm, and wiped away a few drops, binding up the place quickly when he saw that she stirred, while Nyria stood by, plying the fan upon her. He wiped Valeria's lips with distilled spirit, and after a time she opened her eyes. But a long, shuddering sigh shook her, and she seemed like to faint anew.

"Speak to her," said Archimenes. "Tell her that all is well."

Nyria obeyed, and presently Valeria opened her eyes again and gazed from Nyria to the physician and round the room. Then, with a murmur of relief, she turned upon her pillow.

"I do but desire to sleep," she said.

Archimenes had meanwhile mixed a strong cordial. When Valeria had drunk it a faint flush came to her cheeks and she lay and slept like a child. Seeing this, Archimenes signed to Nyria to follow him into the ante-chamber. There Stephanus stood, with a heavy toga folded round him, his bag in his hand. Archimenes greeted his former colleague warmly.

"Methinks thou art not needed to-night. Let the lady rest. Sleep will work wonders. I would now have a few words with this maiden. Do thou divest thyself of that wrapper, Brother." Then he questioned Nyria, who told as meagre a tale as she might, which, however, Archimenes seemed to comprehend.

"Now will I see Paulinus," he said. "Lead thou the way, Nyria. Brother Stephanus, I need not keep thee."

"I thank thee, sir," replied Stephanus. "I will wait here till Nyria returns. Like enough, while she hath been tending others there have been none to tend her."

And though his voice was rougher than its wont, Nyria rejoiced to hear it, for the girl had felt troubled, remembering how Stephanus had turned away from her without speaking in the slave-market that day.

She took Archimenes to her lord's apartments, then hastened back to the ante-chamber, where Stephanus stood, dark, square and gloomy, not having taken off his toga nor set down his bag.

"How dost thou find thyself after thy fatigues?" he inquired in a formal tone.

"Well enough, Stephanus," she answered wistfully.

"Doubtless thou hast been generously served and fed since thou camest hither?" he said.

Then Nyria remembered that she had had no food all day, and even as he spoke a sudden dizziness overpowered her; she swayed, and would have fallen, but that he caught her by the shoulders and placed her on a chair.

"Be seated," he said. "I may not support thee, since thou art no maid of mine. Nevertheless, if thou wert the veriest stranger, yet would I not see thee starve." Then, going to the door of Valeria's chamber, he called softly through the curtains, "Æola! Bring food and wine for Nyria. She doth need them sore."

Æola ran out and Nyria said meekly,—

"Thou art kind, Stephanus." But he answered not, nor did he take the hand she held out.

"Wilt thou have none of me, Stephanus?" she asked. He shook his head, but still he answered nothing.

Nyria began to weep a little. "I am still Nyria," she said, but Stephanus kept silence.

Presently Æola came back with a tray well furnished.

Nyria's faintness was only due to want of food, for when they had cut some morsels, and had fed her and made her drink the wine, she felt strong once more. When she had finished, and Æola had borne off the tray, Stephanus stepped before Nyria with his toga folded closely round him and his bag in his hand.

"Thou hast chosen thine own home," said he. "Notwithstanding, if thou dost ever need a friend, thou canst command Stephanus." And without another word or sign he left her.

Nyria gazed after him with straining eyes.

Two or three days went by, during which Valeria kept her chamber, and Archimenes visited her every day, but Stephanus appeared no more. Paulinus was out a great deal, and 'twas said that Rome was agog with the preparations for war.

Then there came a morning when Valeria looked more like her natural self, save for the constant dread in her eyes. Her women robed her in a simple white stola, and Nyria tired her head, having practised the Greek mode on Æola's curly brown tresses.

Thus Valeria was dressed and in her sitting-room when Nyria gave the doctor entrance.

"Scarcely do I need thy services now, good doctor," the lady said, smiling graciously.

Archimenes made her a spreading bow as he seated himself near her.

"I like to see that tinge of pink on thy face, fair Domina," said he, "for it shews that thou dost still find some charm in life to make thy blood surge swiftly. Yet if I be no longer needed as a doctor, may I, most noble Valeria, speak as a friend to-day. I pray thee, dear lady, hear my words, for they be winged with kindness and desire for thy well-being."

Valeria gave him a startled look, stiffening somewhat.

"I question not their endowment," she answered, "and I am pleased to count Archimenes my friend, for he could say naught that was not kindly meant. Nevertheless, in private concerns a woman's own judgment is her wisest counsellor."

"If she have no other," he replied. "Concede to Archimenes some claim of experience in the complex nature of thy sex, seeing that for the best part of a long and chequered life his dealings have been mainly with the concerns of women."

"Hath it then been thine experience that any two women's natures are alike?" asked Valeria. "If so, I trow, Archimenes"—and she slowly shook her head with a sad smile—"that thou hast not worked with open eyes among the hearts of women."

"Ah! dear Domina, 'tis not for Archimenes to commend his powers of insight. Yet would I not dare approach the sacred precincts of Valeria's heart did I not know full well that on this shrine there burns a different flame from that which lights the breasts of other women—though each be kindled in honour of the same god!"

Valeria seemed at a loss to answer him. Then she exclaimed,—

"A truce to imagery, Archimenes. I tell thee that I know not whether there burns in my heart a fire to any god at all, or if there be aught but ashes consumed to waste."

"Perchance burnt out because too early lit," he said gently. "Ah! Valeria, such as desire to lead child-maidens to the marriage altar would be wiser to wait till they chose their own road thither."

"Some there be who'd fain choose none which led to that common end whither men would hasten them," Valeria replied bitterly.

Archimenes bent forward, folding his hands.

"Alack! the wisdom of men, dear lady, hath not yet taught them that there be women who are by nature vestals. These be they who should serve the virgin goddess—not such as have no vocation for the cloistral life, the vows of which they cannot keep—like yon poor traitress of whom all Rome hath been talking of late."

"Cornelia! Hapless soul! Yet better far to be at peace in the darkness of the tomb than pledged to a lifelong deception. Verily, Archimenes, there be other obligations harder to fulfil than those of the unwilling vestal."

"Ay, bonds from which the virginal soul revolts. The true vestal is she over whom Eros hath no power. But shackles laid by law on women cut deep—eh, Domina?"

"Thou hast learned somewhat of the sex," said Valeria, gazing through the open doorway to where some young green shoots were pushing their way up through the soil. She took no heed of Nyria, who sat upon the steps leading to the terrace, within sight and call, nor did Archimenes appear to notice the slave-girl's presence. He leaned closer to Valeria.

"Wouldst thou be free?" he asked in a low, earnest tone.

Valeria glanced at him in a tremulous way. "What meanest thou, Archimenes?" she faltered.

"Domina," he said, "there are two men to whom a woman should unveil her inmost self—her priest, if she hath faith in him

—and her doctor, who to heal effectually the ills of her body must needs be acquainted with those of her mind."

"Death only can cure mine," Valeria said.

"Talk not of death," Archimenes replied. "Thou knowest not what dread power thou mayest invoke. Men and women who talk of death have small acquaintance with him. Such as have stood beneath the shadow of his wing, and felt his trailing garments brush them by, remain silent with bowed heads. Dear lady, call not death, lest he come at thy call."

"Thinkest thou not that I would welcome him!" cried Valeria, passionately. "Oh, Archimenes, physician as thou art, dost thou not know that death comes often as the manumittor—as the janitor that openeth the door of freedom?"

"Who shall say?" replied the physician. "Even if death unlatch the gate to another world, that portal should be for the aged and worn, not for thee, to whom this life should still be beautiful. Valeria"— his gaze went searchingly over her face—"may I put my finger on the root of thy disease?"

"From what, then, do I suffer?" asked Valeria, and she looked at him as one who would challenge his reply; but seeming to read the answer in his eyes, she shrank.

"This do I know," said Archimenes, solemnly. "Thou art yet young, and many joyous years should lie before thee. But if trouble doth press thus on thee again, haply not all Archimenes's skill may serve to save thee. Yet he might perchance relieve thee now. Wouldst thou be free of that nameless burden which doth beset thee?"

"Ask the prisoner if he would have his fetters removed," replied Valeria in tones of shame and agony. "Oh, Archimenes," and she clasped her hands before her, "if thou canst free me of that from which I thought only death could deliver—if thou wilt—oh, then—oh, then—receive a hapless woman's gratitude!"

Her voice broke. She turned aside in her chair, and burying her face in the cushions shook with sobs.

Archimenes rose and poured some cordial from a flagon into a glass and gave it to her to drink. She took it, saying apologetically, "I am weak."

"Ay, thou art weak," he answered. "But thou wilt soon be strong again. Here is thy faithful little maid. Lean thou on her arm and let her lead thee forth into the sunshine. Take thy mistress, Nyria; she will walk upon the terrace. Show her how the buds begin to burst, and the golden crocus to peep up through the grass. Tell her that though the night of winter hath been long, the morn of spring doth dawn on her to-day."

Then Archimenes bowed once more, and folding his toga round his ample person he withdrew. Nyria ran before along the ante-rooms to lift the curtains that he might pass, and she heard him bid a slave announce him to Paulinus.

Holding Nyria's arm, Valeria walked up and down outside. It was lovely in the garden. The sky was very blue, and the marble of the terrace and of the fountain showed white from having been lately washed by spring rains. Bulbs were pushing forth flowers—the snowdrops in thick patches and the gold and purple cups of the crocus were scattered over the grass, and overhead, in the trees, spread a pale tint of green.

By-and-by one of Paulinus's slaves came along the terrace with a message that his lord craved speech with the Domina.

"Tell thy lord Valeria waits him," she answered; and presently Paulinus himself approached. At sight of her husband Valeria trembled a little and clung closer to Nyria's arm. Dressed in his ceremonial toga, which he swung back impetuously when he advanced, he gazed at her with anger and yet compunction in his face.

"So! my wife!" he said at length, "my lady-wife, to whose presence I must needs request the favour of admittance like any stranger that may chance to call—I trust I see thee better of thine ailment."

"I thank thee," said Valeria, gathering courage. "I am better."

"Doubtless," he exclaimed, with a coarse laugh, "since thou hast gained thy point."

"'Tis scarcely meet that thou shouldst gibe," she said; but he took her up quickly.

"Archimenes hath been with me. It appears thou hast made good thy case to him."

"If he said that to thee, which I can hardly credit, Archimenes misstated fact," she answered. "That which he may have carried came from himself, and since I know not what it chanced to be, haply thou'lt tell me. Nyria, go."

But Nyria, with her hands to her forehead, murmured, "Will it not please thee to be seated, Domina? Thy strength is small as yet."

"I'll walk to a seat," replied Valeria; and, followed by Paulinus, she went to the court and placed herself in the big marble chair, while he took the bench near it.

The conference was not a long one. Paulinus bore himself sulkily, but when he raised his voice in anger a gesture from Valeria quieted him. Presently she called to Nyria to bring her a shawl, which the girl did. Paulinus was saying,—

"It is my pleasure, and that, at least, thou'lt not deny me. I tell thee that if thou wouldst remain my wife in name thou shalt grant me—in the world's eyes at least—such favour as a wife should outwardly accord her husband."

"It is at thy command," Valeria answered. "Acquaint me with thy wishes and preparations shall forthwith be made for welcoming thy friends."

"Thy secretary shall make out a list of guests at my dictation. I'll have this thing done to prove that though I be called hence yet am I master in my own house; and mind no cost be spared. That fellow, Licinius Sura, shall come that I may show Rome that thou and I are in accord, and thus stop all scandalous tales. Likewise would I see"—and Paulinus laughed brutally—"how thou dost comport thyself with him."

Valeria flinched. "Methinks thou scarce keepest to the letter of thy bond."

"Nay! By this I prove my trust in thee. If there be naught but common friendship betwixt thee and the fellow, show me—as I shall show the world—that thou art worthy to bear my name."

Valeria stood up, very pale.

"As thou willest, but leave me now, I beg," she said.

"Ay, I leave thee the honour of my house. 'Tis well for thee, Valeria, that thou hast borne me sons to make thy position surer. Else, notwithstanding the plea of that mealy-mouthed physician, thou hadst like to have gone forth a beggar. Bear that in mind—daughter of Vitellius though thou be. I relinquish a husband's closer claims on thee so long as thou dost hold thyself fittingly before the world as the loyal spouse of Valerius Paulinus and the mother of his sons. But let me hear a whisper that any other stands in the place whence thou wouldst thrust Paulinus, and not the vengeance of Cæsar himself shall equal mine."

He drew his toga round him with a sweeping movement.

"When I seek words with thee again," he said, "thou'lt come to me in the public apartments. These"—and he waved his hand towards her part of the house—"these rooms are sacred unto thee, and to the name thou bearest. See that thou dost keep them so."

XXX

PREPARATIONS for war went on apace, and troops were massing daily for what promised to be a long and arduous campaign in distant Sarmatia, where the rigours of climate and the uncertain prospects of the army made it impossible for even Vitellia to follow her lord.

In Paulinus's household preparations were going on, likewise, for the farewell festivity that he desired. At length the great day of departure came, and from dawn there was bustle at the Valerian villa, for though the guests were not bidden till past noon, many clients thronged the vestibule, and various persons had business to transact with Paulinus ere he went away. Vitellia arrived early, for it had been arranged that the brothers-in-law should start together from the house of Paulinus. She was richly dressed in robes of dull rose, much worked in gold, and wore a quaint girdle set with pink stones. But her plain, earnest face looked worn and saddened.

No greater contrast could have been found to Valeria, who, lovely as a dream, stood passively in her dressing-room while her women put the final touches to her apparel. Her stola of soft mauve was bordered with large purple flowers, raised like velvet. She wore purple shoes latched with silver thongs, and her purple palla, lined with pale green, was stiff with silver threads. Round her neck and arms were chains of magnificent green stones, which Paulinus had sent her that morning, with a scroll, on which he had written: "I do not pray thee to accept these jewels. 'Tis my command, Valeria, that thou wearest them to-day. To-morrow, if thou dost so desire, bestow them in the gutter, or where thou wilt."

Valeria put on the jewels with the same indifference she showed in robing. But, once arrayed, her manner changed, and she took up her part, pledged to play it bravely. The sisters passed to the atrium together, with Nyria and Æola behind. The slave-girls were dressed alike in new white silk-embroidered robes, each with a violet fillet in her hair.

Paulinus looked large and goodly in his armour, which shone like burnished gold.

"Verily the gems do become thee well," he said to Valeria. "My choice hath pleased thee this time—eh?"

She flushed and paled, for his manner was at once suave and truculent, and she was at a loss before his mood. When the company began to arrive Paulinus greeted them with his wife, standing beside Valeria and holding her hand, as the custom was for a newly-wedded pair, or a lord and lady who desired to show their unity of heart.

The scene was a fine one, for the atrium had an air of distinction, and the marble and other works of art were priceless. The Hermes of the central fountain, poised on one winged foot, seemed to inhale the fragrance of spring flowers banked below him. Wreaths of white blossoms twined the pillars, with here and there a band of violets or a knot of mauve or green. Large marble jars bore blossoming orange trees and masses of azalea, and the staircase was festooned with garlands. On either side of the atrium, rooms were opened for refreshments, and about them moved an army of stewards—some in Valeria's personal livery of white and violet: others in Paulinus's flame colour, with bands of two shades of crimson and the crossed swords in gold braiding, which was the badge of his former office as Tribune of the Prætorian Guard.

Vitellia stood near her sister, greeting such as came her way, but Asiaticus went about among the guests, laughing and talking loudly, and showing that the scent of battle was in his nostrils.

The shifting crowd came and went, gathering round the host and hostess, then breaking into knots and strolling through the rooms. It was a representative assemblage of the best of Roman society, though many recently well-known forms were absent—victims to Domitian's treacherous wrath.

Here came the mild-mannered historian, Tacitus, with his wife and her father—that broken-down war-horse, Agricola, a pathetic figure, aged before his time, writhing painfully beneath the slight Domitian had put upon him by offering him no command in the outgoing army, with ears pricked to the sound of battle, yet too proud to show how keenly he resented the Emperor's disfavour. There passed the poetess Sulpicia, plump, alert and smiling, beside the bland Stoic, Euphrates, following his florid, wealthy wife, led by Statius, the writer. Now came Nonius Asprena, the magnificent, with his exquisitely graceful lady, and many others of consular and senatorial rank. Eprius Marcellus, with his beaked nose and thick, grey brows; Regulus, the lawyer, with his keen, yet shifty, glance, on whom Nyria gazed with special interest. There, too, was the poet Martial, apparently much at ease. Galla had gone to Neapolis, and perhaps the poet had forgotten her, since seemingly his former jealousy of Paulinus for supplanting him in the favours of that fickle lady was outworn. It appeared now that he stood on terms of intimacy with Paulinus, to whom he had recently raked up some claim of distant cousinship, based upon his title to the name of Valerius, which Paulinus had not cared to dispute, and which served the sycophantic poet's purpose by fortifying his footing in the villa.

Nyria, gazing round with girlish enjoyment, was surprised to see Martial chatting in a friendly way to Gregorio. The boy was supposed to be in attendance on his master, and was got up in minstrel's garb—a gay tunic, with shoulder-knot of ribbons, and coloured shoe-thongs winding up his legs—but loth that his position should be marked, he had put on a daring familiarity which it pleased Martial to encourage. The two strolled off and drank wine together, as though the lad were an artist of Paris's standing instead of a mere slave-singer.

Presently the steward called a name, at which Valeria, hearing only part, paused nervously in what she was saying to another guest. Paulinus at her side muttered,—

"'Tis not the fellow thou thinkest, but his cousin, Palfurius. Ease thy mind and give the curled dandy greeting. I hear that at last he hath made good his footing on the Palatine."

Palfurius Sura advanced—a short, thick man, dressed in the latest fashion, without the distinction that Marcus possessed, but with the more confident bearing of a pure-blooded patrician. He had an appointment at Court, nominally to superintend the Imperial chamberlains—a barren office, yet coveted on account of the opportunities it afforded of gaining the ear of Cæsar.

"I have the honour to forestall my Judæan cousin, whose litter I passed below thy gate, Paulinus," said he. "I knew not that thou and Marcus Licinius wert on terms of friendship."

"My wife's friends are mine," returned Paulinus, gallantly. "Valeria doth find thy cousin pleasant company. He talks to her of matters beyond such brains as thine and mine, Palfurius."

"The fellow is clever enough—like all half-breeds," murmured Palfurius, contemptuously. "Thou hast gathered all the stars of Rome around thee, Domina," he added, glancing towards a group of celebrities.

Valeria responded formally. Her eyes were on the distant door. Paulinus, talking to a lady near her, watched his wife askance. He heard the announcement of Licinius Sura's name, and at once released himself from his companion.

"I pray thee, excuse me. Here cometh one to whom I'd fain do honour;" and he took Valeria's hand anew, extending his other to Licinius, and hailing him with a marked cordiality that astonished the bystanders.

"Welcome, Licinius, though, alack! for an hour only, seeing that I am called to the wars and that Valeria must mourn in seclusion, as becomes a loyal wife bereaved of her mate."

Licinius, not raising his eyes, bowed low, while Valeria returned his salutation silently.

"Praise Saturn, time's not slow," added Paulinus, with well-assumed warmth. "We shall return ere long and meet as better friends, for there's no union so close as that of hearts which have been severed — whether by distance or by difference. Eh, Licinius?"

Licinius seemed confused. "Paulinus should know better than I," he answered, "seeing he leaves his lady-wife, while I have none to mourn mine absence."

"Ho! ho!" jeered Paulinus, dropping Valeria's hand. "What, then, hath chanced Salome?"

"Paulinus is pleased to speak in riddles," said Licinius, with averted eyes.

"A riddle which Rome hath read long since," returned Paulinus, loudly. "Gossip saith that Salome was Licinius's slave till he became hers."

"Perchance," returned Licinius, "gossip in Rome hath a lying tongue. I heed it not." And he moved aside to let Plinius and Anteia approach.

Valeria had grown very white, but she was forced to perform her part as hostess. Pliny pressed her to pay a visit to his Laurentine villa.

"Not yet," he said; "the season is scarcely enough advanced. Our gardens in town show more sign of spring than those in the country. But when the thorn trees are thick with blossom, thou must come, Valeria. 'Twill be a joy to Anteia."

Valeria accepted the invitation in a mechanical manner.

"I have much to concern me at present," said Pliny. "Several pleadings will keep me in Rome, but we'll spend a happy month later on. I would that my business here were like to be half as pleasurable," he continued. "Of late it hath lain largely in Cæsar's own basilica, for he is troubled at this insurrection in Sarmatia, fearing that others may spring up. Cæsar is superstitious concerning prognostications, and we have had unhappy proof that they for whom the Chaldeans foretell greatness stand in jeopardy—especially such as be connected with Judæa. Domitian hath not forgotten the prediction of a rising in that quarter."

Valeria murmured something indifferently, and Pliny, thinking to interest her, went on,—

"There is one man whom the astrologers thus distinguish, who is too advanced in years to be reckoned dangerous. From what I know of Nerva, methinks they're out in their forecasts. 'Tis strange, in truth, he should be quartered just now at Edessa, but he's not the man to snatch the purple, though others might push him to it."

Valeria's eyes had wandered to Licinius, who stood close, his gaze bent on the ground, seemingly absorbed in what was being said, though Plinius had dropped his voice. Paulinus at that moment turned from another group and laid a heavy hand upon Licinius's shoulder.

"How's this?" he exclaimed. "Art thou also about to deprive Rome of thy presence, as some say?"

"For once," replied Licinius, "some say right."

"Whither goest thou?" The words seemed torn from Valeria's lips.

Licinius flashed a full glance at her, then dropped his eyes, and, folding his arms with a courtly inclination, answered,—

"I go, Domina, to Judæa."

"Ah!" Valeria gasped and swayed. She went so pale that Plinius put out his arm to support her.

"Thou art fatigued," he said kindly. "Be seated, Valeria. Let me bring thee wine."

"Nay . . . nay . . . 'tis naught. Heed me not, I beg," she murmured in evident distress, yet seeming so eager to hide her weakness that Plinius merely put himself between her and the rest till she should recover. Paulinus was talking loudly meanwhile with Licinius.

"Make no excuses, 'tis but natural," he said jovially. "All men do desire to see the land of their birth and blood;" but there was sneering intent in his words, for Judæan blood was not prized in Rome.

Licinius reddened and bit his lip.

"'Tis no sentiment that takes me to Judæa, but certain private business that doth need adjustment."

"'Tis well a man should straighten the road for those that come after him," said Plinius. "Thou hast a son, Licinius, as I've heard, and if there be a flaw in the bond that binds thee to his mother, doubtless thou'lt legitimise the boy."

To Valeria's aching fancy the whole room seemed to listen for Licinius's next words. Embarrassed, yet jesting, he retorted,—

"The laws of Rome are merciful. Were every man compelled to recognise such evidences of folly 'twould render the division of his goods no easy task." At which Paulinus was forced to guffaw noisily. Then he affected to remember Valeria, and turned round to her.

"This test of thy composure hath been too much for thee," he said. "But bear up a little longer, sweet wife. 'Twill soon be over, and then we will think but of meeting again. Verily, friends," he added, glancing round, "I would claim thy kind indulgence for Valeria, seeing that it doth rack a woman sore to see her spouse go forth to war." Valeria stiffened and smiled feebly.

"Methinks, my wife," Paulinus went on, "the time hath come for thee to pledge me in our parting cup. I set store, thou knowest, by our beloved old Roman customs."

As he spoke there sounded from without the shrill blast of military trumpets and the rolling tramp of many feet. It was the legionaries arriving. Paulinus put an arm round Valeria and remained thus till two officers came to tell him that troops lined the portico and the roadway.

"'Tis well," he said. "When Rome calls her sons to arms their part is to obey right willingly, even though they leave behind them ties sweeter and more sacred than those which bind them to their country's service."

At this there burst forth great applause, but Valeria said naught. The crowd, a close-packed throng, pressed into the atrium to see the generals depart. Asiaticus was already buckling on his sword, at which Vitellia assisted him, though beneath his breath he grumbled at her clumsy fingers. Paulinus passed round the circle, giving a farewell word to such of those who stood nearest.

"Do thou keep old Rome sound," he said to Nonius Asprena. "Guide the Conscript Fathers aright, for we who go to strengthen her borders would find it ill to hear that in our absence Rome had cankered at her core."

And to Plinius,—

"I pray Minerva, Pliny, that thou be not so overworked with pleadings as to hinder thee from providing books for posterity, since we, who be not men of brains like thee, do look to such as Plinius for the training of our descendants."

And to Regulus he said,—

"How wilt thou employ thyself whilst so many of thy clients are away?" Regulus smiled disagreeably, and Paulinus added, "I trow a brain like thine will never lack occupation, even though Paulinus doth not afford it thee."

To Licinius Sura he gave an odd, curt nod. "Good luck go with thee to Judæa, and may better luck keep thee there," a joke that made some wonder and others smile.

After moving round, Paulinus returned to Valeria, and his eyes fell on Nyria. "Obey thy lady in all things, Yellow Hair. 'Tis my last behest to thee," he said, and Nyria meekly made obeisance.

"Now last, but not least—my wife!" he cried; "of least account, perchance, before Paulinus's friends, yet reigning proudest, fairest, best beloved, the goddess of his hearth! Come, drink with me, Valeria, the cup wherein from ancient times loyal wives have been wont to pledge their faith with prayers for their departing lords."

He signed to the chief steward, who, already at his orders, had brought a goblet filled with wine. Valeria trembled, clasping and unclasping her hands in nervous distress. She glanced piteously at Paulinus and dropped her eyes again.

"Thy heart is too full for words, sweet wife," he said, loud enough for all to hear. "Seeing that thou art past speech we'll e'en dispense with those last tender sentiments that thou wouldst utter. But quench not thine emotion, Valeria, for the tears shed upon the footsteps of a forthgoing spouse shall keep the path fresh for his return."

Paulinus took the cup from the steward's hand. It was of gold, finely chased, having two handles twined with serpents, and doves sitting on the edge. He held it while Valeria slowly touched the brim with her lips. But the mouthful she took seemed to choke her, for she turned her head away and put up her fan.

Paulinus, with an air of devotion, kissed the spot where her lips had rested, and raised the cup twice round his head; then, lowering it again and holding it before his breast while he bowed to her, he said,—

"By this cup I pledge thee, Valeria. None other lips shall come 'twixt thine and mine until we drink together again."

And with that he quaffed off the wine and handed back the cup to the steward. Then all seemed confusion. The thronging lords present pressed forward, lining the stairway, over which many fair heads peered, leaving a smaller group behind, where Valeria stood white and silent, between her maidens, and beyond her, Licinius Sura, his arms folded in his toga, his eyes bent upon the ground.

At a little distance Martial and Gregorio together watched the departure of Paulinus. The boy's black eyes roved cunningly from his master to Valeria, from her to Sura, and thence back to Martial with a leer. The poet's thumb and forefinger were spread upon his chin, which, bent upon his chest, gave him a thoughtful appearance. His piercing gaze lingered on Valeria, and there was triumph in his look. From the head of the stairs Paulinus waved a brawny arm, girt with broad bands of gold, while cheers rose to greet him from below. Thus he passed down, his helmet gleaming as he descended, and behind him followed Asiaticus, torn from Vitellia's embrace, with his hand upon his sword and impatience in his eyes. The trumpeters blew loudly, arms clanged in salute, and there was a great acclaiming without when the generals went forth and mounted their horses. Then sounded the rhythmic clink of mail, and again the rolling tramp of many feet dying in the distance as the legionaries marched away.

Now the atrium cleared rapidly. The guests filed before Valeria bowing their farewells. To each she returned a mechanical bend and smile, but uttered not a word. When the greater number had passed, she suddenly withdrew to her own rooms, ignoring the remainder, who still stood talking. Nyria and Æola followed at a little distance. Instinct told Nyria that her lady would rather be alone, and so she stayed Æola among the other women, who were congregated in the slaves' ante-chamber, eager to hear how all had gone off, and for the most part full of jealousy against the two favoured attendants who had witnessed the show. Æola's sweet nature took no count of this, and she chattered so pleasantly that the others were won over by her innocent good-humour. Nyria stood apart, keeping the curtains of her lady's sitting-room, when presently there came a rustle of silk and Vitellia passed along from the atrium alone. Seeing the girl, she asked for Valeria, and Nyria went before to announce her coming.

Valeria stood in the middle of the apartment like one who had been struck. She did not appear to hear the entrance of the slave or her sister until Vitellia called softly,—

"Lucia! Lucia!"

Then Valeria turned and a tremor seized her—a long shiver going from her neck to her feet. Nyria, fancying she might be cold, stepped forward to arrange the purple and silver palla which had fallen from her shoulders.

"Ah! 'Tis thou," said Valeria; and putting up her hand she began to remove the circlets of glittering green stones from her neck and arms.

"What dost thou, Lucia?" asked Vitellia, advancing.

"What do I?" said Valeria, slowly. "I—I am taking off my chains;" and with a sudden gesture of repulsion she threw the jewels from her. "Oh! prisoners of Hades!" she cried, "hopeless though ye be—poor souls!—bound for ever in the realms of darkness—which of ye fare worse than I? 'Take off my chains' I said? Alas, that may not be!"

Nyria caught the necklace as she flung it away and laid it on a table.

"Thou art sad and disturbed in mind, Lucia," said Vitellia, tenderly. "But Paulinus made a brave show, and he has gone to fight the enemies of his country. Thou art proud of him, art thou not, Lucia?"

"Proud! Proud!" repeated Valeria. "Proud of what? Oh, ay, Paulinus made a brave show."

"But thy heart is very sad," said Vitellia, pitifully.

"Nay! nay!" cried Valeria, turning sharply, and facing her sister, with one hand clutching her throat, as though she would have choked herself. "Nay, my heart is not sad. I am proud, as thou sayest, Vitellia. What should sadness and Valeria have to do with each other since Paulinus hath gone forth 'mid acclamations to overcome the enemies of Rome? That should not make me sad;" and as she spoke she paced to and fro in the room.

"I understand thee not," said Vitellia, in an injured tone. "Trouble should not derange thee thus, Lucia, though thy heart may well be sad. Is not mine sad also?"

Vitellia moved in the steps of Valeria, who went more rapidly, as though to escape her. "Hath not my lord gone forth likewise?" she said. "Alack! who can say that he hath a better chance than Paulinus to return?"

Valeria stopped suddenly in her walk. "The gods are not so gracious that they should hinder Asiaticus's return. Oh! the gods would be good indeed to thee, Vitellia, did they slay him nobly on the battlefield."

"Speak not so!" cried Vitellia, covering her face with her hands. "Be not thus cruel. Asiaticus is my lord."

"Am I cruel to thee?" said Valeria, more gently. "Cruel because I speak the truth. Why should we two sisters hide from each other that to-day, at least, we are blest in so far that our husbands have gone from us?"

Aghast, Vitellia thrust out her hands to check Valeria's utterance.

"Peace! peace!" she cried. "Speak for thyself, Lucia, if thou must blaspheme the sanctity of marriage. I will neither agree with nor listen to thee. Since I may not go with Asiaticus it will now be my chief duty and my sole joy to plead with the gods for his preservation."

Valeria gave a low, scornful laugh, and pointed to the doorway.

"Go then, Vitellia. I would not detain thee. Go, plead with thy gods for Asiaticus's return. Alack, mine own heart tells me that 'tis the men from whom we women shrink that the gods protect for our destruction."

Vitellia dropped her hands and stared in a troubled way at her sister.

"I cannot go until I have spoken to thee of somewhat which is in my mind," she said. "Thou knowest, Lucia, that, when lords are parted from their wives, gossip is ever rife in Rome concerning the women they leave behind. Paulinus hath of his noble favour extended confiding courtesy towards one whom some perchance would say he had been wiser to forbid his doors. But thou wilt reward thy husband's faith in thee by loyalty in his absence?"

Valeria's eyes flashed from her strained white face. As she made no reply, Vitellia continued confusedly: "Wilt thou not, Lucia? Promise me that while Paulinus is away thou wilt not welcome him of whom I speak."

"Of whom dost thou speak?" asked Valeria, haughtily.

At that moment there was a sound in the ante-room, and while Vitellia hesitated Chabrias drew aside the curtains and announced, in a loud voice,—

"The Honourable Marcus Licinius Sura."

On the instant Valeria answered. "I crave thy courtesy, lord," she said in clear, ringing tones. "For the moment I am engaged. I pray thee to wait without."

Licinius, bowing, withdrew, and Chabrias let fall the curtains. Valeria had turned to Vitellia, who, looking discomposed, was drawing up her palla as though to depart. With an imperious gesture Valeria motioned her to remain.

"Thou canst not go, as thou saidst, Vitellia, until thou hast spoken on this matter. Of what, and with whom, dost thou accuse me?"

"Of naught, of naught," returned Vitellia, awkwardly.

"Nay, explain thyself," repeated Valeria, standing slim and tall before her sister, who seemed huddled in her palla as she bent forward.

Vitellia changed her tone.

"Dear, though the world might misjudge thee, *I* could not. Do I not know that if thou hast erred 'tis in thought only? But ah! Lucia, how can I discredit that of which I've heard thine own lips speak?"

A slight flush came into Valeria's pale cheeks. "What didst thou hear?" she asked.

"When thou wast lying on yonder bed of sickness, not knowing what thou wert uttering, thou didst cry aloud for one Marcus, who methinks must be this Licinius Sura."

Valeria's blush grew deeper. Her expression softened. Yet she spoke lightly.

"It doth oft please the gods to afflict with madness those who are sick. Haply 'twas thus with me. But if it were, the madness hath passed, Vitellia."

Vitellia searched her face with tender, anxious eyes.

"Is that so? Oh! Lucia—I ask it as thy sister—tell me that this man is naught to thee save thy husband's friend."

A faint smile played round Valeria's mouth.

"Methinks Licinius Sura can scarce be called my husband's friend, notwithstanding Paulinus's greeting of him to-day, the purport of which I know not, for Paulinus's moods have long been past my comprehension. But that thou mayst content thyself that the man is naught to me, Vitellia, be present whilst I receive him. Perchance thou'lt then go forth satisfied."

So saying, she struck the silver gong on the table, and Chabrias came to the door.

"Bid Licinius Sura enter," she said.

As the curtains dropped again Vitellia caught her sister's hand and pressed it.

"Thou dost restore my confidence," she exclaimed. "Oh, Lucia, the thought of this hath rankled in my breast! Now I am happy again."

"Verily, it takes not much to make thee so," returned Valeria—"even though Asiaticus be gone to war!"

Her tone was sarcastic, but Vitellia appeared to heed it not. She had sunk upon a chair, and sat there, her palla gathered about her as if she were chilled, her hands closely clasped in her lap, and her eyes fixed upon the doorway. Valeria stood calm, and very dignified. Suddenly, however, she made a movement towards Nyria, and picking up the necklace she had thrown off, hurriedly bade the slave fasten it.

Hardly had Nyria done so when Chabrias ushered in Licinius Sura.

"I crave thy pardon, lord, for having taxed thy grace in waiting," said Valeria, greeting him with stately formality. "My sister and I had much to talk over and to arrange since, as thou knowest, we are both for the time left widowed."

Licinius's brows puckered in a slight frown. With arms folded before him, he bent low, replying, with equal formality,—

"'Tis I, most noble Valeria, who should crave thy pardon for mine intrusion. I ventured, seeing that I had no chance just now to bid thee farewell and that urgent matters call me hence upon a long journey, for I liked not to leave Rome without a word from one who hath extended to me much favour."

He looked with veiled intent at Valeria, who returned his look with cold composure, though Nyria saw the agony in her eyes.

"To-morrow," added Licinius, "I start for Judæa."

"A long journey, truly!" replied Valeria. "And do thy wife and son go with thee?"

Vitellia, listening, could hardly repress an exclamation of surprise, and for a moment Licinius appeared confounded.

"The Domina is pleased to jest," he said. "Journeys to Judæa are not for women and babes."

"Yet my sister here," rejoined Valeria, politely indicating Vitellia, "thinks naught of wandering twice as far in the wake of her devoted lord. Vitellia hath made many a long journey with Asiaticus."

Licinius bowed to Vitellia, as good breeding demanded. She had risen, appearing anxious to leave, perhaps because her mind was now at ease, or possibly because she felt herself an awkward third at the interview—for none counted Nyria in the shadow of the curtains. As Vitellia bade her sister good-bye she drew her a pace or two towards the doorway, and murmured in her ear,—

"Why didst thou not tell me he was wed?"

"In truth I know not," answered Valeria, aloud, as Nyria lifted the curtains for Vitellia to pass out. "Methinks because marriage hath never seemed to me so great a bar to infidelity as thou, Vitellia, dost consider it." She turned with a hard smile to Licinius.

"Of what dost thou speak?" he asked.

Valeria sat down on the wide couch by the window and motioned him to a seat opposite.

"My sister expressed surprise that I had not thought to mention to her that thou wast wedded," she replied.

"Hadst thou done so," he said, crossing firmly one leg over the other, "thou wouldst have told an untruth."

Then he threw aside his stiff manner and bent towards her, his fingers straying to the embroidered edge of her palla caressingly.

"What means this, Valeria? To-morrow I leave thee, and the gods alone know when I shall return. Wherefore art thou cold to me?"

"Cold! Wherefore am I cold to thee?" said Valeria, shrinkingly. "How can I be aught but cold? What of Salome?"

"So thou didst hear!" cried Licinius. "A pest on that loose tongue of Paulinus. His untimely banter had been like to raise a whirlwind, were it of any account. But 'twas not. Thine own heart might have told thee that, Valeria. Why hast thou misjudged me thus unheard?"

"Why hast thou remained unheard? Why not have told me thyself of this Salome and thy son?"

Licinius rose and shrugged his shoulders vexedly. He took two turns along the room, and coming back, stood before Valeria, one foot thrust out, his arms folded, a frown upon his handsome face, and yet a look of tenderness round his lips.

"Why should I have told thee?" he asked. "Is it to such as thee, Valeria, that a man should bring stories of the foolish passions of his youth? Wouldst have me like Paulinus, who pollutes the ears of his latest love with coarse tales of those that have preceded her? This Salome—shall I, then, tell thee who she is?"

Valeria slowly nodded. Her eyes were cast down, and she said no word. He spoke shortly.

"A slave of Jewish blood, who took my fancy when I was scarce more than an impetuous boy; older than I, and with wiles enough to captivate a dozen such fools. I bought and freed her—wherein I was as unwise as many another. The child—well, yes, there's a child. She calls him my son, and I suppose he is. But why need we talk of him? As for the woman—Valeria, dost think she hath been aught to me since I have known thee?"

"Verily my vanity would answer no," Valeria said. "Even now I'd fain believe thee. Yet how may I? Did I not ask thee in those early days if other women had been aught to thee, and thou didst deny the existence of any such?"

"Like enough," replied Licinius, smiling, as he kneeled at her feet. "Thou wouldst not have me remember, sweet, wouldst thou, every lie I have uttered to cover my folly?"

Valeria winced. "I'd have thee truthful," she said—"at least to me."

"And so I am," he returned, "since I desire thee only. If I have ever lied, 'twas no great matter. I spoke truly, Valeria, that Salome was naught to me; 'tis long since she hath been. Dear, when first we learned to love each other I bade Salome leave my house. She hath not been there since, except on trivial business concerning the child. She was never my wife, even according to the Plebs' form of marriage. Dost think, thou dear, unwise lady, that Licinius would link his fate with such as she?"

"I know not," cried Valeria. "All the world is against me, and thou, Marcus, giv'st me naught to lean upon."

"Nay, now—have I not said that mine arm and my heart wait for thee?" And he drew her into his embrace.

"Ay! ay!" cried Valeria, bitterly, rising and pushing him from her. "Thou wouldst silence me with kisses. But when hast thou offered to play the part of loyal lover and to take me from the protection of Paulinus, so that the law may make me justly thine?"

Licinius rose too, and again a vexed look crossed his dark, handsome face. "'Tis impossible," he said. "Valeria, thou knowest not what thou dost demand. There are others bound up with Licinius—their interests his, their plans and ambitions his, their hopes, their fears inextricably mingled with his own. How can Licinius desert those who thus rely on him?"

"'Tis not the first time thou hast talked in such a way," she answered. "What is this part of thy life in which I may not share? What are thine ambitions and thy projects, Marcus? Who are those with whom thou art thus bound? Doth not Valeria stand closer to thee than they?"

"Valeria stands closest of all," he replied, and held her passionately to him, till her head lay upon his shoulder. "Valeria is Licinius's nearest and dearest. She rests within the very sanctuary of his heart, as he would fain rest in hers. Let Valeria be to him a haven from those worldly plots and strivings whereof he may not speak. But let her not demand to know their nature, for that, alas! Licinius may not tell."

"I would not ask it," she answered, clinging to him, "were I not prepared to give up all for thee. This being so, blame me not"—she dropped her face, half hiding it on his breast—"blame me not, as thou hast ofttimes blamed me, in that I have ne'er given thee love's dearest, last, best pledge of all. Have I not told thee that I will follow thee whithersoever thou desirest—that I will be altogether thine, if thou in like manner dost vow thyself to me?"

He stooped over her, and his lips seemed lost in the waving tresses of her hair, which, half uncoiled, lay against his shoulder.

"Tempt me not, Valeria," he said. "If this be the price of thy favour, how can I accept it, seeing, as I have told thee, that my service is not mine to vow? I am bound by ties of honour which I dare not break. These be ill days for a man to fail in obligations such as mine—further reaching than the embraces of love. Life itself might be the forfeit of unreadiness to answer to my bond when the time is ripe for its fulfilling. 'Tis no idle matter this. Oh! sweet, trust me for the future, and give thyself ungrudgingly to me in the present. I swear thou shalt not repent it."

"But thou wouldst leave me, Marcus—"

"To-morrow, duty calls me hence—but to-night is our own," he said, bending his head again on hers.

She trembled exceedingly as she lay in his arms. Then slowly, with a movement of infinite regret, she drew herself from him.

"Nay," she answered, brushing back her hair with hands that shook, "thou sayest 'tis impossible to take me from my husband's house as the law doth permit; and I—how should I urge thee? Yet think not that I could accept any lesser seal of thy love. Haply I am not as other Roman matrons, Marcus—though some there be who do truly regard the sanctity of marriage, like Vitellia, who left me just now; but though I deem all such ties unholy that be not sanctified by love, yet I would not plight myself to one who will not grant me the seemly ratification of my pledge."

"Speak not so, beloved," he cried. "We are at cross-purposes, whose love should make us one. Give thyself to me, Valeria. Be mine to-night in confirmation of that thou hast already granted—for do I not hold thy heart?—and in earnest of future joy. I'll swear thee eternal fealty, and when these matters with which I must concern myself be settled, and a brighter day doth dawn on Rome and on my fortunes, then will Licinius claim thee for his own."

Valeria said nothing at first, then she slowly shook her head.

"When that day hath dawned, Marcus, come and Valeria will give herself to thee."

He snatched her fiercely to him, and kissed her face over and over again, folding his arms about her and pressing her against his breast.

"Thou askest too much of a man, Valeria," he exclaimed. "Thy sweetness maddens me. Wherefore should I wait? Why shouldst thou have kept me all these months on the brink of happiness, tantalising me with gleams of bliss? How know we whether Fate will ever again allow us a chance like this? To-night, opportunity is ours. What should hinder us from making this farewell a union —the sweetest that hath ever been?"

"What should hinder us?" she repeated sadly, loosing herself from his embrace. "Wouldst thou have me tell thee? 'Tis this, beloved," and she gazed round the chamber. "I am Paulinus's wife—not thine. And while I here remain my husband's words ring always in mine ears. 'These rooms,' he said, 'are sacred to thine honour and my name.'"

Licinius had listened to her eagerly. Now he turned angrily away.

"Choose then," he said—"Paulinus and thine honour, or thy love and me."

"I have chosen," she answered mournfully. "Thou canst say naught to move Valeria. Alack! I dare not even desire that thou couldst. My love thou hast, Marcus, as full well thou knowest, and whether thou comest again, or comest never, Valeria will be true to thee. But Paulinus is my lawful spouse—in name only; yet do I eat of his bread—I abide beneath his roof—the service that surrounds me is of his providing. My heart and mind are thine, Marcus, and thine alone, but if thou dost desire me, then take me in the manner befitting one of thy gens, and one of mine."

For a moment she stood, her head upraised, her arms held out, her eyes fixed pleadingly on him, but as he ignored her appeal her arms dropped quickly and all the light went from her face.

Licinius angrily slipped his toga over his shoulder and went towards the door. There he paused and turned.

"Prate not of gens!" he cried. "'Tis the pride of thy gens which stands between us, not this nonsense of Paulinus's honour. I had been wiser never to look for warm woman's blood in such as thee. Thou art graven in stone, Valeria, and wilt yield not a finger, while I have poured out all that man can give, unavailing, at thy feet. Keep thyself thus cold and proud if thou wilt. Thou'lt have time enough to think whether thou wouldst not have done better to warm thy marble heart at the fire which burns in mine. Now I leave thee, and, as I said, only the gods know when I may return. If thou shouldst ever cast a thought my way, let it not be of ice, lest I feel the frigid shaft, e'en on Judæa's sun-baked plains. I have work there in plenty before Rome shall see me again. Do thou fulfil thy duty likewise as fate and thy gens shape it for thee."

Valeria stared after him with wide eyes as though she had not heard him aright. She held out her arms once more, and called, in wild entreaty,—

"Marcus! . . . oh, Marcus, thou canst not leave me thus!"

He paused on the threshold and took three steps back, then stopped anew and cried,—

"Nay! If I leave thee at all to-night, it must needs be thus. I am of flesh and blood, Valeria, not of stone like thee. Nay, nay—touch me not. Stand back! Thou hast bid me go, and I had best begone."

Again he swung his toga round him and strode to the door, past Nyria, who darted to lift the curtain. But she was too late. This time he disappeared.

Valeria stood motionless where he had left her, while Nyria watched her mistress anxiously. Presently Valeria lifted her hand and brushed it across her face, pushing her hair back from her brow. Then with slow steps she crossed the room to the further end and passed through the curtains to her bed-chamber. Thither at first Nyria dared not follow, but at length the strain of silence grew more than the devoted slave-girl could bear, and she softly entered.

A light was in the chamber, and as Nyria approached she saw that the swinging lamp had been kindled above the alcove, from which the silver-fringed violet curtains were drawn apart. Valeria stood in the opening, one hand holding the curtain. But it was not Valeria who enchained Nyria's attention, for she saw above the raised altar within an image of inspiring beauty—the face of some female divinity bent upon Valeria in a look of tenderest and most wondrous human compassion. So sublime was the understanding upon the carven face that it seemed as though goddess and woman were blended in one.

And as Nyria looked Valeria cast herself in abasement before the image, her loosened hair fallen, her purple and silver palla spread behind her, and prayed aloud out of the agony of her spirit.

"Mother," she cried, "mother divine! Thou who, by the anguish of thine own tender heart, dost know the pangs which assail the souls of women, look down upon this suffering soul of mine. Thou who didst search all the world for thy young daughter snatched from thee by the lawless passion of him who stole her into slavery—thou who hast learned how bitter is the bondage where love be not, yet who in thy supreme wisdom dost comprehend the more bitter thraldom of love itself, oh! hear, and in pity soothe this heart which bleedeth at thy feet. Demeter, comfort me."

XXXI

LIFE at the Cœlian villa proceeded for some time without further stirring incident. Of what went on outside Nyria knew little, for Valeria kept her constantly near her own person, and as she herself sought no distraction they scarcely left the house.

It was very difficult at first to rouse the Domina from melancholy; when her patient secretary tried again to interest her in literary work, she only shook her head, answering sadly, "Nay, good Phileros; one who liveth tragedy hath small disposition to write it." A sentiment that seemed natural enough in a wife whose husband was fighting in Sarmatia, and the secretary could only bow and retire.

One day, not long after the departure of Paulinus, Chabrias stated that Martial craved audience of Valeria. This, in her present mood, Valeria would certainly have denied had not Martial taken the precaution to send in a scroll, bearing Paulinus's signet which, in terms not to be gainsaid, requested that she should receive his friend. Accordingly Martial was given entrance.

"I will not crave thy pardon for mine intrusion, most noble Valeria," he remarked unctuously, "since I have Paulinus's permit to visit thee. Thine illustrious husband did commend his spouse to my cousinly care, in as far as one so lowly placed as I, and of so dull a wit, may offer friendly service to the fair and talented Valeria."

"I thank thee," she returned coldly, cutting short his fulsome speech.

"I have brought one or two little poems," continued Martial, "on which I would gladly have thy cultured judgment. Amongst thy household I have discovered a youth with an excellent gift of music, who like myself hath no desire but to serve thee. Mayhap thou wouldst suffer the lad to sing some lines of mine composed in thine honour."

Valeria assented indifferently, whereupon Martial produced some verses, exquisite and subtly eulogistic, which she was forced to admire. When Gregorio appeared and fitted them to music she listened with surprise and pleasure, though it might have been apparent that this was not the first time Gregorio had strung his lyre to Martial's poetry. Nor was it by any means the last, for, the doors once opened to him, Martial came again and again. He guessed that there were only two roads to Valeria's favour—through her rarely-stirred emotions, and through her intellect—and he was adroit enough to approach her along both. It was then easy to throw into desultory conversation allusions to Sura's genius and prowess, which would, so Martial declared, notwithstanding Domitian's jealousy, make for him renown some future day. Thus Martial led Valeria on to talk of the man who was for ever in her thoughts, feeding her starved soul with scraps of news he purported to have obtained by chance of Sura's movements. Valeria's eyes betrayed her eagerness. She had been vainly hoping for a word from Marcus, and Martial's news of him, scant and ill-founded though it were, was as a draught of water to one athirst.

None knew better than Martial how to suit his manners to his company. Seeing him respectful though admiring, unobtrusive yet sympathetic, his taste cultured, and, moreover, apparently devoid of that strain of coarseness which she had inferred from Paulinus's frequent quotations of his witty remarks, Valeria now told herself that her old dislike had been ill-founded and that the coarseness lay in Paulinus, not in the poet. Certainly Martial afforded her pleasant intellectual distraction, besides being almost her only means of hearing anything of Licinius, for Pliny, who might otherwise have spoken of him, divined her secret and therefore purposely refrained from mention of his name. Martial, doubting not that Licinius would soon return from Judæa, and the interrupted relations be renewed, thus giving him ground on which to plot against Valeria for the filling of his empty pockets, was careful not to let her see that he suspected her interest in Sura, but, keeping his malign object in view, he gathered all the clues he could and lost no chance of ingratiating himself with Valeria, the exposure of whom, if successful, was to bring him in two thousand sestertii. Meanwhile, however, months passed and Licinius gave no sign of return, so that Martial began to fear that the rupture was more complete than he had imagined.

But as time went on Nyria succeeded in drawing the Domina to talk of things she had once cared for—the literature and art of Greece and such other matters. Valeria would show her scrolls of pictures, and be faintly amused at her artless comments; and as the lady took no pains to lower her conversation to the slave-girl's level, she unconsciously lifted Nyria's mind nearer her own, so that it expanded like an opening flower.

Thus the girl's life became one of comparative leisure and happiness. One afternoon early in the spring she was sunning herself by the door in the wall when Lucius, the slave who had admitted Domitilla with Stephanus and herself on their visit to Clementus, approached furtively and delivered a message from the bishop. Nyria was to be at the house by the river that evening an hour after sunset, observing, of course, strict secrecy in the matter.

Valeria seemed not pleased when Nyria, for the first time, asked to absent herself.

"Art thou also a gadabout?" she said bitterly. "Go then, but return in time for the unrobing. I like not clumsy fingers. Æola is ever in a dream, and none of the rest serve me as well as thou."

With this grudging permission Nyria was forced to be content. Wrapped in a hooded cloak, she went forth by the deserted Licinian villa, past the flight of steps leading to Julia's great empty house, and by the short cut she had traversed with Stephanus, of whom she now thought longingly.

A crowd was gathered round a group of street mimes as she entered the lower Forum, and Nyria, passing by the outskirts of it, noticed a litter borne by four stalwart slaves in dull red liveries with a narrow white border, evidently belonging to some patrician household. There was a lady in the litter, who appeared to be looking at the performance. Now, ladies of position did not usually exhibit themselves thus, but a gaily-decked head, wearing a scarlet cap, with gossamer veil and gold ornaments hanging low upon the forehead, peered forth from behind the curtains, and in the dark, saucily-attractive face Nyria recognised her former companion, Thanna.

Thanna called her eagerly to the side of the litter, and Nyria ran at the call, though instinct told her directly afterwards that it was not seemly for one of Valeria's household to be seen talking with a woman in Thanna's guise. Thanna, however, was beaming all over with good-nature and self-complacence. She bade her bearers set down the litter so that Nyria might step in beside her. This, however, Nyria refused to do.

"Glad I am to see thee, Thanna," she said. "But I may not delay. Mine errand takes me further."

Thanna pouted crossly. "Dost still trouble thyself over other folks' business, Nyria? Why be thus foolish? I, too, am sent out for certain purposes, yet I enjoy whatsoever I find agreeable on the road. Be advised and do the same, else thou'lt find life but dull."

"Thou art sent forth—*thou!*" cried Nyria; "in a litter like that, with those fine bearers, whom thou orderest as if they were thine own."

"They're mine. And the litter's mine also," replied Thanna. "Said I not that I'd do well for myself? Ay! and I have done well—very well. There is none to scold Thanna now—none to order her about."

"But thou sayest that thou art sent forth! Thy lord? Doth he not command thee?" asked Nyria, puzzled.

Thanna shrugged her silk-clad shoulders, over which she wore a soft crape wrap.

"On occasion—or thinketh he doth. More oft 'tis I that command him."

Nyria stared agape, and Thanna went on, smiling: "'Tis true he doth demand certain offices from me such as a lady-wife might tender, though I would remark that there be few lady-wives in Rome who have the wit of Thanna—as Regulus well knows. The tasks my lord doth set me, do employ the mind, and suit my humour better than tiring heads or draping waxen images in dressing-rooms."

"Thou hast fallen on easy fortunes," said Nyria, wonderingly.

"Ay, verily. Wilt come to see me, Nyria? Thou shouldst be well served in my household."

Nyria hesitated, for she knew that Valeria disliked Regulus.

"Come thou to me instead," she proposed. "I have a room of mine own where I may receive thee."

"And how should I be required to enter?" asked the other, loftily. "Thanna goes by no slaves' gate."

Nyria was nonplussed. "I know not," she said. "The slaves' gate is meet for slaves like thee and me, Thanna."

"Speak for thyself," retorted Thanna. "The slave in heart remains a slave, but *I* have bettered my state. Farewell, Nyria. Haply we'll contrive to meet some day." She signed to her bearers to hoist the litter on their shoulders, and waved a supple jewelled hand as she was borne away.

The Domina Domitilla was with Clementus when Nyria arrived. She spoke graciously to the girl, but left almost immediately. Then Nyria received her first formal instruction from the bishop. After several such visits as a catechumen, she was told that her baptism would take place on an evening near at hand in the chapel used by the Christians for worship. The longer time required for this ceremony compelled Nyria to explain to her mistress the cause of her absence. But she had already learnt that the safety of the whole body of Christians depended largely on the loyal reticence of each member, and therefore besought from the Domina a promise of secrecy.

Valeria conveyed haughtily that she kept no secrets with slaves; then the exquisite humility of the small figure standing there, with bent golden head and folded hands, that had never yet failed at her bidding, melted the woman's proud heart.

"My child," she said, "come hither and tell me what is this wonderful mystery. Thou shouldst know that Valeria breaks faith with none."

"I know it, Domina. Nevertheless, 'twas not for my sake but for Christ and His Church," and kneeling by Valeria's couch Nyria, in rapt tones, told her tale.

"And when thou hast stepped down into this tank of water wilt thou henceforth be made holy?" laughed Valeria.

"Nay, Domina; Christ only is holy. But Nyria will be washed from sin and made meet to serve Him. Christ became man that He might do the rest."

"I trow He knoweth well what He hath found in thee," replied Valeria, half amused, half touched. "But put not flesh and blood upon a pedestal, Nyria, to worship it. Else some day, surely, thou'lt find out thy mistake," and Valeria sighed deeply.

"Nay, Domina. Christ is God and careth for the least of His children—even for me, and thus I fain would worship Him."

"Strange child! How knowest thou that He doth care for thee?" questioned Valeria, cynically. "Methinks thy god hath used thee ill if He be accountable for the stripes of thy past."

"Not so, Domina," cried the girl, flushing deeply. "My suffering hath been naught compared to that of many another, and, in truth, I would it had been greater, since Christ hath borne so much for me. Moreover, hath He not blessed me exceedingly in bringing me to *thee*?" and Nyria's lips fell on the hem of Valeria's robe.

"After that I cannot forbid thee from going where thou wilt, Nyria," said Valeria, smiling. "Be baptised if thou dost so desire," reading. sank back on her couch and took up the scroll she had been and she

Nyria gratefully accepted her dismissal, and went to clothe herself in the manner she had been advised by Domitilla—first in a fair linen undergarment for the immersion, taking with her another into which to change afterwards, and then in a clean white woollen outer robe that could be easily taken off and re-donned. Over all her grey hooded cloak.

As she dressed, Nyria thought anxiously of an unpleasant experience which had troubled her on each of her previous visits to Clementus, wondering if it would be repeated to-night.

The house by the river belonged to Lucius's parents, though it was used by the bishop for receiving and instructing members of his flock, as more secluded and less likely to fall under suspicion of such purposes than his own. Moreover, there led from it, as Nyria learned that night, a carefully-constructed subterranean passage beside the bed of the Tiber to the chapel among the quarries. The street in which this humble dwelling stood was quiet and respectable, but portions of the lower city which must be passed to reach it were far from being so, and Nyria dreaded traversing them alone. Giving form to her terror, she had seen a man following her each night, wrapped in a heavy cloak with a hood concealing his head and face. Sorely frightened, especially when the more populous and better-lighted parts were left behind her and she came to a dark, lonely stretch of road, Nyria had invariably taken to her heels and run breathlessly until the lights in Paulinus's portico assured her of safety. But though her mysterious pursuer quickened his pace also, he had not thus far made any attempt to molest her. Knowing that she must be late returning to-night, Nyria longed for the protection of Stephanus's strong arm. Remembering, however, that she was about to be made one of Christ's children, and that He would surely shield His own, she went forth, casting all her doubts and fears resolutely aside.

There were some half-dozen catechumens assembled in the room where she had been instructed, as well as some other persons previously baptised, who were to present the candidates, and among them the Domina Domitilla and Flavius Clemens. The little company stood in rows while the bishop recited a prayer; then, at a sign from him, the boy Lucius removed a square piece of flooring, usually hidden by the bed, now pushed on one side, and disclosed a trap-door. Lucius descended with a torch, and the rest followed, leaving two only to close the aperture and guard the house against intrusion.

Nyria clung nervously to the hand of Domitilla, who led her down twenty or thirty wooden steps and along a few feet of low-roofed passage, then down more steps, now of rock, into another tunnel, long and low, slimy in places, and lined with great blocks of stone, from which green moisture oozed. Presently they issued through a rude arch into a space where rocks uprose, with grass and shrubs growing between. High cliffs partially enclosed it, and the region seemed wild and lonely. Nyria afterwards learned that above here was the spur where she had been wont to sit, and whence she had often watched the Christians passing down and out of sight. That road led from the city among the unused quarries, and descended by a steep path into the valley between the hills, which the little company now crossed, stumbling over the stones, for only one flickering torch carried by Lucius lighted their steps. Again they entered the cliff and were in a winding passage, which widened presently into a moss-grown alley, partly natural, partly cut by man. Large tablets were set at intervals upon the rock walls, bearing legends that, later, Nyria came to know by heart. One ran, "Oh, Christ! who didst suffer little children, we have sent our son to Thee."

Another, to a maid of fifteen:—"Here, Lord, we lay a lily on Thy shrine;" and for yet another young girl, "Sweet Hermione was about to be led to the marriage altar, but Christ called her, and she followed Him."

Of an aged woman it was written,—

"Full of faith and years, Dulcinea gave herself to God;" and of a beloved parent, "Our mother, Marcia, hath gone home and beckons us thither."

Another inscription there was which Nyria thought exceedingly beautiful. "Behold! Flavia was weary, then did Christ Himself prepare her bed."

The procession wound on through what seemed a labyrinth of passages until at last it turned into a large underground temple, with rough pillars supporting the roof and benches hewn out against the walls, where the aged and infirm might sit, while at the upper end of the chapel stood what Nyria would have called the rostrum, from which she afterwards heard Clementus preach. At this end also was a stone tank of water, approached by a small flight of steps on either side; and beyond, an archway into another cave, where the candidates for baptism might change their garments after immersion.

The place of worship was fashioned out of several large caves now united—its pillars being irregular blocks, which originally divided the cavities, but were now hewn into more or less uniform shape. The columns were curiously carved. They were a first attempt of the Early Church to memorialise its saints, for families of the community, which numbered martyrs among their members, were permitted to engrave here representations of their sufferings. With these Nyria afterwards became familiar, but to-night she was too nervous to gaze about her.

The catechumens were placed near the tank, with their sponsors, and Clementus himself at their head, supported by an elderly presbyter and two deacons or readers. By this time the body of the chapel was filling rapidly. Those of the foremost rank were kneeling, a few weakly ones crouched on the floor or the benches, and a great number stood looking on eagerly. For this ceremony was for them the dedication not only of a soul to Christ's service but of a body to the ordeal of martyrdom.

Indeed, the spirit of these early Christians, with the horror of Nero's persecution still to many a vivid memory, was essentially a martyr spirit. The bulk of them looked forward—in theory at all events—to a martyr's death. Baptism meant for them being sealed with their Saviour's blood, for from the moment they had His mark set upon them they might be called on to suffer for Him. Thus, they were required to keep that grim possibility continually before their eyes. They looked always at Christ crucified. They were always climbing Calvary. Yet when the summit of their Calvary was reached, when martyrdom actually faced them, many flinched who had been wont to speak of it as the goal of their religion, the one blessed sacrifice they might make for Him who died that they should live eternally—pathetic instances, alas, of poor human weakness!

The inaugural sacrament of baptism was therefore considered by the early Christians as of great moment. They felt an intense interest in the catechumens presented at the font, seeing them already figuratively stretched on the cross or tied to the stake. And it was a curious perversion of the religious sentiment, or maybe a survival of Pagan instincts, that the fervent among them took a morbid satisfaction in the youth and beauty by which any particular victim was distinguished. Thus Nyria occasioned much comment amongst the crowd in the church, especially as she was new to most of them. For the Christians dwelt a race apart in Rome, the sect consisting mainly of tradesfolk and small farmers, with a few persons employed in public offices, occasionally a soldier, and a small sprinkling of slaves from Pagan households, besides those belonging to Christian families.

The service began with the singing of a hymn, followed by a simple address from the bishop and one or two prayers, during which these good folk took a childlike and mundane pleasure in the innocent novelty offered them. There was so little amusement in their lives. Their religion debarred them from participating in ordinary Roman enjoyments. They might not enter a theatre, nor attend games, nor might they even witness such harmless sports as wrestling and fencing, because of the company into which these brought them and the evil language of the Gladiatorial Schools. Outside his own community a Christian's social outlook was extremely limited, and as all his chief interests hinged upon the assemblages and ceremonies in his church, he could scarcely be blamed for making the most of them.

Among the spectators in the rear, half screening himself by a pillar—round which he nevertheless contrived to gain a view of what was going on—crouched a man in a dark cloak, with the hood drawn up about his head. His eyes never left the form of Nyria. The girl shivered, partly with cold, partly with apprehension, as she looked down into the black-green depths of the tank, whereat the watcher gnashed his teeth, though powerless to do anything on her behalf. She clung to Domitilla's hand as the service proceeded, glancing up at her from time to time in a frightened sort of way.

"Be not afeared, Nyria," whispered the lady.

"'Tis deep, Domina," replied the girl.

"The water will scarce cover thy head," murmured Domitilla.

But Nyria still shivered when she looked into the depths of the tank. When an old man, the first among the catechumens, entered, she watched him breathlessly as he passed down the steps at one end and up at the other, the water rising gradually around him and lowering again while he issued forth. Two persons stood at either side of the tank and guided the passage of each catechumen, dipping from the shoulders one that happened to be taller than usual, and lifting young children across by an arrangement of ropes, so that they were merely plunged in the middle. Seeing that a woman preceding her had bound her hair upon her head and covered it with her kerchief, Nyria craved permission of Domitilla to do the same. Then, with an almost piteous look at her sponsor, the girl took her place in the rank of those about to descend. They followed one another without delay, the bishop meanwhile reciting repeatedly a short prayer, commending each new-made Christian to the service of the Master.

Nyria could endure pangs that she was accustomed to, but the whole ceremonial affected her overstrained nerves, and there was something peculiarly awesome in the dark, shadowy walls of the tank. She made her first downward step tremblingly; as soon, however, as she felt the cold water rising about her, she advanced with more courage. The next thing she was conscious of were the strong arms guiding her forward, and in a moment she emerged, dripping, and covering her face with her hands, rushed, shamed, through the passage made by the bystanders, to the retiring-room, where the women and children were permitted to dry themselves and change their robes.

Just as she had done this and shaken her hair loose about her shoulders, she was called back to the chapel, where the bishop was about to give a few final words of exhortation. Some of these Nyria never forgot:—

". . . For Christ Himself hath said, 'If ye guard not that which is little, how shall ye be intrusted with that which is great? I say unto ye, that he who would be faithful in much must first be faithful in the least thing.' Keep thyselves, therefore, children of the Cross, pure and unstained, that the seal of this baptism may be without blemish upon ye, when ye are called before men to be known by that Sign—so that whatsoever course ye enter upon, the end may bring ye to the courts of our Heavenly King, whither Christ hath gone before."

The little company remained kneeling during the singing of the last hymn. After this the bishop gave his blessing and the long-looked for rite was over.

It was some time before the chapel was cleared. Many of the congregation had friends or relatives among those just baptised, and stayed to speak to them, while others waited to have speech with the bishop, who went round like a tender father, giving each one personal greeting. On the way back Domitilla admonished the girl on the responsibilities of her new profession, earnestly impressing upon her that a child of Christ must never be disloyal, to which Nyria listened dutifully, praying that she might not prove unfaithful to her trust.

When they had re-traversed the river passage, the girl, whose heart was full, set out alone on her walk to the Cœlian. It was so late that she hoped to be free of her mysterious pursuer; but she had not gone the length of the street before she heard his footsteps again behind her. To-night she was upheld by a special sense of divine protection, and so walked on courageously, her thoughts divided between that Christus she had pledged herself to serve and the earthly mistress to whom she had likewise vowed her devotion. Nevertheless, when she reached the lonely stretch of road between the Licinian and Valerian villas, the certainty that she was again being followed quickened her footsteps to a run. This time, however, she was overtaken. The striding legs behind made short work of her best speed, and a hand fell on her shoulder. Terrified, she gasped and struggled to free herself, when a voice that she knew well said in her ear,—

"Child! Hath it come to this—that I thus frighten thee? Dost not know me, Nyria?"

She turned with a gasp, and in the pale light of the stars saw, looking into hers, the kind, anxious eyes of the goldsmith. So great was the relief, that she sank exhausted against him. He put his arm round her and held her up, though he would have released her when she could stand alone had she not clung to him half laughing, half weeping.

"Oh! Stephanus! 'Tis thou! 'Tis thou! But wherefore hast thou thus affrighted me these many times?"

"Thou hast affrighted thyself, Nyria. Didst dream I'd let thee go unprotected night after night through yon evil streets where foul things stalk? I told thee that if thou hadst need of him thou couldst call on Stephanus. Wherefore didst thou not?"

"I was afeard. Thou wast harsh to me," she murmured.

"Ay! Was I harsh?" he said, supporting her as they walked slowly on. "Mayhap, mayhap. A man is but a man."

"I mind not now," she said, "if thou'lt be kind again."

He held her closer to him, and looked down on her with the old tenderness, but less of passion.

"Ascalaphus hath been calling thee," he said. "The fellow wondereth why thou hast not been near the shop so long. 'Tis dull where thou dost not show thy face."

"I'll come to-morrow if Valeria will let me."

"Is she good to thee, Nyria?" Stephanus asked anxiously.

"Oh, ay!" cried the girl, and as they proceeded she gave him particulars of her life. "How knewest thou that I went forth these nights—and why," she asked.

"That's my secret," he rejoined humorously. "I, like others, have means whereby to inform myself. I saw thee go down into yon cursed water-tank to-night with all thy curls bound up as though thou hadst been the sinful vestal, Cornelia. But for thee, Nyria, methinks such ways are foolishness."

They had reached the villa, and were talking by the little gate, so absorbed in each other, that neither noticed a dark, bent figure flitting by. As they thus stood—the man's arms round the girl, the girl's face lifted in childlike faith to his—there came from out of the shadows a cynical chuckle, which started the pair apart.

"Nay, let me not disturb thee, pretty lovers," cried a voice both recognised. "Such moments are precious, doubtless. Enjoy them while ye may. Who knows what fate may cast between ye?"

Then there stepped forth into the starlight—leaning on her stick—none other than Euphena. She mocked them, her dusky evil face thrust forward between her bent shoulders, and a leering look in her yellow eyes.

"So! ho! Stephanus! Courting still? And still doth Nyria flout thee?" Euphena chuckled again. "Dost still deem yon maid will make a docile wife to set by thy decent hearth? Verily, meseems it might serve to show thee thy mistake. Wouldst see what like in truth hath this spirit-thing that thou wouldst bind in earthly wedlock? Shall I show thee—shall I show thee—eh, good goldsmith?"

Stephanus muttered some vague reply, too startled to protest, as Euphena came nearer and with the point of her stick drew a circle on the ground round Nyria.

"Stand there and stir not," she said. "Remain as thou art with the wall behind thee, while I show to friend Stephanus that which he would fain turn into a house-keeping Roman matron. Come, good goldsmith, hither."

Stephanus advanced, puzzled, but interested. Euphena signed to him where he might stand, a few feet from Nyria. "Thou art a worthy fellow, but thick-headed," she declared. "I'll open now thine eyes, and thou shalt see. Look first upon the maid as thou hast ever pictured her. Then behold Nyria as she is."

While the old woman spoke she had been dipping her hands into a pouch at her side, bringing forth handfuls of what seemed dust or sand, which she threw before Stephanus's face, muttering some unintelligible gibberish. Suddenly she placed one hand over his eyes, and with the other made certain strange significant signs in the air.

"Behold!" she said, and drew herself aside.

Stephanus saw Nyria standing as he had left her, save that the bundle she carried had fallen and rolled away. Her slight frame was relaxed, her arms hung at her sides, her head was lifted, and a rapt expression was on her face. Her eyes gazed straightly before her, though it seemed to Stephanus that she saw him not. The light of the stars shone down upon her. But a more mysterious light, soft, yet brilliant, and full of dazzling radiance, lit up the girl's form. It rose around her in luminous clouds of silvery whiteness, melting into palest blue, which was tinged with exquisitely delicate violet where the glory crowned her head. Transfigured thus, she stood before him for the space of several seconds, and Stephanus, gazing, realised that this was no mere mortal maid, but the eternal soul of Nyria. When the vision faded it was as if a dark curtain fell before him. He put out his arms in a bewildered way, rubbed his eyes, and shook himself to recall his senses.

Nyria stood smiling and held out her hands.

"Why lookest thou thus on me?" she asked, and then the man, approaching, overwhelmed with remembrance, fell dumbly at her feet. She raised him tenderly.

"Oh! Nyria—oh! Nyria!" he cried, when words came to him. "What is't mine eyes have looked upon? 'Twas thee, sweet—and yet 'twas more than thee."

And as Nyria bent wonderingly to him, Euphena passed unheeded on her way, her mocking laugh ascending from the curve of the hill.

XXXII

MONTHS rolled by. The present year was full of happenings, though not such as affected Nyria, whose days flowed on tranquilly in the full enjoyment of the religion which was to her so deep a source of satisfaction, and in devoted attendance on her mistress. Valeria's pride compelled her to bear, at least with outward equanimity, the long absence of Licinius Sura. As time went on, and she received no word from him, she began to believe that he had indeed gone from her for ever, and to turn, at first in despair, afterwards with pathetic persistence, to any available interests that helped her to forget the aching longing she could never wholly still. Throughout this period Martial continued to make good his ground at the Valerian villa, coming frequently in the friendly way that befitted the cousinship which he affected to have discovered between himself and the master of the house, and welcomed warmly by Valeria for the sake of his clever conversation, refined to please her, and especially for the occasional items of news which he contrived to bring concerning Licinius. These were unimportant in themselves, and were for the most part trumped up by Martial, who, in point of fact, could obtain but the vaguest information of Sura's movements; but they served the poet's purpose, for he saw that they were none the less treasured by Valeria, who, beneath her indifferent calm, hungered for tidings of the man she loved.

The visit to Pliny's Laurentine villa duly took place in the spring of that year, and was followed by another during summer to his Tuscan estate, which was a treat to Nyria, who was thus brought again in touch with her former friend, Æmilia. This woman and her husband were very happy. Even Antæia's death, which occurred in child-birth some time later, did not affect their situation, for Pliny would not part with his adored wife's favourite dresser, who, indeed, afterwards waited on his equally adored second wife, Calpurnia.

But for the most part Nyria seldom saw her former friends, as the Domina was always away from Rome in the summer, and in the winter time kept her fully occupied. Nyria sometimes met Alexamenos at the Christian meetings, or going to the barracks of the Equites on the Cœlian. He would fain have renewed his suit had Nyria permitted, but as the young officer belonged to the bodyguard he was usually in attendance on Cæsar, and from association with the court Valeria always shrank.

During the visit to Tuscany her acquaintance with the historian,

Tacitus, a fellow-guest at the time, became strong friendship, and his cultured mind provided just the stimulus to intellectual pursuits which Valeria had lacked. Later on she hired a villa at Nemi for the rest of the hot months, and here, too, Tacitus was staying with his wife and her parents for the health of his father-in-law, which had been failing fast. Crushed by adversity, the broken-hearted general was carried down to the city in August, and there drew his last breath. That was shortly before Cæsar went to join the legions, though he never got as far as Sarmatia. It was during his absence that gossip raged anew among the enemies of the Empress concerning her intimacy with the popular actor, Paris, resulting in Domitian's revenge on his return to Rome, which are matters of history and may be read elsewhere.

By this time the Lady Vitellia had left Rome; for hearing that Asiaticus was becoming too popular with the soldiery in Sarmatia, Domitian, always in dread of a usurper, recalled the warlike general, and, much to Asiaticus's vexation, thrust him into an insignificant post on the Adriatic, whither his lady went to console him. On the whole, that winter began more agreeably for Valeria. There was always in her heart a curtained chamber where she dared not dwell, lest the old longing that lay there, drugged into silence, should break forth and cry aloud that all was desolation without Licinius. Nevertheless, released from the pressure of Paulinus's presence, yet free to enjoy the advantages that his wealth and position afforded her, having at hand the friendship of the most talented men of the times, Valeria found daily fresh food for thought. It was by the suggestion of Pliny that she undertook a project which proved of considerable interest to her during that and the ensuing winter. There was a large circle of cultured people of the upper class in Rome who, before the expulsion of the philosophers, had indulged in literary and philosophical lectures and debates presided over by various professors of light and learning. Of late these public discussions had been discontinued, since it was scarcely safe to air openly any opinion that might be considered heterodox. So the thinkers were obliged to content themselves with occasional meetings in each other's houses. Now the Valerian villa seemed admirably suited to a purpose with which its mistress was in sympathy, and luckily Paulinus, who kept up occasional communication with his wife by the state-runners to and from the seat of war, when applied to, wrote his approval of Pliny's scheme. Once a fortnight, therefore, Valeria's spacious rooms were filled with a fashionable and cultured crowd, when some star in the intellectual firmament would deliver an address.

The first course was inaugurated by Tacitus's brilliant lecture on Oratory. At the next the poetess Sulpicia read a paper; and later, Valeria composed a rival essay on Greek poetry that Martial delivered for her. The wealthy Stoic, Euphrates, and other philosophers of importance lectured on various occasions. And thus Valeria's receptions became a feature of these two winter seasons.

One fine morning, in the early part of the year 95, Nyria went down to the Via Margaritaria to tell Stephanus that the Domina purposed to inspect his goods that afternoon. Seeing several lads amusing themselves with the parrot at the shop door, she guessed that Juvenal was within.

The goldsmith smiled kindly as she entered. There was less of the lover about Stephanus than formerly, a change that was welcome to Nyria, who liked to feel that she had in him a faithful friend not too exacting in his demands. And that was what Stephanus now showed himself to be, though his manner toward the girl had a tender reverence which made her hold him very dear.

She hesitated at the moment to explain her errand, for the philosopher was deep in talk, and merely gave her a brief salutation, taking up his subject again immediately.

"What thinkest thou, Stephanus? Hath Regulus learned aught fresh touching the reputed plot of Apollonius and the Jews? Else wherefore should he have again sent spies to Edessa to report anew on that conference between the Wonder-Worker and Nerva, seeing that Cæsar settled the affair by trial last autumn? Will they have Apollonius up again before him?"

"Nay, the gods alone can explain Regulus's crooked workings," replied Stephanus. "And if they did call Apollonius again before the tribunal, what matter, since it appeareth that his magic hath taught him how to turn himself into air."

"'Twas strange," said Juvenal, meditatively. "The case hath oft perplexed me. Hath this man the power of a god that he could thus remove himself without sign from the midst of the court?"

Stephanus shook his head. "I know naught of witchcr—
whereof it savours. Haply Ascletario could inform — that
Methinks the man must have had a body of disciples about —ed of
who covered his departure." —st, was

"Ay, but he was in bonds," cried Juvenal, "and the between
stood on either side."

Again Stephanus shook his head. "He got away, it — might e'er
verily many a luckless prisoner in Rome would be gla—
secret." —ul, but 'tis wise.

Nyria, who sat near, ventured to break in. —metimes serve thee
him they call the Wonder-Worker?" she asked

"Ay, Apollonius of Tyana, who was ar—nd to let a lie pass unjudgment in last year's Judæan scare."

Nyria, who had heard talk at the tim—thou saidst, else Mercury him-
a conspiracy in Syria, listened int—lie not unless thou need; but if

"'Twas well for Rufus and Orfitus that they got off through the magician's pleading. But Nerva will never again be allowed to enter Rome, whether or not he were veritably concerned. Domitian fears him too much—thanks to the Chaldeans."

"Well may Domitian fear any man," retorted Stephanus, grimly. "So long a list of wrongs as he hath wrought doth surely demand redress. A man will be found some day to wreak vengeance on him, and thus fulfil the Chaldean prophecy; but it needeth one of stouter spirit than Nerva, who is no more than a mouse, and an old mouse too."

"Mice nibble in the dark," sneered Juvenal. "They say that Nerva favours the Christians, whereof the half are Jews; which doth account, mayhap, for this report of Regulus, saying he'll produce conspirators of Jewish blood concerned in this Syrian scheme before he's finished with it. What ails thee, Nyria? Thou look'st aghast."

"Nyria finds the spring weather warm," put in Stephanus, hurriedly. "And thy talk is not over cheering, Juvenal. Let rest such ghoulish tales."

"Nay, maids should know what risks they run. Have naught to do with Christians, Nyria, else thou'lt find thyself concerned in plots and politics whereof thou knowst not much. The Temple and the State be close allied in Rome—each fouler than the other. And these foreign plotters do follow the same tricks, it seems, and hide their treason 'neath the guise of worship."

But Nyria, her white features set, rose up and made her first stand for Christ. Her fingers firmly pressed upon the edge of Stephanus's graving-board, she faced the philosopher.

"I know not what others do, but say not that Christians are schemers, Juvenal. They work naught of treason. *I* should know, who—am—a Christian."

val- An impatient sound escaped Stephanus. Nyria turned to him.
discus "Be not angry," she said simply. "I had to say it. Christ is
openly [aster."
thinker venal stared at the girl in frank surprise. Then he made her
meetings ng bow.
admirably hou wouldst serve thy company, as it seems, warn them
sympathy, nterfere not with Cæsar, whose wrath when once aroused
munication wi n that of other gods. Be thou warned too, Nyria,"
of war, when app aly. "That lap of luxury in which thou'st lain at
a fortnight, therefo is but ill training for the arena, where many
fashionable and cultur."
firmament would deliver a terposed.
The first course was inau he maid. Why take her seriously? 'Tis
on Oratory. At the next the Nyria hath been ill advised, but she
later, Valeria composed a rival essa,

"In truth, I hope not," said the philosopher, with a compassionate glance at the girl, who was now near weeping. "Else worse ills are like to follow than such as beset her in yon Forum. Verily, Nyria, thou'lt do well to avoid these Christians, or thou mayest find thyself at the mercy of some base informer, such as Regulus. I mean it kindly, pretty maid, and do thou take it thus."

So saying, Juvenal swung his cloak round him, nodded gravely to Stephanus, and withdrew.

The goldsmith did his best to comfort Nyria in kindly fashion. "Fret not thyself, child. 'Tis such as were at Edessa at the time of this secret conference with Nerva that Regulus would have his finger on. The Christians in Rome are safe enough—so far. But Juvenal is right in the main, and I would thou wert not one of them."

Horror had struck at Nyria's heart—not for herself, but for the faithful little band with which she worshipped. Stephanus's reiterated assurances, however, soon allayed her fears, and she smiled again. The goldsmith continued thoughtfully,—

"Nay, nay, little one, fear not. No danger shall come nigh thee. This scoundrel Regulus is concerned elsewhere, and there's no murmur against thy brethren. Yet if that had been other than Juvenal before whom thou didst betray thy secret, I could find it in my heart to scold thee for thy folly. But thou art safe enough with him. Nevertheless, 'tis needless and unwise to expose thy friends thus."

His words presented a new aspect of the case to Nyria.

"I could not bear that any should speak ill of them," she said diffidently. "It had seemed I were ashamed of my Master if I held my peace."

"Tush, child! Thou needst not blazon all thou doest. The Christians would not thank thee. Nero's persecutions have taught them to be silent when speech may lead them into peril."

Now Nyria knew well that discovery was the one thing that Christians most dreaded. She had learnt that the direst deed of shame a Christian could commit, next to the denial of Christ, was the betrayal of his fellow-members. How to steer a course between the two sometimes puzzled her.

"Thinkest thou, Stephanus," she inquired, "that it might e'er be lawful to lie?"

He laughed outright. "I know not if 'tis lawful, but 'tis wise. Be not thus tender, Nyria. A round lie may sometimes serve thee well."

"'Tis sin," she murmured sadly. "And to let a lie pass unchecked is lying too."

"What if it be? 'Tis lawful, as thou saidst, else Mercury himself doth oft offend. Nay, Nyria, lie not unless thou need; but if thou must, why—lie freely. 'Tis lesser sin, for sure, than to betray them that trust thee."

"Ay, 'tis so," she answered. "And methinks that were I confident betrayal would follow on my words I could but lie, and pray Christ's pardon, seeing He would know I sinned not of desire."

Stephanus gazed at her with that tender gaze which, ever since Euphena had shown him the mystic light around the maid, had something of a devotee in it.

"Verily, none might impute sin to thee," he murmured. "But tell me, Nyria, wherefore hast thou come to-day? 'Tis not oft I see thee now, child." His heart yearned to hear her say she came for love of him, but Nyria merely rose and explained her errand.

"The Domina doth desire to look over thy gems, and haply may purchase some. I would thou wert prepared for her coming, Stephanus."

The goldsmith gave a grudging assent. He had no mind to receive Valeria, whom he cordially disliked, but business could not be ignored.

They went out together to the shop-door, where Ascalaphus hailed Nyria excitedly. She signed to a passing tray-seller, and bought a packet of sweets, whereat Ascalaphus's excitement increased, and he ambled suggestively on his perch. Nyria laughed at the comical appearance he presented. She put a dainty sweetmeat between her lips, and approaching the cage, made him take it from them between the bars. Stephanus looked on enviously.

"Thou hast thy pouch full of coin, it seems," he remarked.

"Oh, ay! I am a wealthy maid. Valeria spares us plenty. But thou knowest, Stephanus, I love best to spend my money on Christ's poor, since He hath given me so much." And Nyria nodded farewell and ran off, quite happy again.

She had a little litter of her own in which to pay the afternoon call, for Valeria was wont to say it turned her sick to see slave-girls pushed in the streets. So when the Domina was borne along the Via Margaritaria in her sumptuous litter, another, less imposing, but carried by bearers in the same livery, followed it. And when Stephanus went to the lady's assistance, Dinarmid, his apprentice, jestingly offered a shoulder for Nyria's descent.

"Verily, here comes a dame of note," he whispered, and Nyria laughed delightedly. She followed the lady into the shop, proud when Valeria praised the goods and declared 'twas difficult to choose among them. Stephanus had set out a row of gold and silver effigies and some exquisite aqua-marines for her inspection, deeming she might fancy them. Meanwhile, Nyria was fingering admiringly a string of British pearls.

"Dost like those, child?" asked Valeria, who was generous when it cost her naught. "Put them round thy neck. Verily, 'tis browner than when Julia kept thee for her show maid. But thou shalt have the pearls. Good goldsmith, add them to thy count."

Stephanus reddened angrily. "Once 'twas Stephanus's privilege to offer Nyria the best his shop contained. Alack! that day is dead."

Valeria glanced at the slave-girl, amused.

"Maids are not bought with gems," she said, "though thou mayst chain prisoners with them if thou wilt." Then she asked how much she owed, offering to sign for the money, which her steward should bring. Stephanus made out the total, and Valeria seemed surprised it was not more, for she had bought a ruby corselet, and some golden images, and a lustrous chain of aqua-marines.

"I see thou hast no mind to make thy fortune," she remarked.

"A man looketh for sweeter fortune than gold can bring," retorted Stephanus, bitterly. "Of what use to gild the cage if the song-bird be not there?"

She smiled again. "Thou hast a poet's humour—but recount thine items and their cost."

Stephanus ran them through hurriedly.

"Thou hast forgot the pearls," she said.

Stephanus drew back, bowing, but with a frown upon his face.

"Thy pardon, Domina, but when thou didst first command me for Nyria I said I took no payment for the maid. Nor will I—save such as she herself bestoweth in other coin than gold."

The sentiment seemed to commend itself to Valeria. She turned to the girl. "Wilt take the pearls, Nyria, or no? They can be no gift of mine, it seems. 'Tis through this friend of thine thou'lt be the richer."

"Thus have I ever been, Domina," replied Nyria, demurely. "I'll keep the pearls, though such debts as I do owe Stephanus can never be repaid."

"He hath a different mind on that," laughed Valeria, drawing up her palla, and as she went forth to the litter Ascalaphus meekly gibbered from behind the blanket with which Stephanus had taken the precaution to screen his cage.

As they left the Lower Forum they passed Matho's new office in its humble nook, for the lawyer had fallen into disrepute by now and was moved from the corner of the Carinæ. When they reached the broader roads the Domina had Nyria's litter carried alongside her own, that the girl might point out things of interest they passed, and thus she learnt much through the eyes of her handmaid, whom she encouraged to chatter freely.

By-and-by they got out of their litters near the city wall and went along the hillside. During her visits to Tuscany and Nemi each summer Valeria had indulged a fondness of her girlhood for walking, and would often now appoint the litter to await them at one of the gates while she and Nyria wandered outside; or, if her ramble were like to lead her near the Cœlian, she would dismiss her bearers and return home afoot with Nyria, the two usually laden with wild flowers. For Valeria's tastes turned naturally to simple things; and now that life held less stress for her, and the thought of Licinius, though never absent, had become only a treasured memory, she permitted herself such pleasures as she had formerly been too harassed to enjoy.

To-day they walked up to Nyria's old haunt above the quarries, which Valeria now knew well. She seated herself on the edge of the deserted knoll and looked straight over the shadowy hills.

"Truly, meseems," she said, "a soul distraught might well come here for commune with the gods and such as be their messengers."

Nyria, kneeling on the ground beside her, talked in reverent accents of the great God who had spoken in her own heart, and of the promise He had given her that some day she should see His face — a promise which Nyria, having learned the truth of the Gospel tidings, looked not now to see fulfilled on earth. Valeria listened, sometimes touched, sometimes inclined to tease.

"Thou art nearer to the truth, it seems," she said, "than they who do philosophise at our fortnightly meetings. Alack! that so many of the great and wise should torment themselves over problems of life and death which thou in thine innocent assurance hast solved to such satisfaction!"

Nyria longed that Clementus might have answered the Roman lady. Deep in Nyria's heart was a passionate desire to turn her Domina into a Christian. It was for this that she had invariably told Valeria all she could of the Christians' teaching, of their ways, and the hours of meeting, hoping that some day the Domina might be tempted to accompany her. Now she pointed out the path by the quarries, and the ravine from which the cave-chapel was entered —relating also various details concerning the church ceremonies and the exhortations of Clementus to his flock. Valeria appeared unusually interested, and presently she said,—

"Phileros shall make me notes of these doctrines, so that they may be turned to account in the papers on the roots of religion which I am producing for our discussions."

Startled and terrified, Nyria prayed her to bear in mind that these matters should be held in strict secrecy. Valeria somewhat discontentedly conceded the question—though under protest.

"I shall never make thee think enough of the importance of literature," she grumbled laughingly. "Tacitus would tell thee that a man should not shrink from exposing the private details of his life were they needed as material for the books that it be in his power to make. But thou art no historian, Nyria—no writer of romance. Yet," she added earnestly, "there is a story writ in thine eyes, though in language I cannot interpret. Lives there not one who may?"

"I know not of whom thou speakest, Domina," replied Nyria.

"Thy cheeks suspect if thou dost not," replied Valeria. "Say, doth not the worthy goldsmith hold the key to thy life-story?"

"Stephanus is my friend," stammered Nyria.

"A generous friend," cried Valeria, pointing to the necklace. "So thou hast taken Stephanus's British pearls but hast not agreed to pay for them."

"Nyria hath naught with which to pay," replied the girl, pained.

"Hast thou not? Ah! Nyria, thou wast a little maid when Stephanus served thee first, but now thou art a maiden grown, and fairer than thy promise. Know that thou bearest in thy breast a priceless jewel, of the kind men love to wrest from maidens. For men are robbers, Nyria. Avoid them, lest they rob thee."

"Stephanus would scorn to rob a maid," cried Nyria, indignantly.

"Then is he nobler than the noblest," Valeria replied. "There's no lord in Rome that would deny himself the joy of rifling from a maid he desired that which no repentance on his part could restore to her again."

Nyria was silent, not knowing what was meant.

"Avoid such robbers," Valeria repeated, "whether they be in guise of beasts prowling at nightfall or sue humbly, as beseems beggars. Brutes or beggars, lords or plebs, all are alike. And, child, remember this—thy trusting heart once snatched away, thou'lt have naught left for any man. Then should love come to thee in guise of prince or beggar, 'twill be too late to list his plea, for thou canst give thyself but once, and oh, ye gods!—what, then, is left?"

Valeria had risen and stood upon the knoll-edge as she spoke these last words to the air. Now she turned, folding her palla close around her, and signed to Nyria that they would go home.

The two walked almost in silence down the hill, and this brooding Valeria bore little likeness to the gently gay lady who had left her litter by the walls an hour or so previously. But Nyria, used to her mistress's moods, knew how swift were their alternations when Valeria allowed herself to be natural. They had forsaken the wider path winding round the outlying spurs, and now took a steep track that dropped into the high road leading from the Aventine to the Cœlian, close to Licinius Sura's villa. This usually looked deserted, but to-day, as they approached it, Nyria saw, to her surprise, the figure of a man coming out by the smaller entrance beneath the plane trees—a man who stepped with a somewhat furtive air, and who was enveloped in a cloak, with a hood drawn up over his head and falling well below his knees. Though his face was indistinguishable there was something familiar in his gait, and Nyria knew that the same thought had struck her mistress, for Valeria gave a gasp and pressed the girl's hand convulsively against her side, so that Nyria felt the quick flutter of her heart.

There should have been torches kindled outside the house had anyone been in residence, by edict of Domitian—one of whose best innovations had been the better lighting of Rome—but not a gleam showed within or without the house, and though dusk had scarcely deepened into night the trees along the road made it very dark. The man was close upon them before he perceived their nearness, and now he retreated against a plane tree to let them pass, peering at them from beneath his hood. After a moment's hesitation he threw back his cloak and stood before them. It was Marcus Licinius Sura.

Valeria stood still and gazed at him like one transfixed. Licinius held out his arms, at which she, never speaking, dropped Nyria's hand, but still stared, catching her palla together beneath her chin.

Licinius laughed the old musical daring laugh which Nyria so well remembered. "Thou seest," he said, "I have returned. Am I welcome, Valeria?"

Valeria made no answer, but a tremor shot through her body. He drew closer, his arms held out.

"Hast not a word for me, Valeria?" and as she broke into a murmur of delirious joy he caught her to his breast.

Now, just then, Nyria, standing a pace or so apart, saw two figures at the corner of the road where it turned down by one side of the house. They came forward slowly, then slipped back, as if desiring to remain unnoticed. Nyria drew nearer to her mistress.

"May it please thee, Domina, someone cometh."

"Ha! little watch-dog, so 'tis thou," said Licinius. "Follow me, child." He opened the gate and the next moment they were within. Licinius half led, half carried Valeria along the path round the house and through the little door. It closed behind them, and Nyria, shrinking against the creeper-hung porch, waited long for them to re-emerge.

XXXIII

It appeared that Sura had come secretly to Rome, and was in hiding, only going out at nightfall in disguise, and holding no communication with his ordinary friends. The cause of this, he gave Valeria to understand, was some important political business, but he told her nothing of its nature, nor did she, absorbed in the joy of his return, question him at first concerning it. But Nyria, hearing scraps of talk, wondered whether the matter were such as informers might set spies upon, for that first evening was not the only occasion on which she saw cloaked figures hanging furtively round the wall of Licinius's house, and she could not forget Juvenal's suggestions.

The villa was kept closed at the main entrance, unlighted, and deserted-looking as during its master's absence. Only two or three slaves attended to his needs in that part of the building screened from the road wherein were Licinius's private rooms, and to which the jasmine-trellised portico gave access. There were two kinds of jasmine round the porch—the wintry species now abloom that threw out yellow flowers in advance of its leaves, and another with white scented blossoms that was in perfection at the beginning of summer. Thither, during those golden weeks, Valeria came frequently, for her creed of love reckoned no measure. Having once surrendered her capitulation was absolute. The agony of the past two years of separation had wrought that which naught else could have worked, and she, who had before borne herself with all the pride of the Valerian gens, now abased herself as once she would have thought impossible, pouring forth freely all the pent-up passion of her nature, and in the renewed bliss of her lover's presence disregarding all but him. Her visits were usually made between noon and twilight. It became her custom to take her litter daily, for the apparent purpose of some shopping, or to pay a short call, though, as she grew careless of such interests, she fell into the way of neglecting social claims. Soon dismissing her bearers on pretext of a ramble, she and Nyria would, when out of sight, don disguising mantles which they carried, and hasten to Licinius's villa, returning home later afoot. Licinius himself always admitted them with his winning smile of welcome, and once beneath the trellis, Valeria would throw back her shrouding palla and enter joyously, while Nyria, folding it with her own, would seat herself discreetly in the sun. Nyria liked to watch the bulbs shoot and the shrubs thicken with leaf-buds, but these were days when she was very sad. Striving humbly as she did to live by the light of her Christian teaching, the girl bore a burden of intolerable shame for Valeria. Moreover, her heart was heavy with half-defined fears. She knew that Licinius was like other Roman lords who held love lightly, even when they most desired it—as a boon bringing joy and satisfaction, but not to be bought at too dear a cost, lest the price exceed its value. In her astute little fashion she gathered that Licinius cared less for scruples of honour than he feared the exposure of his relationship with Paulinus's wife and this, more for his own sake than Valeria's. Love was not to him the thing it represented to Valeria, who throughout this dreamy springtide was intoxicated with the spell of her passion—thinking shame no longer, but loving because she must as a flower opens to the sun. The sunshine did not mature the blooms more fully and more sweetly than love beautified Valeria. And thus it was that the loyal little handmaiden began to fear lest this strange enchantment on her cherished mistress's face should be observed and wondered at. Gregorio's lynx eyes she felt instinctively noticed every change in Valeria. And there was Martial also to be dreaded, a constant visitor at the Valerian villa, whose ways puzzled the slave-girl, for lords did not usually make friends with slaves of other households. Yet Martial always chatted with Gregorio when they met, and Nyria's distrust of the slave-lad made her distrust the poet.

One afternoon towards the end of spring, Nyria, issuing forth from the side-gate in Licinius's wall was startled to see Martial and Gregorio deep in conversation beneath the plane trees. Nyria hurriedly drew up her hood, but too late to avoid recognition.

"Thou needst not try to hide thyself," Gregorio hissed, his big head thrust forward in his snake-like way. "Yah! thou traitress. I bide my time, Nyria. Soon we shall see who standeth most secure—thou in thy Domina's favour, or I in that of Paulinus."

Nyria paled, and Martial put a hand on the boy's shoulder to restrain him.

"Thou art jealous, eh?" he laughed. "What should Nyria do in the empty house of Licinius if it be not to gossip with some handsome fellow that he hath left in keeping? Dost know aught of the absent master, Nyria? Methought I heard some rumour of Sura being in Rome."

Nyria, taken aback, began to stammer a vague reply, to which Gregorio gave an impatient sneer. Martial rebuked him.

"Thy music, friend Gregorio, is sweeter than thy wit. I'd sooner trust Nyria to bear the message with which I was about to favour thee. Pray tell thy Domina, pretty Nyria, with Martial's greeting, that while I waited on Cæsar this morning there came a laurelled letter from Sarmatia bringing news of a victory, and, better still, of our Illustrious Paulinus's speedy return. Doubtless she will herself receive a missive from her lord, who doth halt at Forum Julii, but fain would I have been the first to speed her these joyful tidings," and with a gallant bow to the girl Martial turned away. Gregorio followed sulkily, leaving her a prey to the keenest apprehension. Instead of going into the city as she had intended, she went back to warn her mistress.

The room where Valeria sat was Licinius's private study, a cheerful apartment, though small, with rugs on the mosaic floor, a writing-table and inlaid chairs and stools. There were always fresh flowers to welcome Valeria, and here she would often arrange the wild ones she brought. In the room were several things she had given him—a small copy in silver of her own Demeter, and an exquisite little piece of sculpture by a famous Greek. This was Love asleep with Psyche, a lamp in her hand, bending over him and gazing intently upon his face. Nyria caught something of the same look on Valeria's face as she gazed at Licinius, unheeding at first the slave-girl's entrance.

The pair were much perturbed at hearing that Paulinus was on his way homeward. Licinius made some bantering attempts to console Valeria and himself, at which she winced.

"The time will come soon," he said, "for me to visit thee openly. Paulinus cannot object after the welcome he gave me."

"Thou knowest well the reason of Paulinus's bearing towards thee then," said Valeria, shivering, "Alack! I've been too happy to remember that Paulinus would return." She sank back as she spoke, but Licinius had risen and stood thinking deeply.

"I fear not Martial, nor this lad of thine," he said. "'Tis Regulus I fear. To him I owe the miscarriage of important plans I am concerned with, and I've learned of late that my spiteful kinsman, Palfurius, is plotting mischief with the knave. They both have Cæsar's ear, which means it is not safe for one they scheme against to be seen abroad as yet. So I must needs keep myself in closer hiding, here or else get me hence. Say, sweet Valeria, which shall it be?"

He sat down beside her and began toying with a small cross of pearls she wore, which he had brought her from Judæa. But Valeria, her anxiety aroused by his words, began to question him.

"Thou hast never told me what mean these plans of thine. Surely now"—she blushed a little, but there was tender confidence in her manner—"*now*, Marcus, I may hear."

"I have never told thee, sweet, because in thy presence I can think of naught save thee," he answered evasively.

"But these affairs hold a large measure of thy mind—that I can see," she persisted; "and since thou art everything to me, fain would I defend thee from all danger."

"*Thou* defend me, sweet!" he rejoined caressingly. "*Thou*, learned Valeria, who hath ever held herself aloof alike from games of dexterity and chance, however high their stakes might be. Thou hast never meddled in State matters."

"Nay—with reason," she replied bitterly. "Better had it been for my father had he abstained from such meddling."

"A man should play life's games," rejoined Licinius, gravely. "What would their stakes be worth without ambition?"

"There would be love," she said reproachfully.

"Ay, ambition fulfilled means love fulfilled likewise. Therefore blame me not, dearest, for risking no chances of defeat. When I have won my game, Valeria, I shall win thee also."

She gazed at him with passionate devotion, but a faintly doubting look in her eyes.

"The gods grant thy game be not the dearer! How couldst thou leave me, Marcus, all those months, not knowing what I suffered?"

"Licinius had his part to play, beloved. There was no place for a woman in it."

"Is that so?" she repeated. "Was there verily no woman in thy life whilst thou wert in Judæa?" She gave him a penetrating glance, and went on hurriedly: "I ask my question of a purpose, though it doth suggest that which I deem dishonour, seeing that even then thou and I were one in heart. And thus the thought hath rankled sorely. Alack! though rumour gave it birth, meseemed it might be true. Jest not, Marcus, I implore thee. Many a time in my dear dreamings of our love there thrusts betwixt thee and me the face"—she reddened and added passionately—"the face of that woman Salome."

"Salome!" he exclaimed. "Where hast thou seen Salome?"

"Twice only—yet each time near thy gate. On the first occasion Martial had just joined me. He saluted her, and in answer to my questioning then told me who she was, adding that she had but lately returned from Judæa, whither she had been—with *thee*."

Licinius looked perplexed and angry. He hesitated, a frown between his handsome brows. Then he turned upon Valeria his engaging smile.

"I tell no lies when truth serves best," he said. "For once, Valeria, thou wert informed correctly."

Cut to the quick, she started up and would have moved away but that he caught her hands.

"Nay, hear me out, beloved. By Aphrodite! 'twas worth the pain to bring that fire to thy face. It maketh thee more goddess in thy beauty than the Vitellian blood itself. Divine Valeria! And thou canst stoop to be jealous—of Salome?"

She turned to him agonised eyes.

"Marcus! Understand me, for I sometimes fear myself. I have given thee my love in all entirety. Let come what may, I have been thine. The gods alone know what this meaneth to a woman like Valeria. Hold me in thine heart, as I hold thee, where none else may dwell, lest Valeria, finding herself dethroned, should cease to be Valeria, but become some hapless puppet of the Furies goaded to revenge. Then who knows what dire deed she'd do and suffer for? Now answer me by that which thou dost hold most sacred—whate'er it be—was Salome ever aught to thee again when thou went'st from me to Judæa?"

Licinius seemed nonplussed once more. Valeria loosed her hands and drew away from him. She rose and stood by a marble tripod whereon lay the sleeping Love, her face revealing, as she said, a new Valeria torn by the wildest emotions. Outraged pride strove with her instinct of self-surrender, while her eyes besought him.

Licinius looked moody for a moment, then he too got up and stood gazing at her. Slowly his face lighted into a smile, pleading, yet exultant. Her bosom heaved as she met his look, she swayed towards him. He flung wide his arms with the gesture that never failed to draw her to him. Then he folded her to his heart, kissing her a hundred times.

"Doth not *that* convince thee?" he cried. "Canst doubt me now, Valeria? What woman could exist for me beneath the sun save *thee*, beloved? Oh! is there need of oaths by gods or gens when every pulse of me throbs for thee, and thee alone? Art satisfied, sweet?" He took his answers from her lips in kisses. "Come then," he said, drawing her to a couch. "I'll tell thee all the truth of this strange matter which hath so long perturbed thee."

He made her seat herself again, and took a place beside her. The pearl cross she wore hung on a thin gold chain on her breast, and he again toyed with it thoughtfully, while that exultant smile still played round his mouth.

Now Nyria, standing apart, since she had not been dismissed after she brought her warning, could not forbear listening when the talk turned on Judæa, seeing it was the land where the Master, Christ, lived and suffered, and of which she longed to know more, but she tried to turn a deaf ear to their ardent passages of love. It mattered not, however, for the pair were too much engrossed in each other to heed the slave-girl's unobtrusive presence.

"I gave thee this cross, Valeria," Licinius said, "as a pledge of my fidelity, for it is a holy symbol among a sect with which I've had dealings of late. Thus let me ease thy mind. When I said but now that rumour in the mouth of Martial had informed thee correctly, I had not time to add that Martial told thee but half the truth, seeing he could have known no more than that. Salome did verily come after me into Judæa, but not at my bidding nor of my desire. She came of her own will to warn me that I should run grievous risk by returning, as I intended at that time, to Rome. Wherefore I thanked her as I should, and did follow her advice, else haply I had not been free to sun me in thy sweetness now."

But Valeria's jealous rage flamed forth anew.

"Then thou didst communicate with *her*, though thou hadst no word for *me*."

"Is the danger in which I stood of no account to thee?" he asked tenderly.

"Ay—thou knowest—but how and why should *she* have been kept in touch with thee if, as thou toldest me long since, thou didst send her hence when first thou hadst learned to love *me!*"

Licinius bit his lip.

"'Tis scarce a subject for our converse, my fair lady, but if thou must be told, a man hath certain natural feeling for his offspring. Since the boy is mine, I scarce can see that he should suffer for his father's faults. Such scant communication as hath passed between his mother and me was to provide for the welfare of the child."

Valeria did not reply at first; then she seemed, with a haughty movement, to reassume control of herself.

"I say naught against thy care for the child—'tis natural, as thou sayest, and not a topic to discuss. For the rest, Valeria will trust thee—since she must. Pray tell me, however, of these plots of thine. Have they aught to do with last year's foolish conspiracy at Edessa, of which 'twas said that Nerva pulled the strings?"

Licinius nodded. "Nay, the strings pulled Nerva, though not enough to get him to the Palatine. The old man is a milk-faced dotard, but there is no better to put forward for our purpose. Moreover, Nerva is superstitious, and the Chaldean's prophecy that Domitian had best beware of him hath implanted some sort of false courage in his timid breast. But the most of all is this—Nerva doth greatly favour the Christians, with whom our chief hope lies."

"But thou art no Christian, Marcus?" said Valeria in surprise.

"Nay. 'Tis a religion for the common folk. But therein lies its power, for the common folk are many and ill-satisfied, whereas this creed of theirs doth seek to exalt the lowly. Nevertheless are they a strange, contradictory set. They would be free, yet will not fight for freedom. Apollonius was right when he told Nerva that they were not educated to the point of revolt. I met the Wonder-Worker at Edessa, Valeria, wherein lies part of my secret, for I was there in disguise during that famous conference with Nerva, concerning which the clever Regulus failed to establish his charge of sedition. Well was it that I thus disguised myself, else would Licinius Sura too have been brought forward at the trial, and since he hath not Apollonius's trick of vanishing, he had like to have fared worse than Rufus and Orfitus, or even Nerva in his Tarentine banishment."

"But that cause surely concerns thee not, since it hath been dismissed," exclaimed Valeria.

"Ay, and justly, so far as touched those three," Licinius replied, "seeing that Apollonius was never in favour of revolt and argued sore against me. As for the other two, they were but targets for Regulus's money-getting ventures."

"He will not turn his scheming now on thee?" inquired Valeria, anxiously.

"I'll see he hath no chance. 'Tis for that I do secrete myself while I have work to do among the Judæan Christians who congregate in Rome."

"I like it not," Valeria said, "for harm may come to thee. What work canst thou find to do among such folk?"

"Nay, nay, sweet lady—have I not told thee enough? Let it suffice thee to remember the augury that out of Judæa shall arise a ruler to whom all nations will be subject. Regulus hath quenched my search once, but he shall not quench it again. 'Tis for this that I have tilled the soil of Judæa, and for this that I do till Judæan Rome. If I can reconcile Jew and Christian in redress of the wrongs of both, and with their aid set some nobler Cæsar on the throne, then need Licinius no longer hide himself in his villa on the Aventine while his cousins sport as they please, winning Imperial favour. 'Twill be thy Marcus's turn then, dear dame, and thine."

Valeria smiled wistfully.

"Oh, dreamer! who would accomplish that which even Apollonius did condemn? Domitian will have died a natural death before thou dost compass thy desire. Valeria seeks no Imperial favour—none save thine—if thou be true to her."

XXXIV

When Paulinus returned to Rome Nyria would hardly have known him for the same who had rescued her in the slave-market. He obviously cared no more for his wife's favour, and his manner when they met conveyed an angry distrust that filled Valeria with nervous dread. The settlement of military details in connection with his Sarmatian command occupied him a good deal, however, and he spent small time at the villa, sedulously avoiding his wife's apartments. Valeria lived in a state in which joy and despair alternated feverishly, snatching every available opportunity for seeing Licinius, and making the most of occasions when Paulinus went up to the Emperor at Albanum, or was otherwise occupied with business.

The white flowers were out now on the jasmine creeper, the roses were all abloom, the datura bells shed heavy fragrance, and the air was laden with summer scents. A brassy glare hung over Rome, and the gilded domes and pediments were as gigantic flames. The heats had come early, and this year the sun was unusually powerful. One day, about the ninth hour, Nyria, having left her Domina at Licinius's house, was returning along an exposed bit of road, when its rays, striking on her head, made her feel sick and giddy. She had been to see the parents of Lucius, who dwelt in the house by the river, and there learned a piece of important news —that no less a person than the Apostle John was coming that summer to Rome and would address the flock. Nyria knew that Clementus was a close personal friend of that holy man, and now, to think that she also should see and hear one who had known the Master in the flesh, seemed happiness too sublime to be possible. Yet amid her joyful anticipation was a sense of uneasiness, for Nyria could not forget the bishop's charge to his catechumens on her baptismal night. Sadly she wondered if indeed she were proving herself faithful, for there was much in Nyria's daily life now of which her tender conscience disapproved. But had she not sworn likewise to serve her mistress—even to the death? And since that vow was also made in heart, at least, to the same great God of all, Nyria could not break it. Besides, her devotion to Valeria was too deep to be foresworn.

She had come up through the narrow short cut from the city, and though the gloom there was grateful it gave her an odd fit of shivering. Thence she turned into the broad road below the Aventine. Here, ahead of her, went a lady's litter, and rounding the curve, Nyria saw Gregorio coming towards it. He walked with his usual jaunty swing, and when he neared the litter he doffed his cap gallantly. The bearers rested the poles on their shoulders while he leaned over the side and chatted familiarly with its occupant. Glancing at the litter as she went by, Nyria saw that Thanna sat therein. She wondered how Thanna had become acquainted with Gregorio, for Thanna had never been to see her at the Valerian villa, though they often met in friendly fashion. Thanna, in a coloured veil, nodded gaily as Nyria passed, but Gregorio only gave his usual scowl. Presently another litter came down the hill, and Nyria, hearing bearers' footsteps behind her, concluded that Thanna had dismissed Gregorio and was following to speak to her, therefore she drew more slowly along the side of the road. In the second litter was the Jewess, Salome, looking black and angry, but very handsome. She sat erect, her hands stretched out grasping the sides of the litter, her dark eyes flashing, and her teeth biting into her red under-lip. Thanna, approaching, called a salutation, at which Nyria, thinking it was for her, stopped and turned just as the litters met. The curtains of both were open, as was customary with women of a certain grade, though in the streets noble ladies invariably rode with them closed. It was evident, as these two women leaned forward in greeting, that they were intimately acquainted. Thanna, forgetting all about Nyria, bade the bearers turn her litter, and she and Salome proceeded down the hill together, bending their heads towards each other, deep in conversation. Salome's shrill, persistent voice was complaining bitterly of some grievance, while Thanna's tinkling tones endeavoured to reassure her. Nyria, watching their progress, perceived Gregorio, a little lower down, halt also and join the litters, swinging along beside that of Salome, with whom he was evidently on equally cordial terms.

This friendship, of which Nyria knew nothing, was due to Thanna's diplomacy, for having discovered that others were after the quarry that she had herself been set to spy upon, she promptly fooled Gregorio and won Salome with offers of sympathy and co-operation—and used both as tools, for Thanna had far too much wit to betray Regulus's purposes.

Her triumphant laughter rang back now, blending with Salome's high-pitched grumbles. In a minute the litters were out of sight, and Nyria went on under the plane trees, drawing up the hood of her mantle and waiting till there was no sign of anyone in the road, before she lifted the latch of Licinius's gate.

Valeria had already put on her palla, and was standing just within the door of the porch. Something had gone wrong—that was easy to be seen—for there were traces of a storm upon her face, while Licinius, at her side, looking worried, uttered assurances to which she listened doubtfully.

"Did I not give thee proof by refusing to see the woman?" he said. "Thou art unreasonable, Valeria. How can I hinder her from calling here? I owe her at least my present security. Sweet! be kind again, and add not to the hardness of our situation by unmerited reproaches."

Valeria looked at him with miserable eyes. "Truly, Marcus, our situation is a hard one. At times it seems that I can bear it no longer. If thou wilt not soon take me from this dishonour, then must I bid thee leave me. I could not live without thee, yet better that sharp death than this long shame and anguish that are destroying me."

He put his arms around her and besought her to be patient, till presently she, somewhat comforted, left him. Drawing her veil over her face, and her palla more closely round her, she took Nyria's arm, and the two went cautiously through the gate, and, mounting the track by Diana's temple, crossed to the hinder part of the hill where Valeria had bidden her litter await her. As she unveiled and removed her outer cloak before rejoining the bearers, a sound of dismay escaped her.

"My cross!" she cried. "Oh, Nyria, I have lost it! Methinks it must have fallen on the road we have come, for it was safe when I went from Marcus. Go, child, search for it! 'Twould be an ill omen for Valeria did she lose that token to-day."

So, seeing the Domina safe into her litter, Nyria flew back, straining her eyes, swiftly over the ground they had traversed, in hope of finding the cross ere dusk fell. By good luck she came upon it close against the temple wall, and being near the main road to Paulinus's house, she decided to return by this direct way instead of cutting across the hill again to overtake her mistress. The girl still felt sick and shivery, and was languidly descending the lonely dip between the Aventine and the Cœlian, taking small heed of anything around her, when a figure on the opposite slope caught her attention. It was Paulinus, whose appearance filled her with sudden alarm. He walked in haste, blind determination in his gait, his toga flung back carelessly so that his big red limbs showed. As he drew near Nyria she saw that his face was of a purplish red and his brows dark with rage.

She stopped, forgetting even to make her obeisance, as he advanced quickly to her. Seizing her by the shoulders he shook her violently, exclaiming, "Where's thy lady? Speak!"

Nyria trembled too much to answer, and he repeated, standing menacingly before her, "Answer me, girl. Where hast thou left the Domina?"

"May it please thee, lord, the Domina is in her litter," stammered Nyria.

"What way went she?" shouted Paulinus.

"May it please thee, methinks the bearers took the road on the Cœlian that leads by the Barracks of the Equites."

Paulinus stared, furious, but baffled.

"Wherefore didst thou leave the Domina?" he asked.

"May it please thee, the Domina sent me back to search for a jewel that she had dropped," answered Nyria.

"Ha!" He put his face forward eagerly. "Where dropped she the jewel? Quick—speak."

"'Twas on the hill-side, by Diana's temple, that I found it, lord."

"And what did thy mistress there?" he asked with a caustic laugh. "Not praying within, I'll warrant."

"Nay, lord, the Domina was walking over the hill, as she often doth."

"Ah!" said he, "I have heard of this fresh fancy of hers to use her feet. Now, Nyria, I'll have the rights of this." He squared himself, big and fierce, so that she trembled anew at his threatening aspect. "Relate to me what the Domina hath done this day. What time went she forth, and whither went she?"

"'Twas about the seventh hour, lord"—and Nyria paused, for a dreadful thought had just come to the girl that she must lie to Paulinus if she would shield Valeria.

"Speak!" he cried. "Thou shalt have no time for prevarication. Where went the Domina?"

"To the Forum first, may it please thee; to the Goldsmiths' Portico, and afterwards to the shop of Trypho."

"Go on—and next?"

"My lady did proceed by the Tuscan Street, and descended from her litter near the gate in the city wall behind the house of Julia, while we walked to gather wild flowers, and bade the bearers wait by the Ostian Gate, whither we came anon," recited Nyria, with pitiful glibness.

Paulinus nodded, but his face was very dark while he stood considering.

"By all the gods," he broke out, "I'll satisfy myself on this matter! A different tale hath been told me, Nyria, and it resteth between thee and another which is the true one. I trust thee, girl." He put his hands again on Nyria's shoulders, and fixed her with a glance like gleaming steel. "Now prove thine oath of fealty. Answer me truly—Hath Valeria been visiting Licinius Sura?"

Nyria met his gaze with eyes distended wide, and intensely blue. Paulinus's words pierced her dazed brain through a roaring sound like that of many waters. Even her own voice, as she spoke, seemed to come from far away, whence echoed with a dull persistence the saying of Stephanus—"A round lie may sometimes serve thee well."

She answered distinctly, "Nay, lord—to my knowledge Valeria hath never visited Licinius Sura."

Paulinus took away his hands, saying slowly,—

"Good! I believe thee, Nyria. Thou'st saved thy mistress and thyself." He turned on his heel and went off, while Nyria, humiliated and heart-broken, crept trembling on her way.

That lie loomed terribly on Nyria's mental horizon. It was a great sin, she knew, and yet it seemed a greater to betray Valeria. She felt sure that if the case were to recur she would lie again. Meanwhile, her head ached with the puzzlement of it all, and she could scarcely attend to her duties that night. Had Valeria been other than Valeria she would have observed the distress upon the girl's face; but Valeria was too absorbed by her own troubled thoughts to notice it, and Nyria dared not obtrude her misery and fears. She would have liked to confess the story to her mistress, and confide her dread of Gregorio, but she shrank from adding to the burden Valeria already bore. Moreover, the Domina took little heed of the characters of those in her household unless their faults were forced on her. She would scorn the idea of a slave's power to injure, unless compelled to realise it; and although she knew that Nyria comprehended her mistress's secret, Valeria's pride would have scorned equally to acknowledge that bond. So Nyria said nothing, hoping that Gregorio's vengeance would prove no more than threats, and that Paulinus's suspicions, allayed by her untruth, might not be re-aroused.

Next morning Nyria was not able to come to the robing, for she had fainted before going to bed, sorely frightening Æola, and in the night grew light-headed. When the matter was reported to Valeria she seemed vexed, yet took but little heed, for her thoughts were evidently elsewhere. She said shortly that Nyria must be tended, and Æola sent for Stephanus.

When Stephanus came he administered potions, and gave stringent directions that Æola alone should wait on Nyria, making excuses that Æola had already nursed fever. His real reason, however, was because Nyria in her wanderings talked much of Clementus, and the Christians, and the coming of the Apostle John, and Stephanus feared trouble were any other of her fellow-slaves—most of whom bore ill-will towards the girl on account of Valeria's favour—to learn that she was a Christian, and to spread the fact abroad. Æola had leanings towards Christianity herself, and would have been baptised ere this but that Crispus had made her promise to wait awhile before changing her faith, on pretext that he himself would look into the matter. Crispus had been much away from Rome of late, for a gladiator, to take first rank in his profession, was obliged to defeat a certain number of noted gladiators at the provincial shows—thereby gaining what was called the silver prize—before he could compete for the golden prize—the crowning honour of the Arena—which must be fought for in Rome, in presence of Cæsar, and meant, beside the gladiatorial championship, a large sum out of the State coffers, and the privilege of retiring, if the victor should so desire. Crispus wanted to win this prize at the next great games arranged to be given by the Emperor, and after that he meant to marry Æola.

Meantime, Æola occasionally attended Christian meetings with Nyria, or with Æmilia, whom Nyria had converted during the visit to Pliny's Tuscan villa, and who now, since Antæia's death, was permitted a long holiday at her father's farm near Tusculum.

Stephanus's thoughts went to Æmilia when Æola bore him a peremptory message from Valeria that she did not wish to be deprived of another handmaiden's service; that Stephanus might hire a capable nurse for Nyria, but that he must leave Æola free. Stephanus growled that it was not likely that the Domina would sacrifice her own convenience for her maid's comfort, though Nyria had formerly sacrificed her skin to serve the lady. He added that he would himself crave audience of Valeria, and, as he crossed the peristyle on this errand, came upon the master of the house. Recognising the goldsmith, who saluted him respectfully—seeing that he had a favour to ask—Paulinus inquired his business, whereat Stephanus informed him of Nyria's condition, and prayed his influence with Valeria. Paulinus was kindly in his way, and indulgent to his slaves when they did not anger him, and he now showed some concern about Nyria's illness, remembering his rough usage of her on the previous day. But he shook his head, frowning, at Stephanus's request. "I interfere not between the Domina and her slaves," said he. "But thou canst hire a skilled nurse in Rome. Chabrias will see to her payment; and if thou dost desire aught else for the sick maid, command it at my cost."

Stephanus bethought him again of Æmilia.

"I thank thee, Illustrious," he said. "With thy permission and the Domina's, I'll hire a litter before the fever gains more hold, and take Nyria to a farm I know of by Tusculum, where the hill air will help to restore her, and she can be well tended by a friend of her own, who was chief dresser to Julia, and whose father owns the farm."

Paulinus readily agreed. "Get an easy litter," said he, "and spare no pains to bring the maid back to health. Nyria is a good child, and did cost me a pretty penny, for which, as thou knowest, worthy fellow, I owe thee a grudge," and Paulinus gave a big harsh laugh and went his way.

So Nyria was laid in a well-cushioned litter and borne away

across the Campania, Æola remaining in her stead. The girl was in a half-delirious, half-comatose state, and had small consciousness of what was happening. She was not aware Stephanus walked beside the litter and closed the curtains so that the sun should not reach her, or opened them that she might have a whiff of air. He went on his feet all the way, though a mule was led behind that he could have ridden had he chosen. By-and-by the bearers stopped at a stream beneath some trees, and Stephanus gave Nyria medicine and milk. Then, as the fresher air of the hills was felt, a more natural sleep came upon her, and she awoke only to the welcoming voice of her old friend Æmilia.

For many weeks Nyria stayed at the farm. Her convalescence was slow, and Stephanus came several times to see her. He told her that Valeria was still in Rome, though most ladies of her position were wont to go away during the summer heats; but he would not consent to Nyria returning yet, and she dared not tell him how much she desired to hear the Apostle speak, lest he should forbid her going. Æmilia had gathered all particulars of John's coming through her husband, who often went into the city on farm business for her father. She and Nyria now settled between them that they would go together to the meeting, but when the day came Æmilia's youngest babe was taken suddenly ill, and seemed nigh to death, so that its parents would not leave it. Thus Nyria was compelled to journey alone.

The sun beat down fiercely after the mists had risen from the great plain, and the air in the city was oppressive. About mid afternoon Nyria was set down at the slaves' gate to the Valerian villa, and went straight to that trellised court from which opened the Domina's apartments. As she pushed back the door of the women's waiting-room, and slipped in from behind the curtain, she heard a sound of talking, and, to her surprise, found facing her the woman Salome and Licinius's son.

This was not the moment to obtrude, so Nyria glided along the fretwork wall—through which she caught a shifting glimpse of scarlet from some lingering slave—to the steps of a pedestal on which stood one of two dancing Fauns guarding the arch, and seated herself to await the Domina's orders.

Valeria sat near a window veiled with thin silk curtains, which threw light into the women's waiting-room. One of her arms rested on the broad marble ledge. The other hung over the side of her chair—soft, round, though slender, clasped with a golden bracelet below the shoulder, from which her stola, of cool, greenish stuff, richly embroidered, fell loosely away. The robe was cut low in the throat, and showed the exquisite moulding of her neck, and at its nape the little rings of hair, which looked dark in the shadow of a great mauve creeper thick with bloom overhead.

The summer seemed to have tried Valeria, for she was much thinner, and her face paler, with violet circles round the eyes, which had a strained look. She sat very still, but her quietness seemed unnatural to the devoted slave-girl watching her.

Salome stood opposite—a plump, comely figure in an over-robe of vermilion hue, and wearing a long gold-edged gossamer veil, which was fastened by jewelled pins to her black wavy hair. A very handsome woman, with her regular Oriental features, her full-lidded dark eyes, and a bold charm of colouring and manner—which last, however, lacked dignity. Her flushed, excited face was in marked contrast with the Domina's marble calm. The child held by one hand to his mother's skirt, glancing in awed admiration at Valeria, and apparently half-frightened at Salome's vehement talk—a pretty boy, with his father's look, dressed simply in a white tunic. The only sign of emotion Valeria showed was when the child, attracted by the pearl tassels of her girdle, put out his hand to finger it. As he touched her knee, Valeria shrank quickly and swept him aside, upsetting a glass of red wine placed with a dish of grapes on a marble tripod near her. The wine poured down over the edge of her robe, staining the green thongs of her sandal, on to the marble floor, where it lay like a pool of blood between her and Salome.

XXXV

THOUGH Nyria knew it not, Salome had called many times of late, craving audience on a private matter, and Valeria, consumed with jealous distrust, had at last consented to receive her.

But Valeria had to keep an iron hand upon herself when she saw the child enter beside his mother and look up with Marcus's eyes from under Marcus's oddly-curved brows. The child smiled at Valeria the frank, engaging smile she knew so well—ah! she fain would have seen that smile on the faces of sons of her own! Those great clumsy lads away at Forum Julii were also so like their father. Had this boy's mother not been present she had it in her heart to snatch the little fellow to her breast.

Her manner, however, gave no sign of such tenderness, and the boy, alarmed at her bearing, shrank against his mother. Salome thrust him pettishly aside. "Go, look at the flowers, Marcus, while I say my say to this lady."

Valeria accorded her a formal salutation. Salome refused the offer of a seat with an attempt at haughtiness that fitted her ill. "The wife of Licinius Sura cares not to come as a guest to the house of Valeria," she muttered darkly.

"Doubtless thou hast cause for holding thyself thus humbly," replied Valeria, "seeing that though thou claimest to be the wife of Licinius Sura he hath not acquainted his friends with thy position, nor introduced thee into Roman society such as I—and he—do naturally frequent. I pray thee, therefore—since my steward put forth thy plea of urgent business—inform me for what reason thou hast thus persistently sought this interview?"

Salome's eyes flashed, and she answered vulgarly,—

"For the reason that I have a better right than thou, Valeria, to Licinius's fidelity, and I come to claim mine own."

There was a momentary silence.

"Surely," said Valeria, icily, "there can be no question of claim between a daughter of Vitellius and *thee*."

Salome burst into a mocking laugh.

"It would seem that Marcus hath been chary of his confidence, which ill becomes a friend so close, towards the fair daughter of a six months' Emperor. Permit that I supply his lack."

Valeria said nothing, and Salome continued, in her shrill voice,—

"Perchance thou'rt not aware that I and the boy I bore Licinius do stand to him in like relation as he and his Jewess mother to that Sura by whom he was adopted into the Licinian gens? My spouse hath long since decided to adopt our son as his lawful first-born heir, in the same manner as his own father did by him. Come hither, Marcus, and bear out my words."

She called to the child, who was watching some gold fish in the fountain. He turned when his mother called, and ran between her and Valeria, whose gaze grew to his face, though she said no word.

"Tell this lady thy name, child," commanded Salome.

"Marcus Licinius Sura," returned he, drawing up his manly little form, with a bow copied in miniature from that other Marcus.

"And who taught thee thy name?" pursued Salome.

"'Twas my father," cried the boy, with more assurance than was usual with Roman children.

"And when didst thou last see thy father?" said Salome, patting his head. "Tell the lady, for she is thy father's friend and would fain hear of him from thee."

The boy smiled again that adorable, wistful smile.

"'Twas this morn, when we ate our prandium together. Shall I tell the Domina that 'tis my birthday?" he asked. His mother nodded, and the boy addressed Valeria.

"He gave me African dates," said the child, "and Syrian plums in coloured sugar; but he was sore grieved that he had not the sweetmeats mother used to love, for they be only made by one in the Campus Martius, and father might not go there to buy them, he said, wherefore he gave me this"—proudly pulling forth a little jewelled purse to show a gold aureus within. "Father bade me buy some sweatmeats for my mother before I bought the ivory bones I did desire. For Marcus must learn to be a man, my father saith. To-morrow he will teach Marcus to throw, for we shall again take our prandium at the villa. To-night we sleep there in our own beds, whereon we used to lie—since 'tis my birthday, Domina, and father said that on his birth-night he could not turn his first-born son away."

Encouraged by the silence with which the lady met his chatter, the child, waxing bold, touched the pearl tassel of Valeria's girdle. It was then that she thrust him back, oversetting the wine, at which the boy began to weep.

"There! there!" said Salome, soothing him. "'Tis not thy fault, Marcus. The lady knoweth that. Get thee hence awhile."

The child ran off, and Salome turned to Valeria, who, after the involuntary movement, seemed struck to stone.

"Thou seest, Valeria, the child is his father's son," said Salome, exultantly. "That bond can be no easy one to break. Licinius Sura will never deal unjustly with the boy, whose case repeateth but his own, since, though I was a slave, thus was Marcus's mother; and he freed me when the child was born. His wife in law should

I now be, save for those three days yearly when, on our joint deciding, I left his roof, but on his solemn pledge that, certain political plans he seeks to carry through being fulfilled, he'll wed me after the Roman law. This have I done for him that he and our son may benefit when fortune calls him to a high estate."

Salome paused, her eyes searching Valeria's face, eager to judge of the effect of her daring. But Valeria stared straight out past the dancing Fauns, through the wide arch where the grape-vine hung its purple clusters. She made no movement. She spoke no word.

"There came a time, two years back," cried Salome, unable to keep silence, "ere Marcus went to Judæa, when his fancy wandered hither, but not for long. Marcus learnt that, after all, 'twas Salome loved him best—Salome, upon whose shrewdness and whose promptitude he could rely in time of need. He owes his safety to Salome, who knoweth all his plans, and thus doth wield a weightier charm than thou with thy fair face and all thy learning—Emperor's daughter though thou be. I am not here to plead, but to proclaim my rights, Valeria, and to warn thee lest thou encroach on them too closely. Wilt share Licinius with Salome—or resign him to her arms? She is his truest mate. None knows Licinius as Salome knoweth him. He may come to thee to while away an idle hour, but 'tis to Salome he will ever turn for counsel and for help in his dearest schemes. Thou canst not contend with the mother of his son, bound to him by ties of race, who shares his closest secrets. Shall I tell thee why Marcus refused thine offer to visit him this evening? 'Tis true that he hath weighty business, on account of which he did excuse himself to thee. He goeth verily, as he said, to yon place of assembly whereof thou knowest to hear the Judæan emissary, and to win him if he may to our country's cause. But *I* shall welcome him on his return."

Salome spoke rapidly, genuine passion evident through the shrill inflexions of her voice. She had staked much on this encounter, yet so small was her self-control that she dealt her stabs recklessly. Her dark eyes watched Valeria through their narrowed lids, and she felt, though Valeria made no sign, that she had struck home.

There did not seem a drop of blood left in Valeria's face; her white lips twitched convulsively. Then the pride of old Latian Vitellians came to her aid, and with a supreme effort she regained her self-command. Stiffening slowly, she sat erect and dignified, her head bent courteously, and said, in clear tones,—

"Right grateful must thou be to know that thy devotion hath met with this requital, since such is thine idea of joy. For mine own part, I hold it folly to barter peace at the price of any man's embraces. Praise Artemis, to me love hath been no more than a pastime wherein I would discover for myself what others found to pleasure them. I own I found but little. Long since I wearied of the task."

Salome dropped her eyes sullenly before Valeria's indifferent gaze as the Domina proceeded.

"Thou hast troubled thyself needlessly if this be all that thou wouldst speak of. Thy relations with Licinius Sura concern me naught, wherein perchance thou hast been misinformed, as in certain matters thou hast mentioned but now, which it boots not to correct. Mine acquaintance with thy lord is but slight, and pertains to a portion of my life which most gladly have I left behind. In the future Valeria is not likely to see him—or thee again. For Roman matrons of ancient gens come not into converse with couples united by the civil marriage of usage. The sacred rite, which is the only one acknowledged in my order, excludes us from such as thine." Valeria bent once more courteously. "I beg thee to excuse me now," she said. "I have an engagement that may not tarry."

She struck the silver gong near her, and when Chabrias appeared, commanded loftily,—

"This lady doth require her litter."

"Marcus!" called Salome, sharply, to the child: and the boy ran forward holding a rose that he had gathered, and looking in a wistful way at the Domina, as if asking her pardon for so doing.

"Put down that flower," said Salome, snatching it from him. "Thou canst have plenty at thy father's house. The gardens of Licinius Sura will grow as fine flowers as these now that I have the ordering of them." She took the boy roughly by the hand, and made a curt drop to Valeria, having no further retort ready. Chabrias held the curtains as they passed.

Now all this time Nyria had crouched on her pedestal, indignant with Salome, whose gibes she was shrewd enough to comprehend, full of concern for Valeria, yet proud of her Domina's bearing, and thankfully considering that this must end all with Licinius. Then again, thought Nyria, the dear Domina would enjoy peaceful pleasures, and haply turn her to the Christian faith.

But meanwhile the Domina sat like a dead woman. Nyria waited until the curtain had dropped behind Salome; then she came forth and made her obeisance. Valeria took no heed. The girl bent respectfully again. "Nyria hath come back," she ventured.

Valeria turned a little. Her eyes, suffused and bloodshot, met the slave's. There came a husky sound from her throat. "Go, I need thee not," she said.

"The Domina hath no orders for this evening?" asked Nyria, with an eager ring in her voice, for she was anxious not to miss the meeting.

Valeria shook her head. "None," she breathed.

"Then, with the Domina's permission, may Nyria absent herself until the morning robing?"

Again Valeria made an impatient, half-strangled sound. "I need thee not," she repeated.

There was devotion in every line of the slave-girl's bending form, and exquisite sympathy in her large blue eyes as she gazed earnestly at her mistress. Her heart yearned over Valeria, but wisely judged that she would be better alone.

"May the Domina's slumbers be sweet," the girl murmured tenderly, using a formula common alike to Pagan and Christian. "May her darkness be turned to eternal day."

With a swift, graceful movement Nyria knelt and kissed Valeria's shoe, stained with the ruby wine. Hastily lifting the hem of her own robe, she tried to wipe the stains away, but they had dried in blood-red patches, and she could not efface them. Regretfully she gave up the attempt, and with one last long look at Valeria, who seemed again unconscious of her presence, she retreated backward to the edge of the court and went out. Afterwards she remembered that the Domina had asked no questions concerning her illness nor the reason of her return. But such forgetfulness was frequent with Valeria.

As Nyria ran out of the court towards the slaves' quarters, she saw Gregorio in a scarlet tunic on the edge of the terrace, where he stood talking eagerly to the poet Martial. It had become Martial's habit, presuming on his new-made intimacy at the villa, to enter by the Domina's gate and get himself announced by any of her personal slaves, instead of by the atrium steward. Nyria wondered if she ought to give Valeria warning of his approach, but after her dismissal she scarcely liked to go back, and concluded that in any case Valeria would decline him audience.

It was not Martial's intention, however, to request it. The result of Gregorio's spying upon Salome's unexpected visit showed him that his only chance of seeing Valeria was to take her by surprise, and he therefore bade Gregorio escort him at once into her presence.

Valeria, still sitting where she had received Salome, did not appear to hear his name, and the poet advanced with the jerky bearing by which he always betrayed excitement. He could play sentimental lyrist, comic epigrammatist, even buffoon, according to occasion, but for the last part he employed a variety of tricksy gestures, which at critical junctures he was apt to perform unconsciously. Thus he now came forward in a curveting fashion, making an exaggerated bow, and paying Valeria one of those fulsome compliments that she disliked.

"Most Exquisite," he began, "to this poor poet who has been tramping the streets of Rome, thou, in thy pale green robes, resting amid flowers, dost verily resemble a goddess." Though he spoke mere words of gallantry, Martial's glance was keen and his wits on the alert. He seized the significance of the scene upon which he had entered—the red stain beside the broken glass on the marble pavement, the scattered rose that Salome had flung upon the floor, and the attitude of Valeria herself, limp and huddled in her chair, her arms hanging loosely by her sides, her neck sunk between her shoulders, her face white and inanimate. The only live thing about her seemed her eyes, staring from between red-rimmed lids, the eyeballs flushed with the look of a ferocious creature rousing slowly to the desire for prey. Martial scrutinised her searchingly, his limbs twitching with eagerness. Was this the opportunity for which he had long watched and waited? He fidgeted with his toga, and laid the cap he had been carrying on a chair. Again he made two or three dancing steps towards her, and performed another bow, while he considered how best to extort for his own advantage a clue to the mental condition in which he found her. He feigned not to notice her silence, but delivered some florid remarks about the contrast her delightful interior presented to the thunderous heat without.

"The atmosphere seems to be in sympathy with the spirit of Rome herself," he said, "for assuredly the seething passions of the city are likewise gathering for a storm."

Valeria's red-rimmed, glassy eyes merely stared blankly at him. Martial went on, the tension of his nerves tightening.

"To thee, Domina, in thy cool retreat, these ferments of the city are of small account. Yet to all thoughtful minds it would be cause for thankfulness did the tempest burst—so it brought about redress of wrongs."

Valeria remained speechless. All Martial's powers of observation were focused upon her. He kept making fussy movements, thus working off his own agitation, but never losing sight of his aim, and deliberately weighing every sentence that he uttered.

"The most noble Valeria must feel with me that Rome owes it to her children that justice shall be paid where justice is due."

There crept the feeblest flicker of comprehension into Valeria's blind, suffused eyes. She murmured heavily one word,—

"Justice!"

He saw that this thought had found an entrance in her mind, and dwelt on it.

"Ay, justice, dear lady. Is it not a decree of the gods that justice must be meted to those who have unjustly suffered?"

"Suffered!"

She spoke in a husky whisper. Martial's lynx eyes never left her face. He continued—enunciating his words with great distinctness.

"The thing which doth move me most, Valeria, is that suffering which comes to a noble heart from having put too great faith in man. Pray the gods they may preserve thee from this anguish of misplaced faith."

Again she repeated after him the one word,—

"Faith!"

It was plain that the chords of her emotion vibrated only on certain notes, and therefore he proceeded, speaking slowly and impressively.

"Thou knowest well, Valeria, that suffering of the kind I name falls oftenest on women. Yet women prate not of their private griefs, but conceal such wounds. In this I honour them, though methinks to endure outrage dumbly is an offence against eternal justice. Compensation is a law of nature, and, for mine own part, gladly would I aid one who had suffered wrongfully to obtain a just revenge."

"Revenge!" she said in that hoarse voice. She was listening intently now, and Martial guessed that the words she had repeated were linking her incomplete chains of thought, though he saw that the awakening intelligence took no heed as yet of himself as an individual. But that perhaps was just as well. Going nearer, he bowed anew, grovelling before her as he exclaimed fervidly,—

"Oh! would that it were in Martial's power to protect those whom he adores from pain—or, if too late to shield them, that he might avenge their wrongs."

This time Valeria made no attempt to answer.

"*Thy* wrongs, for instance, dearest lady," cried Martial, "if by unfortunate chance suffering had fallen on thee through the treacherous cruelty of one whom thou hadst trusted. Then verily mightst thou command Martial's arm to strike a blow, which haply thy hand, being that of a woman, could not have strength to deal."

By some subconscious process his words caused a certain recoil in Valeria. Her nobler self sensed a temptation, against which it rebelled. And this revolt of her soul was translated for the moment into physical revulsion from the cringing creature at her feet. She drew back and raised her arms tremblingly as she uttered a shuddering "A-ah!"

Martial perceived that he had erred, and in an instant was erect again, and a pace or two from her, gesticulating anew.

"'Tis folly to talk so," said he. "How could aught assail Valeria in which even her most devoted friend should find cause for vengeance? Then one must needs choose some other occasion to prove one's loyalty to *thee*."

Valeria's eyes widened in the evident effort to understand.

"Strange that this subject should have arisen," pursued Martial. "I was not thinking of personal revenge, Domina, though my mind hath indeed been charged with the question of political vengeance. Pondering upon that, and then the sight of thee, hath made me realise, dear lady, how ill could I bear that any should render disloyalty to Valeria." He turned as he spoke, and seated himself, talking with an appearance of unconcern, though studying her closely the while.

"I know thou seldom carest to bestow thine attention on State matters, Domina, but all must now be interested in upholding the Augustus, who, whate'er his private life may be, as Cæsar claims the service of all true Romans. Mayhap thou hast heard that he is sore disturbed by rumours of a plot against him, and would fain discover if they be well-founded, though he is prepared to deal most leniently, I'm told, with the offenders. Suspicion pointeth towards the Christians, but I scarce think that among that rabble there can be any person of sufficient note to instigate a conspiracy. However, if a party of Christians were discovered, 'twould be well to learn from them whether there's any truth in these whispers of a rising in that quarter. Most likely the tale is false, and the Christians would find their case the better for their innocence being publicly asserted."

Valeria's brows were knit. Martial waited to see if she would speak before he said tentatively,—

"Such action, if it be but the fluttering of a nest of foolish fanatics, may alarm malcontents and lighten the clouds over Rome. 'Twere well for peaceful citizens to have their minds cleared of doubt. It makes heavy hearts to think that one whom we've held dear, and in close familiar intercourse, may be proved a traitor, having repaid our trust with deceit and the love we gave him with treachery."

This thrust pierced Valeria's torpid brain. A slight moaning sound forced its way from her throat.

"Nevertheless," said Martial, "though great the pain, 'tis best to know the truth, and to wipe out for ever such a traitorous friend or lover from one's life."

Now Valeria made a sudden movement. Drawing herself together in her chair, she put both hands up to her forehead as if to brush something away. Then, clasping them against her breast, she leaned forward, her lips parted. Martial bent forward too, and said, with emphasis, "'Tis in my mind to search out and supply a small body of these Christians for the stilling of Cæsar's fears."

This time Valeria addressed him earnestly.

"What— wouldst—do?" she asked.

"Do, dear lady? Take half a dozen to Cæsar's basilica and there let them answer for themselves."

"But—haply—haply," she gasped. "Cæsar . . . might condemn—"

"Ay! Condemn them to tell the truth, and then pack them off as he did those youths of the house of David—dost remember? Cæsar harms no riffraff of that sort. He doth reserve his vengeance for such as are worth it. Run thy mind, Domina, over the names of those that he hath sent to death, and thou'lt see they were all men of note."

"Ay!" she said. "But if haply there were one among the Christians of more note than the rest?"

Martial shrugged. "He'd receive a lesson, and one deserved, for he should understand that such associations are not befitting a man of position. But Cæsar sickens of severity. Cæsar would but question the fellow and let him go."

She leaned back, her brows closer knitted, deep in thought. Martial affected to dismiss the matter.

"It may not be easy to find a nest of these Christians. And *yet*"—he bent his chin between his thumb and forefinger, his gaze glued to Valeria's face as he affected to consider—"I have bethought me that I might. Their place of meeting is outside the city, report says among the tombs. Methinks I know the whereabouts. One would take the road that passes down—below—below the Esquiline."

"Nay," she interrupted suddenly, putting out her hand and pointing before her, "the path passes down behind the Aventine, where it joins one that circles the hill's base, having come forth from the city nigh the river by a road—but I know it not, for I have not been that way."

"Nay, nay, the noble Valeria doth not, of course, enter those low parts of the city," returned Martial, with forced quietude. "But the path behind the Aventine? Perchance thou'st come upon it in thy rambles?"

"Ay," she answered in an absent voice, her eyes following where her finger slowly pointed. "There is a knoll that few frequent which jutteth out some way beyond the Nævian Gate—thou canst gain it by a goat-track from the steep descent below Diana's Temple."

"Ay—ay—and then?"

"Then mount the knoll, and when thou'rt on the brow which doth face between the Tiber's course and the tombs of the Appian Way, thou'lt see, close beneath, a landslip, and a ledge of crumbling wall over which thou mayst watch the Christians pass."

"And whither—whither go they?" persisted Martial.

"They wind down the path, and disappear among the ancient quarries which are worked no more."

Breathless with excitement, he exclaimed, "And when go they oftenest thither?"

"At nightfall mostly now, methinks," she answered in that dream-like voice.

"And how may a man find their meeting-place?"

Unable to keep still, he had risen, and his questions came thickly as he bent over her; but he tried to keep a level tone, fearing lest, if he should raise his voice, the spell might be broken. She still pointed with her finger, slowly tracing the direction.

"The path doth turn, I have been told, and if thou followest it along the Quarries' side thou'lt reach a little valley betwixt the hills. There the red rocks arise on either hand like walls and strew the open space. Then as thou goest—"

The finger stopped.

"Ay—on—on—as thou goest—is't *there*—the meeting-place?"

"Go where the rocks draw close," she pointed, "thou'lt find a crevice by which a man may enter, though creepers cover it. 'Tis by a twisted thorn. But go not in, lest thou lose thyself amid the labyrinth of caves. For none that have not learned the clues may come out again alive."

She paused, her hand uplifted, her eyes slowly straining as though she saw the scene.

Martial's blood ran free again; he had been like to choke in his anxiety.

"Thou hast told me all but this," he said—"Knowest thou when next the Christians meet?"

"To-night," she answered. "To-night he will be there. He goeth to hear the stranger speak, and haply to enlist his aid. But she—*she* awaiteth his return." Valeria's voice broke in a horrible raucous sound that convulsed her throat.

"Be content," cried Martial, "she will await him long. To-night at least he shall woo solitude within the cells," and Martial burst into a Satanic laugh. For now he understood the nature of the shock which had transformed this proud woman into a puppet to serve his purpose. In his exultation he forgot his part, forgot all but that he had succeeded far better than he had dared to hope, and that she was the instrument by which he might work out his end. He stooped over her, laying his hand upon her arm with more force than he was aware, and bending down said jubilantly in her ear,—

"By Até! we shall secure them now! After this, thou and I, Domina, should stand high in Cæsar's favour, though thou carest less for that than for thine own revenge."

The pressure of his fingers on her bare flesh roused Valeria like a somnambulist from trance. She gave a violent start, and for the first time seemed to recognise the poet. But he delayed no longer. Taking his cap, he made her a flourishing bow, and was gone beneath the grape-hung archway. As her head turned after him she saw her arm and the mark his hand had made—red on the skin. With a stifled shriek she stared at it, and then she rose mechanically and advanced towards the middle of the court, where she watched Martial disappear along the terrace.

There was a dreadful wonder in her gaze. "What . . . have I done?" she whispered brokenly. "*What . . . have I done?*"

Then her face changed. The puzzlement gave place to a lurking look of evil. Motionless she stood—only her blood-shot eyeballs rolled restlessly, as with quickening impulse. The gleam of intelligence grew keener—more alert.

"She waits for him," Valeria said. "Ay! but the waiting will be long."

XXXVI

Nyria went at once to find Æola, and the two girls had a happy half-hour together, chatting over their evening meal. Æola would probably have accompanied Nyria to the Christian meeting, but Crispus had just returned to Rome from Baiæ and was to visit her that evening, and though Æola liked going to the services in the Cave Chapel, Crispus was more dear to her.

Therefore Nyria set off alone. Just ahead she again saw Martial, with Gregorio swinging along beside him, conversing animatedly by the poet's ear. While Nyria watched them, uneasily wondering at the friendship between the two, there approached another pair, also afoot, in whom she recognised Regulus, with knit brows, seemingly absorbed in thoughtful converse with the lady by his side. Decked in gay but tasteful attire, Nyria saw Thanna—handsomer and more radiant than of old, and showing by her assured manner that she considered herself every whit the equal of her lord. As they drew nearer the pair glanced up, and seeing Martial, made as though they would speak to him, whereat the poet paused in the roadway and appeared to command the Greek slave to depart. Gregorio demurred, and being accustomed to following his own will, he seemed inclined to resent the prohibition; but Martial briefly insisted, adding some reason that seemed to carry weight, for Gregorio turned, slouching round, and came slowly back up the hill. Meeting Nyria, he scowled fiercely at her, while he bent and hissed in passing,—

"Mine hour is near. I said thou shouldst go forth at my bidding, and when thou art thrust hence—thou and thy Domina—thou mayst thank Gregorio."

The boy spoke wildly, in a fume of rage. His wrath shone like red fire in his eyes, and gathered in foam upon his lips. His limbs trembled like those of a crouching beast that fain would spring. He was obviously excited beyond the point of self-control, and scarcely knew what he said. For a moment Nyria stood hesitating in the road, wondering whether she, too, should return. Then she remembered that Paulinus was away, and that Valeria would probably deny the boy her presence, so that he could do small harm to-night. And Nyria might never again, perhaps, have a chance of hearing the Apostle speak, so she went on; but as she passed the group of three she saw—again to her surprise—that Martial and Regulus were conversing freely before Thanna, and apparently deferring to her opinion, even though it did not seem altogether to coincide with their own.

"Be not so squeamish," Nyria heard Regulus say. "Thy sympathy with love affairs is well enough, and natural to thy sex. Yet 'tis not like thee, Thanna, to let aught lead thy wit astray. Thou wouldst not surely see the knave escape, now that we've got our finger on him, after all the work he's given us? Thou wouldst not miss thy share of the reward, I trow? 'Tis but banishment that shall be his lot, whither these ardent dames may follow him if they so please. As for the rest of the rabble, they'll serve to amuse Cæsar at the games."

Thanna murmured something in reply. As the three followed on Nyria's steps she caught some mention, in the voice of Martial, of Cæsar being at Albanum.

"No matter," Regulus replied. "I hold the signed permit of Cæsar at mine own discretion; but he will return forthwith. It remaineth only to hear thy clue, friend Martial. Time presses—so thou saidst—therefore speak."

"First double the amount," cried Martial. "Why, man, I'm giving thee a haul. Cæsar hath not had such sport this many a day. Two thousand sestertii, forsooth! I claim that, in passing, from a purse less filled than thine. Thou'lt get ten at least, and must pay me half."

"The Judæan rebel is no man of property," grumbled Regulus. "He beareth the best part of his fortune in that comely visage that enticeth women, and his twice too-subtle brain. 'Twill be by favour of Cæsar if I receive my due fourth."

"*Thou* knowest the way to Cæsar's coffers," sneered Martial. "Five thousand is my price if thou wouldst have a hand in this."

"Hush! hush! I pray," whispered Thanna, becoming suddenly aware of the meek little figure in advance which had passed unnoticed. "Conclude the matter, Regulus, 'tis no time to argue—but speak low."

She hastened on and overtook Nyria close by Licinius Sura's gate. From within came the voice of little Marcus in boisterous play. Thanna, catching the sound, stood on tip-toe and peeped over the wall.

"Haste!" she said to Nyria in a low tone. "I'd speak to thee, but not here—round the curve." Nyria walked on, and Thanna joined her a few yards lower down. Linking her arm in Nyria's she chattered in a friendly way, expressing surprise that it should be so long since they had met. Whereat Nyria told her of her illness, and her visit to the farm.

"And what did thy noble lady without thy care?" asked Thanna, with a meaning look. "Who covered her visits to yon villa?"

Hurt and distrustful, Nyria drew proudly away. "My lady's doings are no concern of thine," she said. But Thanna did not seem to resent her speech. Instead, she answered gently,—

"I would not wound thee; 'tis thy friend I'd be. But tell me, Nyria—for thy devoted care, doubtless thy word hath gained weight ere this with Valeria?" Nyria merely shook her head, unwilling to discuss the matter.

Thanna gazed, half quizzically, half pityingly, at her. "Alack! alack!" she cried. "Did thy gods endow thee at thy birth with any wit? Now, had *I* stood in thy shoes I'd have ruled thy mistress long ere this, even as I rule my lord."

"Thy ways were never mine," said Nyria, simply.

"Thou hadst best adopt them, then, if thou wouldst save Valeria sorrow. 'Tis no secret where her fancy is engaged. But there's another who hath a claim upon Valeria's half-breed lover, and is like to make it good to thy Domina's undoing. Verily, I know not why Valeria, who hath a rich and generous lord, and all she should desire, need link herself to this Judæan upstart with whom Salome hath at least the tie of race. What either see in him is matter for the gods to question. Nevertheless, thy lady had best leave him to Salome. He's a bargain that she need not grudge," added Thanna, dropping her voice, but smiling cynically as she said, "Other arms there be yearning to embrace him. Yet though he hath his value in more ways than one, she who sacrificeth aught for him will find he costs her dear."

Nyria said nothing. Her brain was in a ferment. She had been puzzled by the snatches of talk that she had heard, and knew not how to answer Thanna.

"Take or leave my warning as thou wilt," cried Thanna. "'Tis naught to me. I fly higher than these intriguing dames. But if thou hast a feeling for thy lady, bid her flout all mention of Licinius. The gods alone know why I'm minded to warn thee for the milk-faced fool. Haply because Thanna with all her wisdom hath some spot of folly. Tell me of thine own love-affairs. When doth Stephanus lift thee o'er his lintel? Bid Thanna to the espousals, for though she consorteth now with lords, Thanna forgetteth not old friends. She'll come with hands filled—and bring her own lord likewise—since Regulus goeth where Thanna leads."

But Nyria, absorbed and apprehensive, merely answered that her mind ran not on marriage.

"'Tis time that Thanna's mind should run on it," rejoined the other, gaily. "For these two years past Thanna hath served Regulus right well, and never doth she serve without full price. Now to Regulus, Thanna's price is marriage—and she'll have it, too." The girls glanced at Regulus, who walked with Martial across the way. He was looking at Thanna with an expression that was both proud and tender. Catching her eye, he held forth his hand. "Come hither," he said, "I need thee."

Thanna nodded saucily, as if to say, "I come when I choose." She pressed Nyria's arm. "Fare thee well," she said. "Thou and I walk different roads, but Thanna meaneth well by thee. Be wise, Nyria, urge thy lady off Salome's fields. So shalt thou secure her and thyself."

The three walked hurriedly citywards, Regulus and Martial having apparently come to some mutual arrangement, for they were in eager but amicable converse.

Nyria looked anxiously after them, miserable doubt in her heart, though she knew not what to fear. She would have flown back had danger seemed to threaten her Domina, but with the breaking of the bond between the lovers she deemed Valeria safe, even should disaster befall Licinius. But she was not sure that Regulus's talk had referred to him, and Thanna's warning had merely advised that which was already done, for Nyria felt sure that all must now certainly be at an end between Valeria and Licinius. So she went on her way, cheering herself with the reflection that even Gregorio's threatened betrayal could wreak no harm, since that which he would betray had ceased to be, and none of the other slaves, even Æola, had known of Valeria's ill-timed visits to her lover, nor realised that Licinius stood in such relation towards their lady. Thus reassured Nyria permitted her mind to look forward to the joy of the evening, which was a great event in her life. She took the path which led to that outlying knoll of the Aventine, and thus down towards the Quarries.

Dusk seemed to have gathered quickly, for the sky was lowering with heavy thunder-clouds, and there were intermittent flashes of sheet-lightning, so that Nyria—always a little nervous without Stephanus's escort—was glad when she had descended the hill-side and gained the valley—endeared to her now by many a sweet and solemn association. It was a home-like spot, with its clumps of humble flowers that liked a stony soil rising among the outcrop of red tufa, and its grassy patches kept close by goats. Several people were there—Lucius was leading in his aged mother, and others welcomed her; but it was the custom among Christians to shelter themselves among the great boulders of red rock, taking heed that no spies were visible where the valley opened upon the Campania between the river and the lines of tombs. Thence could they safely slip, by ones and twos, within the crevice. Once inside the walls of rock there was greater safety, for therein lay numerous passages, where any number of pursuers might easily lose their bearings.

The chapel appeared well filled as Nyria entered. Gaius, an old presbyter, accounted a religious man, kept the entrance, allowing none to linger round the doorway where he himself waited to receive the Apostle. Nyria stood in awe of this Gaius, who was reputed to have been favoured by the Apostle John, whom he had served in Ephesus, but who was known to be sterner and less forbearing towards human frailties than the blessed John. So she made her way past him to the best place she could find, not noticing the cloaked and hooded figure of Licinius Sura standing in the shadow of a rough-hewn pillar. The chapel was usually poorly lighted. But to-night a double number of torches had been fixed up, and certain servers carried them as well, in order that the congregation might not fail to see the countenance of the aged Apostle.

The torches, of a common kind, flared smokily, casting wavering shadows upon the rock walls of the chapel, and illuminating the faces of the worshippers with a lurid, flickering light. These phantom shadows beneath the dim, curved roof, and the sense of awed anticipation in the atmosphere, plunged Nyria back into the dream-world of her girlish musings, wherein she scarcely knew how much was real and what might be illusive.

But soon Clementus came, and with him, John. Close behind them followed Flavius Clemens and Domitilla with their two young sons, but Nyria had no eyes save for the saint she had so longed to see. Gaius, the presbyter, prostrated himself before the Apostle, and being raised with a few kindly words, drew to the rear, carrying the Teacher's cloak, while Clementus led the holy man to the head of the little chapel. Then the company sang a hymn about that glorious golden city of which John had written to the churches. It was a long hymn with many verses, and had been composed by Clementus, who called it *The City of Our Souls*. Many of the people knew it by heart, and sang with great fervour, as it portrayed the spiritual gloom and stress through which they were pressing to the light of the land beyond.

> "Exiled in this alien Rome,
> Christ, Thy children sigh for home!"

sang the ill-trained voices with infinite pathos.

> "Steep the path to heights supernal
>   While dread darkness round us rolls,
> But there shines a light eternal
>   In the City of our Souls.
> In that City far away
> Shines the one eternal day."

Licinius Sura, in his obscure corner, unseen, but observant, wondered what was meant by this imagery. There were a few lines in the hymn here and there which seemed to imply that the singers were ready to rebel against the restrictions under which they were forced to exist.

"We are captives in this city,"

so they sang—

"Bound by sin, and slaves to men,
But the freedom of that city
Needs no stroke of Cæsar's pen,
For a stronger far than he
There, will set all captives free."

During the singing of this hymn Clementus led the saintly Bishop of Ephesus round among the eager gathering, turning at the topmost row, and proceeding in a circle from one side to the other, staying him in the centre so that all might see him well. And every eye was strained upon the beloved disciple—the last remaining upon earth who had seen the Saviour in the flesh. A very aged man was he, bowed with the burden and labour of years, and of lowly mien, square-built and rugged—neither so tall nor so polished as the cultured Clement. His worn face was bony and hollow-cheeked, his snow-white hair fell meekly over his shoulders, his frosted beard descended on his breast. Yet his eyes were of the clearest blue, extraordinarily luminous; and the look that sped from them over the attentive crowd was full of a god-like and most bountiful compassion. To Nyria's ready fancy he seemed to be seeing wondrous things from which other eyes were holden.

Licinius Sura watched him with the keenest interest, attracted by the rugged yet majestic simplicity of the saint, surprised that one so old and feeble should seemingly sway the very heart-strings of this curious, mixed multitude. He waited impatiently to hear him address the people, looking to see kindled some fire that should lighten his own quest and prove this aged enthusiast an advocate of more righteous law and the liberty of their nation. "Christus, hail!" rang out the rough, untrained voices, herding veritably like sheep together, and gazing with pathetic dependence upon the worn features of this sole earthly representative of their Lord.

"Christus, hail! our anthem rolls
To the City of our souls;
To that City girt with gold,
And with glories manifold,
From the tyrant walls of Rome,
Master! lead Thy children home."

The echoes died slowly away. Then Clementus, having brought John back to the upper part of the chapel, spoke to the congregation of how this beloved Apostle had nobly borne his share of the suffering and sorrow that had fallen on those whom Christ left to carry on His work. Of the saint's escape from martyrdom at the hands of Nero most of them already knew, and how he had been banished to that island where visions great and wonderful had been vouchsafed him. Now, Clementus said, he had come again, perhaps for the last time, to visit Christ's church in Rome. Whereat all cried with one voice, "Blessed is he that cometh in the name of the Lord," and John, bowing his head, began his address.

His voice thrilled all his listeners, even that critical and keenly disappointed one who had looked to hear the Jewish leader's fulminations against the tyrannical abuses of Domitian's reign; but it was of a greater Ruler than Cæsar that the Apostle spoke—of a fairer city than the Queen of the Seven Hills upon which he had been wont to pour forth the vials of his righteous wrath. With a voice, the louder notes of which rang like some clarion, strangely strong and clear—seeing that it issued from the lips of an enfeebled old man, and yet which in its softer accents could be as distinctly heard, he dilated, in powerful imagery, upon the glories of that golden city of his visions, wherein Christ should reign amid His Elect, and told of those trances when, out of the body, he had foreseen Heaven's judgment upon the persecutors of the Church, and had beheld things which should be. To those who remembered the troublous times of which he spoke, and the man as he was in earlier life—truly a son of Thunder, his nature seemed now a perfected blending of spiritual with those purely human elements that had previously predominated in him. He made no more passionate denunciations against the kings of the earth, though he drew a graphic contrast between that great city called Babylon, Mother of Abominations, drunken with the blood of prophets and saints, and the heavenly Jerusalem, wherein nothing evil might enter—an emblematic place, which, to Licinius Sura's mind, could exist nowhere but in the fervid imagination of an idealist. To Nyria, equally, in her ignorance, many of the Apostle's allusions were not comprehensible, and the effort she made to follow his meaning confused her, so that her thoughts began to drift. When John spoke of those whose faithful witness to Christ had placed them beyond the power of Death and Judgment, Nyria's mind reverted to a question that continually troubled her. How would it be were she herself called upon to bear witness for Christ and maybe to suffer for Him? Was she strong enough to stand firm in the Faith, or, if assailed, would she shrink? She who had once lied, would she in some hour of trial be tempted to deny her Master? The thought was agony. And then the Preacher's words recalled her:—

"The day of the Lord cometh, we have been told, in a way that is unknown, and at a time that shall be unknown. And haply not to all of us shall it come alike. To some of ye it may be soon—for that shall surely be the Lord's day when He shall require ye to testify of Him. And that day and hour shall be of the Lord's sending. Nevertheless, look ye well unto yourselves that there be none among ye who shall betray the brethren unto that hour, even as the Son of Perdition, whose name we may not speak, did betray Christ, his Master. Now that sin of betrayal, my children, is verily a sin unto death, and to be kept far from ye, for Christ hath said that whosoever is ashamed of Him before men, of that one shall Christ Himself be ashamed before His Heavenly Father—and he that betrayeth Christ's flock betrayeth Him. Yet if such an offender there should be among ye, pray for that hapless one, and forgive, as Christ forgave them that tormented Him. For I know of a truth now, little children, that there is but one power by which ye shall conquer in earth or in heaven, and this conquering power is love, which is, as it were, the womb of heaven wherein are contained all good things that shall hereafter be born. And this commandment, which covers all other commandments, whether greater or less, I give unto you, as Christ gave it unto them that stood nearest Him—that ye likewise love one another. For the bonds of men be many, and do wound both flesh and spirit, but the bond of Christ is love, and lendeth wings unto the spirit of your souls. Lay not upon yourselves, therefore, the burden of hatred, which if ye so do, it shall weigh ye down till there be no life in ye, but rise above all evil on the wings of the spirit. . . .

". . . Who shall declare unto you the nature of love? It is as the Breath of God that goeth forth upon the surface of the globes, quickening all things unto life. And love is the only fetter which God doth lay upon the flesh. It is the chain which bindeth all mankind into one body, and linketh it unto that higher body of them that have gone before. Wherefore, my little children, seeing none know how soon we may be called unto the Presence of Him who is Love Itself, shall we not make ready? I would have ye learn that without love all faith and all works be imperfect. If, therefore, aforetime I bade ye look for vengeance on them that suffered you ill, I bid ye now look unto the Cross where no vengeance is, for God shall avenge ye, but ye shall not avenge yourselves. . . . My love have I verily given unto you, whether I know ye or know ye not in the flesh, and the Master's love worketh through me to such as are called to be His. And this love I would that ye shed abroad—for this is that Mystery that bringeth life. Wherefore demand vengeance upon none, but return life unto death, as the Master doeth. . . .

"Now, the loves that a man beareth, what be they but symbols of that Mystery of love unknown? And behold, the love that a man beareth unto his spouse is the symbol whereby Christ hath chosen to set forth His love for them that are His, that shall verily be as Himself. Yet I say unto you that the love a man beareth to a woman is but the faint foreshadowing of eternal love, which

Christ in His human manifestation hath striven to spread amongst us. But the true understanding of love is not yet. They that have approached the Mysteries know somewhat of love, but not all. Nevertheless, ye shall know in that day when we, having attained unto all power and all knowledge, are fitted to be with the Master where He is—when having accomplished all things that He did desire, with the glory that shall be His own upon Him, and the worlds beneath His feet, Christ shall show us of the fulness of the love of God.

"Now, therefore, little children, gather ye yourselves together in the shadow of the Cross which shadoweth the world, for behind it shall arise the light that is greater than the darkness of this present time, so that, though ye be driven through dark ways, yet shall ye be called into light. But cast out all fear from among you, and all hatred and lying, holding yourselves together in a bond which may not be broken, that though the hands of the heathen be raised against ye they shall not prevail. Yet testify ye in word and deed of Him, when men shall call upon your witness to the truth, for herein shall your love be made known. Verily, none can show forth greater love than to lay down his life for a friend, as the Master saith, who Himself forgave much to one that had sinned—in that she loved much. Thus shall it be with ye. Wherefore, I say unto each of ye, little children, betray none, neither call down vengeance upon any, lest it fall on thine own head; but if death or betrayal must needs come, lay down thy life and be free, that the love wherewith thou hast loved may be in Christ, and Christ in thee."

Now Bishop John blessed the people in his Master's name. Nyria, sinking on her knees with the rest, her heart deeply stirred, and still gazing rapturously on the figure of the Saint, seemed to see him surrounded by a veil of milky fire, full of golden stars which rose around his head. Others saw only a weak old man nearing the end of his pilgrimage, but the fanciful, adoring slave-girl thought she saw, for one dazzling moment, a glimpse of two holy ones with radiant wings and mysterious sunshine on their gleaming brows, whose tender arms upheld him reverently.

And while the people knelt, their own bishop, Clementus, prayed earnestly a short prayer for strength and guidance, and then the notes of the last hymn rang out, solemn and slow, from the kneeling company.

"Bare is the Cross, Lord, that points through the gloom;
Painful the path, Lord, that leads to the tomb;
Domine! dirige nos;
Our road we cannot see,
But whither Thou hast gone, oh! Lord,
We fain would follow Thee.
Domine! dirige nos—
Miserere nostri!

Wide on the Cross, Lord, extend Thou Thine Arms,
Lift up Thy Voice, Lord, dispel our alarms;
Domine! dirige nos;
Thy trembling sheep are we,
But Thou dost know each one, oh! Lord,
The Father gavest Thee;
Domine! dirige nos—
Miserere nostri!

High on the Cross, Lord, be Thy glory shed;
Lighten our feet, Lord, where'er Thine have led;
Domine! dirige nos;
Hear Thou our trusting plea
For Thou hast trod this path alone—
We follow after Thee.
Domine! dirige nos—
Miserere nostri!"

Now when the blessing had been pronounced, and the people were risen from their knees, it became clear that many wished to linger in hope of receiving some personal notice from John. But Clementus asked consideration for the Apostle, who was exhausted and needed rest, having only that day arrived from a long journey, and promising that he would receive them all on some subsequent occasion, begged that they would now disperse. This they duly did, going out in their usual quiet manner in small parties, their exit superintended by Gaius, while Clementus kept the Apostle back until the crowd should have melted. Domitilla stayed with them, but Flavius Clemens set the example of departure by leading out his two young sons. Nyria came forth in a state of religious ecstasy, which made her mood abstracted. The night was dark, so that the walls of rock seemed part of the heavy sky, and objects were scarcely distinguishable from the surrounding blackness. The girl picked her way as best she could, while sounds of scuffling and stifled cries came from the advance party, as though some had fallen and hurt themselves. Now, a broad and vivid flash of sheet-lightning illuminated the scene, giving a momentary glimpse of struggling forms, and was followed by a fierce growl of thunder. Almost simultaneously a military signal rang out, and there burst from the rocks around a glare of many torches, that struck upon the curved helmets and glittering breastplates of a band of soldiers. The clang of armour and the rattle of spears resounded, while a noise of imperative voices mingled with cries and shrieks from the frightened herd as the Prætorians thrust flaring torches in and out among the Christians, calling on them in Cæsar's name to surrender, then swiftly overpowering and binding one after another.

It was all so rapid and unexpected, and so great was the terror and turmoil, that for a minute Nyria could not realise what had happened. Then, seeing one or two throw their cloaks over their heads and slink behind the protruding rocks in hope of escaping, she would have done likewise, when on a sudden she remembered the Bishop and the Apostle, who, unless checked in coming forth from the chapel, must inevitably be captured. Her one thought was to save them, and she rushed back to the opening whence she had been allowed to issue unharmed, but found it now guarded by two Prætorians, who lay in waiting to prevent any re-entering the caves. One of these caught Nyria roughly, while the other tore away her hood and thrust his great helmet before her face, crying, "Who's this? Why, 'tis Paulinus's little yellow-haired German maid! How cam'st thou hither, girl?"

"I, too, am a Christian," said Nyria, trembling.

"Then keep thy silly tongue between thy teeth if thou wouldst avoid Cæsar's vengeance," said the man, not unkindly, and pulled her along against the wall of rock. She managed to twist herself from his hold as he turned to secure another prisoner, and meanwhile the noise and confusion got greater.

Every instant the soldiers gagged and bound fresh victims. The old presbyter, Gaius, protested loudly as they fettered him. "Nay—nay, I am a peaceable old man who wishes ye well. Harm me not. I've worked no treason against Cæsar." But another vivid lightning gleam paling the torches showed Nyria his strained face, ghastly with fear, and his gaunt form as he, too, was swept on.

Presently a company of Prætorians pressed forward, lifting torches and shouting, "We've found him not. Where is he—the man we have come for? There can be no Roman lord among this rabble."

Now for the first time that evening Nyria beheld Licinius Sura. He was standing quite near her, against a piece of projecting rock, his cloak wrapped round him and the hood of it drawn over his head. She knew him by his bearing, by the gleam of his eyes beneath his hood, and by the indomitable half smile curling his lips.

A soldier with a torch plucked at his cloak and rudely questioned, "Whom have we here? Speak, fellow—thy name."

"Licinius Sura," he answered boldly, and flung open his cloak. "Is't *he* whom ye seek?"

"Ay," said the soldier. "At least thou'rt no skulk," he laughed, while his comrades buzzed round applauding, whereat one appearing to be in authority came up and said something to Sura in a low tone.

Licinius nodded sharply, and, folding his arms, stood erect and indifferent, but not speaking. The Prætorians closed round him and Nyria saw Licinius no more. Her thoughts flew to the Domina, and Thanna's warning came back to her. The ground seemed to rock beneath her feet, and she would have fallen, but was caught again by the soldier who had captured her.

"Bear up," he said. "'Tis no time to faint. Haply thou'lt not be served so ill. Like enough Cæsar will let thee go, seeing thou art Paulinus's maid. But now thou'lt have to march with these vermin we have trapped." He shook her senses sharply back into her, and she was pushed among some other women, who, like frightened sheep, were driven out of the valley into the road that led citywards. At intervals it lightened and the thunder muttered, and a few drops of rain fell, but the storm was passing away beyond the Tiber, and the night seemed less black than before.

Wearied with the day's excitement, and still weak from her illness, Nyria stumbled dizzily on, walking she knew not how nor whither Beside her in the rank was Lucius's aged mother, who had been jostled and hurt by the soldiery, and who moaned pitiably for her son, not knowing where he was, yet dared not pronounce his name lest it lead to his capture. Nyria tried to help her along, and that was the one conscious thought she had, but her own strength was feeble. The old woman prated childishly of the persecutions under Nero, which she well remembered, making those around her shudder, and set the soldiers rudely jeering. She clung to Nyria's hand.

"The day of doom is near," she said. "Yet would I fain keep touch with young life so long as I may." But there was little life in Nyria then. Her feet struck heavily against the stones; a singing sound came into her ears. At length she staggered and fell, wholly losing knowledge of all that passed around her.

XXXVII

When Nyria awoke to consciousness she was lying on wet stones in some place which she thought must be the caves, for the walls and ceiling were of honeycombed tufa, like that from which the chapel was quarried, and rough projections somewhat resembling pillars abutted, and partially divided the space into several compartments. In the one where she was Nyria saw that many women were huddled, and their wailings told that a terrible calamity had befallen them. By slow degrees memory of the evening's events returned to her.

A faint grey light filtered through a series of gratings set at the outer edge of the cells. Nyria lifted herself and found that she was not lying in a pool, as she had at first fancied, but that the dampness came from her wet clothes and dripping hair, which she at once shook out. The mother of Lucius, who lay groaning by her side, told her that one of the soldiers had dashed water over her when she had fainted on the road, and that, seeing this did not revive her, he had carried her to the prison.

Thus she learnt that they were in prison, and later, that these were the dungeons of the Mamertine. Horror thrilled Nyria, but she soon took courage, believing that when she was missed at the villa, and the arrest of the Christians became known, Valeria would certainly send to obtain her release. The other prisoners might not be so fortunate, and this grieved the girl deeply. Meanwhile, however, she could but do her best for them, and so she set herself to relieve, as far as possible, the suffering around her. It went to her heart to hear the people calling to each other after relatives and friends from whom they had been separated, and bewailing those who would be in suspense concerning them. A good many were in bodily pain, and sorely needed tending. And all were in consternation as to what had brought about their capture, and why they had been molested, seeing that for long past there had been no Christian persecution.

It was after the day was well advanced, while they were talking thus, that old Gaius the presbyter, who had been groaning in a corner by himself, suddenly threw up his hands and exclaimed, in deadly apprehension,—

"The pains of hell have gat hold of me, and the torments of death approach, for lo! we are betrayed into the hands of the wicked, and there is none to deliver us."

The people looked at him in surprise, for they had hid their own murmurings, fearing Gaius as a godly elder, who would condemn their want of faith. Presently the presbyter lifted up his voice again, and said, "The spirit of the Lord is upon me, and behold! there is a traitor amongst us. Let him beware lest the vials of God's wrath be poured upon him who hath betrayed the Elect!"

His words stirred the people, who asked each other, "Who hath done this?" and the men declared that were it a man they would tear him limb from limb, and the women, that if it were a woman they would fall upon her themselves. By-and-by Gaius commanded a drawing together for prayer that the Lord's finger might point out the offender and shew them their enemy; and after the presbyter had thus prayed they sang a hymn. But the blessed Apostle's injunctions were still fresh in Nyria's mind, and though she kneeled with the others, she prayed in her heart that they might be turned from bitterness. When many hours had passed, some vessels of water and cakes of coarse meal were thrust into the dungeon, and the prisoners seized eagerly upon them. Though she could hardly lift the heavy ewers, Nyria carried cakes and water to the weak ones who were unable to serve themselves.

But the water was stale-smelling, and the loaves were such as the poorest city scavenger would not have taken, and she who had been accustomed to good fare could not eat them, though she made a pretence at it, that the mother of Lucius might be encouraged to swallow a few morsels.

This was the only kind of food they were given, and when after a day or two it was found that the meal cakes, if left lying, bred worms, the stomachs of most sickened, and they preferred to starve. Hunger and privation would have seemed of less account could they have known what fate was in store for them. It was conjectured by some that the reason of their being kept in ignorance was because the legal officers were awaiting Cæsar's edict, while several suggested that it was on Licinius Sura's account that they had been attacked. Almost all knew Sura, who had gone freely amongst them on the plea that he also was of Jewish blood and desired to enter their faith. At first they had feared him as a spy, but his frank manner and sympathy with their troubles and ambitions had found him friends, into whose confidence he had contrived to work his way. But then it was remembered that he had refused spiritual teaching from Gaius, who often began the preparation of catechumens for baptism, saying that he was not yet fit for it, and that now made him an object of suspicion, though none could come to any conclusion concerning him.

Meanwhile, the messenger for whom Nyria looked, had not come from the Valerian villa. The Domina must be ill, she feared, for surely nothing else could have kept her from sending to release her slave. Remembering that Licinius probably stood likewise in jeopardy, the girl feared greatly for Valeria's state of mind. Suspense began to tell on Nyria, for she had not yet recovered her strength after her illness, and thinking made her brain dizzy. She lost count of time. The only way to note the days and nights was by the waxing and waning of that dim light penetrating the gratings. No torches were allowed, and the long dark hours increased the prisoners' misery. Nyria knew not how many days had elapsed when at last there appeared one from the outer world. It was Stephanus. Two soldiers brought him to the door, but they let him enter alone, for everyone liked and trusted the goldsmith, who was known not to favour Christian doctrines, and who often obtained permits to visit sick prisoners. Nyria's eyes, used to the gloom of the cells, saw him before he discerned her. He looked grim, and worn, and grey as he advanced, peering into the crowded space. Then came a rush of prisoners, many of whom were his acquaintances, and a torrent of inquiries stormed him, to which he scarce made answer, for Nyria ran up with a heart-breaking cry, and he strained her to his breast.

"What shall I say unto thee?" he groaned. "Child, I never thought to embrace thee thus—in the dungeons of the Mamertine! 'Twas but a chance word of the soldiery that led me here. Oh! sweetheart, wherefore didst thou do this thing? I thought thee safe at Tusculum! Thou hast been unfair to poor friend Stephanus, Nyria. Verily thou hast served me ill."

Then, as he felt Nyria shaking with sobs, Stephanus ceased from reproaches, and soothed her as if she had been a babe.

"There! there! little one. Call up thy courage and trust Stephanus to save thee—ay, though he stand in thy stead. Fret not, sweetheart. This may teach thee wisdom. Now thou'lt heed Stephanus's warning to put no faith in that proud, evil dame of thine."

"Thou art unjust, Stephanus," sobbed Nyria. "Be sure my Domina knoweth not what hath chanced. Go thou and ask her aid. Then will she save me."

Stephanus made a savage sound in his throat. "Sooner would I ask a tigress for the life of a lamb beneath her paw. 'Tis to Valeria thou owest this—to her, and to thine own blind folly."

Keen ears had caught Valeria's name. "Who is she?" the people asked. "What concern hath she with yon maid's plight?"

Now Stephanus, to turn the current of their thoughts, began to speak of such of their kinsfolk who had escaped the Prætorians. Gaius bent his long lean countenance over the goldsmith's shoulder.

"Canst tell me, friend, if the holy Apostle and our dear bishop escaped the marauders?"

"Ay, and are in hiding till John of Ephesus be speeded out of danger, which Clementus thinks of most," Stephanus answered bitterly, but speaking low that the guard might not hear.

"Since the pillars of the Church are preserved the building is secure!" remarked Gaius, devoutly. "May the Lord be praised who preserved them! But how was it, friend?"

"The boy Lucius, who stayed to extinguish the torches, and then ran on before, heard the turmoil and got back to warn them —and my lady likewise," Stephanus said. "But Flavius Clemens is imprisoned on charge of having seduced the Emperor's heirs to worship strange gods, thus contemning Cæsar's divine sovereignty. This hath excited Cæsar's royal wrath against the Christians, and there be many new arrests in Rome."

The company was roused to fresh lamentation. "'Twas *my* place as a presbyter to remain with our blessed heads," moaned Gaius. "Thus I, too, should have been saved to serve the Church. May the Lord count it unto me as righteousness that in my care for those humbler brethren am I cast into tribulation."

Now all began asking Stephanus what more he knew, but he evaded their questions, shaking his head sorrowfully, at which some feared the worst.

"Are the Christians like to be sore pressed again?" inquired Gaius in hollow accents. "What say folk our fate will be? Is it the Arena?"

"Nay—nay—none knoweth," replied Stephanus, hastily; when all cried with one voice, turning on each other, "An enemy hath betrayed us! *Who* hath done this thing?"

Stephanus drew Nyria closer, for she trembled.

"Be silent," he whispered, "and thou shalt be safe. 'Tis but thy confidence that is to blame. The real crime lieth at the door of yon fierce, reckless wanton." Soft as the whisper was, the crowd caught a word or two.

"Stephanus! *thou* knowest whose the crime. Say—else will we serve ye as we'd serve our betrayer."

So great became the tumult that the two soldiers ran in with drawn lances to quell it.

"Back! back! ye vermin," they shouted, thrusting forward their spear-heads, and began to jeer at the cowering mob. "Poor game ye be! When men go forth a-hunting, 'tis to the chase; but women's sport is but to snare their prey. Fit quarry for women are ye, and snared right well, ye white-livered rabbits that shall burrow in holes no more."

"Was't a woman that betrayed us?" demanded the people, and a soldier answered scoffingly,—

"When was there ever a betrayal without a woman at its start? Ay, ay! A woman did betray ye. All know now that Valeria gave up the secret of your hiding-place to wreak her wrath on a faithless lover."

"*Valeria!* Who's Valeria?" shrieked the mob.

"Ye scum! Know ye not the fine lady-wife of Paulinus—Rome's Paulinus—a brave man and a soldier of whom the city's proud, although it seemed his spouse preferred the sneaking son of old Sura by a Judæan slave."

"Sura! Then 'twas Sura! Curses on him for a spy," yelled the crowd.

"He hath done himself no good," laughed the soldier. "He's safe enough betwixt four walls, and when next ye meet 'twill be a merry meeting, bravely set to please the gods and Cæsar. Verily the gods alone know what Sura thought to make of such as ye. For though not rich, he had a certain standing, being by name at least of the Licinian gens. Already there are grabbers at his villa, wherein Palfurius did implant himself last evening, driving out a Jewish woman and her brat that this dream-besotted Marcus harboured."

"Palfurius will not long remain," put in the other Prætorian. "The villa was promised by Titus to Lucius Licinius Sura, failing just heirs to Marcus. Already such as favour Lucius have despatched runners to him in Germany, and soon we shall see him on the Aventine. But ye, good people, will escort to Hades this miscalculating lover of Valeria."

The speech struck many into shuddering silence, then a voice called out, "Was't to this Valeria that Licinius betrayed us?"

Nyria started violently, and made a movement as if to speak, but Stephanus held her back.

"If not Licinius, 'twas this maid," they cried, perceiving her hesitation. "Stephanus said Valeria was her mistress, and an evil dame, whom she did trust too well. Say, Nyria, heard thy lady aught of us from thee?"

Stephanus promptly swung the girl behind him, and clenched his hand upon her mouth. But a fresh outcry followed, in which, this time, the soldiers joined. Gaius vainly exhorted his flock,—

"My children! this turbulence is unseemly. Though trouble comes upon ye, endure as I do—with calmness and fortitude."

Half a dozen appealed to the presbyter. "Shall we not learn who is our enemy, elder? The lot of falsity lies betwixt this maid and Licinius. Question her, that we may know if she be our betrayer."

Thus deferred to, Gaius addressed the goldsmith.

"Friend, remove thy person from before the maid. The Lord would point out the offender. Now, Nyria"—as Stephanus sulkily obeyed—"hast ever spoken to thy lady of our faith?"

Nyria wrung her hands and glanced imploringly from side to side.

"The truth—as thou livest," said Gaius, sternly.

"Ay—the truth," hissed the people.

"I will not hide it," said Nyria, trembling. "My lady knoweth that I am a Christian, for she knoweth all concerning me. Likewise —"

But Stephanus stopped her roughly,

"Seest not that the maid is light-headed with her sore distress?"

"Distress! So are we distressed! And who wrought our distress?" they railed.

"Speak, girl," questioned Gaius. "Hast ever told thy lady of our meeting-place and what hours we keep?"

Nyria felt Stephanus's iron grip upon her, but she spoke out straightly. "Ay, sir, my lady knoweth, for I hid naught from her. But Valeria hath not betrayed us. Valeria would scorn—"

Angry shouts drowned the pleading voice. Such a hubbub was raised that the soldiers who had been looking on amused, drove the crowd back again with their lances. But the presbyter stood gazing at Nyria with black eyes that seemed as swords piercing her.

"'Shall he prosper?'" the old man cried, lifting up his voice sepulchrally. "'Shall he escape that doeth such things? Shall he break the covenant and be delivered? Nay—surely in the midst of Babylon shall he die.'"

Stephanus, at his patience' end, snatched up the girl and bore her to a distant corner beneath one of the gratings. There he comforted her with caresses, whispering, "Lie thee here, sweet, every night and watch for me. I'll make a means of getting speech with thee between the bars. I have much to say, but may not say it now." For the soldiers were calling that it was time for him to go.

After he had left, Nyria sat dismally alone beneath the grating, wondering whether the Christians would make a further attack on her now that there was none to be her friend, but she was past caring what avenge they took. Those near where she sat, however, drew off, and herded with the rest on the opposite side of the cell, casting injured, furious looks at her. Even Lucius's mother, who had depended on her care, dragged her poor old body away as though the girl were plague-infected. But soon the taunts and revilings began to fly fast, and Nyria knew that there was justice in them, since now she saw that she had verily betrayed her companions, having had no right to speak of their customs to any person who took no part in them. Nevertheless, she could not believe Valeria to have done this shameful deed.

During the long hours the poor girl lay stupefied with wretchedness and faint for lack of food. Through the grating overhead she could hear, as night rolled on, the regular tramp of the soldiery, and distant echoes of revelry in the city. But no sound came of Stephanus, nor the next night, nor the next. Nyria had a fresh touch of fever, and drifted into a half-dreaming condition, sometimes scarcely realising where she was. Her fellow-prisoners, too, had lost spirit and strength, but they kept aloof from her. Even Lucius's mother would take naught at her hands—which cut the girl to the quick. She might well have died herself from neglect and starvation had not old Gaius pressed food upon her.

"This suffering is but thy fitting punishment, maiden," he said, accusing her of sullen pride. "Bear thyself meekly and haply thou shalt be forgiven. For the greater vengeance should fall of a truth on yonder evil woman in whom thou didst place too much faith."

"Nay, I alone have sinned," said Nyria. "I will not blame Valeria. 'Tis not she who hath betrayed us. Some error hath caused it to be said that my Domina did this thing, but I know her too well. She hath not done it." Whereat Gaius rebuked the girl solemnly for stiffneckedness, and went away to call the rest to prayer, in which he would not have Nyria join, so she prayed alone silently that God would send light upon her darkness.

At last as she lay one night Stephanus's voice called softly to her through the grating, and they held a whispered talk. He questioned her concerning her health and thrust through the bars a flat bottle containing wine mixed with a drug which he made her drink. He fed her, too, with morsels of tender meat and sweet wholesome bread, which at first she was almost too weak to stand and take from him, but by degrees she grew better, and ate and drank with relish.

"'Tis needful that thou shouldst preserve thy strength," he said. "Treasure it, Nyria, for thou wilt want it sore." She thanked him gratefully, and at his bidding secreted a portion of this good food, and the flat bottle which he refilled from a large leathern one he carried, placing them within the bosom of her robe.

"See thou hide the stuff well," Stephanus whispered, "lest yonder half-starved wretches snatch it from thee. I would I could supply them all, though that is more than any man may do. But thou shalt not lack sustenance, Nyria. I'll bring thee a further store each time I come, only do thou let none see."

"How camest thou?" she whispered.

"With difficulty. I have found a friendly fellow of the guard, whose father I once cured of a fever when others had given him up; and I may stay while he turns his back, but, sweet, the time at best is short, and I have much to say. Hast strength to hear?"

"Ay," she answered, trembling, while all the while he worked away gently, striving to loose the bars above her head.

"I'll save thee, child—think not that I shall fail. If by no other means, then haply by this. Thou art worn to half thy width, and if I can draw two of these irons out, I'll lift thee through, and we'll away to some happier land afar from Rome, where Cæsar's cruel edict may not follow us. Trust me—I've many plans, yet would try them one by one, lest an ill chance should wreck the rest. But 'tis better far that thou shouldst know the worst that may befall. Cæsar's wrath presses on Flavius Clemens for this hapless folly of his in leading his lads to hear John of Ephesus. Else the Emperor might have scorned to bestir himself over this besotted sect. But tampering with the minds of Cæsar's heirs is treason, for the which, alack! all Christians must suffer. Cæsar, insatiate beast that he is, hath decreed to stamp them out. Bear with me for a moment, child—thou shalt not surely be one of these, yet must thou exert thy wit and help Stephanus save thee. The men will fight with gladiators at the games. The women—may their God protect the young and fair!—of the rest they'll be torn down by beasts. Methinks, my dear, Stephanus would verily sooner slay thee himself than see thee in the maw of a lion, or cast to the sweepings of the Palace, as may be. There, there, fret not!" for a faint moan came from below the grating. "Have I not told thee that thou shalt be safe? Stephanus's arm is strong, but look thee, Nyria, 'tis well that thou shouldst know what lies the other way. Thou hast ever fled from me when I would have held thee safe. Know now I would not prison thee—else were I like Cæsar. Nevertheless, thou must trust me to be thine aid. Come to Stephanus's breast, and when he hath secured thee that resting-place, reward him by nestling there."

Nyria stood on tip-toe and tenderly kissed the rough hands working at the bars. "Haply I have been unkind to thee," she murmured, "and that I would not be, for thou hast served me well. But if thou wouldst save me, Stephanus, why not go to Valeria and tell her of my plight? I long to know how she doth fare."

Stephanus swore roughly between his teeth. "She fareth well with her sister fiends, the Furies. May they turn and rend her for her copying of their ways!"

"Oh, oh!" moaned Nyria. "Why hast thou always been unjust to her?"

"Haply I was unjust before, but now no retribution gods or men can call down on her head is too severe. Knowest thou what she hath done? Not content with being faithless to her spouse and treading her evil ways safeguarded by thy purity, she hath ensnared Licinius, and given him over to a fate at the hands of his enemies that should make even Até veil her face, and which, when she sees it, should turn Valeria into stone if she be not that already."

"What mean'st thou?" sobbed Nyria.

"Nay, nay, there's time enough for thee to know. I'll not tell thee needless terrors, but ask me not to seek thy lady. I'd sooner seek Medusa. 'Tis true I went to the Valerian villa, before I knew the worst of her offence, in hope she would redeem thee when she heard thy lot. But there they told me all the horror of her acts and that she had shut herself up and would see not e'en the nearest of her women."

"Whate'er she did, she meant no wrong," cried Nyria. "Think of her sore distress."

"She thought not of thine, nor that of others on whom she's wreaked her unholy wrath. 'Tis not alone thy sufferings, Nyria, that cry her shame, though I concern myself the most with thee. When chance favours I'll appeal to Paulinus on thy behalf. Cæsar kept him at Albanum, where the brute-emperor deviseth pageants for the games, and is practising his gladiators in the amphitheatre. Thus Paulinus, though eager to avenge his honour, did not return until his clever dame had secured her course by searing the tongue that gave evidence against her."

"Oh, what mean'st thou?" cried Nyria, again.

"Nay, nay, child, ask me not—of what avail to know? Thou art safe, at least, from such a fate as that. The vengeance of the Domina cannot follow thee here. But Paulinus may be thy salvation. Rough though he be, he hath a kindly heart, and shows soft towards a suppliant if one approach him cautiously. And thou standest well with Paulinus, Nyria, having ne'er done aught to anger him."

"Nay, nay," said Nyria, ruefully. "Once I lied to Paulinus, and methinks if he knew it he would not forgive me."

"Thou hast lied! Why, how was that?"

Consumed with remorse, Nyria told the tale.

"Alack! alack!" muttered Stephanus. "I would at least that thou hadst lied to save thyself. Paulinus had been liker to overlook thine offence; but pray the gods the truth of it hath never reached his ears. Now must I get me hence, sweet, else will the guard be changed and Stephanus taken prisoner. Keep a brave heart; the gods know thou canst be courageous. Remember that I work for thee—and a dozen longer-headed be plotting on thy behalf as well—though none that love thee better. Juvenal itches to stir up strife against this shameful slaughter, and the Porticus Margaritaria would storm the Mamertine to snatch Stephanus's darling hence if 'twould avail. But first we'll try more secret measures. My hope lies in Paulinus."

The goldsmith busily strewed sand to conceal the effect of his labours. "I have loosed these bars somewhat," he said, "but they are thick as Cæsar's skull, and set in stone that might be Valeria's own bosom. Fare thee well, light of my eyes. Thou shalt shine forth again and gladden poor Stephanus's road."

He kissed the clinging fingers through the grating, and disappeared noiselessly into the night.

Nyria ate a further portion of her food at dawn, and drank a little more wine, feeling wondrously refreshed thereby. But her companions, seeing that she ate not during the day, and yet had regained strength, declared that the devil preserved her, since she was one of his agents to work them ill. Most gladly would she have shared her store with them, but dared not, as it would have gone no way among so many. Moreover, one and all still scorned to receive aught at her hands. Meantime, the dungeons grew more crowded daily, for fresh prisoners were continually being thrust in, who brought reports of another threatened Christian persecution.

XXXVIII

"NYRIA, handmaid in the household of Valerius Paulinus, come forth. Thy lord awaiteth thee."

This summons set Nyria's heart beating wildly. A jailor stood at the prison door, shouting his command, which broke harshly across the feeble strains of a hymn sung by some of the unhappy Christians crouching in a group around the presbyter. As they, too, caught its meaning, their singing ceased, and they stared expectantly at the girl, who rose from her corner. She came forward, sudden joy lighting up her features, and faced, with the innocent pride of the pet slave, these less-favoured prisoners.

"'Tis *I* whose presence is demanded. Paulinus is *my* master. I knew that he would come—oh! I knew." And Nyria clasped her hands in a rapture of gratitude. "I knew he would not leave me long."

There was an unintelligible murmur—derision, wonder, envy mingled. Nyria glanced round pityingly on the uplifted faces.

"I will speak for ye," she said. "Paulinus is kind, and hath much power. Perchance he may save some of ye."

The murmur grew louder. Several poor creatures caught at the girl's skirts imploringly. "Save me!"

"Nay—me!"

"Oh! Nyria, speak for me first."

"Verily, Nyria, *I* never flouted thee; I deserve this at thy hands."

"Nay—now, Nyria, we all deserve it. Bethink thee thou hast wronged us. 'Tis by thy fault that we are here. Therefore thou shouldst engage to free us."

Gaius's sepulchral tones rang out, "Let the Lord's favour fall on those that have served Him best. Nyria, I have reasoned with thee on thy sin. Show thou thy gratitude."

A quavering laugh echoed this suggestion. Lucius's mother, growing silly, shook a shadowy fist.

"Let the maid first free herself. Wait! wait! See in what guise she doth return."

"She'll return quicker than she goeth if she do not hasten her steps," called the jailor. "Paulinus willeth not to wait all day. Rest silent, ye carrion."

Nyria went to the door, but was followed by persistent cries.

"Forgive me—"

"Ay, forgive me, Nyria—"

"Verily, we meant no harm—"

"Have pity on us, Nyria—"

"Pity! Pardon! And if thou canst say a word—"

Nyria paused. "I forgive ye all," she said, "for I, too, sinned, but now will ye see that Valeria is blameless—"

She had no time for more; the jailor pushed her roughly through the door, which clanged behind her, then along a passage, and by a stone stair to an upper floor, where the light of day almost blinded her. A pitiable object she presented in her stained and draggled dress hanging loosely from her sharpened shoulder-blades, and with her golden curls all tangled. But there was a faint flush in her thin cheeks, and confident hope was re-lit in her eyes.

The jailor halted before a room whence rang the sound of a hurried, heavy tread. Nyria was bidden to enter, and stood alone in the presence of her master. One look at him as he stopped in his stride, and she ran forward and crouched at his feet. He scowled down at her sharply, and made a movement as if he would kick off her clasp, but seemed softened by her abasement, and the next moment stooped to pat her head.

"There! there! Yellow Hair, I want to talk with thee awhile. A pretty game thou'st played—to land thyself in the Mamertine! I thought thou hadst more wit."

Nyria rose, full of anxious joy. Paulinus surveyed her with a kindly gaze.

"Poor hapless maid," he said. "Thou has suffered sorely for thy sins."

Her bosom heaved. The note of compassion in his voice well-nigh made her weep, but the brisk decision of his next words stimulated her afresh.

"Choke down thy sobs," said he, "and come to business. Thou'st been ill-served, but thou hast none but thyself to thank for this poor plight. No one asked thee to walk in here. And now, if thou wilt take mine advice, thou wilt walk hence as soon as may be. Dost see that, Yellow Hair?" Paulinus flung a folded paper on the table, with which he had been fidgeting as it stuck lengthwise in his belt. Nyria drew near and glanced at it nervously.

"Open it," he said. "It will not bite. Look at it well." Nyria obeyed with shaking fingers. It was a purple-bordered scroll with Cæsar's seal, which she knew, and likewise her own name at the top, but more than this she could not read. She looked beseechingly at Paulinus, big tears welling in her eyes.

"'Tis an order for thy release," said he.

"Oh, lord!—oh, lord!" Nyria would have fallen at his feet again but he pulled her up.

"Nay, know thou hast not got that gain for naught—nor I neither. From first to last thou'lt have cost me a nice penny, Yellow

Hair. But thou art worth the coin, else should I not spend it thus readily. Nevertheless, there is a price that thou must likewise pay—one well within thy power, but thou must pay it roundly, as I do—and grudge naught. Dost hear?"

"Ay! lord." A rush of grateful blood had dried up Nyria's tears, and her eyes, burning with a slow blue fire, were fixed upon Paulinus. He avoided their steadfast gaze. His heavy brows were knit in a dark frown. There was barely-suppressed excitement in his manner. Great beads of moisture stood out on his forehead, which he impatiently flung off with his fingers. He tramped the length of the room twice, and then stood—broad, red and burly—before the slender girl.

"Thou didst lie to me the other day," he said. "Nay—start not. Thou hast paid the penalty, and shalt escape further punishment. For it's plain to me that thou hadst not courage—poor mouse!—to betray Valeria, who would doubtless have requited thee mercilessly after her manner. I should have seen thou wert protected from her spite before demanding aught of thee that went against her. But we'll better that this time, Yellow Hair. Valeria's vengeance is sharp, but it shall not reach thee—so thou serve Paulinus well."

Something leaped up in Nyria and warned her to be careful. She began to feel afraid of Paulinus while he scanned her with his restless, twinkling eyes.

"So far thou hast not served me over well," he said. "And yet I bought thee at thy desire, and have never—save that once—been harsh to thee. Do Christians deem it well to deceive good masters who give trust and no unkindly words?"

Nyria was silent. His speech pierced her like a winged shaft, cutting deep. She dared not answer, lest in her unwisdom she might commit a further crime. Her blue eyes met his with a dumb, helpless look that touched him.

"There—there—I would not taunt thee, child, only bid thee have a care. See now, Nyria, thou mayest retrieve thy wrong, but no more lies—as thou valuest thy life and liberty." Turning to the table, he laid his hand upon the order for her release.

"Thou art free," he said, "just so soon as thou hast told me all I need to know of Valeria's dealings with her lover. Speak out and fear naught. She's cast him off to a worse fate than any flesh-and-blood woman would have dreamed of, methinks—and haply it may stir her when she sees him endure the fruits of her betrayal. 'Tis thus she rewards such as sue for her favours—poor, doting fools!—whereof thou and I are twain, Yellow Hair, seeing we've both striven to serve her well. But her reign is over. It is my purpose to divorce Valeria. Though the Flamen himself tied the knot, by Juno! I'll wrench it asunder, were every pleader in Rome against me."

His voice grew thick and rasping, his red face purpled. Veins in his forehead, already full, swelled like knotted cords. Nyria gazed at him in fear and wonder. He gave a laugh that made her shiver.

"Bacchus aid me with his Mænad crew! For I swear no base-born Jew shall worst Paulinus. Charon will have some work, I trow, to collect the comely members of Licinius Sura when Valeria's lover doth cross the Styx to woo fair women's shades in Tartarus. By all the gods! And did he think he'd turn Paulinus into the laughing-stock of Rome and ne'er regret the deed?"

Nyria's frightened look recalled the outraged man. With an effort he regained some self-control.

"Now tell me how this affair began, and when, and how long I have been thus duped? The fact I know—scarce more, since I was loth to listen when ready spies crawled at mine ear. Would I had been less scrupulous—but wiser, for the sharpest of them now is silenced and shipped away by yon ruthless fiend, who thus avenged herself on the poor lad while yet I tarried at Albanum to pleasure Cæsar. But *thou* canst stand to my need, Nyria. Know that to prove my case before the Pontifices I must bring evidence which thou canst well supply. Thou art the only one of Valeria's women who knows enough, it seems; but thou wast ever at her side, and should be steeped to the finger-tips in such acquaintance with her guilt as I do now require."

Paulinus leaned heavily on the table, from which Nyria shrank away trembling violently.

"Well, hast thou naught to say?" he asked.

Twice—thrice she tried to speak, but her cold lips only moved without a sound.

"Thou'st become besotted with thy troubles, Yellow Hair," he put in impatiently. "But trust me for thy future. Think now of my affairs."

And Nyria thought—but not of him. Her thoughts flashed back to her first meeting with Clementus on the hill, and how she agreed to bear whatever might come upon her if Valeria's life were spared. She thought of Valeria in her desolation, baited by jealous foes eager to triumph in her downfall. Of the bishop's words on her baptismal night:—"*If ye guard not that which is little, how shall ye be intrusted with that which is great. He who would be faithful in much must first be faithful in the least thing;*" and again of what the blessed Apostle had said, giving the words of Christ Himself: "*None can show forth greater love than to lay down his life for a friend.*"

Life or liberty, or Valeria? Nyria hesitated no longer.

"Lord," she said, and there was a ring of new strength in her tone, "Nyria hath naught to say, for there is naught that she can tell thee against her lady's honour."

"How—what saidst thou? Naught! *Naught!*" Paulinus spluttered furiously. "Have a care! Have a care!" he cried. "'Tis not safe for thee to trifle."

Nyria trembled anew, but she put forth her hands in an attitude of exquisite submission.

"Lord! slay me if thou wilt, yet can I say no word against my lady."

For a moment Paulinus was speechless. Then he drew himself up with an angry sound, though there was something like admiration in his eyes.

"So it was not fear that prompted that lie! Thou wouldst be faithful to yon fiend? By what magic hath she bewitched thee?"

Nyria answered not, but there crept into her face a look that puzzled Paulinus.

"Dost know the sort of woman she is?" he asked, bending forward. "Dost know that she betrayed the Christians to serve her spite upon Licinius? Dost know that had she sent to snatch thee hence at once she might have saved thee, but that she was too well occupied venging herself upon Gregorio—hapless lad!—because he busied himself about mine ends, and was ass enough to bray over it? Dost know all this, and *yet* canst bear the burden of her sin?"

Nyria merely bent her head. The look of unwilling admiration deepened in Paulinus's eyes.

"By the gods! there's some spirit in that sickly frame of thine. Thou art well worth thy chance. But thou must overcome thy scruples, child. Say but the word and we'll have thee forth from that tomb, where verily they've sucked so much life from thee as to leave thee like a shade. Thou shalt be tended carefully, and wilt soon regain thy pretty looks. Mayhap a handsome husband will come and beg thee of me. Then, if thou dost favour him, right cheerfully will I give thee, with thy freedom, a well-filled purse. Eh, what say'st thou, Nyria?"

"Lord, thou art good indeed. Nevertheless, Nyria hath naught to say."

His brows drew together again in that heavy frown. A fierce oath rose, but was checked upon his lips.

"Thou art right to show thy fealty, but the laws of Rome remit it, child, in such a case as this. Thou shalt be forgiven all. Dost not desire to be free?"

Nyria's glance strayed longingly towards the order of release. Paulinus saw the look.

"Ay, 'tis thy price," he said. "Hard won, I do assure thee, for Cæsar hath no mind to let go the puppets that hop at his bidding, and he hath promised himself a fine day's sport over all mad Christians. But since 'tis won, why scruple to take it, Yellow Hair? Valeria hath proved that she cares not a sesterce for thee.

Thou hast served her purpose, like others—ay! even Licinius—and now thou mayest afford a meal for the lions. She'll not sleep the worse!"

Nyria quivered indignantly. Her whole soul rose in passionate defence of Valeria, but she dared say no word. Quietly she harboured her strength for repeated denial, if it were needed.

Paulinus's patience and his temper, sternly leashed, both began to fail.

"Come! Speak up, Yellow Hair. Time presses. Say what thou hast to say and we'll go hence and lay thy statement before the lawyer who conducts my case."

"My lord," replied Nyria, "I thank thee for thy kindness. Naught else have I to say, save this—I may not purchase freedom thus, for the price is that which Nyria cannot pay."

Paulinus started forward and glared at her, but the blue eyes faced him dauntlessly. This time they exasperated him. He seized her by the shoulders and shook her till the poor little bones shivered in their sockets.

"Am I to be defied by *thee*—a toothful of carrion to be thrown to the beasts?"

Nyria cowered with a faint cry wrung from her terror and despair. He flung her from him with an oath. Her head struck against the corner of the table, and the blow half stunned her.

"Get up," he said, "and listen to reason, if thou canst. I've told thee what's at stake. Go into the Arena if thou willest—'tis all the same to me—but know this—thou shalt not save Valeria one pang—nay, nor the scurvy rogue who toyed with her. Licinius will play a pretty part in Cæsar's Games, and Valeria shall watch the venture by Domitian's command. Think not to win him back to her, or e'en to protect thyself if thou persistest in this folly. Whether thou dost own the truth or not thou'lt not mend matters for Valeria. Save thy skin if thou dost so desire, but mark!—when thou art once in the lion's jaws not Cæsar himself can do it for thee. Choose!"

He stood over her, fierce, large, insistent, unable to believe, even now, that he could not bend her to his will. But Nyria had forgotten herself in a tempest of feeling for Valeria—more desolate than she—since above the dark waves that engulfed her Nyria's star of faith shone true, but to Valeria all must be darkness.

"Speak, girl," cried Paulinus, in blind fury. "Choose!"

"Lord! Nyria hath no choice, for there is naught for her to tell."

He staggered back, and sinking into a chair put his arms across the table and slowly drew the paper towards him, as though he would tear it across. A wild sob broke from Nyria. She made an involuntary movement forward. She could not help thinking what that paper meant to her. Paulinus was back at her side in an instant.

"Thou little fool! She is not worth it. Come, Nyria, why should we care—either of us? Let her go."

But Nyria gulped down her sobs, and tried to push his hand away. He kept it on her chin, however, and tilted up her face. The blue eyes, drowned in tears, met his. There was anguish in their depths, but no sign of wavering.

"Answer me," he said. "By Jupiter! I'll force confession from thee. Didst thou never go with Valeria to Sura's house, nor admit him to her private apartments?"

Nyria tried to shake her head, but it was held as in a vice. "Speak up!" cried her tormentor.

"Never!" she whispered hoarsely.

"Didst ne'er see aught to awaken thy suspicions of thy lady's loyalty?"

"Never!" The lie came more clearly.

"Nor carry letters from Valeria to her lover?"

"Nay."

Paulinus suddenly loosed his hold and pushed Nyria off, while he crushed the parchment in his hand.

"Am I to understand that this is all I can get from thee? Wilt thou learn sense if thou hast time?"

"Nay, lord, there is no more that I can say."

And then Paulinus went beside himself, and raged like one insane, swearing that the gods should aid him work his will upon Valeria, seeing that his revenge was lawful, and not like to be thwarted by a wretched slave. Stopping short, he tore Cæsar's order into pieces and flung them at Nyria's feet.

"There's thy liberty!" he said. "The Christians are champion liars, and well deserve the Arena. Go back to thy dungeon, and may the woman for whom thou art weak enough to sacrifice thyself grant thee thy reward."

He strode past through the doorway. One of the soldiers outside called to Nyria, who stood stupefied. The man came in, and pushed her in front of him along the passage towards the steps to the cells. She was half dazed, but it was with a heart-breaking sense of finality that she heard Paulinus's heavy tread sound in the opposite direction.

The soldier thrust Nyria whence she had come, making mock of her.

"Ah! thou bold fledgeling, who would release thy fellows—back to thy cage! 'Tis not so easy—seest thou—to fly from Cæsar's keeping."

Light-blinded by her brief absence, Nyria staggered through the fœtid gloom to her accustomed corner. The prisoners, crouching in various melancholy attitudes, stirred at her approach. Despair was too deeply rooted in the hearts of most for them to expect much from her intervention, and they had settled down to their misery directly she had left. Her return re-awakened some faint hope in a few who looked up anxiously, but this was speedily quenched by the sight of her, and for the most part they were aroused only to rude jeers, embittered by their disappointment.

"How's this?" they cried in affected surprise. "Here's that fine dame who left us to greet the noble Roman lord who came to fetch her forth from prison—so she said."

"Can this be Nyria who returns amongst us, sad of countenance! What, then, hath happed the great Paulinus?"

"Came he but to crave thy pardon, Nyria, for the accident by which thou wert brought hither with the other victims of his lady's whim?"

"Nay! surely he did somewhat to amend it!"

"Haply he forgot to command thy litter. Hath he gone, perchance, to order one?"

"Nay, nay! A litter be not grand enough for Nyria. Paulinus would petition the Senate for a gilded chariot to bear yon wronged maiden hence, with a splendid team of horses, and fitting retinue, a palm-embroidered robe, and offerings for Capitoline Jupiter."

"Meanwhile, no doubt he bade thee wait what time thy triumph be prepared."

"'Tis strange and sad, sweet maid, thou hast no brighter tarrying-place. Wherefore not await thy lord in the room where he received thee?"

"Nyria would take tender farewell of her poor companions. Be sure she thought of us."

"'Tis our last converse, Nyria. No more wilt thou hold commune with misguided Christians."

"Cheer thee, Nyria. Thou shalt see us when thou accompaniest Paulinus to the Games, where we shall make sport for Cæsar."

But Nyria, with her head bowed on her hands, answered not. The gibing voices sounded to her but as voices in a dream.

Yet they must have hurt her, for by-and-by, when the scoffers had grown tired of scoffing, and were otherwise occupied once more, some praying, others moaning and murmuring amid themselves, Nyria became aware that old Gaius was sitting by her side, with his hand on hers, bidding her not weep, and though she had not known that she was weeping she now saw the tears falling on her lap.

"Heed not those who thus revile thee, Nyria," he said gently. "Christ, too, was mocked, remember, and He did no wrong. But thou hast sinned against these poor brethren, and must bear meekly with their taunts and their revilings. Kneel with me now, and we will pray the Lord to put this burden on Valeria, of whose making it is, and thus to ease thy shoulders."

"Nay, sir, I may not pray thus, though greatly do I grieve for mine own sin. But Valeria's, if 'twere done, 'twas done in some strange madness which doth lie betwixt herself and God. Naught shall make me say my lady sinned."

"Doth not thine own heart cry shame on thee?" said Gaius, severely. "To screen a sinner is to share his sin. Verily, Nyria, it would be my lot to demand thine expulsion from the Church if we were free."

Nyria could but mournfully bend her head again. To reason was beyond her powers. Her faith in Valeria was sorely shaken, but she still clung to it, and moreover was filled with so great a pity for Valeria that, even had she caused the evil imputed to her, Nyria longed the more to be her shield. Nyria felt, too, that Clementus and the holy Bishop John, though condemning sin, would scarcely have judged a sinner thus harshly. John's teaching had all been of love. Had he not bidden them look unto the Cross where no vengeance was? And as the gloom of her surroundings deepened it was to the Cross alone that Nyria looked.

Stephanus came again that night as he had come for many nights, carrying on his endeavour to loosen the bars of the grating.

"'Tis well-nigh a hopeless task," Nyria heard him mutter as he loomed darkly above her. By the wrenching movement of his hands, and the groan in his voice, she knew that he was angry and despairing.

"May Vulcan be accurst that forged such bolts! 'Tis work for gods to break them—if gods there be—and not for mortal man. And yet if I do not snatch thee through the stone and metal by sheer force from out thy dungeon, thou wilt not come hence! Of what avail to toil and scheme and petition for thy rescue since when the prison doors are set open for thee thou let'st them swing again upon thy face?"

Nyria stood beneath the grating, one small, thin hand thrust through towards him. He snatched and kissed it passionately, but dropped it the next minute to continue his work.

"How couldst thou thus gainsay Paulinus?" he whispered, hoarse with emotion.

She gave a broken sigh, but answered not.

"I met him when he left the prison," went on Stephanus. "I had sought him fruitlessly at the villa, and elsewhere, and having heard he had come here, waylaid his steps, and prayed him of his mercy, for thy service in his household, to save thee if he could. But he laughed in my face, with looks black as thunder, and said he had offered thee life, liberty and rich reward—of the which thou hadst rejected all. Knowing thy sad case I could not believe his words, but when he swore to me 'twas true meseemed child thou hadst been stricken with madness and knew not what thou didst."

"Did he tell thee what he would have had of me?" inquired Nyria, sadly.

"Ay! ay! he told me all, seeing he was nigh distraught—and no wonder, when thou hadst thus disappointed him. He needs thine evidence before the Pontifices to divorce Valeria—and he'll do it without thine aid, even though others refuse him, as hath Plinius, gossip saith, to whom he did apply to conduct his case."

"And have any else refused?" asked Nyria, eagerly.

"Oh, ay, till there be fuller proof. Whereby Paulinus is in somewhat of a strait—for which doubtless he did call on thee. But Matho is ever ready for a job, and questions none, and though engrossed just now in certain legal business of Regulus—who, while dabbling in mire, would fain keep his fingers clean—Matho awaits Paulinus's commands. Matho is of poor repute, 'tis true, but he's a worthy weapon to drive forth yon Vitellian dame from her violated hearth. I'd gladly see Paulinus win and deal Valeria such sorrow as she hath dealt to thee."

Nyria's hands clung to the bars.

"Oh, be more kind!" she cried. "Thou wast ever tender-hearted to me, but for Valeria thou hast had no mercy."

"Hist! Quiet!" he whispered. "Here comes the guard," and instantly Stephanus lay motionless along the grating.

They waited, breathless, till the tramp had passed. Then Stephanus put his lips close down to Nyria, and continued, in a rapid undertone,—

"I love thee—that's why. Valeria hath ever stood between us, for thine and my undoing. She hath had her chance with thee, and hath made ill use of it. But thou art free from her now, and canst show Stephanus if thou hadst ever aught of feeling for him. If thou hast, thou wilt save thyself by giving evidence in favour of Paulinus."

"I cannot—oh! I cannot. I were unworthy thee if I betrayed my mistress."

"She is no longer thy mistress. Thou art in Cæsar's custody. That which she did changed all. Hath she not delivered thee to a worse fate than any thou couldst wreak on her? And not thee only, but all yon hapless crowd, whose doom lies at her door. Thinkest thou that there is a woman amongst it who would not gladly buy her life on such easy terms as these? 'Tis but to tell the truth—which thy preachers command."

"Nay, then—I am wicked," murmured Nyria, "for I have told many lies for Valeria. Yet would I—if needs must—tell them all again."

"The gods bear me witness," Stephanus groaned, "I understand thee not. Dost deem it no sin to lie when 'tis to save Valeria, who deserveth naught from man nor immortal, yet verily a dread, dark sin to tell the truth, when by it thou canst save thyself and me? Is Valeria of more account to thee than this Christus, whom Domitilla saith is a god of truth?"

"Nay, Christ is greatest of all," answered Nyria, wearily. "Christ will understand; myself—*I* know but little. This only I know—never could I deny Christ, and likewise I could not deny Valeria."

"Nay, only this poor friend of thine," retorted Stephanus, stifling an oath, which broke into a bitter sob. He made an inarticulate struggle, his body writhing. She saw him shake as he lay upon the grating, and she put her hand through again to comfort him, but he turned from it gasping.

"Alack!" she said. "What shall I do if thou, too, fail me?"

Then he drew her fingers to his heaving breast.

"By all the gods of Greece! never will I fail thee, Nyria. If I might die for thee I would, but that also is denied me. Yet Hades's darkness closes round my vision. All have I done to save thee that man may do. Yet have I failed, and now am at the end, and know not where to turn. To all have I gone who perchance might aid thee—ay! even to old Euphena, and to Ascletario—but none avail me aught. Euphena scoffs and cries that she prophesied truly concerning thine end, and that none may save a fool from the fruits of his folly. Ascletario prateth only of some distant day when in another life thou and I shall meet and love each other unrestrained. Alack! I need thee now. Yet 'tis not for my desires I'd strive, but for thy safety. Naught remains but to pray the gods to work a miracle. Not the Roman ones—for they are like these people who feast on human torture. But in the old Greek gods there was some strength and justice. Artemis did interpose for Iphigenia when the altar was laid and the knife lifted, and Agamemnon's daughter was not more pure than thou! Oh! had I never prayed before, now night and day I'll pray for thee."

"Fear not for me, Stephanus," she said softly. "Christ is mine aid."

"Alack! then why doth He not take heed of thee?" Stephanus cried. "I fear, sweetheart, He is too far hence to trouble Him concerning one poor little maid in Rome. In truth, my dear, I'd sooner trust mine own right arm to save thee than leave the task to any god, whether Greek or Christian. For gods may be false or true—and we know not—but a man who loves a maid as I love thee can ne'er be aught than true to her."

Nyria's hand fondled his face.

"Thy love was ever too great for me," she said. "Nevertheless, Christ's love is greater. Dost mind, Stephanus, how

Clementus said before I was baptised that Christ would seal me with His blood so that I might enter on eternal life?"

"Ay! I could well-nigh curse Clementus, and even my Lady Domitilla, who hath led thee like the little lamb they prated of to the shambles of the butcher."

"I shall not feel the knife," said Nyra, raptly; "even though it fall Christ will give me strength to endure. But be at peace, Stephanus. Harbour not such thoughts. I would that thou couldst feel, as I do, that all must needs be well with one who goes to Christ."

"And hast thou no regrets, my dear? Ah! me, what kind of faith is this?"

"Nay, my regrets be many," said Nyria, her voice trembling. "I long to know thee happy, and I would—I would that I might see my lady once again." Here she broke down and sobbed bitterly.

Stephanus covered her hands with kisses, but he answered, in stern tones,—

"I desire not to share thy regrets with her. Know, Nyria, the woman she is. List while I tell thee what she did command as part of her vengeance on such as had offended her. I would not soil thine ears with the tale, seeing thou art sensitive and the boy was thy fellow-slave. But 'tis well that thou shouldst know Valeria. Yon hapless Gregorio forgot himself, it seems, and sought her presence unbidden, pouring forth some mad tale what time she was in wrath, though he knew it not at first. Then did she have him put in chains, and sent for the public brander, who with hot irons seared the singing-bird's tongue, so that he should neither sing nor tell tales any more. He was an evil lad, and a spy, whom doubtless she feared on his self-committal—but what think'st thou of her vengeance, Nyria? 'Twas neatly planned and carried out. The boy, being bound, was borne to a ship and far down the coast e'er any knew. But Æola chanced to see him seared, and screamed and fainted at the sight. The girl hath horror in her eyes since then. And thou—what think'st thou, Nyria?"

Nyria, who had stilled her sobs and grown completely silent, made no answer at first, then a heart-broken cry escaped her.

"Valeria did that—*that*?"

"Ay, 'tis true. I'd not lie to thee. Thus haply would she have served thee too—hadst thou crossed her. But thou shouldst be safer. Since thou couldst no longer wait on her thou needst not return to the Cœlian. Paulinus promised thee thy freedom, and would give thee in marriage to any suitor thou didst favour. Sweet! Stephanus waits. Only give evidence for Paulinus."

"I cannot, oh! I cannot! Valeria may have done these

things—yet will I be true to her, for I loved—nay! nay! I love her still. Besides, it is too late. Paulinus destroyed the order for my release."

"Ay, but 'tis not too late. Thou shalt have another chance to-morrow, Paulinus said. Oh, Nyria! favour it, for my heart is breaking."

"Alas! what can I say?" she murmured.

"Nay, I know not, but when thou art questioned tell the truth—'tis all I ask of thee. The gods of all time compel thy lips. I go now to implore their aid. Lend thou thyself to it, and await to-morrow, sweet, in confidence. May it bring thee wisdom and good fortune, for after to-morrow—"

Stephanus could say no more, but went silently away.

XXXIX

NEXT day the jailor came again and called Nyria forth. This time her fellow-prisoners watched her exit with indifference. She was taken to the quarters of one of the prison officials, whose wife received her with some show of kindly interest.

"Thou must wash and dress thyself," said this woman, and she took the girl to a bathroom, where she helped her to put on clean undergarments and a fresh white outer robe, and combed and brushed her matted hair.

"A fine thing to have a fair skin and yellow curls like thine, since thus men think it worth their while to save thee," said the jailor's wife. "For mine own part, I like a ruddy cheek, and see small beauty in a moon-faced shade. Thou art fit only to stand in stead of one of the sculptured figures in a temple. But men's tastes be queer."

Nyria wondered dizzily what these preparations on her behalf could mean, but she was too weak and weary to care very much as to what was about to happen to her. Presently the woman set her down to food and wine and roughly bade her eat and drink. This made her feel less weak and dazed, and she was looking more like her former self when Paulinus entered. The girl started up in surprise, fearing a repetition of the scene which had so exhausted her. But Paulinus merely looked her over grimly, though without unkindness.

"So thou art in better case," he said. "Perchance I was over hard on thee. Doubtless thy brain was addled by prison fare, else wouldst thou not have spurned mine offer of release. Know, Nyria, that the mandate was obtained with difficulty and only for the reason that thine evidence is necessary to the ends of justice. On no other ground could I secure thy freedom."

"I thank thee, lord," she answered meekly. "But Nyria hath no evidence to give."

Paulinus shrugged incredulously. "I am not come to plead with thee for that which others can command. Thou shalt now hear what Cæsar hath to say upon the matter. Thou'lt follow me to the Palatine."

Hearing that she was to be taken before Domitian, Nyria's limbs began to shake, and her heart felt like water within her. Her old horror of the Emperor came back, and she thought that she would rather face death than enter that hated presence. She tried to implore Paulinus's mercy, but speech forsook her; the room went round, and everything turned to blackness. When she recovered, the jailor's wife was holding a cup of wine to her lips, and Paulinus stood by, hardly able to control his impatience. "Come, come, girl, art better?" he said. "If so, hasten—Cæsar waits for no man."

In desperation Nyria flung herself at her master's feet.

"Lord! lord! I dare not go. Greatly do I fear Cæsar. Oh! I pray thee leave me to any other fate than this."

But Paulinus only grew more impatient. "Have done, Nyria. 'Twill not be the first time thou hast stood before Cæsar. Obey his will and he may not be severe with thee, though that none can vouch for. Rise—rise, and come thou after me."

He went out, and two soldiers led her behind him. But she still felt faint, and when they got outside, to where Paulinus's litter waited, another had to be procured for her, since it was plain that she could not walk to the Palatine. Paulinus fumed at the delay, but presently they set forth, and like one in a dream Nyria was borne over the heads of the people in the wake of her master, down the hill, along the familiar road below the Capitol, and up the great marble stairs which in bygone days she had so often trod, toiling after Julia's bearers. The sun shone brightly, and the heat, the light and the fresh air at first made her more giddy. The noises from the city beat like waves upon her confused brain, and yet gave her consciousness of well-known things—the scent of flowers from the stalls of sellers on the Sacred Way; the frowning rocks of the Capitol; the white pillars and gilded dome of the great temple, whither some procession was mounting; the glittering vista of the Forum, with its busy throngs and innumerable statues; the cries of hawkers; the sun-chariot of Apollo outlined against the sky, and here a set of mimes playing antics; she knew it all—this cruel, sumptuous pageant of Rome, of which she seemed a part no more. It was as a picture now that she beheld the well-known scenes, feeling herself to have reached some other stage of being, whence she looked back on what had been her life as though verily it were no more than the play-acting of mimes.

She was in a half-dreaming state as they went along, but when they had passed the Court of the Danaids and entered the colonnade of the Palace, between the gleaming white columns that to Nyria's fancy had always resembled the teeth of some dreadful monster waiting to devour her, sheer terror quickened the girl's numbed senses, and she realised that she must collect her powers in order that she might not bring discredit on the faith she professed, nor on Valeria.

The litters were set down long before they had reached that large ante-room where Julia had been wont to alight. Thither, between rows of soldiers, Nyria walked behind Paulinus, keeping her eyes to the ground.

Cæsar did not receive to-day in the State presence-chamber, but in a smaller room, the entrance to which was guarded by Prætorians. Paulinus made her a sign to wait as he himself went in, the doors closing behind him.

Presently they opened again, and two more Prætorians came out and led Nyria in between them, through the double row of lictors and a small company of officers of the guard stationed below where Cæsar sat, his face half hidden by the bulky form of Paulinus, who stood before the Emperor.

Suddenly there was the sound of a stifled groan, and of the sharp jingle of mail, causing Nyria to glance up bewilderedly, and she saw Alexamenos. His movement had been involuntary, and now he stood at attention, perfectly rigid, though deathly pale, his handsome features drawn and his horrified gaze fixed on Nyria. Not till now had he known that she was among the Christian prisoners, and to Alexamenos those blue eyes staring piteously from the thin white face were as the eyes of one who had already walked the ways of death. He could say nothing—he could do nothing. His heart was rent, but before all else he was a soldier, and his training stood him now in good stead.

At that moment the Emperor motioned Paulinus aside, and said, in that voice which had ever struck fear to Nyria's soul,—

"Come hither, girl."

She advanced, making a profound obeisance, and stood before Domitian with drooped head, a slender figure in her white robe, her long yellow hair waving over her shoulders, her wasted arms folded on her breast. When she heard again those dreaded tones, and realised in blind fashion the imposing personality, the bloated face, the short-sighted eyes peering at her from between almost lashless lids, the bull neck and thick, extended hand, Nyria shuddered from head to foot and seemed about to sink to the ground. But she had Christ's and her lady's honour to uphold, and with the thought of that her courage rose.

Domitian addressed her in strangely gentle fashion.

"Nyria! I recall thy name, and I grieve—not to see thee here, but to learn that thou wouldst disobey the commands of thy kindly master, and that thou shouldst be brought before me on so grave an accusation as that of treason against the State religion, and thus against Cæsar himself as its head." He paused, and beneath his outward calm the arrogance of his mien was terrible to the hapless girl. But his voice was soft as he went on: "Methinks that there must be some error on the part of thine accusers, and in my clemency towards the humblest of my people I would give thee a chance to disprove this double charge. First tell me, Nyria, wherefore not obey thy lord?"

The girl trembled but answered clearly,—

"My lord commanded of me that which 'tis not in Nyria's power to fulfil."

"Tush! Thou quibblest, child," returned Cæsar in quick tones.

"Thy lord knows well the truth of that which he did demand of thee. He but needs thy statement to bear him out, and thou wilt provide it in due course if thou hast an ounce of brain. But the other matter is of more serious moment, seeing that if thou art in heresy thou'lt meet a fate in the Arena that will for ever seal thy lips. All Christians suffer at the Games to-morrow—didst know that, Nyria?"

A shudder shook the girl from head to foot.

"I knew it not," she said.

"Nay? Then mark the news I give thee well, and think before thou answerest me. For I must know the truth concerning thee if thou art to be a witness in the illustrious Paulinus's case against his lady, which I purpose shall be tried before me. Say then, Nyria—hast thou been faithless to the gods of Rome?"

Nyria made the conventional reverence, her hands to her forehead, then looked at the Emperor with unabashed eyes.

"I am indeed the humblest of Cæsar's slaves," she answered. "Nevertheless, Nyria serves no god but one."

An angry flame leaped in Domitian's eyes.

"Then 'tis true, as I am informed, that thou hast been fool enough to join that mischievous sect which calleth itself Christian?"

"'Tis true, oh, Cæsar! that Nyria serveth Christ."

Domitian frowned and snapped his thumb and finger, a well-known sign that he was wroth. But as he looked at the girl his anger appeared to die down, and he smiled as might a giant at some pigmy's pranks.

"Now, Curly Locks, thou knowest that Cæsar hath ever been a loving father to his people, and would be lenient to the folly of a babe. 'Tis to this thou trustest, I can see. Well, well, it shall not fail thee. For how shouldst thou be fit to judge in matters of faith? What canst thou know of these pernicious doctrines? The scoundrels trapped thee in thine ignorance—did they not? Disown the lot and thou shalt be forgiven."

Nyria bent again, but there was pride in her humility.

"Thy slave thanks thee, oh, great Cæsar! But I had been well instructed in the Christian doctrine before I was permitted baptism, else would Nyria have been unfit to enter the fold of Christ. Truly, my lord, I am no child, but of years sufficient to know my mind. Of mine own judgment I chose this faith, and therein must I abide."

To the astonishment of the bystanders Domitian appeared pleased at this reply. He laughed as though he meant to humour her.

"Well spoken, Curly Locks! It seems those dogs have taught thee oratory, for that's a lengthy speech to come from so small a maid. Nay, nay, child, I like to see thou hast both wit and will. In truth I had forgot the flight of time and that thou'rt not the milk-faced babe thou look'st. Nevertheless, thy wit is folly, Nyria, and Cæsar of his clemency would deign to show thee reason. Dost know aught of certain dark ceremonies to which thou hast pledged thyself? These cunning Christians would not call at once, mayhap, on a votary so fair and young to drink the blood of murdered babes, and revel in foul orgies that put to shame the feasts of Mithras and all forbidden rites. I'll wager, Nyria, thou'rt not instructed in practices such as these?"

"Nay, my lord! Cæsar hath been misinformed. The Christians practise naught save what is pure and holy."

Domitian frowned anew. A crimson flush overspread his face, and fading, gave place to a livid pallor. He looked at Nyria attentively, then uttered an ironic laugh.

"Verily, here's wisdom that can correct e'en Cæsar! Didst learn it from thy god—the ass?"

It was Nyria's turn now to flush deeply, and from her face, too, the flush quickly faded, leaving her deadly pale. She reared herself and answered,—

"Oh, great Cæsar! Nyria hath naught of wisdom save that which the one true God hath taught her—to know and worship Him who made the world, to whom all men be subject—even all rulers—and His only Son, our Lord and Saviour Jesus Christ."

Everyone was amazed to see Domitian silent, a faint smile on his lips, as if he were considering how to reply. Paulinus, no longer able to control himself, ground his foot in the carpet, and leaning towards the Emperor, beside whom he stood, exclaimed,—

"'Tis the most obstinate and ungrateful minx that ever had the chance to abuse great Cæsar's kindness. I pray thee, command the tortures, August. Naught else will shake her stubbornness."

But Domitian demurred. "Nay, there are better ways to deal with women. Besides," he said, "this maid hath brain beyond the run of them, and is worth argument, if but for the front she showeth." And he turned to the girl again. "Thou art courageous, Nyria. Nevertheless, Cæsar would not shackle thy tongue. He is interested in this reasoning, and would know why it is that thou wilt not worship the gods of Rome, which are good enough for other folk. What hast thou to say concerning our Roman gods?"

Emboldened by his gentleness, and sustained by that spirit within which bade her—since chance offered—defend her faith, Nyria spoke out bravely again.

"My lord, I have oft heard stories of the Roman gods, concerning strange and cruel doings by which they showed no wiser, and less merciful, than men, and were most hard to understand. Meseemed, therefore, that the god I wished to worship should be of loftier kind, whom I could learn to know and love."

Domitian stooped forward and looked intently at her. There was an odd smouldering fire in his eyes.

"Men worship *me*," he said suddenly. "Wilt have me for thy god, Nyria?"

The blue eyes shot at him an indignant glance. She thought he was making mock of her.

"'Tis natural that a maid of thine intelligence should wish to know and love the god she worships. On the word of divine Cæsar, Curly Locks, if thou wilt choose me for thy god, thou shalt have sufficient knowledge to warrant thy worship."

Incapable of grasping his freakish mood, Nyria stood with bent head, keeping silence.

"Come closer," said he, and put forth his hand, with the finger bent, as she remembered it, like the paw of a tiger with the claw hidden. Reluctantly she drew nearer.

Domitian, bending still towards her, pressed for her answer.

"Think thyself highly favoured, Curly Locks. Thou dost admit that thou hast joined a false sect now under penalty of law, and thus art thou guilty of blasphemy against the State religion. Roman justice demandeth that thou, like all the rest, shouldst suffer for thy crime. Even Cæsar may not pardon thee without some proof of recantation. Come, give me but this. Kneel here before me, in the presence of Paulinus, and hail me as thy god. Thou hast but to worship Cæsar and thou shalt be free."

Nyria saw now that he was deeply in earnest; she saw, too, that he desired to befriend her, but underneath the apparent goodwill she was conscious of something which made her shiver with fear and loathing.

"My lord," she said, "thou art great Cæsar and Nyria is a slave. To thee, as Emperor, will I gladly kneel. Yet verily thou art no god, though thou art Cæsar. And to a man I may not offer worship."

Again, to the surprise of those present, Cæsar made no demonstration of wrath, but seemed deep in thought, his eyes fixed on Nyria, with a look in them which frightened her more than violence. Paulinus angrily interposed.

"The girl is mad, Cæsar. Let me take her out and have some sense whipped into her;" but Domitian silenced him as before.

"Thine experience, friend, hath not instructed thee how best to deal with women. Retire, I will treat with the maid alone."

He gave the signal of dismissal, and Paulinus strode forth stormily, followed by the Prætorians and lictors, Alexamenos casting a gaze of anguish at Nyria before the door closed upon them.

Paulinus betook himself at once to a side-room, where Regulus, in company of Palfurius Sura, awaited an audience with Cæsar. The officers in the ante-chamber exchanged sniggering glances, except Alexamenos, who stood apart, pale and unnerved.

"Didst note how Domitian looked at her?" whispered one. "I marvel that he should care to take up with another man's slave-girl!"

"What sees our sapient Cæsar in the maid?" said another. "Her face is that of a scared ghost that hath already been dead a week."

"She hath wondrous golden hair—and saw'st thou ever eyes so blue? That little proud way of hers whets Domitian's fancy."

"Domitian always admired the girl," put in a fourth. "She used to come here in Julia's time. 'Twas only the temper of the mistress that kept him from making eyes at the maid."

"What will be the outcome of it?" resumed the first speaker, idly. "If the wench be over-bold she'll suffer. These Christians are contumacious folk. Think ye, will she deny her god?"

"Nay!" exclaimed Alexamenos, turning suddenly on them. "Nyria will be true to her faith, at all costs."

"What sayst *thou*, Alexamenos?" cried some. "Wouldst like thyself to be put to the test? 'Tis well for thee that we've no informers amongst us."

Alexamenos turned away again. "A soldier's duty is to obey," he muttered, striving to comfort himself with the reflection that the Church preached submission to rulers.

"A maid betwixt Cæsar and the lions! Well, well, it needs no wizard to tell the result," laughed another. "I hold that the girl will gladly buy her life and liberty at the price, and she may indeed deem herself favoured to be given the choice."

Alexamenos groaned.

Alone with Nyria, the Emperor smiled a smile intended to be reassuring, and pointed to a stool at his feet. "Place thyself there, child," he said.

Nyria shook her head, and with her pathetic gesture of humility replied, "Cæsar is gracious, but his slave will stand."

He did not urge the point, and she remained in a reverent attitude before him, strong in spirit, though with shaking limbs.

"Fear not, Nyria," Domitian said caressingly. "For though thou art a captive brought here to plead with Cæsar for thy life, verily it seems that Cæsar doth plead with thee instead. Dost understand, child, that I'd fain make thy trouble light if thou wouldst have it so. Be thankful that Cæsar's heart inclineth ever to mercy—else would things have gone harder with thee. There is but one way now in which thou canst be saved. What I could do publicly that have I tried in vain. Now, Nyria, since thou hast rejected Cæsar the god, Cæsar the man will plead with thee."

Nyria felt his eyes burning upon her face, but she did not raise her own.

"Carest thou not for liberty, Nyria?" he went on in his smoothly rolling voice. "Carest thou not for life? Hath it been so little joy to thee that thou art ready to relinquish it?"

"Nay, lord," she stammered, seeing that he expected her to speak.

"Then wherefore hold it lightly? Be not unhappy, child. They told me that 'twas of thine own desire thou didst enter the household of Paulinus. Had I given a thought then to thy case thou shouldst have entered mine. But thou knowest, Nyria, that before aught else Cæsar doth concern himself with his country's welfare, and at that time troublous State matters engrossed me. Nevertheless, Cæsar hath not forgotten thee. Though I lost thee then, yet, having found thee again, fain would I keep thee at my side. When as a little maid, Nyria, thou camest here with thy mistress, Julia, who now dwelleth with the gods, Cæsar discerned the strength and sweet fidelity which made thee different from thy kind. To-day I see the child become a woman, with a fairer beauty and a nobler spirit. When I heard thee answer in defence of that which thou holdest dear, then thought Cæsar, 'Did Nyria pour at Domitian's feet such love and faith, at least I'd know one loyal heart was true to me'—though methinks in all mine empire there'd be none other!"

The ruler of the known world heaved a sigh of self-commiseration, and as he went on his tones lowered impressively.

"Perchance, child, thou didst deem great Cæsar happy! Ay, verily, great is he! Acclaimed divine by gods and men! Supremely powerful, and feared wherever Roman Eagles spread their sway—and yet of all men Domitian is most wretched. He hath no true friends—each one bears a hidden dagger. He hath no loyal kinsfolk—all of his gens conspire against him. He hath no faithful wife—Rome's Empress preferred a mime to Cæsar! Doom dogs my steps, and treason shadows me. They call me tyrant! Alack! I strike lest I be stricken."

He threw up his arms in a theatrical gesture, but his voice thrilled with such genuine emotion that Nyria, marvellous though it seemed, pitied the Emperor, and gazed at him with the quick sympathy of her tender soul.

"Speak to me, child!" he said. "Speak from thy heart, Nyria."

Clasping her hands in a supplicatory movement, she answered,—

"Oh, my lord! To hear such words from thee! Great as thou art, and I a humble slave! Thou art Cæsar, and all nations of the earth obey thy command. Fair women there be in plenty who would doubtless give devotion to Cæsar. 'Tis not for Nyria, oh, my lord! to serve thee thus."

"Ay, 'tis for Nyria," he answered; and there came into his accents a roughness which told of the fierce animal nature beneath. "Cæsar hath had a wide choice of women, and hath found none true—save *thee*." His rasping tones grew suave again. "Had I thy faithful breast to lean upon, thy loyal love to comfort me, I'd be again that which I strove to be when first I wore the purple—

generous, high-aimed, loth to shed my people's blood. 'Tis strange, child, that I should sue to thee—I, who am the Emperor, and thou, as thou sayest, a slave. Yet I, whose word is law, do stoop to beg from thee that which from others I would compel. I ask not that thou shouldst renounce thy faith. Let the world think that thou hast knelt to me and 'tis enough. Thou shalt be free to worship as thou wilt, for thou saidst the truth—a man is Cæsar, not a god. 'Tis as a man I woo thee. Give me thy love and fealty, then verily will Cæsar worship *thee*."

He had risen from his chair, and stood over her as she shrank back terrified, yet fascinated by his extraordinary gentleness. Was this the mighty Cæsar of whom she had always thought as of some fierce creature, ruthless in seizing that which he desired, and, when he had wearied of it, insatiate still. He made no attempt now to snatch at the thing he wanted, but stood quite quiet, majestic in his scarlet toga, the gold chaplet binding his thin fringe of reddish hair, and his tall stature adding to his imperial mien. His eyes were misty, his face flushed, his manner tremulous. He held his passions rigorously under curb while he watched, waiting for some more subtle delight than woman's swift surrender was wont to yield him. The girl made a profound prostration, her face hidden by her hands.

"Nay, fear not, Nyria. Cæsar's favour is thine. Rise, sweet maid, and look at me."

She lifted herself and glanced wildly up at him, her blue eyes half-blinded by terror and tears, her thin frame shaking.

"Oh, my lord!" she cried. "How may Nyria answer thee? She hath no words in which to speak. . . . 'Tis verily beyond her power. . . . Nyria knoweth naught of love."

Her answer did not seem to displease Domitian. He smiled at her. "Ay, 'tis ever so with nymphs; and thou art child of woods and streams. Daphne, too, refused the nuptial torch. And yet, methinks, had Phœbus shed his glorious beams upon the maid, she, dazzled by his splendour, would not have fled the god's embraces. So let Apollo lack his laurel, but grant, oh, Zeus, my Daphne be immortal!"

The Emperor laughed softly to himself, proud of his rhetorical aptitude, as when he had competed for the poetic bays.

"Cæsar will not thus err in wisdom, for thou, Nyria, shalt behold somewhat of the glory that thou mayst share with him. Nymph or Christian thou mayst be, yet likewise art thou woman, and surely hast a woman's vanity. So, Curly Locks, thou shalt enjoy some foretaste of the gifts which Cæsar will bestow on one he favours." Thus saying, Domitian struck a silver gong beside him, making a peculiar triple call, and almost at once an inner door opened and several Nubian slaves appeared, prostrating themselves with their heads upon the ground.

He gave a rapid order, and they retreated swiftly backwards, leaving the Emperor and the girl alone once more. Domitian curbed his impatience, while Nyria stood with bent head praying silently for release. The strain did not last long, however, for the Nubians returned, having fulfilled their errand in an incredibly short space of time, and now bearing, for the gratification of the Emperor's new favourite, an array of riches which might have been the spoil of an Eastern magician's store. Some carried open coffers piled with silver and gold, or heaped with gems, while from open trays balanced on their heads hung long strings of pearls and chains and girdles of all manner of precious stones, such as Julia had loved to wear. Other slaves showed, outspread over their arms, magnificent embroidered robes, and tissues of silk gauze in exquisite tints. Two tiny black boys waved immense plumes of snowy feathers set in long gold staves. Two more held coloured baskets containing smaller fans made of the wings of tropical birds set in carved ivory with gemmed handles; and two others bore branching screens of peacocks' plumage. Besides all these were innumerable articles of attire, treasures from India and every part of the known world.

At a sign from Cæsar the Nubians laid their burdens on tables and about the floor, till the room glittered with the costly profusion. They were dismissed impatiently, and, bending low, retreated backwards again.

"The dogs have brought but a small sample of what hereafter thou canst command, sweet nymph," said the Emperor. "By Venus's zone! not Jove himself showered gold on Danaë more plenteously than I will shower it on thee." He turned to Nyria, who stood bewildered by the splendour, her blue eyes' piteous gaze wandering round. Domitian's own eyes were brighter. He looked triumphant. He was confident of having gained his point, and now he flushed and paled quickly, as was his way when excited. Swinging his toga back, he stepped forward, showing his great bare knees and the gold thongs that came up his legs, while he stretched out his big hairless arms over the trays of coins and coffers of ornaments, picking out one thing after another and holding it forth.

"See, Curly Locks! this golden belt doth match thy hair, but thine eyes are bluer than these sapphires, and give out a deeper light. Not Helen had such eyes and hair as thine. Here's coral for thy cheek when thou art fed more daintily than they have served thee in the Mamertine, poor maid! These rubies shall lend thy lips their hue when rich Falernian sends thy blood again free-coursing through its veins."

He played with the jewels for a minute, looking from them to her, then flung them capriciously back into the coffer.

"Nay, nay! No rubies for thee, nor coral either. Thou shalt

wear pearls—naught but pearls—coils of pearls, which shall make thy skin show fairer. For thou art thyself a pearl, my Nyria, set in virgin gold—Domitian's choicest pearl. But thou shalt grow plumper ere Domitian seeks thine arms. Verily that slender form needs tending. Archimenes shall serve thee. He is skilled with maids and matrons, and by his care thou shalt speedily grow comely for thy nuptials. 'Tis true that wanness lends thee a rare charm, so that thou dost look a thing ethereal—made of moonbeams or of sea-foam—pale Aurora rising from the sea ere the sun-god's kiss had turned her rosy. But thy sun-god loves rounded limbs and roses, Nyria."

He drew nearer with fawning gentleness, which gave the suggestion of immense self-restraint. And in truth this licentious potentate, who had supped on all delights, feared to spoil by over-eagerness a fresh sensation which might prove supremely exquisite. His cat-like caress, behind which she sensed instinctively the cruel claw, was horrible to the girl. Yet she did not move. In his thick fingers he held a long chain of especially fine pearls, and threw it dexterously over her head, so that it made a fetter by which he bound her to him.

The pressure of the chain roused Nyria from the fascination he had cast on her, and she started back, trying to wrench off the string of pearls; but seizing her wrist, he checked her, smiling masterfully. Then she forgot that it was the Emperor to whom she spoke—forgot all but her fear and her repugnance.

"Touch me not! Oh, I cannot bear it!"

"Foolish child! Be not affrighted, Nyria, since thou hast Cæsar's love."

"Nay, nay!" she shrieked. "I have told thee I love thee not—I know not love."

"Seest thou that I can make thee richest of all women in Rome?" he said, pointing to the jewels scattered around, while loosing her wrist he tossed playfully the chain of pearls as it hung over her. She took advantage of his movement to struggle anew, and broke the string, so that the pearls rolled on to the ground. Domitian scowled, and then laughed.

"So, Curly Locks, thou dost flout what would have bought the kisses of every Roman lady, matron or maid!"

"Then seek them, lord. Thou art great Cæsar, and canst buy whom thou wilt—save Nyria."

"'Tis for that I want thee." The smile had left Domitian's face; he spoke with strong passion. "Well do I know women may be bought—that is their flesh, but not their minds and souls, if any do possess such, save those. Could I cage thy spirit, Nyria, to companion mine, neither sword of man nor fiat from Olympus would affright Domitian, for in thy love he would have found Elysium."

"I love thee not! Sooner let me die!" cried Nyria, all her courage rising in her despair. "Kill my body, Cæsar, but thou canst never cage my spirit. Man hath no power over that which Christ doth claim."

A moment passed. Then there sounded in Domitian's throat a strange sound, inarticulate in its fury. The muscles of his bull-neck knotted, foam gathered on his lips, blood suffused his eyes, his face was crimson. He made gurgling attempts to speak, each ending in a savage growl. At last he found words—hoarse, stammering.

"I . . . stooped to thee, and thou . . . thou hast dared defy me! Am I not Cæsar? Dost think thou canst escape me? I'll take by force what from choice thou wouldst not give. Then may Christ claim His own—when Cæsar and the beasts have done with thee."

But Nyria stood motionless, and now she was unafraid. Spiritual strength upheld her, for had she not called on Christ, and was He not all-powerful to save, even from this greater horror than any of the Arena?

Domitian took a stride towards the girl, his arms upraised, his cruel hands twitching, his breath coming hot and fast. He tossed his great head in a gesture of supreme arrogance.

"Who is lord-god in Rome?" he cried. "Is it Christ or Cæsar?"

Suddenly, as he spoke, a change came over the Emperor. His step was arrested, his hands dropped to his sides, his foaming lips gaped apart. Some unseen power controlled him.

And while the Emperor of the world stood thus, seeming paralysed, the slave-girl, confident and calm, faced him, her blue eyes full of a courage that was divine—before which he shrank, confounded, though trembling with rage and impatience.

Christ had triumphed.

For the space of several seconds they stood thus—slow seconds, tense with silent conflict between forces of hell and heaven. Then sharp revulsion took Cæsar, and slew alike his fury and his desire. He turned from blood-colour to a corpse's hue. The fire in his eyes went out and left them dull and glassy. An expression of peevish, cold distaste soured his face.

"Begone!" he muttered. "I want thee not." He turned to the table and struck one fierce stroke on the silver gong. At the signal, lictors and Prætorians flocked within. Domitian made a contemptuous sign towards Nyria.

"Back to the dungeons!" he said. "She shall be food for the beasts to-morrow."

And at his words two soldiers laid rude hands on Nyria's shoulders, and drove her before them from the Palace.

XL

NYRIA was taken away from the Palace by another route, but so weak and dazed was she, after the scene she had just gone through, that she did not at first observe the difference. It was not until she saw the Colossus, and the great fountain in front of the enormous oval amphitheatre of the Flavians, that she realised it was not to the Mamertine, but to the dungeons of the Coliseum, that she was being led.

The knowledge gave her a sudden sense of relief, for now she knew that the end must be near; but her dulled brain was not capable of realising the further ordeal that lay before her.

They had to pass through a circle of guards stationed round the building, and within the belt of soldiers all was uproar and confusion. An army of workmen thronged the openings. Ladders and scaffoldings were being mounted by bands of sailors, who rehearsed the adjustment of the velarium overhead. Great waggons and covered vans stood in process of discharging their contents. Forests of greenery were being borne in, and slaves were wreathing the pillars of the State portico. Flower-sellers and provision hucksters had already established their stalls round the pillars of the great colonnade. Cartloads of blossoms were being unladen. Crimson and purple draperies waited to be put in place, and richest carpets lay piled in heaps at the doors. It seemed impossible that all could be in readiness for the morrow.

To Nyria these details were already familiar. She had often gone past the Coliseum when preparations for games were in progress. Often, too, in Julia's time, had she been compelled to attend these games, standing behind her mistress's chair in Cæsar's podium, and enduring their barbaric course with averted gaze, purposely abstracting her consciousness from horrible actualities. But on none of these occasions had there been the wholesale slaughter that was promised this time; and Nyria, even though she felt an extraordinary detachment from the painfully suggestive facts surrounding her, was forced to remember that she would now form a part of them. Yet she was well-nigh indifferent. She was as one who, dreaming, knows that it is but an evil dream through which she must pass, but which will leave her free once more. For Nyria the stress of realities had ceased with Cæsar's change of mood.

The soldiers hurried her between them to a door near to that exit known as the Gate of Death, because it was the one through which bodies of slain gladiators were carried to the mortuary.

This door led to a winding stair, by which were reached the cells and corridors lying under the great pillared space below the first gallery.

Down here, as above, all was bustle. Jailors, attendants, and soldiers jostled each other along the dim passages. There were slaves carrying planks and trestles. These they were setting down by another door at the end of the passage guarded by Prætorians, and through which Nyria was now thrust. She found herself in a low, large room, a segment of the vast substructure of the oval theatre, half across which a couple of huge curving buttresses ran, extending inwards. Between these, and immediately opposite to the entrance by which she came, were wide double doors leading into the Arena itself, but now securely closed. On either side of the buttresses, set high in the wall, were grated windows, letting in streams of soft afternoon light, and showing distantly, between their bars, glimpses of the raised tiers of seats in the amphitheatre. The upper balconies were garlanded with ivy; the lower boxes, the Senatorial benches and the Emperor's podium, which—gorgeous with gilding and rich draperies—was set almost opposite, were festooned with roses, long wreaths of which florists were now affixing. Their delicious scent floated into the ante-chamber of doom, and was an ironic reminder of the joys of life and liberty to the unfortunates condemned to die. From the interior of the amphitheatre came a continuous noise made by carpenters, decorators, sand-strewers, setters of the machinery and accessories required for certain mythologic pageants which were to be represented, and the voices of these various workmen busy over their preparations, the uproar pierced from time to time by wails or shrieks from the prisoners.

Nyria stood, stupefied, gazing blankly at the scene before her. In her fresh white robe she looked like a visitant from another sphere entering some horrible pandemonium, but no one noticed her at first. The other poor victims were too intent upon their own misery—for the dread significance of their removal hither had just burst upon them. This place was much better lighted than the dungeons of the Mamertine, and the captives could be clearly distinguished—a crowd of wretched creatures looking more like animals than human beings as they huddled together in torn, befouled garments, with matted hair, bony limbs and emaciated faces—the gleam of hunger as well as of despair in their staring eyes. Their removal from the Mamertine had taken place while Nyria was at the Palace. All her former companions were here, and there were many unfamiliar faces among them, showing that additional prisoners had been brought in. Immediately after her own entrance a fresh batch appeared.

The new arrivals were a party of young woman, who shrieked

and laughed hysterically, half distraught with terror. They had been walking innocently along the Vicus Sandalarius together when some soldiers had set upon them, saying that certain of their number had been known to frequent the Christian place of worship; and amongst these was Æola. Nyria was attracted by a quick call, and turned just as the poor little maid rushed sobbing to her friend's arms. The girls clung together in anguish that was too great for speech. Æola was the first to utter clear syllables.

"Oh! 'Tis thou! 'Tis thou!" she muttered shudderingly. "I had been wondering whither they had taken thee. Oh! Nyria! Hold me—hold me tight. I am afeard—I am afeard."

"Christ is with us," whispered Nyria. "Be not afeard. Trust in Jesus. He will give thee strength."

"But I am no Christian," sobbed the little maid. "Nay, Nyria, blame me not. I would serve Christ, but thou knowest that I have not been baptised. Will Christ protect such as are not wholly His? And oh! doth His protection extend even to the dungeon?"

"Ay, Christ will lead us to the tomb, and beyond it," said Nyria solemnly.

"But I want not to die," and a terrified fit of shivering seized Æola. "Think of Crispus! He knows not that I am here. Oh! Nyria, pray Christ to save us."

Nyria bent her head, folding Æola closely in her arms and trying to comfort her. She too had prayed urgently that if it were her Master's will she might not suffer martyrdom. Now she had ceased to pray this for herself, believing that He who called her to it must know best. But for Æola it was different.

"How wast thou taken?" she asked, and then Æola told her.

"None would listen when I said I was not baptised," cried she. "'Thou, too, went with them,' they said. "But will not Christ release me, seeing I am not yet sealed with His sign? He sent an angel to open Peter's prison-doors. Oh! pray, Nyria, that an angel may come to us—or if one could be sent to warn Crispus—he is at Neapolis, knowing naught, save that he is entered for the Games."

"Then he will be here," said Nyria, compassionately. But Æola shook her head.

"Cæsar hath hastened on the Games, and haply Crispus may not arrive in time. He was to fight Balbus Plautius the Mirmillo. As thou knowest, Crispus is champion net-thrower, and looked to vanquish Balbus. But if he hears we are in custody—that haply—haply we have gone to our death—Crispus will have no heart to do well."

"Should he be vanquished," said Nyria, softly, "thou and Crispus, Æola, may clasp hands again across Death's river."

Æola fell to fresh shuddering.

"Nay! I want him here," she moaned. "If Crispus knew my plight he'd surely save me."

"Cease thy caterwauling!" cried a brutal soldier, and roughly shook her as he passed. "Thou'lt make e'en the beasts sicken with thy whining, so that they'll turn from their sport. 'Tis old women's work to shepherd squalling babes like ye."

Æola stared up at him in the gathering twilight; she was half crazy with fright. Nyria dragged her back into the shelter of a buttress, where she tried to soothe and calm her. The sun had gone down now behind the high walls of the Coliseum, and in the shadowy recess they were less likely to be seen. They had scarcely placed themselves out of notice, within the sheltering curve, when the door was flung open again and a guard of soldiers advanced with lances thrust before them, shouting, "Silence!"

The wailing and shrieking ceased, and the prisoners looked expectantly round.

"Make way—ye rats—make way!" cried the soldiers, clearing a space with their spear-heads. "Here cometh Matho to read ye a proclamation from Cæsar."

A shiver ran through the assembly. Some hoped for a reprieve, but most feared the worst at the mention of Cæsar's name.

"Mercy! mercy!" yelled half the hapless crowd, raising their arms, while several cried ecstatically, "Cæsar sendeth death, but Christ deliverance."

"Silence!" roared the soldiers anew, and Matho, preceded by two slaves bearing torches, and attended by a couple of clerks, came forward in a fidgety, uneasy sort of way, for, in truth, the task was not to his liking, and he scarcely cared to trust himself amid such a crowd—even with a bodyguard of Prætorians. But he could not decline Cæsar's command, especially as he was far less flourishing than when he had conducted the sale of Julia's slaves. His toga was shabby. His person, formerly obese, was shrunken; the skin of his face was drawn tightly over his cheek-bones and hung in yellow wrinkles round his chin. In his hand he carried a purple-bordered parchment, which he now unrolled, casting contemptuous looks around him, while the torch-bearers placed themselves on either hand, so that he should have sufficient light by which to read.

"Listen!" he called out in a dictatorial voice. "Listen, ye malefactors, and ye shall learn Cæsar's leniency towards a set that of a surety deserve naught at his hands."

It appeared that the ruler of the world, in his humane consideration for all men, desired that even these offenders against the State and its religion should be given a chance of life. Thus some

His gaunt arms raised, he tried to make a way to the head of the board, but the people took no heed save to push him back when he obstructed their onslaught.

"List to your preacher!" shouted a soldier. "He bids ye give thanks to Cæsar, ye thankless brood!"

Another soldier laughed. "Does the old fellow think the hounds will heed him while they have their prey? As well preach to the beasts to-morrow."

Gaius's own eyes showed the ravening gleam, his under-lip trembled and the moisture ran from it, though he strove to maintain a dignified demeanour. But his exhortations were in vain. The people spared no time, even to scoff, but ate and drank recklessly. One wasted youth, who had not been able to get near the food, lay embracing the base of a wine-jar, from which he had imbibed too freely for his starved stomach. A Prætorian, approaching it, kicked him contemptuously over.

"What! Drunk already? Here, Petronius! Antiachus! hither. Let us save these bestial fools from overlading—this one is full to his gullet. If they drink more, Charon will have to dip them head first in the Styx to cool their brains."

Riotously the soldiers' strong arms seized the jar, and half a dozen swung it aloft, when twenty of the mob bore down on them dreading to lose a drop.

"Hence! hence!" cried the Prætorians, enjoying what was to their minds a joke. "How many of ye have thought to pour libations to your god? None—verily, methinks. Shame—shame on such an impious sect! Here's then to those who'll see ye hence safely. Stand back, foolish folk—unless ye would be re-baptised in Cæsar's good red wine." Thus saying, they tilted the jar, scattering cupfuls hither and thither amid hoots from the thirsting prisoners who pressed round, holding their mouths to catch the falling liquid.

"To Jove, the Liberator! whom ye have scorned, wherefore will he liberate ye from his rule, and speed ye by the hand of Libitina through Death's door to those domains where the light of day shines never. Gird up yourselves, glad travellers, and fall in line. But first—here's to Hercules, that he may lend ye his own prowess to-morrow—and chiefly may he aid the Bacchanals."

A crazy laugh rang out.

"Ay! ay! call on him—we shall need his aid. Verily, never have I rent a man of flesh before."

The dancing-girl of the Suburra darted across the cell. She had been leaning over a brimming amphora to drink, and her face was wet with the wine which fell in red streams over the front of her robe as she ran past, laughing wildly, followed by two or three other damsels whom she had infected with her unnatural merriment.

"So ho! ye lusty Mænads!" called the soldiers. "'Twill be a fine sight when ye set on Pentheus Sura."

Again the laughter echoed—derision mixed with horror—a laugh to send men mad.

"Cæsar will revel in the Sura show," declared a soldier. "Cæsar always hated Marcus Licinius, and his dispatch will be the pick of the entertainment to Domitian. And someone else will see it, too, who haply may not like it half so well. Cæsar hath commanded every dame of quality in Rome to attend the Games on pain of his imperial displeasure—wherefore, perforce, Valeria must come and witness the sport she hath herself so generously afforded."

Now, at the name of Valeria, Nyria in her corner, where she was still tremulously trying to calm Æola, leaned forward, listening intently. She had been longing for news of Valeria, but Æola was too excited and too miserable to be able to tell her much. Æola was crouching in an angle of the buttress beside Nyria, and moaning in her terror, which had been increased by the sight of the orgy round her. Her features were contorted. Her pretty brown eyes, round and frightened, were protruding from their sockets. She grew light-headed, and called repeatedly on Crispus, while she clutched Nyria's arm and asked at intervals, "Why do they shout and fight thus? Oh! Nyria, is Satan among them? Are they Satan and his evil ones come to take us hence?"

And in truth the half-frantic figures, leaping and raiding in the lurid light of the torches, and then crouching over their hardly-gotten plenty, might have been fierce ghouls from some nether plane of doom. Scarcely human they looked, worn almost to shadows, showing only by the pitiful appetites they sought to slake, some link with humanity. The sight of good food, after their long starvation, had maddened many, sweeping aside alike the martyr's hopes and fears, and turning men and women of nobler aims into ravening wretches, with no thought save to satisfy themselves ere death came. Round the huge room there stood a certain number seeming to shrink against the walls, and who, while suffering like pangs, yet turned in loathing from the scene. Some remained in silent prayer. Others cast longing looks at the tables, wondering whether the food and drink would last out till they might lawfully obtain a share, for great pieces of meat and bread were flung hither and thither, and the stone floor ran with spilled wine. Some weak ones, fearing to be trampled on if they strove with the rest, leaned over and licked up the red streams that ran near where they lay, and eagerly snatched scraps of meat from under passing feet, devouring them in haste lest they be snatched away again.

Now Gaius came to Nyria's side. She, full of her own thoughts, did not at first observe his gaunt, emaciated frame in the shadows where she sat. He laid his lean hand on her shoulder, and it would be permitted to fight unarmed against young gladiators, as yet scarcely trained. To others would be given blunt staves of wood for use in combat with African beasts. Others would be allowed to emulate the feats of Grecian heroes; and for a number of young women was reserved the highest privilege of all—that of playing the parts of Bacchanals by whom impious Pentheus, in the person of Licinius Sura, should be rent limb from limb.

"Such," said Matho, "is the fitting sentence of our divine ruler upon this blasphemous traitor who hath not only conspired against the State, but hath dared to flout the godship of Cæsar—even as Pentheus in his folly flouted that of the divine Dionysus. Most fitting is it, too," he added, "that he who hath falsely requited women's favours—as all know to have been the way of this Sura—should meet his well-merited end at the hands of women."

Now, at first the meaning of Matho's announcement with regard to Licinius Sura was not plain to the Christians, and they looked at each other in a puzzled way. Most of them knew nothing of Greek drama, being poorly educated, and reading but little—nor were they permitted by their religion to frequent the theatres where it was performed. But presently there came a piercing shriek from the rear, where a young woman sat—a chorus and dancing-girl of the Suburra, recently converted to Christianity, who had formerly seen Paris act the part of Dionysus, and who had herself taken a share in the destruction of the waxen image substituted for Pentheus, to be torn by Agave and her Mœnad crew from the pine tree on Cithœron. This girl knew now the fate that was intended for herself and her companions, and her horror was quickly communicated to the rest.

"Better far the lions!" they cried. "In mercy, cast us to the lions rather than drive us to this deed of blood."

Old Gaius, gaunt and worn, arose.

"Let Cæsar hear the prayer of his servants. Verily have we done no wrong. Nevertheless, if it be Cæsar's will that we should perish—perish we must. But lay not this sin upon the innocent. I pray thee, command not these blameless maids to pass to their own doom with blood-guiltiness upon them.'

And the wretched girls pressed forward and threw up their arms, crying, "Have pity on us, for how shall we slay a man?"

Matho's small, squeamy eyes glanced from side to side.

"Hold thy peace, old rat!" he said scornfully. "The maids have tongues of their own, though verily they do not otherwise resemble their sex. Ye spiritless she-mice," he went on to the hapless women, "is there none among ye that will show teeth to her assailant? Know ye not that this Sura is the cause of your present plight? Had he not wormed his way by treachery into the counsels of your brethren, discovery and punishment might have been long in overtaking ye, even though ye practised that pernicious Christian heresy."

"The lawyer speaketh truth," groaned one of the Christians, a huge fellow, who had been a contented goatherd on the Sabine Hills, but who was now worn to skin and bone, and whose protruding cheek-bones and famished eyes gave him a savage appearance. "The fellow Sura doth deserve his fate, for oft hath he tempted me and many others to sedition against Cæsar. Nevertheless are these maids blameless, as the elder saith, and 'tis not meet that such a task should be dealt to women."

"Dictate not thou to Cæsar," cried Matho, sharply. "Doubtless thou, good friend, wouldst lend a lusty hand in chastisement of Licinius Sura to secure thee the women's chance of life. For know, ye white-hearted maids, that Cæsar doth ordain that those among the Mœnads who play their part best may haply be rewarded with life and liberty. The Most August doth put no limit to the number of his Bacchanals, so that all ye, maids and young matrons, who can prove stout enough to launch retribution at yon impious plotter may find freedom when ye have requited Cæsar's wrongs—as Roman women should be ready to do. Were ye pure-blooded Romans, ye'd applaud great Cæsar for the service he permitteth ye, and not stand whining thus. But what can one expect of paltry wretches in whose veins runs some mawkish diluted stream? Warm your hate, women—warm your blood—if ye have either. Cæsar in his munificence sends ye good red wine and food—ha! ha! Methought that sound would stir ye to valour! Eat and drink now, and to-morrow show what ye can do to serve Cæsar while ye have life and strength. Softly! softly! good people. The meal is coming. Quench your ardour for the moment while I get me hence. Never were malefactors fed as by Cæsar's generous decree ye favoured rascals shall be. Hearten ye, poor spineless vermin! Put blood in your veins, and sharpen well your teeth and claws, but see none faint nor fail to-morrow."

Thus saying, Matho gathered up his toga, and signing to the soldiers to clear his path, followed them hastily, scarce waiting for the torch-bearers to light his way.

A burst of anguished sound pursued him, piteous prayers mingling with execrations—to all of which he closed his ears, thankful to secure himself a safe exit.

The hapless throng, seeing their last hope disappear, turned in their misery upon each other—some raising wrathful cries against their persecutors, some in their madness still imploring aid; while some, clinging together, drew apart and prayed shudderingly. The air was full of wailing, in the midst of which rose here and there a cry of faith from some ecstatic, half-maddened soul; but for the most part, those who called on their Master in this dark hour did so silently, and, like Nyria, drew into some secluded corner where only by their shut eyes and softly-moving lips could it be seen that they prayed.

Gaius went from group to group, striving to exhort, to calm and counsel his miserable flock, but his attempts were ill-received. Such as clung the closest to their crucified Lord, and desired only to follow in His steps, scarce needed the presbyter's well-meant, but not always well-chosen, advice; while others, to whom martyrdom held only terrors which they were not fitted to endure, openly scoffed at the poor old man of whom formerly they had stood in awe—seeing that now he had come to like plight with themselves. Many of the people thought only of Matho's promise of a feast. They would have prayed to any gods could their prayers have brought them food and wine. And now the suggestion of it made the saliva run in their dry mouths, and set the few poor thoughts of their befogged brains circling round this possibility—shutting out the certainty that lay beyond.

Into this vortex of human woes was presently brought the evidence of Cæsar's favour—his munificence towards those who else had been too weak to make worthy sport for him and his associates upon the morrow.

Directed by some soldiers, a company of slaves appeared, bearing huge baskets, and the planks and trestles which Nyria had seen them carrying when she entered. They arranged the trestles, and laid the planks across them to make tables, while some fixed up a torch or two, which, however, only served to accentuate the gloom. Out of the shadows gleaming eyes watched the slaves anxiously, while some of the eager crowd dragged their famished frames nearer over the stone-floor—only to be thrust aside with rude jeers by the soldiers.

"Keep back till the board is spread, ye greedy rabble! Saw ye never food before?" they cried.

"Such scum have never fed on food like this," cried others, while the slaves lifted out huge joints and trays full of crisp brown cakes. Silence had fallen on the prisoners. They waited in well-nigh breathless suspense, while many a nostril quivered, inhaling the rich scent that reeked from the baskets—the odour of fresh-cooked meat, of sweet, new-baked bread. Here came piles of pasties exuding savours, and showing, where some broke, a close stock of meat or fruit within. Here, sausages in stacks, brown and steaming, and strewn with olives swimming in oil, as poorer folk loved them. There, a pig's head crowned with laurel. Now a great side of beef in a deep dish, half hidden by its wreath of many-coloured nasturtium flowers, with pungent green berries —fit for a patrician's table. There, too, was the big bowl—nay, several—full of frumenty—dear to the heart of all the lower ranks in Rome—a mixture of grain boiled in milk and seasoned with strong spirit distilled from other grain. There were great jars, too, each half as high as a man, brimming with red wine, and borne shakingly by two slaves apiece, and lesser flagons full of spirits of various kinds.

Now more torches were brought and fixed upon the walls, spluttering smokily, and casting long lurid flames across the scene. Then a sound arose like the long-drawn breathing of a pack of wolves. It began by fits and starts, then gradually fell into rhythmic cadence. And the slaves, comparatively well-nourished, glanced at each other nervously and hurried their movements, anxious to be gone. The soldiers jeered and laughed, but they too, glanced from side to side, and keeping their lances set drew back in a file towards the door. And the starving wretches stirred spasmodically at first—one stretching out a lean hand here, another wriggling nearer an inch or two there; this shadowy figure slipping stealthily forward from the hindmost ranks; there a pair of bony arms extended, once fair and round, now no more than a skeleton's; then the quavering cry of a helpless old woman who could not move and feared to be downtrodden in the rush.

The soldiers meant to give the signal, but it was accorded unintentionally by a hapless slave, who slipped on some spilt gravy, and fell, upsetting the dish he bore—a famous stew of sheep's tongues and liver, cooked with mushrooms, and a sauce of plums and wine. The luscious mess was scattered all about him till the stones reeked of its savour, and one hungrily thrust out a fleshless claw and snatched a piece, and then another and another did likewise, falling over each other on the slippery stones, till none could see the slave. Then swiftly, while the soldiers laughed, two or three sped to the tables and snatched at the first thing they saw, gnawing what they seized with furtive looks and backs bent to the rest. Others came behind them, and pounced over the shoulders of the foremost, till a seething mass of beings surged round the food. The soldiers watched and gibed.

"Come on!" they cried, seeing the saner among the crowd standing meekly back. "Fall to, ye starvelings, likewise. 'Tis Cæsar's royal decree that none need go with empty stomachs to meet old Charon on the river's brink. Ye need sound stuff to stay ye through to-morrow. Come, then, and take your fill. We are not paid to apportion bones to dogs such as ye."

But against these taunting commands the voice of Gaius might be heard, grown weak with long fasting, yet sternly condemnatory, and exhortant as ever.

"My people! ye are men—not beasts. Abstain! Abstain! Give thanks first to Him who hath vouchsafed ye this boon, and thrust none aside, for all should share equally. Place yourselves in order, brethren, and I, being chief among ye, will dispense the food—to the ailing first—then to all in due course."

burned through her thin robe, seeming like fingers of fire pressing upon her.

"In Christ's name," he murmured, "Nyria, get me food. Thou art small and slender, and canst slip between those sons of Belial, but they drive me back, and I—*I starve.*"

Nyria's ready sympathy was at once aroused.

"Ay, sir," she said. "Sit thee here beside my friend, and I will serve thee." She sped away, while the old man watched her, too eager to sit down. "Anything thou canst get," he called. "It matters not, only somewhat, in Christ's name."

Nyria had not thought of obtaining food for herself, for she had eaten well that day, and Æola had refused to take any, saying she too had well fed before her afternoon walk which had brought her to such disaster, but now Nyria thought that if she could persuade her to drink a little wine and to eat a morsel it might strengthen her. So she filled a flagon from one of the large amphoræ, and was carrying it with two cups, when someone pulled her skirt.

Looking down, Nyria saw that it was the aged mother of Lucius, almost past speech. She signed feebly for food and drink. Happy to be permitted to serve her again, Nyria knelt beside the poor old woman, and pouring wine into a cup, held it to her lips, and fed her with morsels of sweet soaked bread. The nourishment revived her, but when she saw from whose hands she had taken it, she pushed the girl aside.

"Oh, mother, canst thou not pardon when Christ forgave much more?" Nyria said, and softly kissed the enfeebled hand raised against her.

But the old woman gave no answer save a groan, and Nyria was forced to go away. She hastened back to the presbyter as quickly as she could, having secured him a portion of beef and half a fruit pasty for Æola. The elder took the food and ate voraciously, thankfully screening himself in a corner of the buttress, while Nyria poured wine for both and tempted Æola with morsels.

Presently she went forth again in search of more food, serving many a weak one on the way, and returning well supplied, so that Gaius had enough. The tables were easier to reach now, as the foremost feasters had satisfied their needs and drawn off, giving place to that more decorous division of the throng who had waited patiently; but several on the outskirts still fell like wolves upon the provender, tearing strips of flesh with teeth and fingers from the bones that fell near them, and contending for a drink from every flagon borne past. The soldiers, tired of amusing themselves with the scene, had gone without and locked the prison doors, so there were no longer any to check the license of the people. Gaius bethought himself of this, and remembering his office as presbyter, cast regretful glances from his corner.

"I thank thee, Nyria," he said. "I have been well served, and feel again the spirit of the Lord strong within me. Now will I go and command those sinful revellers, as one having authority in the Church, to desist from this wanton rioting and to wallow no more in gluttony and drunkenness."

He rose from the spot where he had partaken of his own meal unmolested, and stalked up the cell with a fresh show of confidence. But he was met by shouts of ribald laughter. Thick voices maunderingly excused themselves when he reproved them. It was vain for him to entreat or to chide such as these. They heeded not, save to laugh or scowl as they would; but others there were who would fain have spent their last night on earth fittingly, and to whom new courage had come with the comforting sustenance of the food and wine. These he gathered round him, and in earnest, if monotonous, tones, he prayed earnestly that the Master, unseen but ever near, would be in the midst of them to-night, and lead them all alike, the sinless and the erring, through their dark and terrible way upon the morrow.

And by degrees on each face peace settled. Tired eyes grew glad again with the joy of looking for that which lay beyond the gate of death. Strained features relaxed. The dreaded Arena was thought of calmly as the path—painful, indeed, but short—that should lead them to their Saviour's welcoming arms. And then it would not matter what the way had been, save, indeed, that the sharper the trial, the brighter would be the joy beyond. Thus, when the voice of Gaius ceased, one and another put tender arms about each other, and spoke of that tenderer embrace that should be theirs upon the morrow. Then, while the wings of God's angel of Sleep hovered over them, bearing balm for their aching eyelids and blessed forgetfulness to shed for the space of a few hours, drowsiness overtook them all and they slept.

XLI

There were no sounds in the dungeon except the gasping breaths of those that were more weary than the rest, the spluttering of torches burning to their sockets, and the gurgles of expiring lamps. Darkness deepened in the cell as, one by one, the lights went out. A miasmatic reek filled the place, hot mist rising from the damp stones, the stench of smoking oil, the odour of spilled wine and broken meats, acrid exhalations from human bodies. The atmosphere would have been intolerable were it not that through the high windows came breaths of pure night air and that mocking fragrance of summer roses.

Æola slumbered like a tired child, her head on Nyria's knee. Prayers and revilings passed her by unheeded; the wave of passion had rocked her to rest, and she lay dreaming sweetly of her lover. And as Nyria, fearing to move lest she should awaken her, looked down on the little white face, like some storm-swept flower, with dark tendrils of hair lying limply round it, an immense wrath and sorrow welled in her bosom for poor Æola, for kind, brave Crispus, for the misery and injustice of it all. She longed that Æola might be spared the awful ordeal of the morrow, and, impossible though it seemed, that she might be given back to Crispus.

Then her mind went to Stephanus—loyal, patient Stephanus, so strong and so true. He had suffered cruelly through Nyria, whom he loved with such fidelity. Happier for him, perhaps, that she was going to die, for thus she could not continue to cause him pain. Nyria wished that she had been kinder to Stephanus—that it had been in her power to reward his devotion. Now it was too late for regrets. But though she had been sorely tempted to save herself for Stephanus's sake, she knew that she could not have rested in the shelter of his arms at the cost of harm to Valeria. She knew, too, that this made it all the harder for Stephanus. He had never understood her feeling for her Domina. He had always grudged her to Valeria. He had always thought ill of Valeria. And the stab of it was that he had been right. No longer could Nyria uphold Valeria, nor believe that public opinion traduced her. In the slaying of her faith in Valeria lay the fiercest agony of martyrdom for Nyria.

Thus to-night it was long before the Angel of Sleep brought Nyria soothing balm. She sat staring out into the shadows. It was the hour of her Gethsemane. Rising in fierce array, doubt, scorn, hatred, unforgivingness assailed her spirit. All the strongest forces of her own nature seemed drawn up against her. And worst adversary of all, love likewise had become her foe; that which had once been her crown and joy was now a deadly thing, like some coiled serpent stirring in her breast, poisoning all sweet and holy thoughts. For though her faith in Valeria was dead, her love, pierced by a thousand shafts, lived on, and could not be destroyed even by this deed of irredeemable wrong. Yet Nyria realised that she could not forgive Valeria—her heart must bear that gall even to the Master's feet; and while bitterness envenomed her soul she could never know the rapture of union with her Lord.

On the eve of martyrdom this thought brought black despair. With the instinct of the religious devotee Nyria strained wildly through her starless night for some ray of hope, some refulgence from the Cross which she had been taught would lighten all spiritual gloom—the Cross on which Christ had borne more agonising griefs than hers for the redemption of mankind. But the dark hour was still dark to Nyria. Loss of trust in Valeria had weakened her trust in Christ, and now she asked herself—Of what avail was it to love? Of what avail to be loyal? Was there truth, justice, or mercy anywhere? Had not Christ, too, forsaken her? Or was Christ not that which she had believed Him to be? Then a heart-broken sense of shame overcame the slave-girl. Surely to-day Christ had saved her, as by a miracle, from a fate worse than could be devised for the tortures of the Arena. She had called to Him, and He had put out His power against Domitian. Was not that proof that though His kingdom was not of earth, and though the gates of death must be passed to reach its fulness, yet still that He would shield His children from injury to their souls. Christ, too, had suffered; Christ too, had seemed forsaken. But the All-Father did not really desert His own. Oh! could she but receive some sign to show that though love on earth had turned to bitterness, Christ's love remained all-comprehending, all-enfolding, embracing and atoning for poor human frailty—the doubt, the weakness, the wrath, even the lies told for love's sake forgiven, human bitterness melted in the flood of divine tenderness. Ah! then, thought Nyria, the sting of death would be withdrawn.

She bowed herself in anguished silence, waiting for succour in this onslaught of spiritual powers that did battle for her soul—waiting as many an anguished soul has waited for the help that never fails the pure in spirit and the hearts that truly love.

And as she waited, Nyria's thoughts went wandering back through misty scenes of her past, as the minds of those in peril or distress are wont to do. She saw the huge overarching trees of her forest-land. She saw the stately Queen Veleda—the virgin priestess who, aloft on her lonely tower, had smiled on the yellow-haired babe of her own royal lineage. She saw the legions of rough soldiers who had borne them captive from their northern home, and again she trod the long and weary march to Rome.

She saw herself as the child-princess whose German tongue and very name she had forgotten—the tiny slave-princess that had played about the Ethiopian's door. And now she was a maiden serving Julia, and the splendour and the misery of that service, the luxury and the privations, the taunts and blows, the pain of Bibbi's lashings—all swept along the shadow-sheet before her. She saw Sabinus in the purple laticlave, calm and steadfast to the end. Oh, that she might prove as calm and brave! She saw dead Julia lying in her rose silk robes, and heard Euphena's scoffings, and those strange prophecies concerning herself, which now she understood. Verily for Nyria there would be no carrying forth and no burying.

Then came the scene in the slave-market, and Paulinus—how kind he was then. And the first night in Valeria's house, when she had sworn by the bread and wine and salt to serve her mistress even to the death—ay! even to the death. She saw the jasmine-creepered porch, and heard Licinius Sura's mocking voice call her "little watch-dog."

And as her memories followed each other in irregular sequen e she was again upon the knoll above the Quarries. Once more she felt the western sun and the soft breeze upon her face. The grey day of storm and sorrow came back to her, when the shades had roamed across the Aventine and the sun had sunk redly behind the Latian mountains. Did she know now who drew the soft night-curtains around the tired earth? Ah! did she know? Was all naught but a dream and a passing—like that of the shades, who might be mere cloud-forms or departed souls of dead men unresting? She saw Clementus outlined against the sunset sky in his long grey cloak and purple vestment, with his grave, far-seeing eyes and dignified mien. Nyria's thoughts went out in tender gratitude to Clementus as she realised that he must be sharing in heart and mind the sufferings of his martyred flock—his own burden the greater because that for the Church's sake he might not come and lay down his life with theirs. Nyria wished she could have seen him just once more, to show him that she did not shrink from the baptism of blood. She remembered how she had shrunk from descending into the tank of water, and prayed piteously that she might be more courageous on the morrow.

The image of Clementus brought a sense of stay and comfort. When he had bidden her question herself concerning the extent of that which she would give up to purchase the life of Valeria, had she not been ready to give up all? She had pledged herself without reserve. She had not bargained for any requital. Surely, therefore, it was not for her to rail against justice now that God demanded from her the fulfilment of her pledge. And had not the loving All-Father promised her, through the mouth of Clementus, that her strength should not fail, and that in the hour of trial He Himself would be her succour? "Love covereth all things," Clementus had said. And the blessed Bishop John had spoken much of love that night when the Christians were first taken. As she thought over the Apostle's words, some dim sense of the might of Love and Sacrifice came to the lonely slave-girl. She began to realise the presence of that all-pervading God upon whose bosom her own small self lay, girdled in a care she could not comprehend. And to her quickened soul there sounded a whisper, "Nyria, Nyria!"

She started and listened. Long years ago she had heard that Voice—heard it in her early girlhood 'mid the silence of the hills, and now she knew the time had come for its promise to be fulfilled.

"Some day, Nyria, thou shalt see My face."

A rush of tears swept like a refreshing shower over her tortured heart. Words she had none, but her whole being lay open to the divine influence that flooded her. Gone were the doubts and fears, gone was the passion of distrust and anger; only love filled her to the full, while the sense of love surrounding, sustaining her, was soothing beyond all human expression to the poor bruised spirit bound in its wearied flesh. Forgiveness seemed a small matter now. Who could speak of it in the circle of that Unutterable Love?

When Nyria woke the sun was already up in the sky and cast two long yellow beams filled with dancing motes across the dungeon, revealing the remains of the previous night's orgy. The sunshine fell on the tables strewn with the remnants of the feast, upon broken amphoræ and pools of spilled wine, upon scattered meat-bones which huge rats were gnawing greedily, and upon the disordered forms of men and women stretched along the stone floor. It shone on pallid faces and tangled hair. The limbs of some of the sleepers twitched, while others ground their teeth, tormented by nightmare phantoms. But many lay like logs, all consciousness deadened. The expression of some of the faces was extraordinarily peaceful, though others were contorted as with a dreadful memory. The last batch brought in lay together, and were distinguishable by their cleaner clothes and plumper appearance. Among them the dancing-girl from the Suburra made fierce distressed sounds in her sleep, her fingers knotting in restless clutches at something she could not grasp. Æola still slept profoundly, notwithstanding that a continuous roar of noise came from the amphitheatre, where preparations for the day's festivities were in final progress. Nyria glanced affrightedly round, then seeing that Æola was sleeping she laid her gently down and ran across to find out how it fared with the poor old mother of Lucius.

One look at the wan, shrivelled face told Nyria that the old woman's sufferings were over, and that she, at least, had escaped the terrors of the amphitheatre. Reverently Nyria bent and arranged the poor frail hands, and drew over the worn frame the folds of her own cloak. "She hath forgiven me," thought the girl. "Soon we shall meet, and then haply she will tell me so." Nyria's sole care now was for Æola, and she ran back to her side.

At that moment there was a grating rumble close at hand; the prison bolts were being withdrawn. The inner door swung open on creaking hinges, and a jailor's strident voice called the unhappy captives roughly back to their brief span of life.

"Ho! ho! good Christians! Ye sleep late after your revels. Come, rouse up. Let this mess be cleared, and prepare ye for the merry-making."

Advancing among them he kicked unceremoniously one of the inert forms lying at his feet. It was that of the goatherd, who sprang up, startled, and standing half stupefied uttered the peculiar cry with which shepherds on the Sabine hills were wont to call their flocks. The jailor laughed. "'Tis another pack thou'lt follow to-day, my friend," he said, and the goatherd, groaning sharply, staggered against the wall, his forehead upon his hands, where he remained silent.

Gradually the sleepers awoke, making drowsy sounds and mechanical gestures; some moaning drearily, some sitting up, and staring round with astonished eyes; mothers hushing babes of whom they had been dreaming; the smile of maidens changing to a stare of horror; men who had been sailors mistaking the din which assailed their ears for the boom of the sea surge, and muttering incoherently in nautical language; others yawning and rolling heavy heads while they called for water to cool their throats, parched from last night's indulgence.

"Nay! ye had drink enough to float a galley!" answered a soldier, entering; and another grumbled as he swept out some rubbish. "We've other work than to wait on ye, who'll soon make food for beasts;" while a third, who was helping to take away the planks and trestles, exclaimed, "A fine thing that Cæsar should deign to feast such folk! Pray Hercules it hath put some courage in ye."

Presently there came a prison official, followed by several slaves bearing piles of skins—the spotted hides of fawns and panthers—also great stacks of ivy.

"By Cæsar's command," he shouted, "here's robing for the Bacchanals. Maids! stand forth. Great Cæsar orders that the lustiest and fairest be chosen for the off-send of Licinius Sura."

Now there went up shrieks and reproaches. Several women passionately refused to do the bloody work. Some wildly entreated that they might be given to the lions; others rushed off, striving to hide themselves in the darker corners of the dungeon. But the soldiers went after them.

"Since Roman ladies find pleasure in fighting gladiators, why should not ye, to save your lives, destroy a man?" they said, selecting the tallest and strongest of the younger women till about fifty were collected. The official flung to each a spotted skin, a slender spear, and a bundle of ivy sprays.

"Go, deck yourselves!" said he, contemptuously. "But surely more spiritless Mænads were never called to serve their god."

Each of the women was ordered to gird a dappled skin upon her, to wreath her thyrsus, and to twine herself a crown of ivy. Then they were all given some instructions as to the manner in which, upon a certain signal, they should make their entrance into the Arena. Having delivered other directions concerning the rest of the unhappy prisoners, this official departed, leaving the Bacchanals as if turned to stone.

A soldier roused them roughly.

"Come, haste! 'Tis Cæsar's will, and ye must do the deed. Put the skins about your shoulders and gird your waists and brows with ivy. Set creepers on the thyrsi and be thankful they are spears. Come! come! 'Twill soon be over. Better sure to kill a man, and have a chance of life, than to meet death within a lion's jaw."

"Nay! if ye will not robe yourselves, ye must be robed," another soldier cried, and knotted a fawn skin by the paws around the neck of one, but she tore it off.

At that moment an insane laugh rang out. There was a stir among the women, who made way with a show of repugnance as one of their number came to the front with dancing steps and arms waving. It was the chorus-girl from the Suburra.

"*Evoe! Evoe!*" she cried. "To the hills! To the hills! ye daughters of madness." Then she burst into a Corybantic song which Paris had made popular in the theatres:—

> "'Iacchos, oh! Iacchos, come!
> Until thou callest all are dumb;
> Lo! the godlike Bromius comes!
> Iacchos, Jove-born, comes!
> His cleansing feet are passing o'er the hills;
> Beneath his footsteps burst a thousand rills;
> Fresh streams of honey fall from every vine—'"

Seizing a trail of ivy, she wound it round her head with practised fingers, and snatching up a fawn skin held it against her bosom and kissed it ecstatically, then draped it round her waist. Brandishing her spear in one hand, she wove ivy swiftly up it, dancing a mad measure the while, her body swaying in wanton gestures. There was grace in her movements, but frenzy in her eyes.

Her mania infected many of the others. Several began singing and wildly waving ivy-wreaths.

"Verily the gods avenge themselves!" cried one of the soldiers in awed amazement. "Behold! Ceres hath struck madness on these blaspheming women."

For even those who had held back seemed inspired now with desperate courage. Slowly they came up to the piles of skins and the stacks of ivy. Slowly, but with grim resolution, they arrayed themselves for the part they had to play.

Meanwhile, officers, carrying out their orders, were drafting forth those men who were to open the gladiatorial contests by fightiwith tyros from the schools, and who, having to enter the Arena by a different gate, were taken from this cell, which thus discharged a considerable portion of its contents.

Nyria and Æola cowered in their shadowy corner between a buttress and the projecting frame of the great iron-bound door. Æola had awakened, but could only cling convulsively to Nyria, who held her close. They were thankful not to have been chosen as Bacchanals, an office for which both were deemed too slight and weak. But in the midst of all the turmoil, sublime calm enwrapped Nyria. The sense of that overshadowing Presence which had revealed itself in the dark hour of her agony had never for an instant left her. She feared no longer; she shrank no longer. Pain might rend her mortal frame, but for her the real anguish of martyrdom was overpast.

The roar in the amphitheatre increased in volume, and was like the rolling of waves upon a rocky strand, every now and then swelling out with resonance in volleys of acclaimings from some eighty thousand throats. Now the sweet shrilling of silver trumpets and long reverberating shouts, taken up again and again by the excited multitude, announced the Emperor's arrival. These last salvos were followed by a lull, for the performance had begun, the minor items preluding the more magnificent effects. As usual, there were sports with lesser beasts; the chariot races of harnessed Molossian dogs, culminating in one wherein dwarfs were the charioteers, in which Domitian took an especial interest, for it was his whim that the combatants should be distinguished by his own two new colours—the gold and the purple. There were also matches between the most famous boxers, wrestling, and exhibitions of performing horses, the more sensational features of the programme being reserved till after the noonday meal. Meanwhile, the doomed crowd in the dungeons waited, knowing that every new sound from the amphitheatre meant the nearer approach of death. The luncheon hour came and passed. During part of it the noise had been deafening, for Cæsar, in a generous mood, caused hampers of food to be distributed among the poorer spectators, and in each hamper was concealed a lottery ticket, with the names of the champion gladiators who were to prove themselves in single combat, so that each possessor of a ticket ran the chance of winning gifts or gold pieces. This added to the fire of expectation, and to the interest in the combatants.

The prisoners had no knowledge of the order of events, and were for the most part bowed down by despair, or else in a state of religious exaltation that made them oblivious of earthly happenings, and deaf to the chatter of the soldiers and officials, of whom a great number thronged the outside corridor and pressed into the dungeon to catch what was going on in the Arena. Old Gaius, a pathetic spectacle of spiritual fortitude oppressed by physical weakness, roused himself from his misery to try to console and exhort his brethren, as he deemed that duty required of him. But his voice broke, and it was a few faithful women who led the short prayers and uttered such words of comfort as they could command. The Bacchanals sat twisting their ivy-trails, some in horror, some in half-crazed enthusiasm, while the mad dancing-girl sang snatches of Pagan invocations mingled with Christian hymns. Nyria and Æola had not stirred from their corner in the curve of the buttress at one side of the great doors through which they must pass to go to their doom.

Suddenly Æola lifted herself from Nyria's arms. A moment since she had seemed almost bereft of reason and, except for her convulsive shudderings, in a state bordering on coma. Now she stared and made a chattering sound with her teeth, but could not speak. She sat up, leaning forward, her ears strained, an expression of agonised expectancy upon her face. She had heard a long, low, rhythmic clang of steel, and the regular muffled sound of drilled feet tramping on sand. The trumpets gave a loud blare, which startled the soldiers and made a stir in the cell. The tramping came nearer, and stopped. Then, through a significant hush in the swell of sound without, there thrilled a sort of chant, fierce, impassioned, sad, solemn—the death-salute of the gladiators.

Æola pointed through the closed doors, but Nyria was past realising what she meant, past shrinking even, when two Prætorians, who had darted from the guard at the entrance, brushed by the girls, and vaulting the buttress, sprang to a ledge beneath one of the high windows which looked into the Arena. Here, clinging to the bars, they put their faces to the grating, and shouted excitedly across to their companions, telling them the number of gladiators, commenting on their appearance, and, naming the champions, offering to bet on those they favoured.

"The Gauls against the Thracians . . . fifties to fifties . . . Mirmillones to the Net-throwers . . . and the champions single-handed . . ."

"A Thrax for me!"

"Nay! a Samnite."

"One thousand sestertii on the Thracians!"

"Nay! nay! *I* back the Fishes. Two thousand on Mirmillones."

"A big sesterce on the champion Net-thrower! *I* stake on Crispus Sabinus."

"Nay! A fig for these provincials! Balbus Plautius for *my* money."

"Five hundred on Balbus Plautius."

"Ay, if the match comes off. They said an hour ago that Crispus was not back in Rome."

"Ay! ay! he's there."

"Nay! 'tis not Crispus."

"Yes, verily, '*tis* Crispus! A big sesterce on Crispus Sabinus who won the palm at Baiæ."

"By Hercules! I swear it's not Crispus. That man can scarce lift his trident."

"Who'll fetch us news of Crispus?"

So the ball of conjecture was flung. Some of the Prætorians were possessed of lottery tickets, and these forgot everything but the chances of the betting. Other soldiers crowded the spaces beneath the windows, but the two first held the positions they had seized. Then there came a shout from the guard at the door.

"Here comes one who knoweth the talk of Rome. Stephanus! Nay, thou shalt not pass till thou hast answered. Where's Crispus Sabinus, who won the silver prize at Antium and took the palm at Baiæ? Is't true the match is off? Say, man! will Crispus fight with Balbus Plautius?"

The Prætorians jestingly made a barrier with their lances to stay the goldsmith's step across the dungeon threshold.

Stephanus stood outside. There was a great change in him. His chin dropped between his bent shoulders. His features looked twisted, and his skin was grey. Great streaks of white patched his short dark beard. He gazed at the guards glassily, shaking his head without a word. When they opposed his entrance he merely raised his arms with a staggering gesture, thrusting them before him, and making a butting movement with his forehead. A Prætorian pushed up from behind—it was the one who had befriended him at the Mamertine.

"Make way!" he cried. "Stephanus holds the Prefect's order."

The soldiers lowered their lances and let the goldsmith go by. Then they eagerly questioned the newcomer.

"Dost know, comrade," cried one, "if Crispus Sabinus is entered to-day for single combat with Balbus Plautius? I've drawn him in the lottery."

"Ay, ay!" was the answer. "That match comes off, but thou'lt lose thy prize, friend. I advise none to back Crispus. The man's distraught. He hath a Christian sweetheart, whom yesterday some who were too eager took, and to-day she feeds the lions. Cæsar, they say, is wroth that Crispus was not kept in ignorance, for he himself hath backed the Net-thrower."

"A plague on Christian sweethearts! Didst mark Stephanus?" said another soldier.

"Ay, what hath happed the goldsmith?" queried a third. "Doth he, too, love a Christian?"

"'Tis yon pale maid with the yellow hair," was the reply. "Eheu!" added the friendly Prætorian. "'Tis ordered she's to be the first to flesh the lions' teeth when the Bacchanals have dealt with Sura."

He spoke in a low tone, and with a warning glance. But

Stephanus seemed neither to see nor hear anyone. The Christians who knew him crowded round, whispering piteous entreaties.

"Oh, Stephanus! Hast brought a drug, good doctor? Give us somewhat that shall deaden pain; or hast thou poison to work quickly? Give it—give it—good Stephanus."

But he thrust out his hands again, pushing them all aside, and there was that in his face which made them leave him. He stood alone, blinded, a blur upon his eyeballs. Stephanus seemed no longer Stephanus. His bluff assurance was gone; his customary readiness of speech had failed him. There was nothing for him to say, nothing for him to do; he scarcely even dared to look for that which he sought. To gaze on Nyria, and know himself helpless on her behalf, was agony almost greater than he could endure. Nothing remained for Stephanus but despair. He had not yet considered that if he could not save Nyria a day might arrive when he should avenge her.

Till the last moment he had been rushing hither and thither in frantic endeavours to influence some great personage in her favour, but to no purpose. He had tried by means of a friend of his—Maximus, the freedman of Parthenius, the Chamberlain—to reach Cæsar himself, but at the Palace he learned that which made the jaws of the beasts seem preferable to Domitian's favour. All, then, was over. Entreaties, offerings to gods and men alike, were unavailing, since Christ would not shield His own, and the gods of Greece were deaf, or powerless, or haply—Stephanus thought—the gods desired that one so fair and pure as Nyria should dwell henceforth amongst themselves. There came back to him the fancy he had often had concerning her—that she was no child of mortal parents, but the offspring of divinities, who had lent her for a little while to earth. Now, doubtless, they would fain recall her to heavenly realms.

As a group of Prætorians divided in front of the great doors he saw the slender, white-clad form and golden head, with chin slightly raised, and innocent blue eyes gazing dreamily from out the pale, thin face. So motionless sat Nyria, so strangely calm, so aloof and inexpectant of terrors, so like that thing of air and sunlight which she had seemed when in happy times they had roamed the hills together, gathering flowers, that to Stephanus she appeared as though her soul had already passed the border-land of earth and was in keeping of the gods. Then poignant regret pierced him.

"Nyria!" he cried hoarsely. But the next instant he struck his breast with his clenched hand in passionate self-reproach. How dared he rouse her from her dreams and draw her back to consciousness for his own selfish sake? Stephanus knew the look in Nyria's eyes. He had seen it in the eyes of dying persons upon whom the gods had cast a merciful glamour, so that Thanatos, Sleep's brother, might hush them gently to their rest. Haply Artemis had heard his prayers when last night he had writhed agony before the virgin goddess's shrine, imploring the maiden daughter of Latona to extend her hand and preserve this blameless maid from pain. Stephanus went over to Nyria, dumb with anguish. She smiled upon him in a strange, sweet way—a smile that had less of earth than heaven. She put her hand on his bent head as he knelt beside her, his throat convulsed.

"Weep not," she whispered. "All is well with me, Stephanus."

"Methought—to—slay thee—child," he said, "or—at least—to soothe thee with a potion that should make thee—forget—reality." He spoke in broken gasps. "And yet—I cannot—unless—unless—thou bid'st me, dear." He stopped. His whole frame quivered in voiceless torment.

"Fear not for me," said Nyria. "Naught matters now, since Christ Himself upholdeth me, and in my heart there's only joy—save for thee." She laid her hand in Stephanus's, and thus they stayed, no word passing—how long they did not know.

Outside, in the Arena, the hellish din went on. Fifties by fifties the gladiators fought and killed each other—brave men pouring forth their lives to slake a tyrant's thirst for slaughter; and the reek of carnage rose, and Rome looked on, laughing, and grew drunk with blood.

Within the cell, the trembling prayers had well-nigh ceased. Wails were drowned by the eager betting of the soldiers. Æola's head lay again on Nyria's knees. She had fallen, fainting, at the clash of javelins and the shouting of her lover's name. The fight between Crispus Sabinus, the Net-thrower, and Balbus Plautius, the Mirmillo—last item in that portion of the programme—had begun.

Here in the dungeon, among the guards and jailors, the fever of interest ran fierce as in the galleries of the amphitheatre. Soldiers crowded the ledges of the little windows, and swung themselves from projections in the roof, while others below leaped up every instant, straining at the bars in frantic efforts to get glimpses of the contest. Moment by moment the excitement grew intenser, as the backers of Crispus found to their delight that the Net-thrower was inspired to almost superhuman skill. So that while the spectators at the windows called out the progress of the fight, in answer to the questions of those behind, fresh wagers were laid, and tablets with the amounts inscribed were flung like missiles from one to another.

"Now Venus Victrix aid thee, Crispus!"

"A feint! a feint! He flieth!"

"Ha! bear on, Crispus. . . . Well done! Well done! Was ever such adroitness?"

"By Neptune! the net nigh caught the fish! Strike, Balbus! Strike!"

Thus screamed the partisans of each.

"Mercury doth lend yon clever rascal his winged feet!"

"A splendid cast! Well done, my Crispus! By Eros! 'twas well done."

"'Tis Eros aids him. He hath a lover's cunning."

"Should he vanquish Balbus, he may beg a boon of Cæsar."

"Heu! Heu! 'Tis the life of a maid, then, that hangs in the net!"

For the mere matter of a girl's life the soldiers and jailors cared no jot. They counted only on the money they might make through one or other of the champions. Crispus was the favourite, since Cæsar himself had backed him. So when the net-thrower drew his adversary with tricksy throws, advancing and retiring on tactics calculated to ensnare the gigantic Balbus and to confuse his more sluggish brain, the galleries—and the dungeon likewise—rang with laughter and applause. And when Balbus, wielding his heavy weapons, appeared to be gaining an advantage over his lighter opponent, the plaudits echoed with less enthusiasm. After each round the betting went up on Crispus.

The excitement was long and tense, but presently it culminated.

"Habet! Habet! Well caught! Well caught! The Fish is down!"

Shouts and cheers followed each other in quick succession. Then came a breathless silence. Tens of thousands waited for Cæsar's signal. And then there was another tumultuous shout as the fiat went forth against the Mirmillo. The backers of Balbus Plautius lowered themselves from the windows and turned away discontentedly. They had lost their money and their lottery tickets were worthless. Balbus Plautius had paid a heavy penalty for the lashes which, at Julia's bidding, he had once dealt Nyria.

The name of Crispus Sabinus resounded from every part of the amphitheatre, but Æola heard it not. She was still lying unconscious, her head on Nyria's knees. Nyria, too, appeared to have no understanding of what had taken place, and might already have been dead, but that her eyes were opened wide as she gazed into space, and once or twice her lashes flickered. Only Stephanus grasped the significance of the victory, and he lifted up his face and listened while one of the soldiers at the window told his comrades how Crispus had been summoned before the Emperor's podium and told that he might ask a boon in reward for his prowess.

"Verily Venus hath favoured Crispus!" cried a soldier. "He kneeleth now to receive the Augustus's grace. . . . Nay, I hear not what boon he craveth, save that—as one might suppose—it doth concern a maid."

"More than one, it seems!" another soldier added, with a chuckle.

Following on some remarks of Cæsar's, a ripple of merriment had passed over the Senatorial benches; and now Domitian's loud laugh sounded through the silence of the assemblage, which held its breath while the ruler of the world deigned to make an utterance.

"Maidens!—saidst thou? Eh, verily, my amorous friend, how many? Dost thou, like Pentheus, claim service of fair women by the score? What number, then, of maidens may it please thee to require?"

Fresh mirth crackled, and meaning jests were bandied in the Imperial circle. Then Crispus's voice became audible again.

"But two, most great and glorious Cæsar. She of whom thy slave did speak—that one who was taken yesterday, and who hath ne'er been baptised into the Christian sect—is my betrothed—Æola."

"Thy betrothed! Ho! ho! It seems that one betrothed doth not content thee, lusty Crispus. What saith Æola to this other maid—how callest thou the other?"

"She is named Nyria, Most August. Æola is her friend."

Crispus's words, clearly spoken, with their ring of agonised suspense, penetrated even to the dungeon. The soldiers murmured in curiosity, and Stephanus's breath came fast and uneven. He half turned to Nyria, but she sat as though she heard naught.

"Cæsar answers not," cried a soldier at the window. "Now, Venus, favour still yon faithful lover."

"Belike he hath been over bold. Domitian doth not even laugh!"

"See—Cæsar whispers to Norbanus!"

"Ay, ay! he giveth the order for the herald."

"Eros preserve thee, brave Crispus!"

And then the herald's voice rang out, loud and clear.

"Crispus Sabinus! 'Tis our lord-god Cæsar's generous will that the life of thy betrothed Æola be given thee in reward for thy skill and valour. Therefore thou may'st forthwith take her hence. But for the maid called Nyria—she having been already brought before the tribunal of Cæsar—our sovereign lord will of his noble leniency send an officer of the bodyguard to acquaint this prisoner with his gracious pleasure concerning her release."

"All hail to Cæsar!" yelled the populace. "The palm for Crispus! Crown our champion! Crispus is conqueror! He cometh! He cometh!"

The soldiers pressed their faces to the bars that they might see the hero as he passed on his victorious progress down the Arena. "For Crispus the Triumphal Gate!" they cried. "Hail! hail to thee, Crispus!"

Plaudits rose and fell, following the gladiator as he went round the amphitheatre to the door by which those who won the palm had right of exit when, after certain formalities, they were free for private business. Soon a blast of horns diverted public attention to the distribution of baskets containing cakes and sweetmeats—a further proof of Cæsar's generosity. There was a brief interlude.

Now machinery rumbled more loudly below, while a fresh commotion started. The soldiers and jailors sprang again to their posts of vantage and criticised the scenes, as the floor of the Arena opened and the rocks and pines of Cithæron mounted into view. The masque of the Bacchanals was looked forward to with keen interest, for it suggested a novel refinement of cruelty which all thought worthy of Domitian.

"Ay! ay! the serpents are deadly," said a soldier in answer to inquiries from the rest. "See how the snake-men from Libya keep them charmed by that soft playing of the pipes! Be sure there's magic in it."

"Mænads of olden time did deck themselves with poisonous serpents," remarked another. "Bacchic votaries may ne'er be harmed by any serpent's fang."

"But this hapless crew be not true Bacchic votaries!" cried a third.

"Nay, but 'tis a fair challenge of divinities. If Christ wields stronger magic than the son of Jove and Semele, let Him deliver His worshippers when the snakes run loose amongst them."

"Ay! ay! that's the ordinance of our Bacchus-Cæsar. Such as the snakes harm not shall be spared. But methinks 'twill be brief work to count those they leave untouched."

Meanwhile the name of Crispus resounded along the vaulted corridors, and reached at last the ears of Æola, calling her back to consciousness. With some instinctive sense of her lover's nearness she gave a start, and, opening her eyes, gazed across the dungeon to where, between the files of soldiers in the doorway, Crispus appeared, exultant, yet trembling now with the strain of the ordeal through which he had passed. He still wore his short tunic in which he had fought in the Arena; his bared limbs were shining, the palm-crown was on his brows, the wooden sword he had received in token of release from future gladiatorial service was clutched in his hand. His gaze searched the cell. With an exceeding glad cry Æola called his name. He darted forward and, dropping his trophy, gathered her in his arms and kissed her passionately. Then his joyous glance fell on Nyria as she sat, white, motionless, her blue eyes wide and blank. Crispus paused a moment.

"I did not forget thee, Nyria," he cried. "I prayed for thy life as for Æola's. But though I may not lead thee forth myself, take heart of grace, dear little friend, for Cæsar saith that he will send thee thy release. Here's good Stephanus to protect thee. Courage, man! Why look so sad? 'Twill yet be well with Nyria."

But Nyria answered not, nor did Stephanus.

Out in the theatre the masque had begun with discordant clash of cymbals, the heavy beat of ox-hide drums and the screaming of Phrygian flutes. The officer by whom the Bacchanals had been selected was already in the dungeon with his attendants, inspecting the band, to see that all were duly clad in dappled skins, their brows ivy-wreathed and a thyrsus in each woman's hand. The crazy chorus-girl was shouting a Bacchic drinking-song:—

"'From Phrygia's and from Libya's hills
Lo! I am come—oh! hear me.
Ye maids of Rome!
Bring home—bring home
The Bromian god to cheer ye.'"

Gaius, his gaunt limbs scarcely able to bear him, his speech broken with agitation, strove to silence her. But the soldiers laughed and applauded, and bade him keep silence himself, for that the song put heart into the maids, and that they would soon enough be silent. Vainly the presbyter implored—vainly he tried to calm and counsel such as would listen. His words were drowned by the shrilling of trumpets. The gates swung open to a blare of sound and a glitter of white, crimson and gold. From the sky, as it were, there came a voice, clear and immensely loud—an effect produced by acoustic contrivance.

"*What! ho! my Bacchanals. Ho! Hear my call. The son of Zeus and Semele bids ye to his rites.*"

At this signal, guards drove the women forth and the doors were closed. Gaius sank on his knees, tears running down his stern face, and, with shaking hands held heavenward, prayed audibly, "Lord! lay not this sin to their charge."

Now, from the passages of the prison, mocking shouts flowed in as two lines of soldiers advanced, and between them a tall, male figure attired in the white linen robes of a woman, garlanded with ivy, and carrying a thyrsus. It was Licinius Sura.

The wave of derision died down, subdued by the personality of the man, in which there was nothing craven, as he stood between two guards, habited in the guise befitting their parts, who were waiting for the sign on which to lead him into the Arena. The light from the high windows fell upon Licinius, showing him erect, but very pale, his handsome features furrowed by suffering, and his whole body worn and looking grotesquely tragic in the woman's garb.

At first his gaze passed unheeding round the crowd; then it stopped suddenly at Nyria, who, with Stephanus kneeling by her, crouched to one side of the doorway, her form bent, her blue eyes with their blank look fixed on Licinius, her thin hands clasped before her breast.

"Ah! little watch-dog!" Sura cried. "So thou dost guard the portal still?" and he laughed the light laugh which had so strange a charm. "Alack! poor watch-dog. Here and now I may not say 'Well met,' but haply an hour hence, when thou and I have crossed the Styx, it may be better met in Hades's Halls."

He had hardly spoken when again the clarion voice summoned from above,—

"*Come, impious mortal, who hast dared blaspheme Divinity. The god thou didst deny now calls thee to thy fate.*"

The roar of voices swelled and the flood of light poured in afresh as the gates swung back, and the whole multitude in the amphitheatre, with faces turned to the Emperor's box, shouted, "Hail! Bacchus-Cæsar!" Licinius Sura braced his frame; his nostrils dilated. There flashed a look of indomitable defiance into his eyes. He went out with unfaltering steps, and on his lips a smile.

As the gate swung to again, the thunder of acclamation changed to a storm of hooting and of horror-stricken yells. But through the clamour, came another note—deeper, fiercer, longer-drawn, indescribably terrifying to the remaining prisoners in the dungeon. It was the howling of the beasts, which were being brought up in iron cages from their subterranean dens. The last dread moment was at hand. This sound reached Nyria's brain. She started, and leaned forward, listening intently, with her hand raised. Stephanus uttered a choking cry, and snatching her in his arms he strained her to his breast. There he held her, pressing her head against him, and bending over her strove with both hands to deafen her ears to those shrill screams and the mad music that filled the amphitheatre while the tragedy was being enacted within it—and to those resonant roars that reverberated through all other sounds.

Then, with the courage of despair, he released her a little and whispered,—

"I brought the drug. Wilt take it, Nyria?"

She did not seem to hear him, and he repeated his question. She raised herself. Her face, after that momentary stress, had regained its calm. There was no tremor in her voice as she answered gently,—

"Nay. Fain would I go by the road Christ chooseth for me. Grieve not, Stephanus. Christ will not let me suffer."

She leaned against her faithful friend, the soft smile on her lips, the dreamy, distant look in her eyes. A kind of awe came over Stephanus as he watched her abstraction from earthly surroundings. He felt as though a curtain had already fallen between them.

Meanwhile, the rest of the prisoners, realising that the end was very near, broke forth anew into prayer. Gaius's earnest though quavering tones led an anguished litany. Outside, the tumult had lessened. One by one the soldiers watching at the windows turned away and sprang down, many of them wearing expressions of disgust. Yet the thirst for blood still raged, and preparations for further slaughter went on. The rumbling of machinery in the vaults below could be again heard, while the Arena was swept, cleaned and re-strewn with fresh sand and perfumes.

Suddenly the guards at the dungeon door saluted a Prætorian officer who had entered, a splendid figure in the gleaming mail of the bodyguard. It was Alexamenos, pale and excited. All eyes turned to him as he advanced swiftly to where Nyria sat.

Stephanus, startled, loosed his arms from about her and drew ck, wondering what this might mean, and fearful for the issue. ıt Nyria remained unmoved. Regardless of the bystanders, lexamenos flung himself on his knees before her.

"Nyria! I bear thee word of Cæsar's clemency. It is the nperor's will that thou be saved."

Stephanus made an incredulous sound. He stared at Alexa- enos, a faint flicker of hope in his face, the lines of which were ghtened by the intensity of his suffering. Nyria's absent gaze ıd turned slowly to the eager messenger. Her smile faded.

"Alas! Cæsar's clemency is not unconditional," Alexamenos ent on in low, anxious tones, "but I implore thee reject not this ace, Nyria, lest the Emperor's mood should change. I have riven for thee. Didst thou not know that I should strive, sweet? y every means in my power have I endeavoured to save thee— nce yesterday, when first I knew thy peril. When thou wert ken from the Presence I claimed an audience, and entreated esar, telling him of my love for thee—of how I had long desired ee for my wife. Alack! 'twas of no avail. He would not then nsent. Yet, when yon gladiator sued him for thy life he served for me the boon that Crispus asked. 'Twas but just now ıat Cæsar sent for me. 'Go, see the maid thou lov'st,' he id. 'Take to Nyria Domitian's message of deliverance. Tell ır that Cæsar grants her life, and will extend to her his Imperial vour.' One thing—but one thing—doth he require. It is com- anded that thou go forth alone—alone thou'lt walk the Arena ıto his podium. Beyond it lie the cages, but fear naught, for esar hath decreed that the doors be not opened till thou hast gone n paces past the podium—but thou'lt *not* pass it, Nyria, thou ilt obey Cæsar's behest. 'Tis but to pause and kneel before the ırone, and call aloud, 'I hail thee lord-god, Cæsar.' Then will ıe cage doors be kept closed till thou art in safety."

"And *this* thou callest Cæsar's clemency?" cried Stephanus.

Alexamenos heeded not the remonstrance, but continued ırnestly, "Well I know what Cæsar meaneth by these terms. nd yet, I pray thee, yield. I love thee, as thou hast learned long nce, and yet I bid thee buy thy life, for that once secured thou ayest trust the rest to Alexamenos. Thou'lt be sent to the alace, but *I* will take thee hence. Fear naught, Nyria. Thou ıst blamed me ere this in that I put my duty as a soldier before l else. I'll do that no more. For thee, I'm first the man that ves thee, and Cæsar's soldier next. Ay, even though the legions se." Alexamenos lowered his voice to a husky whisper. "Domi- an shall not stretch his lustful arm too far. The Prætorians, as told thee, are no man's slaves—not even Cæsar's. Let him oppose ıem if he dare."

Alexamenos's eager whisper paused, and Stephanus, dumb and

frenzied, looking from one to the other, would fain have snatched his treasure back to his breast again, but rigidly restrained himself, and remained silent.

The girl said not a word. Her blue eyes wore a pained and faintly puzzled look. She still seemed to be gazing beyond the world, and this recalling her to earthly matters was difficult, since she had left them far behind.

"Nyria!" cried the young Prætorian, passionately. "Dost thou not know me, sweet? Dost thou not remember Alexamenos who hath loved thee ever, and would gladly give his life for thee? Why seem'st thou thus far away? List to my pleadings! Say that thou wilt do that which Alexamenos prayeth of thee. Why hesitate? Is it that thou fearest to deny the Master Christ? He knoweth all that is in thy heart, Nyria, and will pardon any thought of ill. But of a truth this is no denial of the Christ, since Cæsar asketh not that of thee. Do *I* deny him when I implore thee to save thyself? Nay! nay! Even though I wear this livery"—and he struck his breastplate with his clenched hand—"not less am I, Alexamenos, a soldier of Cæsar, still a servant of the Most High God. And yet I bow the knee to Cæsar! The good Clementus teaches that Christians must submit to earthly rulers. And did not Christ Himself command that the things which are Cæsar's be rendered unto Cæsar?"

Still Nyria answered not. And still Alexamenos pleaded urgently,—

"'Tis but a small thing that is required of thee—only to accord openly unto Domitian this tribute to his greatness which Pagan and Christian do alike acknowledge. Confound not this lawful homage to Rome's Emperor with the worship of thy soul, which Christ alone can claim. Yield but the outward symbol, Nyria. In thy heart thou mayst maintain, as I do, Christ's supremacy."

At that moment there came a clang of heavy spear-butts on the pavement—the sound of a salute from the guard. Alexamenos instinctively started to his feet. There had entered another officer of the bodyguard, one who had also stood in the podium behind the Emperor.

"Verily, Alexamenos, art practising for the rostrum? Time fails thee, friend! Cæsar sends to know the maid's decision."

"Nyria! Oh! speak, beloved!" cried Alexamenos. "Say that thou wilt kneel to Cæsar."

Almost with his words there came the sweet high note of the trumpet signal. Four soldiers, two on either hand, went towards the great doors to fling them open, while Alexamenos, his hand upon his sword, sprang between them and Nyria.

"Come, maiden! Thou must know thy mind by now," exclaimed the other officer, and he signed to two more soldiers to

lead her forth. But Alexamenos waved them back, fo
was rising.

Stephanus knelt a pace distant. His yearning eyes n
her. She turned to him, tottering slightly, and held out he
but ere he could clasp them the soldiers had flung wide th
and Stephanus saw on Nyria's face a look which made h
his breath in awe and shrink from touching her. It
upward look, a look of faith and rapture, of joy ineffable
her those great gates might have been wreathed in ros
opened by angelic hands welcoming to Paradise. For her
came the rushing of a thousand silver wings, faces of tend
transcendent, leading her on. Others, half dazed by the str
light that poured in, and by the floods of gorgeous colour, c
glimpses of the dazzling half circle of the amphitheatre, saw
the cruel concourse arrayed in snowy togas, rich-hued pallas
glittering jewels, with gay garlands festooning all; saw, too
Imperial podium, where Cæsar sat enthroned amid purple and
and saw between the wide-set doors a single figure passing
slender, white-clad, with falling golden hair and blue eyes
with ecstasy. But Stephanus saw a fleeting vision of the t
figured form that he had seen in starlight on the Cœlian, and
it for no mere mortal maid going to martyrdom, but the passi
an eternal soul over whom death had no power. For this tin
least, horror, grief, desire of revenge—all went from Stepha
heart, and upon his face shone a reflection of the light on Nyri

Row after row, tier above tier of bloodthirsting faces l
thrilling with interest, on that one small figure walking a
across the sand-strewn space—one little slave-girl holding
breathless check the pomp and power of Rome. Every gaze
fixed on Nyria. Lips were silent, but every heart cried, "I
Christ or Cæsar?"

From the plebeians in the topmost gallery to the patric
benches the vast assemblage hung upon the moment.
Emperor stooped forward from beneath his gold and pu
canopy. His face grew livid as Nyria approached the podium.

She advanced slowly, yet unshrinkingly, her hands clasped
her breast, her head uplifted, but she saw not Cæsar. Her b
eyes' worshipping gaze went far beyond, unto Glory beneath wh
Domitian in his pride and splendour was as naught. As she dr
near the Emperor leaned closer—closer, with extended hand, re
to make the sign of mercy.

But Nyria passed on.

THE END

Colston & Coy. Limited, Printers, Edinburgh.

T. FISHER UNWIN'S NEW NOVELS.

THE DAYSPRING—A Romance. By WILLIAM BARRY, D.D., Author of 'The Wizard's Knot,' etc., etc.

This is the life story of an eager, earnest young soul, rising at length above the illusion of the senses to the clear heights of faith. Noble aims, misconstrued in the mirage of modern Paris, under the charm of a deluding spirituality, bring us to the moment of choice between two paths, one that of so-called Free Love, the other that of supreme self-sacrifice. The dreamy mysticism, the sparkling humour, the sudden brilliances, the delicate fancies which characterise the work of the author of 'The New Antigone' are to be found in this newest and perhaps most fascinating of Dr. Barry's books. A background of adventure is set by the last days of the Second Empire and the Commune of 1871.

A DRAMA OF SUNSHINE—Played in Homburg. By MRS. AUBREY RICHARDSON. (First Novel Library).

A dramatic episode of life in Homburg, at the height of the English season. The characters represent types of men and women actually to be met with in the high social and political world of to-day. A Society Beauty and a Sister of an Anglican Community personify the red Rose of Love, Pride and Gaiety, and the pale Lily of Purity, Aspiration and Repression. In the heart of the Rose, a lily bud unfolds, and in the calyx of the Lily, a rose blossoms. The incidents of the story succeeds each other swiftly, reaching a strong *dénouement*, and working out to a satisfying termination.

THE SITUATIONS OF LADY PATRICIA: A Satire for Idle People. By W. R. H. TROWBRIDGE, Author of 'The Letters of Her Mother to Elizabeth.'

Lady Patricia is an Englishwoman of a noble but impoverished family, whose girlhood has been spent on the Continent. Left an orphan she comes to England with the independent intention of seeking her own living. Sometimes under her own, sometimes under an assumed name, she takes various situations in England and France, and is brought in contact with many different sets of society both in the upper and the middle classes. In this volume she relates her experiences, and comments upon them with caustic wit. The plan of the work affords the author of 'The Letters of Her Mother to Elizabeth' an excellent opportunity of satirising the aristocracy and the *bourgeois gentilshommes* of England and France, and readers of the earlier volume will be prepared for a book full of piquancy and daring.

THAT FAST MISS BLOUNT. A Novel. By ROY HORNIMAN, Author of 'The Living Buddha,' 'The Sin of Atlantis,' etc.

There is nothing easier for a girl who has been born in a garrison town of hard-up Service parents than to drift, especially if, as in the case of Philippa, she has been disappointed in her first romance and is left a little soured and hardened. It is so easy to enjoy the tawdry amusements that come her way; and if, like Philippa, she is beautiful, flirtation follows flirtation, men come and go, till it becomes the habit to talk of her as 'that fast Miss Blount.' She is not the sort of girl as a rule who gets married. There is something in the atmosphere about her which makes marrying men fight shy of her. Philippa, however, is saved from social shipwreck by marrying in such a way as to rouse the envy of all those who have been her traducers. The background of the story is concerned with the family life of Captain and Mrs. Blount's household. There are also some exciting chapters dealing with the South African war.

ANGLO-AMERICANS. By LUCAS CLEEVE.

The main theme of this story is the fundamental antagonism existing between two characters—an American girl educated in ideas of freedom and independence, and of the subservience of man to woman, and her husband, an English Lord, who expects his wife to regard his career and interests as her own, and to devote herself to them even to the obliteration of herself. The girl's father is a millionaire, and the story tells incidentally of the illicit means by which his pile was made.

Lightning Source UK Ltd.
Milton Keynes UK
UKHW022358270721
387819UK00002B/183